Samuel Johnson, George Birkbeck Norman Hill

Letters

Collected and Edited by George Birkbeck Hill. Vol. 1

Samuel Johnson, George Birkbeck Norman Hill

Letters

Collected and Edited by George Birkbeck Hill. Vol. 1

ISBN/EAN: 9783337327026

Printed in Europe, USA, Canada, Australia, Japan

Cover: Foto ©Andreas Hilbeck / pixelio.de

More available books at **www.hansebooks.com**

LETTERS

OF

SAMUEL JOHNSON, LL.D.

COLLECTED AND EDITED

By GEORGE BIRKBECK HILL, D.C.L.

PEMBROKE COLLEGE, OXFORD

EDITOR OF BOSWELL'S 'LIFE OF JOHNSON'

IN TWO VOLUMES: VOL. I

Oct. 30, 1731 — Dec. 21, 1776

OXFORD

AT THE CLARENDON PRESS

M DCCC XCII

PREFACE

How extensive was Johnson's correspondence, and how much of it has been preserved, is not perhaps generally known. He wrote unwillingly. 'I know not how it happens,' he told Dr. Taylor in the year 1756, 'but I fancy that I write letters with more difficulty than some other people who write nothing but letters; at least I find myself very unwilling to take up a pen only to tell my friends that I am well; and indeed I never did exchange letters regularly but with dear Miss Boothby[1].' Seven years later he wrote to Boswell: 'I love to see my friends, to hear from them, to talk to them, and to talk of them; but it is not without a considerable effort of resolution that I prevail upon myself to write[2].' In this he was like Goldsmith who, apologising for his neglect in correspondence, said, 'No turnspit dog gets up into his wheel with more reluctance than I sit down to write[3].' I have seen in an Auction Catalogue an extract from a letter by Grainger, the author of the *Sugar Cane*, in which he says: 'When I taxed little Goldsmith for not writing as he promised me, his answer was that he never wrote a letter in his life; and faith I believe him, unless to a bookseller for money.'

Nevertheless, however indolent a man may be with his correspondence, if he lives to the age of seventy-five, and if his letters are thought worth keeping, a great mass will be preserved. Happily, there was one person to whom Johnson wrote eagerly enough. His letters to Mrs. Thrale are more than 300 in number. When he was away from Streatham,

---

[1] *Post*, i. 64. [2] *Life*, i. 473.
[3] Forster's *Life of Goldsmith*, ed. 1871, i. 433.

when

when he was not. to use his own words to her, 'reposing at that place which your kindness and Mr. Thrale's allows me to call my *home*[1],' he longed for news. He once reproached Boswell for indulging 'in an uneasy apprehension' about his wife and children who were 400 miles away in Edinburgh. 'Sir,' said he, 'consider how foolish you would think it in them to be apprehensive that you are ill[2].' His trade might, as Baretti said, be wisdom; but 'there was never yet philosopher that could bear the tooth-ache patiently,' and Johnson was just as foolish himself about 'My Master' and 'My Mistress' as Boswell was about his wife and children. One June when he was at Oxford, he was left a few days without any news from Streatham. On the 5th he complains to his 'Mistress' that three days had gone by without a letter. On the 6th he writes: 'If I have not a little something from you to-day, I shall think something very calamitous has befallen us.' On the 7th his apprehension is still rising. 'I grieve and wonder and hope and fear about my dear friends at Streatham. But I may have a letter this afternoon. Sure it will bring me no bad news. If I have a letter to-day I will go away as soon as I can; if I have none, I will stay till this may be answered, if I do not come back to town.' On the afternoon of the same day he is comforted. 'Your letter, which ought to have come on Tuesday, came not till Wednesday. Well, now I know that there is no harm, I will take a chaise and march away towards my own country[3].' He delighted in the letters which Mrs. Thrale sent him. 'Never imagine,' he wrote, 'that they are long; they are always too short for my curiosity. I do not know that I was ever content with a single perusal[4].' Had he wished it he could have kept up a correspondence with men famous in almost every path of life, discussing those great questions that so long occupied Rasselas and his friends, which they left with 'a conclusion in which nothing is concluded.' It was not that kind of letter-writing that he loved. He neglected the members of his famous

[1] *Post*, i. 129.   [2] *Life*, iii. 4.   [3] *Post*, i. 324-7.   [4] *Post*, i. 216.

Club,

Club, a set of men who, he maintained, were sufficient worthily
to fill all the chairs of a University[1]. So far as we know he did
not write a single letter to Edmund Burke ; he wrote more than
300 to the wife of a Southwark brewer. With such ardour did
he keep up the correspondence that in nine weeks of the summer
of 1775 he wrote to her thirty times. Let us for once be thankful for the old abuse of the franking system, by which these
letters were carried free of postage. Had he had to pay the
usual charge of fourpence on each he would, I fear, have
remembered, as he once bade Mrs. Thrale remember, that 'three
groats make a shilling[2],' and he would have written far less
frequently.

If we would judge of her share in the correspondence we must
not look so much to those of her letters which she has printed
as to the one which by some lucky chance came into Boswell's
possession. 'I shall present my readers,' he says, 'with one of
her original letters to Johnson, which will amuse them probably
more than those well-written but studied epistles which she has
inserted in her collection[3].' The insinuation which he casts on
their genuineness can be shown to be well founded. There is no
doubt that some of them are fabrications, and clumsy fabrications too[4]. She was far too inaccurate to make a successful
forger. It was not 'studied epistles' that she sent to her old
friend, or he would have speedily cried out, 'Fiddle-de-dee, my
dear.' What it was that delighted him in her letters we learn
from one of his answers, where he says : 'Such tattle as filled
your last sweet letter prevents one great inconvenience of
absence, that of returning home a stranger and an enquirer.
The variations of life consist of little things. Important innova-
tions are soon heard, and easily understood. Men that meet to
talk of physicks or metaphysicks, or law or history, may be
immediately acquainted. We look at each other in silence, only

---

[1] *Life*, v. 109.   [2] *Post*, i. 161.   [3] *Life*, iii. 421.
[4] For a curious instance see *post*, ii. 258, *n.* 3. For another apparent instance of her fabrication see ii. 210, *n.* 1.

for

for want of petty talk upon slight occurrences. Continue, therefore, to write all that you would say[1].'

Two other series of letters we owe to that strong feeling which
Johnson ever preserved for the friends of his youth—a feeling
which grew stronger and stronger as life ebbed away. 'If he
ever took delight in anything,' said Baretti, 'it was to converse
with some old acquaintance[2].' It was this feeling which more
than anything else attached him to Dr. Taylor, that heavy
pluralist whose thoughts were ever running on preferments,
'whose size and figure and countenance and manner were that
of a hearty English 'Squire with the parson superinduced[3].' It
was not, as some suspected, his hope of being Taylor's heir
which kept the friendship alive. He clung in the same kind of
way to his old schoolfellow, Henry Jackson, 'a low man, dull
and untaught, who wore a coarse grey coat, black waistcoat,
greasy leather breeches, and a yellow uncurled wig; whose countenance had the ruddiness which betokens one who is in no
haste to "leave his can."' He gave him his guineas, and when
he died he wrote: 'His death was a loss, and a loss not to be
repaired, as he was one of the companions of my childhood[4].'
Had this worthy been as ready with his pen as he was in
devising that new scheme of dressing leather by which he hoped
to mend his fortune, Johnson doubtless would have corresponded
with him too. To his old playfellow, Edmund Hector, the
Birmingham surgeon, he wrote: 'I am now grown very solicitous
about my old friends, with whom I passed the hours of youth
and cheerfulness, and am glad of any opportunity to revive the
memory of past pleasures. I therefore tear open a letter with
great eagerness when I know the hand in which it is super-
scribed[5].' With him also he not unfrequently corresponded.
Taylor docketed the letters which he received. The last is
numbered 108. Of these Boswell had been allowed to publish
but four. In the present collection sixty-two additional letters

[1] *Post*, ii. 19.   [2] *Post*, i. 388, *n.* 2.   [3] *Life*, ii. 474.
[4] *Life*, ii. 463; iii. 131.   [5] *Post*, i. 73.

are

are given; twenty-three of which, if I am not mistaken, have never been in print before. Forty-two, therefore, remain unpublished; some may have been lost, but most I suspect are hidden away in the desks of collectors.

There are great and curious gaps in Johnson's general correspondence. Of the four years, 1745, 6, 7 and 8, not a single letter, so far as I know, has been preserved. For 1755 we have as many as 22, and for 1760 only two. He wrote most copiously in the last few months of his life, when he was seeking relief from his sufferings at Lichfield and Ashbourne. Deserted by Mrs. Thrale and deprived by death of his domestic companions, overwhelmed with disease and looking with horror on the grave into which he was sinking, lonely and solitary, he sought on all sides for encouragement, kindness and sympathy. Sixteen years earlier, when distressed by illness, he had written: ' To roll the weak eye of helpless anguish, and see nothing on any side but cold indifference, will, I hope, happen to none whom I love or value; it may tend to withdraw the mind from life, but has no tendency to kindle those affections which fit us for a purer and a nobler state[1].' This cold indifference was what he seems at this time to have been dreading. By the frequency of his letters he strove to keep himself alive in the memory and the affections of his friends.

In the present collection will not be found those of his letters which were included by Boswell in the *Life*. In number they are not far short of 340. For each of them I give in the proper place the briefest notice of the person to whom it was addressed, the date at which it was written, and the volume and page where it will be found[2]. All the other letters which I have been able to collect I am now publishing. I have not thought it right to pass over any on account of their insignificance. Those which were already in print I have found mainly in the two volumes of Correspondence published by Mrs. Piozzi in 1788, in the

[1] *Post*, i. 141.
[2] The references are in all cases to my edition of the *Life*, published by the Clarendon Press.

editions

editions of the *Life* by Malone and Croker, in the *Miscellanies of the Philobiblon Society* and in *Notes and Queries*. To the last of these publications, a storehouse of curious and interesting matter, I would once more express my obligations—obligations shared in by every student of the literature, history, and antiquities of our country[1]. The letters in these various publications are about 570 in number.

In addition to this, through the kindness of collectors of autographs, and dealers, my collection is enriched with a large number of hitherto unpublished letters. A few of them indeed are already in print in costly private catalogues, such as Mr. Alfred Morrison's noble volumes. These, however, are not within the reach of the general reader. With the inclusion of these, and of the fifteen letters which were first given in my edition of the *Life*, the new letters, unless I am mistaken, amount to between ninety and a hundred. If we add to them the large number which are known only to the readers of *Notes and Queries* and of the *Miscellanies of the Philobiblon Society* it will be seen that the present Collection makes a great and important addition to Johnsonian literature.

In my eager search after letters I have examined in the Bodleian many hundreds of auctioneers' catalogues. This part of my task would have been greatly lightened had those catalogues which contain descriptions of autographs been bound up separately. As it was, I found them scattered among long lists, not only of books, but also of musical instruments, bins of wine, and cigars. If librarians would keep apart the catalogues in which autographs and manuscripts in general are described, students of literature and history would have at their command a great amount of curious material. Those of Johnson's letters of which I found mention in these lists I have entered in their proper places, giving moreover such abstracts of their contents as were published by the auctioneers. Some future editor may perhaps

---

[1] Many of these letters we owe to Professor John E. B. Mayor, who sent to *Notes and Queries* most careful copies of the originals.

be fortunate enough in many cases to get complete copies. One series of letters I am greatly disappointed at not being able to include in my collection. In Messrs. Sotheby and Co.'s Catalogue of Mr. F. Perkins's Library, which was sold in July, 1889, lot 1134 is 'a series of twenty autograph letters of Johnson to Mr. Perkins, Southwark, together with one from Boswell to Perkins.' They were sold for £81. It is possible that among these twenty letters are found the five which Perkins allowed Boswell to publish. Of none of them have I been able to get a copy. This I the more regret as they would have thrown light on a side of Johnson's character that is little known, and would have let us see him engaged in what his biographer calls 'the real business of life[1].' Perkins, it will be remembered, was 'the worthy superintendent of Thrale's Brewery[2].' On his master's death he became the junior partner of the wealthy Quakers who purchased the business. After the lapse of more than a century, when the secret letters and papers of kings and ministers have been given to the world, it might have been thought that the private correspondence of a great scholar with a superintendent of a brewery could with propriety be divulged. Expectation must, however, be still kept waiting. Perhaps a second hundred years must pass away before it shall be ascertained what was the part that Johnson took in founding the new firm of Barclay and Perkins. Something however can even now be known. One letter, it seems, had got separated from the rest and this I am able to publish[3]. A passage too in one of Johnson's letters to Mrs. Thrale[4] throws further light on the secret transactions by which, in the year of grace 1781, Mr. Perkins the man was changed into Mr. Perkins the master.

My chief labour has been spent on the two volumes of correspondence published by Mrs. Piozzi. In themselves they required far more annotation than the other letters, for in writing to her Johnson touched on a much greater variety

---

[1] *Life of Johnson*, iv. 85.   [2] *Life*, ii. 286, *n.* 1.   [3] *Post*, ii. 222.
[4] *Post*, ii. 216.

of

of persons and subjects. He frequently introduced quotations and literary allusions. She was a lady of some learning and many pretensions, who had more wit and more literature, he maintained, than even the great Mrs. Montagu[1]. In his letters to his other friends these quotations and allusions are as rare as in those to her they are abundant. I have traced and explained them so far as I have been able, but some have hitherto baffled my search. I have had besides to supply the names which Mrs. Piozzi either left in blank or merely indicated by the first letter. The frequent errors into which she has fallen have caused me a great deal of trouble. Many of these arose from that habit of inaccuracy of which Johnson in vain tried to work a cure; but some were clearly intentional. Of his letters not a few are carelessly inserted in the wrong places, but of her own some, as I have already said, are fabrications. In this part of my work I have made use of the curious marginal notes which Baretti wrote in his copy of the Correspondence[2]. In his conjectures, when he fills up the blanks, he is not always right. Nevertheless, whenever he was not under the influence of his feelings, his remarks are often of service. The malignity which he exhibits towards Mrs. Piozzi renders it needful to receive his general statements with caution. He had no doubt cause for anger in the attacks which she made on him through Johnson[3], but the savageness of his reply far exceeded the offence. Nevertheless in his remarks there is often a good deal of truth. If they did nothing else they would throw light on a man who was not the least interesting of the little group which gathered round the Thrales at Streatham.

I cannot but think that now that Johnson's letters are collected he will take a far higher rank among letter-writers than he has as yet filled. Admirable as many of those are which are published by Boswell, nevertheless in the *Life* they are

[1] *Post,* ii. 153. [2] The book is in the British Museum.
[3] *Post,* i. 350, 354-5.

overshadowed.

overshadowed, as it were, by his superlative merit as a talker. We hurry through them, or even skip over them, to arrive at the passages where the larger type and the inverted commas give signs that there we shall have good talk. His letters may be good but his talk has no rival. But when we no longer have it to tempt us, we shall not fail to recognise how admirable he was in his correspondence. What a variety, moreover, does it exhibit! We have those fine and weighty passages in which he treated of the greatest of all arts—the art of living, and taught, as few philosophers have better taught, the management of the mind, whether it is troubled by cares or well-nigh broken with grief. We have that strong common-sense set forth in vigorous English, on which his friends could always draw in their perplexities. We have, moreover, above all in his letters to Mrs. Thrale, a playfulness and lightness of touch which will surprise those who know him only by his formal writings. How pleasantly, for instance, does he laugh at his friend Taylor whose 'talk was of bullocks,' who bred cattle almost as eagerly as he hunted after preferments, and who was famous, it was said, for having the largest bull in England and some of the best sermons'. The sermons were Johnson's, and the bull Johnson has almost made his own by the humorous way in which from time to time he introduces him in his letters. 'I have seen the great bull,' he writes, 'and very great he is. I have seen likewise his heir-apparent, who promises to enherit all the bulk and all the virtues of his sire. I have seen the man who offered an hundred guineas for the young bull, while he was yet little better than a calf.' A year later he writes: 'There has been a man here to-day to take a farm. After some talk he went to see the bull, and said that he had seen a bigger. Do you think he is likely to get the farm?' Fifteen months later he returns to the subject: 'Our bulls and cows are all well; but we yet hate the man that had seen a bigger bull².'

The gem of my collection is a letter from Johnson to his wife,

¹ *Life*, iii. 181, *n.* 3.   ² *Post*, i. 166, 178, 197.

which

which I owe to the liberality of Mr. William R. Smith, Barrister-at-Law, of the Inner Temple, and of Greatham Moor, West Liss, Hampshire, a descendant of the Rev. George Strahan, to whose vicarage at Islington Johnson in the last years of his life now and then went for the benefit of good air. In this letter, full of tenderness, the fond and youthful husband addresses his wife who was but four days short of fifty-one as 'my dear girl,' 'my charming love,' and as 'the most amiable woman in the world.' Well! she was twenty years older than Johnson, and no doubt deserved some of the ridicule which Lord Macaulay has so lavishly cast upon her. Nevertheless at the time of her marriage she was of just the same age as was Barbara, Duchess of Cleveland, when our great historian describes her as 'no longer young, but still retaining some traces of that superb and voluptuous loveliness which twenty years before overcame the hearts of all men.' For all we know, it was Mrs. Johnson's 'superb and voluptuous loveliness which overcame the heart' of the lamented Mr. Porter, the Birmingham mercer, and it was the traces of it which overcame young Samuel Johnson. She was only a decent married woman; had she been a royal harlot Macaulay, instead of mocking her 'ceruse bloom,' might himself have laid on the colours with an ardour and a skill scarcely surpassed by Sir Peter Lely.

Wherever I have been able to see the originals or to get exact copies, I have retained Johnson's spelling. In these days of examinations, when an excessive importance is attached to a somewhat mean art, it may bring comfort to those who fail in it to know that the man who by his Dictionary first set orthography on a sure footing was not always careful to comply with his own rulings. Thus in the following letters we find 'persuance,' 'I cannot butt,' 'council' (those who plead a cause), 'happyest,' 'Fryday,' 'solicite,' 'defense,' 'pamflets,' 'harrassed,' 'do's' and 'dos' (does), 'inventter,' 'barels,' 'cloaths' (clothes), 'acknowlegement,' 'distresful,' 'personale,' 'Plimouth,' 'imbecillity,' 'enervaiting,' and 'devide.' Johnson frequently omitted
the

the sign of the genitive case, as, 'Bankers book,' 'Doctors prescription.' In writing proper names he often left out the second final consonant, as 'Boswel[1],' 'Cadel,' 'Gastrel,' 'Wraxal,' 'Dod,' 'Pot.' This perhaps he did by rule; in like manner he frequently wrote 'ilness.' In his letters to John Nichols he spells his correspondent's name ' Nichols.' ' Nicols,' ' Nichol,' and ' Nicol.'

The information which I have given, in all cases where I could obtain it, of the prices paid at public sales for Johnson's letters will be of interest to collectors of autographs[2].

I have now the pleasant task of expressing my acknowledgments for the help which I have received in my work. To the owners of the original letters I have in each case done this in a footnote. But there are two gentlemen among them, Mr. Alfred Morrison and Mr. William R. Smith, to whom I would more particularly express my gratitude for the liberality which has led them to allow me to make the freest use of their large and valuable collections of *Johnsoniana*. To Mr. Falconer Madan, Fellow of Brasenose College and Assistant-Librarian of the Bodleian, I am indebted not only for general assistance, but also more particularly for the communication of two unpublished anecdotes of Johnson, which he found among Dr. Philip Bliss's notes[3]. Mr. J. L. G. Mowat, Fellow and Bursar of Pembroke College, Oxford, I have to thank for the aid which he gave me in deciphering, copying and collating a collection of Johnson's letters which is kept in the Library of that Society. Mr. G. K. Fortescue, the Superintendent of the Reading Room of the British Museum, has once more laid me under obligation by the kindness with which he has allowed me to draw on his wide knowledge of books, and by the facilities which he has given me in my visits to the Library. To Mrs. Raine Ellis I am indebted both for the information contained in the accurate notes of her admirable edition of the *Early Diary of Frances Burney*, and

---

[1] I cannot recall a single instance in which he wrote *Boswell*.
[2] See in the Index, ' JOHNSON, autograph letters.'   [3] *Post*, ii. 438.

also

also for the help which she has given me in clearing up difficulties in the correspondence with Mrs. Thrale. It is greatly to be wished that she should complete her task by publishing a new edition of Madame D'Arblay's *Diary*. She alone knows how much Madame D'Arblay altered what Miss Burney had written, and how much after her death her editor contributed to this work of mischievous and misleading revision [1]. Mr. G. J. Campbell, Solicitor, of Inverness, I have to thank not only for a curious fragment of an autograph letter of Johnson but also for the trouble which he kindly took in gathering what information there was still to be had about Johnson's route from Loch Ness to Glenelg. To Mr. C. E. Doble, M.A., of the Clarendon Press, I am once more deeply indebted for the care with which he has read through my proof-sheets, and for the corrections and suggestions which he has made.

One acknowledgment comes alas too late. To a young dealer in autographs, the late Mr. Samuel J. Davey, I owe not only many unpublished letters, but also the original of a curious note taken by Dr. Brocklesby of a conversation with Johnson and Boswell on the evening of the day on which the famous physician,

---

[1] To Mrs. Ellis I owe the following little incidents connected with Johnson. I received them too late to insert in their proper places in my notes. In a pretty little book which she published a few years ago under the title of *Sylvestra* she recounts how one day, in his lodgings at Oxford, he was heard calling out :— 'Wench, I gave thee my shirt to be air'd, and thou hast brought me thy mistress's smock' (vol. i. p. 27). Mrs. Ellis tells me that it was from her husband's great-uncle that the anecdote comes. He was lodging in the same house, and heard the cry. Kettel Hall is most likely the scene of the story, where Johnson had rooms in 1754 [*]. One of her correspondents, who was born at the end of last century and who died two years ago, a sister of Dean Peacock, writing to her said, 'I remember hearing a good deal of a Mr. Harrison of Stub House, near Kirby Hill, in Yorkshire. He was a gentleman-farmer and country squire, notorious for swearing and overbearing conduct. He was said to be a clever man and a relation of Dr. Johnson. He had a son called Cornelius.' This man was most likely a descendant of the Rev. Cornelius Harrison, perpetual curate of Darlington, 'who was,' said Johnson, 'the only one of my relations who ever rose in fortune above penury or in character above neglect [†].'

[*] *Life*, i. 270, n.

[†] *Post*, i. 225.

William

William Hunter, died[1]. I know no man who carried on the gentle craft of an autograph dealer with more generous ardour than Mr. Davey. His manuscripts were not to him mere articles of traffic. He prized them also as materials of literature. Whatever he had he was ready to place freely at the service of the student. I can only record my deep regret that a career so full of good promise was brought to so untimely an end.

I have done my best to make my work as accurate and as complete as possible, but errors and omissions are sure to be discovered. It will be shown, I fear, that in spite of all my anxious care, letters which are in print have been left unnoticed, and that others which I enter as new have been already published. I have been encouraged in my task by the kind, I might even say the generous treatment which my edition of the *Life of Johnson* received both from readers in general, and more especially from men familiar with the literature and history of the eighteenth century. I cannot but hope that this laborious addition to Johnsonian lore and to literary history will meet with the same friendly welcome. It is my wish to complete my task by a new edition of the *Lives of the Poets*. For that, the third and final part of my work, I have already laid the foundations. To finish the whole building will require a long course of study and work.

G. B. H.

February 8, 1892.

[1] *Post*, ii. 436.

ERRATA.

Vol. I. p. 92, date of letter, *for* 1781 *read* 1761.
„ p. 221, l. 22, *for* talk *read* task.

TABLE OF CONTENTS

———•———

The Letters published by me for the first time, whether in my edition of Boswell's *Life of Johnson* or in this Collection, are marked * in the following Table.

Those now first collected from Magazines and from works printed for private circulation are marked †.

Those quoted in part or merely mentioned in Auctioneers' Catalogues and elsewhere are marked ‡.

Italics are used to show that the Letter is to be found not here but in the *Life of Johnson*.

VOLUME I.

b 2

              VOLUME II.

Dear Sir

I apprehend
...I have...
with neither...
that may...
dy suffered
more than...
... I have
our troubles...
does not easily...
as call in...
have two or...
to be the best...
to part with
you instantly...
this night. I

To Mrs Johnson at Mrs Evans'
in Earl Marsham Carsdowch
Square : 1

LETTERS OF DR. JOHNSON.

1.

TO GREGORY HICKMAN[1].

SIR, Lichfield, Oct. 30, 1731.

I have so long neglected to return you thanks for the favour and assistance received from you at Stourbridge, that I am afraid you have now done expecting it. I can, indeed, make no apology, but by assuring you, that this delay, whatever was the cause of it, proceeded neither from forgetfulness, disrespect, nor ingratitude. Time has not made the sense of obligation less warm, nor the thanks I return less sincere. But while I am acknowledging one favour, I must beg another—that you would excuse the composition of the verses you desired. Be pleased to consider, that versifying against one's inclination is the most disagreeable thing in the world ; and that one's own disappointment is no inviting subject ; and that though the desire of gratifying you might have prevailed over

[1] First published in the *Manchester Herald* (see *Gentleman's Magazine*, 1813, p. 18).

Nichols (*Literary Anecdotes*, viii. 416) says that this letter was written 'on the occasion of the writer's being rejected on his application for the situation of Usher to the Grammar School at Stourbridge.' Johnson had been a pupil of the school about the years 1725-6. *Life*, i. 50. According to a writer in *Notes and Queries*, 5th S. i. 249, Hickman—whose Christian name was Gregory—was by his mother's side connected with Johnson. See *post*, Letter of July 8, 1771, for Johnson's desire to revisit Stourbridge and 'recall the images of sixteen.'

my dislike of it, yet it proves, upon reflection, so barren, that to attempt to write upon it, is to undertake to build without materials. As I am yet unemployed, I hope you will, if any thing should offer, remember and recommend,

Sir,

Your humble servant,

SAM: JOHNSON.

2.

To ——.

Lichfield, July 27, 1732. Malone states that he had seen a letter of Johnson's to a friend dated as above, in which he says that 'he had recently left Sir Wolstan Dixey's house. He then had hopes of succeeding either as master or usher in the school of Ashbourne.' Boswell's *Johnson*, ed. 1824, i. 53, *n.* 2.

For Johnson's miserable life at this Leicestershire baronet's house, see *Life*, i. 84.

3.

TO EDWARD CAVE.

[Birmingham], November 25, 1734. Published in the *Life*, i. 91.

This Letter was sold by Messrs. Christie and Co. on June 5, 1888, for £3 3s.

4.

TO EDWARD CAVE.

Greenwich, July 12, 1737. Published in the *Life*, i. 107.

This Letter was sold by Messrs. Christie and Co. on June 5, 1888, for £4 15s.

5.

TO EDWARD CAVE.

Castle Street, Wednesday Morning, —, [1738]. Published in the *Life*, i. 120.

6.

TO EDWARD CAVE.

6 Castle Street, Monday, —, [1738]. Published in the *Life*, i. 121.

This Letter was sold by Messrs. Christie and Co. on June 5, 1888, for £4 15s.

To

7.

To EDWARD CAVE.

[London, 1738]. Published in the *Life*, i. 122.

This Letter was sold by Messrs. Christie and Co. on June 5, 1888, for £4 10s.

8.

To EDWARD CAVE.

[London, 1738]. Published in the *Life*, i. 123.

9.

To EDWARD CAVE.

[London], Wednesday, —, [1738]. Published in the *Life*, i. 136.

10.

To EDWARD CAVE.

[London, 1738]. Published in the *Life*, i. 137.

This Letter was sold by Messrs. Christie and Co. on June 5, 1888, for £46. This extraordinary price was due to one word only. Johnson had signed himself—'Your's *impransus*.' 'It is remarkable,' writes Boswell, 'that this letter concludes with a fair confession that he had not a dinner.'

11.

To EDWARD CAVE.

[London, 1738]. First published in the *Life*, i. 138.

12.

To JOHNSON's WIFE [1].

DEAREST TETTY [2],

After hearing that you are in so much danger, as I apprehend from a hurt on a tendon, I shall be very uneasy

---

[1] From the original in the possession of Mr. William R. Smith of Greatham Moor, West Liss, Hants.

This Letter was probably written during Johnson's visit to Staffordshire and Derbyshire recorded in the *Life*, i. 82. In August or September of 1739 he had, it seems, gone to Appleby in Leicestershire, as a candidate for the mastership of the school (*ib.* p. 132). His visit was prolonged for some months.

[2] 'Johnson used to name Mrs. Johnson by the familiar appellation of *Tetty* or *Tetsey*, which, like *Betty* or *Betsey*, is provincially used as a contraction for *Elizabeth*, her Christian name.' *Ib.* i. 98.

till

till I know that you are recovered, and beg that you will omit
nothing that can contribute to it, nor deny yourself any thing
that may make confinement less melancholy[1]. You have
already suffered more than I can bear to reflect upon, and
I hope more than either of us shall suffer again. One part
at least I have often flatterd myself we shall avoid for the
future, our troubles will surely never separate us more. If
M [   ][2] does not easily succeed in his endeavours, let
him not [   ] to call in another Surgeon to consult with
him, Y [   ] have two or three visits from Ranby[3] or
Shipton, who is [   ] to be the best, for a guinea, which you
need not fear to part with on so pressing an occasion, for I can
send you twenty pouns[4] more on Monday, which I have received
this night ; I beg therefore that you will more regard my
happiness, than to expose yourself to any hazards. I still
promise myself many happy years from your tenderness and
affection, which I sometimes hope our misfortunes have not
yet deprived me of. David[5] wrote to me this day on the affair
of Irene, who is at last become a kind of Favourite among the

---

[1] Mrs. Desmoulins told Boswell
that 'Mrs. Johnson indulged herself
in country air and nice living at an
unsuitable expense, while her husband
was drudging in the smoke of London.' *Life*, i. 238.

[2] The original is torn.

[3] John Ranby, principal serjeant
surgeon to George II. Horace Walpole, writing on June 29, 1743, about
the French at the battle of Dettingen,
says : 'I fancy their soldiery behaved
ill, by the gallantry of their officers ;
for Ranby, the King's private surgeon,
writes that he alone has 150 officers
of distinction desperately wounded
under his care.' *Letters*, i. 255.
Ranby was surgeon also to Sir
Robert Walpole. *Ib.* p. 332.

[4] I am not quite sure of this word.
It looks as if Johnson had written *puns*
at first, and then inserted *o*, forgetting *d*.

[5] 'David,' no doubt, is David

Garrick. It was not till October 19,
1741, that he stirred up the London
world by his first appearance at
Goodman's Fields. Nevertheless, at
the date of Johnson's letter he was
intimate with the actors. He was
just dissolving partnership as a wine-
merchant with his eldest brother
Peter. 'Foote used to say, he remembered Garrick living in Durham
Yard, with three quarts of vinegar in
the cellar, calling himself a wine-
merchant. It is certain, however,'
adds Murphy, 'that he served all the
houses in the neighbourhood of the
two play-houses, and at those places
was a member of different clubs with
the actors of the time.' Murphy's
Garrick, pp. 11–16. Chetwood in
his *History of the Stage*, p. 158,
says that 'Garrick's facetious good-
humour gained him entrance behind
the scenes two or three years before
he commenced actor.'

Players,

Players, Mr. Fletewood promises to give a promise in writing that it shall be the first next season, if it cannot be introduced now, and Chetwood the Prompter is desirous of bargaining for the copy, and offers fifty Guineas for the right of printing after it shall be played [1]. I hope it will at length reward me for my perplexities.

Of the time which I have spent from thee, and of my dear Lucy[2] and other affairs, my heart will be at ease on Monday to give Thee a particular account, especially if a Letter should inform me that thy[3] leg is better, for I hope you do not think so unkindly of me as to imagine that I can be at rest while I believe my dear Tetty in pain.

Be assured, my dear Girl[4], that I have seen nobody in these rambles upon which I have been forced, that has not contribute [*sic*] to confirm my esteem and affection for thee, though that esteem and affection only contributed to encrease my unhappiness when I reflected that the most amiable woman in the

---

[1] 'Mr. Peter Garrick told me,' writes Boswell, 'that Johnson and he went together to the Fountain tavern, and read *Irene* over, and that he afterwards solicited Mr. Fleetwood, the patentee of Drury Lane Theatre, to have it acted at his house ; but Mr. Fleetwood would not accept it, probably because it was not patronised by some man of high rank ; and it was not acted till 1749, when his friend, David Garrick, was manager of that theatre.' *Life*, i. 111. For an account of Fleetwood, see Davies's *Life of Garrick*, i. 66. William Rufus Chetwood published in 1749, *A General History of the Stage*; on the title-page he describes himself as having been twenty years prompter at Drury Lane. He mentions (p. 46) that Voltaire, during his residence in England, came frequently to the theatre. 'I furnished him every evening with the play of the night, which he took with him into the *Orchestre*, his accustomed seat.'

Johnson, in September, 1741, tried to dispose of the copyright of his play by the help of his friend, Edward Cave, who wrote :—'I have put Mr. Johnson's play into Mr. Gray's [a bookseller] hands, in order to sell it to him, if he is inclined to buy it. . . He [Johnson] and I are very unfit to deal with theatrical persons. Fleetwood was to have acted it last season, but Johnson's diffidence or [there is a blank in the original] prevented it.' *Life*, i. 153. In the end he did better than he had hoped, for Dodsley gave him £100 for the copyright, while he made £195 by the representation. *Ib.* p. 198.

[2] Mrs. Johnson's daughter by her first husband. She was living either ' with her relations in the country,' or else with Johnson's mother. *Ib.* i. 110.

[3] He had at first written *your*.

[4] As Mrs. Johnson was born on Feb. 4, 1688-9, she was only four days short of fifty-one.

world

world was exposed by my means to miseries which I could not relieve.

I am

My charming Love

Yours

SAM: JOHNSON.

Jan. 31st, 1739-40[1].

Lucy always sends her Duty and my Mother her Service.

To Mrs. Johnson at Mrs. Crow's in Castle Street near Cavendish Square, London[2].

13.

TO LEWIS PAUL[3].

St. John's Gate, January 31st, 1740-41.

SIR,

Dr. James presses me with great warmth to remind you of your promise, that you would exert your interest with Mr. Warren to bring their affairs to a speedy conclusion ; this you

---

[1] 'The new style was adopted in England by 24 Geo. II (1751), which enacted,(1) That the year 1752 should begin on January 1 instead of March 25, which was then the *legal* commencement. (2) That the 3rd day of September, 1752, should be called the 14th. Accordingly the [*legal*] year 1751 had no January, February, nor March up to the 24th inclusive, and September wanted eleven complete days.' *Penny Cyclo.*, first ed. xxiii. 178. Johnson recorded in his Diary:— ' Jan. 1, 1753, N.S. which I shall use for the future.' Jan. 1 had been always popularly kept as the first day of the year. Thus Swift wrote to Stella on Jan. 1, 1711-12 :—'Now I wish my dearest little MD many happy new years.' Swift's *Works*, ed. 1803, xxii. 45.

[2] Johnson had been lodging in 6 Castle Street since the spring of 1738. *Life*, i. 121. It is now called Castle Street East.

[3] First published in Croker's *Boswell*, p. 43.

This Letter was sold by Messrs. Sotheby and Co. on May 10, 1875, for £5 7s. 6d.

In a paper by the late Robert Cole, F.S.A., read before the British Association at Leeds in September, 1858, quoted in Gilbert French's *Life of Samuel Crompton*, 2nd ed. p. 244, an interesting account is given of Lewis Paul. Baines, in his *History of the Cotton Manufacture*, ed. 1835, p. 119, had stated that 'Arkwright was generally believed to have invented the machine for spinning cotton and wool by rollers, but that the process had previously been described in the specification of the machine invented by John Wyatt.' Mr. Cole proves that 'to Paul alone must be awarded the honour of the invention.' He was the son of a Dr. Paul, and the ward of the third Earl of Shaftesbury. Between 1729 and 1738 he invented a machine for pinking crapes, &c. A daughter of Johnson's godfather, Dr. Swinfen, (afterwards Mrs. Desmoulins) learnt

know,

know, Sir, I have some right to insist upon, as Mr. Cave[1] was, in some degree, diverted from attending to the arbitration by my assiduity in expediting the agreement between you; but I do not imagine many arguments necessary to prevail upon Mr. Warren to do what seems to be no less desired by him than the Doctor. If he entertains any suspicion that I shall endeavour to enforce the Doctor's arguments, I am willing, and more than barely willing, to forbear all mention of the question. He that desires only to do right, can oblige nobody by acting, and must offend every man that expects favours. It is perhaps for this reason that Mr. Cave seems very much inclined to resign the office of umpire; and since I know not whom to propose in his place equally qualified and disinterested, and am yet desired to propose somebody, I believe the most eligible method of determining this vexatious affair will be, that each party should draw up in a narrow compass his own state of the case, and his demand upon the other; and each abate somewhat, of which himself or his friends may think due to him by the laws of rigid justice. This will seem a tedious method, but will, I hope, be shortened by the desire, so often expressed on each side, of a speedy determination. If either party can make use of me in

the art as his pupil. His first patent for spinning is dated June 24, 1738, and was for fourteen years. To meet the expenses he borrowed money from Warren, the Birmingham bookseller; £200 from Dr. Swinfen's daughter, and various sums from Dr. James, the inventor of the powder. He granted licenses to use his spindles; thus in April, 1740, he granted a license to Warren for 50 spindles, in consideration of the debt owing to him amounting to £1000; and to Cave a license for 250 spindles in consideration of a large sum. Dr. James wrote to Warren on July 17, 1740:—'Yesterday we went to see Mr. Paul's machine, which gave us entire satisfaction. I am certain that if he could begin with £10,000 he must, or at least might, get more money in twenty years than the City of London is worth.' Paul, who was desirous of getting the machinery used in the Foundling Hospital, addressed to the President, the Duke of Bedford, a letter, the draft of which is in Johnson's handwriting[a]. In the course of twenty years or so his machine, he said, had gained him, as patentee, above £20,000. He made considerable improvements in it, and in 1758 obtained a new patent. He died the following year.

[1] Edward Cave was the printer of St. John's Gate, Clerkenwell, the proprietor of the *Gentleman's Magazine*. *Life*, i. 111.

[a] See Appendix A.

this

this transaction, in which there is no opportunity for malevo-
lence or prejudice to exert themselves, I shall be well satisfied
with the employment.

Mr. Cave, who knows to whom I am writing, desires me to
mention his interest, of which I need not remind you that it is
complicated with yours ; and therefore cannot be neglected by
you without opposition to motives, far stronger than the per-
suasions of,

Sir,

Your humble servant,

SAM: JOHNSON.

14.

TO LEWIS PAUL [1].

At the Black Boy, over against Durham Yard, Strand [2],
March 31st, 1741.

SIR,

The hurry of removing and some other hindrances, have
kept me from writing to you since you left us, nor should I
have allowed myself the pleasure of doing it now, but that
the Doctor [3] has pressed me to offer you a proposal, which I

---

[1] First published in Croker's *Boswell*, p. 44. This Letter was sold by
Messrs. Sotheby and Co. on May 10,
1875, for £6.

[2] On Durham Yard about the
year 1772 the Adelphi was erected
by the Scotch architects, the brothers
Adam. *Life*, ii. 325, *n*. 3. Johnson
twice lodged in the Strand. *Ib.* iii.
405, *n*. 6.

[3] Dr. James, the inventor of the
famous powder. His 'skill in physic'
Johnson celebrated in the *Lives of
the Poets. Life*, i. 81. They had
been schoolfellows, and saw a good
deal of each other in London. *Ib.*iii.4.

Thomas Warren was the Birmingham bookseller in whose house
Johnson lived for some months in
the year 1733, and who in 1735
published his translation of Lobo's
Voyage to Abyssinia. Ib. i. 85-7.
In 1743 Warren became bankrupt,

as is shown by an advertisement in
Aris's Birmingham Gazette of Feb.
21, 1743, offering for sale by his
assignees a license for working fifty
of Paul's spindles. Two years afterwards a second attempt was made to
sell. (See the *Gazette* of April 29,
1745.) *The Life of Crompton*, 2nd
ed. p. 293. See *post*, Letter of April 15,
1755, where Johnson writes to
Hector :—'What news of poor Warren ? I have not lost all my kindness
for him.' 'Dr. James and Warren
appear to have contracted, James to
supply pills and vulnerary balsam,
and Warren to publish in numbers
The Rational Farmer, with an *Her-
bal*; and also the *American Traveller*,
of which book Dr. James would
seem to have been the author.'
Messrs. Puttick and Simpson's *Auction Catalogue* for July 29, 1867 ;
Lot 708 : 'Paul Papers.'

know

know not why he does not rather make himself; but his request, whatever be the reason of it, is too small to be denied.
He proposes,—1. To pay you immediately, or give you satisfactory security for the speedy payment of £100. 2. To exchange general releases with Mr. Warren. These proposals he
makes upon the conditions formerly offered, that the bargain
for spindles shall be vacated. The securities for Mr. Warren's
debts released, and the debt of £65 remitted, with the addition of this new article, that Mr. Warren shall give him the
books bought for the carrying on of their joint undertaking.
What difference this new demand may make, I cannot tell,
nor do I intend to be understood in these proposals to express any of my own sentiments, but merely to write after a
dictation. I believe I have expressed the Doctor's meaning, but being disappointed of an interview with him, cannot
shew him this, and he generally hints his intentions somewhat
obscurely.

He is very impatient for an answer, and desires me to im-
portune you for one by the return of the post. I am not willing,
in this affair, to request anything on my own account ; for you
know already, that an agreement can only be made by a communication of your thoughts, and a speedy agreement only by
an expeditious communication.

I hope to write soon on some more agreeable subject ; for
though, perhaps, a man cannot easily find more pleasing employment than of reconciling variances, he may certainly amuse
himself better by any other business, than of interposing in con-
troversies which grow every day more distant from accommodation, which has been hitherto my fate ; but I hope my
endeavours will be, hereafter, more successful.

I am, Sir,

Yours, &c.,

SAM: JOHNSON.

To Mr. Lewis Paul. In Birmingham.

15.

TO EDWARD CAVE.

[London, 1742.] Published in the *Life*, i. 155.

To

16.

To Edward Cave.

[London, 1742.]   Published in the *Life*, i. 156.

17.

To the Reverend Dr. Taylor [1].

DEAR SIR,

The Brevity of your last Letter gives me expectation of a longer, and I hope you will not disappoint me, for I am always pleased to hear of your proceedings.   I cannot but somewhat wonder that Seward [2] should give his Living for the prospects or advantages which you can offer him, and should be glad to know your treaty more particularly.   I think it not improper to mention that there is a slight report of an intention to make Lord Chesterfield Lieutenant [3], of which, if I hear more, I will inform you farther.

---

[1] Published in *Notes and Queries*, 6th S. v. 303, by Professor John E. B. Mayor, with the following note by Mr. M. M. Holloway :—'These MSS. were purchased by Sir John Simeon, Bart., in 1861, from a descendant of the Pierpoint family in Devonshire ; three only appear to have been known to Boswell [*Life*, i. 238 ; iv. 228, 270], and about twelve have been privately printed for the Philobiblon Society by Sir John Simeon, from whom I bought the collection, and sold this portion to the Lord Overstone.'   In the reprints in the Philobiblon Society (vol. vi) I have discovered blunders, and therefore I feel the more grateful to Professor Mayor for the trouble he has taken to secure an accurate reprint.   I have been fortunate enough to obtain copies of other letters of the same series ; but there are many which I have not seen. For Dr. Taylor see *Life*, ii. 473.

[2] The Rev. Thomas Seward, Rector of Eyam, Derbyshire, and of Kingsley, near Cheadle in Stafford-

shire, and Canon Residentiary of Lichfield.   Boswell describes him as 'a genteel well-bred dignified clergyman, who had travelled with Lord Charles Fitzroy, who died when abroad.' *Life*, ii. 467.   According to Horace Walpole, when Lord Charles fell ill, Seward, thinking that his life was saved by the treatment used, 'began a complimentary Ode to his physician ; but was called down before it was finished on his pupil's relapse, who did die ; however the bard was too much pleased with the *début* of his poem to throw it away, and so finished it.' *Letters*, viii. 415.   He was the father of 'the celebrated' Anna Seward (*Life*, ii. 467), an affected, tiresome, spiteful and mendacious creature, who wrote bad verses, and disgraced Walter Scott by being one of his correspondents.   Nay, even he went so far as to write a preface to what is called her Poetical Works.

I have not ascertained the nature of Seward's 'treaty' with Taylor.

[3] Sir Robert Walpole's Ministry

I propose

I propose to get *Charles of Sweden*[1] ready for this winter, and shall therefore, as I imagine, be much engaged for some months with the Dramatic Writers, into whom I have scarcely looked for many years[2]. Keep *Irene* close, you may send it back at your leisure.

You have never let me know what you do about Mr. Car's affair or what the official has decided. Eld[3] is only neglected, not forgotten.

---

had come to an end in February of this year. On March 6, Lord Chesterfield wrote to Dr. Chenevix:— 'The public has already assigned me different employments, and among others that which you mention ; but I have been offered none, I have asked for none, and I will accept of none till I see a little clearer into matters than I do at present. I have opposed measures not men.' Chesterfield's *Misc. Works*, iv. 226. The employment mentioned was the Lord-Lieutenancy of Ireland. *Ib.* i. 195. He did not receive the appointment till 1745. *Ib.* p. 254. The phrase 'measures not men' is earlier by 23 years than any instance I have seen quoted. Mr. E. J. Payne, in his note on 'the cant of *Not men but measures*' in Burke's *Present Discontents* (1770), quotes Dr. John Brown's *Thoughts on Civil Liberty* (1765), p. 124, and Goldsmith's *Good-Natured Man* (1768), Act ii, where Lofty says:—'Measures, not men, have always been my mark.' Payne's *Burke*, i. 274.

[1] This no doubt was a play. The two and thirty lines in *The Vanity of Human Wishes* in which 'Swedish Charles' is drawn, have lived till now, and are likely to live for many an age yet. The play, had it been written, would be as much forgotten as *Irene*.

[2] In his edition of *Shakespeare* (published in 1765), vol. vi. 159, he says:—'I was many years ago so shocked by Cordelia's death, that I know not whether I ever endured to read again the last scenes of the play till I undertook to revise them as an editor.' According to a writer in the *Gentleman's Magazine*, 1843, i. 482, Steevens says:—'Dr. Johnson once assured me that when he wrote his *Irene* he had never read *Othello*; but meeting with it soon afterwards, was surprised to find that he gave in one of his characters a speech very strongly resembling that in which Cassio describes the effects produced by Desdemona's beauty on such inanimate objects as the *guttered rocks and congregated sands* [Act ii. sc. 1. l. 69]. The Doctor added that on making the discovery, for fear of imputed plagiarism he struck out the accidental coincidence from his own tragedy.' That Johnson, who was now but thirty-two years old, should for many years have scarcely looked into the dramatic writers, is a clear proof that his friend Gilbert Walmsley was wrong in hoping that he would 'turn out a fine tragedy-writer.'

[3] Eld perhaps was the man mentioned in the following passage in the *Life*, iii. 326 :—'BOSWELL. "I drank chocolate, Sir, this morning with Mr. Eld ; and, to my no small surprise, found him to be a *Staffordshire Whig*, a being which I did not believe had existed." JOHNSON. "Sir, there are rascals in all countries." BOSWELL. "Eld said, a Tory was a creature generated between a non-

[If

[If the time of the Duke's government should be near ex-
piration, you must cling close and redouble your importunities,
though if any confidence can be placed in his Veracity, he may
be expected to serve you more effectually when he is only a
Courtier, than while he has so much power in another Kingdom[1].]

I am well informed that a few days ago Cardinal Fleury sent
to an eminent Banker for Money, and receiving such a reply as
the present low state of France naturally produces, sent a party
of the Guards to examine his Books and search his House, such
is the felicity of absolute Governments, but they found the
Banker no better provided than he had represented himself,
and therefore broke part of his furniture and returned[2].

It is reported that the peace between Prussia[3] and Hungary
was produced wholly by the address of Carteret, who having
procured a copy of Broglio's orders at the very time that they
were despatched, and finding them to contain instructions very
inconsistent with a sincere alliance, sent them immediately to
the King of Prussia, who did not much regard them, till he
found that he was in persuance [*sic*] of them exposed without

---

juring parson and one's grandmother."
JOHNSON. "And I have always
said, the first Whig was the Devil."

[1] This passage is erased in the
original. The 'Duke' was no doubt
the third Duke of Devonshire, who
was Lord-Lieutenant of Ireland from
1737 to 1744. Burke's *Peerage*, ed.
1864, p. 335. 'Taylor had a considerable political interest in the
county of Derby, which he employed
to support the Devonshire family;
for, though the schoolfellow and
friend of Johnson, he was a Whig.'
Life, ii. 474. It is likely that Taylor
hoped to receive from the Duke one
of the valuable Irish deaneries or
bishoprics which were so commonly
given to Englishmen. Confidence
could be placed in his Grace's veracity,
for it was this Duke whom Johnson
commended for a 'dogged veracity.'
Life, iii. 378.
For Taylor's greed of preferments

see *post*, Letters of May 16, 1776, and
July 8, 1782.

[2] Voltaire describes Cardinal Fleury
as a minister, 'ne comprenant abso-
lument rien à une affaire de finance.'
Œuvres de Voltaire, ed. 1819-25.
xix. 38. A writer in the *Gentleman's
Magazine* for March, 1742, p. 165,
speaking of the oppressive taxation
in France says:—'The people are
everywhere ripe for rebellion; the
Ministry have demanded a loan of
ten millions of livres of the financiers,
to be paid the first of July.'

[3] In *Notes and Queries* this is
printed 'Russia,' but Johnson certainly meant, and most probably
wrote, *Prussia*. Horace Walpole
wrote four days later:—'We were
surprised last Tuesday [the 8th] with
the great good news of the peace
between the Queen [Maria Theresa]
and the King of Prussia.' Walpole's
Letters, i. 175.

assistance

assistance to the hazard of the late battle, in which it is generally believed that he lost more than twice as many as the Austrians. He would then trust the French no longer[1]. You see that I am determined to write a letter, for I never was authour of so much political Intelligence before.

I am, if the relief of uneasiness can produce obligations, more obliged to you, for what I imagine you have now sent Miss[2], than for all that you have hitherto done for me.

Thurloe's papers which cost here £8 9s. 6d.[3], are intended to be reprinted in Ireland at four guineas. Methinks you should send orders to Faulkener[4] to subscribe.

I am, Dear Sir,

Yours very affectionate, &c.,

SAM: JOHNSON.

Have you begun to write out your Letters?

June 10, 1742[5].

To the Reverend Dr. Taylor
at Market Bosworth, Leicestershire[6].

[1] In the *Gentleman's Magazine* for July, 1742, p. 389, much the same account is given, though Carteret's name is not mentioned. According to Carlyle the King of Prussia learnt of the orders given to Broglio from one of his prisoners, an Austrian general who had been mortally wounded. This man had seen a letter from Fleury to the Queen of Hungary, and got the King a sight of it. *History of Friedrich II*, ed. 1862, iii. 580. The 'late battle' was that of Chotusitz or Czaslau, in which Frederick, though he gained the victory, lost in killed 1905, to 1052 on the side of the Austrians. *Ib.* p. 574. The peace was signed at Breslau on June 11. The news of it had reached London on the 8th; but in England the dates still followed the Old Style.

[2] 'Miss,' no doubt, was Johnson's step-daughter, Lucy Porter. See *post*, p. 18.

[3] In the Register of Books for May, 1742, in the *Gentleman's Magazine*, p. 280, I find :—' *A Collection of the State Papers of John Thurloe, Esq., Secretary to Oliver Cromwell, &c.*, price £8 14s. in sheets. Woodward and Davis.'

[4] George Faulkner, 'the prince of Dublin printers,' as Swift called him (Swift's *Works*, ed. 1803, xviii. 288); the associate and correspondent of Lord Chesterfield (Chesterfield's *Misc. Works*, iv. 291). Boswell describes him as ' the famous George Faulkner.' *Life*, v. 44. Richardson charged him with joining with other Dublin booksellers in pirating *Sir Charles Grandison*. *Sir Charles Grandison*, 2nd ed. vi. 412.

[5] Horace Walpole, writing on the same day, thus dates his letter :— ' June 10, the Pretender's birthday, which, by the way, I believe he did not expect to keep at Rome this year, 1742.' *Letters*, i. 173.

[6] 'Taylor went to Christ Church with a view to the study of the law,

TO

18.

To the Reverend Dr. Birch.

[London], September 29, 1743. Published in the *Life*, i. 160.

19.

To John Levett.

December 1, 1743. Published in the *Life*, i. 160.

20.

To John Levett[1].

SIR.

I am obliged to trouble you upon an affair which I have hardly time to explain, but in which I must beg that you will assist as a few words will enable you to understand it better than I do; and the Humanity and Generosity which appeared in your last letter give me no reason to doubt of your Compliance with my Request.

When I married Mrs. Johnson who was her first husband's executrix, we by the advice of his chief Creditor made a resignation (I suppose legal) of all his affairs to Mr. Perks an Attorney of Birmingham. Soon afterwards Mr. Perks died, as was supposed, without any effects, and therefore We thought no more of the affair, but were lately accidentally informed that a Composition is offered, and then I wrote to Birmingham for

---

but entering into holy orders was presented to the valuable Rectory of Market Bosworth in 1740, on the death of Mr. Beaumont Dixie. He was supposed to have got it by purchase. Gisborne, the banker of Derby, suspecting somewhat from the sums Taylor drew from him, marked some of the pieces; which presently came back, in part of the same sum, from the worthy Patron, who had reason afterwards for saying "that a broken attorney made a notable parson." He found that he had met with his match.' Nichols's

Lit. Anec. ix. 58.

[1] From the original, in the possession of the Rev. F. R. Jefferson, Noman's Heath Vicarage, Tamworth.

Boswell mentions Mr. Levett among Johnson's early friends belonging to the best families in Lichfield. *Life*, i. 81. In 1761 Mr. John Levett was returned for Lichfield, but on petition was declared to be not duly elected. *Parl. Hist.* xv. 1088. Johnson, in a letter dated a month earlier, had apologised to Mr. Levett for his delay in paying the interest of a mortgage. *Life*, i. 160.

Directions

Directions how to act, and received yesterday a Letter by which I am informed that the accounts are to be irrevocably settled on Thursday. Having not the papers at London, there is great danger, as I apprehend, that they cannot arrive soon enough. I have however sent Miss Porter directions to open a Cabinet, and bring it to you, and beg that you will find a Messenger to make the Demand in form[1].

Be pleased to inform Me where I may see you when you come to town, for not to have the satisfaction of waiting upon one for whom, on account of a long series of kindness to my Father and myself, I have so much Respect will be a great and uneasy Disappointment to,

Sir,

Your most humble Servant,

SAM: JOHNSON.

I had forgot to inform you that your Messenger may apply to Mr. Willm Ward, Mercer in Birm. for directions where to go.

Jan. 3, 1743–4.

To Mr. Levett in Lichfield.

21.

TO [? JOHN LEVETT[2].]

SIR,

I have been hinderd from writing to you by an imagination that it was necessary to write more than I had time for,

---

[1] Light is thrown on this letter by the following passage in a paper by Mr. Samuel Timmins, published in the *Transactions of the Archaeological Section of the Birmingham and Midland Institute,* 1876 :—' My friend, Mr. Joseph Hill, says, A copy of an old deed which has recently come into my hands, shews that a hundred pounds of Mrs. Johnson's fortune was left in the hands of a Birmingham attorney named Thomas Perks, who died insolvent ; and in 1745, a bulky deed gave his creditors 7s. 4d. in the pound. Among the creditors for £100 were " Samuel Johnson, gent., and Elizabeth his wife, executors of the last will and testament of Harry Porter, late of Birmingham aforesaid, woollen draper, deceased." Johnson and his wife were almost the only creditors who did not sign the deed, their seals being left void. It is doubtful, therefore, whether they ever obtained the amount of the composition, £36 13s. 4d.' See also the *Life,* i. 95, *n.* 3.

[2] From the original, in the possession of Mr. J. H. Hodson of Lichfield.

It was most likely written to Mr. Levett of that town, to whom Johnson, as is shown by his Letter of

but

but recollecting that business may be despatched much more expeditiously by conversation, I beg to be informed when I can wait on you with most convenience to yourself. I believe I shall find means of accommodating the affair so as to give you valuable satisfaction. You forgot to send me word what interest is due, which I mention that you may examine, for though Mr. Aston[1] has a receipt for interest which I got him to pay to your Father, I cannot conveniently wait on him about it.

I am, Sir,

Your most humble servant,

SAM: JOHNSON.

Golden Anchor, Holborn[2]. Sat. Morning.

22.

To [? JOHN LEVETT[3].] No date.

SIR,

I am very ill, and unable to wait on you or meet with you. I have been disappointed by two to whom I applied, and either of whom might have done it without inconvenience. The gentleman whom I have desired to come with this has (?) offered it on terms which may make a little longer delay, but if you have any one with whom you can have the things necessary it may now be done.

I am, Sir,

Your humble friend,

SAM: JOHNSON.

I had sent to you but I had forgot your lodging which you have not mentioned in your notes.

23.

To MR. 'URBAN.'

August, 1744. Published in the *Life*, ii. 164.

Dec. 1, 1743 (*Life*, i. 161), owed the interest of a mortgage.

[1] Mr. Aston probably belonged to the family of Sir Thomas Aston. *Life*, i. 83. He is mentioned again, *post*, p. 30.

[2] Johnson twice lodged in Holborn between the years 1741 and 1749. *Life*, iii. 405, *n*. 6.

[3] From the original, in the possession of Mr. J. H. Hodson of Lichfield.

To

24.

To James Elphinston [1].

SIR,

I have for a long time intended to answer the Letter which you were pleased to send me, and know not why I have delayed

[1] First published in *Memoirs of the Life and Writings of Dr. Johnson*, 1785, p. 166.

James Elphinston most likely became known to Johnson through William Strahan, the printer, who had married his sister. The year after the date of this letter 'he suggested and took the charge of an edition of the *Rambler* at Edinburgh.' *Life*, i. 210. About the year 1753 he opened a school at Brompton; moving later on to Kensington, where Boswell and Johnson one day dined with him (*ib.* ii. 226), in 'a noble mansion opposite to the King's gardens, with an elegant ball-room with handsome bow-windows at the top of the eastern division of the house.' Nichols's *Lit. Anec.* iii. 32. Jeremy Bentham describes it as 'a spacious mansion,' having dined there 'on a summer's day' with Burkarti, the Resident from the Free City of Hamburgh, who occupied in it 'a comfortable and pleasant apartment.' Bentham's *Works*, x. 58. In the fourth edition of the *Rambler*, published in 1756, the reader is informed in a foot-note on the first page, that 'Mr. Elphinston, to whom the author of these papers is indebted for many elegant translations of the mottos which are inserted from the Edinburgh edition, now keeps an academy for young gentlemen at Brompton, near Kensington.' Johnson, who by his own failure knew the difficulty of starting an 'academy,' was willing, it seems, in this curious way, to give his friend, the young Scotchman, a helping hand. He thus described

him twenty years later :—'His inner part is good, but his outer part is mighty awkward. . . . I would not put a boy to him, whom I intended for a man of learning. But for the sons of citizens who are to learn a little, get good morals, and then go to trade, he may do very well.' *Life*, ii. 171. He had been abroad in his youth with Carte, the Jacobite historian, who believed in the royal touch, and he was himself a Nonjuror. Johnson in 1754 had recommended his school for the son of his friend, Fitzherbert, but was told that 'the *Scotchman* and *Non-juror* would be insuperable objections.' *An Account of the Life of Dr. Johnson*, 1805, p. 66.

In 1778 Elphinston published that translation of *Martial* which provoked Burns's epigram :—

'O thou whom Poetry abhors,
    Whom Prose has turned out of
        doors,
    Heard'st thou that groan—proceed no further,
    'Twas laurell'd Martial roaring
        murder.'

'His brother-in-law Strahan sent him a subscription of fifty pounds, and said he would send him fifty more, if he would not publish.' *Life*, iii. 258. Of his skill as a translator the following may be taken as a sample :—

'To Sabidius.

'I love thee not, nor can the cause
    display;
    I love thee not, poor Sab: I still
        may say.'

it so long; but that I had nothing particular either of enquiry or information to send you; and the same reason might still have the same consequence, but that I find, in my recluse kind of life, that I am not likely to have much more to say at one time than another, and that therefore I may endanger, by an appearance of neglect long continued, the loss of such an Acquaintance as I know not where to supply. I therefore write now to assure you how sensible I am of the kindness you have always expressed to me, and how much I desire the cultivation of that Benevolence which perhaps nothing but the distance between us has hindered from ripening before this time into Friendship. Of myself I have very little to say, and of any body else less; let me, however, be allowed one thing, and that in my own favour; that I am,

Dear Sir,
Your most humble servant,

April 20, 1749.   SAM: JOHNSON.

25.

TO MISS PORTER [1].

Goff Square [2], July 12, 1749.

DEAR MISS,

    I am extremely obliged to you for your letter, which I would have answered last post, but that illness prevented me.

He introduced a new system of orthography, and quarrelled over it with Strahan, who, no doubt, refused, as King's Printer, to follow his brother-in-law in a mode of spelling of which the following is a specimen. It is taken from his 'Deddicacion To' Dhe King' of his *Propriety Ascertained in her Picture*, (two quarto volumes of about 650 pages):— 'Yoor Madjesty haz dained by fixing Inglish Speech in Inglish Orthoggraphy to' secure dhe unfading luster ov Truith, and dhe unfailing succession ov a Horrace, a Boileau, and a Pope.' Strahan nevertheless bequeathed to him an annuity of £100.

He lived till the age of eighty-seven, dying in 1809; to the last he wore the dress which had been in fashion early last century—'the coat with flaps and buttons to the pockets and sleeves, the powdered bag-wig with a high toupee, a cocked hat, shoe-buckles and an amber-headed cane.' Nichols's *Lit. Anec.* iii. 35.

[1] First published in Croker's *Boswell*, p. 62.

[2] In Dodsley's *London and its Environs*, 1761, iii. 53, this place is called Gough's Square, and is described as 'a very small oblong square, with a row on each side of handsome buildings.' In what year

I have

I have been often out of order of late, and have very much neglected my affairs. You have acted very prudently with regard to Levett's affair, which will, I think, not at all embarrass me, for you may promise him, that the mortgage shall be taken up at Michaelmas, or, at least, some time between that and Christmas; and if he requires to have it done sooner, I will endeavour it [1]. I make no doubt, by that time, of either doing it myself, or persuading some of my friends to do it for me.

Please to acquaint him with it, and let me know if he be satisfied. When he once called on me, his name was mistaken, and therefore I did not see him; but, finding the mistake, wrote to him the same day, but never heard more of him, though I entreated him to let me know where to wait on him. You frighted me, you little gipsy, with your black wafer, for I had

Johnson took the house is not known; he resided in it till March 23, 1759. *Life*, iii. 405, *n.* 6. It is likely that the money which he received for *Irene* in February, 1749, enabled him to live in more comfort than hitherto, and that it was then that he moved. It was in this house that he wrote the main part of his Dictionary, his *Ramblers*, *Adventurers*, many of his *Idlers*, and *Rasselas*. It was here that he mourned over the loss, first of his wife and then of his mother. It still stands, with a tablet on it to tell its history. 'It is the first or corner house on the right hand, as you enter through the arched way from the North-west.' *Ib.* i. 188, *n.* 1.

[1] On December 1, 1743, Johnson wrote to Levett to ask his forbearance with respect to the interest due on a mortgage. Money no doubt had been borrowed on the security of the freehold house at Lichfield which had belonged to his father, and in which his mother was still living. Mr. J. H. Hodson of Lichfield has in his interesting collection of autographs the following unaddressed letter of Johnson's step-daughter, referring to the same affair:—

'I shall take it as a particular favour if you will not mention the ejectment, or cause it to be deliver'd to Mrs. Johnson till I have spoke to you again, which I shall be glad to do the first opportunity. She has been very poorly for some time, and is too weak at present to bear the shock of such a thing, and I believe the very knowing of it would almost destroy her. I hope you need not be under any apprehension concerning the Money, as I will do my utmost endeavour to procure it as soon as I can. Your complying with the above request will infinitely oblige

'Your humble Servant,

'LUCY PORTER.

June 7.'

See *post*, Letter of March 7, 1752.

On Johnson's death his house was sold for £235. Hawkins's *Johnson*, p. 599. On October 20, 1887, it was sold for £800 to Mr. G. H. Johnson of Southport. *Daily News*, Oct. 21, 1887. Mr. Johnson with a noble spirit is preserving it as a memorial of its great owner.

forgot

forgot you were in mourning, and was afraid your letter had brought me ill news of my mother, whose death is one of the few calamities on which I think with terror[1]. I long to know how she does, and how you all do. Your poor mamma is come home, but very weak[2]; yet I hope she will grow better, else she shall go into the country. She is now up-stairs, and knows not of my writing.

I am, dear Miss,

Your most humble servant,

SAM: JOHNSON.

26.

To ——[3].

I am very much obliged to you for your commission, which though, I think, not absolutely necessary to me, will be extremely convenient, as it will rescue me from the necessity of soliciting a favour, which, you know, all mankind is apt to rate not according to its real value, but to the exigence of him that asks it. I have all the assurance that human life allows, of being able by the time you mention of setling [*sic*] the affair without any trouble, and shall consider this exemption from the pain of borrowing as a very considerable favour to,

Sir,

Your humble servant,

SAM: JOHNSON.

Will you spend an evening with me? as you mention nothing of my coming to you, I suppose it is not convenient. May I have the pleasure of seeing you? I am almost always at home.

---

[1] Carlyle, who in many ways was like Johnson, writing about his mother not long before her death, said :— 'The thing I have dreaded all my days is perhaps now drawing nigh.' *Correspondence of Emerson and Carlyle*, ed. 1883, ii. 226.

[2] 'Mrs. Johnson, for the sake of country air, had lodgings at Hampstead.' *Life*, i. 192.

[3] From the original in the possession of the Rev. Clement Price, Selby Oak Vicarage, Birmingham. The address and date are torn off. It is possible that this letter was written to Mr. Levett, and refers to the mortgage mentioned in the letter to Miss Porter.

TO

27.

To the Printer of the General Advertiser.

[London, April 4, 1750.]   Published in the *Life*, i. 227.

28.

To the Reverend Mr. Birch.

Gough Square, May 12, 1750.   Published in the *Life*, i. 226.

29.

To James Elphinston.

[London, 1750.]   Published in the *Life*, i. 210.

30.

To James Elphinston.

[London], September 25, 1750.   Published in the *Life*, i. 211.

31.

To Samuel Richardson [1].

DEAR SIR,   March 9, 1750-1.

Though Clarissa wants no help from external splendour, I was glad to see her improved in her appearance [2], but more glad to find that she was now got above all fears of prolixity, and confident enough of success to supply whatever had been hitherto suppressed. I never indeed found a hint of any such defalcation, but I regretted it ; for though the story is long, every letter is short [3].

---

[1] Published in the *Correspondence of Samuel Richardson*, v. 281.

[2] The first edition of *Clarissa* (1748) was in small print, in seven volumes duodecimo. The fourth edition (1751) was in large print, in seven volumes octavo ; each containing a table of contents, while at the end of the last volume is ' a collection of many of the Moral and Instructive Sentiments in this History made by an Ingenious Gentleman and presented to the Editor.'

[3] In the Preface to the first two volumes Richardson says :—' It was resolved to present to the World the Two First Volumes by way of Specimen ; and to be determined with regard to the rest by the Reception those should meet with. If that be favourable, Two others may soon follow ; the whole Collection being ready for the Press : That is to say, If it be not found necessary to abstract or omit some of the Letters, in order to reduce the Bulk of the Whole.' In the Preface to the fourth edition he says :—' It is proper to

I wish

I wish you would add an *index rerum* [1], that when the reader recollects any incident, he may easily find it, which at present he cannot do, unless he knows in which volume it is told; for Clarissa is not a performance to be read with eagerness, and laid aside for ever; but will be occasionally consulted by the busy, the aged, and the studious [2]; and therefore I beg that this edition, by which I suppose posterity is to abide, may want nothing that can facilitate its use.

I am, Sir,

Yours, &c.,

SAM: JOHNSON.

32.

To JOHN NEWBERY [3].

DEAR SIR,

I have just now a demand upon me for more money than I have by me: if you could conveniently help me with two pounds it will be a favour to

Sir,

Your most humble servant,

April 18, 1751.   SAM: JOHNSON.

Endorsed—' 20th April. Received of Mr. Newbery the sum of two guineas for the use of Mr. Johnson, pʳ me.

' THOS. LUCY.'

[1] observe with regard to the *present Edition* that it has been thought fit to restore many Passages, and several Letters which were omitted in the former merely for shortening-sake. These are distinguished by Dots or inverted Full-points. And it is intended to print them separately, for the sake of doing justice to the Purchasers of the former Editions.'

[2] Richardson's last novel, *Sir Charles Grandison*, very likely in consequence of Johnson's request, repeated as it was in his letter of September 26, 1753, was furnished with a copious 'Index, Historical and Characteristical,' as well as with one to the 'Similes and Allusions.' In this latter we find such entries as the following:—'GRANDISON, *Sir Charles*, His look, *To* a sun-beam, v. 332. His friends in the nuptial procession, *To* the Satellites attending a primary planet.'

[3] Lord Macaulay had read *Sir Charles Grandison* so often that 'he thought it probable that he could re-write it from memory.' Trevelyan's *Macaulay*, ed. 1877, i. 133. A curious proof of the popularity of *Clarissa* in France is shown by the fact that *Lovelace* is given in Littré's *Dictionary* as a French word. It is defined as *élégant séducteur.*

[3] This and the next two Letters

To

33

To JOHN NEWBERY.

SIR,

I beg the favour of you to send me by the bearer a guinea, for which I will account to you on some future production.

I am, Sir,

Your humble servant,

SAM: JOHNSON.

July 29, 1751.

Endorsed—' 29th July. Received of Mr. Newbery the sum of one guinea for the use of Mr. Johnson.

' THOS. LUCY.'

The following entry is in Newbery's hand: 'Lent Mr. Johnson, July 30, £1 1.'

---

were first published in Prior's *Life of Goldsmith*, ed. 1837, i. 340.

Goldsmith pleasantly introduces John Newbery in the *Vicar of Wakefield*, ch. xviii, as a traveller who came up to a little ale-house in which the Vicar was detained by illness and by want of money. 'This person was no other than the philanthropic bookseller in St. Paul's Churchyard, who has written so many little books for children : he called himself their friend, but he was the friend of all mankind. He was no sooner alighted, but he was in haste to be gone ; for he was ever on business of the utmost importance, and was at that time actually compiling materials for the history of one Mr. Thomas Trip. I immediately recollected this good-natured man's red pimpled face ; for he had published for me against the Deuterogamists of the age, and from him I borrowed a few pieces to be paid at my return.' According to a writer in the *European Magazine* for August, 1793, p. 92, 'Dr. Goldsmith used to tell many pleasant stories of Newbery, who, he said, was the patron of more distressed

authors than any man of his time.' He is that 'great philosopher Jack Whirler' of *The Idler*, No. 19, 'whose business keeps him in perpetual motion, and whose motion always eludes his business.' Hawkins writes of him as 'a man of a projecting head, a good understanding, and great integrity ; who by a fortunate connection with Dr. James, the physician, and the honest exertions of his own industry became the founder of a family.' Hawkins's *Johnson*, p. 364. He was the vendor of Dr. James's famous powder, in which Goldsmith had such faith that he took it in his last illness, in defiance of his doctors, and probably thereby increased the violence of the attack. Forster's *Goldsmith*, ii. 418. Horace Walpole, who had no less faith in it, thought that 'Goldsmith might have been saved, if he had continued it, but his physician interposed.' *Letters*, vi. 72. Fielding praises it in *Amelia*, Bk. viii. ch. 9, and Cowper felt 'bound to honour it.' Southey's *Cowper*, v. 226. See also *ib.* p. 126. For an interesting account of Newbery and his connection

To

34.

To John Newbery.

DEAR SIR, Aug. 24, 1751.

I beg the favour of you to lend me another guinea, for which I shall be glad of any opportunity to account with you, as soon as any proper thing can be thought on, or which I will repay you in a few weeks.

I am, Sir,

Your most humble servant,

SAM : JOHNSON.

Endorsed—' 24th August. Received of Mr. Newbery the sum of one guinea for the use of Mr. Johnson, pᵣ me,

' THOS. LUCY.'

with Dr. James see *A Bookseller of the Last Century*, by Charles Welsh. London, 1885.

It is likely that the first of the three sums was an advance and not a loan, for Johnson was at this time contributing a *Life of Cheynel* to *The Student*, a Monthly Miscellany published by Newbery. This *Life* appeared in three successive numbers, probably those for May, June and July, 1751. In some of the numbers the name of the month is omitted. In 1758 Johnson was again working for Newbery, who was the proprietor, in whole or in part, of the *Idler*. The advances or the loans began again, as the two following entries show :—

' May 19, 1759.

I promise to pay to Mr. Newbery the sum of forty-two pounds nineteen shillings and ten pence on demand, value received.

£42 19s. 10d. SAM : JOHNSON.'

' March 20, 1760.

I promise to pay to Mr. Newbery

the sum of thirty pounds upon demand.

£30 0s. 0d. SAM : JOHNSON.'

Prior's *Goldsmith*, i. 341.

From April 15, 1758 to April 5, 1760 Johnson wrote his *Idlers* for a weekly newspaper in which Newbery had some part. *Life*, i. 330. According to Hawkins, 'a share in the profits of this paper was Johnson's inducement to write.' Hawkins's *Johnson*, p. 364. When the *Idlers* were collected in volumes they were published by Newbery, one-third of the profits going to him and two-thirds to the author. In an account between the two men of the sale of an edition in two volumes of 1500 copies Newbery took £42 1s. 2d. and Johnson £84 2s. 4d. *Life*, i. 335. It is probable that the money for which the receipt is given in the text was an advance on future profits. See the Introduction to my edition of Johnson's *Essays* in ' The Temple Library,' p. 36.

TO

35.

To William Strahan [1].

Dearest Sir,

Nov. 1, 1751.

The message which you sent me by Mr. Stuart [2] I do not consider as at all your own, but if you were contented to be the deliverer of it to me, you must favour me so far as to return my answer, which I have written down to spare you the unpleasing office of doing it in your own words. You advise me to write, I know with very kind intentions, nor do I intend to treat your counsel with any disregard when I declare that in the present state of the matter 'I shall *not* write'—otherwise than the words following :—

'That my resolution has long been, and is *not* now altered, and is now *less* likely to be altered, that I shall *not* see the Gentlemen Partners [3] till the first volume is in the press, which they may forward or retard by dispensing or not dispensing with the last message.'

[1] From the original in the possession, first, of Mr. Frederick Barker, of 41 Gunterstone Road, West Kensington, W., and subsequently of the late Mr. S. J. Davey, of 47 Great Russell Street, W. C.

William Strahan, who was born in Edinburgh in 1715, at an early age established himself as a printer in London. In 1770 he purchased from Mr. George Eyre a share of the patent for King's Printer; he was a member of Parliament from 1774 to 1783, and he died in 1785. In conjunction either with Millar or Cadell he was the publisher of works of Blackstone, Blair, Gibbon, Hume, Johnson, Robertson, and Adam Smith; and he was the printer of Johnson's Dictionary.

[2] Francis Stuart, or Stewart, was one of the five Scotchmen whom Johnson employed as amanuenses in the work of his *Dictionary. Life,* i. 187. He died early, as is shown by the next letter but one. In 1780 Johnson writing about him said :—'The memory of him is yet fresh in my mind; he was an ingenious and worthy man.' *Ib.* iii. 421. According to a writer in the *Gent. Mag.* for 1799, p. 1171, who had been employed in Strahan's printing works, Stewart in a night ramble in Edinburgh in 1736 with some of his companions 'met with the mob conducting Captain Porteous to be hanged; they were next day examined about it before the Town Council, when, as Stewart used to say, "we were found to be too drunk to have any hand in the business." He gave an accurate account of it in the *Edinburgh Magazine* of that time.' This last statement throws doubt on the whole narrative, for the *Scots Magazine,* the first published at Edinburgh, did not begin till 1739.

[3] 'The Gentlemen Partners' in the *Dictionary* were R. and J. Dodsley, L. Hawes, C. Hitch, J. and P. Knapton, T. and T. Longman, and A. Millar.

Bc

Be pleased to lay this my determination before them this morning, for I shall think of taking my measures accordingly to-morrow evening, only this that I mean no harm, but that my citadel shall not be taken by storm while I can defend it, and that if a blockade is intended, the country is under the command of my batteries, I shall think of laying it under contribution to-morrow Evening [1].

I am, Sir,

Your most obliged, most obedient,

and most humble servant,

SAM: JOHNSON.

To Mr. Strahan.

36.

To ——.

[London], December 10, 1751.

In Messrs. Sotheby and Co.'s Auction Catalogue for May 10, 1875, Lot 83 is 'an autograph Letter of Dr. Johnson, one page quarto, dated December 10, 1751. "I thought it necessary to inform you how it happened that I seemed to give myself so little trouble about my Book, when I gave you so much." He speaks of Lord Orrery's favourable opinion of " our Charlotte's Book [2]," and mentions other matters connected with literary subjects.' It sold for £2 5s.

[1] Johnson was to receive for the *Dictionary* £1575 in all, paying his assistants himself. Boswell says that 'he was often goaded to dispatch, more especially as he had received all the copy-money by different drafts a considerable time before he had finished his task.' *Life*, i. 287. It seems probable that the partners had threatened 'a blockade' by refusing the weekly contribution. To this, Johnson replied that he was the real master of the position ; if he were to throw up the work in the middle the loss which would be incurred would fall on them and be very heavy. By the evening of the next day therefore they must let him have some money, or he would strike work.

[2] 'Our Charlotte' was Mrs. Lennox. She had published in the previous winter a novel under the title of *The Memoirs of Harriet Stuart*. 'One evening at the Club,' writes Hawkins, 'Johnson proposed to us the celebrating the birth of her first literary child, as he called her book, by a whole night spent in festivity. Our supper was elegant, and he had directed that a magnificent hot apple-pie should make a part of it, and this he would have stuck with bay-leaves, because, forsooth, Mrs. Lennox was an authoress, and had written verses ; and further, he had prepared for her a crown of laurel, with which, but not till he had invoked the Muses by some ceremonies of his own invention, he encircled her brows. About five his face shone with meridian splendour, though his drink had been only lemonade.' Hawkins's *Johnson*, p. 286.

In Messrs. Sotheby and Co.'s Auc-

To

37.

To William Strahan [1].

Dear Sir,

What you tell me I am ashamed never to have thought on—I wish I had known it sooner—Send me back the last sheet; and the last copy for correction. If you will promise me henceforward to print a sheet a day, I will promise you to endeavour that you shall have every day a sheet to print, beginning next Tuesday.

I am, Sir,

Your most, &c.

SAM: JOHNSON.

To Mr. Strahan.

38.

To William Strahan [2].

Dear Sir,

I must desire you to add to your other civilities this one, to go to Mr. Millar [3] and represent to him the manner of going on, and inform him that I know not how to manage. I pay three and twenty shillings a week to my assistants, in each instance having much assistance from them, but they tell me they shall

tion Catalogue for November 27, 1889, Lot 102 is a letter of Mrs. Lennox dated November 21, 1751, in which she writes: 'Mr. Johnson has informed me of the generous concern you exprest for the severity of my critics, and your good intentions to rescue my book from their censures, and restore me to Mr. Millar's good opinions.'

[1] From the original in the possession of Mr. Frederick Barker, of 41 Gunterstone Road, West Kensington. First published in my edition of Boswell's *Life of Johnson*, vol. vi. *Addenda*, p. xxv.

In all likelihood Johnson is writing about the *Dictionary*. As the first edition was in folio, a sheet consisted

of four pages. Johnson writing on April 3, 1753, says, 'I began the second vol. of my *Dictionary*, room being left in the first for Preface, Grammar, and History, none of them yet begun.' *Life*, i. 255. As the book was published on April 15, 1755 (*ib.* i. 290, *n.* 1), the printing must have gone on very rapidly, when a start was once made. By *copy* he means his *manuscript for printing*.

[2] This and the next letter are from the original in the possession of Mr. John Waller, of 2 Artesian Road, Westbourne Grove. First published in my edition of Boswell's *Life of Johnson*, vol. vi. *Addenda*, p. xxv.

[3] For Andrew Millar, see *post*, p. 30.

he

be able to pull better in method, as indeed I intend they shall. The point is to get two Guineas[1].

Sir,

Your humble servant,

SAM: JOHNSON.

To Mr. Strahan.

39.

TO WILLIAM STRAHAN.

SIR,

I have often suspected that it is as you say, and have told Mr. Dodsley of it. It proceeds from the haste of the amanuensis to get to the end of his day's work. I have desired the passages to be clipped close, and then perhaps for two or three leaves it is done. But since poor Stuart's[2] time I could never get that part of the work into regularity, and perhaps never shall. I will try to take some more care, but can promise nothing ; when I am told there is a sheet or two I order it away. You will find it sometimes close ; when I make up any myself, which never happens but when I have nobody with me, I generally clip it close, but one cannot always be on the watch.

I am, Sir,

Your most, &c.,

SAM: JOHNSON.

40.

TO — LEVETT, ESQ., in Lichfield[3].

SIR,

I am extremely obliged to you for the long credit and kind forbearance which I have received from you. I have sold a property principally to satisfy you, and in consequence of that

---

[1] The writer in the *Gent. Mag.* quoted *ante*, p. 25, says that after the printing had gone on some time 'the proprietors of the *Dictionary* paid Johnson through Mr. Strahan at the rate of a guinea for every sheet of MS. copy delivered. The copy was written upon quarto post, and in two columns each page. Johnson wrote in his own hand the words and their explanation, and generally two or three words in each column, leaving a space between each for the authorities, which were pasted on as they were collected by the different amanuenses; and in this mode the MS. was so regular that the sheets of MS. which made a sheet of print could be very exactly ascertained.'

[2] See *ante*, p. 25, n. 2.

[3] From the original in the possession of Mr. J. H. Hodson of Lichfield.

sale

sale can now give you a Draught of one hundred pounds upon a Bookseller of credit payable on the first of May and realizable in the meantime [1]. If you have not any evidence of the money paid for me by Mr. Aston I know not how to ascertain it, for though I could make oath to a payment I cannot certainly tell of how much, though I think, of twelve pounds [2]. Would you be pleased to terminate the affair with Mr. J. Sympson [3]? I have not mentioned it to him, because I neither would employ any one you may not desire to be employed, nor oblige you to confess any dislike. I know not indeed that anybody needs to be employed, for I do not doubt your candour.

I am, Sir, with great respect,

Your humble servant,

SAM: JOHNSON.

For any money above one hundred pounds I must beg you to accept my Note for six months.

March 7, 1752.

41.

To the Reverend Dr. Taylor.

[London], March 17, 1752. Mentioned in the *Life*, i. 238.

42.

To the Reverend Dr. Taylor.

March 18, 1752. Published in the *Life*, i. 238.

[1] I have little doubt that the property which Johnson sold was his share, or part of his share in *The Rambler*, the last number of which was published a week after the date of this letter. On April 1 of the previous year he had entered into an agreement with Cave about the sale of the second edition of the first seventy numbers. (Nichols's *Lit. Anec.* viii. 415, where the year 1759 is clearly a misprint for 1751, for it is described as the 24th George II.) That Johnson subsequently sold the whole of his share in the future profits we know from Chalmers. *Biog. Dict.* xix. 58.

This letter darkens the gloom in which we see the *Rambler* bring his paper to its close. His wife was on her death-bed, and now we learn that he was harassed for the payment of a debt which he had incurred for the sake of his mother.

[2] In a letter to Levett dated Dec. 1, 1743, he says: 'I will pay the interest (I think twelve pounds) in two months.' *Life*, i. 160. See *ante*, p. 16, for mention of a receipt which Mr. Aston had.

[3] For Joseph Simpson, one of Johnson's schoolfellows, who became a barrister but 'fell into a dissipated course of life,' see *Life*, iii. 28.

To

43.

To the Reverend Mr. Birch [1].

Sir,

I beg the favour that if you have any catalogue by you such as the Bibl. Thuaneana [2], or any other of value, that you will lend it for a few days to

Sir,

Your most humble servt,

SAM: JOHNSON.

Nov. 4, 1752.

If you leave it out directed, we will call for it.

To the Reverend Mr. Birch.

44.

To Andrew Millar [3].

Sir,   July 11.

You seem to have entirely mistaken Mr. Macbean's errand by objecting want of money—no money was asked—the whole affair is that Mr. Macbean and Mr. Hamilton want to wager as you and I have done, and so lay the money in your hand, you have therefore to put the money into Macbean's hand to be put back into yours. I have no share in the matter but that I lend Macbean the money, that is you lend on my account. You may easily see my end in it, that it will make both

---

[1] From the original in the British Museum :— *Sloane MSS.*, 4310. 300.

[2] The *Catalogus Bibliothecæ Thuanæ* was published in Paris in 1679. The library had belonged to the historian De Thou (Thuanus), whose *Historia sui Temporis* in 138 books Johnson towards the close of his life had thoughts of translating. *Life*, iv. 410. He inspired, it seems, his young friend Windham to undertake the task, who however did not make much progress. *Diary of the Right Hon. W. Windham*, pp. 21, 50. ‘En mourant de Thou laissait une bibliothèque qui est restée célèbre.’ *Nouv. Biog. Gén.* xlv. 259. Johnson mentions the *Thuanian Catalogue* in his

Account of the Harleian Library, *Works*, v. 189.

[3] From the original in the possession of Mr. Alfred Morrison of Fonthill House.

Andrew Millar was ‘a bookseller in the Strand, who took the principal charge of conducting the publication of Johnson's *Dictionary*. When the messenger who carried the last sheet to him returned, Johnson asked him, “Well, what did he say?”—“Sir, (answered the messenger) he said, thank GOD I have done with him.” “I am glad (replied Johnson, with a smile) that he thanks GOD for any thing.”’ *Life*, i. 287. See also *Letters of Hume to Strahan*, p. xxiii.

M—

M— and H— push on the business, which is all that we both
wish.

It is therefore my advice that it be complied with, since, as
you see, there is no expense in it, but remember that I don't
care, and will not have it mentioned as any obligation on me,
but as done for the common interests [1].

When I sent back your books I returned by mistake to you
a *Young upon Opium* [2], which I had from Mrs. Strahan ; please to
let me have it back.

Pray be so kind as to procure me the three following books—

    Law's Serious Call.   8vo. [3]

    Helsham's Philosophy [4].

    Present State of England—last [5].

          I am, Sir, &c.

                SAM: JOHNSON.

To Mr. Millar.

---

[1] Johnson had two Macbeans among his amanuenses, one of whom he befriended in his old age. *Life*, i. 187. Mr. Hamilton was most likely Archibald Hamilton, the printer, 'who had kept his coach (Mrs. Williams said) several years sooner than Mr. Strahan. *Johnson.* "He was in the right. Life is short. The sooner that a man begins to enjoy his wealth the better."' *Ib.* ii. 226. Hamilton, it seems from this letter, had some share in printing the *Dictionary*, though a great deal of it was done by Strahan. *Ib.* iv. 321. Apparently for the sake of getting the work hastened, some kind of wager had been made by the author and the publisher. Johnson perhaps had wagered that he could supply copy or manuscript faster than Millar could get it set up in type. Macbean, who perhaps was at the head of Johnson's assistants, now wished to wager against the printer. Millar was to hold the stakes. Macbean had no money, and Johnson had no money, but Millar could trust Johnson and therefore was to advance it on his account. He was to put the amount of the wager into Macbean's hands, who would at once pay it back to him as the holder of the stakes. If Macbean lost, Millar, who would hand over the stake to Hamilton, would come on Johnson, who, in his turn, would no doubt deduct the money from Macbean's weekly wages.

[2] *A Treatise on Opium.* By Geo. Young, M.D. Published by Millar in 1753. *Gent. Mag.* 1753, p. 202.

[3] 'When I was at Oxford,' said Johnson, 'I took up Law's *Serious Call to a Holy Life*, expecting to find it a dull book (as such books generally are) and perhaps to laugh at it. But I found Law quite an overmatch for me.' *Life*, i. 68.

[4] *A Course of Lectures in Natural Philosophy*, by the late Rich. Helsham, M.D. *Gent. Mag.* 1739, p. 276.

[5] Chamberlayne's *Present State of Great Britain*—the last edition.

                  To

45.

To the Reverend Mr. Birch [1].

Sir,

I beg the favour of you to lend me Blount's Censura Scriptorum [2]. I shall send my servant for it on Monday.

I am, Sir,

Your most humble servant,

SAM: JOHNSON.

Jan. 20. To the Reverend Mr. Birch.

Endorsed—20 Jan. 1753.

46.

To the Reverend Joseph Warton.

[London], March 8, 1753. Published in the *Life*, i. 253.

47.

To William Strahan [3].

Sir,

I have enclosed the Scheme [4] which I mentioned yesterday in which the work proposed is sufficiently explained.

The Undertaker, Mr. Bathurst [5], is a Physician of the University of Cambridge, of about eight years standing, and will per-

[1] From the original in the British Museum :—*Sloane MSS.* 4310. 302.

[2] Sir Thomas Pope Blount's *Censura Celebriorum Authorum*. London, 1690, folio. 'It is a bibliographical dictionary of a peculiar kind, and may be described as a record of the opinions of the greatest writers of all ages on one another.' Among the *celebriores authores* passed over in silence are Spenser, Shakespeare and Milton. *Dict. Nat. Biog.*, v. 256.

[3] From the original in the possession of Mr. Frederick Barker, of 41 Gunterstone Road, West Kensington. First published in my edition of the *Life*, vol. vi. *Addenda*, p. xxi.

[4] The Scheme, which if not written by Johnson was certainly revised by him, is given in the Addenda to my edition of the *Life*, vi. xxii. It was

for a comprehensive *Geographical Dictionary*.

[5] Bathurst was Johnson's beloved friend, of whom 'he hardly ever spoke without tears in his eyes.' *Life*, i. 190, *n*. 2. He took his degree of Bachelor of Medicine at Peterhouse, Cambridge, in 1745, and did not, it should seem, proceed to the higher degree. By 1753 he would have been of eight years' standing. In 1757 he was at the Havannah, where 'he fell a sacrifice to the destructive climate.' Johnson wrote to Beauclerk : 'The Havannah is taken ;—a conquest too dearly obtained ; for Bathurst died before it. *Vix Priamus tanti totaque Troja fuit.' Ib.* i. 242, *n*. 1. The quotation is from Ovid, *Heroides*, i. 4.

form

form the work in such a manner as may satisfy the publick. No advice of mine will be wanting, but advice will be all that I propose to contribute unless it should be thought worth while that I should write a preface, which if desired I will do and put my name to it. The terms which I am commissioned to offer are these :—

1. A guinea and half shall be paid for each sheet of the copy.

2. The authour will receive a Guinea and half a week from the date of the contract.

3. As it is certain that many books will be necessary, the Authour will at the end of the work take the books furnished him in part of payment at prime Cost, which will be a considerable reduction of the price of the Copy; or if it seems as you thought yesterday no reduction, he will allow out of the last payment fifty pounds for the use of the Books and return them.

4. In two months after his first demand of books shall be supplied, he purposes to write three Sheets a week and to continue the same quantity to the end of the work, unless he shall be hindered by want of Books. He does not however expect to be always able to write according to the order of the Alphabet but as his Books shall happen to supply him, and therefore cannot send any part to the press till the whole is nearly finished.

5. He undertakes as usual the Correction.

I am, Sir,

Your most humble servant,

SAM: JOHNSON.

March 22nd [probably 1753].

To Mr. Strahan.

48.

TO SAMUEL RICHARDSON [1].

DEAR SIR,   May 17, [1753].

As you were the first that gave me any notice of this paragraph, I send it to you with a few little notes, which I wish

---

[1] First published in *Original Letters*, edited by Rebecca Warner, 1817, p. 209. Published in Croker's *Boswell*, p. 95, under the date of May 17, 1755.

This letter was written when a

you would read. It is well when men of learning and penetration busy themselves in these enquiries; but what is *their* idleness is *my* business. Help indeed now comes too late for me [1], when a large part of my book has passed the press.

I shall be glad if these strictures appear to you not unwarrantable; for whom should he who toils in settling a language desire to please but him who is adorning it [2]? I hope your new book is printing. *Macte nova virtute.*

I am, dear Sir,

Most respectfully and most affectionately,

Your humble servant,

SAM: JOHNSON.

49.

TO SAMUEL RICHARDSON [3].

DEAR SIR,   September 26, 1753.

I return you my sincerest thanks for the volumes of your new work; but it is a kind of tyrannical kindness to give only so much at a time, as makes more longed for; but that will probably be thought, even of the whole, when you have given it.

I have no objection but to the preface, in which you first mention the letters as fallen by some chance into your hands,

---

large part of one of Johnson's books had passed the press, and when a new book by Richardson was likely to be printing. This suits May, 1753. On April 3 of that year Johnson recorded :—'I began the second vol. of my *Dictionary*, room being left in the first for Preface, Grammar, and History, none of them yet begun.' *Life*, i. 255. The first edition of *Sir Charles Grandison* bears the date of 1754, but the first four of the six volumes were published before the remaining two, and were reviewed in the *Gentleman's Magazine* for November, 1753, p. 511. Johnson, as his next letter shows, had received a present of some of the volumes as early as September 26, and Miss Talbot was reading them still earlier.

Carter and Talbot Corres. ii. 131, 9.

[1] 'Well might Johnson say that "the English Dictionary was written with little assistance of the learned," for he told me that the only aid which he received was a paper containing twenty etymologies, sent to him by a person then unknown, who he was afterwards informed was Dr. Pearce, Bishop of Rochester.' *Life*, i. 292.

[2] Johnson's admiration of Richardson was very great. He was one of the very few men whom he 'sought after.' *Ib.* iii. 314. In an introductory note to the *Rambler*, No. 97, he describes him as 'an author who has enlarged the knowledge of human nature.'

[3] Published first in the *Richardson Correspondence*, v. 283.

and

and afterwards mention your health as such, that you almost despaired of going through your plan. If you were to require my opinion which part should be changed, I should be inclined to the suppression of that part which seems to disclaim the composition [1]. What is modesty, if it deserts from truth? Of what use is the disguise by which nothing is concealed [2]?

You must forgive this, because it is meant well.

I thank you once more, dear Sir, for your books; but cannot I prevail this time for an index?—such I wished, and shall wish, to Clarissa [3]. Suppose that in one volume an accurate index was made to the three works—but while I am writing an objection arises—such an index to the three would look like the preclusion of a fourth, to which I will never contribute; for if I cannot benefit mankind, I hope never to injure them.

I am, Sir,

Your most obliged and most humble servant,

SAM: JOHNSON.

50.

TO THE REVEREND DR. BIRCH [4].

SIR,

If you will be pleased to lend me Clarendon's History for a few days, it will be a favour to,

Sir,

Your most humble servant,

SAM: JOHNSON.

To the Rev^d Dr. Birch.

Endorsed—January, 1754.

---

[1] In the *Richardson Correspondence* this is printed *competition*.

[2] In the preface Richardson says:—'How such remarkable collections of private letters fell into the editor's hands he hopes the reader will not think it very necessary to enquire.' After describing how he had in *Pamela* 'exhibited the beauty and superiority of virtue in an innocent and unpolished mind,' and in *Clarissa* in 'a young lady of higher fortune and born to happier hopes,' he continues:—'Here the editor apprehended he should be obliged to stop by reason of his precarious state of health and a variety of avocations which claimed his first attention.'

[3] See *ante*, p. 22.

[4] From the original in the British Museum:—*Sloane MSS.*, 4310. 304.

51.

To the Reverend Joseph Warton [1].

DEAR SIR,　　　　　　　　　　　　March 8th, 1754.

I cannot but congratulate you upon the conclusion of a work, in which you have borne so great a part with so much reputation. I immediately determined that your name should be mentioned, but the paper having been some time written, Mr. Hawkesworth, I suppose, did not care to disorder its text, and therefore put your eulogy in a note. He and every other man mention your papers of Criticism with great commendation, though not with greater than they deserve [2].

But how little can we venture to exult in any intellectual powers or literary attainments, when we consider the condition of poor Collins. I knew him a few years ago full of hopes and full of projects, versed in many languages, high in fancy, and strong in retention. This busy and forcible mind is now under the government of those who lately would not have been able to comprehend the least and most narrow of its designs. What do you hear of him? are there hopes of his recovery? or is he to pass the remainder of his life in misery and degradation? perhaps with complete consciousness of his calamity [3].

[1] First published in Wooll's *Memoirs of Dr. Joseph Warton*, p. 219.

[2] On March 8, 1753, Johnson, writing for 'the authors and proprietors of *The Adventurer*,' offered Mr. Warton two guineas for each paper that he should contribute. *Life*, i. 253. In the last number, published on March 9, 1754, the day after the date of Johnson's letter, Hawkesworth, the editor, stated in a note :— 'The pieces signed Z are by the Rev. Mr. Warton, whose translation of Virgil's *Pastorals* and *Georgics* would alone sufficiently distinguish him as a genius and a scholar.'

[3] Johnson thus described Collins's state in 'the character' which he wrote of him in 1763 :— 'The latter part of his life cannot be remembered but with pity and sadness. He languished some years under that depression of mind which enchains the faculties without destroying them, and leaves reason the knowledge of right without the power of pursuing it. These clouds which he perceived gathering on his intellects he endeavoured to disperse by travel, and passed into France ; but found himself constrained to yield to his malady, and returned. He was for some time confined in a house of lunatics, and afterwards retired to the care of his sister in Chichester, where death, in 1756, came to his relief.' Johnson's *Works*, viii. 402. Johnson was mistaken in the year of his death. He died on June 12, 1759, unnoticed either by the *Gentle-*

You

You have flattered us, dear Sir, for some time, with hopes of seeing you; when you come you will find your reputation increased, and with it the kindness of those friends who do not envy you; for success always produces either love or hatred. I enter my name among those that love, and that love you more and more in proportion as by writing more you are more known; and believe, that as you continue to diffuse among us your integrity and learning, I shall be still with greater esteem and affection,

Dear Sir,
Your most obedient and most humble servant,
SAM: JOHNSON.

52.

To WILLIAM STRAHAN[1].

[Perhaps written at Oxford in July, 1754.]

SIR,

I shall not be long here, but in the meantime if Miss Williams wants any money pray speak to Mr. Millar and supply

---

man's Magazine or the *Annual Register*. Goldsmith, writing of him a few weeks earlier, had described him as 'happy if insensible of our neglect, not raging at our ingratitude.' *Enquiry into the Present State of Polite Learning*, ch. x. To this account Johnson added the following in his *Lives of the Poets*:—'Such was the fate of Collins, with whom I once delighted to converse, and whom I yet remember with tenderness. . . . His disorder was not alienation of mind, but general laxity and feebleness, a deficiency rather of his vital than intellectual powers. What he spoke wanted neither judgment nor spirit; but a few minutes exhausted him.' *Works*, viii. 403. See *post*, Letter of April 15, 1756. Johnson thus mentions him in a note on *Cymbeline* in his edition of Shakespeare (vii. 358) :—'For the obsequies of Fidele a song was written by my unhappy friend, Mr. William Collins

of Chichester, a man of uncommon learning and abilities. I shall give it a place at the end in honour of his memory.'

[1] From the original in the possession of Mr. Frederick Barker, of 41 Gunterstone Road, West Kensington. First published in my edition of the *Life*, vol. vi, *Addenda*, p. xxvii; where in a note I state :—'Miss Williams (the blind lady) came to live with Johnson after his wife's death in 1752 (*ib.* i. 232). The fact that Strahan is asked to supply her with money after speaking to Mr. Millar seems to show that this letter was written some time before the publication of the *Dictionary* in April 1755. Millar "took the principal charge of conducting its publication,' and Johnson "had received all the copy-money, by different drafts, a considerable time before he had finished his task" (*ib.* i. 287).

'His "journey" may have been his

her

her, they write to me about some taxes which I wish you would pay.

My journey will come to very little beyond the satisfaction of knowing that there is nothing to be done, and that I leave few advantages here to those that shall come after me.

I am, Sir, &c.,

SAM: JOHNSON.

My compliments to Mrs. Strahan.

To Mr. Strahan.

53.

TO THE REVEREND THOMAS WARTON.

[London], July 16, 1754.   Published in the *Life*, i. 270.

54.

TO ROBERT CHAMBERS.

[London], November 21, 1754.   Published in the *Life*, i. 274.

55.

TO THE REVEREND THOMAS WARTON.

[London], November 28, 1754.   Published in the *Life*, i. 275.

56.

TO THE REVEREND THOMAS WARTON.

[London], December 21, 1754.   Published in the *Life*, i. 276.

57.

TO THE REVEREND JOSEPH WARTON [1].

DEAR SIR,   [London], Dec. 24th, 1754.

I am sat down to answer your kind letter, though I know not whether I shall direct it so as that it may reach you ; the

visit to Oxford in the summer of 1754. He went there, because, " I cannot," he said, "finish my book [the Dictionary] to my mind without visiting the libraries" (*ib.* i. 270). According to Thomas Warton "he collected nothing in the libraries for his *Dictionary*" (*ib. n.* 5). It is perhaps to this failure that the latter part of the letter refers.'

Since writing this note I have discovered that Johnson visited Oxford in July or early in August, 1755.

An Account of the Life of Dr. Johnson, p. 109. That he had intended to pay a visit there that summer is shown by his letter to T. Warton dated June 24. *Life*, i. 290. His letter to the same friend, dated August 7, leads one to think that he had examined manuscripts during his stay. On the whole I am inclined to assign this letter to July, 1754, though it may belong to the following year.

[1] First published in Wooll's *Memoirs of Dr. Joseph Warton*, p. 229.

miscarriage

miscarriage of it will be no great matter, as I have nothing to send but thanks, of which I owe you many; yet, if a few should be lost, I shall amply find them in my own mind; and professions of respect, of which the profession will easily be renewed while the respect continues: and the same causes which first produced can hardly fail to preserve it. Pray let me know, however, whether my letter finds its way to you.

Poor dear Collins!—Let me know whether you think it would give him pleasure if I should write to him[1]. I have often been near his state[2], and therefore have it in great commiseration.

I sincerely wish you the usual pleasures of this joyous season, and more than the usual pleasures, those of contemplation on the great event which this festival commemorates.

I am, dear Sir,
Your most affectionate
and humble servant,
SAM: JOHNSON.

58.

To the Reverend Thomas Warton.

[London], February 4, 1755. Published in the *Life*, i. 278.

59.

To the Reverend Thomas Warton.

[London], February 4, 1755. Published in the *Life*, i. 278.

60.

To the Reverend Thomas Warton.

[London], February 13, 1755. Published in the *Life*, i. 279.

[1] Johnson wrote to Thomas Warton on November 28, 1754:—'Poor dear Collins! Would a letter give him any pleasure? I have a mind to write.' T. Warton says in a note on this passage:—'Collins was at this time on a visit to Mr. Warton; but labouring under the most deplorable languor of body and dejection of mind.' *Life*, i. 276, *n*. 2. Warton in a letter to William Hymers says:—'In 1754 he came to Oxford for change of air and amusement, where he stayed a month; I saw him frequently, but he was so weak and low that he could not bear conversation. Once he walked from his lodgings opposite Christ Church to Trinity College [Warton's College], but supported by his servant.' N. Drake's *Gleaner*, iv. 475.

[2] Boswell describing Johnson's hypochondria says: 'I am aware that he himself was too ready to call such a complaint by the name of madness.' *Ib.* i. 65. 'I inherited,' Johnson said, 'a vile melancholy from my father, which has made me mad all my life, at least not sober.' *Ib.* v. 215.

To

61.

To the Earl of Chesterfield.

[London], February 7, 1755.   Published in the *Life*, i. 261.

62.

To the Reverend Thomas Warton.

[London], February, 1755.   Published in the *Life*, i. 279.

63.

To the Vice-Chancellor of Oxford.

London, February 26, 1755.   Published in the *Life*, i. 282.
This Letter was sold by Messrs. Sotheby and Co. on May 10, 1875,
for £6 6s.

64.

To the Reverend Thomas Warton.

[London], March 20, 1755.   Published in the *Life*, i. 282.

65.

To the Reverend Thomas Warton.

[London], March 25, 1755.   Published in the *Life*, i. 283.

66.

To the Reverend Dr. Birch.

[London], March 29, 1755.   Published in the *Life*, i. 285.

67.

To Mr. Burney.

Gough Square, April 8, 1755.   Published in the *Life*, i. 286.

68.

To the Reverend Dr. Taylor [1].

Sir,

I think your draught better than Mr. Ballard's; and the
case quite clear on Mr. B—'s side; at least so far as that Dr.
Wilson [2] can have no money till the debts due out of that money
which he claims are paid.   The law or custom of the Church

---

[1] From the original in the possession of Mr. Frederick Barker, of 41 Gunterstone Road, West Kensington.
It was sold by Messrs. Christie and Co. on June 5, 1888, for £3 3s.

[2] There were at this time two Wilsons, Thomas and Christopher, Prebendaries of Westminster. Le Neve's *Fast. Ecc. Angl.* iii. 366. Taylor, who was also a prebendary, might have had some dispute with one of them. He succeeded Thomas Wilson in one of his livings in 1784. *Post*, Letter of May 13, 1784.

must

must determine the rest. It seems equitable enough that he should claim that money which was received for him, and only wanted to be divided, if there were no prior claim, or debt due from it.

What is the matter that one never sees you? I am moved [1], and I fancy I shall move again, but how oftensoever I move, I shall be with great constancy,

Your affectionate, &c.,

SAM: JOHNSON.

April 11, 1755.

To the Rev^d Dr. Taylor.

69.

TO EDMUND HECTOR [2].

DEAR SIR,

I was extremely pleased to find that you have not forgotten your old friend, who yet recollects the evenings which we have passed together at Warren's [3] and the (illegible [4]). As Nature, I suppose, operates very uniformly, I believe you as well as I are come now to that part in which the gratifications and friendships of younger years operate very powerfully on the

[1] Johnson, writing this word at the end of one line and the beginning of the next, divides it 'mo-ved.' By 'move' he seems to imply change of residence; but there seems no doubt that from about 1749 to 1759 he lived in Gough Square. *Life*, iii. 405, *n*. 6. The next letter moreover, written only four days later, is dated Gough Square. It is possible that the move was from one house to another in the same Square.

[2] First published in *Notes and Queries*, 6th S. iii. 301.

Edmund Hector was a medical man in practice at Birmingham, the son, it is probable, of George Hector of Lichfield. 'My mother,' writes Johnson of his own birth, 'had a very difficult and dangerous labour, and was assisted by George Hector, a man-midwife of great reputation. I was born almost dead, and could not cry for some time. When he had me in his arms he said, "Here is a brave boy."' *An Account of the Life of Dr. Johnson*, 1805, p. 9. Johnson recorded in his *Diary* in 1781:—'Hector is an old friend, the only companion of my childhood that passed through the school with me. We have always loved one another.' *Life*, iv. 135. Hector's sister, Mrs. Careless, was, said Johnson, 'the first woman with whom I was in love. It dropt out of my head imperceptibly. If I had married her,' he afterwards added, 'it might have been as happy for me.' *Ib.* ii. 460–1.

[3] See *ante*, p. 8, *n*. 3.

[4] 'Swan' is suggested by the publisher of this letter, and with great probability. For Warren's house, where Johnson and Hector had lodged, was 'over against the Swan Tavern in High Street.' *Ib.* i. 85, *n*. 3.

mind.

mind. Since we have again renewed our acquaintance do not let us intermit it so long again.

The Books I think to send you in a strong box by the carrier, and shall be obliged if you will remit the money to my mother, who may give you a receipt in my name[1].

I wish, come of wishes what will, that my work may please you, as much as it now and then pleased me, for I did not find dictionary making so very unpleasant as it may be thought[2].

Mr. Baskevill[3] called on me here. I suppose you visit his printing house, which will I think be something very considerable.—What news of poor Warren? I have not lost all my kindness for him, for when I remember you I naturally remember all our connexions, which are more pleasing to me for your sake.

I am, Sir,

Your humble servant,

Sam: Johnson.

Gough Square, Fleet Street, Apr. 15, 1755.

To Mr. Hector in Birmingham.

[1] The books were probably the two volumes of the *Dictionary* which were published about the day on which this letter was written. *Life*, i. 290, *n*. 1. See *post*, Letter of Oct. 7, 1756, where Johnson refers to Hector's kindness in this matter.

[2] When Stockdale expressed his surprise that Johnson 'in his easy circumstances should think of preparing a new edition of a tedious scientific dictionary, "Sir," said he, "I like that muddling work."' *Ib*. ii. 203, *n*. 3. See *post*, Letter of Oct. 6, 1772.

[3] W. Hutton in his *History of Birmingham*, ed. 1795, p. 120, gives an interesting account of John Baskerville, the famous Birmingham printer. Born in 1706, he was first a stone-cutter, then a writing-master, next a japanner. 'His inclination for letters induced him to turn his thoughts towards the press. He sunk £600 before he could produce one letter to please himself. His first attempt in 1756 was a quarto edition of Virgil, price one guinea. He died in 1775. No one could be found to buy his types. They were refused by both Universities, and they lay a dead weight till purchased by a literary society at Paris in 1779 for £3700.' From them were printed the great editions of Voltaire's Works published in 1785-9. Johnson in 1769 gave to the Library of Trinity College, Oxford, a copy of the Virgil which he had promised, he said, many years before. *Life*, ii. 67. Macaulay, in the third chapter of his *History* (ed. 1874, i. 356), describes how 'the magnificent editions of Baskerville went forth to astonish all the librarians of Europe.' I doubt much whether anything could have astonished Bodley's Librarians during the latter half of the eighteenth century. The Library shows signs of great neglect during that period.

To

70.

To Bennet Langton.

[London], May 6, 1755. Published in the *Life*, i. 288.

71.

To the Reverend Thomas Warton.

[London], May 13, 1755. Published in the *Life*, i. 289.

72.

To the Reverend Thomas Warton.

[London], June 10, 1755. Published in the *Life*, i. 290

73.

To the Reverend Thomas Warton.

[London], June 24, 1755. Published in the *Life*, i. 290.

74.

To Miss ——[1].

MADAM,   July 19, 1755.

I know not how liberally your generosity would reward those who should do you any service, when you can so kindly acknowledge a favour which I intended only to myself. That accidentally hearing that you were in town, I made haste to enjoy an interval of pleasure which I found would be short, was the natural consequence of that self-love which is always busy in quest of happiness; of that happiness which we often miss when we think it near, and sometimes find when we imagine it lost. When I had missed you, I went away disappointed; and did not know that my vexation would be so amply repaid by so kind a letter. A letter indeed can but imperfectly supply the place of its writer, at least of such a writer as you; and a letter which makes me still more desire your presence, is but a weak consolation under the necessity

---

[1] First published in the *Piozzi Letters*, ii. 400.

Mrs. Piozzi says that it was 'addressed to a lady who desires that her name may be concealed.' *Ib.* p. 385. Baretti states in a marginal note that the lady—'with whom I brought him acquainted'—was Miss Cotterell, one of the two daughters of Admiral Cotterell, who lived opposite Johnson in Castle Street, Cavendish Square (*Life*, i. 244).

For Baretti, see *Life*, i. 302.

of

of living longer without you: with this however I must be for a time content, as much content at least as discontent will suffer me; for Mr. Baretti being a single being in this part of the world, and entirely clear from all engagements, takes the advantage of his independence, and will come before me; for which if I could blame him, I should punish him; but my own heart tells me, that he only does to me, what, if I could, I should do to him.

I hope Mrs. ——[1], when she came to her favourite place, found her house dry, and her woods growing, and the breeze whistling, and the birds singing, and her own heart dancing. And for you, Madam, whose heart cannot yet dance to such musick, I know not what to hope; indeed I could hope every thing that would please you, except that perhaps the absence of higher pleasures is necessary to keep some little place vacant in your remembrance for,

Madam,

Your, &c.,

SAM: JOHNSON.

75.

TO THE REVEREND THOMAS WARTON.

[London], August 7, 1755. Published in the *Life*, i. 290.

76.

TO THE REVEREND DR. BIRCH[2].

SIR,

If you can lend me for a few days Wood's Ath. Ox.[3], it will be a favour. My servant will call for it on Monday.

I am, Sir,

Your most humble servant,

SAM: JOHNSON.

Saturday.

To the Reverend Dr. Birch.
Endorsed—Nov. 8, 1755.

[1] Mrs. Porter the actress, according to Baretti, who says, 'Johnson esteemed her much, whatever Mrs. Piozzi may insinuate of his contempt for theatrical folks. She lived at High-wood-ill' [*sic*]. Johnson wrote to Baretti on July 20, 1762:—'Miss Cotterell still continues to cling to Mrs. Porter.' *Life*, i. 369; and on Dec. 21 of the same year:—'Miss Cotterell is still with Mrs. Porter.' *Ib.* p. 382.

[2] From the original in the British Museum:—*Sloane MSS.* 4310.

[3] Wood's *Athenæ Oxonienses*.

TO

77.

To Lewis Paul[1].

DEAR SIR,

I would not have you think that I forget or neglect you. I have never been out of doors since you saw me. On the day after I had been with you, I was seized with a hoarseness, which still continues ; I had then a cough so violent, that I once fainted under its convulsions. I was afraid of my lungs. My Physician bled me yesterday and the day before, first almost against his will, but the next day without any contest[2]. I had been bled once before, so that I have lost in all 54 ounces[3]. I live on broaths, and my cough, I thank God, is much abated, so that I can sleep. You [*sic*] find it impossible to fix a time for coming to you, but as soon as the physician gives me leave, if you can spare a bed, I will pass a week at your house[4]. Change of air is often of use, and, I know, you will let me live my own way. I have been pretty much dejected.

I am, Sir,

Your most humble servant,

SAM: JOHNSON.

Monday, Dec. 23[5], 1755.

To Mr. Paul.

78.

To Miss Boothby[6].

Dec. 30, 1755.

DEAR MADAM,

It is again midnight, and I am again alone. With what meditation shall I amuse this waste hour of darkness and

---

[1] First published in Croker's *Boswell*, p. 100. Corrected by me from the original in the possession of the late Mr. S. J. Davey, of 45, Great Russell Street, London. For Lewis Paul, see *ante*, p. 6.

[2] In Mr. Croker's edition this is printed ' without my [word wanting].' The word is not wanting, but difficult to decipher.

[3] For Johnson's use of bleeding see *Life*, iii. 152, *n*. 3.

[4] Paul's house was perhaps at Kensington. His death on April 25, 1759, is recorded in the *Gentleman's Magazine* for that year (p. 242) as taking place at Kensington Gravel Pits.

[5] Monday was the 22nd.

[6] This and the five other letters to Miss Boothby were first published in the *Piozzi Letters*, ii. 391-400.

Hill Boothby, only daughter of Brooke Boothby and Elizabeth Fitz-herbert, and sister of the sixth baronet, Sir Brooke Boothby, was

vacuity ?

vacuity? If I turn my thoughts upon myself, what do I perceive but a poor helpless being, reduced by a blast of wind to

born Oct. 27, 1708, died Jan. 16, 1756. Johnson had become acquainted with her on his visit to Derbyshire, mentioned *ante*, p. 3, when the daughters of some of the Derbyshire squires showed their good taste and good sense by desiring the company of the young genius, poor and unpolished as he was. *Life*, i. 83. Her friend Miss Meynell, of whom 'Johnson said that she had the best understanding he ever met with in any human being' (*ib.*), had married Miss Boothby's relation, William Fitzherbert, father to the first Lord St. Helens ; a man more 'generally acceptable' than any known to Johnson. *Ib.* iii. 148. Nevertheless in the year 1772, in some fit of despondency, after going one morning to see the convicts executed, 'he went to his own stable and hanged himself with a bridle.' *Ib.* ii. 228, *n.* 3. His wife died in 1753, 'in the flower of her age, distinguished for her piety and fine accomplishments,' as we read in the *Gentleman's Magazine* for that year (p. 148) in a notice likely enough written by Johnson. He told Mrs. Thrale, if we can trust that lady's account, that 'her husband felt at once afflicted and released.' Her virtues had been almost oppressive. Piozzi's *Anecdotes*, p. 160. Her six motherless children for the next three years were under Miss Boothby's care. *An Account of the Life of Dr. Johnson*, 1805, p. 36. She and Johnson kept up a long correspondence; thirty-two of her letters were preserved and published, and but six of his. *Ib.* pp. 33-144. 'I never did exchange letters regularly,' he wrote to Dr. Taylor, 'but with dear Miss Boothby.' *Post*, p. 64. Mrs. Piozzi gives the following account of her,

but how much of it is true cannot be known. There is surely, to say the least, great exaggeration in it. ' Dr. Johnson told me she pushed her piety to bigotry, her devotion to enthusiasm; that she somewhat disqualified herself for the duties of this life by her perpetual aspirations after the next ; such was however the purity of her mind, he said, and such the graces of her manner, that Lord Lyttelton and he used to strive for her preference with an emulation that occasioned hourly disgust, and ended in lasting animosity: " You may see (said he to me when the *Poets' Lives* were printed) that dear Boothby is at my heart still. She *would* delight in that fellow Lyttelton's company though, all that I could do ; and I cannot forgive even his memory the preference given by a mind like hers.' Piozzi's *Anecdotes*, p. 160. ' Did you not tell him he was a rascal ?' Mrs. Piozzi might have been asked in his own words (*Life*, iv. 10) by any one who had any belief in the latter part of her story. That Miss Boothby was a lady of some learning is shown by 'a Hebrew Grammar, or the sketch of one, composed for her own use, and written in a character eminently beautiful that was preserved by her family.' *Piozzi Letters*, ii. 379.

She is the original of Miss Sainthill in *The Spiritual Quixote* (ed. 1773, iii. 99-183), while Sir William and Lady Forester, with whom 'this very sensible maiden lady' was staying, are drawn from the Fitzherberts. ' Her Ladyship,' we are told, ' was a little inclined to the mystic, or rather the seraphic theology.' *Ib.* p. 101. Boswell, who quotes with approval the third of Johnson's letters to Miss Boothby, says 'that the excellence

weakness

weakness and misery? How my present distemper was brought upon me I can give no account, but impute it to some sudden succession of cold to heat; such as in the common road of life cannot be avoided, and against which no precaution can be taken.

Of the fallaciousness of hope, and the uncertainty of schemes, every day gives some new proof; but it is seldom heeded, till something rather felt than seen, awakens attention. This illness, in which I have suffered something and feared much more, has depressed my confidence and elation; and made me consider all that I have promised myself, as less certain to be attained or enjoyed. I have endeavoured to form resolutions of a better life; but I form them weakly, under the consciousness of an external motive. Not that I conceive a time of sickness a time improper for recollection and good purposes, which I believe diseases and calamities often sent to produce, but because no man can know how little his performance will answer to his promises; and designs are nothing in human eyes till they are realised by execution [1].

Continue, my Dearest, your prayers for me, that no good resolution may be vain. You think, I believe, better of me than I deserve. I hope to be in time what I wish to be; and what I have hitherto satisfied myself too readily with only wishing.

Your billet brought me what I much wished to have, a proof that I am still remembered by you at the hour in which I most desire it!

The Doctor is anxious about you. He thinks you too negligent of yourself; if you will promise to be cautious, I will exchange promises, as we have already exchanged injunctions [2].

of the others is not so apparent.' *Life*, iv. 57, *n.* 3. They are in truth in an unnatural strain. They were all written when Johnson was depressed by a severe illness and when she was dying. He seems moreover to affect a style that would have better become a spiritual novel.

I have not followed Mrs. Piozzi's arrangement of these letters. I have little doubt that they were all written within a few days, and that Johnson in dating two of them Jan. 1 and 3,

1755, mistook the year.

[1] On his birthday, nine years later, he recorded:—'I have now spent fifty-five years in resolving; having from the earliest time almost that I can remember been forming schemes of a better life. I have done nothing.' *Life*, i. 483.

[2] In her 'billet' dated Sunday night (Dec. 28),—endorsed by Johnson 'December, 1755,'—she said:—'I beg you would be governed by the good Doctor while you are sick;

However,

However, do not write to me more than you can easily bear; do not interrupt your ease to write at all.

Mr. Fitzherbert sent to-day to offer me some wine; the people about me say I ought to accept it. I shall therefore be obliged to him if he will send me a bottle [1].

There has gone about a report that I died to-day, which I mention, lest you should hear it and be alarmed. You see that I think my death may alarm you; which for me is to think very highly of earthly friendship. I believe it arose from the death of one of my neighbours. You know Des Cartes's argument, 'I think, therefore I am.' It is as good a consequence, 'I write, therefore I am alive.' I might give another, 'I am alive, therefore I love Miss Boothby', but that I hope our friendship may be of far longer duration than life [2].

I am, dearest Madam,

with sincere affection,

Your, &c.,

SAM: JOHNSON.

79.

To Miss Boothby.

MY SWEET ANGEL,　　　　　　　　　Dec. 31, [1755].

I have read your book [3], I am afraid you will think without any great improvement; whether you can read my notes I know not. You ought not to be offended; I am perhaps as sincere as the writer. In all things that terminate here I shall be much guided by your influence, and should take or leave by your direction; but I cannot receive my religion from any human hand [4]. I desire however to be instructed, and am far from thinking myself perfect.

when you are well, do as you please.' *An Account*, &c., p. 129. The 'good Doctor' was Lawrence—Johnson's 'physician and friend,' sprung from Milton's 'Lawrence, of virtuous father virtuous son.' *Life*, ii. 296, *n.* 1.

[1] 'I am glad you sent for the hock,' she replied. 'Mr. Fitzherbert has named it more than once.' *An Account*, &c., p. 130.

[2] 'Had she lived some years longer

Johnson would in all probability have become quite an enthusiast in point of religion, and have gone mad with it. He was so strongly inclined to it.'—BARETTI.

[3] She had written in her last letter :—'As an answer to one part of your letter I have sent you a little book.' *An Account*, &c., p. 130.

[4] 'He would have certainly taken

I beg

I beg you to return the book when you have looked into it. I should not have written what is in the margin, had I not had it from you, or had I not intended to shew it you.

It affords me a new conviction, that in these books there is little new, except new forms of expression; which may be sometimes taken, even by the writer, for new doctrines.

I sincerely hope that God, whom you so much desire to serve aright, will bless you, and restore you to health, if he sees it best. Surely no human understanding can pray for any thing temporal otherwise than conditionally. Dear Angel, do not forget me. My heart is full of tenderness.

It has pleased God to permit me to be much better; which I believe will please you.

Give me leave, who have thought much on medicine [1], to propose to you an easy, and I think a very probable remedy for indigestion and lubricity of the bowels. Dr. Lawrence has told me your case. Take an ounce of dried orange-peel finely powdered, divide it into scruples, and take one scruple at a time in any manner [2]; the best way is perhaps to drink it in a glass

---

it from her without ever suspecting he did.'—BARETTI.

'I would be a Papist if I could,' he said to Boswell. 'I have fear enough; but an obstinate rationality prevents me.' *Life*, iv. 289. She wrote to him in an earlier letter :—'I am desirous that in the great and one thing necessary you should think as I do ; and I am persuaded you sometime will.' *An Account*, &c., p. 100. It is probable that her views were somewhat the same as the poet Cowper's, who wrote shortly before Johnson's death :—'We rejoice in the account you give us of Dr. Johnson. His conversion will indeed be a singular proof of the omnipotence of Grace ; and the more singular the more decided.'— Southey's *Cowper*, xv. 150.

[1] 'Dr. Johnson,' writes Boswell with justice, 'was a great dabbler in physic.' *Life*, iii. 152. 'My know-

ledge of physic (he said) I learnt from Dr. James, whom I helped in writing the proposals for his *Dictionary* and also a little in the *Dictionary* itself. I also learnt from Dr. Lawrence, but was then grown more stubborn.' *Ib.* iii. 22. See *post*, Letters of May 23, 1773, and June 19, 1783.

[2] 'Next morning [April 1, 1775] I won a small bet from Lady Diana Beauclerk, by asking Dr. Johnson as to one of his particularities, which her Ladyship laid I durst not do. It seems he had been frequently observed at the Club to put into his pocket the Seville oranges, after he had squeezed the juice of them into the drink which he made for himself. Beauclerk and Garrick talked of it to me, and seemed to think that he had a strange unwillingness to be discovered. We could not divine what he did with them ; and this was the bold question to be put.

of hot red port¹, or to eat it first and drink the wine after
it. If you mix cinnamon or nutmeg with the powder, it were
not worse; but it will be more bulky, and so more troublesome.
This is a medicine not disgusting, not costly, easily tried, and if
not found useful, easily left off.

I would not have you offer it to the Doctor as mine.
Physicians do not love intruders; yet do not take it without his
leave. But do not be easily put off, for it is in my opinion very
likely to help you, and not likely to do you harm; do not take
too much in haste; a scruple once in three hours, or about five
scruples a day, will be sufficient to begin, or less, if you find any
aversion. I think using sugar with it might be bad; if syrup,
use old syrup of quinces: but even that I do not like. I should
think better of conserve of sloes. Has the Doctor mentioned
the bark? in powder you could hardly take it; perhaps you
might take the infusion.

Do not think me troublesome, I am full of care. I love you
and honour you; and am very unwilling to lose you.

*A Dieu je vous recommande*².

I am, Madam,

Your, &c.,

Sam: Johnson.

My compliments to my dear Miss³.

I saw on his table the spoils of
the preceding night, some fresh peels
nicely scraped and cut into pieces.
"O, Sir, (said I) I now partly see
what you do with the squeezed
oranges which you put into your
pocket at the Club." Johnson. "I
have a great love for them." Boswell. "And pray, Sir, what do you
do with them? You scrape them it
seems, very neatly, and what next?"
Johnson. "Let them dry, Sir."
Boswell. "And what next?"
Johnson. "Nay, Sir, you shall know
their fate no further." Boswell.
"Then the world must be left in the
dark. It must be said (assuming a
mock solemnity) he scraped them,
and let them dry, but what he did
with them next he never could be

prevailed upon to tell." Johnson.
"Nay, Sir, you should say it more
emphatically:—he could not be prevailed upon, even by his dearest
friends, to tell."¹ *Life*, ii. 330.

¹ *Port* is not in Johnson's *Dictionary*, though he gives *claret, hock*,
and *sherry*. I have often in my
boyhood heard port offered to a
guest as 'red wine,' while sherry was
spoken of as 'white wine.'

² 'The true phrase is Je vous recommande à Dieu.'—Baretti. Once
when Dr. Johnson was himself very
ill he broke out into French. 'Ah,
priez Dieu pour moi,' he exclaimed
suddenly to Miss Burney, grasping her
hand. Mme. D'Arblay's *Diary*, ii. 295.

³ No doubt Mr. Fitzherbert's eldest
daughter.

To

80.

To Miss Boothby [1].

January 1, 1755 [1756].

DEAREST MADAM,

Though I am afraid your illness leaves you little leisure for the reception of airy civilities, yet I cannot forbear to pay you my congratulations on the new year; and to declare my wishes, that your years to come may be many and happy. In this wish indeed I include myself, who have none but you on whom my heart reposes [2]; yet surely I wish your good, even though your situation were such as should permit you to communicate no gratifications to,

Dearest, dearest Madam,

Your, &c.,

SAM: JOHNSON.

81.

To Miss Boothby.

Jan. 3, 1755 [1756].

DEAREST MADAM,

Nobody but you can recompense me for the distress which I suffered on Monday night. Having engaged Dr. Lawrence to let me know, at whatever hour, the state in which he left you; I concluded when he staid so long, that he staid to see my dearest expire. I was composing myself as I could to hear what yet I hoped not to hear, when his servant brought me word that you were better. Do you continue to grow better? Let my dear little Miss inform me on a card. I would not have you write lest it should hurt you, and consequently hurt likewise,

Dearest Madam,

Your, &c.,

SAM: JOHNSON.

---

[1] This letter is quoted by Boswell, *Life*, iv. 57, *n*. 3.

[2] Four years later, on the death of his mother, he wrote to Lucy Porter, his step-daughter: — 'Every heart must lean to somebody, and I have nobody but you.' *Post*, Letter of Feb. 6, 1759.

To

82.

To Miss Boothby.

DEAREST DEAR.   Saturday, [Jan. 3, 1756].

I am extremely obliged to you for the kindness of your enquiry. After I had written to you, Dr. Lawrence came, and would have given some oil and sugar, but I took Rhenish[1] and water, and recovered my voice. I yet cough much, and sleep ill. I have been visited by another Doctor to-day; but I laughed at his Balsam of Peru[2]. I fasted on Tuesday, Wednesday, and Thursday, and felt neither hunger nor faintness[3]. I have dined yesterday and to-day, and found little refreshment. I am not much amiss; but can no more sleep than if my dearest lady were angry at,

> Madam,
> Your, &c.,
> SAM: JOHNSON.

83.

To Lewis Paul.

January 6, 1756.

In Messrs. Sotheby and Co's. Auction Catalogue for May 10, 1875, Lot 86 is an autograph Letter of Johnson to Lewis Paul, dated Jan. 6, 1756, with the post-mark 'Peny Post.' Says that he is better, 'but cannot yet go into the cold air.' It sold for £2 18s.

84.

To Miss Boothby.

HONOURED MADAM,   January 8. 1756.

I beg of you to endeavour to live. I have returned your *Law*, which however I earnestly entreat you to give me[4]. I am

---

[1] *Rhenish* is not defined in Johnson's Dictionary, but he defines *Hock* as *Old strong Rhenish*.

[2] This doctor was, I suspect, James, who dealt in balsams. *Ante*, p. 8, *n.* 3.

[3] 'As to regular meals (said Johnson), I have fasted from the Sunday's dinner to the Tuesday's dinner without any inconvenience.' *Life*, iii. 306.

[4] On October 11, 1755, she wrote to him :—'Have you read Mr. Law? not cursorily but with attention? I wish you would consider him. *His Appeal to all that doubt* I think the most clear of all his later writings.' *An Account*, &c., p. 127. It was probably this book of hers which he had borrowed and was now returning. Law's *Serious Call to a Holy Life* he had read at Oxford. *Ante*, p. 30, *n.* 1.

in

in great trouble ; if you can write three words to me, be pleased
to do it. I am afraid to say much, and cannot say nothing
when my dearest is in danger.

The all-merciful GOD have mercy on you.

I am, Madam,

Your, &c.,

SAM: JOHNSON[1].

85.

TO THE REVEREND DR. BIRCH[2].

SIR,   Jan. 9, 1756.

Having obtained from Mr. Garrick a benefit for a gentlewoman of [*word illegible*[3]], distressed by blindness, almost the
only casualty that could have distressed her, I beg leave to
trouble you, among my other friends, with some of her tickets[4].

---

[1] She died on the 16th of this
month. 'I have heard Baretti say,'
writes Mrs. Piozzi, 'that when this
lady died Johnson was almost dis-
tracted with his grief.' Piozzi's
Anecdotes, p. 161.

In writing to him Miss Boothby
now and then quoted passages from
his letters to her. I have gathered
the following fragments from the
missing correspondence.

'Few are so busy as not to find
time to do what they delight in
doing.' *An Account*, &c., p. 42.

'The best intention may be troublesome.' *Ib*. p. 55.

'Those whom we condescend to
call Great.' *Ib*.

'The effect of education is very
precarious. But what can be hoped
without it? Though the harvest
may be blasted, we must yet cultivate
the ground.' *Ib*. p. 73.

'The common dialect of daily correspondence.' *Ib*. p. 121.

[2] First published in Croker's *Boswell*, p. 101.

'Of Dr. Birch Johnson said he
had more anecdotes than any man.'
Life, v. 255. 'He was,' says Haw-

kins, 'but a dull writer. Johnson
was used to speak of him in this
manner :—"Tom is a lively rogue ;
he remembers a great deal, and can
tell many pleasant stories ; but a pen
is to Tom a torpedo, the touch of it
benumbs his hand and his brain :
Tom can talk, but he is no writer."'
Hawkins's *Life of Johnson*, p. 209.
Horace Walpole describes him as a
worthy, good-natured soul, full of
industry and activity, and running
about like a young setting-dog in
quest of anything, new or old, and
with no parts, taste, or judgment.'
Letters, vii. 326. He ran about in
more senses than one, for he once
walked round London, crossing the
Thames twice so as to take in Southwark. The excursion took him six
hours, 'and he computed the circuit
at above twenty miles.' Hawkins,
p. 208.

[3] This word, which is something
like *Lournitz*, is, perhaps, the name
of the place in South Wales whence
Miss Williams came.

[4] Seven years later Boswell, in
the account which he gives of his
first meeting with Johnson, says:—
Your

Your benevolence is well known, and was, I believe, never
exerted on a more laudable occasion.

I am, Sir,

Your most humble servant,

Sam: Johnson.

86.

To Lewis Paul[1].

Tuesday, Jan. 13, 1755 [1756][2].

Sir,

I am much confused with an accident that has happened.
When your papers were brought me, I broke open the first
without reading the superscription, and when I had opened
it, found it not to belong to me. I did not read it when I found
my mistake. I see it is a very full paper, and will give you
much trouble to copy again, but perhaps it will not be necessary, and you may mend the seal. I am sorry for the mischance.
You will easily believe it was nothing more. If you send it me
again, the child[3] shall carry it.

For bringing Mrs. Swynfen[4], I know not well how to attempt

'He then addressed himself to
Davies: "What do you think of
Garrick? He has refused me an
order for the play for Miss Williams,
because he knows the house will be
full, and that an order would be
worth three shillings." Eager to
take any opening to get into conversation with him, I ventured to say,
"O Sir, I cannot think Mr. Garrick
would grudge such a trifle to you."
"Sir," said he, with a stern look, "I
have known David Garrick longer
than you have done: and I know no
right you have to talk to me on the
subject."' Boswell adds in a note:
—'That this was a momentary sally
against Garrick there can be no
doubt; for at Johnson's desire he
had, some years before, given a
benefit-night at his theatre to this
very person, by which she had got
two hundred pounds.' *Life*, i. 392.

[1] First published in Croker's *Boswell*, p. 101.

This Letter was sold by Messrs.
Sotheby and Co. on May 10, 1875,
for £3 4s.

[2] This conjectural date, which is
given by Mr. Croker, I have adopted,
as well as his arrangement of the
other undated letters of the same
series. For Lewis Paul, see *ante*,
p. 6.

[3] The child was perhaps his black
servant who had entered his service
in 1752. *Life*, i. 239. *Post*, p. 66, he
is described as 'my boy.'

[4] See *ante*, p. 6, *n.* 3, where it
is stated that 'a daughter of Johnson's Godfather (Dr. Swynfen), afterwards Mrs. Desmoulins, learnt the
art of pinking crapes by Paul's
machine as his pupil.' He borrowed
£200 from her, 'for which he gave a
bond (afterwards repaid, and the
bond given up and cancelled).'
French's *Life of S. Crompton*, p. 255.
How nearly Mrs. Swynfen was related to this lady I do not know.

it.

it. I am not sure that her husband will be pleased, and I think it would look too much like making myself a party, instead of acting the part of a common friend, which I shall be very ready to discharge. I should imagine that the best way would be to send her word when you will call on her, and perhaps the questions on which she is to resuscitate her remembrance, and come to her at her own house. I really know not how to ask her husband to send her, and I certainly will not take her without asking him.

I am, Sir,

Your most humble servant,

SAM: JOHNSON.

87.

TO MISS CARTER [1].

MADAM,

From the liberty of writing to you, if I have hitherto been deterred by the fear of your understanding, I am now encouraged to it by the confidence of your goodness.

I am soliciting a benefit for Miss Williams, and beg that if you can by letters influence any in her favour, and who is there whom you cannot influence? you will be pleased to patronise her on this occasion. Yet, for the time is short, and as you were not in town, I did not till this day remember that you might help us, and recollect how widely and how rapidly light is diffused.

To every joy is appended a sorrow. The name of Miss Carter introduces the memory of Cave. Poor dear Cave!

[1] First published in Pennington's *Memoirs of Mrs. Elizabeth Carter*, ed. 1816, i. 40.

Miss Elizabeth Carter, commonly known in later life as 'the learned Mrs. Carter,' was one of the three ladies—Hannah More and Fanny Burney being the other two—with whom Johnson dined one day, when he said :—'Three such women are not to be found ; I know not where I could find a fourth, except Mrs. Lennox, who is superior to them all.' *Life*, iv. 275.

He had addressed to her an epigram both in Greek and Latin in the *Gentleman's Magazine* for 1738, p. 210 (Johnson's *Works*, i. 170), and also the following, which, I believe, is only to be found in Pennington's *Memoirs*, i. 398 :—

'Quid mihi cum Cultu? Probitas inculta nitescit,

Et juvat Ingenii vita sine arte rudis.

Ingenium et mores si pulchra probavit Elisa,

Quid majus mihi spes ambitiosa dabit?'

I owed

I owed him much; for to him I owe that I have known you[1]. He died, I am afraid, unexpectedly to himself, yet surely unburthened with any great crime; and for the positive duties of religion, I have yet no right to condemn him for neglect[2].

I am with respect, which I neither owe nor pay to any other,

Madam,

Your most obedient

and most humble servant,

SAM: JOHNSON.

Gough Square,

Jan. 14, 1756.

88.

TO JOHN RYLAND[3].

SIR,   [London, January, 1756.]

I have obtained a benefit play for Miss Williams, which yet will not be for her benefit without the concurrence of her friends, among which she numbers you, and therefore has troubled [you] with tickets which she begs you will try to dispose among your acquaintance. We both send our compliments to Mrs. Ryland, and to the young Scholar.

I am, dear Sir,

Your affectionate humble servant,

SAM: JOHNSON.

To Mr. Ryland.

[1] Under the signature of *Eliza* she had been an early contributor to the *Gentleman's Magazine,* of which Cave was editor and proprietor. Pennington's *Memoirs,* p. 37.

[2] Cave died on January 10, 1754. In the Memoir which Johnson wrote of him he says:—'He fell into a kind of lethargic insensibility, in which one of the last acts of reason which he exerted was fondly to press the hand that is now writing this little narrative.' Johnson's *Works,* vi. 433.

[3] From the original in the possession of the late Mr. S. J. Davey, of 47 Great Russell Street, London.

'It is remarkable,' writes John Nichols, 'that Mr. Ryland should nowhere have been mentioned in Mr. Boswell's communicative Life of Johnson.' *Lit. Anec.* ix. 502. He is twice mentioned, but no more than mentioned; nevertheless he was one of Johnson's oldest and closest friends. Perhaps Boswell passed him over in silence, in return for his keeping from him the letters which he had received from Johnson. He was Hawkesworth's brother-in-law, and Hawkesworth Boswell attacked for his 'provoking effrontery.' *Life,* i. 252. An interesting paper might be written on the intentional omissions in the *Life of Johnson.*

John Ryland was a merchant, a

TO

89.

To Mr. Cave[1].

DEAR SIR, [London, January, 1756.]

I find this Gentleman knows more of Tickets than either you or I ; and I wish you would be so good as to settle with him. I fancy printed ones may serve, on good strong paper. Let them be dated right. There should be for Box, Pit, and Galleries.

I am, Sir,

Your, &c.,

SAM: JOHNSON.

To Mr. Cave.

90.

To Samuel Richardson[2].

DEAR SIR, Tuesday, Feb. 19, 1756.

I return you my sincerest thanks for the favour which you were pleased to do me two nights ago[3]. Be pleased to accept of this little book, which is all that I have published this winter[4]. The inflammation is come again into my eye[5], so that I can write very little.

I am, Sir,

Your most obliged

and most humble servant,

SAM: JOHNSON.

To Mr. Richardson.

good scholar, a staunch Whig of the old school, and a dissenter. He was a contributor to the *Gentleman's Magazine.* He constantly visited Johnson during his last illness, and supplied Nichols with several of the particulars in the article on Johnson in the *Gentleman's Magazine*, 1784, p. 957.

[1] First published in the *Gentleman's Magazine* for 1793, p. 19. Mr. Nichols conjectures with great probability that this letter refers to Miss Williams's benefit. Cave was either the brother or the nephew of the founder of the *Gentleman's Magazine* who had died in 1754.

[2] First published in the *Richardson Correspondence*, v. 285.

[3] The nature of the favour may probably be inferred from his next letter to Richardson (*post*, p. 61). By his severe illness which affected his sight he must have been kept from earning money by his pen.

[4] 'The little book' was either the *Abridgment of the Dictionary*, advertised in the *Gentleman's Magazine* for January, 1756, p. 45, or Sir Thomas Browne's *Christian Morals with Life*, advertised in the *Gentleman's Magazine* for March, p. 139.

[5] Four days earlier he had thought the inflammation cured, for on

To

To Lewis Paul [1].

Sir,   [London], Wednesday, [1756].

I this morning found a letter, which as you sent when my eye was out of order, I had never read to this hour, and therefore, now I have read, I make haste to tell you that if I understand it right, that is, if Mr. Cave [2] be your landlord, I believe I can favour you, and, if the difficulty still continues, will endeavour it. They do not, I fancy, want the money, and then they may as well seize, if they must seize, for more or less, the property, I suppose, being equivalent to much more, and in no danger of being removed. I am very sorry I did not read the letter among the first things that, upon recovery, I was able to read; but having put it aside, it had the fate of other things for which the proper time has been neglected. Let me know what I shall do, or whether any thing at all is to be done.

I am now thinking about Hitch [3]. I am yet inclined to believe that he will rather lend money upon spindles, a security which he has found valid, than upon a property to be wrung by the law from Dr. James, who will not pay for three box tickets which he took [4]. It is a strange fellow. Hitch has a dislike of

February 15 he composed a prayer entitled, 'When my Eye was restored to its Use.' *Prayers and Meditations*, p. 27. According to Boswell, 'he did not see at all with one of his eyes, though its appearance was little different from that of the other.' *Life*, i. 41. This seems borne out by his letter to Mrs. Thrale of May 24, 1773, where he says:— 'My fever has left me a very severe inflammation in the seeing eye.' See also *Life*, ii. 264, where he says, 'By an inflammation in my eye I could not for some time read your letter.' Nevertheless writing to Miss Porter on May 29, 1770, he says:—'I am very sorry that your eyes are bad; mine continue pretty good, but they

are sometimes dim.' According to Malone, speaking to Dr. Burney of his bad eye he said, 'the dog was never good for much.' *Life*, i. 41, n. 2.

[1] First published in Croker's *Boswell*, page 101.

[2] Probably William Cave, Edward Cave's younger brother, 'who inherited from him a competent estate.' Johnson's *Works*, vi. 434, note.

[3] Perhaps Charles Hitch, one of the original proprietors of Johnson's *Dictionary*. *Life*, i. 183.

[4] Paul had granted a license to Dr. James for the use of his invention (*Life of Crompton*, p. 256, and *ante*, p. 6), for which, it should seem, money was still due, though

James;

James; perhaps another might think better of him, but where
to find that other I know not.   I can, I believe, by a third hand
have Hitch sounded; but if it had not the appearance of de-
clining the office, I should tell you, that your own negotiation
would effect more than mine.   However, in both these affairs,
I am ready to do what you would have me.

I am, Sir,

Your most humble servant,

SAM: JOHNSON.

92.

To LEWIS PAUL[1].

SIR,

I am still of opinion that they will hear me at the gate[2],
and I have no difficulty to speak to them, but though I hope
I can obtain a forbearance, I am confident that I shall get
nothing more, nor would any attempt to borrow of them or
sell to them have any other effect than that of disabling me
from proceeding in my just request.   You may easily believe
that spindles are there in very little credit.

I will propose to a friend to speak to Mr. Hitch, you well
know it is impossible to guess what [may] be the answer when
money is to be sought.   If my friend refuses the errand, what
shall we do? that must be considered.   Will you then write to
him by me, as a preparative, and then see him if he gives any
countenance to the affair?   You are much more skilful in these

payment apparently was resisted.
The three box-tickets had no doubt
been taken for Miss Williams's
benefit.

[1] First published in Croker's *Boswell*, page 101.   An exact transcript
of the original letter, now in the
Patent Office Library, has been sent
me by the kindness of Mr. W. E.
Milliken of that Office, who writes to
me :—' Dr. Johnson was often a guest
in the house of Kenneth Mackenzie,
seventh and last Earl of Seaforth,
whose only child, Caroline, born
1767, was my mother's mother.
Johnson took a great fancy to Lady

Caroline as a child — would fondle
her, and call her " his little Jacobitish
mistress "—by no means repelled, we
may be sure, by the well-known
sympathies of her house, and by the
fact of her lineal descent, through her
mother, from Charles II's son, the
Duke of Grafton.   Thus it comes
about that I, as an infant, have been
nursed in the arms of one who, as a
little child, had herself been petted
by Dr. Johnson.'

[2] St. John's Gate, Clerkenwell,
where the *Gentleman's Magazine*
was published.

transactions

transactions than I, and might much sooner find out a proper person to deal with, for my friends have not much money.

Would it be wrong if you wrote a short letter for me to show at Cave's as a kind of Credential, containing only a few lines to mention the value of the stock, the certainty of the security, and your desire of my interposition. That I may not seem to thrust myself needlessly between Cave and payment, let the letter be without dejection as if the delay was a thing rather convenient than necessary to you. Cave cannot, I think, want forty pounds, nor perhaps has he twice forty to spare.

I will do my best for you in both negociations, with Hitch my best can be very little, with Cave I expect to succeed, at least for so short a delay as to Midsummer, and think it would [*sic*] as well in your letter to refer payment to Michaelmass, or Christmass. If they will grant the whole of our request (for I shall make it mine too) they may more easily grant part. But once more—you know all these things better than I.

> I am, Sir,
>> Your most humble servant,
>>> SAM: JOHNSON [1].

March 12, 1756.
To Mr. Paul.

93.
To Dr. HAWKESWORTH [2].

DEAR SIR,   [March, 1756.]

I have been looking into the Book here and there and I think have read a pretty fair specimen. It is written with

[1] While Johnson was thus busying himself for his friend, he was, as the next letter but one shows, in difficulties himself.

[2] From the original in the possession of the late Mr. S. J. Davey, of 47 Great Russell Street, London.

Boswell describes Hawkesworth as living in great intimacy with Johnson about the year 1752. *Life*, i. 234. This letter was enclosed by Hawkesworth to Fulke Greville in another dated Bromley, Kent, March 14, 1756. It refers to Greville's

Maxims, Characters, and Reflections, which had just been published—'a book,' according to Boswell, 'which is entitled to much more praise than it has received.' *Life*, iv. 304. Hawkesworth wrote to Greville:— 'I enclose you Johnson's letter, it will cost you threepence, but I dare say you will think it worth twice the money. It is an original, and (as I told you it would be) expressed in general terms, without referring to particular passages as new, striking, delicate or recherché. You see in

uncommon

uncommon knowledge of mankind, which is the chief excellence of such a book. The sentences are keenly pointed, and vigorously pushed, which is their second excellence. But it is too Gallick [1], and the proper names are often ill-formed or ill-chosen. To use a French phrase, I think the good *carries it over* the bad [2]. The good is in the constituent, the bad in the accidental parts.

We cannot come to-morrow, but I purpose to be with you on the Saturday following, to see the Spring and Mrs. Hawkesworth [3].

I am, Sir,

Your most humble servant,

SAM: JOHNSON.

Miss W——[4] sends her compliments.

94.

TO SAMUEL RICHARDSON [5].

SIR,

I am obliged to entreat your assistance. I am now under an arrest for five pounds eighteen shillings. Mr. Strahan, from

the first place that he has not read the book through ; he never reads any book through. . . Take his own testimony in his own words, they are written indeed not in letters but in pothooks, a kind of character which it will probably cost you some time to decipher, and perhaps at last you may not succeed.' It is amusing to find Johnson long afterwards, when looking through the manuscripts which Hawkesworth had left behind him, asking :—' Who was his Amanuensis? that small hand strikes a reader with terrour. It is pale as well as small.' *Post*, Letter of April 12, 1777.

According to Mme. D'Arblay, Greville never met Johnson till about twenty years after the date of the Letter in the text. For the curious scene which she then witnessed see *Life*, iv. 304, *n.* 4, and *Early Diary of Frances Burney*, ii. 285. For

Johnson's habit of rarely reading books through, see *Life*, i. 71; ii. 226.

[1] For his dislike of Gallicisms, see *ib.* iii. 343. It is strange that in the next sentence in his letter he should himself, to use his own words, ' babble a dialect of France.'

[2] Le bon l'emporte sur le mal.

[3] Hawkesworth was living at Bromley, where Johnson four years earlier had buried his wife; ' to which,' writes Boswell, ' he was probably led by the residence of his friend at that place.' *Life*, i. 241.

[4] Blind Miss Williams.

[5] First published in the *Gentleman's Magazine*, 1788, p. 479, and a second time in Murphy's *Essay on Johnson*, ed. 1792, p. 87. ' On the margin of this letter,' says Murphy, ' there is a memorandum in these words :—" March 16, 1756. Sent six guineas. Witness, Wm. Richardson." ' My friend Mr. Arthur John Butler, whom

whom I should have received the necessary help in this case, is not at home; and I am afraid of not finding Mr. Millar. If you will be so good as to send me this sum, I will very gratefully repay you, and add it to all former obligations.

I am, Sir,

Your most obedient

and most humble servant,

SAM: JOHNSON.

Gough Square, March 16, [1756].

95.

TO THE REVEREND DR. BIRCH[1].

Mr. Johnson returns Dr. Birch thanks for his book which sickness has obliged him to keep beyond the time intended, and desires his acceptance of the Life of Sir Thomas Browne, by way [of] interest for the loan[2].

To Dr. Birch.

Endorsed—March 20, 1756.

96.

TO THE REVEREND JOSEPH WARTON[3].

DEAR SIR,   April 15th, 1756.

Though when you and your brother[4] were in town you did not think my humble habitation worth a visit, yet I will not so far give way to sullenness as not to tell you that I have lately seen an octavo book which I suspect to be yours, though I have not yet read above ten pages[5]. That way of publishing, without

who has done so much to make Dante known to English readers, has seen in the old books of Jacob Tonson the younger, a correspondence of about this period, ' beginning with a letter from Johnson to the effect that he was in difficulties and required assistance. The difficulty, he added, was not likely to recur, "as I have no other debts except to friends." There are besides a receipt from him and an extract from Tonson's ledger—"To your note of hand when you was arrested for debt . . . £40."'

[1] From the original in the British Museum :— *Sloane MSS.*, 4310. 311.

[2] See *ante*, p. 57, *n.* 4.

[3] First published in Wooll's *Memoirs of Dr. Joseph Warton*, p. 238.

[4] Thomas Warton. Johnson felt very grateful to him for 'the uncommon care which he had taken of his interest' in procuring him the degree of Master of Arts. *Life*, i. 275.

[5] The 'octavo book' was Warton's *Essay on the Genius and Writings of Pope*. Dodsley, the publisher, wrote to Warton on April 8 :—' Your Essay is published, the price 5s. bound. I

acquainting

acquainting your friends, is a wicked trick[1]. However, I will not so far depend upon a mere conjecture as to charge you with a fraud which I cannot prove you to have committed.

I should be glad to hear that you are pleased with your new situation[2]. You have now a kind of royalty, and are to be answerable for your conduct to posterity. I suppose you care not now to answer a letter except there be a lucky concurrence of a post-day with a holiday. These restraints are troublesome for a time, but custom makes them easy, with the help of some honour, and a great deal of profit, and I doubt not but your abilities will obtain both.

For my part, I have not lately done much. I have been ill in the winter, and my eye has been inflamed; but I please myself with the hopes of doing many things, with which I have long pleased and deceived myself.

What becomes of poor dear Collins[3]? I wrote him a letter which he never answered. I suppose writing is very troublesome to him. That man is no common loss. The moralists all talk of the uncertainty of fortune, and the transitoriness of beauty; but it is yet more dreadful to consider that the powers of the mind are equally liable to change; that understanding may make its appearance and depart, that it may blaze and expire.

Let me not be long without a letter, and I will forgive you the omission of the visit; and if you can tell me that

have a pleasure in telling you that it is liked in general, and particularly by such as you would wish should like it. But you have surely not kept your secret : Johnson mentioned it to Mr. Hitch [the bookseller, no doubt] as yours.' Wooll's *Memoirs of Dr. Warton*, p. 237. The second volume was not published till 1782, though 200 pages of it, as we are told in the preface, had been printed more than twenty years. When Boswell in 1763 expressed his wonder at the delay, Johnson replied :— 'Why, Sir, I suppose he finds himself a little disappointed in not having been able to persuade the world to be of his opinion as to Pope.' *Life*, i. 448.

[1] Johnson himself for the most part did not print his name on the title-page, though in most cases, to quote his own words, 'he expected it to be known' (*post*, Letter of Jan. 20, 1759). The authorship of the *Rambler*, however, he tried to keep secret. *Life*, i. 209, *n.* 1.

[2] 'In 1755 Warton was elected second master of Winchester School, with the management of a boarding house.' Wooll's *Memoirs*, p. 30.

[3] See *ante*, p. 36.

you

you are now more happy than before, you will give great
pleasure to,

                    Dear Sir,

                        Your most affectionate

                            and most humble servant,

                                SAM: JOHNSON.

                    97.

            TO THE REVEREND DR. BIRCH[1].

SIR,

Being, as you will find by the proposal, engaged in a work
which requires the concurrence of my friends to make it of
much benefit to me, I have taken the liberty of recommending
six receipts to your care, and do not doubt of your endeavour
to dispose of them.

I have likewise a further favour to beg. I know you have been
long a curious collector of books. If therefore you have any
of the contemporaries or ancestors of Shakespeare, it will be
of great use to lend me them for a short time; my stock of
those authours is yet but curta supellex[2].

                    I am, Sir,

                        Your obliged humble servant,

                                SAM: JOHNSON.

June 22, 1756.

    To the Reverend Dr. Birch.

                    98.

            TO THE REVEREND DR. TAYLOR[3].

DEAR SIR,

I promised to write to you, and write now rather to keep
my promise than that I have anything to say, that might not be
delayed till we meet. ⟨I know not how it happens, but I fancy
that I write letters with more difficulty than some other people,
who write nothing but letters, at least I find myself very unwilling to take up a pen, only to tell my friends that I am
well, and indeed I never did exchange letters regularly but
with dear Miss Boothby[4].

[1] From the original in the British
Museum:—*Sloane MSS.*, 4310. 312.
    The work on which Johnson was
engaged was his edition of *Shakespeare. Life*, i. 318, and *post*, p. 68.

[2] 'Tecum habita, et noris quam sit
tibi curta supellex.' *Persius*, iv. 52.
    [3] First published in *Notes and
Queries*, 6th S., v. 304.
    [4] Johnson wrote to Boswell on

                                However

However let us now begin, and try who can continue punctuality longest.. There is this use in the most useless letter, that it shews one not to be forgotten, and they may, at least in the beginning of friendship, or in great length of absence, keep memory from languishing, but our friendship has been too long to want such helps, and I hope our absence will be too short to make them necessary.

My life admits of so little variety, that I have nothing to relate, you who are married, and a magistrate, may have many events to tell both foreign and domestick[1]. But I hope you will have nothing to tell of unhappiness to yourself.

[I was glad of your prospect of reconciliation with Mouseley (?)[2], which is, I hope, now completed; to have one's neighbour one's enemy is uncomfortable in the country where good neighbourhood is all the pleasure that is to be had. Therefore now you are on good terms with your Neighbours, do not differ about trifles[3].]

I am, dear Sir,
Your most affectionate servant,
Sam: Johnson.

My compliments to your Lady.

July 31, 1756.

To the Rev^d Dr. Taylor, at Market Bosworth, Leicestershire[4].

99.

To Lewis Paul[5].

Sir.

I would not have it thought that if I sometimes transgress the rules of civility, I would violate the laws of friendship. If

December 8, 1763:—'I love to see my friends, to hear from them, to talk to them, and to talk of them; but it is not without a considerable effort of resolution that I prevail upon myself to write.' *Life*, i. 473. Goldsmith, apologising to one of his friends for his neglect in correspondence, said: 'No turnspit dog gets up into his wheel with more reluctance than I sit down to write.' Forster's *Goldsmith*, i. 433. Wordsworth had the same reluctance. Wordsworth's *Life*, ed. 1851, i. 260.

[1] Before long Taylor's 'domestick events' supplied correspondence enough. See *post*, Letter of August 13, 1763.

[2] See *post*, Letter of November 18, 1756.

[3] The passage enclosed in brackets is erased in the original.

[4] Taylor was Rector of this town.

[5] First published in Croker's *Bos-*

I had heard anything from the gate[1] I would have informed you, and I will send to them lest they should neglect to transmit any accounts that they receive. I have been many times hindered[2] from coming to you, but if by coming I could have been of any considerable use, I would not have been hindered. They are so cold at the gate both to the landlord and to you, that if I could think of any body else to apply to, I would trouble them no more. I am thinking of Dicey.

                    I am, Sir,
                        Your humble servant,
                                        SAM: JOHNSON.

Sept. 25, 1756.

To Mr. Paul.

100.

To Lewis Paul[3].

SIR,   Wednesday, [1756].

You will think I forgot you, but my boy is run away[4], and I know not whom to send. Besides, nothing seemed to require much expedition, for Mr. Cave has left London almost a fortnight. They intimate at the Gate some desire to know your determination. I will be with you in a day or two.

                    I am, Sir,
                        Your humble servant,
                                        SAM: JOHNSON.

101.

To Lewis Paul.

DEAR SIR,   Saturday, [1756].

I have been really much disordered,—when your last message came I was on the bed, and had not resolution to rise,

---

well, p. 102; corrected by me from the original in the possession of the late Mr. S. J. Davey, of 47 Great Russell Street, London.

It was sold by Messrs. Christie and Co., on June 5, 1888, for £4.

[1] St. John's Gate. *Ante*, p. 59.

[2] Johnson has not written this word very clearly, but both here and just below he has, if I mistake not, written *hindred*.

[3] This and the next two letters were first published in Croker's *Bos-*

well, p. 102.

[4] The boy is no doubt Francis Barber (*ante*, p. 54, *n.* 3), who 'continued' in Johnson's service from 1752 till Johnson's death, with the exception of two intervals; in one of which, upon some difference with his master, he went and served an apothecary in Cheapside, but still visited Dr. Johnson occasionally; in another he took a fancy to go to sea.' *Life*, i. 239, *n.* 1.

                                        having

having had no sleep all night. I indeed had for two days no audible voice, but am now much better, though I cannot hope to go out very quickly.

I am, Sir,

Your humble servant,

SAM: JOHNSON.

102.

To LEWIS PAUL.

[No date.]

SIR,

I am astonished at what you tell me. I cannot well come out to-night, but will wait on you on Monday evening. I have been very busy, but have now some leisure. I repeat again that I am astonished. Henry[1] is just gone out of town, but I could send to him, if there was any likelihood of advantage from it. I am certain it is not done with his privity, for he has no interest in it,—and he is too wise to do ill without interest!

I am. Sir,

Your humble servant,

SAM: JOHNSON.

I am ready to do on this occasion any thing that can be done.

103.

To EDMUND HECTOR [2].

Oct. 7, 1756.

DEAR SIR,

After a long intermission of our correspondence you took some time ago a very kind method of informing me that there was no intermission of our friendship[3], yet I know not why, after the interchange of a letter or two, we have fallen again into

---

[1] David Henry, an Aberdeenshire man, was born in 1710. He came up to London at an early age, where as a journeyman printer he lived on terms of intimacy with Benjamin Franklin and William Strahan. He married Cave's sister. In 1754 his name appears as a partner at St. John's Gate, where he lived for many years, possessing the freehold property of it at his death in 1792. He was an author as well as a printer and publisher. Patrick Henry, the American statesman, was the son of his first cousin. Nichols's *Lit. Anec.* iii. 423, 759.

[2] First published in *Notes and Queries*, 6th S. iii. 301.

[3] See *ante*, p. 42, *n.* 1.

our former silence.   I remember that when we were nearer each other we were more diligent in our correspondence, perhaps only because we were both younger, and more ready to employ ourselves in things not of absolute necessity.   In early life every new action or practice is a kind of experiment, which when it has been tried. one is naturally less eager to try again.   Friendship is indeed one of those few states of which it is reasonable to wish the continuance through life, but the form and exercise of friendship varies, and we grow to recollect (?) to show kindness on important occasions without squandering our ardour in superfluities of empty civility [1].

It is not in mere civility that I write now to you but to inform you that I have undertaken a new Edition of Shakespeare [2], and that the profits of it are to arise from a subscription, I therefore solicit the interest of all my friends, and believe myself sure of yours without solicitation.   The proposals and receipts [3] may be had from my mother, to whom I beg you to send for as many as you can dispose of, and to remit to her money which you or your acquaintances shall collect.   Be so kind as to mention

[1] 'This passage is very difficult to decipher.' Note in *Notes and Queries.*

[2] 'It is remarkable that at this time his fancied activity was for the moment so vigorous that he promised his work should be published before Christmas, 1757. Yet nine years elapsed before it saw the light.' *Life,* i. 319.

[3] In a copy of Harwood's *History of Lichfield* in the Bodleian Library one of these receipts has been inserted at p. 487 :—

'No. 27.
    Received of The Revd. Mr. Seward One Guinea, being the First Payment for a Copy of SHAKE-SPEARE'S WORKS which I promise to deliver according to the Proposals.
                    'SAM. JOHNSON.'
The signature has been pasted on; the receipt is in print with the exception of Mr. Seward's name, which is written, but not by Johnson.   In a volume of pamphlets in the Bodleian Library (No. 141) I have found the following entry in Malone's handwriting :—

'The Proposals in 1756 were entitled thus :—
    " Proposals for printing
            by Subscription
    The Dramatick Works
                of
    William Shakspeare.
    Corrected and Illustrated
                by
        Samuel Johnson.
            Conditions.
    1. That the book shall be elegantly printed in eight volumes in octavo.
    2. That the price to subscribers shall be Two Guineas ; one to be paid at subscribing, the other on the delivery of the book in sheets.
    3. That the work shall be published in or before Christmas, 1757."'

my

my undertaking to any other friends that I may have in your part of the kingdom, the activity of a few solicitors may produce great advantages to me.

I have been thinking every month of coming down into the country, but every month has brought its hindcrances [1]. From that kind of melancholy indisposition which I had when we lived together at Birmingham, I have never been free, but have always had it operating against my health and my life with more or less violence [2]. I hope however to see all my friends, all that are remaining, in no very long time, and particularly you whom I always think on with great tenderness.

I am, Sir,

Your most affectionate servant,

SAM: JOHNSON.

To Mr. Hector, in Birmingham.

104.

To LEWIS PAUL [3].

SIR, Oct. 8, 1756.

You think it hard by this time you cannot have a letter.

I engaged Mr. Newbery [4], who sent me on Monday night the note enclosed, and appeared to think the matter well settled. On Tuesday I wrote to Mr. Henry [5], but soon heard he was out of town. I knew not what to do.—I then had recourse to young Mr. Cave [6], who very civilly went about the business, and came to me yesterday in the evening with this account.

Mr. Cave [7] seized, and has a man in possession.

He made a sale, and sold only a fire-shovel for four shillings.

The goods were appraised at about eighty pounds.

[1] Johnson let more than twenty years go by without visiting his native town, being hindered no doubt mainly by his poverty. *Life*, i. 340, *n*. 1. In the last seventeen years of his life he visited it a dozen times. *Ib*. iii. 452.

[2] See *ib*. i. 64, 87 for his 'melancholy indisposition.'

[3] First published in Croker's *Boswell*, p. 102.

The original was sold by Messrs.

Sotheby and Co., on May 10, 1875, for £3 3s.

[4] See *ante*, p. 22.

[5] See *ante*, p. 67.

[6] Richard Cave, Edward Cave's nephew, 'who from 1754 to 1760 was the printer of the *Gentleman's Magazine* in conjunction with David Henry.' Nichols's *Lit. Anec.* v. 58.

[7] William Cave. *Ante*, p. 58, *n*. 2.

Mr. Cave

Mr. Cave will stay three weeks without any further motion in the business, but will still keep his possession.

He expects that you should pay the expence of the seizure; how much it is I could not be informed.

He will stay to Christmas upon security. He is willing to continue you tenant, or will sell the mill to any that shall work or buy the machine. He values his mill at a thousand pounds [1].

He did not come up about this business, but another.

Mr. Barker [2], as young Mr. Cave thinks, is at Northampton.

These, Sir, are the particulars that I have gathered.

I am, Sir,
Your very humble servant,
SAM: JOHNSON.

105.

To LEWIS PAUL [3].

SIR,   [No date.]

I am no less surprised than yourself at the treatment which you have met with, and agree with you that Mr. Cave must impute to himself part of the discontent that he shall suffer till the spindles are produced.

If I have any opportunity of dispelling the gloom that overcasts him at present, I shall endeavour it both for his sake and yours; but it is to little purpose that remonstrances are offered to voluntary inattention or to obstinate prejudice. Cuxon in one place and Garlick in the other leave no room for the unpleasing reasonings of

Your humble servant,
SAM: JOHNSON.

106.

To DR. TAYLOR [4].

DEAR SIR,

You have no great title to a very speedy answer, yet I did not intend to have delayed so long. I am now in doubt whether

---

[1] The mill, I conjecture, was the place in which the 250 spindles were worked for which Paul had granted a license to Edward Cave. *Ante*, p. 6.

[2] Perhaps Johnson wrote *Bowker*, for with a man of that name Paul had been connected in business.

Life of S. Crompton, p. 265.

[3] First published in Croker's *Boswell*, p. 103.

The original was sold by Messrs. Sotheby and Co., on May 10, 1875, for £2 19s.

[4] First published by the *Philobiblon*

you

you are not come to town, if you are double postage is a proper fine [1].

There is one honest reason why those things are most subject to delays which we most desire to do. What we think of importance we wish to do well, to do anything well requires time, and what requires time commonly finds us too idle or too busy to undertake it. To be idle is not the best excuse, though if a man studies his own reformation it is the best reason he can allege to himself, both because it is commonly true, and because it contains no fallacy, for every man that thinks he is idle condemns himself and has therefore a chance to endeavour amendment, but the busy mortal has often his own commendation, even when his very business is the consequence of Idleness, when he engages himself in trifles only to put the thoughts of more important duties out of his mind, or to gain an excuse to his own heart for omitting them.

I am glad however that while you forgot me you were gaining upon the affections of other people.

It is in your power to be very useful as a neighbour, a magistrate, and a Clergyman, and he that is useful, must conduct his life very imprudently not to be beloved. If Mousley (?) [2] makes advances, I would wish you not to reject them. You once esteemed him, and the quarrel between you arose from misinformation and ought to be forgotten.

When you come to town let us contrive to see one another more frequently, at least once a week. We have both lived long enough to bury many friends, and have therefore learned to set a value on those who are left. Neither of us now can find many whom he has known so long as we have known each other. Do not let us lose our intimacy at a time when we ought rather to think of encreasing it. We both stand almost single in the world, I have no brother, and with your sister you have little correspondence [3]. [But if you will take my advice, you

Society, vi. 15; also in *Notes and Queries*, 6th S. v. 324. It is endorsed: 'The best Letter in the World.'

[1] Johnson directed the letter to Market Bosworth; if Taylor were in London it would have to be forwarded to him there.

[2] The editor of this Letter in *Notes and Queries* says that the name may be Morley or Moresby. It is no doubt the person mentioned *ante*, p. 65.

[3] Johnson writing to Hector many

will

will make some overtures of reconciliation to her. If you have
been to blame, you know it is your duty first to seek a renewal
of kindness. If she has been faulty, you have an opportunity
to exercise the virtue of forgiveness. You must consider that
of her faults and follies no very great part is her own. Much
has been the consequence of her education, and part may
be imputed to the neglect with which you have sometime
treated her. Had you endeavoured to gain her kindness and
her confidence, you would have had more influence over her[1].]
I hope that before I shall see you, she will have had a visit or
a letter from you. The longer you delay the more you will
sometime repent. When I am musing alone, I feel a pang for
every moment that any human being has by my peevishness
or obstinacy spent in uneasiness[2]. I know not how I have fallen
upon this, I had no thought of it, when I began the letter, [yet]
am glad that I have written it.

I am, dearest Sir,

Your most affectionate

Nov. 18, 1756.   SAM: JOHNSON.

To the Rev^d Dr. Taylor, at Market Bosworth, Leicestershire.

107.

To CHARLES O'CONNOR.

London, April 9, 1757.   Published in the *Life*, i. 321.

108.

To EDMUND HECTOR [3].

DEAR SIR,

My mother informs me that you have lately remitted her

---

years later said :—' You and I should
now naturally cling to one another :
we have outlived most of those who
could pretend to rival us in each
other's kindness. . . . You indeed
have a sister with whom you can
divide the day : I have no natural
friend left.' *Life*, iv. 147.

[1] 'The sentences in brackets have
been carefully erased in much darker
ink, probably by Taylor, and the

words "You will forgive her and"
here inserted, not (apparently) in
Johnson's hand, also in much darker
ink.' Note in *Notes and Queries*.

[2] 'I am always sorry (said Dr.
Johnson) when I make bitter speeches,
and I never do it but when I am
insufferably vexed.' Mme. D'Arblay's
Diary. i. 131. See *Life*, ii. 256.

[3] First published in *Notes and
Queries*, 6th S. iii. 321.

some

some money for the receipts¹. I am very sensibly touched by your kindness. The Subscription though it does not quite equal perhaps my utmost hope, for when was hope not disappointed? yet goes on tolerably, and the undertaking will I think be some addition to my fortune, whatever it may be to my reputation².

I rather take it unkindly that you do not from time to time let me hear from you. I am now grown very solicitous about my old friends, with whom I passed the hours of youth and cheerfulness, and am glad of any opportunity to revive the memory of past pleasures. I therefore tear open a letter with great eagerness when I know the hand in which it is super-scribed. Your letters are always so welcome, that you need not increase their value by making them scarce.

I am, Sir,

Your most affectionate friend,

SAM: JOHNSON.

London, Apr. 16, 1757.
  To Mr. Hector in Birmingham.

109.

TO THE REVEREND THOMAS WARTON.

[London], June 21, 1757. *Life*, i. 322.

110.

TO BENNET LANGTON.

[London], June 28, 1757. Published in the *Life*, i. 337.

111.

TO [THOMAS WARTON³].

DEAR SIR,   Oct. 27, 1757.

I have been thinking and talking with Mr. Allen⁴ about some literary business for an inhabitant of Oxford. Many

¹ See *ante*, p. 68, *n.* 3.
² Johnson wrote to Mr. Burney on December 24, 1757:—'How my new edition [of Shakespeare] will be received I know not ; the subscription has not been very successful.' *Life*, i. 323.
³ Published in Croker's *Boswell*, page 108, with the following note :— 'This letter was found by Mr. Peter

Cunningham, in the papers of Allen, the printer, and was intended, no doubt, for Thomas Warton, though perhaps, from some change of opinion, not forwarded to him.'
⁴ Edmund Allen, afterwards 'John-son's landlord and next neighbour in Bolt Court, for whom he had much kindness.' *Life*, iii. 141.

schemes

schemes might be plausibly proposed, but at present these may be sufficient. 1. An Ecclesiastical History of England. In this there are a great many materials which must be compressed into a narrow compass. This book must not exceed 4 vols. 8vo. 2. A History of the Reformation, (not of England only, but of Europe;) this must not exceed the same bulk, and will be full of [*a word omitted*] and very entertaining. 3. The Life of Richard the First. 4. The Life of Edward the Confessor.

All these are works for which the requisite materials may be found at Oxford, and any of them well executed would be well received. I impart these designs to you in confidence, that what you do not make use of yourself shall revert to me un-communicated to any other. The schemes of a writer are his property and his revenue, and therefore they must not be made common.

I am, Sir,

Your most humble servant,

SAM: JOHNSON.

112.

TO MR. BURNEY.

Gough Square, December 24, 1757. First published in the *Life*, i. 323.

113.

TO MR. BURNEY.

London, March, 8, 1758. Published in the *Life*, i. 327.

114.

TO THE REVEREND THOMAS WARTON.

[London], April 14, 1758. Published in the *Life*, i. 335.

115.

TO THE REVEREND THOMAS WARTON.

[London], June 1, 1758. Published in the *Life*, i. 336.

116.

TO BENNET LANGTON.

[London], September 21, 1758. Published in the *Life*, i. 338.

117.

TO BENNET LANGTON.

January 9, 1759 [misdated 1758]. Published in the *Life*, i. 324.

To

118.

To Mrs. Johnson (Johnson's mother [1]).

Honoured Madam,

The account which Miss [2] gives me of your health pierces my heart. God comfort and preserve you and save you, for the sake of Jesus Christ.

I would have Miss read to you from time to time the Passion of our Saviour, and sometimes the sentences in the Communion Service, beginning '*Come unto me, all ye that travail and are heavy laden, and I will give you rest* [3].'

I have just now read a physical [4] book, which inclines me to think that a strong infusion of the bark would do you good. Do, dear mother, try it.

Pray, send me your blessing, and forgive all that I have done amiss to you. And whatever you would have done, and what debts you would have paid first, or anything else that you would direct, let Miss put it down; I shall endeavour to obey you.

I have got twelve guineas [5] to send you, but unhappily am

[1] The first seven of these Letters to Mrs. Johnson and Miss Porter (excluding No. 128) were published by Malone in the fourth edition of the *Life*; the remaining five by Croker in his *Boswell*, pages 114, 115, 118.

'In 1759, in the month of January, Johnson's mother died at the great age of ninety, an event which deeply affected him; not that "his mind had acquired no firmness by the contemplation of mortality," but that his reverential affection for her was not abated by years, as indeed he retained all his tender feelings even to the latest period of his life. I have been told that he regretted much his not having gone to visit his mother for several years, previous to her death. But he was constantly engaged in literary labours which confined him to London; and though he had not the comfort of seeing his aged parent, he contributed liberally to her support.' *Life*, i. 339.

[2] Lucy Porter, his step-daughter.

[3] Johnson mingles the version in the Communion Service — 'Come unto me all that travail and are heavy-laden, and I will refresh you,' with that in the Bible—'Come unto me, all ye that labour and are heavy-laden, and I will give you rest.' *St. Matthew*, xi. 28.

[4] Johnson defines *physical* in its second signification, *pertaining to the science of healing*. For his 'dabbling in physic,' see *ante*, p. 49, *n.* 1.

[5] 'I find in his Diary,' writes Hawkins, 'a note of the payment to Mr. Allen, the printer, of six guineas, which he had borrowed of him, and sent to his dying mother.' Hawkins's *Johnson*, p. 366. Johnson, in all his money difficulties, never seems to have turned to his old pupil Garrick, who could easily have helped him, and no doubt would. Seven years earlier, however, Johnson had drawn

at

at a loss how to send it to-night.   If I cannot send it to-night, it will come by the next post[1].

Pray, do not omit any thing mentioned in this letter: God bless you for ever and ever.

I am your dutiful son,

Jan. 13, 1758[2].   SAM: JOHNSON.

To Mrs. Johnson in Lichfield.

119.

TO MISS PORTER.

MY DEAR MISS,

I think myself obliged to you beyond all expression of gratitude for your care of my dear mother.   God grant it may not be without success.   Tell Kitty[3] that I shall never forget her tenderness for her mistress.   Whatever you can do, continue to do.   My heart is very full.

I hope you received twelve guineas on Monday.   I found

him in Prospero (*The Rambler*, No. 200), and had ended his paper by saying:—'I left him without any intention of seeing him again, unless some misfortune should restore his understanding.'   Reynolds, moreover, was in great prosperity, for in 1758 he had one hundred and fifty sitters (Taylor's *Reynolds*, i. 157). From him he did at one time borrow thirty pounds, which, on his death-bed, he requested him to forgive. *Life*, iv. 413.

[1] Jan. 13, on which day Johnson was writing, was Saturday.   He wrote again on Tuesday, the 16th; Thursday, the 18th; and Saturday, the 20th, for it was on the evenings of those days of the week that mails left London 'for all parts of England.' There were at this time only 123 places to which letters were sent six times a week.   Dodsley's *London and its Environs*, ed. 1761, v. 219. As is shown by Johnson's next letter, the mail that left London for Lichfield on Saturday evening was delivered on Monday—in the morning, as we learn from the *Life*, ii. 468,

where a London letter is received at breakfast-time.

[2] Written by mistake for 1759. Johnson had not yet got accustomed to the change of style, which he had first used six years before (*ante*, p. 6, *n*. 1).   Even in a letter written so far on in the year as March 1, he falls into the same blunder (*post*, p. 86).

'On the outside of this letter was written by another hand—" Pray acknowledge the receipt of this by return of post without fail."'—MALONE.

[3] Catherine Chambers, Mrs. Johnson's maid-servant. Johnson recorded in his Diary on 'Sunday, Oct. 18, 1767. Yesterday, Oct. 17, at about ten in the morning, I took my leave for ever of my dear old friend, Catharine Chambers, who came to live with my mother about 1724, and has been but little parted from us since.   She buried my father, my brother, and my mother.   She is now fifty-eight years old. . . . We kissed, and parted.   I humbly hope to meet again, and to part no more.' *Life*. ii. 43.

a way

a way of sending them by means of the postmaster, after I had written my letter, and hope they came safe[1]. I will send you more in a few days. God bless you all.

> I am, my dear,
>> Your most obliged
>>> and most humble servant,

Jan. 16, 1759.   SAM: JOHNSON.

Over the leaf is a letter to my mother.

To Miss Porter, at Mrs. Johnson's, in Lichfield.

120.

To Mrs. Johnson.

DEAR HONOURED MOTHER,

Your weakness afflicts me beyond what I am willing to communicate to you. I do not think you unfit to face death[2], but I know not how to bear the thought of losing you. Endeavour to do all you [can] for yourself. Eat as much as you can.

I pray often for you; do you pray for me. I have nothing to add to my last letter.

> I am, dear, dear mother,
>> Your dutiful son.

Jan. 16, 1759.   SAM: JOHNSON.

121.

To Mrs. Johnson.

DEAR HONOURED MOTHER,

I fear you are too ill for long letters; therefore I will only tell you, you have from me all the regard that can possibly

---

[1] The difficulty of sending money is shown in a letter of Cowper's dated Olney, Nov. 10, 1767:—'I shall be glad if you will find an opportunity of sending me six guineas in a parcel by the Olney waggon which sets out from the George, in Smithfield, early on Tuesday morning, therefore it must be sent to the inn on Monday night.'—Southey's *Cowper*, xv. 21.

[2] How Johnson's truthfulness stands forth here! No flattering at that dread hour. 'I do not think you unfit to face death' is all that he dared say even to his mother. ' "Don't compliment now," he replied warmly,' on his own death-bed to a friend who praised too highly the life which he had led. *Life*, iv. 410, n. 2.

subsist

subsist in the heart. I pray God to bless you for evermore, for Jesus Christ's sake. Amen.

Let Miss write to me every post [1], however short.

I am, dear mother,

Your dutiful son,

Jan. 18, 1759.   SAM: JOHNSON.

To Mrs. Johnson, in Lichfield.

122.

To MISS PORTER.

DEAR MISS,

I will, if it be possible, come down to you [2]. God grant I may yet [find] my dear mother breathing and sensible. Do not tell her lest I disappoint her. If I miss to write next post, I am on the road.

I am, my dearest Miss,

Your most humble servant,

Jan. 20, 1759.   SAM: JOHNSON.

To Miss Porter, at Mrs. Johnson's, in Lichfield.

123.

To MRS. JOHNSON [3].

DEAR HONOURED MOTHER,

Neither your condition nor your character make it fit for me to say much. You have been the best mother, and I believe the best woman in the world. I thank you for your indulgence to me, and beg forgiveness of all that I have done ill, and all that I have omitted to do well [4]. God grant you his Holy

---

[1] Every letter which he received would have cost him fourpence. In the last year of Johnson's life the charge was raised to fivepence. By 1812 it had gone up to ninepence, where it remained for nearly thirty years. *Penny Cyclo.*, ed. 1840, xviii. 455.

[2] Travelling was still very slow. Fielding, in *Tom Jones* (bk. xi. ch. 9), published in 1749, describes a nobleman in his coach and six taking two days to perform a journey of ninety miles, though he started at seven in the morning. Johnson in 1772, by which time a great deal had been done to render travelling more rapid, took twenty-six hours in going in the coach from London to Lichfield—a distance of 116 miles. *Post*, Letter of Oct. 19, 1772.

[3] 'This letter was written on the second leaf of the preceding.'— MALONE.

[4] In a prayer which Johnson wrote, dated 'Jan. 23. The day on which my dear mother was buried,' he says :— 'Forgive me whatever I have done

Spirit,

Spirit, and receive you to everlasting happiness, for Jesus Christ's sake. Amen. Lord Jesus receive your spirit. Amen.

I am, dear, dear mother,

Your dutiful son,

SAM: JOHNSON.

Jan. 20, 1759.

124.

To WILLIAM STRAHAN [1].

SIR,

When I was with you last night I told you of a story which I was preparing for the press. The title will be

'The Choice of Life

or

The History of . . . . . Prince of Abissinia.'

unkindly to my mother, and whatever I have omitted to do kindly.' *Pr. and Med.*, p. 37. On Easter Day of the same year he wrote in a prayer:—'Forgive me, O Lord, whatever my mother has suffered by my fault. . . . And, O Lord, so far as it may be lawful I commend unto thy fatherly goodness my father, brother, wife, and mother, beseeching thee to make them happy for Jesus Christ's sake.' Croker's *Boswell*, p. 823. In this commendation, in giving their names, he mentions them in the order in which they had died.

[1] From the original in the possession of Mr. Frederick Barker, of 41 Gunterstone Road, West Kensington. First published in my edition of the Life, vol. vi; *Addenda*, p. xxviii.

'The late Mr. Strahan,' writes Boswell, 'told me that Johnson wrote *Rasselas* that with the profits he might defray the expense of his mother's funeral, and pay some little debts which she had left. He told Sir Joshua Reynolds, that he composed it in the evenings of one week, sent it to the press in portions as it was written, and had never since read it over. Mr. Strahan, Mr. Johnston,

and Mr. Dodsley purchased it for a hundred pounds, but afterwards paid him twenty-five pounds more, when it came to a second edition. . . . Voltaire's *Candide*, written to refute the system of Optimism, which it has accomplished with brilliant success, is wonderfully similar in its plan and conduct to Johnson's *Rasselas;* insomuch, that I have heard Johnson say, that if they had not been published so closely one after the other that there was not time for imitation, it would have been in vain to deny that the scheme of that which came latest was taken from the other.' *Life*, i. 341. That Johnson sent *Rasselas* to the press in portions, as it was written, does not seem consistent with this letter, and Sir Joshua's memory probably failed him on this point.

His friend Baretti said that 'any other person with his reputation would have got £400 for it, but he never understood the art of making the most of his productions.' Prior's *Life of Malone*, p. 160.

Candide, it should seem, was published in the latter half of February, 1759. Grimm in his letter of March 1 speaks of its having just appeared.

It

It will make about two volumes like little Pompadour[1], that is about one middling volume. The bargain which I made with Mr. Johnson was seventy five pounds (or guineas) a volume, and twenty-five pounds for the second edition. I will sell this either at that price or for sixty[2], the first edition of which he shall himself fix the number, and the property then to revert to me, or for forty pounds, and I share[3] the profit, that is retain half the copy. I shall have occasion for thirty pounds on Monday night when I shall deliver the book which I must entreat you upon such delivery to procure me. I would have it offered to Mr. Johnson[4], but have no doubt of selling it, on some of the terms mentioned.

I will not print my name, but expect it to be known[5].

I am, dear Sir,

Your most humble servant,

SAM: JOHNSON.

Jan. 20, 1759.

Get me the money if you can.

He does not mention it in his previous letter of Feb. 15. *Corres. Lit.* (ed. 1829), ii. 296. This letter proves that *Rasselas* was written before *Candide* was published. See also the Introduction to my edition of *Rasselas*, Clarendon Press, 1887, p. 24.

[1] By 'little Pompadour' Johnson, I conjecture, means the second and cheaper edition of *The History of the Marchioness de Pompadour.* The first edition was published by Hooper in one volume, price five shillings (*Gentleman's Magazine* for Oct. 1758, p. 493), and the second in two volumes for three shillings and sixpence (*Gentleman's Magazine* for Nov. 1758, p. 543). It is strange however that Johnson should refer to this book, as it is scandalous and almost indecent.

[2] In the original 'fifty - five pounds' written first and then scored over.

[3] In my edition of the *Life, share*

is misprinted *have.*

[4] Mr. Johnson, the bookseller, was, I conjecture, W. Johnston, who, with Strahan and Dodsley, purchased the book. He lived in Ludgate Street. See Nichols's *Lit. Anec.,* iii. 727.

[5] Johnson did not generally 'print his name.' He published anonymously his translation of *Lobo's Voyage to Abyssinia; London; The Life of Savage; The Rambler* and *The Idler,* both in separate numbers and when collected in volumes; *Rasselas; The False Alarm; Falkland's Islands; The Patriot;* and *Taxation no Tyranny;* (when these four pamphlets were collected in a volume he published them with the title of *Political Tracts by the Authour of the Rambler*). He gave his name in *The Vanity of Human Wishes, Irene,* the *Dictionary,* his edition of *Shakespeare,* the *Journey to the Western Islands,* and the *Lives of the Poets.*

Fielding at one time of his life

To

To Miss Porter.

You will conceive my sorrow for the loss of my mother, of the best mother. If she were to live again, surely I should behave better to her. But she is happy, and what is past is nothing to her; and for me, since I cannot repair my faults to her, I hope repentance will efface them. I return you and all those that have been good to her my sincerest thanks, and pray God to repay you all with infinite advantage. Write to me, and comfort me, dear child. I shall be glad likewise, if Kitty will write to me. I shall send a bill of twenty pounds in a few days, which I thought to have brought to my mother; but God suffered it not. I have not power or composure to say much more. God bless you and bless us all.

I am, dear Miss.

Your affectionate humble servant,

SAM: JOHNSON.

Jan. 23, 1759 '.

To Miss Porter in Lichfield.

126.

To Miss Porter.

(The beginning is torn and lost.)

.   .   .   .

You will forgive me if I am not yet so composed as to give any directions about any thing. But you are wiser and better than I, and I shall be pleased with all that you shall do. It is not

boasted that he had never published even a pamphlet without setting his name to it, and adds :—'For the sake of men's characters I wish all other writers were by law obliged to use the same method ; but till they are I shall no longer impose any such restraint on myself.' Fielding's *Works*, ed. 1806, v. 413.

' In a prayer which Johnson composed on this event he speaks of himself as 'now about to return to the common comforts and business of the world.' *Pr. and Med.*, p. 38. In a note on this (*Life*, i. 514) I speak of this prayer as being composed on the day on which his mother was buried, and add :—'After his wife's death he had allowed forty days to pass before his "return to life."' On looking once more at the passage in *Prayers and Meditations*, I see that I may have been mistaken. For he adds that the prayer was 'repeated on my fast with the addition.' The addition is likely enough the second part of the prayer, and it is in it that this statement is found. When the fast was held we are not told.

of any use for me now to come down ; nor can I bear the place. If you want any directions, Mr. Howard[1] will advise you. The twenty pounds I could not get a bill for to-night, but will send it on Saturday.

I am, my dear,

Your affectionate servant,

SAM: JOHNSON.

Jan. 25, 1759.

127.

TO MISS PORTER.

DEAR MISS,

I have no reason to forbear writing, but that it makes my heart heavy, and I had nothing particular to say which might not be delayed to the next post ; but had no thoughts of ceasing to correspond with my dear Lucy, the only person now left in the world with whom I think myself connected[2]. There needed not my dear mother's desire, for every heart must lean to somebody, and I have nobody but you ; in whom I put all my little affairs with too much confidence to desire you to keep receipts, as you prudently proposed.

If you and Kitty[3] will keep the house, I think I shall like it best. Kitty may carry on the trade for herself, keeping her own stock apart, and laying aside any money that she receives for any of the goods which her good mistress has left behind her.

[1] Mr. Howard, whose Christian name was Charles, 'was in the law, and resided in the Close.' Boswell mentions him among Johnson's early friends and patrons. *Life*, i. 80. Writing of him in a letter to Dr. Taylor (*post*, August 18, 1763), Johnson says :—'His profession has acquainted him with matrimonial law, and he is in himself a cool and wise man.' His daughter Mary married in December, 1757, Dr. Erasmus Darwin. Their third son was Robert Waring Darwin, the father of Charles Robert Darwin. It is very likely that from Johnson's friend, 'the cool and wise man,' the great naturalist indirectly derived his Christian name. He was named, it is believed, after Erasmus Darwin's favourite son Charles, who died from a dissection wound at Edinburgh ; who, in his turn, was named, we may assume, after his mother's father, Johnson's friend. It is interesting to find Charles Darwin's great-grandfather described by Johnson as 'a cool and wise man'; for no man in a higher degree deserved that character than Charles Darwin himself.

[2] He had some distant relations to whom he left legacies. *Life*, iv. 401, n. 3 ; 402, n. 2.

[3] Catherine Chambers, Mrs. Johnson's old servant. *Ante*, p. 76, n. 3.

I do

I do not see, if this scheme be followed, any need of appraising the books [1]. My mother's debts, dear mother, I suppose I may

[1] His mother had carried on her husband's trade as a bookseller; the books were the stock in her shop. *Life*, i. 90, *n.* 3 ; 175, *n.* 1. In the Johnson MSS. at Pembroke College are the following documents relating to the trade as carried on by her husband, her son Nathanael and herself:—

To the Hon^d Gilb. Walmesley Esqr.

		£	s	d
1	Memoires of Literature for feb. and March .	o	2	o
May 10, 1726. 1 Dit. Ap. and May		o	2	o
1	Dit. June	o	1	o
1	Swift's Cadenus &c. . .	o	1	o
1	memoires July, Aug. Sept. Oct.	o	4	o
1	Phyical [*sic*] Dict. . .	o	6	o
1	moyle's Works. 3 vol.	o	17	o
1	Gullivers Travels. 2 vol.	o	9	6
1	Glew [? 1 lb. of glue] .	o	o	5
1	memoirs for Nov. and Dec.	o	2	o
Jan. 27, 1726^7. 1 Hederici Lexicon		o	13	6
1	Aliffs Canon and Civill Law	1	4	o
		4	2	5

Jan. 27, 1726-7.

Received then the contents of this Bill four pound two shillings two-pence in full of all Accounts

MICH. JOHNSON.

To the Hon^d Mr. Walmesly.

		£	s	d
1	Holland on ye smallpox	o	2	9
1	Republick, Aug. Sept. Oct.	o	3	o
1	—— Nov. Decemb. . .	o	2	o
1	Norfolk Congress . .	o	o	9
1	Cornel. Nepos, De[cember]	o	4	6
1	Republick, Jan. feb. March, Ap. May . .	o	5	o
1	Letter from Rome . .	o	1	6

		£	s	d
1	Tryal of witnesses . .	o	1	6
1	Republick, June, July, Aug.	o	3	o
1	—— Sept. Oct. . . .	o	2	o
		1	6	o
		o	3	9
		1	2	3

Last Bill, query where it ended.

		£	s	d
Human Understanding .		o	5	6
Republ. May and June .		o	2	o
Dunciade and Key . . .		o	2	o
July		o	1	o

Here I suppose the former bill ended.

Decemb. ye 28, 1729.

Recev^d then the Contents of this Bill and all Acct.

M. JOHNSON.

SIR,

I here send you the Books togeather with an account of the Charge of them; the whole is 26. 6. 4, rec'd 21—so that there remains due to me 5. 6. 4, which you will please to remit att your Convenient time.

I am your humble Servt

D. JOHNSON.

Swarkstone, Aug. 21, 1733.

On Monday and Tuesday the third and fourth of Septr will be ye last day's of our attending the sale, and on which day's we shall return half a Crown in the Pound, for all books that may be bought on those two day's. I shall be glad to have your company.

For Gilb^t Walmesley

Esq. at His House

In Lichfield.

pay

pay with little difficulty; and the little trade may go silently forward. I fancy Kitty can do nothing better; and I shall not want to put her out of a house, where she has lived so long, and with so much virtue. I am very sorry that she is ill, and earnestly hope that she will soon recover; let her know that I have the highest value for her, and would do any thing for her advantage. Let her think of this proposal. I do not see any

To the Hon^d Gilbert Walmesley Esqr.

	£	s.	d.
17 Republicks of Letters from May 1732 to November 1733	0	17	0
1 Lock on ye Longitude	0	0	6
	0	17	6

Nov. 10th, 1733.

Rec^d then in full of this Bill and all Accts.

         SARAH JOHNSON.

To Gilbert Walmesley Esqr.

	£	s.	d.
12 Republicks of Letters from Oct. 1733 to Nov. 1734	0	12	0
Feb. 21st. An Almanack bound in vell.	0	1	9
1734, May 20. The Bishops Charge	0	1	0
Oct. 2. A Play	0	0	6
	0	15	3

Rec^d Feb. 3, 1734/5 ye contents of this Bill in full of all accounts, I say rec^d by me,

         NATH: JOHNSON.

Febru. ye 3d, 1734-5

	£	s.	d.
Mr. Walmsley paid all but	0	0	3
October was the last Republick he had then recev^d			
June 30th. Popes Letters .	0	6	0
12 Republicks since . .	0	12	0
	0	18	3

Jan. 10, 1735.

Rec^d then in full of this Bill and all Act's.

         SARAH JOHNSON.

         'Ashby, Jan. 31, 1735.

SIR,

My sister Johnson desiars me to wright in her behalf to you, there being due to her for the parcell of books you had of her at Swarkstone five pund six shillings and foure pence, you had a perticuler acount sent you with the books, as she wase obliged to sell of the studey of books at a loe rate to turn it into money, she hoped you would have paid the bill which she sent to Mr. Newton, some time agoe. He returned the bill and said you mentiond some mestake, which if there wase my sister desiard him to let you so [sic] she would desiare you to paye him the rest, and deduct the mestake for she desiars no moore than is justly due to her, the interest that might have been maid in this time will help towards a smal mestake. She begs you will paye the money to Mr. Newton who will soon come to Ashby and will i dare saye help it to my sister Johnson. I am y^r

         Humble sarvant,

         JAMES BATE.'

At the foot is written in another hand :— 'N.B. I paid Mr. Newton £5; but I believe s^d [?] I rectify the mistakes in Mrs. Johnson's bill, there will be something due, tho' a trifle, to

         G. WALMESLEY.'

                   likelier

likelier method by which she may pass the remaining part of her life in quietness and competence.

You must have what part of the house you please, while you are inclined to stay in it; but I flatter myself with the hope that you and I shall some time pass our days together [1]. I am very solitary and comfortless, but will not invite you to come hither till I can have hope of making you live here so as not to dislike your situation. Pray, my dearest, write to me as often as you can.

I am, dear Madam,

Your affectionate humble servant,

Feb. 6, 1759.   SAM: JOHNSON.

128.
To Miss Porter [2].

MY DEAR MISS,

I am very much pleased to find that your opinion concurs with mine. I think all that you propose is right and beg that you would manage every thing your own way, for I do not doubt but I shall like all that you do.

Kitty shall be paid first, and I will send her down money to pay the London debts afterwards, for as I have had no connexion with the trade, it is not worth while to appear in it now. Kitty may close her mistress's account and begin her own. The stock she shall have as you mention. I hope she continues to recover.

I am very much grieved at my Mother's death, and do not love to think nor to write about it. I wish you all kinds of good, and hope sometime to see you.

I am, dear Miss,

Your affectionate servant,

London, Feb. 15, 1759.   SAM: JOHNSON.

[1] Miss Porter lived on, it should seem, in Johnson's house in Lichfield till she had built one of her own. *Life*, i. 110, *n.* 3. She died without ever visiting London. *Ib.* ii. 462.

[2] I have carelessly failed to record the name of the correspondent to whose kindness I am indebted for this unpublished letter. It is endorsed :—'An original letter of Dr. Johnson—given to me by Geo. Pearson, St. John's Coll. Cam. G.W.' George Pearson was probably the son of the Rev. Mr. Pearson, of Lichfield (*Life*, ii. 471; iv. 256), whom Mr. Croker describes, in one place, as the legatee of Lucy Porter, and in another place as the husband of the lady who inherited her fortune. Croker's *Boswell*, Preface, p. xiv. and p. 492.

To

129.

To Miss Porter.

DEAR MADAM,   March 1, 1758[9] [1].

I thought your last letter long in coming; and did not require or expect such an inventory of little things as you have sent me. I could have taken your word for a matter of much greater value. I am glad that Kitty is better; let her be paid first, as my dear, dear mother ordered, and then let me know at once the sum necessary to discharge her other debts, and I will find it you very soon.

I beg, my dear, that you would act for me without the least scruple, for I can repose myself very confidently upon your prudence, and hope we shall never have reason to love each other less. I shall take it very kindly if you make it a rule to write to me once at least every week, for I am now very desolate, and am loth to be universally forgotten.

I am, dear sweet,
Your affectionate servant,
SAM: JOHNSON.

130.

To Miss Porter.

DEAR MADAM,   March 23, 1759.

I beg your pardon for having so long omitted to write. One thing or other has put me off. I have this day moved my things, and you are now to direct to me at Staple Inn, London [2]. I hope, my dear, you are well, and Kitty mends. I wish her success in her trade. I am going to publish a little story book,

[1] See *ante*, p. 76, *n.* 2.
[2] He had left Gough Square, where he had lived since 1749. *Life*, iii. 405, *n.* 6. On January 9 of this year (in a letter misdated 1758) he wrote to Langton, who had sent him some game: 'I have left off house-keeping, and therefore made presents of the game.' *Life*, i. 326.

Apparently he had dispersed his household, sleeping probably in his old house, but having no cooking done there. His chambers in Staple Inn are not known. I made enquiries about them, but was informed that the books of the Society had been destroyed in a fire.

which

which I will send you when it is out [1]. Write to me, my dearest girl, for I am always glad to hear from you.

I am, my dear,

Your humble servant,

SAM: JOHNSON.

131.

To Miss Porter.

DEAR MADAM,   May 10, 1759.

I am almost ashamed to tell you that all your letters came safe, and that I have been always very well, but hindered, I hardly know how, from writing. I sent, last week, some of my works, one for you, one for your aunt Hunter, who was with my poor dear mother when she died, one for Mr. Howard [2], and one for Kitty.

I beg you, my dear, to write often to me, and tell me how you like my little book.

I am, dear love,

Your affectionate humble servant,

SAM: JOHNSON.

132.

To Mrs. Montagu [3].

MADAM,   June 9, 1759.

I am desired by Mrs. Williams to sign receipts with her name for the subscribers which you have been pleased to pro-

---

[1] The little story book was *Rasselas*. It was reviewed in the *Gentleman's Magazine* for April (p. 184), and was no doubt published in that month. *The Gentleman's Magazine* at this time was published at the end of the month, or even later. Thus the number for April, 1759, contains news as late as April 30.

[2] See *ante*, p. 82, *n*. 1.

[3] This and the following letter were first published in Croker's *Boswell*, page 118.

For an account of Mrs. Montagu, see Boswell's *Johnson*, ii. 88. In 1775 she gave Mrs. Williams a small annuity. Croker's *Boswell*, p. 458,

and *post*, Letter of Sept. 22, 1783. The subscriptions were perhaps for Mrs. Williams's *Miscellanies*, though that volume was not published till seven years later. *Life*, ii. 25.

Johnson once censured Mrs. Montagu's mode of conferring charity. 'If,' said he, 'a wench wants a good gown, do not give her a fine smelling-bottle, because that is more delicate; as I once knew a lady lend the key of her library to a poor scribbling dependant, as if she took the woman for an ostrich that could digest iron.' Piozzi's *Anecdotes*, p. 271. We learn from Hayward's *Piozzi*, i. 154, that this lady was Mrs. Montagu.

cure,

cure, and to return her humble thanks for your favour, which
was conferred with all the grace that elegance can add to
beneficence.

I am, Madam,

Your most obedient and most humble servant,

SAM: JOHNSON.

133.

To MRS. MONTAGU.

MADAM,   Gray's Inn[1], Dec. 17, 1759.

Goodness so conspicuous as yours will be often solicited,
and perhaps sometimes solicited by those who have little pre- ·
tension to your favour.   It is now my turn to introduce a
petitioner, but such as I have reason to believe you will think
worthy of your notice.   Mrs. Ogle, who kept the music-room
in Soho Square[2], a woman who struggles with great industry
for the support of eight children, hopes by a benefit concert to
set herself free from a few debts, which she cannot otherwise
discharge.   She has, I know not why, so high an opinion of me
as to believe that you will pay less regard to her application
than to mine.   You know, Madam, I am sure you know, how
hard it is to deny, and therefore would not wonder at my compliance, though I were to suppress a motive which you know
not, the vanity of being supposed to be of any importance to
Mrs. Montagu.   But though I may be willing to see the world
deceived for my advantage, I am not deceived myself, for I know
that Mrs. Ogle will owe whatever favours she shall receive from
the patronage which we humbly entreat on this occasion, much

---

[1] Johnson, who had moved to Staple Inn on March 23 of this year, had resided there but a short time, and was now occupying chambers in Gray's Inn, whence in a few months he moved to Inner Temple Lane. I am informed by Mr. W. R. Douthwaite, Librarian of Gray's Inn and author of *Gray's Inn, its History and Associations*, that 'he does not seem to have held chambers *directly* from the Society.'

[2] Horace Walpole in 1771 mentions a Madame Cornelys who 'took Carlisle House in Soho Square, enlarged it, and established assemblies and balls by subscription.' She had apparently been there some years, as in 1764 he had said that 'she had enlarged her vast room.' *Letters*, iv. 302 ; v. 283. She got into difficulties and died in the Fleet Prison. Cunningham's *Handbook of London*, ed. 1850, p. 456. Perhaps Mrs. Ogle had occupied the same house.

more

more to your compassion for honesty in distress, than to the request of,

Madam,

Your most obedient and most humble servant,

SAM: JOHNSON.

134.

TO JOSEPH SIMPSON.

[London, 1759?] Published in the *Life*, i. 346.

Boswell ascribes this undated letter to 1759. In a note on it I have shown that it probably belongs to a later date.

135.

TO BENNET LANGTON.

[London], October 18, 1760. Published in the *Life*, i. 357.

136.

TO THE REVEREND THOMAS PERCY[1].

DEAR SIR,

I went this morning to Mr. Millar[2], and found him very well disposed to your project. I told him the price of 3 vols. was an hundred guineas, to which he made no objection[3]. I said nothing of advancing any money, for he was in great haste, and I did not at once recollect it. There is only one thing which I

[1] From the original in the Dyce and Forster Libraries, Science and Art Department, South Kensington, communicated to me by Mr. R. Forster Sketchley.

[2] Andrew Millar, the great bookseller, whom Johnson called 'the Maecenas of the age.' *Life*, i. 287, n. 3.

[3] In 1761 Percy published a translation from the Portuguese of a Chinese novel, *Hau Kiau Chooan*, in four volumes, and in 1762 *Miscellaneous Pieces relating to the Chinese*, in two volumes. His *Reliques of Ancient English Poetry* did not appear till 1765; nevertheless it is no doubt this work which was the subject of this letter. It was in three volumes, and Johnson, as Percy tells us in his Preface, had seen some of the manuscript and had urged its publication. Shenstone wrote on March 1, 1761 :—'You have perhaps heard me speak of Mr. Percy; he was in treaty with Mr. James Dodsley for the publication of our best old ballads in three volumes. . . . I proposed the scheme for him myself.' Shenstone's *Works*, iii. 321. 'Mr. Shenstone,' writes Percy in his Preface, 'was to have borne a joint share in the work had not death unhappily prevented him.' (He died on Feb. 11, 1763.) The bargain with Millar dropped through, for it was Dodsley who had the high honour of publishing the *Reliques*.

dislike.

dislike.　He wants the Sheets that are in my hands to shew to I know not whom.　In that there is yet some danger.　If we had not had this Specimen I think we should have immediately bargained.　Perhaps after all the bargain is made.　You will know from his own Letter, which he promised me to write to-night, and which, if he writes it, will make this superfluous.　But, this business being of moment, I would not appear to neglect it.　Make all compliments to Mrs. Percy [1], for

Sir,

Your most humble servant,
SAM: JOHNSON.

Nov. 29, 1760.

　　To the Rev^d Mr. Percy.

137.

To Miss Porter [2].

Inner Temple Lane [3], Jan. 13, 1761.

DEAREST MADAM,

　　I ought to have begun the new year with repairing the omissions of the last, and to have told you sooner, what I can

---

[1] It was to his young wife that Percy, two years earlier, had addressed those pretty lines beginning :-

'O Nancy, wilt thou go with me,
　Nor sigh to leave the flaunting town ?
Can silent glens have charms for thee ?
　The lowly cot and russet gown ? '

Dodsley's *Collection of Poems*, ed. 1758, vi. 233, and H. B. Wheatley's edition of the *Reliques*, i. Preface, p. 72.

[2] First published in Croker's *Boswell*, 8vo. ed., p. 122.

[3] Johnson had moved into Inner Temple Lane in 1760.　'I have been told,' says Hawkins, 'by his neighbour at the corner, that during the time he dwelt there, more inquiries were made at his shop for Mr. Johnson than for all the inhabitants put together of both the Inner and Middle Temple.'　Hawkins's *Life of Johnson*, p. 383.　In Dodsley's *London*, published in 1761, the side of the Temple fronting the Thames is described as 'lying open and airy, and enjoying a delightful prospect into Surrey.' vol. vi. p. 104.　Boswell, thirty years after Johnson, had chambers on the same staircase, and here 'he was forcing himself to sit some hours a-day,' at the very time that he was bringing out his *Life of Johnson*. *Letters of Boswell*, p. 335, and Croker's *Boswell*, p. 830.

According to the *Gentleman's Magazine* for 1857, part ii, p. 552, Johnson had occupied the first floor of No. 1.　On October 8 of that year there was a sale by auction of the floor, windows, doors, and panel partition.　They fetched £10 5*s*.　The entire staircase and the outside door with its pilasters were withdrawn from the sale, as the Benchers wished to preserve them as relics.　The house was pulled down.　It

always

always tell you with truth, that I wish you long life and happiness, always increasing till it shall end at last in the happiness of heaven.

I hope, my dear, you are well; I am at present pretty much disordered by a cold and cough; I have just been blooded, and hope I shall be better.

Pray give my love to Kitty. I should be glad to hear that she goes on well.

I am, my dearest dear,
Your most affectionate servant,
SAM: JOHNSON.

138.

To JOSEPH BARETTI.

London, June 10, 1761.   Published in the *Life*, i. 361.

139.

To the Reverend Thomas Percy[1].

DEAR SIR,

The kindness of your invitation would tempt me to leave pomp and tumult behind, and hasten to your retreat; however, as I cannot perhaps see another coronation[2] so conveniently as

stood on the site of what is now called Johnson's Buildings.

To the kindness of Mr. H. W. Lawrence, Sub-Treasurer of the Inner Temple, I owe the following copy of a 'Bench Table Order':—

'Inner Temple, Bench Table,
'Tuesday, Nov. 10, 1857.

'Ordered that the Staircase, &c. of Dr. Johnson's Staircase be presented to the Crystal Palace Company.'

Mr. W. Gardiner, the Secretary of the Crystal Palace Company, informs me that no trace of it can be found. He does not think that it was ever set up, but that it was stored in a part of the building which was destroyed by fire in 1866.

Charles Lamb, who in 1809 took chambers at No. 4 of the same Lane, says :—'I have two rooms on the third floor and five rooms above, with an inner staircase to myself, and all new painted &c., and all for £30 a year!' *Letters of Charles Lamb*, ed. by A. Ainger, i. 252.

[1] From the original in the possession of Mr. Alfred Morrison, of Fonthill House.

This Letter was sold for £5 10s. by Messrs. Christie & Co. on June 5, 1888. Lot 48.

[2] The Coronation took place on Sept. 22. Horace Walpole wrote on Sept. 28 :—'What is the finest sight in the world? A Coronation. What do people talk most about? A Coronation. What is delightful to have passed? A Coronation. Indeed, one had need be a handsome young peeress not to be fatigued to this,

this, and I may see many young Percies, I beg your pardon for staying till this great ceremony is over, after which I purpose to pass some time with you, though I cannot flatter myself that I can even then long enjoy the pleasure which your company always gives me, and which is likewise expected from that of Mrs. Percy, by,

Sir,
Your most affectionate
SAM: JOHNSON.

Sept. 12, 1781.

To the Rev^d Mr. Percy, at Easton Mauduit, Northamptonshire, by Castle Ashby.

140.

TO DR. STAUNTON.

[London], June 1, 1762.   Published in the *Life*, i. 367.

141.

TO A LADY.

[London], June 8, 1762.   Published in the *Life*, i. 368.

142.

TO JOSEPH BARETTI.

London, July 20, 1762.   Published in the *Life*, i. 369.

143.

TO THE EARL OF BUTE.

[London], July 20, 1762.   Published in the *Life*, i. 376.

144.

TO MISS PORTER [1].

DEAR MADAM,

If I write but seldom to you it is because it seldom happens that I have anything to tell you that can give you pleasure, but last Monday I was sent for by the chief Minister [2] the Earl of

death with it.' *Letters*, iii. 444. Johnson visited Percy at his Vicarage at Easton Maudit in 1764. *Life*, i. 486.

[1] From the original in the possession of the late Mr. Stamford Raffles, 13 Abercromby Square, Liverpool.

[2] Neither *Premier* nor *Prime Minister* is in Johnson's *Dictionary*. In 1775 he used the term *Prime Minister*. *Life*, ii. 355. Hume in 1742 speaks of Walpole as Prime Minister. Hume's *Essays*, ed. 1742, ii. 204. For Johnson's pension see *Life*, i. 372.

Bute,

Bute, who told me that the King had empowered him to do something for me; and let me know that a pension was granted me of three hundred a year. Be so kind as to tell Kitty.

I am, dearest Madam,
Your most affectionate
SAM: JOHNSON.

July 24, 1762.

To Miss Porter, Lichfield.

145.

TO THE EARL OF BUTE.

Temple Lane, November 3, 1762.   Published in the *Life*, i. 380.

146.

TO MISS REYNOLDS [1].

DEAR MADAM,   Dec. 21, 1762.

If Mr. Mudge should make the offer you mention, I shall certainly comply with it, but I cannot offer myself unasked [2].   I am much pleased to find myself so much esteemed by a man whom I so much esteem.

Mr. Tolcher [3] is here; full of life, full of talk, and full of enterprise. To see brisk young fellows of seventy-four, is very surprising to those who begin to suspect themselves of growing old.

---

[1] First published in Croker's *Boswell*, page 129.
Boswell says that he had seen Johnson's letters to Miss Reynolds (Sir Joshua's sister), but that ' her too nice delicacy would not permit them to be published.'—*Life*, i. 486, *n.* 1.

[2] 'To be a godfather.' — MISS REYNOLDS. Mr. Mudge was most likely one of the sons of the Rev. Zachariah Mudge, either John, 'the celebrated surgeon,' or Thomas, who in 1793 or 1794 received a reward of £3,000 from Parliament for his improvement in the construction of chronometers. William Mudge, John Mudge's son, famous for the part he took in the trigonometrical survey of

Great Britain and Ireland, was born in 1762. It is probable therefore that it was about him that the offer was made. See Boswell's *Johnson*, i. 378, and Knight's *Cyclo. of Biog.* iv. 373.

[3] 'An alderman of Plymouth, he to whom Johnson exclaimed in his mock enthusiasm, "I hate a Docker."'—CROKER. See the *Life*, i. 379, *n.* 2. Northcote in Hazlitt's *Conversations* (p. 288) said :—' Old Mr. Tolcher used to say of the famous Pulteney—" My Lord Bath always speaks in blank verse."' He gave young Northcote an introduction to Reynolds. Leslie and Taylor's *Life of Reynolds*, i. 406.

You

You may tell at Torrington that whatever they may think, I have not forgot Mr. Johnson's widow [1], nor school—Mr. Johnson's salmon—nor Dr. Morison's Idler. For the widow I shall apply very soon to the Bishop of Bristol [2], who is now sick. The salmon I cannot yet learn any hope of making a profitable scheme, for where I have inquired, which was where I think the information very faithful, I was told that dried salmon may be bought in London for a penny a pound; but I shall not yet drop the search.

For the school, a sister of Miss Carwithen's has offered herself to Miss Williams, who sent her to Mr. Reynolds, where the business seems to have stopped. Miss Williams thinks her well qualified, and I am told she is a woman of elegant manners, and of a lady-like appearance. Mr. Reynolds must be written to, for, as she knows more of him than of me, she will probably choose rather to treat with him.

Dr. Morison's Books shall be sent to him with my sincere acknowledgements of all his civilities.

I am going for a few days or weeks to Oxford, that I may free myself from a cough, which is sometimes very violent; however, if you design me the favour of any more letters, do not let the uncertainty of my abode hinder you, for they will be sent after me, and be very gladly received by,

Madam,

Your most obliged humble servant,

SAM: JOHNSON.

147.

To Joseph Baretti.

London, December 21, 1762. Published in the *Life*, i. 380.

[1] 'A clergyman's widow—to procure a pension for her.'— MISS REYNOLDS. Johnson and Reynolds on their tour to Devonshire in the summer of this year had visited at Torrington Reynolds's brother-in-law, Mr. Johnson. Leslie and Taylor's *Life of Reynolds*, i. 215.

[2] Thomas Newton, a Lichfield man. Johnson hearing his *Dissertations on the Prophecies* described as his great work, said : — 'Why, Sir, it is Tom's great work : but how far it is great, or how much of it is Tom's, are other questions.'—*Life*, iv. 286.

To

148.

To George Strahan [1].

DEAR GEORGE,   Feb. 19, [1763].

I am glad that you have found the benefit of confidence, and hope you will never want a friend to whom you may safely disclose any painful secret. The state of your mind you had not so concealed but that it was suspected at home, which I mention that if any hint should be given you, it may not be imputed to me, who have told nothing but to yourself, who had told more than you intended [2].

I hope you read more of Nepos, or of some other book, than you construe to Mr. Bright [3]. The more books you look into for your entertainment, with the greater variety of style you will make yourself acquainted. Turner I do not know; but think that if Clark [4] be better, you should change it, for I shall never be willing that you should trouble yourself with more than one book to learn the government of words. What book that one shall be, Mr. Bright must determine. Be but diligent in reading and writing, and doubt not of the success. Be pleased to make my compliments to Miss Page and the gentlemen.

> I am,
> > Dear Sir,
> > > Yours affectionately,
> > > > SAM: JOHNSON.

149.

To George Strahan [5].

DEAR SIR,   March 26, 1763.

You did not very soon answer my letter, and therefore cannot complain that I make no great haste to answer yours.

---

[1] First published in Croker's *Boswell*, page 129.

George Strahan, the son of William Strahan the printer, became Vicar of Islington. He attended Johnson on his death-bed, and published his *Prayers and Meditations. Life*, iv. 376. He was at this time at the Abingdon Grammar School.

[2] See *post*, Letter of Aug. 19, 1782.

[3] Mr. Bright was the Master of Abingdon School.

[4] I think that John Clarke is meant, the author of books on Latin Grammar and Composition. I do not know who Turner was.

[5] First published in Croker's *Boswell*, page 130.

I am

I am well enough satisfied with the proficiency that you make, and hope that you will not relax the vigour of your diligence. I hope you begin now to see that all is possible which was professed. Learning is a wide field, but six years spent in close application are a long time; and I am still of opinion, that if you continue to consider knowledge as the most pleasing and desirable of all acquisitions, and do not suffer your course to be interrupted, you may take your degree not only without deficiency, but with great distinction.

You must still continue to write Latin. This is the most difficult part, indeed the only part that is very difficult of your undertaking. If you can exemplify the rules of syntax, I know not whether it will be worth while to trouble yourself with any more translations. You will more increase your number of words, and advance your skill in phraseology, by making a short theme or two every day; and when you have construed properly a stated number of verses, it will be pleasing to go from reading to composition, and from composition to reading. But do not be very particular about method; any method will do, if there be but diligence. Let me know, if you please, once a week what you are doing.

I am,
Dear George,
Your humble servant,
SAM: JOHNSON.

150.

To Miss Porter [1].

MY DEAR,   April 12, 1763.

The newspaper has informed me of the death of Captain Porter [2]. I know not what to say to you, condolent [3] or consolatory, beyond the common considerations which I suppose you have proposed to others, and know how to apply to yourself. In all afflictions the first relief is to be asked of God.

---

[1] First published in Croker's *Boswell*, page 130.

[2] 'Miss Porter's brother, a Captain in the Navy, left her a fortune of ten thousand pounds; about a third of which she laid out in building a stately home, and making a handsome garden in an elevated situation in Lichfield.' *Life*, ii. 462.

[3] *Condolent* is not in Johnson's *Dictionary*.

I wish

I wish to be informed in what condition your brother's death has left your fortune; if he has bequeathed you competence or plenty, I shall sincerely rejoice; if you are in any distress or difficulty, I will endeavour to make what I have, or what I can get, sufficient for us both.

I am,
Madam,
Yours affectionately,
SAM: JOHNSON.

151.

To GEORGE STRAHAN [1].

DEAR SIR,   April 16, 1763.

Your account of your proficience is more nearly equal, I find, to my expectations than your own. You are angry that a theme on which you took so much pains was at last a kind of English Latin; what could you expect more? If at the end of seven years you write good Latin, you will excel most of your contemporaries: Scribendo disces scribere. It is only by writing ill that you can attain to write well. Be but diligent and constant, and make no doubt of success.

I will allow you but six weeks for Tully's Offices. Walker's Particles [2] I would not have you trouble yourself to learn at all by heart, but look in it from time to time, and observe his notes and remarks, and see how they are exemplified. The translation from Clark's history will improve you, and I would have you continue it to the end of the book.

I hope you read by the way at loose hours other books, though you do not mention them; for no time is to be lost; and what can be done with a master is but a small part of the whole. I would have you now and then try at some English verses. When you find that you have mistaken any thing, review the passage carefully, and settle it in your mind.

---

[1] First published in Croker's *Boswell*, page 130.

[2] *Treatise of English Particles, shewing how to render them according to the proprietie and elegance of the Latine.* London, 1655. By William Walker, B.D.

Be pleased to make my compliments, and those of Miss Williams, to all our friends.

> I am, dear Sir,
>> Yours most affectionately,
>>> SAM: JOHNSON.

152.

To The Right Hon. George Grenville [1].

SIR,   July 2, 1763.

Be pleased to pay to the bearer seventy-five pounds, being the quarterly payment of a pension granted by his Majesty, and due on the 24th day of June last to, Sir,

> Your most humble servant,
>> SAM: JOHNSON [2].

153.

To Miss Porter [3].

MY DEAREST DEAR,   July 5, 1763.

I am extremely glad that so much prudence and virtue as yours is at last awarded [4] with so large a fortune, and doubt not but that the excellence which you have shewn in circumstances of difficulty will continue the same in the convenience of wealth.

I have not written to you sooner, having nothing to say,

[1] Published in the *Grenville Papers*, ii. 68.

George Grenville was Chancellor of the Exchequer. For the payment of Johnson's pension see *Life*, i. 376, *n.* 2.

[2] Four days before the date of this letter the following note had been sent, which, in its result, affected Johnson's life scarcely less than his pension. I owe this copy of it to the kindness of Mrs. Thomas, of Eyhorne House, Hollingbourne, near Maidstone, who possesses the original :—

'Mr. Thrale presents His most respectfull compliments to Mrs. and Miss Salusbury and wishes to God He could have communicated His Sentiments to Them last night, which is absolutely impossible for Him to

do to any other Person breathing ; He therefore most ardently begs to see Them at any Hour this afternoon, and He will at all Events immediately enter upon this very interesting Subject, and when once begun, there is no Danger of His wandering upon any other : in Short, see Them, He must, for He assures Them, with the greatest Truth and Sincerity, that They have *murder'd* Peace and Happiness at Home.

'Southwark, 28 June, 1763.'

Mr. Thrale married Miss Salusbury on the following Oct. 11. *Gentleman's Magazine*, 1763, p. 518.

[3] First published in Croker's *Boswell*, page 144.

[4] Perhaps he wrote *rewarded*.

which

which you would not easily suppose—nothing but that I love
you and wish you happy; of which you may be always assured,
whether I write or not.

I have had an inflammation in my eyes; but it is much better,
and will be, I hope, soon quite well.

Be so good as to let me know whether you design to stay at
Lichfield this summer; if you do, I purpose to come down.
I shall bring Frank[1] with me; so that Kitty must contrive to
make two beds, or get a servant's bed at the Three Crowns[2],
which may be as well. As I suppose she may want sheets, and
table linen, and such things, I have sent ten pounds, which she
may lay out in conveniences. I will pay her for our board
what you think proper; I think a guinea a week for me and the
boy.

Be pleased to give my love to Kitty.

I am, my dearest love,
Your most humble servant,
SAM: JOHNSON.

154.

To Miss Porter[3].

MY DEAREST LOVE,   July 12, 1763.

I had forgot my debt to poor Kitty; pray let her have the
note, and do what you can for her, for she has been always very
good. I will help her to a little more money if she wants it, and
will write. I intend that she shall have the use of the house as
long as she and I live[4].

That there should not be room for me at the house is some
disappointment to me, but the matter is not very great. I am
sorry you have had your head filled with building, for many
reasons. It was not necessary to settle immediately for life at
any one place; you might have staid and seen more of the
world. You will not have your work done, as you do not understand it, but at twice the value. You might have hired a house

---

[1] His black servant.

[2] 'The good old-fashioned inn, the very next house to that in which Johnson was born and brought up,' where he and Boswell stayed in 1776. *Life*, ii. 461. It is still stand-ing.

[3] First published in Croker's *Bos-well*, page 145.

[4] See *ante*, p. 82.

at half the interest of the money for which you build it. if your house cost you a thousand pounds. You might have the Palace for twenty pounds¹, and make forty of your thousand pounds; so in twenty years you would have saved four hundred pounds, and still have had your thousand.

> I am, dear Dear,
> Yours, &c.,
> SAM: JOHNSON.

155.

To GEORGE STRAHAN ².

DEAR GEORGE,

To give pain ought always to be painful, and I am sorry that I have been the occasion of any uneasiness to you, to whom I hope never to [do] any thing but for your benefit or your pleasure. Your uneasiness was without any reason on your part, as you had written with sufficient frequency to me, and I had only neglected to answer them, because as nothing new had been proposed to your study, no new direction or incitement could be offered you. But if it had happened that you had omitted what you did not omit, and that I had for an hour, or a week, or a much longer time, thought myself put out of your mind by something to which presence gave that prevalence, which presence will sometimes give even where there is the most prudence and experience, you are not to imagine that my friendship is light enough to be blown away by the first cross blast, or that my regard or kindness hangs by so slender a hair as to be broken off by the unfelt weight of a petty offence. I love you, and hope to love you long. You have hitherto done nothing to diminish my good will, and though you had done much more than you have supposed imputed to you, my good will would not have been diminished.

I write thus largely on this suspicion, which you have suffered to enter your mind, because in youth we are apt to be too

---

¹ When Boswell visited Lichfield in 1776 the Bishop's Palace was occupied by Miss Seward's father. *Life*, ii. 467. Bishop Selwyn, who was appointed in 1867, was, I was told, the first prelate who made it his permanent abode.

² First published in Croker's *Boswell*, page 146; corrected by me from the original in the possession of Mr. W. R. Smith, of Greatham Moor, West Liss, Hants.

rigorous

rigorous in our expectations, and to suppose that the duties of life are to be performed with unfailing exactness and regularity; but in our progress through life we are forced to abate much of our demands, and to take friends such as we can find them, not as we would make them.

These concessions every wise man is more ready to make to others, as he knows that he shall often want them for himself; and when he remembers how often he fails in the observance or cultivation of his best friends, is willing to suppose that his friends may in their turn neglect him, without any intention to offend him.

When therefore it shall happen, as happen it will, that you or I have disappointed the expectation of the other, you are not to suppose that you have lost me, or that I intended to lose you; nothing will remain but to repair the fault, and to go on as if it never had been committed.

I am, Sir,

Your affectionate servant,

SAM: JOHNSON.

Thursday, July 14, 1763.

156.

To THE REVEREND DR. TAYLOR[1].

DEAR SIR,

You may be confident that what I can do for you either by help or counsel in this perplexity shall not be wanting, and I take it as a proof of friendship that you have recourse to me on this strange revolution of your domestick life.

I do not wonder that the commotion of your mind made it difficult for you to give me a particular account, but while my knowledge is only general, my advice must be general too.

Your first care must be of yourself and your own quiet. Do not let this vexation take possession of your thoughts, or sink too deeply into your heart. To have an unsuitable or unhappy

[1] First published in *The Miscellanies of the Philobiblon Society*, vi. 19; afterwards by Professor J. E. B. Mayor in *Notes and Queries*, 6th S., v. 324. It is the first of a series of letters about a quarrel between Dr. Taylor and his wife which ended in a separation. Boswell seems to have known nothing of this matter. According to Nichols (*Lit. Anec.* ix. 58) Taylor was twice married.

marriage

marriage happens every day to multitudes, and you must endeavour to bear it like your fellow sufferers by diversion at one time and reflection at another. The happiness of conjugal life cannot be ascertained or secured either by sense or by virtue, and therefore its miseries may be numbered among those evils which we cannot prevent and must only labour to endure with patience, and palliate with judgement. If your condition is known I should [think] it best to come from the place, that you may not be a gazing-stock to idle people who have nobody but you to talk of. You may live privately in a thousand places till the novelty of the transaction is worn away. I shall be glad to contribute to your peace by any arrangement in my power.

With respect to the Lady I so little understand her temper that I know not what to propose. Did she go with with [*sic*] a male or female companion? With what money do you believe her provided? To whom do you imagine she will recur for shelter? What is the abuse of her person which she mentions? What is [the] danger which she resolves never again to incur? The tale of Hannah I suppose to be false, not that if it be true it will justify her violence and precipitation, but it will give her consequent superiority in the publick opinion and in the courts of Justice, and it will be better for you to endure hard conditions than bring your character into a judicial disquisition.

I know you never lived very well together, but I suppose that an outrage like this must have been preceded by some uncommon degrees of discord from which you might have prognosticated some odd design, or that some preparations for this excursion must have been made, of which the recollection may give you some direction what to conjecture, and how to proceed.

You know that I have never advised you to any thing tyrannical or violent, and in the present case it is of great importance to keep yourself in the right, and not injure your own right by any intemperance of resentment or eagerness of reprisal. For the present I think it prudent to forbear all persuit [*sic*], and all open enquiry, to wear an appearance of complete indifference, and calmly wait the effects of time, of necessity, and of shame. I suppose she cannot live long without your money, and the confession of her want will probably humble her.

Whether

Whether you will inform her brother, I must leave to your discretion, who know his character and the terms on which you have lived. If you write to him, write like a man ill treated but neither dejected nor enraged.

I do not know what more I can say without more knowledge of the case, only I repeat my advice that you keep yourself cheerful, and add that I would have [you] contribute nothing to the publication of your own misfortune. I wondered to see the note transcribed by a hand which I did not know.

I am, dear Sir,

Your most affectionate

SAM: JOHNSON.

August 13, 1763.

To the Rev^d Dr. Taylor in Ashbourn, Derbyshire.

157.

TO THE REVEREND DR. TAYLOR [1].

DEAR SIR,

I have endeavoured to consider your affair according to the knowledge which the papers that you have sent me, can afford, and will very freely tell you what occurs to me.

Who Mr. Woodcock is I know not, but unless his character in the world, or some particular relation to yourself, entitle him to uncommon respect, you seem to treat him with too much deference by soliciting his interest and condescending to plead your cause before him, and imploring him to settle those terms of separation which you have a right to prescribe. You are in my opinion to consider yourself as a man injured, and instead of making defence, to expect submission. If you desert yourself who can support you? You needed not have confessed so much weakness as is made appear by the tale of the half-crown and the pocket picked by your wife's companion. However nothing is done that can much hurt you.

You enquire what the fugitive Lady has in her power. She has, I think, nothing in her power but to return home and mend her behaviour. To obtain a separate maintenance she must prove either cruelty to her person or infidelity to her bed, and

---

[1] First published in *The Miscellanies of the Philobiblon Society*, vi. 22 ; afterwards in *Notes and Queries*, 6th S., v. 342.

I suppose

I suppose neither charge can be supported. Nature has given women so much power that the law has very wisely given them little[1].

The Letter for Mr. Wakefield I think you do not want; it is his part to write to you, who are ill treated by his sister. You owe him, I think, no obligations, but have been accustomed to act among your wife's relations with a character of inferiority which I would advise you to take this opportunity of throwing off for ever. Fix yourself in the resolution of exacting reparation for the wrong that you suffer, and think no longer that you are to be first insulted and then to recompense by submission the trouble of insulting you.

If a separate alimony should come to be stipulated I do not see why you should by an absurd generosity pay your wife for disobedience and elopement. What allowance will be proper I cannot tell, but would have you consult our old friend Mr. Howard[2]. His profession has acquainted him with matrimonial law, and he is in himself a cool and wise man. I would not have him come to Ashbourne nor you go to Lichfield; meet at Tutbury[3] or some other obscure and commodious place and talk the case at large with him, not merely as a proctor but as a friend.

Your declaration to Mr. Woodcock that you desired nothing to be a secret was manly and right; persist in that strain of talking, receive nothing, as from favour or from friendship; whatever you grant, you are to grant as by compassion, whatever you keep, you are to keep by right. With Mr. Wakefield you have no business, till he brings his sister in his hand, and desires you to receive her.

I do not mean by all this to exclude all possibility of accommodation; if there is any hope of living happily or decently, cohabitation is the most reputable for both.

[1] 'Men,' said Johnson, 'know that women are an over-match for them, and therefore they choose the weakest or most ignorant. If they did not think so, they never could be afraid of women knowing as much as themselves.' *Life*, v. 226.

[2] See *ante*, p. 82, *n*. 1.

[3] Tutbury is nearly half-way between Ashbourne and Lichfield, lying a little off the main road. Here in 1569, and again in 1585, Mary Queen of Scots was imprisoned. Froude's *History of England*, ed. 1870, ix. 33; xi. 529.

Your

Your first care must be to procure to yourself such diversions as may preserve you from melancholy and depression of mind, which is a greater evil than a disobedient wife.   Do not give way to grief, nor nurse vexation in solitude ; consider that your case is not uncommon, and that many live very happily who have like you succeeded ill in their . . . .¹ connexion.

I cannot butt [*sic*] think that it would be prudent to remove from the clamours, questions, hints, and looks of the people about you, but of this you can judge better than,

Dear Sir,
Your affectionate

Aug. 18, 1763.   SAM: JOHNSON.

To the Reverend Dr. Taylor in Ashbourne, Derbyshire.

158.

TO THE REVEREND DR. TAYLOR ².

DEAR SIR,

Having with some impatience reckoned upon hearing from you these two last posts, and been disappointed, I can form to myself no reason for the omission but your perturbation of mind, or disorder of body arising from it, and therefore I once more advise removal from Ashbourne as the proper remedy both for the cause and the effect.

You perhaps ask, whither should I go? any whither where your case is not known, and where your presence will cause neither looks nor whispers.   Where you are the necessary subject of common talk, you will not safely be at rest.

If you cannot conveniently write to me yourself let somebody write for you to

Dear Sir,
Your most affectionate

SAM: JOHNSON.

August 25, 1763.

To the Reverend Dr. Taylor in Ashbourne, Derbyshire.

---

¹ 'This word I cannot decipher. It looks like "uplier." ' Professor Mayor, *Notes and Queries*.

² From the original in my possession ; first published in my edition of the *Life*, i. 472.

TO

To the Reverend Dr. Taylor [1].

DEAR SIR,   Sept. 3, 1763.

Mr. Woodcock, whatever may be his general character, seems to have yielded on this occasion a very easy admission to very strong prejudices. He believes every thing against you and nothing in your favour. I am therefore glad that his resolution of neutrality, so vehemently declared, has set you free from the obligation of a promise made with more frankness than prudence to refer yourself to his decision. Your letters to him are written with great propriety, with coolness and with spirit, and seem to have raised his anger only by disappointing his expectations of being considered as your protector, and being solicited for favour and countenance. His attempts to intimidate you are childish and indecent; what have you to dread from the Law? The Law will give Mrs. Taylor no more than her due and you do not desire to give her less.

I wish you had used the words *pretended* friendship and would have [you] avoid on all occasions to declare whether, if she should offer to return, you will or will not receive her. I do not see that you have any thing more [to do] than to sit still, and expect the motions of the Lady and her friends. If you think it necessary to retain Council [*sic*], I suppose you will have recourse to Dr. Smallbrook [2], and some able Man of the common Law or chancery, but though you may retain them provisionally, you need do nothing more; for I am not of opinion that the Lady's friends will suffer her cause to be brought into the Courts.

I do not wonder that Mr. Woodcock is somewhat incredulous when you tell him that you do not know your own income; pray take care to get information, and either grow wiser or conceal your weakness. I could hardly believe you myself when I heard

[1] First published in *The Miscellanies of the Philobiblon Society*, vi. 28; afterwards in *Notes and Queries*, 6th S., v. 343.

[2] 'About this time [1738] Johnson applied to Dr. Adams to consult Dr. Smalbroke of the Commons, whether a person might be permitted to practice as an advocate there without a doctor's degree in Civil Law.' *Life*, i. 134.

that

that a wrong letter had been sent to Woodcock by your servant who made the packet. You are the first man who, being able to read and write, had packets of domestick quarrels made by a servant. Idleness in such degree, must end in slavery, and I think you may less disgracefully be governed by your Lady than by Mr. Hint [?]. It is a maxim that no man ever was enslaved by influence[1] while he was fit to be free.

I cannot but think that Mr. Woodcock has reason on his side when he advises the dismission of Hannah. Why should you not dismiss her? It is more injury to her reputation to keep her than to send her away, and the loss of her place you may recompense by a present or some small annuity conveyed to her. But this I would have you do not in compliance with solicitation or advice, but as a justification of yourself to the world; the world has always a right to be regarded[2].

In affairs of this kind it is necessary to converse with some intelligent man, and by considering the question in all states to provide means of obviating every charge. It will surely be right to spend a day with Howard. Do not on this occasion either want money or spare it.

You seem to be so well pleased to be where you are, that I shall not now press your removal, but do not believe that every one who rails at your wife, wishes well to you. A small country town is not the place in which one would chuse to

---

[1] The word *influence* was much in men's mouths at this time. Hume in his *History of England* (ed. 1773, viii. 319), writing of the reign of Charles II, says:—'The Crown still possessed considerable power of opposing parliaments, and had not as yet acquired the means of influencing them.' Cf. also *ib.* vi. 163. The elder Pitt, in 1766, said in Parliament:—'I have had the honour to serve the Crown, and if I could have submitted to influence might have still continued to serve.' *Parl. Hist.* xvi. 98. Burke in 1770, in his *Thoughts on the Cause of the Present Discontents*, writes:—'The power

of the Crown, almost dead and rotten as Prerogative, has grown up anew, with much more strength, and far less odium, under the name of *Influence.*' Payne's *Burke*, i. 10. Johnson perhaps had in mind the following lines in *The Castle of Indolence* (ii. 29):—

'But in prime vigour what can last for ay?
That soul-enfeebling wizard Indolence,
I whilom sung, wrought in his works decay;
Spread far and wide was his curs'd influence.'

[2] See *Life*, ii. 74, *n.* 3.

quarrel

quarrel with a wife; every human being in such places is a spy.

I am, dear Sir,

Yours affectionately,

SAM: JOHNSON.

To the Rev^d Dr. Taylor in Ashbourne, Derbyshire.

160.

TO GEORGE STRAHAN [1].

DEAR SIR,

I should have answered your last letter sooner if I could have given you any valuable or useful directions, but I know not any way by which the composition of Latin verses can be much facilitated. Of the grammatical part which comprises the knowledge of the measure of the foot, and quantity of the syllables, your grammar will teach you all that can be taught, and even of that you can hardly have any thing by rule but the measure of the foot. The quantity of syllables even of those for which rules are given is commonly learned by practice and retained by observation. For the poetical part, which comprises variety of expression, propriety of terms, dexterity in selecting commodious words, and readiness in changing their order, it will all be produced by frequent essays, and resolute perseverance. The less help you have the sooner you will be able to go forward without help.

I suppose you are now ready for another author. I would not have you dwell longer upon one book, than till your familiarity with its style makes it easy to you; every new book will for a time be difficult. Make it a rule to write something in Latin every day, and let me know what you are now doing, and what your scheme is to do next. Be pleased to give my compliments to Mr. Bright, Mr. Stevenson, and Miss Page.

I am, dear Sir,

Your affectionate servant,

SAM: JOHNSON.

Sept. 20, 1763.

To Mr. Strahan at the Reverend Mr. Bright's in Abingdon, Berks.

---

[1] First published in Croker's *Boswell*, page 161; corrected by me from the original in the possession of Mr. W. R. Smith, of Greatham Moor, West Liss, Hants.

TO

To the Reverend Dr. Taylor [1].

DEAR SIR,

The alterations which you made in the letter, though I cannot think they much mended it, yet did no harm, and perhaps the letter may have the effect of reducing the Lady and her friends to terms truly moderate and reasonable by shewing what slight account you make of menaces and terror. I no more desire than you to bring the cause before the Courts, and if they who are on the Lady's side can prove nothing, they have in reality no such design. It is not likely that even if they had proof of incontinency they would desire to produce it, or make any other use of it, than to terrify you into their own Conditions.

Of the letter which you sent me I can form no judgement till you let me know how it came into your hands. If the servant who received it produced it voluntarily, I suspect that it was written on purpose to be shewn you; if you discovered it by accident, it may be supposed to be written that it might be shewn to others. I do not see that it deserves or requires any notice on either supposition.

You suspect your housekeeper at Ashbourn of treachery, and I doubt not that the Lady has her lower friends and spies behind her. But let your servant be treacherous as you suppose, it is your own fault if she has any thing to betray. Do your own business, and keep your own secrets, and you may bid defiance to servants and to treachery.

Your conduct with regard to Hannah has, I think, been exactly right; it will be fit to keep her in sight for some months, and let her have directions to shew herself as much as she can.

Your ill health proceeds immediately from the perturbation of your mind. Any incident that makes a man the talk and spectacle of the world without any addition to his honour is naturally vexatious, but talk and looks are all the evils which this domestick revolution has brought upon you. I knew that you and your wife lived unquietly together, I find that provocations

[1] First published in the *Miscellanies of the Philobiblon Society*, vi. 32; afterwards in *Notes and Queries*, 6th S., v. 382.

were greater than I had known, and do not see what you have to regret but that you did not separate in a very short time after you were united. You know, however, that I was always cautious when I touched on your differences, that I never advised extremities, and that I commonly softened rather than instigated resentment. What passes in private can be known only to those between whom it passes, and they who [are] ignorant of the cause and progress of connubial differences, as all must be but the parties themselves, cannot without rashness give any counsel concerning them. Your determination against cohabitation with the Lady I shall therefore pass over, with only this hint, that you must keep it to yourself; for as by elopement she makes herself liable to the charge of violating the marriage contract, it will be prudent to keep her in the criminal state, by leaving her in appearance a possibility of return, which preserves your superiority in the contest, without taking from you the power of limiting her future authority, and prescribing your own conditions.

I cannot but think that by short journeys, and variety of scenes, you may dissipate your vexation, and restore your health, which will certainly be impaired by living where every thing seen or heard impresses your misfortunes on your mind. .

I am. dear Sir,

Your most &c. &c.,

Sept. 29, 1763.   SAM: JOHNSON.

To the Rev^d Dr. Taylor in Ashbourn, Derbyshire.

162.

TO MISS REYNOLDS [1].

Oxford, October 27, [1763].

Your letter has scarcely come time enough to make an answer possible. I wish we could talk over the affair. I cannot go now.

[1] First published in Croker's *Boswell*, page 161. Mr. Croker says in a note that 'Captain, afterwards Sir George Collier, was about to sail to the Mediterranean, and offered Miss Reynolds a passage; and she appears to have wished that Johnson might be of the party. Johnson was not aware that Captain Collier's *lady* was also going. Sir Joshua had gone to the Mediterranean in a similar way with Captain Keppel.'

Sir George Collier in 1779 was the commander of the English Fleet in the war against America. *Annual Register*, 1779, p. 188.

I must

I must finish my book[1]. I do not know Mr. Collier. I have not money beforehand sufficient. How long have you known Collier, that you should have put yourself into his hands? I once told you that ladies were timorous, and yet not cautious.

If I might tell my thoughts to one with whom they never had any weight, I should think it best to go through France. The expense is not great; I do not much like obligation, nor think the grossness of a ship very suitable to a lady. Do not go till I see you. I will see you as soon as I can.

I am. my dearest,

Most sincerely yours,

SAM: JOHNSON.

163.

To JAMES BOSWELL.

London, December 8, 1763. Published in the *Life*, i. 473.

164.

To MISS PORTER[2].

MY DEAR, London, Jan. 10, 1764.

I was in hopes that you would have written to me before this time, to tell me that your house was finished, and that you were happy in it. I am sure I wish you happy. By the carrier of this week you will receive a box, in which I have put some books, most of which were your poor dear mamma's, and a diamond ring, which I hope you will wear as my new year's gift. If you receive it with as much kindness as I send it, you will not slight it; you will be very fond of it.

Pray give my service to Kitty[3], who, I hope, keeps pretty well. I know not now when I shall come down; I believe it will not be very soon. But I shall be glad to hear of you from time to time.

---

[1] If this letter is assigned to the right year the book must have been his edition of Shakespeare, which was begun in 1756 and completed in 1765.

[2] First published in Croker's *Boswell*, page 163.

[3] Catherine Chambers. *Ante*, p. 76, *n*. 3.

I wish

I wish you, my dearest, many happy years; take what care you can of your health.

> I am, my dear,
>> Your affectionate humble servant,
>>> SAM: JOHNSON.

165.

DEAR SIR,

I congratulate you upon the happy end of so vexatious an affair, the happyest [*sic*] that could be next to Reformation and Reconcilement. You see how easily seeming difficulties are surmounted.

That your mind should be harried, and your spirits weakened, it is no wonder; your whole care now should be to settle and repair them. To this end I would have you make use of all diversions, sports of the field abroad, improvement of your estate or little schemes of building, and pleasing books at home; or if you cannot compose yourself to read, a continual succession of easy company. Be sure never to be unemployed, go not to bed till you sleep, and rise as soon as you wake, and give up no hours to musing and retrospect. Be always busy.

You will hardly be quite at rest till you have talked yourself out to some friend or other, and I think you and I might contrive some retreat for part of the summer where we might spend some time quietly together, the world knowing nothing of the matter [2].

I hear you talk of letting your house at Westminster. Why should you let it? Do not shew yourself either intimidated or ashamed, but come and face mankind like one that expects not censure but praise. You will now find that you have money enough. Come and spend a little upon popular hospitality. Your low spirits have given you bad counsel: you shall not give your wife, nor your wife's friends, whose power you now find to be nothing, the triumph of driving you out of life. If

---

[1] First published in the *Miscellanies of the Philobiblon Society*, vi. 37; afterwards in *Notes and Queries*, 6th S., v. 382.

[2] Johnson spent some weeks of this summer at Easton Maudit, in Northamptonshire (*Life*, i. 486). It is possible that Taylor met him somewhere in the neighbourhood, and 'talked himself out to him.'

you

you betray yourself who can support you? All this I shall be glad to dilate with you in a personal interview at some proper place, where we may enjoy a few days in private.

I am, dear Sir,

Yours affectionately,

SAM: JOHNSON.

May 22, 1764.

To the Reverend Dr. Taylor in Ashbourn, Derbyshire.

166.

TO JOSHUA REYNOLDS.

Easton Maudit, August 19, 1764. Published in the *Life*, i. 486.

167.

TO WILLIAM STRAHAN [1].

SIR,

I think I have pretty well disposed of my young friend George, who, if you approve of it, will be entered next Monday a Commoner of University College, and will be chosen next day a Scholar of the House. The Scholarship is a trifle, but it gives him a right, upon a vacancy, to a Fellowship of more than sixty pounds a year if he resides, and I suppose of more than forty if he takes a Curacy or small living [2]. The College is almost filled with my friends, and he will be well treated [3]. The Master is

---

[1] First published in my edition of Boswell's *Johnson*, volume vi, *Addenda*, p. xxx, from the original in the possession of Mr. Frederick Barker, of 41 Gunterstone Road, West Kensington.

[2] In the College records is the following entry :—

'Oct. 30-31, 1764. Candidatis examinatis electi sunt Gulielmus Jones et Georgius Strahan in vacuas Exhibitiones D^{ui} Simonis Benet Baronetti.'

Gulielmus Jones is the famous oriental scholar, Sir William Jones, whose portrait adorns the Hall of his ancient College. *Life*, ii. 25, *n.* 2.

On April 16, 1767, is found the election of 'Georgium Strahan, so-

phistam in perpetuum hujus Collegii Socium.'

He vacated his fellowship in 1773.

Jones had been elected Fellow on August 7, 1766. *Life of Sir William Jones*, p. 45. His fellowship is described as 'not exceeding, upon an average, one hundred pounds.'

[3] Among Johnson's friends belonging either then or later on to the College were the Master, Dr. Wetherell; William Scott (afterwards Lord Stowell); John Scott (afterwards Earl of Eldon); Robert Chambers (afterwards Sir Robert Chambers, one of the Judges in Bengal); the Right Hon. William Windham; and Mr. Coulson, whose guest he was in June, 1775 (*post*, Letter of June 1,

informed

informed of the particular state of his education, and thinks, what I think too, that for Greek he must get some private assistance, which a servitour of the College is very well qualified and will be very willing to afford him on very easy terms.

I must desire your opinion of this scheme by the next post, for the opportunity will be lost if we do not now seize it, the Scholarships being necessarily filled up on Tuesday.

I depend on your proposed allowance of a hundred a year, which must the first year be a little enlarged because there are some extraordinary expenses, as

Caution [1] (which is allowed in his last quarter) .	7	0	0
Thirds [2] (He that enters upon a room pays two thirds of the furniture that he finds, and receives from his successor two thirds of what he pays ; so that if he pays £20 he receives £13 6s. 8d., this perhaps may be)	12	0	0
Fees at entrance, matriculation, &c., perhaps .	2	0	0
His gown (I think) .	2	10	0
	£23	10	0

If you send us a Bill for about thirty pounds we shall set out commodiously enough. You should fit him out with cloaths and linen, and let him start fair, and it is the opinion of those whom

1775). In the Common Room there is an engraving of him with this inscription: 'Samuel Johnson, LL.D. in hac camera communi frequens conviva. D.D. Gulielmus Scott nuper socius.' 'I have drunk,' said Johnson, 'three bottles of port without being the worse for it. University College has witnessed this.' *Life*, iii. 245.

See Appendix B for A. Macdonald's Letter to David Hume about an Oxford education.

[1] The 'caution' is the sum deposited by an undergraduate with the College Bursar or Steward as a security for the payment of his 'battells' or account. Johnson in 1728 had to pay at Pembroke College the same sum (seven pounds) that George

Strahan in 1764 had to pay at University College. *Life*, i. 58, *n.* 2.

[2] An undergraduate who entered Queen's College in 1778 wrote to his father :—'My furniture is pretty good, and the thirds will run low, I believe.' *Letters of Radcliffe and James*, p. 45. Bentham, who entered Queen's College in June, 1760, calls them 'thirdings.' He paid £8 for his 'caution'; £1 12s. 6d. for his gown (which, being a commoner's, would be cheaper than Strahan's), and 7s. for his cap and tassel.

Less than a year before the date of Johnson's Letter he had been attending Blackstone's lectures on law, and detecting the lecturer's fallacy about natural rights. Bentham's *Works*, x. 36, 39, 45.

I consult,

I consult, that with your hundred a year and the petty scholarship he may live with great ease to himself, and credit to you [1].

Let me hear as soon as is possible.

In your affair with the university, I shall not be consulted, but I hear nothing urged against your proposal [2].

I am, Sir,
Your humble servant,
SAM: JOHNSON.

Oct. 24, 1764.

My compliments to Mrs. Strahan.

To Mr. Strahan, Printer, in New Street, Shoe-lane, London.

[1] Dr. Wetherell wrote to Mr. Strahan on May 20, 1767 :—'I think myself peculiarly happy in being so nearly connected with your son George, whose amiable temper will always render him a valuable member of society, and whose studies will, I hope, benefit mankind.' *From an original letter in the possession of Mr. Frederick Barker.*

[2] When in February, 1767, Johnson had his interview with George III, 'the King asked him what they were doing at Oxford. Johnson answered, he could not much commend their diligence, but that in some respects they were mended, for they had put their press under better regulations, and were at that time printing Polybius.' *Life*, ii. 35. He overstated the case. By that time not even an editor had been secured; one was found by the end of the year. Advances were made to him till 1787 for work done, when they came to an end, and the edition of Polybius too. It does not appear that a single page of type had been set up. More than a hundred years after the last payment was made, in the *Selections from Polybius* of Mr. Strachan-Davidson, Johnson's statement was in part made good. Nevertheless the press had been put under better regulations, and the first steps had been taken in advancing it from a state of degradation to the proud position which it now holds. In the 'Orders of the Delegates of the Press, 1758,' there is the following entry, bearing date but six days later than that of Johnson's letter :—

'Tuesday, Oct. 30, 1764. At a meeting of the Delegates of the Press.

'Ordered,

'That the following articles be made the foundation of the new lease to be granted of the moiety of the Printing House; that a copy of them be delivered to Mr. Baskett and Mr. Eyre, and that they be desired to give in their respective proposals at a meeting to be held on Tuesday the sixth of November.' (p. 41.)

The chief part of the lease consisted of the privilege to print Bibles and Prayer Books. Mark Baskett and members of his family before him had long been tenants. His lease was to expire at Lady Day, 1765. It seems probable that Strahan had hoped to get a share in the lease. Six years later he purchased from Eyre 'a share of the patent for King's Printer.' Nichols's *Lit. Anec.* iii. 392. From a curious manuscript volume in the possession of the Delegates I have been allowed to extract the following abbreviated account of what took place :—

To

168.

To David Garrick [1].

DEAR SIR,   May 18, 1765.

I know that great regard will be had to your opinion of an

'In November 1764, Mr. Basket came to Oxford, and petitioned for a renewal of his lease. Mr. Eyre, a printer of London, made a somewhat better offer. Mr. Basket's offer was accepted by the Delegates out of regard to the fact that he and members of his family had long been tenants, and a note of agreement was signed by the Vice-Chancellor on the one part and by Mr. Basket on the other. Mr. Eyre dispersed a Memorial, dated Nov. 28, 1764, to the Common Rooms setting forth the Hardships of his Case. His partisans maintained that Mr. Basket did not deserve any Preference, as he had even forfeited his Former Lease by his great Neglect and shamefull manner of Printing. There was great Truth in this last Argument. Mr. Basket lived upon a Genteel Private Fortune, and neither understood nor gave any Attention to the Business of Printing. He left it therefore to the Care of his Servants, who employed the Presses in printing a Great Number of small Prayer-Books in 12mo. for Foreign Sale: So that what Mr. Eyre alledged in his Memorial was an indisputable Fact—"That most of the Chapells in Oxford were supply'd with Folio and Quarto Prayers Book [*sic*] from Cambridge." The Under Serv[ts] and Press-men were a set of Idle Drunken Men, and the House appeared more like an Ale House than a Printing Room.

'It was very evident that a great Majority of the Members of Convocation would declare against fullfilling the Agreement. The Opinion of Councill was taken whether having been signed by the Vice-Chancellor it was absolutely binding. The answers returned by Mr. Wilbraham were so confused and perplexed that very little knowledge or satisfaction was to be obtained from them. Mr. Norton [afterwards Sir Fletcher Norton, first Lord Grantley ; *Life*, ii. 91, 472, *n.* 2] return'd an Answer favourable to the Friends of Mr. Eyre who consulted him. The lease, partly owing to the illness of the Vice-Chancellor, was not brought before Convocation till his successor entered into office.

'On Oct. 21, 1765, a New Occasional Delegacy for Leasing out the House &c. was appointed. On Oct. 29, the Lease was brought before Convocation. The Seal was refused by a great Majority. On Nov. 6 a new Delegacy was appointed, who examined the Proposals of different Printers, and in the end appointed Messrs. Gill and Wright, Stationers in Abchurch Lane, London, who undertook to give a Bond to indemnify the University from the Costs of any Suit which Mr. Basket should commence against them: On Dec. 10 the several Proposals were read in Convocation. There was against Mr. Basket's being Tenant, a great Majority. Against Mr. Eyre a great Majority. For Messrs. Wright and Gill a great Majority.' Their tenancy lasted till the end of 1788. They both became Aldermen of London ; each was supposed to have left a fortune of £300,000. Nichols's *Lit. Anec.* iii. 604.

[1] Published in the *Private Corre-*

Edition

Edition of Shakspeare. I desire, therefore, to secure an honest prejudice in my favour by securing your suffrage, and that this prejudice may really be honest, I wish you would name such plays as you would see, and they shall be sent you by,

Sir,

Your most humble servant,

SAM: JOHNSON [1].

169.

To DAVID GARRICK [2].

DEAR SIR,

You have many requests, and many of them must be

spondence of David Garrick, i. 183, and Croker's *Boswell*, p. 167.

[1] Johnson's edition was published in the following October. He did not go the way to secure Garrick's good-will, for in his Preface he reflected on him in the following passage :—' I collated such copies as I could procure, and wished for more, but have not found the collectors of those rarities very communicative.' *Life*, ii. 192. Dr. Warton writing on Jan. 22, 1766, said :—' Garrick is entirely off from Johnson, and cannot, he says, forgive him his insinuating that he withheld his old editions, which always were open to him.' Wooll's *Warton*, p. 313. See the *Life*, v. 244, *n.* 2 for Johnson's doubt whether Garrick had ever examined one of Shakespeare's plays from the first scene to the last. What answer Garrick sent to Johnson's letter is not known; the following letter which he wrote to him nearly a fortnight later is given in the *Garrick Correspondence*, i. 186 :—

'May 31, 1765.

'DEAR SIR,

'My brother greatly astonished me this morning, by asking me "if I was a subscriber to your Shakspeare?" I told him, yes, that I was one of the first, and as soon as I

heard of your intention; and that I gave you, at the same time, some other names, among which were the Duke of Devonshire, Mr. Beighton, &c. I cannot immediately have recourse to my memorandum, though I remember to have seen it just before I left England. I hope that you will recollect it, and not think me capable of neglecting to make you so trifling a compliment, which was doubly due from me, not only on account of the respect I have always had for your abilities, but from the sincere regard I shall ever pay to your friendship.

'I am, Sir, your most obedient humble servant,

'DAVID GARRICK.'

It is a curious fact that in the edition of Shakespeare which Johnson and Steevens published jointly in 1773, while in Johnson's Preface, which comes first, the reflection on Garrick remains, in Steevens' Advertisement to the Reader which follows it is stated that 'Mr. Garrick's collection of plays, curious and extensive as it is, derives its greatest value from its accessibility.'

[2] From the original in the possession of Mr. Alfred H. Huth, Bolney House, Ennismore Gardens, London. There is nothing to show in what year this Letter was written. It was

denied.

denied[1], but I hope this will not be of the number, by which you are desired to order your Boxkeeper, to reserve four places for Dr. Bell of Westminster[2], any night on which you intend to appear, before Friday.

I am, Sir,

Your most humble servant,

May 25.   SAM: JOHNSON.

[Written in pencil—To David Garrick, Esq., Adelphi[3].]

170.

TO GEORGE STRAHAN[4],
University College, Oxford.

DEAR SIR,   May 25, 1765.

That I have answered neither of your letters you must not impute to any declension of good will, but merely to the want of something to say. I suppose you pursue your studies diligently, and diligence will seldom fail of success. Do not tire yourself so much with Greek one day as to be afraid of looking on it the next; but give it a certain portion of time, suppose four hours, and pass the rest of the day in Latin or English. I would have you learn French, and take in a literary journal once a month, which will accustom you to various subjects, and inform you what learning is going forward in the world. Do not omit to mingle some lighter books with those of more importance; that which is read *remisso animo* is often of great use, and takes great hold of the remembrance. However, take what course you will, if you be diligent you will be a scholar[5].

I am, dear Sir,

Yours affectionately,

SAM: JOHNSON.

sold by Messrs. Sotheby and Co., on May 10, 1875, for £2 15s.

[1] Boswell at his first meeting with Johnson heard him complain that 'Garrick had refused him an order for the play for Miss Williams.' *Life,* i. 392.

[2] See *Life,* ii. 204, *n.* 1 for the Rev. Dr. Bell, Prebendary of Westminster.

[3] Garrick moved to the Adelphi about 1770 or 1771, so that the letter belongs to a later year.

[4] First published in Croker's *Boswell,* page 168.

[5] G. Strahan's fellow-student William Jones, in the first two or three years after matriculation, not only read 'with great assiduity all the Greek poets and historians of note,

To

To the Reverend Dr. Taylor [1].

DEAR SIR,

It is so long since I heard from you that I know not well whither to write. With all your building and feasting you might have found an hour in some wet day for the remembrance of your old friend. I should have thought that since you have led a life so festive and gay you would have [invited] me to partake of your hospitality. I do not [know] but I may come, invited or uninvited, and pass a few days with you in August or September, unless you send me a prohibition, or let me know that I shall be insupportably burthensome. Let me know your thoughts on this matter, because I design to go to some place or other and would be [loth] to produce any inconvenience for my own gratification.

Let me know how you go on in the world, and what entertainment may be expected in your new room by,

Dear Sir,

Your most affectionate Servant,

SAM: JOHNSON.

Temple [2], July 15, 1765.

To the Reverend Dr. Taylor in Ashbourn, Derbyshire.

To Mrs. Thrale [3].

London, Aug. 13, 1765.

MADAM,

If you have really so good an opinion of me as you express, it will not be necessary to inform you, how unwillingly I miss

and the entire works of Plato and Lucian, with a vast apparatus of commentaries on them, and the best authors in Italian, Spanish and Portuguese,' but also studied deeply Arabic, Persian and Hebrew. He brought to Oxford a native of Aleppo who spoke Arabic fluently, in the hope that some of his brother-collegians would take lessons from this man and help to bear the expense of his maintenance. *Life of Sir William Jones.* p. 40.

[1] First published in the *Miscellanies of the Philobiblon Society*, vi. 39; afterwards in *Notes and Queries*, 6th S. v. 383.

[2] Johnson was still living in Inner Temple Lane, where he had resided for more than five years. Writing to Taylor on the following October 2, he dates his letter 'Johnson's Court.'

[3] First published in the *Piozzi Letters*, i. 1. For Johnson's first acquaintance with the Thrales, see the *Life*, i. 490. 520.

the

the opportunity of coming to Brighthelmstone[1] in Mr. Thrale's company; or, since I cannot do what I wish first, how eagerly I shall catch the second degree of pleasure, by coming to you and him, as soon as I can dismiss my work from my hands[2].

I am afraid to make promises even to myself; but I hope that the week after the next will be the end of my present business. When business is done, what remains but pleasure? and where should pleasure be sought, but under Mrs. Thrale's influence?

Do not blame me for a delay by which I must suffer so much, and by which I suffer alone. If you cannot think I am good, pray think I am mending, and that in time I may deserve to be,

Dear Madam,

Your most obedient and

most humble servant.

SAM: JOHNSON.

173.

TO MR. OR MRS. THRALE.

Autumn of 1765.

'Mr. Johnson in the autumn of the next year [1765] followed us to Brighthelmstone, whence we were gone before his arrival; so he was disappointed and enraged, and wrote us a letter expressive of anger which we were very desirous to pacify, and to obtain his company again if possible. Mr. Murphy brought him back to us again very kindly.'

[1] Brighthelmstone, or Brighton, was still a small place, but was growing rapidly. Defoe in 1722 says that Bright Helmston was commonly called Bredhemston. Defoe's *Tour*, Vol. I, Letter ii, p. 61. In 1761 it was described as 'being bounded on the west by a large corn field, and on the east by a fine lawn called the Steine, which runs winding up into the country among hills to the distance of some miles. Though,' it was added, 'the town is well supplied with provisions, yet some inconveniencies are experienced from the want of a regular and daily market.' *Gentleman's Magazine*, 1761, p. 249. Five years later in the same Magazine (1766, p. 59) we read that 'it is a small ill-built town, containing six principal streets, East Street, Black Lion Street, Ship Street, Middle Street, West Street and North Street. It is become one of the principal places in the kingdom for the resort of the idle and dissipated, as well as of the diseased and infirm.' See also Wooll's *Memoirs of Dr. Warton*, p. 347.

[2] His edition of Shakespeare.

Piozzi

Piozzi Anecdotes, page 126.   This letter is not in Mrs. Piozzi's Collection.

174.

To [THE REV. EDWARD LYE[1]].

DEAR SIR,

I think you may be encouraged by the liberality of the Archbishop to hope for more Patrons of your undertaking, and therefore advise you to open your Subscription.   The method may perhaps be not at first to advertise but to send your proposal with a letter to such of the Bishops and others as you hope to find favourers of literature, sending at the same time to all your inferiour [?] friends, particularly to our Club[2].   When you see how far your personal interest will carry you, an estimate may be easily made of the probability of success, and the measures will be easily adjusted.   I would have the whole price paid at once, which all will readily comply with, and much trouble will be saved.   In contracting with your printer, oblige him to a certain number of Sheets weekly.   If you print at London, you will like Mr. Allen the printer better than most others. He is a Northamptonshire Man[3].   Go on boldly, I doubt not your Success.

[1] From the original in the possession of Mr. Frederick Barker, of 41 Gunterstone Road, West Kensington.

Though this letter has no address I have no doubt that it was written to the Rev. Edward Lye, Vicar of Yardley Hastings, Northamptonshire, the editor of Junius's *Etymologicum Anglicanum* to which Johnson had gone for some of his etymologies.   Lye for many years before 1765 had been engaged on an *Anglo-Saxon and Gothic Dictionary*, but had almost relinquished the design from a dread of the labour and expense.   On June 25, 1765, Archbishop Secker urged him to print it by subscription, and promised to subscribe £50.   On July 5, Lye replied that with this encouragement he would go on with his work.   He lived to print about thirty sheets, but died on August 16, 1767, leaving its completion to his friend, the Rev. Owen Manning, who published it in 1772, from the press of Mr. Allen of Bolt Court.   Nichols's *Lit. Anec.* ix. 751.

[2] Johnson wrote to Boswell on March 9, 1766 :—'Mr. Lye is printing his Saxon and Gothick Dictionary; all THE CLUB subscribes.' *Life*, ii. 17.

[3] Mr. Lye's living was in Northamptonshire, near Easton Maudit, Dr. Percy's vicarage, where Johnson had spent some weeks the year before.   *Life*, i. 486.   Allen the printer Johnson described as 'one of his best and tenderest friends.' *Ib.* iv. 354.

Please

Please to make Mrs. Calvert the compliments of Mrs. Williams, and of,

Dear Sir,

Your most humble Servant,

SAM: JOHNSON.

We have Gothick types at London.

Aug. 17, 1765.

175.

To the Reverend Dr. Taylor [1].

DEAR SIR,

You need be no longer in pain, for I received your letter, but though when I wrote to you I expected soon to have had it in my power to go to you, yet, as it often happens, one thing or another has obstructed my purpose.

My Shakespeare is now out of my hands, and I do not see what can hinder me any longer. When I find that I can come I will write to you, for I suppose you will meet me at Derby [2]. I think it time that we should see one another, and spend a little of our short life together.

I am, dear Sir,

Yours affectionately,

Oct. 2, 1765.

SAM: JOHNSON.

Johnson's Court, Fleet Street [3].

176.

To the Reverend Joseph Warton [4].

DEAR SIR, Oct. 9th, 1765.

Mrs. Warton uses me hardly in supposing that I could forget so much kindness and civility as she showed me at Winchester [5]. I remember, likewise, our conversation about St. Cross [6]. The

---

[1] First published in the *Miscellanies of the Philobiblon Society,* vi. 41.

[2] Johnson did not pay his visit to the Midland Counties before the summer of 1767.

[3] For Johnson's Court, see the *Life,* ii. 5, 229, 427.

[4] First published in Wooll's *Life of Dr. Joseph Warton,* page 309.

[5] Johnson had spent two nights at Winchester in August, 1762, on his way to Devonshire with Reynolds. Leslie and Taylor's *Life of Reynolds,* i. 214. He visited it again in 1778. *Life,* iii. 367.

[6] The ancient and beautiful Hospital for aged brethren about a mile from Winchester.

desire

desire of seeing her again will be one of the motives that will bring me into Hampshire.

I have taken care of your book; being so far from doubting your subscription, that I think you have subscribed twice: you once paid your guinea into my own hand in the garret in Gough Square. When you light on your receipt, throw it on the fire; if you find a second receipt, you may have a second book[1].

To tell the truth, as I felt no solicitude about this work, I receive no great comfort from its conclusion; but yet am well enough pleased that the public has no farther claim upon me. I wish you would write more frequently to,

Dear Sir,
Your affectionate humble servant,
SAM: JOHNSON.

177.

To CHARLES BURNEY.

[London], October 16, 1765. Published in the *Life*, i. 500.

178.

To THE REVEREND DR. LELAND[2].

SIR,

Among the names subscribed to the degree which I have had the honour of receiving from the University of Dublin, I find none of which I have any personal knowledge but those of Dr. Andrews and yourself.

---

[1] Johnson had opened his subscription list for his edition of Shakespeare in 1756. *Ante*, p. 68.

[2] First published in Malone's edition of the *Life*.

Johnson had received from Trinity College, Dublin, the degree of Doctor of Laws. *Life*, i. 489. Dr. Leland was the author of a *History of Ireland*. *Ib.* ii. 255; iii. 112. He was a frequent correspondent of Edmund Burke, whom he addressed as 'My dear Ned.' Dr. Francis Andrews was the Provost, the only layman who had held that office since the Restoration. Leland writing to William Burke on July 27 of this year says:—'I am First Lord of the Treasury and Paymaster-General of the forces to my lawful and rightful sovereign King Andrews the Great. John Rooney, the porter, is my private-secretary; and I have every morning a levee of chimney-sweepers, paviours, carpenters, junior fellows, &c. I take bribes of hares and wild-fowl from the brewer. I do jobs; and in all respects am perfectly a ministerial man in this little kingdom.' *Burke Correspondence*, i. 82, 462.

Men

Men can be estimated by those who know them not. only as they are represented by those who know them ; and therefore I flatter myself that I owe much of the pleasure which this distinction gives me, to your concurrence with Dr. Andrews in recommending me to the learned society.

Having desired the Provost to return my general thanks to the University, I beg that you, Sir, will accept my particular and immediate acknowledgments.

I am, Sir,
Your most obedient and most humble servant,
SAM: JOHNSON.

Johnson's Court, Fleet Street,
   London, Oct. 17, 1765.

179.

TO EDMUND HECTOR [1].

DEAR SIR,

I am very glad of a letter from you upon any occasion, but could wish that when you had despatched business, you would give a little more to friendship, and tell me something of your self.

The books must be had by sending to Mr. Tonson the receipts and second payment which belongs to him [2]. Any bookseller will do it, or any correspondent here. It would be extremely inconvenient, and uncustomary for me to charge myself with the distribution.

I never refuse any subscriber a new receipt when he has lost that which he had. You have three by which you may supply the three deficiencies. When the former receipts are found they must be destroyed.

If Mr. Taylor [3] be my old friend, make my kindest compliments.

[1] First published in *Notes and Queries*, 6th S. iii. 321.

[2] The first payment for the new edition of Shakespeare (a guinea) had been made to Johnson, as is shown by his receipt (*ante*, p. 68). The second payment was the booksellers' share. Had Johnson followed the usual custom of printing the list of subscribers we should have known how much he received for his labours. ' I have two very cogent reasons,' he said, ' for not printing any list;—one that I have lost all the names, the other that I have spent all the money.' *Life*, iv. 111. J. and R. Tonson stand first in the list of booksellers on the title-page of his *Shakespeare*.

[3] John Taylor, ' who by his in-

By

My heart is much set upon seeing you all again, and I hope
to visit you in the spring or summer, but many of my hopes have
been disappointed. I have no correspondence in the country,
and know not what is doing. What is become of Mr. Warren [1]?
His friend Paul has been long dead [2]. And to go backwarder,
what was the fate of poor George Brylston [3]?

A few years ago I just saluted Birmingham, but had no time
to see any friend, for I came in after midnight with a friend,
and went away in the morning [4]. When I come again I shall
surely make a longer stay; but in the mean time should think it
an act of kindness in you to let me know something of the
present state of things, and to revive the pleasure which your
company has formerly given to,

Dear Sir,

Your affectionate and most humble servant,

SAM: JOHNSON.

Dec. 8, 1765.

To Mr. Hector, in Birmingham.

180.

To Miss Porter [5].

Johnson's Court, Fleet Street, Jan. 14, 1766.

DEAR MADAM,

The reason why I did not answer your letters was that I
can please myself with no answer. I was loth that Kitty should

---

genuity in mechanical inventions
and his success in trade acquired an
immense fortune.' *Life*, i. 86.

'John Taylor, Esq. may justly be
deemed the Shakespeare or Newton
of Birmingham. He rose from
minute beginnings to shine in the
commercial hemisphere, as they in
the poetical or philosophical. To
this uncommon genius we owe the
gilt button, the japanned and gilt
snuff-box, with the numerous race
of enamels; also the painted snuff-
box. . . . He died in 1775 at the age
of 64, after acquiring a fortune of
£200,000.' W. Hutton's *Brief History of Birmingham*, 1797, p. 9.

[1] The Birmingham bookseller who
printed his translation of Lobo's
Abyssinia. *Life*, i. 86. *Ante*, p. 8.

[2] Lewis Paul, Johnson's corre-
spondent, died on April 25, 1759.
Gentleman's Magazine, 1759, p. 242.
See *ante*, p. 6.

[3] Of 'poor George Brylston' and
his fate nothing, I fear, can ever be
known.

[4] No doubt he passed through it
on his way to Lichfield, where he
spent five days in the winter of
1761-2. *Life*, i. 370.

[5] First published in Croker's *Boswell*, page 173.

Miss Porter had probably finished
her new house, and was now on the
point of leaving Johnson's, in which

leave

leave the house till I had seen it once more, and yet for some reasons I cannot well come during the session of parliament[1]. I am unwilling to sell it, yet hardly know why. If it can be let, it should be repaired, and I purpose to let Kitty have part of the rent while we both live; and wish that you would get it surveyed, and let me know how much money will be necessary to fit it for a tenant. I would not have you stay longer than is convenient, and I thank you for your care of Kitty.

Do not take my omission amiss. I am sorry for it, but know not what to say. You must act by your own prudence, and I shall be pleased. Write to me again; I do not design to neglect you any more. It is great pleasure for me to hear from you; but this whole affair is painful to me. I wish you, my dear, many happy years. Give my respects to Kitty.

I am, dear Madam,

Your most affectionate humble servant,

SAM: JOHNSON.

181.

To JAMES BOSWELL.

Johnson's Court, January 14, 1766. Published in the *Life*, ii. 3.

182.

To BENNET LANGTON.

Johnson's Court, March 9, 1766. Published in the *Life*, ii. 16.

183.

To BENNET LANGTON.

Johnson's Court, May 10, 1766. Published in the *Life*, ii. 17.

184.

To WILLIAM DRUMMOND.

Johnson's Court, August 13, 1766. Published in the *Life*, ii. 27.

185.

To JAMES BOSWELL.

London, August 21, 1766. Published in the *Life*, ii. 20.

she had been living with his mother's old servant Kitty (Catherine Chambers). Kitty died in the following year, having, it seems probable, stayed on in the old house.

[1] For an explanation of this see the *Life*, i. 518.

To

186.

To David Garrick [1].

Oct. 10, 1766.

Dear Sir,

I return you thanks for the present of the Dictionary, and will take care to return you other books.

I have had it long in my mind to tell you that there is a hundred pounds of yours in Mr. Jonson's [2] hands, if you have not received it. I know not whether any other paper than what I gave you be necessary. If there is anything more to be done, I am ready to do it.

Please to make my compliments to Mrs. Garrick.

I am, Sir,

Your obliged, &c.,

Sam: Johnson.

187.

To Miss Porter [3].

Dear Madam,

Soon after I had received your letter I went to Oxford [4], and did not return till last Saturday. I do not very clearly understand what need there is of my coming to Lichfield. It is now too late in the year to repair the poor old house, if the reparation can be delayed. Nor can I very easily discover what I can do towards it when I come, more than pay the money which it shall cost. The days are now grown short, and a long journey will be uncomfortable, and I think it better to delay doing whatever is to be done till Spring. I will come down, however, if you desire it.

I am sorry to have no better account of poor Kitty's health. I hope she will be better. Pray give my love to her, and desire her not to forget my request.

I should take it kindly if you would now and then write to me,

[1] Published in the *Garrick Correspondence*, i. 245.

[2] The editor of the *Garrick Correspondence* suggests ' Tonson.' It is very likely that Jacob Tonson the younger published some of Garrick's plays.

[3] From the original in the possession of the Rev. W. E. Buller, The Vicarage, Chard.

[4] For this visit to Oxford see *Life*, ii. 25.

and

and give me an account of your own health, and let me know how you go on in your new house.

I am, dear Madam,

Your most affectionate humble servant,

Nov. 13, 1766. SAM: JOHNSON.

To Mrs. Lucy Porter, Lichfield.

188.

TO MRS. SALUSBURY [1].

MADAM, February 14, 1767.

I hope it will not be considered as one of the mere formalities of life, when I declare, that to have heard nothing of Mrs. Thrale for so long a time has given me pain. My uneasiness is sincere, and therefore deserves to be relieved. I do not write to Mrs. Thrale, lest it should give her trouble at an inconvenient time [2]. I beg, dear Madam, to know how she does; and shall honestly partake of your grief if she is ill, and of your pleasure if she is well.

I am, Madam,

Your most obliged and

most humble servant,

SAM: JOHNSON.

189.

TO WILLIAM DRUMMOND.

Johnson's Court, April 21, 1767. Published in the *Life*, ii. 29.

190.

TO MRS. THRALE [3].

MADAM, Lichfield, July 20, 1767.

Though I have been away so much longer than I purposed or expected, I have found nothing that withdraws my affections

---

[1] *Piozzi Letters*, i. 3. Mrs. Salusbury was Mrs. Thrale's mother, wife of John Salusbury of Bachy-craig, and daughter of Sir Thomas Cotton of Combermere. For Johnson's Latin epitaph on her see his *Works*, i. 152.

[2] On March 3 of this year Henry Salusbury Thrale was christened at St. Saviour's, Southwark.

[3] *Piozzi Letters*, i. 4.

desirous

from the friends whom I left behind, or which makes me less desirous of reposing at that place which your kindness and Mr. Thrale's allows me to call my *home* [1].

Miss Lucy [2] is more kind and civil than I expected, and has raised my esteem by many excellencies very noble and resplendent, though a little discoloured by hoary virginity. Every thing else recals to my remembrance years, in which I proposed what, I am afraid, I have not done, and promised myself pleasure which I have not found [3]. But complaint can be of no use ; and why then should I depress your hopes by my lamentations? I suppose it is the condition of humanity to design what never will be done, and to hope what never will be obtained. But among the vain hopes, let me not number the hope which I have, of being long,

Dear Madam,

Your, &c.,

SAM: JOHNSON.

[1] See *post*, Letter of Oct. 15, 1773. D. Lysons, describing the house at Streatham, says :—' On the side of the small common between Streatham and Tooting is a villa which belonged to the late Henry Thrale, Esq. . . . The kitchen-gardens are remarkably spacious, and surrounded by brick walls fourteen feet in height, built for the reception of forcing-frames. Adjoining the house is an enclosure of about 100 acres, surrounded with a shrubbery and gravel walk of nearly two miles in circumference.' *Environs of London*, ed. 1800, iii. 482. Mrs. Piozzi later on fronted the house, so as to make it look ' wholly new.' Hayward's *Piozzi*, ii. 140. This interesting spot has unhappily been swept over by the advance of London.

[2] His step-daughter, Lucy Porter. Five years earlier, in a letter to Baretti, he had written : — ' My daughter-in-law [step-daughter], from whom I expected most, and whom I met with sincere benevolence, has lost the beauty and gaiety of youth, without having gained much of the wisdom of age.' *Life*, i. 370. She was born in January, 1717, and was only seven years younger than her step-father.

[3] In his *Annales* (*Life*, i. 74) he recorded :—' In '67, when I was at Lichfield, I went to look for my nurse's house ; and inquiring somewhat obscurely was told, " this is the house in which you were nursed." I saw my nurse's son, to whose milk I succeeded, reading a large Bible, which my nurse had bought, as I was then told, some time before her death.' *An Account of the Life of Dr. Johnson*, 1805, p. 12.

191.

To Mrs. Thrale [1].

DEAR MADAM,   Lichfield, Oct. 3, 1767.

You are returned, I suppose, from Brighthelmstone, and this letter will be read at Streatham.

—Sine me, liber, ibis in urbem [2].

I have felt in this place something like the shackles of destiny. There has not been one day of pleasure, and yet I cannot get away [3]. But when I do come, I perhaps shall not be easily persuaded to pass again to the other side of Styx, to venture myself on the irremeable road [4]. I long to see you, and all those of whom the sight is included in seeing you. *Nil mihi rescribas*; for though I have no right to say, *ipsa veni*, I hope that *ipse veniam* [5]. Be pleased to make my compliments.

I am, &c.,

SAM: JOHNSON.

192.

To Bennet Langton.

Lichfield, October 10, 1767. Published in the *Life*, ii. 45.

193.

To William Drummond.

Johnson's Court, October 24, 1767. Published in the *Life*, ii. 30.

[1] *Piozzi Letters*, i. 5.

[2] Ovid, *Tristia*, i. i. 1. Johnson often quotes Latin in his letters to Mrs. Thrale. Comparing her with her husband he said:—'She is more flippant, but he has ten times her learning; he is a regular scholar, but her learning is that of a school-boy in one of the lower forms.' *Life*, i. 494.

[3] In August he recorded at Lichfield in his Diary:—'I have been disturbed and unsettled for a long time, and have been without resolution to apply to study or to business, being hindered by sudden snatches.' *Pr. and Med.*, p. 73. The fol-

lowing spring he told Boswell that 'he had lately been a good while at Lichfield, but had grown very weary before he left it. BOSWELL. "I wonder at that, Sir; it is your native place." JOHNSON. "Why so is Scotland *your* native place."' *Life*, ii. 52.

[4] 'The keeper charmed, the chief without delay

Passed on and took the irremeable way.'

Dryden's *Æneid*, vi. 424. See also Pope's *Iliad*, xix. 312.

See *post*, Letter of July 8, 1784, 'for the irremeable stream.'

[5] Ovid, *Heroides*, i. 2.

To

194.

To Mrs. Aston [1].

MADAM,

Nov. 17, 1767.

If you impute it to disrespect or inattention, that I took no leave when I left Lichfield, you will do me great injustice. I know you too well not to value your friendship.

When I came to Oxford I inquired after the product of our walnut-tree, but it had, like other trees this year, but very few nuts, and for those few I came too late. The tree, as I told you, Madam, we cannot find to be more than thirty years old, and, upon measuring it, I found it, at about one foot from the ground, seven feet in circumference, and at the height of about seven feet, the circumference is five feet and a half; it would have been, I believe, still bigger, but that it has been lopped [2]. The nuts are small, such as they call single nuts; whether this nut is of quicker growth than better I have not yet inquired; such as they are, I hope to send them next year.

You know, dear Madam, the liberty I took of hinting that I did not think your present mode of life very pregnant with happiness. Reflection has not yet changed my opinion. Solitude excludes pleasure, and does not always secure peace [3]. Some communication of sentiments is commonly necessary to give vent to the imagination, and discharge the mind of its own flatulencies. Some lady surely might be found, in whose conversation you might delight, and in whose fidelity you might repose. *The World*, says Locke, *has people of all sorts* [4]. You will forgive me this obtrusion of my opinion; I am sure I wish you well.

Poor Kitty has done what we have all to do, and Lucy has

---

[1] First published in Croker's *Boswell*, page 188.

Mrs. (or rather Miss) Elizabeth Aston was the daughter of Sir Thomas Aston, Bart. *Life*, i. 83; ii. 466, 9.

[2] It seems impossible that a walnut-tree, fast growing though it is, should have attained to such a size in so short a time.

[3] 'The life of a solitary man will be certainly miserable, but not certainly devout.' *Rasselas*, ch. 21.

[4] *The Rambler*, No. 160, opens with this quotation.

K 2

the

the world to begin anew [1] : I hope she will find some way to more content than I left her possessing.

Be pleased to make my compliments to Mrs. Hinckley [2] and Miss Turton.

I am, Madam,
Your most obliged and most humble servant,
SAM: JOHNSON.

195.

TO MRS. THRALE [3].

DEAR MADAM,   [New Inn Hall, Oxford [4]], March 3, 1768.

I thought Mr. W— had been secured. Since what I have done is ineffectual, I doubt the power of my solicitation ; but, to leave nothing undone, I have written to him.

[1] Kitty Chambers, with whom Lucy Porter had lived in Johnson's house, had lately died.

[2] She was related to Miss Seward. *Letters of Anna Seward*, iv. 113, 378.

[3] *Piozzi Letters*, i. 6. This and some of the following letters refer chiefly to the General Election of 1768. Horace Walpole wrote on March 8 :—' Our, and my last, Parliament will be dissolved the day after to-morrow.' *Letters*, v. 89. Mr. Thrale had been elected for Southwark at a bye-election in Dec. 1765 (*Parl. Hist.* xv. 1089) and sat till the dissolution of 1780 *Life*, iii. 442. He had stood, I believe, for Abingdon in 1754, for in the fragment of a manuscript diary in the possession of Mr. Mathews of St. Giles's, Oxford, I have seen the following entry :—' 1754, April 15. Mr. Morton was chosen for Abingdon, after a long opposition of first Collington, Esq., who left ye town and his Debts unpaid. Next Thrale, Esq., who notwithstanding ye Superfluity of his money was rejected to ye Honour of Abingdon.'

[4] Johnson was visiting ' his friend Mr. Chambers, who was now Vinerian Professor, and lived in New Inn Hall.' *Life*, ii. 46. As Principal of the Hall he had succeeded Blackstone, the author of the *Commentaries*, in 1766; he held the post till his death in 1803, in spite of his long absence in India as Chief-Justice of Bengal. But as there do not seem to have been any students this mattered little. He was succeeded by Blackstone's son William, who was Principal till 1831, ' himself generally non-resident, without a single member on the books but himself. There were no rooms in the Hall except the Head's dwelling-place.' Cox's *Recollections of Oxford*, ed. 1870, pp. 64, 193. Hearne, writing in 1732, tells how George Wigan, who was elected Principal in 1726, 'hath not had so much as one gownsman entered at it ever since he had it, but shutting up the gate altogether wholly lives in the country.' Bliss's *Remains of Thomas Hearne*, iii. 84. After 1831 students, or rather undergraduates, were once more admitted. In 1887 the Hall, in virtue of a statute made by the University Commissioners, became completely united with Balliol College.

Mr. Pennick

Mr. Pennick I have seen, but with so little approach to intimacy that I could not have recollected his name ; yet to him I have inclosed a letter, which, after this information, you may use as you think is best.   I suppose it can do no harm.

Do you think there is any danger, that you are thus anxious for a single vote?   Pray let me know, as often as you can find a little time ; for I love to see a letter.

Be pleased to make my compliments to Mr. Thrale and Mrs. Salusbury, and Miss Hetty, and every body.   How does the poor little maid [1] ?

I am, &c.,

SAM: JOHNSON.

196.

TO THE REVEREND RICHARD PENNICK [2].

SIR,

I am flattered by others with an honour with which I dare not presume to flatter myself, that of having gained so much of your kindness or regard, as that my recommendation of a Candidate for Southwark may have some influence in determining your vote at the approaching election.

As a man is willing to believe well of himself, I now indulge

---

[1] Miss Hetty was Mrs. Thrale's eldest daughter, Esther, the *Queeney* of these letters. In 1808 she married Admiral Lord Keith. Allardyce's *Life of Lord Keith*, p. 348. In 1854 it was stated that she was the last survivor of all the persons mentioned in Boswell. *Gentleman's Magazine*, 1854, ii. 322. She died on March 31, 1857. 'The poor little maid' is mentioned again, *post*, p. 134.

[2] *Piozzi Letters*, i. 7 ; republished with corrections from the original in *Notes and Queries*, 5th S. vii. 101.

'The Rev. Richard Pennick was chaplain to the Earl of Bristol in his embassy to Spain in 1760, and Rector of Abinger in Surrey from 1764 to 1803.   He had also the living of St. John, Southwark [which would give him his vote], and was Keeper of the Reading Room in the British

Museum; *ob.* Jan. 29, 1803.' *Ib.* p. 102.

Miss Burney (who spells his name Penneck) writing of him in 1775 says :—' He took so violent a passion for a Miss Miller, an actress, that upon suspecting Mr. Colman was his rival, this pious clergyman, who is twice the heightt [*sic*] at least of Mr. Colman, one night, in the streets, knocked him down when he was quite unprepared for any attack. . . . He is half a madman ; he looks dark and designing and altogether *ill-favoured.'   Early Diary of Frances Burney*, ii. 2, 9, where in an interesting note the editor shows the better side of this divine's character. Horace Walpole wrote on Feb. 11, 1773 : —' Colman has been half-murdered by a divine out of jealousy, who keeps Miss Miller.' *Letters*, v. 435.

my

my vanity, by soliciting your vote and interest for Mr. Thrale, whose encomium I shall make very compendiously, by telling you that you would certainly vote for him if you knew him.

I ought to have waited on you with this request, even though my right to make it had been greater. But, as the election approaches, and I know not how long I may be detained here, I hope you will not impute this unceremonious treatment to any want of respect in, Sir,

Your most obedient and most humble servant,

SAM: JOHNSON.

New Inn Hall, Oxford, March 3, 1768.

To the Rev. Mr. Pennick at the Museum.

197.

To Mrs. Thrale [1].

MADAM,   [Oxford], March 14, 1768.

My last letter came a day after its time, by being carried too late to the post. This I mention, that you may not suspect me of negligence. I wrote at the same time to Mr. W. in more forcible terms than perhaps he thinks I had a right to : he has not answered me. He and his wife are on such terms, that I know not whether his inclination can be inferred from hers.

If I can be of any use, I will come directly to London; but if Mr. Thrale thinks himself certain, I have no doubt. That they all express the same certainty, has very little effect on those who know how many men are confident without certainty, and positive without confidence. We have not any reason to suspect Mr. Thrale of deceiving us or himself.

I hope all our friends at Streatham are well; and am glad to hope that the poor maid will recover. When the mind is drawn toward a dying bed, how small a thing is an election? But on death we cannot be always thinking, and, I suppose, we need not [2]. The thought is very dreadful!

This little dog does nothing, but I hope he will mend; he is

---

[1] *Piozzi Letters*, i. 8.

[2] 'If one was to think constantly of death,' he said, 'the business of life would stand still.' *Life*, v. 316.

now reading Jack the Giant-killer [1]. Perhaps so noble a narrative may rouse in him the soul of enterprise.

I am, &c.,

SAM: JOHNSON.

198.

To —— APPERLEY [2].

Sir,

I do not think that you can live anywhere without gaining influence, and therefore believing that you cannot be without it in Oriel College, I take the liberty of entreating you to employ it at the approaching election of a Fellow, in favour of Mr. Crosse, a gentleman of great merit both literary and social, and one on whom some such benefaction is necessary in the prosecution of his studies.

This address to you I make merely from zeal to serve him, without any solicitation, and as he is a man whom I have a desire to forward, you will, by doing what you can for him, and doing it speedily, bestow a very great favour upon,

Sir,

Your most obedient and most humble servant,

SAM: JOHNSON.

Oxford, March 17, 1768.

To —— Apperley, Esq., at Sir W. W. Wynne's, Bart., in Grosvenor Square, London.

---

[1] 'This little dog' is of course himself. For his uses of the term *dog* see *Life*, vi. 298, and for his defence of *Jack the Giant-killer* as a book for children, *Ib.* iv. 8, *n.* 3. 'It is,' said Northcote in his old age, 'the first book I ever read, and I cannot describe the pleasure it gives me even now. I cannot look into it without my eyes filling with tears. I do not know what it is (whether good or bad), but it is to me, from early impressions, the most heroic of performances. I remember once not having money to buy it, and I transcribed it all out with my own hand.' *Conversations of Northcote*, p. 96.

[2] From the original in the possession of Mr. George Pritchard, 1, Connaught Street, Hyde Park.

Who were Apperley and Crosse I do not know for certain, but most probably they are found in the following list :—

Apperley, Anthony, Jesus College, B.A. 1733, M.A. 1735.

—————— James, Jesus College, B.A. 1728, M.A. 1731, B.M. 1734.

Crosse, John, of St. Martin's-in-the-Fields, St. Edmund Hall, matric. Oct. 21, 1762 ; B.A. Dec. 1, 1768.

Crosse was not elected Fellow of

TO

199.
To Mrs. Thrale [1].

MADAM,   [Oxford], March 18, 1768.

No part of Mr. Thrale's troubles would have been trouble-some to me, if any endeavours of mine could have made them less. But I know not that I could have done more for him, than, in your approaching danger, I can do for you. I wish you both well, and have little doubt of seeing you both emerge from your difficulties.

When the election is decided, I entreat to be immediately informed ; and when you retreat to Streatham, if I shall not have returned to town, I hope that Mrs. Salusbury will favour me now and then with an account of you, when you can less conveniently give it of yourself. To be able to do nothing in the exigence of a friend is an uneasy state, but in the most pressing exigencies it is the natural state of humanity, and in all has been commonly that of,

Dear Madam,
Your, &c.
Sam: Johnson.

200.
To James Boswell.

Oxford, March 23, 1768. Published in the *Life*, ii. 58.

201.
To Mrs. Thrale [2].

DEAR MADAM,   Oxford, March 24, 1768.

You serve me very sorrily. You may write every day to

Oriel. He was not qualified for 'the approaching election,' which was held on the Friday after Easter, as he was not a B.A.; but from his standing he might have qualified had he wished. No doubt he would have done so had he had any chance of success.

[1] *Piozzi Letters*, i. 9.

Two days before this letter was written six followers of John Wesley were expelled from St. Edmund Hall for their active Methodism. Johnson justified their expulsion. 'BOSWELL. "But, was it not hard, Sir, to expel them ; for I am told they were good beings ?" JOHNSON. "I believe they might be good beings ; but they were not fit to be in the University of Oxford. A cow is a very good animal in the field, but we turn her out of a garden."' *Life*, ii. 187.

[2] *Piozzi Letters*, i. 10.

this

this place¹; and yet I do not know what is the event of the Southwark election, though, I am sure, you ought to believe that I am very far from indifference about it². Do let me know as soon as you can.

Our election was yesterday. Every possible influence of hope and fear was, I believe, enforced on this occasion ; the slaves of power, and the solicitors of favour, were driven hither from the remotest corners of the kingdom, but *judex honestum prætulit utili*³. The virtue of Oxford has once more prevailed.

The death of Sir Walter Bagot, a little before the election⁴, left them no great time to deliberate, and they therefore joined to Sir Roger Newdigate their old representative, an Oxfordshire gentleman, of no name, no great interest, nor perhaps any other merit, than that of being on the right side. Yet when the poll was numbered, it produced

For Sir R. Newdigate	352
Mr. Page	296
Mr. Jenkinson	198
Dr. Hay	62 ⁵

¹ In the list of daily posts (Sundays excepted) established on Oct. 10, 1763, Oxford is entered. The charge was threepence for a single letter of one sheet. *Court and City Register for* 1765, p. 130. It was raised to fourpence in 1784; fivepence in 1797; sixpence in 1801; sevenpence in 1805 ; and eightpence in 1812. *Penny Cyclo.,* article *Post-Office.*

² The poll had closed the day before with the following result :—

Henry Thrale 1248
Sir Joseph Mawbey . . 1159
William Belcher . . . 994
Jackson's Oxford Journal, March 26, 1768.

³ Horace, 4 *Odes,* ix. 41.

⁴ Five days after Bagot's death, on Jan. 25 of this year, a new writ had been ordered, when Sir William Dolben was returned. *Parl. Hist.* xv. 1085.

⁵ The contest had been between

the High Church party, which in the reign of the first two Georges had been the Jacobite party, and the new party of the King's Friends. 'The Court,' wrote Horace Walpole, 'had set up Jenkinson, one of the favourite cabal, for Oxford, where he had been bred, but he lost the election by a considerable majority, though the favours of the Crown were now showered on that University.' *Memoirs of the Reign of George III,* iii. 191. In his *Letters* (vi. 282) Walpole describes Newdigate as a man who 'formerly would have been proud to be chief mourner at the Pretender's funeral.' Jenkinson had been Lord Bute's private secretary,— 'one of the Jesuits of the Treasury,' as Walpole calls him. He rose through royal favour to be Earl of Liverpool. *Life,* iii. 146. Hay (afterwards Sir George Hay) was a Fellow of St. John's College. He had taken his degree of D.C.L. in 1741-2, and

Of

Of this I am sure you must be glad ; for, without enquiring into the opinions or conduct of any party, it must be for ever pleasing to see men adhering to their principles against their interest, especially when you consider that these voters are poor, and never can be much less poor but by the favour of those whom they are now opposing.

> I am, &c.,
>
> SAM: JOHNSON.

202.

TO MISS PORTER [1].

MY DEAR, DEAR LOVE,   Oxford, April 18, 1768.

You have had a very great loss [2].   To lose an old friend, is to be cut off from a great part of the little pleasure that this life allows.   But such is the condition of our nature, that as we live on we must see those whom we love drop successively, and find

---

was known as Dr. Hay. He was one of the Lords of the Admiralty (with a brief interval) from 1756 to 1765, when he was made Dean of the Arches. Both men, in spite of their defeat, were returned to this Parliament, Jenkinson being elected for two places. *Parl. Hist.* xvi. 432, 442, 445. In Balliol, Brasenose, Pembroke, University, and Worcester not a single vote was given against Newdigate. In Christ Church, and in Merton which had always been a Hanoverian stronghold, Jenkinson had a large majority. Hay's stronghold was St. John's, where he received double as many votes as Newdigate. On the list of voters is entered Jeremy Bentham, M.A., of Queen's College, with a 'Q' [query] against his name, for his right to vote was disputed. Though he had taken the degree of M.A. he was under age. He voted for Jenkinson and Hay. As there was no scrutiny the legality of his vote was never settled. He had been engaged, he says, partly in reading Montesquieu and partly in watching a chemical experiment, when the Archbishop of York called on him to solicit his vote for these two candidates. Bentham's *Works*, x. 48, 54. Johnson's name is not given in the polling-list, and it is clear that he had no vote. By his diploma of M.A. he was entitled to 'one, so long as he paid the yearly University dues. He was doubtless hindered by his poverty. In the Bodleian a list of the poll is preserved, from which I have got much of this information. Among the 493 voters I noticed only three names of any great distinction—Blackstone, Bentham, and William Scott, afterwards Lord Stowell. Only 14 of the voters had two Christian names—not quite 1 in every 35.

[1] First published in Malone's edition of *Boswell*.

[2] 'The death of her aunt, Mrs. Hunter, widow of Johnson's schoolmaster.' CROKER. 'She was with my poor mother when she died,' wrote Johnson. *Ante*, p. 87.

our

our circle of relation grow less and less, till we are almost unconnected with the world; and then it must soon be our turn to drop into the grave. There is always this consolation, that we have one Protector who can never be lost but by our own fault, and every new experience of the uncertainty of all other comforts should determine us to fix our hearts where true joys are to be found [1]. All union with the inhabitants of earth must in time be broken; and all the hopes that terminate here, must on [one] part or other end in disappointment.

I am glad that Mrs. Adey and Mrs. Cobb [2] do not leave you alone. Pay my respects to them, and the Sewards, and all my friends. When Mr. Porter [3] comes, he will direct you. Let me know of his arrival, and I will write to him.

When I go back to London, I will take care of your reading-glass. Whenever I can do anything for you, remember, my dear darling, that one of my greatest pleasures is to please you.

The punctuality of your correspondence I consider as a proof of great regard. When we shall see each other, I know not, but

[1] '—that so, among the sundry and manifold changes of the world, our hearts may surely there be fixed where true joys are to be found.' *Collect for the Fourth Sunday after Easter.*

[2] 'Mrs. Cobb and her niece, Miss Adey, were great admirers of Dr. Johnson.' *Life*, ii. 466. Miss Seward (unhappily one of the most untruthful of writers) says that Johnson exclaimed: 'How should Moll Cobb be a wit? Cobb has read nothing, Cobb knows nothing; and where nothing has been put into the brain nothing can come out of it to any purpose of rational entertainment.' Anna Seward's *Letters*, iii. 330. It is probable that Mrs. Cobb and Mrs. Adey had been with their brother joint-owners of Edial Hall when Johnson rented it for his academy.

[3] Her surviving brother, who died in 1783. *Life*, iv. 256. Miss Seward in April, 1764, describes him as 'a thin, pale personage, somewhat below the middle height, with rather too much stoop in the shoulders, and a little more withered by Italian suns than are our English sober bachelors after an elapse of only forty years, in a black velvet coat, and a waistcoat richly embroidered with coloured flowers upon gold tissue; a bag wig in crimp buckle powdered white as the new-shorn fleece.' Miss Porter she describes on the same occasion as 'rustling into the drawing-room in all the pomp of blue and white tissue and Brussels lace, with the most satisfied air.' Anna Seward's *Poetical Works*, ed. 1810, i. cxv. There was this excuse for the finery, that Mr. Porter was paying a formal call on Miss Sarah Seward, to whom he was engaged.

let us often think on each other, and think with tenderness. Do not forget me in your prayers. I have for a long time back been very poorly ; but of what use is it to complain ?

Write often, for your letters always give great pleasure to

My dear,

Your most affectionate

and most humble servant,

SAM : JOHNSON.

203.

TO MRS. THRALE [1].

MADAM,   Oxford, April 19, 1768.

If I should begin with telling you what is very true, that I have of late been very much disordered, you might perhaps think that in the next line I should impute this disorder to my distance from you ; but I am not yet well enough to contrive such stratagems of compliment. I have been really very bad, and am glad that I was not at Streatham, where I should have been troublesome to you, and you could have given no help to me.

I am not, however, without hopes of being better, and therefore hear with great pleasure of the welfare of those from whom I always expect to receive pleasure when I am capable of receiving it, and think myself much favoured that you made so much haste to tell me of your recovery.

I design to love little Miss Nanny very well ; but you must let us have a Bessy some other time [2]. I suppose the Borough bells rung for the young lady's arrival [3]. I hope she will be happy. I will not welcome her with any words of ill-omen. She will certainly be happy, if she be as she and all friends are wished to be by, Madam,

Your, &c.,

SAM: JOHNSON.

---

[1] *Piozzi Letters*, i. 12.

[2] On the 17th the child had been christened Anna Maria. No doubt Johnson had asked that one of Mrs. Thrale's daughters should bear the name of his wife—Elizabeth. The next child was named Lucy Elizabeth and he was godfather.

[3] Mr. Thrale's brewery and town-house were in the Borough of Southwark.

To

204.

To Mrs. Thrale[1].

MADAM,
                                              Oxford, April 28, 1768.

It is indeed a great alleviation of sickness to be nursed by a mother, and it is a comfort in return to have the prospect of being nursed by a daughter, even at that hour when all human attention must be vain. From that social desire of being valuable to each other, which produces kindness and officiousness, it proceeds, and must proceed, that there is some pleasure in being able to give pain[2]. To roll the weak eye of helpless anguish, and see nothing on any side but cold indifference, will, I hope, happen to none whom I love or value; it may tend to withdraw the mind from life, but has no tendency to kindle those affections which fit us for a purer and a nobler state.

Yet when any man finds himself disposed to complain with how little care he is regarded, let him reflect how little he contributes to the happiness of others, and how little, for the most part, he suffers from their pains. It is perhaps not to be lamented, that those solicitudes are not long nor frequent, which must commonly be vain; nor can we wonder that, in a state in which all have so much to feel of their own evils, very few have leisure for those of another[3]. However, it is so ordered, that few suffer from want of assistance; and that kindness which could not assist, however pleasing, may be spared.

These reflections do not grow out of any discontent at C—'s[4] behaviour: he has been neither negligent nor troublesome; nor do I love him less for having been ill in his house[5].

---

[1] *Piozzi Letters*, i. 13.

[2] He means, I suppose, that there is some pleasure in finding that one's sufferings are a cause of pain to another.

[3] Adam Smith in his *Theory of Moral Sentiments*, published in 1759, had said (ed. 1801, ii. 27):—'Before we can feel much for others we must in some measure be at ease ourselves.' Cf. *ib.* i. 281, where he attacks 'those whining and melancholy moralists who are perpetually reproaching us with our happiness, while so many of our brethren are in misery,' and *Life*, ii. 94, where Johnson maintains that an excess of sympathy 'would be misery to no purpose.'

[4] Chambers.

[5] 'Johnson said, "How few of his friends' houses would a man choose to be at when he is sick." He mentioned one or two. I recollect only Thrale's.' *Life*, iv. 181. He would not have been a troublesome patient any-

There

There is no small degree of praise. I am better, having scarce eaten for seven days. I shall come home on Saturday.

I am, &c.,
SAM: JOHNSON.

205.

TO MRS. THRALE [1].

MADAM,   [Oxford], May 23, 1768.

Though I purpose to come home to-morrow [2], I could not omit even so long, to tell you how much I think myself favoured by your notice. Every man is desirous to keep those friends whom he is proud to have gained, and I count the friendship of your house among the felicities of life.

I thank God that I am better, and am at least within hope of being as well as you have ever known me. Let me have your prayers.

I am, &c.,
SAM: JOHNSON.

206.

TO F. A. BARNARD [3].

SIR,   May 28, 1768.

It is natural for a scholar to interest himself in an expedition, undertaken, like yours, for the importation of literature;

where, for, according to Mrs. Piozzi (*Anec.* p. 275), 'he required less attendance, sick or well, than ever I saw any human creature.'

[1] *Piozzi Letters*, i. 15.

[2] For his arrival in London and his surprising Boswell one morning with a visit at his lodgings see *Life*, ii. 59. He might have returned either by the Oxford Post-Coach, which left at 8 a.m. ; fare 15*s.*, no outside passengers ; or by the Oxford Machine which left the Bear Inn, High Street, every Monday, Wednesday, and Friday at 6 a.m. What time these coaches reached London we are not told. The Machine was licensed by the Vice-Chancellor ; carried six inside passengers at 10*s.*

each ; outside passengers half-price. Each inside passenger was allowed 20 lbs. of luggage ; above that weight a penny per lb. was charged. Had Johnson had heavy luggage he might have sent it by the University Old Stage Wagon, which left Oxford every Tuesday morning at one o'clock [i.e. one hour after midnight], and arrived at the Oxford Arms in Warwick Lane every Wednesday at three. It returned on Thursdays at nine [in the morning], and was at Oxford on Friday evenings. *Jackson's Oxford Journal*, Feb. 20, 1768.

[3] First published in the *Report of the Committee on Papers relating to the Royal Library which his Majesty*

and

and therefore, though, having never travelled myself, I am very little qualified to give advice to a traveller ; yet, that I may not seem inattentive to a design so worthy of regard, I will try whether the present state of my health will suffer me to lay before you what observation or report have suggested to me, that may direct your inquiries, or facilitate your success. Things of which the mere rarity makes the value, and which are prized at a high rate by a wantonness rather than by use, are always passing from poorer to richer countries ; and therefore, though Germany and Italy were principally productive of typographical curiosities, I do not much imagine that they are now to be found there in great abundance. An eagerness for scarce books and early editions, which prevailed among the English about half a century ago, filled our shops with all the splendour and nicety of literature ; and when the Harleian Catalogue [1] was published, many of the books were bought for the library of the King of France.

I believe, however, that by the diligence with which you have enlarged the library under your care, the present stock is so nearly exhausted, that, till new purchases supply the booksellers with new stores, you will not be able to do much more than glean up single books, as accident shall produce them ; this, therefore, is the time for visiting the continent.

What addition you can hope to make by ransacking other countries we will now consider. English literature you will not seek in any place but in England. Classical learning is diffused everywhere, and is not, except by accident, more copious in one

has presented to the Nation. See *Gentleman's Magazine,* 1823, part i. p. 347. ·

In a note in Croker's *Boswell,* p. 196, Barnard is described as 'Mr., afterwards Sir Francis, Barnard, Librarian to King George III.' According to Nichols his name was not Francis, but Frederick Augustus. See Nichols's *Lit. Hist.* iv. 699. I learn from Mr. R. R. Holmes, the Librarian at Windsor Castle, that Nichols also is mistaken, for he was

not Frederick Augustus, but Frederick Augusta. So he is given in the first volume of the Catalogue of the Royal Library.

Boswell had been shown this letter, but had been refused leave to print it. *Life,* ii. 33, *n.* 4. It was Barnard who arranged Johnson's interview with the King. *Ib.* There can be little question that the present letter was written to be shown to the King.

[1] See *Life,* i. 153.

part

part of the polite world than in another. But every country has literature of its own, which may be best gathered in its native soil. The studies of the learned are influenced by forms of government and modes of religion ; and, therefore, those books are necessary and common in some places, which, where different opinions or different manners prevail, are of little use, and for that reason rarely to be found.

Thus in Italy you may expect to meet with canonists and scholastic divines, in Germany with writers on the feudal laws, and in Holland with civilians. The schoolmen and canonists must not be neglected, for they are useful to many purposes ; nor too anxiously sought, for their influence among us is much lessened by the Reformation. Of the canonists at least a few eminent writers may be sufficient. The schoolmen are of more general value. But the feudal and civil law I cannot but wish to see complete [1]. The feudal constitution is the original of the law of property, over all the civilised part of Europe ; and the civil law, as it is generally understood to include the law of nations, may be called with great propriety a regal study. Of these books, which have been often published, and diversified by various modes of impression, a royal library should have at least the most curious edition, the most splendid, and the most useful. The most curious edition is commonly the first, and the most useful may be expected among the last. Thus, of Tully's Offices, the edition of Fust is the most curious, and that of Graevius the most useful [2]. The most splendid the eye will discern. With the old printers you are now become well acquainted ; if you can find any collection of their productions to be sold, you will undoubtedly buy it ; but this can scarcely be hoped, and you must catch up single volumes

[1] Johnson wrote to Boswell on Aug. 31, 1772 :—'The leisure which I cannot enjoy, it will be a pleasure to hear that you employ upon the antiquities of the feudal establishment. The whole system of ancient tenures is gradually passing away ; and I wish to have the knowledge of it preserved adequate and complete ; for such an institution makes a very important part of the history of mankind. Do not forget a design so worthy of a scholar who studies the law of his country, and of a gentleman who may naturally be curious to know the condition of his own ancestors.' *Life,* ii. 202. See also *ib.* iii. 414.

[2] Fust's edition was published in 1465, and Graevius's in 1688.

where

where you can find them. In every place things often occur where they are least expected. I was shown a Welsh grammar written in Welsh, and printed at Milan, I believe, before any grammar of that language had been printed here [1]. Of purchasing entire libraries, I know not whether the inconvenience may not overbalance the advantage. Of libraries connected with general views, one will have many books in common with another. When you have bought two collections, you will find that you have bought many books twice over, and many in each which you have left at home, and, therefore, did not want; and when you have selected a small number, you will have the rest to sell at a great loss, or to transport hither at perhaps a greater. It will generally be more commodious to buy the few that you want, at a price somewhat advanced, than to encumber yourself with useless books. But libraries collected for particular studies will be very valuable acquisitions. The collection of an eminent civilian, feudist [2], or mathematician, will perhaps have very few superfluities. Topography or local history prevails much in many parts of the continent. I have been told that scarcely a village of Italy wants its historian [3]. These books may be generally neglected, but some will deserve attention by the celebrity of the place, the eminence of the authors, or the beauty of the sculptures [4]. Sculpture has always been more cultivated among other nations than among us. The old art of cutting on wood, which decorated the books of ancient impression, was never carried here to any excellence; and the practice of engraving on copper, which succeeded, has never been much employed among us in adorning books. The old books with wooden cuts are to be diligently sought; the designs were often made by great masters, and the prints are such as cannot

[1] In the *Brit. Mus. Catalogue* is entered:—'Welsh Grammar. By G. Roberts. Milan (?), 8°. 1567.' See also William Rowlands' *Cambrian Bibliography*, p. 22.

[2] *Feudist* is not in Johnson's *Dictionary*. He formed the word, I conjecture, from the French *feudiste*.

[3] Johnson is thinking of a passage in Baretti's *Italian Library*, ed.

1757, p. 177, where it is stated that 'there is scarce a village in Italy but there is a particular history of it.' It is strange that Johnson, who generally would not listen in silence to an exaggeration, here circulates one so gross.

[4] Johnson does not give this use of *sculptures* in his *Dictionary*.

be made by any artist now living. It will be of great use to collect in every place maps of the adjacent country, and plans of towns, buildings, and gardens. By this care you will form a more valuable body of geography than can otherwise be had. Many countries have been very exactly surveyed, but it must not be expected that the exactness of actual mensuration will be preserved, when the maps are reduced by a contracted scale, and incorporated into a general system.

The king of Sardinia's Italian dominions are not large, yet the maps made of them in the reign of Victor fill two Atlantic folios[1]. This part of your design will deserve particular regard, because, in this, your success will always be proportioned to your diligence. You are too well acquainted with literary history not to know that many books derive their value from the reputation of the printers. Of the celebrated printers you do not need to be informed, and if you did, might consult Baillet, Jugemens des Sçavans[2]. The productions of Aldus are enumerated in the Bibliotheca Graeca[3], so that you may know when you have them all ; which is always of use, as it prevents needless search. The great ornaments of a library, furnished for magnificence as well as use, are the first editions, of which, therefore, I would not willingly neglect the mention. You know, sir, that the annals of typography begin with the Codex, 1457[4]; but there is great reason to believe, that there are latent, in obscure corners, books printed before it. The secular feast, in memory of the invention of printing, is celebrated in the fortieth year of the century; if this tradition, therefore, is right, the art had in 1457 been already exercised nineteen years[5].

[1] *Théâtre des États du Duc de Savoie*, published in 1700 at the Hague. Johnson gives as one of the meanings of *Atlas*, 'a large square folio.' By 'Atlantic folios' he means folios of this large square size. They are still called 'Atlas folios.'

[2] Adrien Baillet's *Jugements des savants sur les principaux ouvrages des auteurs*, 9 vols., 1685-6.

[3] J. A. Fabricius's *Bibliotheca Graeca*, ed. 1726; xiii. 606.

[4] Johnson most likely got his information from Maittaire's *Annales Typographici*, 1719. On p. 35 we find given as the first printed book, '*Psalmorum Codex;* per Joannem Fust et Petrum Schoeffer. Moguntiae, 1457.' Moguntia is Mainz.

[5] Early in 1740 'the third hundred year's feast of the noble art and mystery of printing, discovered

There

There prevails among typographical antiquaries a vague opinion, that the Bible had been printed three times before the edition of 1462, which Calmet calls 'La première édition bien avérée.' One of these editions has been lately discovered in a convent, and transplanted into the French king's library[1]. Another copy has likewise been found, but I know not whether of the same impression, or another. These discoveries are sufficient to raise hope and instigate inquiry. In the purchase of old books, let me recommend to you to inquire with great caution, whether they are perfect. In the first edition the loss of a leaf is not easily observed. You remember how near we both were to purchasing a mutilated Missal at a high price.

All this perhaps you know already, and, therefore, my letter may be of no use. I am, however, desirous to show you, that I wish prosperity to your undertaking. One advice more I will give, of more importance than all the rest, of which I, therefore, hope you will have still less need. You are going into a part of the world divided, as it is said, between bigotry and atheism : such representations are always hyperbolical, but there is certainly enough of both to alarm any mind solicitous for piety and truth ; let not the contempt of superstition precipitate you into infidelity, or the horror of infidelity ensnare you in super-stition.—I sincerely wish you successful and happy, for

I am, Sir,

Your affectionate humble servant,

SAM: JOHNSON.

207.

TO FRANCIS BARBER.

[London], May 28, 1768.   Published in the *Life*, ii. 62.

in 1440, was celebrated in Strasburg.' *Gentleman's Magazine*, 1740, p. 95. 'Nineteen years' seems a mistake for '*seventeen* years.'

[1] Augustin Calmet published at Paris in 1709-16 *Commentaire sur tous les livres de l'ancien et du nouveau Testament*, in 25 vols.

quarto. In the Bodleian there are two Bibles earlier than the edition of 1462, one published as early as 1456, and the other in 1460-1. The copy in the French King's library Johnson saw when he visited Paris in 1775, but he had doubts about it. *Life*, ii. 397.

208.

To Mrs. Thrale [1].

Madam,   [Johnson's Court, London,] June 17, 1768.

I know that you were not displeased to find me gone abroad, when you were so kind as to favour me with a visit. I find it useful to be moving; but whithersoever I may wander, I shall not, I hope, leave behind me that gratitude and respect, with which your attention to my health, and tenderness for my weakness, have impressed my heart. May you be long before you want the kindness which you have shown to,

Madam,
Your &c.,
Sam: Johnson.

209.

To Miss Porter [2].

My Love,

It gives me great pleasure to find that you are so well satisfied with what little things it has been in my power to send you. I hope you will always employ me in any office that can conduce to your convenience. My health is, I thank God, much better; but it is yet very weak; and very little things put it in a troublesome state; but still I hope all will be well. Pray for me.

My friends at Lichfield must not think that I forget them. Neither Mrs. Cobb, nor Mrs. Adey, nor Miss Adey, nor Miss Seward, nor Miss Vise, are to suppose that I have lost all memory of their kindness. Mention me to them when you see them. I hear Mr. Vise [3] has been lately very much in danger. I hope he is better.

When you write again, let me know how you go on, and what company you keep, and what you do all day. I love to think

---

[1] *Piozzi Letters*, i. 15.

[2] First published in Croker's *Boswell*, page 197; corrected by me from the original in the possession of Mr. Frederick Barker, of 41 Gunterstone Road, West Kensington.

One of Johnson's letters of this date, probably this very one, was sold at Mr. A. Hayward's sale on March 21, 1890, for £8 5s. *The Times*, March 22, 1890.

[3] Boswell, who writes the name *Vyse*, speaks of him as 'the respectable clergyman at Lichfield, who was contemporary with Johnson.' *Life*, iii. 124.

on

on you, but do not know when I shall see you. Pray, write very often. I am, ·

Dearest,

Your humble Servant,

June 18, 1768.   SAM: JOHNSON.

210.

To MRS. THRALE [1].

MADAM,   [Johnson's Court, London], Nov. 11, 1768.

I am sincerely sorry for you both ; nor is my grief disinterested ; for I cannot but think the life of Mrs. Salusbury some addition to the happiness of all that know her. How much soever I wish to see you, I hope you will give me no pleasure at the expence of one to whom you have so much reason to be attentive.

I am, &c.,

SAM: JOHNSON.

211.

To MRS. THRALE [2].

MADAM,   Dec. 2, 1768.

I can readily find no paper that is not ruled for juridical use [3]. You will wonder that I have not written, and indeed I wonder too ; but I have been oddly put by [4] my purpose. If my omission has given you any uneasiness, I have the mortification of paining that mind which I would most wish to please. I am not, I thank God, worse than when I went ; and you have no hope that I should grow better here. But I will show myself to-morrow, and only write in hope that my letter will come before me, and that you will have forgiven the negligence of,

Madam,

Your, &c.,

SAM: JOHNSON.

---

[1] *Piozzi Letters*, i. 16.

Mrs. Salusbury, whose life seems to have been in great danger, lived till 1773.

In Messrs. Puttick and Simpson's *Auction Catalogue* of March 16, 1852, Lot 437 is as follows :—' In Dr. Johnson's Autograph. "Liber Memorabilis [? Memorialis]. Nov. 14, 1768.

To write to W, Lucy, Zolcher [? Tolcher. See *ante*, p. 93, *n.* 3] Boswell." '

[2] *Piozzi Letters*, i. 17.

[3] Perhaps Johnson was visiting his friend Mr. Welch, the Magistrate. *Life*, iii. 216.

[4] '*Put by ;* to turn off, to divert.' Johnson's *Dictionary*.

To

212.

To David Garrick.

Jan. 17, 1769.

In Messrs. Sotheby's Auction Catalogue of May 10, 1875, Lot 89 is an autograph letter of Johnson to David Garrick, 1½ pages quarto, dated Jan. 17, 1769. 'He speaks of his kind promise of a benefit for Mrs. Williams; asks him to select an appropriate play, and hopes he will continue to make his favour as efficatious as he can.' 1769, I suspect, is a misprint for 1756, for in January of that year Garrick gave Miss Williams a benefit. I find no mention of a second.

213.

To Miss Flint[1].

MADEMOISELLE, A Londres, Mars 31, 1769.

Il faut avouer que la lettre que vous m'avez fait l'honeur de m'ecrire, a eté long-tems sans réponse. Voici mon apologie. J'ai eté affligé d'une maladie de violence peu supportable, & d'un lenteur bien ennuiant. Tout état a ses droits particuliers. On compte parmi les droits d'un malade ce de manquer aux offices de respect, et aux devoirs de reconoissance. Géné par ses douleurs, il ne scait veiller qu'à soi-même. Il ne pense qu'à se soulager, et à se retablir, peu attentif à tout autre soin, et peu sensible à la gloire d'etre traduit d'une main telle que la vôtre.

Neanmoins, Mademoiselle, votre merite auroit exigé que je m'efforcasse à vous rendre graces de vos egards, si je l'aurois pu faire sans y meler des querelles. Mais comment m'empescher

---

[1] *Piozzi Letters*, i. 18. Mrs. Piozzi says in a note:—'Miss Flint was a *very* young lady, who had translated Johnson's Strictures at the end of Shakespeare's Plays.' Miss Reynolds had accompanied her to Paris. According to Northcote, 'she subsequently married a M. de Reveral; being left a widow she was guillotined with her only son in the Reign of Terror.' Northcote's *Reynolds*, i. 201. Whatever may have been the fate of her son, she escaped the guillotine. In a list of the English prisoners I find her name entered as follows:—'Louise Mather Flint Rivarol, wife of the royalist pamphleteer. Arrested as wife of emigré. At Luxembourg, Austin Convent and Port Royal, April 22, 1794 to July 23, 1794. Her father was a teacher of languages. She died 1821.' *Englishmen in the French Revolution*, by John G. Alger, 1889, p. 345.

de

de me plaindre de ces appas par lesquelles vous avez gagné sur l'esprit de Mademoiselle Reynolds jusqu'a ce qu'elle ne se souvient plus ni de sa patrie ni de ses amis. C'est peu de nous louer, c'est peu de repandre nos ouvrages par des traductions les plus belles, pendant que vous nous privez du plaisir de voir Mademoiselle Reynolds & de l'ecouter. Enfin, Mademoiselle, il faut être moins aimable, afin que nous vous aimions plus.

Je suis,

Mademoiselle,

Vôtre tres humble &

Obeissant Serviteur,

SAM: JOHNSON.

214.

To Mrs. Thrale [1].

MADAM,   [London], May 18, 1769

Now I know you want to be forgetting me, but I do not want to be forgotten, and would rather send you letters, like *Presto's* [2], than suffer myself to slip out of your memory That I should forget you, there is no danger; for I have time enough to think both by night and day; and he that has leisure for any thing that is not present, always turns his mind to that which he likes best.

One reason for thinking on you is, that I must for a while be content with thinking, for our affairs will not suffer me to come home till Saturday.

I am, &c.,

SAM: JOHNSON.

215.

To the Reverend Thomas Warton.

[London], May 31, 1769.   Published in the *Life*, ii. 67.

[1] *Piozzi Letters*, i. 19.
[2] 'August 2, 1711. The Secretary and I have been walking three or four hours to-day. The Duchess of Shrewsbury asked him, was not that Dr. Dr., and she could not say my name in English, but said *Dr. Presto*, which is Italian for Swift.' Swift's *Journal to Stella, Works*, ed. 1803, xxi.270. Johnson said that the Letters which composed this Journal 'have some odd attraction.' *Life*, iv. 177, *n.* 2. By Deane Swift's edition of Swift's Letters (1768) *Presto* had lately become known as Swift's name.

To

216.

To Mrs. Thrale [1].

DEAR MADAM,   New Inn Hall, [Oxford,] June 27, 1769.

I had your note sent hither ; and can easily spare the pine-apple, and be satisfied with the reason for which it was sent. Though I hope I shall never want any new memorials to keep you in my mind, yet I am glad to find you solicitous not to be forgotten, though I should not deserve to be remembered if there could be any reason for such solicitude.

The pain and sickness which you suffer, you may bear to feel and I to think on with less impatience on your part, and less grief on mine, because the crisis is within view.   I will not encrease your uneasiness with mine. I hope I grow better. I am very cautious, and very timorous [2].   Whether fear and caution do much for me, I can hardly tell.   Time will perhaps do more than both.

I purpose to come to town in a few days, but I suppose I must not see you.   I will, however, call on Mr. Thrale in the Borough, and shall hope to be soon informed that your trouble is over, and that you are well enough to resume your care for that which yet continues, and which your kindness may sometimes alleviate.

I am, &c.,

SAM: JOHNSON.

217.

To Mrs. Thrale [3].

MADAM,   Oxford, June 29, 1769.

Hesiod, who was very wise in his time, though nothing to such wise people as we, says, that the evil of the worst times has some good mingled with it [4].   Hesiod was in the right.   These

---

[1] *Piozzi Letters*, i. 20.

Johnson had been at Oxford almost a month, perhaps longer (*Life*, ii. 67), so that it is probable that some of his letters to Mrs. Thrale are missing.   He was the guest no doubt of Chambers (*ante*, p. 132, *n.* 4).

[2] 'During this visit he seldom or never dined out.' *Life*, ii. 68, *n.* 1.

On September 18 he recorded in his journal :—'This year has been wholly spent in a slow progress of recovery.' *Pr. and Med.*, p. 85.

[3] *Piozzi Letters*, i. 21.

[4] 'ἀλλ' ἔμπης καὶ τοῖσι μεμίξεται ἐσθλὰ κακοῖσιν.' HESIOD, *Works and Days*, l. 179.

times

times are not much to my mind ; I am not well; but in these times you are safe, and have brought a pretty little Miss. I always wished it might be a Miss, and now that wish is gratified, nothing remains but that I entreat you to take care of yourself; for whatever number of girls or boys you may give us, we are far from being certain that any of them will ever do for us what you can do; it is certain that they cannot now do it, and the ability which they want, they are not likely to gain but by your precepts and your example ; by an example of excellence, and by the admonitions of truth.

Mr. Thrale tells me, that my furlough is shortened ; I am always ready to obey orders ; I have not yet found any place from which I shall not willingly depart to come back to you.

I am, dearest Lady,

Your, &c.,

SAM: JOHNSON.

218.

To MR. THRALE [1].

SIR,   New Inn Hall, Oxford, June 29, 1769.

That Mrs. Thrale is safely past through her danger is an event at which nobody but yourself can rejoice more than I rejoice. I think myself very much honoured by the choice that you have been pleased to make of me to become related to the little maiden [2]. Let me know when she will want me, and I will very punctually wait on her.

I am, &c.,

SAM: JOHNSON.

219.

To MRS. THRALE [3].

DEAREST MADAM,   July 6, 1769.

Though I am to come home to-morrow, I would not let the alarming letter which I received this morning be without notice. Dear Madam, take all possible care of your health. How near

---

[1] *Piozzi Letters*, i. 23.

[2] She was born on June 22, and christened Lucy Elizabeth. He had asked that he might have a Bessy.

Ante, p. 140. For her death, see *post*, Letter of Nov. 18, 1773.

[3] *Piozzi Letters*, i. 23.

we

we always are to danger! I hope your danger is now past; but that fear, which is the necessary effect of danger, must remain always with us. I hope my little Miss is well. Surely I shall be very fond of her. In a year and half she will run and talk. But how much ill may happen in a year and half! Let us however hope for the better side of possibility, and think that I may then and afterwards continue to be,

Madam,

Your, &c.,

SAM: JOHNSON.

220.

To MRS. THRALE [1].

MADAM,   Lichfield, August 14, 1769.

I set out on Thursday morning, and found my companion, to whom I was very much a stranger, more agreeable than I expected. We went cheerfully forward, and passed the night at Coventry [2]. We came in late, and went out early; and therefore I did not send for my cousin Tom [3]; but I design to make him some amends for the omission.

Next day we came early to Lucy, who was, I believe, glad to see us. She had saved her best gooseberries upon the tree for me; and, as Steele says, *I was neither too proud nor too wise* to gather them. I have rambled a very little *inter fontes et flumina nota* [4], but I am not yet well. They have cut down the trees in George Lane [5]. Evelyn, in his book of Forest Trees,

---

[1] *Piozzi Letters*, i. 24.

[2] Coventry is ninety miles from London; Lichfield is twenty-six miles farther. Paterson's *British Itinerary*, i. 149.

[3] Johnson mentions his cousin, Tom Johnson, in his Letters of May 1, 1770, where he calls him 'my nearest relation,' of Dec. 6, 1774, and May 29, 1779. In his will he left a bequest to his descendants. *Life*, iv. 403, 440.

[4]   'Hic inter flumina nota
    Et fontes sacros frigus captabis
    opacum.'
        VIRGIL. *Eclogues*, i. 52.

Johnson again quotes these lines inaccurately, *post*, Letter of July 8, 1771. In 1783 he said :—' I have this year read all Virgil through; the *Eclogues* I have almost all by heart.' *Life*, iv. 218.

[5] 'I was,' says Johnson, 'by my father's persuasion put to one Marclew, commonly called Bellison, the servant, or wife of a servant of my father, to be nursed in George Lane, where I used to call when I was a bigger boy, and eat fruit in the garden, which was full of trees. Here it was discovered that my eyes were bad. . . . My mother visited me every day,
tells

tells us of wicked men that cut down trees, and never prospered afterwards[1]; yet nothing has deterred these audacious alder-men from violating the Hamadryads of George Lane. As an impartial traveller I must however tell, that in Stow-street, where I left a draw-well, I have found a pump ; but the lading-well in this ill-fated George Lane lies shamefully neglected.

I am going to-day or to-morrow to Ashbourne ; but I am at a loss how I shall get back in time to London. Here are only chance coaches, so that there is no certainty of a place. If I do not come, let it not hinder your journey. I can be but a few days behind you ; and I will follow in the Brighthelmstone coach. But I hope to come.

I took care to tell Miss Porter, that I have got another Lucy. I hope she is well. Tell Mrs. Salusbury, that I beg her stay at Streatham, for little Lucy's sake.

I am, &c.,

SAM: JOHNSON.

221.

To MRS. ASTON [2].

MADAM,   Brighthelmstone, August 26, 1759.

I suppose you have received the mill : the whole apparatus seemed to be perfect, except that there is wanting a little tin spout at the bottom, and some ring or knob, on which the bag that catches the meal is to be hung. When these are added, I hope you will be able to grind your own bread, and treat me with a cake made by yourself, of meal from your own corn of your own grinding [3].

I was glad, Madam, to see you so well, and hope your health will long increase, and then long continue.

I am, Madam,

Your most obedient servant,

SAM: JOHNSON.

and used to go different ways, that her assiduity might not expose her to ridicule, and often left her fan or glove behind her that she might have a pretence to come back un-expected ; but she never discovered any token of neglect.' *Annals,* p. 10.

[1] *Silva : or a Discourse of Forest Trees.* By John Evelyn, ed. 1776, pp. 633-643.

[2] First published in Croker's *Boswell,* page 198.

For Mrs. Aston, see *ante*, p. 131, *n.* 1.

[3] In the April number of the *Gentleman's Magazine* for this year

TO

222.

To James Boswell.

Brighthelmstone, September 9, 1769. Published in the *Life*, ii. 70.

223.

To the Reverend Dr. Taylor [1].

Dear Sir,

I got very well to London, and went on the next Monday to Brighthelmston, from which I am now returned. I think you might write to me, and let me know what became of your demand of the living [2], and other occurrences of your life. I am not fully determined against coming this winter again into your corner of the world, but I have got no settled plan. Write to me however.

I am, Sir,

Your most, &c.,

Oct. 5, 1769.   Sam: Johnson.

224.

To the Reverend Thomas Percy [3].

Sir,

I am desired by some Ladies who support a Charity School on Snow hill, to solicit you for a Charity Sermon, to be

(p. 177) there are a print and description of a hand-cornmill invented by Samuel and Sampson Freeth of Birmingham.

[1] From the original in the possession of Mr. Alan Stenning of St. Stephen's Club.

It was franked by Mr. Thrale.

[2] Johnson, writing to Mrs. Thrale about Taylor on May 16, 1776, says :—'Livings and preferments, as if he were in want with twenty children, run in his head.' Taylor seems to have been successful in his demand, for I find in the *Gentleman's Magazine* for October of this year (p. 511), under Ecclesiastical Preferments, 'Rev. Dr. Taylor—to the living of St. Botolph, Aldersgate.'

[3] From the original in the Dyce and Forster Libraries, South Ken-sington Museum, sent me by Mr. R. F. Sketchley.

The Ladies' Charity School which was founded in King Street, Snow Hill, in 1702, still flourishes, having been transferred first to John Street, Bedford Row, next to Queen Square, Bloomsbury, and lastly to Powis Gardens, Notting Hill. Boswell mentions Johnson's old friend Mrs. Gardiner, the wife of a tallow-chandler, 'not in the learned way, but a worthy good woman,' as very zealous for its support (*Life*, i. 242 ; iv. 246). So also was Miss Williams, who 'left her little substance to the school' (*ib.* iv. 241)—amounting, as the old books of the Institution still show, to £357. In it are preserved her tea-spoons and portrait ; also a set of spoons which in all likelihood

preached

preached either the last Sunday of this month, or the first of the next. This application had been made sooner if you had been in town, but I hope it is not yet too late, and that if you can comply without great inconvenience you will not refuse. They meet on Wednesday, and desire to know your determination to-morrow. I hope you will not refuse them, for I have a great esteem of some of them, and I think you may appear with great propriety on such occasions.

I am, Sir,

Your most humble servant,

SAM: JOHNSON.

Nov. 5, 1769.

Please to send your answer to Mrs. Williams, for I shall not be in town.

To the Reverend Mr. Percy.

225.

To JAMES BOSWELL.

London, November 9, 1769. Published in the *Life*, ii. 110.

226.

To THE REVEREND HENRY BRIGHT [1].

SIR, Johnson's Court, Fleet Street, Jan. 9, 1770.

I would gladly be informed if you are willing to take

were Johnson's. He was one of the subscribers from the year 1777 till his death. 'It afforded a hint for the story of *Betty Broom* in the *Idler*, Nos. 26 and 29' (*ib*. iv. 246). On March 12, 1783, as the Minutes show :—'Dr. Johnson, having turn, presents Mary Ann Austin, daughter of Charles and Amey Austin, living at the top of Goswell Street, at one Mr. Mason's, near the prison bar.' Mrs. Thrale was both a subscriber and a manager. See an article in *The Speaker* for March 22, 1890, in which I have given an account of Johnson's connection with this institution.

The following extracts from the Minute Book of the Institution shew the result of Johnson's application :—

'Vicarage House, St. Sepulchre's, Nov. 8, 1769.

The Rev. Mr. Percy, Chaplain to his Grace the Duke of Northumberland and the Rev. Mr. Butler of Charlotte Street Chapel, have promised to preach for these children on Sunday, 26 instant.'

'Vicarage House, St. Sepulchre's, Dec. 13, 1769.

Mr. Treasurer reported that there was collected at the Charity Sermons preached (Nov. 26 last) by the Rev. Mr. Percy and the Rev. Mr. Butler £23 16s. 10d.'

I am indebted for these extracts to Miss Anne C. Moore, the Honorary Secretary of the Charity.

[1] From the original in the British Museum :—*Stowe MSS.*, 685.

Henry Bright was Master of another

another pupil, in the same manner as Mr. Strahan was taken. You will, I think, have more trouble with him, and therefore ought to have a higher price.

I shall [be] at Oxford on Fryday [*sic*] and Saturday next[1], when if you cannot come over, I shall expect a letter from you.

I am, Sir,

Your most humble servant,

SAM: JOHNSON.

227.

TO THE REVEREND DR. FARMER.

Johnson's Court, March 21, 1770.   Published in the *Life*, ii. 114.

228.

TO MISS PORTER[2].

DEAREST MADAM,   May 1, 1770.

Among other causes that have hindered me from answering your last kind letter, is a tedious and painful rheumatism, that has afflicted me for many weeks, and still continues to molest me[3]. I hope you are well, and will long keep your health and your cheerfulness.

One reason why I delayed to write was, my uncertainty how to answer your letter. I like the thought of giving away the money very well; but when I consider that Tom Johnson[4] is my nearest relation, and that he is now old and in great want; that he was my playfellow in childhood, and has never done any thing to offend me; I am in doubt, whether I ought not rather give it him than any other.

Of this, my dear, I would have your opinion. I would willingly please you, and I know that you will be pleased best with what you think right. Tell me your mind, and do not

Abingdon Grammar School. *Ante,* p. 95.

[1] Of this visit to Oxford there is no mention elsewhere.

[2] First published in Croker's *Boswell,* page 214.

[3] He describes his sufferings from this illness in his Diary, and ends by saying:—'The pain harasses me much; yet many have the disease perhaps in a much higher degree, with want of food, fire, and covering, which I find thus grievous, with all the succours that riches and kindness can buy and give.' (He was staying at Mr. Thrale's.) *Pr. and Med.* p. 94.

[4] *Ante,* p. 154, *n.* 3.

learn

learn of me to neglect writing ; for it is a very sorry trick, though it be mine.

Your brother [1] is well ; I saw him to-day, and thought it long since I saw him before : it seems he has called often, and could not find me.

> I am, my dear,
> Your affectionate humble servant,
> SAM : JOHNSON.

229.

To Miss Porter [2].

MY DEAREST DEAR,   London, May 29, 1770.

I am very sorry that your eyes are bad ; take great care of them, especially by candlelight. Mine continue pretty good, but they are sometimes dim [3]. My rheumatism grows gradually better. I have considered your letter, and am willing that the whole money should go where you, my dear, originally intended. I hope to help Tom some other way. So that matter is over.

Dr. Taylor has invited me to pass some time with him at Ashbourne ; if I come, you may be sure that I shall take you and Lichfield in my way. When I am nearer coming, I will send you word.

Of Mr. Porter I have seen very little, but I know not that it is his fault, for he says that he often calls, and never finds me ; I am sorry for it, for I love him. Mr. Mathias [4] has lately had a great deal of money left him, of which you have probably heard already.

> I am, my dearest,
> Your most obedient servant,
> SAM : JOHNSON.

230.

To the Reverend Thomas Warton.

London, June 23, 1770. Published in the *Life*, ii. 114.

---

[1] Miss Porter's second brother, who died in 1783. *Life*, iv. 256.

[2] First published in Croker's *Boswell*, page 214.

[3] See *ante*, p. 57, *n.* 5.

[4] Johnson mentions him again, *post*, Letter of April 8, 1780. A gentleman of this name and his sister are more than once mentioned in Miss Seward's *Correspondence*. Miss Burney mentions also a Mr. Mathias as paying her at the end of 1786 her salary at Court. Mme. D'Arblay's *Diary*, iii. 257.

231.

TO THE REVEREND DR. TAYLOR [1].

DEAR SIR,

I hope the danger that has threatened you is now over, and that you have nothing now to overcome but that languor which must necessarily succeed a disorder so violent as yours. Recovery is a state which requires great caution, and I entreat you not to be negligent of yourself.

I am now at Lichfield, and if my company can afford you either help or entertainment I am ready to come to you. If you can write let me know from yourself the state of your health ; if writing is difficult, let me hear by some other hand. Be very careful of yourself.

I am, dear Sir,

Your most humble servant,

Lichfield. July 2, 1770.   SAM: JOHNSON.

232.

TO MRS. THRALE [2].

DEAR MADAM,   Lichfield, July 7, 1770.

I thought I should have heard something to-day about Streatham ; but there is no letter ; and I need some consolation, for Rheumatism is come again, though in a less degree than formerly. I reckon to go next week to Ashbourne, and will try to bring you the dimensions of the great bull [3]. The skies and the ground are all so wet, that I have been very little abroad ; and Mrs. Aston is from home, so that I have no motive to walk. When she is at home, she lives on the top of Stow Hill [4], and I

[1] First published in the *Miscellanies of the Philobiblon Society*, vi. 42.

[2] *Piozzi Letters*, i. 26.

[3] See *post*, p. 166.

[4] Boswell describes Mrs. Aston and her widowed sister Mrs. Gastrell as having each 'a house and garden and pleasure-ground, prettily situated upon Stow Hill, a gentle eminence, adjoining to Lichfield.' *Life*, ii. 470. It was in a pleasant house 'in the little green valley of Stow, that slopes from the east end of the Cathedral, and forms with its old grey tower on the banks of its lake so lovely a landscape,' that Thomas Day, the author of *Sandford and Merton*, was at this time educating an orphan girl of thirteen with the intention of fitting her to be his wife. He had given her the name of Sabrina Sidney, in honour of the river Severn and Algernon Sidney. Johnson might well have seen her, for 'all the ladies of the place kindly

commonly

commonly climb up to see her once a day. There is nothing there now but the empty nest. I hope Streatham will long be the place[1].

To write to you about Lichfield is of no use, for you never saw Stow-pool, nor Borowcop-hill. I believe you may find Borow or Boroughcop-hill in my Dictionary, under *cop* or *cob*[2]. Nobody here knows what the name imports.

I have taken the liberty to enclose a letter ; for, though you do not know it, three groats make a shilling[3].

I am, dearest Madam,
Yours, &c.,
SAM: JOHNSON.

233.

TO MRS. THRALE[4].

MADAM,   Lichfield, July 11, 1770.

Since my last letter nothing extraordinary has happened. Rheumatism, which has been very troublesome, is grown better. I have not yet seen Dr. Taylor, and July runs fast away. I shall not have much time for him, if he delays much longer to come or send. Mr. Grene, the apothecary[5], has found a book, which

took notice of her.' The education which Day gave her was successful, but she went counter to some of his fancies, and he would not marry her. Seward's *Memoirs of Dr. Darwin*, p. 22, and *Memoirs of R. L. Edgeworth*, pp. 135, 150, 218.

Johnson wrote some Latin verses on the little stream that flows in the valley, which begin :—

'Errat adhuc vitreus per prata virentia rivus,
    Quo toties lavi membra tenella puer.'   *Works,* i. 163.

[1] The sentence seems imperfect.

[2] Johnson defines *Cop* as *The head, the top of anything; anything arising to a head.* He does not instance Borowcop Hill. In the *Ann. Reg.* for 1775, part 1, p. 134[a], mention is made of Cop's Hill in Boston, whence the Americans fired on the English troops.

[3] 'The postage on a letter to Lichfield, a place more than 80 and less than 140 miles from London, was at this time fourpence. Dodsley's *London,* v. 211. On the letter enclosed by Johnson an extra charge of the same amount would have been made; but the packet no doubt was directed to Mr. Thrale, who, being a member of Parliament, would receive it free of charge. The enclosed letter, being franked by Thrale, would also go free. A groat therefore was saved either to Johnson, or more probably to his correspondent, for letters were very rarely prepaid ; a groat, he seems to say, is of some importance, for three make a shilling.

[4] *Piozzi Letters,* i. 27.

[5] For Mr. Green and his Museum

[a] In this volume of the *Ann. Reg.* there are three pages each numbered 134.

tells who paid levies in our parish, and how much they paid, above an hundred years ago. Do you not think we study this book hard? Nothing is like going to the bottom of things. Many families that paid the parish rates are now extinct, like the race of Hercules [1]. *Pulvis et umbra sumus* [2]. What is nearest us touches us most. The passions rise higher at domestic than at imperial tragedies. I am not wholly unaffected by the revolutions of Sadler-street [3]; nor can forbear to mourn a little when old names vanish away, and new come into their place.

Do not imagine, Madam, that I wrote this letter for the sake of these philosophical meditations; for when I began it, I had

see *Life*, ii. 465. Erasmus Darwin, writing on December 17, 1790, says:—'I remember Mr. Green of Lichfield, who is now growing very old, once told me his retail business [as an apothecary] by means of his show-shop and many-coloured window produced him £100 a year.' C. Darwin's *Life of Erasmus Darwin*, p. 38. In the same letter, speaking of a young man who was thinking of settling at Lichfield as an apothecary or surgeon, and of the means of getting acquainted with people, Darwin says:—'Fourthly card assemblies,—I think at Lichfield surgeons are not admitted as they are here [Derby]; but they are to dancing assemblies.'

[1] 'Ut tamen Herculeae supcressent semina gentis,' &c.
   OVID, *Fasti*, ii. 237.

[2] HORACE, 4 *Odes*, vii. 16.

[3] At the corner of Sadler Street, now known as Market Street, Johnson's house stood. Among the revolutions of the town the watchmen's bills had not disappeared. In a note in his *Shakespeare* on Dogberry's charge to the Watch, 'only have a care that your bills be not stolen'

(*Much Ado About Nothing*, Act iii. scene 4), he says:—'A bill is still carried by the watchmen at Lichfield.' The Watch, as I was informed at Lichfield, used to be called "dozeners [a]." The twelve bills they bore were always carried till very lately in the Court of Array; they are still preserved in the Guild Hall. This Court of Array was a survival of old times. 'The Statutes of Array by which Commissioners were empowered to take in each county a review of all the freemen able to bear arms, &c. were repealed in the reign of James I. Notwithstanding the Bailiffs have constantly held a manorial court on Green Hill at the same time as the view of men and arms according to ancient charter and prescription.' Harwood's *History of Lichfield*, p. 354.

John Howard, who visited the City Gaol three years later, describes it as having 'the rooms too small and close. No yard, no water, no straw. Allowance 1s. 6d. a week.' Out of this allowance the wretched prisoner had to buy all that he needed. *State of the Prisons*, &c., ed. 1777, p. 329.

[a] In Jersey there are in each parish several *vinteniers*, each of whom has the charge of a particular *vintaine* into which the parishes are divided. *Cæsarea: The Island of Jersey*, ed. 1840, p. 126.

neither

neither Mr. Grene, nor his book, in my thoughts; but was resolved to write, and did not know what I had to send, but my respects to Mrs. Salusbury, and Mr. Thrale, and Harry [1], and the Misses.

I am, dearest Madam,

Yours, &c.,

SAM: JOHNSON.

234.

TO MRS. THRALE [2].

DEAR MADAM,   Lichfield, July 14, 1770.

When any calamity is suffered, the first thing to be remembered is, how much has been escaped. The house might have been entered by ruffians when Mrs. Salusbury had been in it, and who can tell what horrours might have followed!

I thought you would in time compliment your compliments away. Nothing goes well when I am from you, for when I am from you the house is robbed [3]. You must therefore suppose, that if I had been with you, the robbery would not have been. But it was not our gang [4]. I should have had no interest.

Your loss, I am afraid, is very great; but the loss of patience would have been greater.

My rheumatism torments me very much, though not as in the winter. I think I shall go to Ashbourne on Monday or Tuesday.

You will be pleased to make all my compliments.

I am, &c.,

SAM: JOHNSON.

235.

TO MRS. THRALE [5].

DEAR MADAM,   Lichfield, July, [1770].

Do not say that I never write to you, and do not think that I expected to find any friends here that could make me

---

[1] Mrs. Thrale's son who died suddenly six years later when Johnson was in Lichfield. *Life*, ii. 468.

[2] *Piozzi Letters*, i. 28.

[3] 'Mrs. Salusbury's house in town was robbed of goods and linen to a large amount, while she was absent at Streatham.' Note by Mrs. Piozzi.

[4] Johnson's 'gang' must have been a *cant* word of the Streatham set. Baretti belonged to it, as Mrs. Thrale's answer showed. *Piozzi Letters*, i. 30.

[5] *Piozzi Letters*, i. 289.

This Letter Mrs. Piozzi carelessly inserts among those of 1775, though wish to prolong my stay. For your strawberries, however, I have no care. Mrs. Cobb has strawberries, and will give me as long as they last; and she has cherries too. Of the strawberries at Streatham I consign my part to Miss and Harry. I hope Susy grows, and Lucy begins to walk. Though this rainy weather confines us all in the house, I have neither frolicked nor fretted.

In the tumult, whatever it was, at your house, I hope my countrywomen either had no part, or behaved well. I told Mr. Heartwell, about three days ago, how well Warren was liked in her place.

I have passed one day at Birmingham with my old friend Hector—there's a name—and his sister, an old love [1]. My mistress is grown much older than my friend.

> ——O, quid habes illius, illius
> Quæ spirabat amores,
> Quæ me surpuerat mihi [2].

Time will impair the body, and uses us well if it spares the mind.

I am, &c.,

SAM: JOHNSON.

236.

To Mrs. Thrale [3].

DEAR MADAM, Ashbourne, July 20, 1770.

I hope your complaint [4], however troublesome, is without danger; for your danger involves us all. When you were ill before, it was agreed that if you were lost, hope would be lost with you; for such another there was no expectation of finding.

I came hither on Wednesday, having staid one night at a

---

in it is mention of Johnson's little god-daughter, Lucy, who died in 1773. It belongs no doubt to July, 1770, when the child was thirteen months old, and might be beginning to walk.

[1] Mrs. Careless, a clergyman's widow. *Post*, p. 202, and *Life*, ii. 459.

[2] 'Of her, of her what now remains, Who breathed the loves, who charmed the swains, And snatched me from my heart?'
FRANCIS, Horace, *Odes*, iv. 13. 18.

[3] *Piozzi Letters*, i. 31.

[4] She had suffered from 'an odious sore throat.' *Ib.* p. 30.

lodge

lodge in the forest of Needwood [1]. Dr. Taylor's is a very pleasant house, with a lawn and a lake, and twenty deer and five fawns upon the lawn [2]. Whether I shall by any light see Matlock I do not yet know [3].

Let us not yet have done rejoicing that Mrs. Salusbury was not in the house. The robbery will be a noble tale when we meet again.

That Baretti's book would please you all I made no doubt. I know not whether the world has ever seen such Travels before [4].

[1] 'June 6, 1785. There are not, I apprehend, less than a thousand acres of oak timber now standing in Needwood Forest : a quantity of which few other forests of the kingdom can at present boast.' W. Marshall's *Rural Economy of the Midland Counties*, ii. 357. In 1798 the forest was said to cover nearly ten thousand acres. Shaw's *History of Staffordshire*, p. 65. Landor in one of his *Imaginary Conversations* makes Johnson say :—'In my English travels I saw gossamer formerly in Needwood Forest, five miles from Lichfield ; latterly my travels were in Scotland, where there was no plant to support it.' Landor's *Works*, ed. 1876, iv. 221.

[2] For Boswell's description of Dr. Taylor's house see *Life*, ii. 473. In Nichols's *Lit. Anec.*, ix. 62, there is the following note :—

'Inscription by Dr. Johnson on Dr. Taylor's house at Ashbourn :—
"Stet domus hæc donec Testudo perambulet orbem,
    Et donec fluctus ebibat Formica marinos."
This is false metre ; read
"Ebibat et donec fluctus formica marinos."'

I am informed by the Rev. Francis Jourdain, Vicar of Ashbourne, that 'Dr. Taylor's house is practically as he left it, the coat of arms still remaining in the entrance hall. The garden, however, has been altered, the lake has been filled up, and the stream diverted.'

[3] Mrs. Thrale in a letter which he had just received had said : 'Mr. Thrale particularly vexes lest you should not see Matlock on a moonlight night.' *Piozzi Letters*, i. 31. He visited it in their company four years later. *Life*, v. 430.

[4] Baretti's *Journey from London to Genoa*, in four small volumes, is noticed in the *Gentleman's Magazine* for July of this year (p. 323). It must have met with a quick sale, for at least two more editions were published before the end of the year. In his Preface he says :—'I have spared no pains to carry my reader in some measure along with me ; to make him see what I saw, hear what I heard, feel what I felt, and even think and fancy whatever I thought and fancied myself. Should this method prove agreeable, and procure the honour of a favourable reception to my work, I shall owe it in a great part to my most revered friend, Dr. Samuel Johnson, who suggested it to me, just as I was setting out on my first journey to Spain.' In a marginal note on Johnson's letter Baretti says : — 'Johnson does not tell it, but he never could think that the petty adventures told in it were true : they are however all true to a tittle in spite of his incredulity.'

Those

Those whose lot it is to ramble can seldom write, and those who know how to write very seldom ramble. If Sidney had gone, as he desired, the great voyage with Drake, there would probably have been such a narrative as would have equally satisfied the poet and philosopher[1].

I have learned since I left you, that the names of two of the Pleiades were Coccymo and Lampado[2].

> I am, &c.,
> SAM: JOHNSON.

237.

To Mrs. Thrale[3].

DEAREST MADAM,   Ashbourne, July 23, 1770.

There had not been so long an interval between my two last letters, but that when I came hither I did not at first understand the hours of the post.

I have seen the great bull; and very great he is. I have seen likewise his heir apparent, who promises to inherit all the bulk and all the virtues of his sire. I have seen the man who offered an hundred guineas for the young bull, while he was yet little better than a calf[4]. Matlock, I am afraid, I shall not see, but I

Johnson told Boswell that 'writers of travels were more defective than any other writers.' *Life*, ii. 377. See also *post*, Letter of August 12, 1773.

[1] 'The next step which Sir Philip Sidney intended into the world was an expedition of his own projecting, wherein he fashioned the whole body, with purpose to become head of it himself. I mean the last employment but one of Sir Francis Drake to the West Indies.' Fulke Grevil's *Life of Sir Philip Sidney*, ed. 1652, p. 81.

[2] 'The allusion,' writes Mrs. Piozzi, 'is to a search made at that time by the Streatham coterie for female names ending in O.' 'I never heard a word of that Coterie.'— BARETTI. In the list of the Pleiades given by the scholiast of Theocritus (xiii. 25) are found Coccymo and Lampatho. Smith's *Clas. Dict.*

[3] *Piozzi Letters*, i. 32.

[4] 'Dr. Taylor was remarkable for having the finest breed of milch cows in Derbyshire or perhaps in England; he sold one some time before his death for 160 guineas, and a heifer for 70 guineas. Mr. Marshall [*Rural Economy*, &c., i. 18] says, "In the Midland District, where the land is titheable, the tithe is seldom taken in kind. I met with only one instance, Bosworth Field, by Dr. Taylor." He had frequently talked of leaving his fortune to Johnson. He died February 29, 1788, worth about £1,200 a year, besides personalities to a very considerable amount.' Nichols's *Lit. Anec.* ix. 63. See *Life*, iii. 150.

purpose

purpose to see Dovedale; and after all this seeing, I hope to see
you.

I am, &c.,

SAM: JOHNSON.

238.

TO FRANCIS BARBER.

London, September 25, 1770. Published in the *Life*, ii. 115.

239.

TO THE REVEREND DR. JOSEPH WARTON.

[London], September 27, 1770. Published in the *Life*, ii. 115.

240.

TO MR. AND MRS. THRALE[1].

Mr. Johnson flatters himself that there is no need of informing
Mr. Thrale that the application required was made to Mr.
Burke, or Mrs. Thrale, that he wishes her every thing that friend-
ship can wish her. He has sent her a pamphlet to amuse her in
her confinement, which he would not have shown to more than
Mr. Thrale, and Mrs. Salusbury.

Johnson's Court, Oct. 2, [1770].

241.

TO FRANCIS BARBER.

[London], December 7, 1770. Published in the *Life*, ii. 116.

242.

TO MR. SMITH[2].

SIR,

I beg leave to give you again the trouble which you were so

[1] From the original in the possession of Mrs. Thomas, of Eyhorne
House, Maidstone.

It seems probable that this letter
was written in 1770. Mrs. Salusbury died on June 18, 1773. If
the pamphlet was, as seems likely,
one of Johnson's, it was *Falkland's
Islands*, which was published in
March, 1771. It was neither *The
Patriot* nor *Taxation no Tyranny*,
both of which were written after

1773; neither could it have been
The False Alarm, which was written
at the Thrales' house, and read to Mr.
Thrale the moment it was finished.
Life, ii. 111. I am surprised to find
that *Falkland's Islands* was written
so long before its publication, though
Johnson does speak of 'the much
lingering of my own and much of
the ministry' in getting it out. *Ib.*
ii. 135.

[2] From the original in the posses-

kind

kind as to take last year of cashing [?] these bills and paying them.

Be pleased to send me some Irish Cloath for 12 Shirts at 4 yards to a shirt, the price may be from 3*s*. 6*d*. to 4*s*. the yard. The piece which you sent in the summer to Mrs. Williams, you may charge to me.

I inclose, as I did last year, a bill of £50 which I beg to know whether you receive. You need send back no money, but a state of the account between us.

I am, Sir,

Your most humble servant,

SAM: JOHNSON.

As I remember, there was a surplus of about ten pounds in your hands last year.

January 25, 1771.

To Mr. Smith.

243.

To JOHN RIVINGTON [1].

SIR,

When Mr. Steevens treated with you about the new impression of Shakespeare, he agreed with [*sic*] the additions now made should be printed by themselves for the benefit of former purchasers. As some of my subscribers may think themselves ill treated, it is proper to advertise our intention, and I shall be glad to see it done in one or more of the papers next week.

I am, Sir,

Your humble servant,

SAM: JOHNSON.

Feb. 2, 1771.

To Mr. Rivington, Bookseller.

sion of Mr. Alfred Morrison, of Fonthill House.

This Letter was sold by Messrs. Sotheby and Co., on May 10, 1875, for £2 10*s*. (Lot 90), and on June 5, 1888, by Messrs. Christie and Co., for £4 10*s*. (Lot 43).

Mr. Smith was perhaps Henry Smith, Thrale's relation and executor. *Post*, Letters of April 5 and 17, 1781.

[1] From the original in the possession of Messrs. Robson and Karslake, 23 Coventry Street, Haymarket.

Johnson's *Shakespeare*, which was first published in 1765 and had reached a second edition, was republished by George Steevens in 1773. *Life*, ii. 204. Rivington was one of the proprietors, and no doubt acted for the others. At the end of

To

244.

To the Rev. Dr. Richard Farmer [1].

Sir,

Some time ago Mr. Steevens and I took the liberty of sending a catalogue in hope of some improvement and augmentation. Mr. Steevens, who undertakes the whole care of this impression, begins to fancy that he wants it.

I have done very little to the book; but by the plunder of your pamphlet, and the authorities which Mr. Steevens has very diligently collected, I think it will be somewhat improved. If you could spare us any thing we should think your communication a great favour. I hope amongst us all Shakespeare will be better understood. You have already done your part, and when you have finished what I am told you are now projecting will leave I believe much fewer difficulties to future criticks.

I am, Sir,

Your most humble servant,

Sam: Johnson.

Johnson's Court, Fleet Street, Feb. 18, 1771.

245.

To Henry Thrale [2].

[London], March, 1771.

Dear Sir,

In the Shrewsbury, an East India ship, commanded by

vol. x is an Appendix of 45 unpaged leaves. Very possibly it was printed separately and sent to the subscribers to the two earlier editions. No copy of such a separate publication is in the British Museum.

[1] From the original in the possession of Mr. Thomas Thring, of 2 Thornhill Villas, Weymouth. 'I bought it,' he informs me, 'of a bookseller at Salisbury some fifty years ago.'

Though it bears no address, there is no doubt that it was written to the Rev. Dr. Farmer, Master of Emanuel College, Cambridge. Boswell publishes a second letter to him written a month later, in which Johnson says:—'Mr. Steevens, a very ingenious gentleman, lately of King's College, has collected an account of all the translations which Shakspeare might have seen and used. He wishes his catalogue to be perfect, and therefore intreats that you will favour him by the insertion of such additions as the accuracy of your inquiries has enabled you to make.' *Life*, ii. 114. Farmer had published in 1767 *An Essay on the Learning of Shakespeare*, which Johnson praised. *Ib.* iii. 38, *n.* 6. Steevens in the Advertisement to the Reader in his and Johnson's *Shakespeare* acknowledges Dr. Farmer's assistance. Appendix ii of vol. x consists of many pages of his 'Observations.'

[2] *Piozzi Letters*, i. 33.

Captain

Captain Jones, there is one Thomas Coxeter, who lately enlisted as a soldier in the Company's service [1]. He repents of his adventure, and has written to his sister, who brings this letter, to procure him his discharge. He is the son of a gentleman, who was once my friend [2]; and the boy was himself a favourite with my wife. I shall therefore think it a great favour, if you will be pleased to use your influence with Sir George Colebrook [3], that he may be discharged. The request is not great; for he is slight and feeble, and worth nothing but to those who value him for some other merit than his own [4].

I am, &c.,
Sam: Johnson.

246.

To Bennet Langton.

[London], March 20, 1771. Published in the *Life*, ii. 135.

[1] The Company must have had difficulty in raising troops in England, for in the *Gentleman's Magazine* for March of this year (p. 141) it is stated that one of their recruiting officers had returned from Germany 'bringing with him five hundred men from the Duchy of Wirtemburg only.'

[2] See *Life*, iii. 158, for the collection of the minor poets which Coxeter had made. He was educated at Trinity College, Oxford, and coming to London worked for the booksellers. He died on April 19, 1747. Johnson assisted his orphan daughter. Nichols's *Lit. Anec.* ii. 512. Among the 'Promotions' announced in the *Gent. Mag.* I find his name in the list for the February before his death (p. 103) entered for a very poor piece of preferment:—' Tho. Coxeter Esq.; elected secretary to the committee of subscribers for purchasing materials for Mr. Carte's History of England.'

[3] ' May 1, 1774. Sir George Colbrooke, a citizen, and martyr to what is called *speculation*, had his pictures sold by auction last week.' Walpole's *Letters*, vi. 81. ' I professed myself sincerely grieved when accumulated distresses crushed Sir G. Colebrook's family, and I was so. "Your own prosperity," said Johnson, "may possibly have so far increased the natural tenderness of your heart that for aught I know you may be a little sorry; but it is sufficient for a plain man if he does not laugh when he sees a fine new house tumble down all on a sudden, and a snug cottage stand by ready to receive the owner, whose birth entitled him to nothing better, and whose limbs are left him to go to work again with.' Piozzi *Anecdotes*, p. 89.

[4] See *post*, Letter of December 1, 1776, for Johnson's attempt to get the young man admitted into a hospital.

To

To Miss Langton [1].

MADAM,   London, April 17, 1771.

If I could have flattered myself that my letters could have given pleasure, or have alleviated pain, I should not have omitted to write to a lady to whom I do sincerely wish every increase of pleasure, and every mitigation of uneasiness.

I knew, dear Madam, that a very heavy affliction [2] had fallen upon you; but it was one of those which the established course of nature makes necessary, and to which kind words give no relief. Success is, on these occasions, to be expected only from time [3].

Your censure of me, as deficient in friendship, is therefore too severe. I have neither been unfriendly, nor intentionally uncivil. The notice with which you have honoured me, I have neither forgotten, nor remembered without pleasure.

The calamity of ill health, your brother will tell you that I have had, since I saw you, sufficient reason to know and to pity [4]. But this is another evil against which we can receive little help from one another. I can only advise you, and I advise you with great earnestness, to do nothing that may hurt you, and to reject nothing that may do you good. To preserve health is a moral and religious duty: for health is the basis of all social virtues; we can be useful no longer than while we are well [5].

If the family knows that you receive this letter, you will be pleased to make my compliments.

[1] First published in the *Gentleman's Magazine* for 1800, page 915.

Miss Langton was Bennet Langton's sister. She died in 1791. *Ib.*

[2] It is possible that Johnson refers to the death of her father, old Mr. Langton, which had taken place in 1769, as I learn from the *Gentleman's Magazine*, 1824, part ii. p. 8.

[3] 'While grief is fresh every attempt to divert only irritates. You must wait till grief be digested, and then amusement will dissipate the remains of it.' *Life*, iii. 28.

[4] He recorded on his next birthday (Sept. 18):—'For the last year I have been slowly recovering both from the violence of my last illness, and, I think, from the general disease of my life.' *Pr. and Med.* p. 104.

[5] See *post*, Letter of March 15, 1777, where he says: 'Gaiety is a duty when health requires it.'

I flatter

I flatter myself with the hopes of seeing Langton after Lady Rothes's recovery [1]; and then I hope that you and I shall renew our conferences, and that I shall find you willing as formerly to talk and to hear; and shall be again admitted to the honour of being,

Madam,

Your most obedient

and most humble servant,

SAM: JOHNSON.

248.

To the Countess de Boufflers.

May 16, 1771. Published in the *Life*, ii. 405, and *Piozzi Letters*, i. 34. For the date, see note in the *Life*.

249.

To Mrs. Thrale [2].

DEAR MADAM,   [London], June 15, 1771.

It seems strange that I should live a week so near you, and yet never see you. I have been once to enquire after you, and when I have written this note am going again. The use of the pamphlet the letter will shew, which lies at the proper page. When Mr. L—— shews so much attention, it cannot become me to shew less. What to think of the case I know not; the relation has all appearance of truth; and one great argument is, that the only danger is in not believing. The water can, I think, do no harm; Dr. Wall thinks it may do good [3]. If Mrs. Salusbury

[1] 'Langton' which Johnson hoped to see was not his friend of that name, but the Lincolnshire village. His letter to Bennet Langton dated August 29 of this year (*Life*, ii. 142) shews that he had been expected there. Lady Rothes, who had been married on May 24, 1770 (*Gentleman's Magazine*, 1770, p. 278), was expecting to be confined; it was after her recovery that the visit was to be paid. There is no need for Mr. Croker's conjectural alteration of the date of the letter.

[2] *Piozzi Letters*, i. 35.

Mrs. Salusbury, Mrs. Thrale's mother, to whom the letter refers, died of cancer on June 18, 1773. *Pr. and Med.*, p. 128. Probably the disorder had begun its attack.

[3] The water was laurel-water; *post*, p. 179. Dr. Wall was not Martin Wall the Oxford physician with whom Boswell and Johnson drank tea in 1784 (*Life*, iv. 292), for he had not by this time taken his degree in medicine; but his father, Dr. John Wall, of Worcester. See *Gentleman's Magazine*, 1756, p. 572, for his *Treatise on the Malvern Waters*.

should

should think fit to go before you can go with her, I will attend her, if she will accept of my company, with great readiness, at my own expence, and if I am in the country will come back.

I need not tell you, that I hope you are with the necessary exceptions all well, or that

I am, &c.,
SAM: JOHNSON.

250.

To James Boswell.

London, June 20, 1771. Published in the *Life*, ii. 140.

251.

To Mrs. Thrale [1].

Thursday, June 20, 1771.

DEAR MADAM,

This night, at nine o'clock, Sam. Johnson and Francis Barber Esquires, set out in the Lichfield stage; Francis is indeed rather upon it. What adventures we may meet with who can tell?

I shall write when I come to Lichfield, and hope to hear in return, that you are safe, and Mrs. Salusbury better, and all the rest as well as I left them.

I am, &c.,
SAM: JOHNSON.

252.

To Mrs. Thrale [2].

Lichfield, June 22, 1771.

DEAR MADAM,

Last night I came safe to Lichfield; this day I was visited by Mrs. Cobb. This afternoon I went to Mrs. Aston, where I found Miss T——[3], and waited on her home. Miss T—— wears spectacles, and can hardly climb the stiles. I was not tired at all, either last night or to-day. Miss Porter is very kind to me. Her dog and cats are all well.

In all this there is nothing very memorable, but *sands form*

---

[1] *Piozzi Letters*, i. 36.
The journey to Lichfield by the stage-coach—a distance of 116 miles—took twenty-six hours; *post*, p. 191. Barber was Johnson's black servant.

[2] *Piozzi Letters*, i. 37.
[3] Perhaps Miss Turton whose death is mentioned in the Letter of August 13, 1777.

the

the mountain[1]. I hope to hear from Streatham of a greater event, that a new being is born that shall in time write such letters as this, and that another being is safe that she may continue to write such.   She can indeed do many other things; she can add to the pleasure of many lives, and among others to that of

Her most obedient and
most humble servant,
SAM: JOHNSON.

253.

To MRS. THRALE [2].

DEAR MADAM,   [Lichfield], June 25, 1771.

All your troubles, I hope, are now past, and the little stranger safe in the cradle. You have then nothing to do but survey the lawn from your windows, and see Lucy try to run after Harry.

Here things go wrong. They have cut down another tree[3], but they do not yet grow very rich. I enquired of my barber after another barber; that barber, says he, is dead, and his son has left off, to turn maltster. Maltsters, I believe, do not get much money. The price of barley and the king's duty are known, and their profit is never suffered to rise high[4].—But there is often a rise upon stock.—There may as well be a fall—.Very seldom. There are those in this town that have not a farthing less this year than fifty pounds by the rise upon stock[5]. Did you think there had been yet left a city in England, where the gain of fifty pounds in a year would be mentioned with emphasis?

I am, &c.,
SAM: JOHNSON.

---

[1] ' Think nought a trifle, though it small appear ;
Small sands the mountains, moments make the year,
And trifles life.'
YOUNG'S *Love of Fame*, Satire vi.

[2] *Piozzi Letters*, i. 38.

[3] See *ante*, p. 154.

[4] Adam Smith says that 'the opportunities of defrauding the revenue are much greater in a brewery than in a malt-house.' He adds that 'the different taxes upon malt amount to six shillings a quarter.' *Wealth of Nations*, iii. 356-7.

[5] Johnson refers, I suppose, to the rise in value of the stock of malt. He may however be speaking of the funds. The Three per Cents. Reduced which on Jan. 4 were at 77⅜ had risen by June 26 to 88. *Gentleman's Magazine*, 1771, pp. 48, 288.

To

To Mrs. Thrale [1].

Dear Madam,   Ashbourne, July 3, 1771.

Last Saturday I came to Ashbourne; the dangers or the pleasures of the journey I have at present no disposition to recount; else might I paint the beauties of my native plains; might I tell of 'the smiles of nature, and the charms of art [2]:' else might I relate how I crossed the Staffordshire canal, one of the great efforts of human labour, and human contrivance; which, from the bridge on which I viewed it, passed away on either side, and loses itself in distant regions, uniting waters that nature had divided, and dividing lands which nature had united [3]. I might tell how these reflections fermented in my mind till the chaise stopped at Ashbourne, at Ashbourne in the Peak. Let not the barren name of the Peak terrify you; I have never wanted strawberries and cream. The great bull [4] has no disease but age. I hope in time to be like the great bull; and hope you will be like him too a hundred years hence.

I am, &c.,

Sam: Johnson.

To Mrs. Thrale [5].

Dear Madam,   Ashbourne, July 7, 1771.

No news yet of * * * * *. Our expectations were premature. Poor Dr. Taylor is ill, and under my government; you know

---

[1] *Piozzi Letters*, i. 39.

[2] 'But what avail her unexhausted stores,
Her blooming mountains and her sunny shores,
With all the gifts that heaven and earth impart,
The smiles of nature and the charms of art,
While proud oppression in her valleys reigns,
And tyranny usurps her happy plains?'
Addison. *A Letter from Italy*, *Works*, i. 35.

[3] In the *Gentleman's Magazine* for July of this year (p. 296) there is a plan of the Grand Canal from the Trent to the Mersey, of which about 45 miles had been completed, from the mouth of the Derwent in Derbyshire to Stone in Staffordshire. It was this portion that Johnson crossed. When the canal was completed in all its length the waters of the Irish Sea and the German Ocean were united.

[4] See *ante*, p. 160.

[5] *Piozzi Letters*, i. 40.

that

that the act [1] of government is learned by obedience; I hope I can govern very tolerably.

The old rheumatism is come again into my face and mouth, but nothing yet to the lumbago; however, having so long thought it gone, I do not like its return.

Miss Porter was much pleased to be mentioned in your letter, and is sure that I have spoken better of her than she desired. She holds that both Frank and his master are much improved. The master, she says, is not half so *lounging* and *untidy* as he was, there was no such thing last year as getting him off his chair.

Be pleased to make my compliments to every body.

I am, &c.,

SAM: JOHNSON.

256.

To MRS. THRALE [2].

DEAR MADAM,   Lichfield, July 7 [?], 1771.

Once more I sit down to write, and hope you will once more be willing to read it.

Last Sunday an old acquaintance found me out, not, I think, a school-fellow, but one with whom I played perhaps before I went to school. I had not seen him for forty years, but was glad to find him alive. He has had, as he phrased it, *a matter of four wives* [3], for which neither you nor I like him much the better; but after all his marriages he is poor, and has now, at sixty-six, two very young children.

Such, Madam, are the strange things of which we that travel come to the knowledge. We see *mores hominum multorum* [4].

---

[1] Johnson, I believe, wrote not *act* but *art*, and not *desired* but *deserved*.

[2] *Piozzi Letters*, i. 41.
There is an error in the date of this letter. On July 7 of this year Johnson, as the last letter shews, was not at Lichfield but Ashbourne.

[3] Perhaps 'the old acquaintance' was one Jackson mentioned by Boswell, *Life*, ii. 463.
Johnson in his *Dictionary* defines

matter when thus used as *space or quantity nearly computed*. We may compare Launcelot's ' Here's a small trifle of wives,' in *The Merchant of Venice*, Act ii. sc. 2.

[4] Horace, *Ars Poetica*, l. 142:—
' Qui mores hominum multorum vidit, et urbes.'
' Manners and towns of various nations viewed.'
FRANCIS, Horace, *Ars Poet.* l. 142.

You

You that waste your lives over a book at home, must take life upon trust.

I am, &c.,

SAM: JOHNSON.

257.

TO MRS. THRALE[1].

DEAREST MADAM,   Ashbourne, July 8, 1771.

Indifference is indeed a strange word in a letter from me to you[2]. Which way could it possibly creep in? I do not remember any moment, for a very long time past, when I could use it without contradiction from my own thoughts.

This naughty baby stays so long that I am afraid it will be a giant, like king Richard. I suppose I shall be able to tell it, 'Teeth hadst thou in thy head when thou wert born[3].' I wish your pains and your danger over.

Dr. Taylor is better, and is gone out in the chaise. My rheumatism is better too.

I would have been glad to go to Hagley, in compliance with Mr. Lyttelton's kind invitation, for beside the pleasure of his conversation, I should have had the opportunity of recollecting past times, and wandering *per montes notos et flumina nota*, of recalling the images of sixteen, and reviewing my conversations with poor Ford[4]. But this year will not bring this gratification

[1] *Piozzi Letters*, i. 42.

[2] *Indifference* does not occur in any previous letter. She referred, perhaps, to a passage in Letter 260, which is, I suspect, misdated.

[3] 'When thou *wast* born.'

    3 *Henry VI*, Act v. sc. 6.

[4] Mr. Lyttelton was William Henry Lyttelton, created Lord Westcote in 1776, and Lord Lyttelton in 1794. He was living at this time at a house called Little Hagley. Johnson visiting him in September, 1774, in company with the Thrales, recorded :—'We went to Hagley, where we were disappointed of the respect and kindness that we expected. . . . We made haste away from a place where all were offended.'

Life, v. 456–7. See *post*, Letter of Aug. 13, 1777. Johnson at the age of fifteen, 'by the advice of his cousin, the Rev. Mr. Ford,' had been sent to school at Stourbridge, two or three miles from Hagley. There he remained a little more than a year. *Life* i. 49. Speaking of Ford he said :—' Sir, he was my acquaintance and relation, my mother's nephew. He had purchased a living in the country, but not simoniacally. I never saw him but in the country. I have been told he was a man of great parts; very profligate, but I never heard he was impious.' *Ib.* iii. 348.

For the Latin quotation in the text, see *ante*, p. 154, *n.* 4.

within my power. I promised Taylor a month. Every thing is done here to please me; and his ill health is a strong reason against desertion.

I return all the compliments, and hope I may add some at last to this wicked, tiresome, dilatory bantling [1].

I am, &c.,

SAM: JOHNSON.

258.

To Mrs. Thrale [2].

DEAREST MADAM, Ashbourne, July 10, 1771.

I am obliged to my friend Harry, for his remembrance; but think it a little hard that I hear nothing from Miss.

There has been a man here to-day to take a farm. After some talk he went to see the bull, and said that he had seen a bigger [3]. Do you think he is likely to get the farm?

Toujours strawberries and cream [4].

Dr. Taylor is much better, and my rheumatism is less painful. Let me hear in return as much good of you and of Mrs. Salusbury. You despise the Dog and Duck; things that are at hand are always slighted. I remember that Dr. Grevil, of Gloucester, sent for that water when his wife was in the same danger; but he lived near Malvern, and you live near the Dog and Duck [5]. Thus, in difficult cases, we naturally trust most what we least know.

Why Bromfield [6], supposing that a lotion can do good, should

---

[1] Johnson in his *Dictionary* introduces a conjectural and absurd derivation of this word by a sentence which would make the modern philogist smile—'If,' he says, 'it has any etymology.'

[2] *Piozzi Letters*, i. 43.

[3] See *ante*, p. 166.

[4] Johnson no doubt is thinking of *toujours perdrix*. Swift in the Preface to *A Tale of a Tub*, describing how 'a poor poet may ring the changes as far as it will go,' adds:—'but the reader quickly finds it all pork.' In a note Plutarch is referred to. Swift's *Works*, iii. 58.

[5] Lysons mentions a mineral spring at Streatham 'the water of which is sent,' he says, 'in considerable quantities to some of the hospitals in London.' *Environs of London*, ed. 1800, iii. 491.

[6] Bromfield is mentioned *post*, Letter of June 14, 1779. Johnson recorded in his *Diary* on March 27, 1782:—'In the evening Dr. Bromfield and his family—Merlin's steelyard given me.' *Pr. and Med.* p. 209. In the *Gentleman's Magazine* for 1786, p. 270, among the deaths I find, 'March 24, in Gerrard Street, Soho, in his 65th year, Robert Bromfield, M.D., F.R.S.'

despise

despise laurel-water in comparison with his own receipt, I do not
see; and see still less why he should laugh at that which Wall
thinks efficacious. I am afraid philosophy will not warrant much
hope in a lotion.

Be pleased to make my compliments from Mrs. Salusbury to
Susy.

> I am, &c.,
> SAM: JOHNSON.

259.

To Mrs. Thrale [1].

DEAR MADAM,   Ashbourne, July 15, 1771.

When we come together to practise chymistry [2], I believe
we shall find our furnaces sufficient for most operations. We
have a gentleman here reading philosophical lectures, who per-
forms the chymical part with furnaces of the same kind with
ours, but much less; yet he says, that he can in his little furnace
raise a fire that will melt iron. I saw him smelt lead; and shall
bring up some ore for our operations. The carriage will cost
more than the lead perhaps will be worth; but a chymist is very
like a lover;

> 'And sees those dangers which he cannot shun.'

I will try to get other ore, both of iron and copper, which are all
which this country affords, though *feracissima metallorum regio.*

The doctor has no park, but a little enclosure behind his
house, in which there are about thirty bucks and does; and
they take bread from the hand. Would it not be pity to kill
them? It seems to be now out of his head.

> I am, &c.,
> SAM: JOHNSON.

260.

To Mrs. Thrale [3].

MADAM,   Ashbourne, July 17, 1771.

At Lichfield I found little to please me. One more of my

---

[1] *Piozzi Letters,* i. 45.

[2] 'It was about this time that a
laboratory was fitted up at Streatham for Mr. Johnson's amusement.'
Note by Mrs. Piozzi. See *post,* p.
183. For Johnson's love of che-

mistry—'an enchanting study' as he
called it—see *Life,* i. 140, 436; iii.
398; iv. 237.

[3] *Piozzi Letters,* i. 46.

Perhaps this letter is misdated, for
it seems to have been written very

few

few school-fellows is dead ; upon which I might make a new reflection, and say, *Mors omnibus communis*[1]. Miss Porter was rather better than last year ; but I think Miss Aston grows rather worse. I took a walk in quest of juvenile images, but caught a cloud instead of Juno.

I longed for Taylor's chaise[2] ; but I think Lucy did not long for it, though she was not sorry to see it. Lucy is a philosopher ; and considers me as one of the external and accidental things that are to be taken and left without emotion. If I could learn of Lucy would it be better ? Will you teach me ?

I would not have it thought that I forget Mrs. Salusbury ; but nothing that I can say will be of use ; and what comfort she can have, your duty will not fail to give her.

What is the matter that Queency[3] uses me no better ? I should think she might have written to me ; but she has neither sent a message nor a compliment. I thank Harry for remembering me.

Rheumatism teazes me yet.

> I am, &c.,
> SAM : JOHNSON.

261.

To SIR JOSHUA REYNOLDS.

Ashbourne, July 17, 1771. Published in the *Life*, ii. 141.

262.

To MRS. THRALE[4].

DEAR MADAM,   Ashbourne, July 20, 1771.

Sweet meat and sour sauce.—With your letter which was

---

soon after Johnson's departure from Lichfield. He left it on June 29.

[1] Baretti says that this was a saying of Pero Grulla (Verdad de Pero Grulla). 'SHALLOW. Certain, 'tis certain ; very sure, very sure : death, as the Psalmist saith, is common to all : all shall die.' 2 *Henry IV*, Act iii. sc. 2. ' 'Tis an inevitable chance, the first statute in *Magna Charta*, an everlasting Act of Parliament, all

must die.' *Anatomy of Melancholy*, ed. 1660, p. 344.

[2] For Taylor's 'large roomy post-chaise, drawn by four stout plump horses, and driven by two steady jolly postillions,' see *Life*, ii. 473.

[3] 'A kind of nickname given to Mrs. Thrale's eldest daughter, whose name being Esther she might be assimilated to a Queen.' *Ib.* iii. 422.

[4] *Piozzi Letters*, i. 47.

kind,

kind, I received another from Miss • • • • •', to let me know with what *frigidity* I have answered her; and to tell me, that she neither hopes nor desires to excite greater warmth. That my first salutation *Madam* surprised her, as if an old friend, newly meeting her, had thrown a glass of cold water in her face; and that she does not design to renew our conversations when I *condescend* to visit them, after • • • gets up.

> 'Tis not for nothing that we life persue².

I have certainly now such a letter as I never had before, and such as I know not how to answer. I dare neither write with *frigidity*, nor with fire. Our intercourse is something

> Which good and bad does equally confound,
> And either horn of fate's dilemma wound³.

There was formerly in France a *cour de l'amour*; but I fancy nobody was ever summoned before it after threescore: yet in this court, if it now subsisted, I seem likely to be nonsuited.

I am not very sorry that she is so far off. There can be no great danger in writing to her.

Of long walks I cannot tell you; for I have no companion; and the rheumatism has taken away some of my courage: but last night I slept well.

To strawberries and cream which still continue, we now add custard and bilberry pye.

Our two last fawns are well; but one of our swans is sick. Life, says Foresight, is chequer-work⁴.

I am, &c.,

SAM: JOHNSON.

---

¹ Miss Porter I think is meant. See *post*, p. 184, where Johnson expresses his surprise that she detained him at Lichfield, and p. 191.

² 'Johnson wrote *pursue*, but many women will write *persue*.' BARETTI.

³ ' Hope, whose weak being ruined is

> Alike if it succeed, and if it miss;
> Whom good or ill does equally confound,

> And both the horns of fate's dilemma wound.'
> COWLEY, *The Mistress: Against Hope.*

⁴ 'FORESIGHT. Nay I have had some omens. I got out of bed backwards too this morning without premeditation; pretty good that too. But then I stumbled coming down stairs and met a weasel; bad omens those. Some bad, some good; our lives are checquered.' Congreve, *Love for Love* Act ii. sc. 1.

To

263.

To Mrs. Thrale [1].

DEAR MADAM,　　　　　　　　　　[Ashbourne], July 22, 1771.

Nothing new has happened, and yet I do not care to omit writing. Last post I had four letters, all female. Besides yours, I had one from Mrs. Hervey [2], Miss • • • •, and Mrs. Williams. Mrs. Hervey must stay; and what to say to • • • • I cannot devise.

My rheumatism continues to persecute me most importunately; and how to procure ease in this place, where there are no hot rooms, I do not see; but I always hope next day, or next night, will be better, and am not always disappointed.

Queeney has not written yet; perhaps she designs that I should love Harry best.

　　　　　　　　　　　　　　I am, &c.,

　　　　　　　　　　　　　　　　SAM: JOHNSON.

264.

To Mrs. Thrale [3].

DEAR MADAM,　　　　　　　　　　Ashbourne, July 24, 1771.

We have no news here but about health and sickness. I am miserably harassed. Dr. Taylor is quite well. The sick swan is dead: and dead without an elegy [4], either by himself or his friends. The other swan swims about solitary, as Mr. Thrale, and I, and others should do, if we lost our mistress.

The great bull, and his four sons, are all well. We call the first of the young bulls the Dauphin; so you see, *non deficit alter aureus* [5]. Care is taken of the breed.

Naughty Queeny! no letter yet. I hope we shall teach little Lucy better.

---

[1] *Piozzi Letters*, i. 49.

[2] She was of the Aston family and the widow of Johnson's friend the Hon. Henry Hervey. *Life*, i. 83, *n.* 4.

[3] *Piozzi Letters*, i. 50.

[4] 'So on Mæander's banks when death is nigh
　　The mournful swan sings her own elegy.'
DRYDEN; quoted in Johnson's Dictionary.

[5] ' Primo avulso non deficit alter Aureus, et simili frondescit virga metallo.'
　　　　VIRGIL, *Æneid*, vi. 143.
' The first thus rent, a second will arise,
　And the same metal the same room supplies.'
　　　　DRYDEN.

　　　　　　　　　　　　　　　　　　　　　Be

Be pleased to make my compliments to Mr. Thrale; and desire that his builders will leave about a hundred loose bricks. I can at present think of no better place for chymistry, in fair weather, than the pump-side in the kitchen garden [1].

I am, &c.,

SAM: JOHNSON.

265.

TO HENRY THRALE [2].

DEAR SIR,   July 31, 1771.

I am this morning come to Lichfield, a place which has no temptations to prolong my stay; but if it had more, would not have such as could withhold me from your house when I am at liberty to come to it. I hope our dear mistress is got up, and recovering [3]. Pray tell her to mind, whether I am not got quite wild for want of government. My thoughts are now about getting to London. I shall watch for a place; for our carriages are only such as pass through the place, sometimes full, and sometimes vacant [4].

I am, &c.,

SAM: JOHNSON.

[1] Mrs. Piozzi says :—'We made up a sort of laboratory at Streatham one summer, and diverted ourselves with drawing essences and colouring liquors. But the danger Mr. Thrale found his friend Dr. Johnson in one day, when he got the children and servants round him to see some experiments performed, put an end to all our entertainment.' *Piozzi's Anecdotes*, p. 236. A writer in the *Gentleman's Magazine* (1830, part i. p. 295) gives the following anecdote, which he had about twenty-five years earlier from Bishop Watson of Llandaff, who was Professor of Chemistry in Cambridge at the time of Johnson's visit in 1765. Johnson coming to the laboratory was asked by Watson whether there was any experiment in particular which he wished to see performed. He replied :—' I have been told that there are two cold fluids which when mixed will take fire ; I do not credit it.' Watson made his assistant pour into one crucible rectified spirit of turpentine and into the other concentrated vitriolic acid with due proportion of the nitric. They were fastened to the end of long rods, held out of the window, and then mixed. The flame which ensued was such as to induce Johnson to be thankful that the explosion was on the outside.'

[2] *Piozzi Letters*, i. 51.

[3] On July 23 she had given birth to a daughter—Sophia, who married Henry Merrick Hoare and died on Nov. 8, 1824.

[4] Lichfield was on the London and Chester Road that passed through Dunstable, Coventry, and Stafford. For the difficulty in getting a place in the passing carriages both here

To

266.

To Mrs. Thrale [1].

Dear Madam,   Lichfield, Sat. Aug. 3, 1771.

If you were well enough to write last Tuesday, you will surely be well enough to read on Monday; and therefore I will now write to you as before.

Having stayed my month with Taylor, I came away on Wednesday, leaving him, I think, in a disposition of mind not very uncommon, at once weary of my stay, and grieved at my departure [2].

My purpose was to have made haste to you and Streatham; and who would have expected that I should be stopped by Lucy [3]? Hearing me give Francis orders to take us places, she told me that I should not go till after next week. I thought it proper to comply; for I was pleased to find that I could please, and proud of shewing you that I do not come an universal outcast. Lucy is likewise a very peremptory maiden; and if I had gone without permission, I am not very sure that I might have been welcome at another time.

When we meet, we may compare our different uses of this interval. I shall charge you with having lingered away, in expectation and disappointment, two months [4], which are both physically and morally considered as analogous to the fervid and vigorous part of human life: two months, in which Nature exerts all her powers of benefaction, and graces the liberality of her hand by the elegance of her smile; two months, which, as Doodle says, 'you never saw before [5],' and which, as La Bruyere says, ' you shall never see again.'

and at Oxford see *post*, Letters of June 6, and July 26, 1775.

[1] *Piozzi Letters*, i. 52.

[2] 'Dr. Johnson said to me of Dr. Taylor, "Sir, I love him; but I do not love him more; my regard for him does not increase. As it is said in the Apocrypha, "his talk is of bullocks:" I do not suppose he is very fond of my company. His habits are by no means sufficiently clerical: this he knows that I see;

and no man likes to live under the eye of perpetual disapprobation."' *Life*, iii. 181.

[3] Miss Porter. See *ante*, p. 181, *n.* 1.

[4] Johnson, writing to Bennet Langton on Aug. 29, said:—'The Queen and Mrs. Thrale, both ladies of experience, yet both missed their reckoning this summer.' *Life*, ii. 142.

[5] Doodle, an Alderman of London,

But

But complaints are vain; we will try to do better another time.—To-morrow and to-morrow [1].—A few designs and a few failures, and the time of designing will be past.

Mr. Seward left Lichfield yesterday, I am afraid, not much mended by his opium [2]. He purposes to wait on you; and if envy could do much mischief, he would have much to dread, since he will have the pleasure of seeing you sooner than,

Dear Madam,

Your, &c.,

SAM: JOHNSON.

267.

TO MRS. THRALE [3].

DEAR MADAM,   Lichfield, Aug. 5, 1771.

Though I have now been two posts without hearing from you, I hope no harm has befallen you. I have just been with the old Dean [4], if I may call him old who is but seventy-eight; and find him as well, both in mind and body, as his younger

---

is a character in *The London Cuckolds* by Edward Ravenscroft; first acted in 1682. Till the year 1752 it was commonly acted on Lord Mayor's Day 'in contempt and to the disgrace of the city. Mr. Garrick set the example of decorum by omitting to perform it on the ninth of November in 1752, though it was acted at Covent Garden that and the following year; but on that day, in 1754, the King commanded *The Provoked Husband* at Covent Garden, which, we believe, gave the death-blow to this obscenity.' Baker's *Biog. Dram.*, ed. 1812, ii. 375. See also *Gentleman's Magazine*, 1752, p. 535, and 1754, p. 532.

[1] Johnson perhaps has in his thoughts the line in *Macbeth* (Act v. sc. 5):—'To-morrow, and to-morrow, and to-morrow.'

[2] Johnson speaking of the Rev. Mr. Seward said:—'Sir, he is a valetudinarian, one of those who are always mending themselves.' *Life*, iii. 152. Johnson one evening at Mr. Seward's house heard "Me miserable!" in *Paradise Lost* (Bk. iv. l. 73) commended as highly pathetic. He left the house with a Mr. Price. 'They had walked some way in silence, when Johnson suddenly stopped, and turning to his companion exclaimed, "Sir, don't you think that 'Me miserable!' is miserable stuff?"' On another occasion he said to him:—'If I saw a Whig and a Tory drowning, I would first save the Tory; and when I saw that he was safe, not till then, I would go and help the Whig; but the dog should duck first; the dog should duck," laughing with pleasure at the thought of the Whig's ducking.' Cary's *Lives of English Poets*, ed. 1846, p. 87.

[3] *Piozzi Letters*, i. 54.

[4] Addenbroke, who had been Dean since 1745. See *post*, Letters of November 30, 1774, and August 27, 1777.

---

neighbours.

neighbours. I went with my Lucy this morning to a philosophical lecture[1]; and have been this evening to see Mr. Green's curiosities, both natural and artificial[2]; and I am come home to write to my dear lady.

So rolls the world away[3].

The days grow visibly shorter.—*Immortalia ne speres monet annus*[4].—I think it time to return. Do you think that after all this roving you shall be able to manage me again? I suppose, like • • • •, that you are thinking how to reduce me; but you may spare your contrivances; and need not fear that I find any reception that gives me pleasure equal to that of being,

Madam,

Your, &c.,

SAM: JOHNSON.

268.

To BENNET LANGTON.

[London], August 29, 1771. Published in the *Life*, ii. 142.

269.

To DAVID GARRICK[5].

DEAR SIR,   Streatham, Dec. 12, 1771.

I have thought upon your epitaph but without much effect. An epitaph is no easy thing.

[1] See *post*, Letter of September 21, 1773, for his being 'owned at table in Scotland by one who had seen him at a philosophical lecture' at Lichfield.

[2] See *ante*, p. 161, *n.* 5.

[3] 'So runs the world away.' *Hamlet*, Act iii. sc. 2, l. 285.

[4] HORACE, 4 *Odes*, vii. 7.
'Those circling hours and all the various year
Convince us nothing is immortal here.' FRANCIS.

[5] Published in the *Garrick Correspondence*, i. 446, and again from the original in Croker's *Boswell* (p. 225), apparently more correctly.
Garrick wrote to Dr. John Hoadley on January 4, 1772 :—'Mrs. Hogarth having desir'd me to write an

Epitaph for her Husband our most Excellent friend—I have done it, as well as I can, and I am lucky enough to have it approv'd by those I w^d wish to please—here it is for you :—

EPITAPH.

Farewell! great Painter of Mankind!
    Who reach'd the noblest point of Art,
Whose pictur'd Morals charm ye mind,
    And thro' the Eyes correct ye heart.

If *Genius* fire thee, Reader, stay,
    If *Nature* touch thee, drop a tear,
If Neither move thee, turn away,
    For HOGARTH's honoured dust lies here.

What say you?'
From the facsimile in Mr. Alfred

Of

Of your three stanzas, the third is utterly unworthy of you. The first and third together give no discriminative character. If the first alone were to stand, Hogarth would not be distinguished from any other man of intellectual eminence. Suppose you worked upon something like this :

> ' The Hand of Art here torpid lies
>   That traced the essential form of Grace :
> Here Death has closed the curious eyes
>   That saw the manners in the face.

> ' If Genius warm thee, Reader, stay,
>   If Merit touch thee, shed a tear ;
> Be Vice and Dulness far away !
>   Great Hogarth's honour'd dust is here.'

In your second stanza, *pictured morals* is a beautiful expression, which I would wish to retain ; but *learn* and *mourn* cannot stand for rhymes. *Art and nature* have been seen together too often. In the first stanza is *feeling*, in the second *feel*. *Feeling* for *tenderness* or *sensibility* is a word merely colloquial, of late introduction, not yet sure enough of its own existence to claim a place upon a stone[1]. *If thou hast neither*, is quite prose, and prose of the familiar kind. Thus easy is it to find faults, but it is hard to make an Epitaph[2].

When you have reviewed it, let me see it again : you are

Morrison's *Collection of Autographs*, ii. 162.

' Dr. Johnson,' writes Mrs. Piozzi, ' made four lines on the death of poor Hogarth, which were equally true and pleasing : I know not why Garrick's were preferred to them.

' The hand of him here torpid lies
    That drew th' essential form of grace ;
Here closed in death th' attentive eyes
    That saw the manners in the face.'

Piozzi's Anecdotes, p. 135.

In the *Gentleman's Magazine* for 1772, p. 336, is given ' the inscription on Hogarth's mausoleum in Chiswick Churchyard.' It agrees with Garrick's in all but the fifth line, which runs : —

' If *thou hast genius*, Reader, stay.'

[1] Nevertheless Johnson in his *Dictionary* gives as the second meaning of *feeling*, *sensibility; tenderness*, and quotes examples from Shakespeare and Bacon. See *Life*, ii. 95, for his contempt for ' very feeling people. " They *pay* you by *feeling*," he said.'

[2] See Appendix C. for two sets of verses by Garrick.

welcome

welcome to any help that I can give, on condition that you make my compliments to Mrs. Garrick.

I am, dear Sir,

Your most, &c.,

SAM: JOHNSON.

270.

To [? THOMAS CADELL].

1771.

In Mr. Fletcher's *Auction Catalogue* of May 30, 1845, Lot 115 is a 'Note of Johnson to his Publisher to bind two copies of *False Alarm* and *Falkland Islands.* 1771.'

271.

To SIR JOSHUA REYNOLDS.

[Johnson's Court], February 27, 1772. Published in the *Life*, ii. 144.

272.

To JOSEPH BANKS.

Johnson's Court, February 27, 1772. Published in the *Life*, ii. 144.

273.

To BENNET LANGTON.

[London], March 14, 1772. Published in the *Life*, ii. 146.

274.

To JAMES BOSWELL.

[London], March 15, 1772. Published in the *Life*, ii. 145.

275.

To THE REVEREND DR. TAYLOR [1].

DEAR SIR,

When I promised to dine with you to-morrow I did not sufficiently consider what I was promising. On the last day of Lent I do not willingly go out, and shall be glad to change to-

---

[1] First published in the *Miscellanies of the Philobiblon Society*, vi. 43. Dr. Taylor, 'whose habits were by no means sufficiently clerical' (*ante*, p. 184, *n.* 2), in giving a dinner in Passion Week had the example of at least two Bishops of his age. See the *Life*, iv. 88, for Johnson's 'admirable sophistry' in his defence of his dining with them.

morrow

morrow for Monday, or any other day except Thursday next
week.

I am, Sir,

Your most, &c.,

SAM: JOHNSON.

April 17, 1772.

276.

TO JAMES BOSWELL.

[London], August 31, 1772. Published in the *Life*, ii. 201.

277.

TO THE REVEREND DR. TAYLOR [1].

DEAR SIR,

I am sorry to find both from your own letter and from Mr.
Langley [2] that your health is in a state so different from what
might be wished. The Langleys impute a great part of your
complaints to a mind unsettled and discontented. I know that
you have disorders, though I hope not very formidable, independent of the mind, and that your complaints do not arise
from the mere habit of complaining. Yet there is no distemper, not in the highest degree acute, on which the mind
has not some influence, and which is not better resisted by a
cheerful than a gloomy temper. I would have you read when
you can force your attention, but that perhaps will be not so
often as is necessary to encrease the general cheerfulness of
Life. If you could get a little apparatus for chimistry or ex-
perimental philosophy it would offer you some diversion, or if
you made some little purchase at a small distance, or took
some petty farm into your own hands, it would break your
thoughts when they become tyrannous and troublesome, and
supply you at once with exercise and amusement.

You tell me nothing of Kedlestone [3], which you went down
with a design of visiting, nor of Dr. Butler [4], who seems to be

---

[1] First published in *Notes and Queries*, 6th S., v. 383.

[2] The Head Master of Ashbourne School. *Life*, iii. 138. He and Taylor, it seems, were at variance later on. *Post*, Letters of July 12, 1775, and September 18, 1777.

[3] Lord Scarsdale's mansion near Derby, which Johnson and Boswell visited in Dr. Taylor's chaise on September 19, 1777. *Life*, iii. 160.

[4] Johnson, no doubt, wrote Butter. A Scotch physician of that name living at Derby was visited by him and Boswell in 1776 and 1777. *Life*, iii. 1, 163.

a very

a very rational man, and who told you with great honesty that your cure must in the greatest measure depend upon yourself.

Your uneasiness at the misfortunes of your Relations, I comprehend perhaps too well. It was an irresistible obtrusion of a disagreeable image, which you always wished away but could not dismiss, an incessant persecution of a troublesome thought neither to be pacified nor ejected. Such has of late been the state of my own mind. I had formerly great command of my attention, and what I did not like could forbear to think on. But of this power, which is of the highest importance to the tranquillity of life, I have been some [*sic*] much exhausted, that I do not go into a company towards night, in which I foresee any thing disagreeable, nor enquire after any thing to which I am not indifferent, lest something, which I know to be nothing, should fasten upon my imagination, and hinder me from sleep[1]. Thus it is that the progress of life brings often with it diseases, not of the body only, but of the mind. We must endeavour to cure both the one and the other. In our bodies we must ourselves do a great part, and for the mind it is very seldom that any help can be had, but what prayer and reason shall supply.

I have got my work so far forward that I flatter myself with concluding it this month[2], and then shall do nothing so willingly as come down to Ashbourne. We will try to make October a pleasant month.

I am, Sir,

Yours affectionately,

SAM: JOHNSON.

August 31, 1772.

I wish we could borrow of Dr. Bentley the Preces in usum Sarum[3].

To the Rev[d] Dr. Taylor in Ashbourn, Derbys.

---

[1] See *Life*, ii. 440, for Johnson's directions for 'the management of the mind.'

[2] He was engaged on the fourth edition of his *Dictionary*. On Easter Eve of the following year he re-corded :—' Of the spring and summer I remember that I was able in those seasons to examine and improve my *Dictionary*.' *Pr. and Med.* p. 123.

[3] Dr. Bentley was Richard Bentley, D.D., nephew of the great

To

278.

To the Reverend Dr. Taylor [1].

Dear Sir,

Now you find yourself better consider what it is that has contributed to your recovery, and do it ever again. Keep what health you have and try to get more.

I am now within a few hours of being able to send the whole dictionary to the press, and though I often went sluggishly to the work, I am not much delighted at the co[mpletion] [2]. My purpose is to come down to Lichfield next week. I will send you word when I am to set out, and hope you will fetch me. Miss Porter will be satisfied with a very little of my company [3].

I am, dear Sir,

Your affectionate Servant,

Oct. 6, 1772.　　　　　　　　　　　　Sam: Johnson.

The Revd Dr. Taylor in Ashbourn, Derbys.

279.

To Mrs. Thrale [4].

Dear Madam,　　　　　　　[Lichfield], October 19, 1772.

I set out on Thursday night at nine, and arrived at Lichfield on Friday night at eleven, no otherwise incommoded than with want of sleep, which however I enjoyed very comfortably the first night. I think a stage coach is not the worst bed [5].

Bentley, Rector of Nailstone, Leicestershire, and Senior Fellow of Trinity College, Cambridge. On his death his library was sold by auction at Leicester in December, 1786. The Catalogue of the Sale is in the Bodleian Library. The book which Johnson wished to borrow was perhaps Lot 114, described as 'Romish Rituale, very elegantly bound in morocco, printed at Paris by Francis Reynault, in red and black, and adorned with a number of curious wood-cuts, 1536.' It was sold apparently for half-a-crown ; the present price, I am told, of such a work would be from £15 to £20.

[1] First published in *Notes and Queries*, 6th S., v. 422. Franked 'Free' by Mr. Thrale.

[2] Johnson, I believe, found relief in the somewhat mechanical work of revising his *Dictionary*. Percival Stockdale records in his *Memoirs*, ii. 179, that about 1774 Johnson offered to edit a new edition of Chambers's *Dictionary of the Arts and Sciences*. When Stockdale expressed his surprise that in his easy circumstances he should be ready to undertake so tedious a task, ' Sir (said he) I like that muddling work.'

[3] See *ante*, p. 181, *n.* 1.

[4] *Piozzi Letters*, i. 55.

[5] See *post*, Letter of May 6, 1776.

I am

I am here at present a little wind-bound, as the paper will show you, and Lichfield is not a place of much entertainment; yet, though I have some thoughts of rambling a little, this is to be my home long enough to receive a letter, which will, I hope, tell me that you are busy in reformation, that dear Mrs. Salusbury is easy, that all the young people are well, and that Mr. Thrale brews at less expence than fourteen shillings a quarter. They have had in this country a very prosperous hay-harvest [1], but malt is five-and-sixpence a strike [2], or two pounds four shillings a quarter. Wheat is nine-and-sixpence a bushel. These are prices which are almost descriptive of a famine. Flesh is likewise very dear [3].

[1] 'Aug. 3, 1772. We have had and have the *summerest* summer that I have known these hundred years. We had really begun to fancy that some comet had brushed us a little out of the sun's way.' Walpole's *Letters*, v. 403.

[2] 'Strike. A bushel; a dry measure of capacity.' Johnson's *Dictionary*.

[3] In the Letters of October 24, November 9, 19, we have further mention of Mr. Thrale's difficulties. 'In a marginal note Mrs. Piozzi says: "Mr. Thrale was a very merry talking man in 1760; but the distress of 1772, which affected his health, his hopes, and his whole soul, affected his temper too."' Hayward's *Piozzi*, i. 42. In her *Autobiographical Memoirs* she gives a further account of these troubles. Her 'extreme inaccuracy'—to use the term Boswell justly applies to her (*Life*, i. 416, *n.* 2)—renders it however untrustworthy. She says that 'a vulgar fellow, by name Humphrey Jackson (*post*, p. 213), had long practised on poor Thrale's credulity.' He had led him into enormous expense in the manufacture of a stuff which should preserve ships' bottoms from the worm, and in brewing by some new process. Hayward's *Piozzi*,

i. 257. In June of this year the failure of the great banking-house of Neal, Fordyce & Co. was the beginning of a commercial panic. 'An universal bankruptcy was expected. The whole city was in an uproar; many of the first families in tears.' *Gentleman's Magazine* for 1772, pp. 292-3. 'Will you believe in Italy,' wrote Horace Walpole to Sir Horace Mann, 'that one rascally and extravagant banker had brought Britannia, Queen of the Indies, to the precipice of bankruptcy!' *Letters*, v. 395. See *post*, Letter of August 12, 1773. 'A sudden run,' writes Mrs. Piozzi, 'threatened the house of Thrale, and death hovered over the head of its principal.' Her mother, Mrs. Salusbury, showed great firmness. 'Fear not,' said Johnson, 'the menaces of suicide; the man who has two such females to console him never yet killed himself, and will not now. Of all the bankrupts made this dreadful year, none have destroyed themselves but married men, who would have risen from the weeds undrowned, had not the women clung about and sunk them, stifling the voice of reason with their cries.' Mrs. Piozzi adds that Mrs. Salusbury lent Thrale all her savings, £3,000, and

In

In this wide-extended calamity let us try what alleviation can be found in our kindness to each other.

I am, &c.,

SAM: JOHNSON.

280.

TO MRS. THRALE[1].

MADAM,   Lichfield, October 24, 1772.

I would have you consider whether it will not be best to write to Sir T——[2], not taking notice of any thing proposed to Mr. B——; and only letting him know, that the report which terrified you so much has had little effect; and that you have now no particular need of his money. By this you will free him from solicitude; and, having nothing to fear from you, he will love you as before. It will abate any triumph of your enemies, and dispose them less to censure, and him less to regard censure.

When you wrote the letter which you call injudicious, I told

that three other friends lent £17,000 among them. 'Our debts were £130,000, besides borrowed money. Yet in nine years was every shilling paid.' Hayward's *Piozzi*, i. 258.

To add to the distress, there had been in late years a great rise in the price of grain. Hume writing in 1755 says that thirty-two shillings a quarter for wheat, and sixteen for barley, which were regarded as low in the reign of James I, 'would rather pass for high by our present estimation.' In a note added to the edition of 1770 he says:—'In the short period of the last fifteen years prices have perhaps risen more than during the preceding hundred and fifty.' *History*, ed. 1773, vi. 177. Adam Smith writing in the year 1775 attributes the high price of corn during the ten or twelve years past to the unfavourable seasons through the greater part of Europe. *Wealth of Nations*, ed. 1811, i. 275. For the bad seasons see *post*, the second Letter of July, 1775. By 1776 good times had returned, with 'the best

brown malt laid in at thirty shillings and sixpence.' *Post*, Letter of May 18, 1776. The price for wheat given by Johnson does not agree with that given in the *Gentleman's Magazine*, 1772, p. 442. The average price in Staffordshire from October 5 to October 10 is stated to be seven shillings and sevenpence—one shilling and twopence dearer than in London. Perhaps Johnson was speaking of the best wheat. In Staffordshire wheat was dearer than in any other county. For the dearness of flesh, remedies were sought in London. In May 'the Committee at the Chapter Coffee-house sold beef from $3\frac{1}{2}d$. to $4d$. and mutton from $3\frac{1}{2}d$. to $4\frac{1}{2}d$. per pound for ready money by the carcase.' *Ib.* p. 244.

[1] *Piozzi Letters*, i. 56.

[2] Sir Thomas Salusbury, Mrs. Thrale's uncle. It had been expected that she would inherit his property, but he married a second time, and disappointed her. *Piozzi Letters*, i. 201, 4, and Hayward's *Piozzi*, i. 251.

you that it would bring no money; but I do not see how, in that tumult of distress, you could have forborn it, without appearing to be too tender of your own personal connections, and to place your uncle above your family. You did what then seemed best, and are therefore not so reasonable as I wish my mistress to be, in imputing to yourself any unpleasing consequences. Your uncle, when he knows that you do not want, and mean not to disturb him, will probably subside in silence to his former stagnation of unactive kindness.

Do not suffer little things to disturb you. The brewhouse must be the scene of action, and the subject of speculation. The first consequence of our[1] late trouble ought to be, an endeavour to brew at a cheaper rate; an endeavour not violent and transient, but steady and continual, prosecuted with total contempt of censure or wonder, and animated by resolution not to stop while more can be done. Unless this can be done, nothing can help us; and if this be done, we shall not want help.

Surely there is something to be saved; there is to be saved whatever is the difference between vigilance and neglect, between parsimony and profusion.

The price of malt has risen again. It is now two pounds eight shillings the quarter[2]. Ale is sold in the public houses at sixpence a quart, a price which I never heard of before[3].

This weather, if it continues, will certainly save hay[4]; but it can but little balance the misfortune of the scanty harvest. This, however, is an evil which we only share with the whole nation, and which we did not bring upon ourselves.

---

[1] Johnson's use of the words *we* and *our* here and in other Letters shows that not only was Streatham his *home*, but that he was indeed one of the household in its troubles and triumphs.

[2] Writing to Mrs. Thrale on October 7 of the following year he calls forty shillings 'a frightful price for malt.'

[3] By the Mutiny Act the innkeeper was required to find each soldier quartered on him lodging, diet, and five pints of small beer for fourpence a day. This was the law in 1741, and I believe in 1772. With the great rise in the price of malt-liquor this must have become a heavy tax on the publicans. *Life*, iii. 9, *n.* 4.

[4] It would save hay by making the grass grow so that there would be feed for the stock. See *post*, p. 198.

I fancy

I fancy the next letter may be directed to Ashbourne. Pray write word how long I may have leave to stay.

I sincerely wish Mrs. Salusbury continuance and increase of ease and comfort; and wish all good to you all.

I am, &c.,
SAM: JOHNSON.

281.

TO MRS. THRALE[1].

DEAR MADAM,   Ashbourne, October 29, 1772.

In writing to your uncle you certainly did well; but your letter was hardly confident enough. You might have ventured to speak with some degree of indifference, about money which you know that you shall not have. I have no doubt of the present perverseness of his intention; but, if I mistake not his character, his intention and execution are not very near each other; and, as he acts by mere irritation, when the disturbance is over, he will lie still.

What have I committed that I am to be left behind on Saturdays? The coach, I think, must go twice with the rest; and at one of the times you might make room for me, if you cared for me. But so am I served, that sit thinking and thinking of you, and all of you.

Poor dear Mrs. Salusbury! Is the place then open[2]? I am however glad to hear that her vigour of mind is yet undiminshed. I hope she will now have less pain.

We are here as we used to be. Our bulls and cows, if there is any change, seem to grow bigger.

That you are to go to the other house I am inwardly pleased, however I may pretend to pity you; and I am of Mamma's opinion, that you may find yourself something to do there, and something of importance[3].

I am, &c.,
SAM: JOHNSON.

---

[1] *Piozzi Letters*, i. 59.
[2] She was dying of cancer.
[3] The other house was Mr. Thrale's house in the Borough close to his Brewery, 'the scene of so many literary meetings,' where Johnson had his own room as well as at Streatham. *Life*, i. 493; ii. 286, *n.* 1. 'It stood,' says Mrs. Piozzi, 'in what is now Park Street, Southwark, but

O 2

TO

282.

To Mrs. Thrale [1].

MADAM,   [Ashbourne], October 31, 1772.

Though I am just informed, that, by some accidental negligence, the letter which I wrote on Thursday was not given to the post, yet I cannot refuse myself the gratification of writing again to my mistress [2]; not that I have any thing to tell, but that by showing how much I am employed upon you, I hope to keep you from forgetting me.

Doctor Taylor asked me this morning on what I was thinking? and I was thinking on Lucy [3]. I hope Lucy is a good girl. But she cannot yet be so good as Queeney. I have got nothing yet for Queeney's cabinet [4].

I hope dear Mrs. Salusbury grows no worse. I wish any thing could be found that would make her better. You must remember her admonition, and bustle in the brewhouse [5]. When I come you may expect to have your hands full with all of us.

then Deadman's Place; so called because of the pest houses which were established there in the Great Plague of London.' Hayward's *Piozzi*, ii. 107. In Dodsley's *London and its Environs*, ii. 220, we find 'Deadman's Place, near Dirty Lane, Southwark.' There were ten Dirty Lanes in London at this time. *Ib.* p. 234. Johnson in 1779 reproached Mrs. Thrale with 'her despicable dread of living in the Borough.' *Post*, Letter of November 16, 1779.

[1] *Piozzi Letters*, i. 60.

[2] Johnson used to call Mrs. Thrale *Madam* or *My mistress*, and Mr. Thrale *Master* or *My master*. *Life*, i. 494. She called her second husband *My master*. Hayward's *Piozzi*, ii. 69.

[3] His god-daughter. *Ante*, p. 155.

[4] See *post*, Letter of November 3, 1773. What has become of the curiosities which Johnson collected for Mrs. Thrale's little girl?

[5] Mrs. Piozzi says that her mother and Johnson 'had disliked one another extremely.' She worried herself and him by 'her superfluous attention to foreign politics. He teased her by writing in the newspapers concerning battles and plots which had no existence. She was exceedingly angry, and scarcely, I think, forgave the offence till the domestic distresses of the year 1772 reconciled them, and taught them the true value of each other; excellent as they both were, far beyond the excellence of any other man and woman I ever yet saw.' *Anecdotes*, p. 128. *Bustle* was a favourite word of Johnson's. See *post*, Letters of April 25 and June 6, 1780. He did not however like the thing, and in the Isle of Skye was displeased at Boswell's bustling. 'It does not hasten us a bit,' he said. 'It is getting on horseback in a ship. All boys do it; and you are longer a boy than others.' Boswell adds:—'He himself has no alertness.' *Life*, v. 307.

Our

Our bulls and cows are all well ; but we yet hate the man that had seen a bigger bull [1]. Our deer have died ; but many are left. Our waterfall at the garden makes a great roaring this wet weather [2].

And so no more at present from, Madam,

Your, &c.,

SAM: JOHNSON.

283.

TO MRS. THRALE [3].

DEAR MADAM,   Ashbourne, Nov. 4, 1772.

We keep writing to each other when, by the confession of both, there is nothing to be said ; but, on my part, I find it very pleasing to write ; and what is pleasing is very willingly continued.

I hope your prescriptions have been successful, and Mr. Thrale is well. What pity it is that we cannot do something for the dear lady ! Since I came to Ashbourne I have been out of order. I was well at Lichfield. You know sickness will drive me to you ; so perhaps you very heartily wish me better : but you know likewise that health will not hold me away ; and I hope you think that, sick or well,

I am, &c.,

SAM: JOHNSON.

284.

TO MRS. THRALE [4].

DEAR MADAM,   Ashbourne, Nov. 7, 1772.

So many days and never a letter !—*Fugere fides, pietasque pudorque* [5]. This is Turkish usage. And I have been hoping and hoping. But you are so glad to have me out of your mind.

I think you were quite right in your advice about the thousand pounds, for the payment could not have been delayed long ; and

[1] *Ante*, p. 178.
[2] Boswell describes this artificial waterfall. *Life*, iii. 190.
[3] *Piozzi Letters*, i. 62.
[4] *Piozzi Letters*, i. 63.

[5] This quotation seems to be a reminiscence of Ovid, *Metamorphoses*, i. 129, which runs 'fugere pudor, verumque, fidesque,' and of vii. 72, which runs 'rectum, pietasque, pudorque.'

a short

a short delay would have lessened credit, without advancing interest. But in great matters you are hardly ever mistaken.

We have here very rainy weather; but it makes the grass grow, and makes our waterfall roar. I wish Queeney heard it; she would think it very pretty. I go down to it every day, for I have not much to do; and have not been very well; but by physick am grown better. You and all your train may be supposed to keep me company in my walks. I wish I could know how you brew, and how you go on; but you tell me nothing.

I am, &c.,

SAM: JOHNSON.

285.

To MRS. THRALE [1].

DEAR MADAM,   [Ashbourne], Nov. 9, 1772.

After I had sent away my last letter, I received yours, which was an answer to it; but, being not fully directed, had lain, I think, two days at the office.

I am glad that you are at last come home, and that you exert your new resolution with so much vigour. But the fury of housewifery will soon subside; and little effect will be produced but by methodical attention and even frugality; nor can these powers be immediately attained. You have your own habits, as well as those of others, to combat: you have yet the skill of management to learn, as well as the practice to establish. Do not be discouraged either by your own failures, or the perverseness of others; you will, by resolution frequently renewed, and by perseverance properly excited, overcome in time both them and yourself.

Your letter to Sir • • • • [2] will, I doubt not, have the effect intended. When he is not pinched he will sleep.

Mr. Thrale's money, to pay for all, must come from the sale of good beer. I am far from despairing of solid and durable prosperity. Nor will your success exceed my hopes, or my opinion of your state, if, after this tremendous year, you should

---

[1] *Piozzi Letters,* i. 64.

[2] Sir Thomas Salusbury. *Ante,* p. 193, *n.* 2.

annually

annually add to your fortune three thousand pounds. This will soon dismiss all incumbrances; and, when no interest is paid, you will begin annually to lay up almost five thousand. This is very splendid; but this, I think, is in your power.

Dear mamma, I hope, continues to be cheerful. Do the ————s take her house furnished? I think it a very proper habitation for them, out of the smoke of the city, and yet not in the blaze of the court.

I am much obliged to you for your desire of my return; but if I make haste, will you promise not to spoil me? I do not much trust yet to your new character, which I have had only from yourself.

Be pleased to direct your next letter to Lichfield; for I shall, I think, be contriving to find my way back.

> I am, &c.,
> SAM: JOHNSON.

286.

To Mrs. Thrale [1].

DEAR MADAM,   [Ashbourne], Nov. 19, 1772.

I longed for your letter to-day; for till that came I could not make any promises, or form any determinations. You need not doubt my readiness to return, but it is impossible to foresee all occasions of interruption, or all necessities of compliance.

Be pleased to tell poor dear Mrs. Salusbury, that I wish her better; and to wish is all the power that we have. In the greatest exigencies we can only regret our own inability. I think Mrs. Queeney might write again.

This year will undoubtedly be an year of struggle and difficulty; but I doubt not of getting through it; and the difficulty will grow yearly less and less. Supposing that our former mode of life kept us on the level, we shall, by the present contraction of expence, gain upon fortune a thousand a-year, even though no improvements can be made in the conduct of the trade. Every two thousand pounds saves an hundred pound interest, and therefore as we gain more we pay less. We have a rational hope of success; we have rather a moral certainty, with life and

---

[1] *Piozzi Letters*, i. 66.

health.

health. Let us therefore not be dejected. Continue to be a housewife, and be as frolicksome with your tongue as you please.

I am, dearest Lady, &c.,

SAM: JOHNSON.

287.

To Mrs. Thrale[1].

DEAR MADAM,　　　　　　　[Ashbourne], Nov. 23, 1772.

I am sorry that none of your letters bring better news of the poor dear lady. I hope her pain is not great. To have a disease confessedly incurable and apparently mortal is a very heavy affliction ; and it is still more grievous when pain is added to despair.

Every thing else in your letter pleased me very well, except that when I come I entreat I may not be flattered, as your letters flatter me[2]. You have read of heroes and princes ruined by flattery, and I question if any of them had a flatterer so dangerous as you. Pray keep strictly to your character of governess.

I cannot yet get well; my nights are flatulent and unquiet, but my days are tolerably easy, and Taylor says that I look much better than when I came hither. You will see when I come, and I can take your word.

Our house affords no revolutions. The great bull is well. But I write not merely to think on you, for I do that without writing, but to keep you a little thinking on me. I perceive that I have taken a broken piece of paper, but that is not the greatest fault that you must forgive in, Madam,

Your, &c.,

SAM: JOHNSON.

288.

To Mrs. Thrale[3].

DEAR MADAM,　　　　　　　[Ashbourne], Nov. 27, 1772.

If you are so kind as to write to me on Saturday, the day on which you will receive this, I shall have it before I leave

[1] *Piozzi Letters*, i. 67.
[2] Johnson again complains of her flattery, *post*, Letters of May 23 and 24, 1773. Boswell describes 'a coarse mode of flattery which she frequently practised.' *Life*, ii. 349. See also *ib.* v. 440.
[3] *Piozzi Letters*, i. 68.

Ashbourne.

Ashbourne. I am to go to Lichfield on Wednesday, and purpose to find my way to London through Birmingham and
Oxford.

I was yesterday at Chatsworth[1]. It is a very fine house.
I wish you had been with me to see it ; for then, as we are apt
to want matter of talk, we should have gained something new
to talk on. They complimented me with playing the fountain,
and opening the cascade. But I am of my friend's opinion,
that when one has seen the ocean, cascades are but little things.

I am in hope of a letter to-day from you or Queeney, but the
post has made some blunder, and the packet is not yet distributed. I wish it may bring me a little good of you all.

I am, &c.,
SAM: JOHNSON.

289.

TO MRS. THRALE[2].

DEAR MADAM, Lichfield, Dec. 3, 1772.

I found two letters here, to recompense my disappointment
at Ashbourne. I shall not now be long before I hope to settle,
for it is a fine thing to be settled. When one parts from friends
it is uncertain when one shall come back, and when one comes
back it is not very certain how long one shall stay. But hope,
you know, was left in the box of Prometheus[3].

Miss Aston claims kin to you, for she says she is somehow a-kin to the Cottons[4]. In a little time you shall make
them all yet prouder of their kindred. Do not be depressed.
Scarce years will not last for ever ; there will sometime be
good harvests[5]. Scarcity itself produces plenty by inciting

---

[1] He visited it with the Thrales in
1774, and alone in 1784. *Life*, iv.
357 ; v. 429.

[2] *Piozzi Letters*, i. 69.

[3] Epimetheus.

[4] Sir Robert Cotton of Combermere, Cheshire, who was made a
baronet in 1677, married Hester,
heiress of Sir Thomas Salusbury,
Bart., of Llewenny, Denbighshire.
Mrs. Thrale was their great-granddaughter. Burke's *Peerage*, article

Viscount Combermere, and Hayward's *Piozzi*, i. 241.

[5] John Wesley in an interesting
letter dated 'Dover, December 9,
1772,' examines the causes of the
general scarcity. 'I ask,' he writes,
'why are thousands of people starving, perishing for want, in every part
of England? The fact I know ; I
have seen it with my eyes in every
corner of the land. I have known
those who could only afford to eat
cultivation.

cultivation. I hope we shall soon talk these matters over very seriously, and that we shall talk of them again much less seriously many years hence.

> My love to all,
> Both great and small.

These verses I made myself, though perhaps they have been made by others before me.

> I am, &c.,
> SAM: JOHNSON.

290.

To Edmund Hector [1].

DEAR SIR,

When I came down into this country, I proposed to myself the pleasure of a few days passed in your company, but it has happened now as at many former times that I proposed enjoyments which I cannot obtain. I have a hasty summons to London, and can hope for little more than to pass a night with you and Mrs. Careless [2].

I purpose to come to you on Monday, and to go away next day, if I can get a place in the Oxford coach. If by this notice you can secure a place for Tuesday to Oxford, it will be a

a little coarse food every other day. I have known one picking up stinking sprats from a dunghill, and carrying them home for herself and her children. I have known another gathering the bones which the dogs had left in the streets, and making broth of them to prolong a wretched life.' Among the causes of the scarcity he places—(1) 'The immense quantities of bread-corn consumed by distilling—converted into a deadly poison.' (2) 'The monopolising of farms. The land which was formerly divided among ten or twenty little farmers is now engrossed by one great farmer. Every one of those little farmers was glad to send his bacon, or pork, or fowls and eggs to market continually. But the great, the gentleman farmers, are above attending to those little things

Hence in the same town, where within my memory eggs were sold eight or ten a penny, they are now sold six or eight a groat [fourpence].' (3) 'The enormous taxes which are laid on almost everything that can be named. Not only abundant taxes are raised from earth, fire and water, but in England the ingenious statesmen have found a way to tax the very light. The taxes are so high on account of the national debt.' *Scots Magazine*, 1772, p. 665.

[1] First published in *Notes and Queries*, 6th S., iii. 361.

[2] Hector's widowed sister. 'She was,' said Johnson, 'the first woman with whom I was in love. It dropped out of my head imperceptibly, but she and I shall always have a kindness for each other.' *Life*, ii. 459.

favour.

favour. I hope we shall meet again with more leisure, and revive past images, and old occurrences.

I am, dear Sir,

Your faithful humble servant,

Lichfield, Dec. 5, 1772. SAM: JOHNSON.

To Mr. Hector, in Birmingham.

291.

To Edmund Hector [1].

DEAR SIR.

I got hither last night, full of your kindness and that of Mrs. Careless, and full of the praises of Banstay (?), which though I had not many days before seen Chatsworth, keeps, I think, the upper place in my imagination. I return all my friends sincere thanks for their attention and civility.

Yet perhaps I had not written so soon had I not had another favour to solicite (*sic*). Your case of the cancer and mercury has made such impression upon my friend [2], 'that we are very impatient for a more exact relation than I could give, and I therefore entreat, that you will state it very particularly, with the patient's age, the manner of taking mercury, the quantity taken, and all that you told or omitted to tell me. To this request I must add another that you will write as soon as you can.

I am, dear Sir,

Your affectionate servant,

Dec. 12, 1772. SAM: JOHNSON.

To Mr. Hector, in Birmingham.

292.

To the Rev. James Granger [3].

SIR, [London, Dec. 15, 1772.]

When I returned from the country I found your letter; and would very gladly have done what you desire, had it been in my

---

[1] First published in *Notes and Queries*, 6th S., iii. 361.

[2] Mrs. Salusbury. *Ante*, p. 195, n. 2.

[3] Published in Croker's *Boswell*, page 471. Mr. Croker states in a note that 'this letter was found by Mr. P. Cunningham among Granger's, with the date of December 15, 1772.' He does not explain

power.

power. Mr. Farmer[1] is, I am confident, mistaken in supposing that he gave me any such pamphlet or cut. I should as soon have suspected myself, as Mr. Farmer, of forgetfulness; but that I do not know, except from your letter, the name of Arthur O'Toole[2], nor recollect that I ever heard of it before. I think it impossible that I should have suffered such a total obliteration from my mind of any such thing which was ever there. This at least is certain, that I do not know of any such pamphlet; and equally certain I desire you to think it, that if I had it, you should immediately receive it from,

    Sir,
     Your most humble servant,
        SAM: JOHNSON.

   293.

TO MRS. THRALE[3].

       [London,] Tuesday, Jan. 26, 1773.

MADAM,

  The inequalities of human life have always employed the meditation of deep thinkers, and I cannot forbear to reflect on the difference between your condition and my own. You live upon mock turtle, and stewed rumps of beef; I dined yesterday upon crumpets. You sit with parish officers, caressing and caressed, the idol of the table, and the wonder of the day[4].

why he inserted it under the date of 1775. Johnson speaking of Granger said :— 'His *Biographical History* is full of curious anecdote, but might have been better done. The dog is a Whig. I do not like much to see a Whig in any dress; but I hate to see a Whig in a parson's gown.' *Life*, v. 255.

[1] Farmer was Dr. Richard Farmer, Master of Emanuel College, Cambridge. *Ante*, p. 169.

[2] In Granger's *Biographical History of England* (ed. 1779, i. 397) in Class vii, under 'Men of the Sword,' is the following description of a print of O'Toole :— 'Arthurus Severus Nonesuch O'Toole. *Æt.* 80. 1618. An old man in armour, with a sword in his hand, on the blade of which are many crowns,' &c. 'I am informed,' Granger continues, 'that this print was prefixed to Taylor, the Water Poet's *Honour of the noble Captain O'Toole*, first edition, 1622.'

Johnson was careless about his own documents, and those of others. G. Steevens speaks of certain annotations being 'in Dr. Johnson's chaos of papers.' *Garrick Corres.* i. 586.

[3] *Piozzi Letters*, i. 71.

[4] Mr. Thrale, as member for Southwark, had to give treats to the electors. Mrs. Piozzi writing of this time says :—'I grew useful now, *almost* necessary; wrote the adver-

          I pine

I pine in the solitude of sickness, not bad enough to be pitied, and not well enough to be endured. You sleep away the night, and laugh or scold away the day[1]. I cough and grumble, and grumble and cough. Last night was very tedious, and this day makes no promises of much ease. However I have this day put on my shoe, and hope that Gout is gone. I shall have only the cough to contend with, and I doubt whether I shall get rid of that without change of place. I caught cold in the coach as I went away, and am disordered by very little things. Is it accident or age?

I am, dearest Madam, &c.,

SAM: JOHNSON.

294.

TO MRS. THRALE[2].

MADAM,

Feb. 19, 1773.

I think I am better, but cannot say much more than that I think so. I was yesterday with Miss Lucy Southwell and Mrs. Williams, at Mr. Southwell's. Miss Frances Southwell is not well[3].

tisements, looked to the treats, and people to whom I was till then unknown admired how happy Mr. Thrale must be in such a *wonder* of a wife.' Hayward's *Piozzi*, i. 257.

[1] 'She was oftener scolding their children than laughing with her friends.' BARETTI.

[2] *Piozzi Letters*, i. 72.

[3] The Southwells were, I conjecture, of the same family as Johnson's friend, the second Lord Southwell, whom he described as 'the highest-bred man without insolence that I ever was in company with; the most *qualitied* I ever saw.' *Life*, iv. 173. According to a story told by Horace Walpole (*Letters*, iii. 403) Lucy Southwell was little better than a card-sharper. Writing on May 14, 1761, he says:—'Jemmy Lumley last week had a party of whist at his own house; the combatants, Lucy Southwell, that curtseys like a bear, Mrs. Prijean, and a Mrs. Mackenzy. They

played from six in the evening till twelve next day; Jemmy never winning one rubber, and rising a loser of two thousand pounds. How it happened I know not, nor why his suspicions arrived so late, but he fancied himself cheated, and refused to pay. However, *the bear* had no share in his evil surmises; on the contrary, a day or two afterwards he promised a dinner at Hampstead to Lucy and her virtuous sister.' There he met Mrs. Mackenzy, who, on his refusing to pay her, horsewhipped him 'in the garden at Hampstead. Jemmy cried out murder; his servants rushed in, rescued him from the jaws of the lioness, and carried him off in his chaise to town. The Southwells, who were already arrived, and descended on the noise of the fray, finding nobody to pay for the dinner, and fearing they must, set out for London too without it, though I suppose they had prepared tin

I have

I have an invitation to dine at Sir Joshua Reynolds's on Tuesday. May I accept it?

Do not think I am going to borrow the Roller. I have undertaken to beg from you the favour of lending to Miss Reynolds Newton on the Prophecies[1], and to Miss Williams Burney's Musical Journey[2]. They are, I believe, both at Streatham.

Be pleased to make my most respectful compliments to dear Mrs. Salusbury. I wish I could send her any thing better.

Diversas hominum sortes. Here am I, sitting by myself, uncertain whether I shall dine on veal or mutton; and there are you with the top dish and the bottom dish, all upon a card, and on the other side of the card Tom Lisgow[3]. Of the rest that

pockets to carry off all that should be left.' *Letters,* iii. 403.

Neither did Lord Southwell bear a good reputation. Mrs. Osborn wrote on June 29, 1751:—'The town says Lord Tilney is gone with Lord Southwell and Strickland to Spaa, and that they will fill their pockets before they part with him.' Mrs. Osborn, *Political and Social Letters of a Lady of the Eighteenth Century,* p. 107.

Hawkins gives a curious account of Edmund Southwell, Lord Southwell's younger brother, 'one of Johnson's distressed friends,' who had quitted the army, 'and trusted to Providence for a support. He was a man of wonderful parts, of lively and entertaining conversation, and well-acquainted with the world. His practice was to wander about the streets of London, and call in at such coffee-houses, for instance, the Smyrna and Cocoa-tree [*Life,* v. 386, *n.* 1] in Pall Mall, and Child's and Batson's [*Ib.* iii. 355, *n.* 2] in the City, as were frequented by men of intelligence, or where anything like conversation was going forward; in these he found means to make friends from whom he derived a precarious support. Mr. Bates, the master of the Queen's Arms Tavern [*Ib.* iv. 87], suffered him, as often as

he pleased, to add to an ideal account subsisting between them the expense of a dinner.' Hawkins's *Johnson,* p. 405.

[1] 'Tom's great work,' as Johnson described Bishop Newton's book. *Life,* iv. 286.

[2] *The Present State of Music in France, Italy, and Germany,* 3 vols., 1771-3.

'Dr. Johnson gave much praise to his friend Dr. Burney's elegant and entertaining travels, and told Mr. Seward that he had them in his eye, when writing his *Journey to the Western Islands of Scotland.*' *Life,* iv. 186.

[3] 'Tom Lisgow was a voter at the Southwark election. Mr. K—— was another. When they were entertained at Mr. Thrale's table, the Editor of these letters used to write the bill of fare on one side of a large blank card in a small character, the names of the company on the other side, and refer to it from time to time as it lay by her plate, that no mistakes might be made, or offence given from ignorance or forgetfulness; to this practice Mr. Johnson laughingly alludes.'—NOTE BY MRS. PIOZZI.

See *post,* Letter of January 2, 1775. Mr. K—— was perhaps the

dwell

dwell in darker fame why should I make mention ?   Tom Lisgow is an assembly.   But Tom Lisgow cannot people the world. Mr. K—— must have a place.   The lion has his jackall.   They will soon meet.

> And when they talk, ye gods ! how they will talk[1].

Pray let your voice and my master's help to fill the pauses.

I am, &c.,

SAM: JOHNSON.

295.

To JAMES BOSWELL.

London, February 24, 1773.   Published in the *Life*, ii. 204.

296.

To THE REVEREND DR. TAYLOR[2].

DEAR SIR,

Is it not a strange thing that we should visit, and meet, and live kindly together, and then part without any enquiry after each other?   This is surely not quite right, and therefore I will this day put an end to it, by desiring you to inform me about

Mr. Keep on whom she has the following marginal note :—'When he heard I was a native of North Wales he told me that *his* wife was a Welsh woman, and desired to be buried at Ruthyn.   "So," says the man, " I went with the corpse myself, because I thought it would be a pleasant journey, and indeed I found Ruthyn a very beautiful place."'   Hayward's *Piozzi*, i. 308.

[1] 'What can be more natural, more soft, or more passionate than that line in Statira's speech where she describes the charms of Alexander's conversation :—

" Then he would talk :—Good Gods ! how he would talk !"'

ADDISON, *The Spectator*, No. 39.

The following is the passage in which this famous line is found :—

'STATIRA.

From every pore of him a perfume falls,

He kisses softer than a southern wind,

Curls like a vine, and touches like a God.

SYSIGAMBIS.

When will thy spirits rest, these transports cease ?

STATIRA.

Will you not give me leave to warn my sister ?

As I was saying—but I told his sweetness,

Then he will talk, Good Gods, how he will talk !'

The Rival Queens ; or Alexander the Great, by Nathanael Lee, Act I.

[2] From the original in the possession of Messrs. J. Pearson & Co., of 5 Pall Mall Place, S.W.

This letter was sold by Messrs. Christie & Co., on June 5, 1888, for £5 5s.

your

your health and your quiet, of both which I shall willingly hear the improvement and encrease.

As to my own health it has been pretty much interrupted by a cough which has hung on me about ten weeks, and for six a fever has been very violent. I have been sometimes near fainting, but have never fainted. My quiet nobody tries to interrupt, or if they try, I seldom hear of it.

When I had left you, I passed some days at Lucy's, and *lent* Mr. Greene the axe and lance[1]. I then went to Birmingham, and was a while with Hector.

About three weeks ago the Schoolmaster who has dedicated his Spelling-book to you, came to me with a request that I would put my name to a printed recommendation, which was to stand before it[2]. This, you see, was not fit for me to do. He was not importunate, but, I suppose, was not pleased. You will sometime let him see the impropriety of his request, that a man, who considers you as his friend, may not think himself unkindly treated.

My cold was once so bad that I began to think of country air, but then what country. I doubt Derbyshire is not the place that cures coughs. While I deliberated, I grew better, but perceive myself now not the match that I once was for wind and weather[3]. Dr. Lawrence[4] laughs at me when he sees me in a great coat.

Infirmity has come somewhat suddenly, at least unexpectedly upon me, and I am afraid that I suffer myself to be corroded with vain and idle discontent.

Let me hear from you.

> I am, dear Sir,
>> Your affectionate humble servant,

London, Feb. 27, 1773.   SAM: JOHNSON.

To the Reverend Dr. Taylor in Ashbourne, Derbyshire.

[1] Johnson had left Taylor's house at Ashbourne for Lichfield about the end of November. *Ante*, p. 201. Mr. Green had a Museum at Lichfield. *Life*, ii. 465.

[2] In the list of books in the *Gentleman's Magazine* for January of this year (p. 38) is *The Rational Spelling-book*. By John Clarke of Grantham.

[3] Ten years earlier, when Boswell shivered from the coldness of the night-air as he and Johnson sailed up the Thames from Greenwich, 'Johnson,' he writes, 'whose robust frame was not in the least affected by the cold, scolded me, as if my shivering had been a paltry effeminacy, saying, "Why do you shiver?"' *Life*, i. 462.

[4] *Ante*, p. 47, *n.* 2.

To

297.

To Mr. B——.

Johnson's Court, March 4, 1773.   Published in the *Life*, ii. 207.

298.

To the Reverend Mr. White.

Johnson's Court, March 4, 1773.   Published in the *Life*, ii. 207.

299.

To the Reverend W. S. Johnson, LL.D.[1]

Sir,

Of all those whom the various accidents of life have brought within my notice, there is scarce any man whose acquaintance I have more desired to cultivate than yours.   I cannot indeed charge you with neglecting me, yet our mutual inclination could never gratify itself with opportunities.   The current of the day always bore us away from one another, and now the Atlantic is between us.

Whether you carried away an impression of me as pleasing as that which you left me of yourself, I know not ; if you did, you have not forgotten me, and will be glad that I do not forget you.   Merely to be remembered is indeed a barren pleasure, but it is one of the pleasures which is more sensibly felt as human nature is more exalted.

To make you wish that I should have you in my mind, I would be glad to tell you something which you do not know ; but all public affairs are printed ; and as you and I have no common friend, I can tell you no private history.

The Government, I think, grow stronger ; but I am afraid the

---

[1] First published in the *Gentleman's Magazine* for 1825, part ii. p. 320.
'William Samuel Johnson of Connecticut spent several years in England about the middle of the last century. He received the degree of Doctor of Civil Law from the University of Oxford ; and this circumstance, together with the accidental similarity of name, recommended him to the acquaintance of Dr. Samuel Johnson.   Several letters passed between them, after the American Dr. Johnson had returned to his native country ; of which, however, it is feared that this is the only one remaining.' *Ib.*   W. S. Johnson is described in *Alumni Oxonienses* as M.A. by diploma April 21, 1756 ; D.C.L. by diploma, Jan. 23, 1766, 'a Missionary.'

next general election will be a time of uncommon turbulence, violence, and outrage.

Of Literature no great product has appeared, or is expected ; the attention of the people has for some years been otherwise employed [1].

I was told a day or two ago of a design which must excite some curiosity. Two ships are in preparation, which are under the command of Captain Constantine Phipps, to explore the Northern Ocean ; not to seek the north-east or the north-west passage, but to sail directly north, as near the pole as they can go. They hope to find an open ocean, but I suspect it is one mass of perpetual congelation [2]. I do not much wish well to discoveries, for I am always afraid they will end in conquest and robbery [3].

I have been out of order this winter, but am grown better. Can I never hope to see you again, or must I be always content to tell you that in another hemisphere,

I am, Sir,
Your most humble servant,

Johnson's Court, Fleet Street, London,   SAM: JOHNSON.
          March 4, 1773.
     To W. S. Johnson, LL.D., Stratford, Connecticut.

300.

TO MRS. THRALE [4].

DEAREST MADAM,   Johnson's Court, Fleet Street,
                        March 9, 1773.

Dr. James called on me last night, deep, I think, in wine [5]. Our dialogue was this :

[1] Adam Smith was writing his *Wealth of Nations* and Gibbon his *Decline and Fall*, though neither work was published till three years later.

[2] Captain Phipps (afterwards Baron Mulgrave) set sail in the following May, and in the neighbourhood of Spitzbergen reached the latitude of more than 80°. He returned to England in the end of September. *Gentleman's Magazine*, 1774, p. 420. 'Talking of Phipps's voyage to the North Pole, Dr. Johnson observed, that it was conjectured that our former navigators have kept too near land, and so have found the sea frozen far north, because the land hinders the free motion of the tide ; but, in the wide ocean, where the waves tumble at their full convenience, it is imagined that the frost does not take effect.' *Life*, v. 236.

[3] See *ib.* ii. 479.

[4] *Piozzi Letters*, i. 74.

[5] 'I knew a physician,' said John-

—You

—You find the case hopeless?—Quite hopeless.—But I hope you can procure her an easier dismission out of life?—That, I believe, is in our power.

The rest of his talk was about other things.

If it can give the dear lady any comfort, be pleased to let her know that my grief for her is very serious and very deep. If I could be useful as you can be, I would devote myself to her as you must do. But all human help is little; her trust must be in a better Friend.

You will not let me burst in ignorance of your transaction with A——[1]. Surely my heart is with you in your whole system of life.

I am, dear Madam, &c.,

SAM: JOHNSON.

I had written this letter before yours came. God bless you all.

301.

To MRS. THRALE[2].

[Johnson's Court],
March 11, 1773.

DEAR MADAM,

Your negotiation will probably end as you desire. I wish your pious offices might have the same success, but death is necessary, and your tenderness will make it less painful. I am sorry that I can do nothing. The dear lady has my wishes, and

son, 'who for twenty years was not sober; yet in a pamphlet which he wrote upon fevers he appealed to Garrick and me for his vindication from a charge of drunkenness.' *Life*, iii. 389. It has been stated, and perhaps rightly, that this physician was James. Mrs. Piozzi at Boulogne recalled 'the story she once heard of Miss Ashe, speaking of poor Dr. James, who loved profligate conversation dearly—"That man should set up his quarters across the water (said she); why Boulogne would be a seraglio to him."' Piozzi's *Journey*, &c., i. 6. He disapproved of riding, for 'he once told a Prebendary of Canterbury that if God had meant men should ride so constantly he would have sent them into the world booted and spurred.' G. M. Berkeley's *Poems*, Preface, p. 426. See also *Life*, i. 81, 159.

[1] A—— is, I conjecture, the man mentioned in the following passage in Mrs. Thrale's letter of November 11, 1779:—'Do you remember when Mr. Perkins told us of that fellow A—r, who would force us into a lawsuit and then lost his cause—how I asked in what manner he looked? Why, says Perkins, *he looked like a man that was nonsuited.*' *Piozzi Letters*, ii. 87.

In an undated letter belonging to 1773 she speaks of his 'callous cruelty.' *Ib.* i. 87.

[2] *Piozzi Letters*, i. 75.

sometimes

sometimes my prayers. I hope our prayers will be heard for her, and her prayers for herself.

I am, &c.,

SAM: JOHNSON.

302.

To Mrs. Thrale [1].

DEAR MADAM,   [Johnson's Court], March 17, 1773.

To tell you that I am sorry both for the poor lady and for you is useless. I cannot help either of you. The weakness of mind is perhaps only a casual interruption or intermission of the attention, such as we all suffer when some weighty care or urgent calamity has possession of the mind. She will compose herself. She is unwilling to die, and the first conviction of approaching death raised great perturbation. I think she has but very lately thought death close at hand. She will compose herself to do that as well as she can, which must at last be done [2]. May she not want the Divine assistance.

You, Madam, will have a great loss; a greater than is common in the loss of a parent. Fill your mind with hope of her happiness, and turn your thoughts first to Him who gives and takes away, in whose presence the living and dead are standing together. Then remember, that when this mournful duty is paid, others yet remain of equal obligation, and, we may hope, of less painful performance. Grief is a species of idleness [3], and the necessity of attention to the present preserves us, by the merciful disposition of Providence, from being lacerated [4] and devoured by sorrow for the past. You must think on your husband and your children, and do [for them] what this dear lady has done for you.

---

[1] *Piozzi Letters*, i. 76.

[2] Johnson talking of dying said :— 'A man knows it must be so, and submits. It will do him no good to whine.' *Life*, ii. 107.

[3] 'All unnecessary grief,' said Johnson, 'is unwise, and therefore will not be long retained by a sound mind.' *Ib.* iii. 136.

[4] Of the word *lacerate* Mrs. Piozzi says in her *British Synonymy* (ed. 1794, i. 345), 'that it should be so seldom used in conversation, though eminently pleasing, one might inquire long and find no cause, unless its familiarity with the surgeon's profession may be deemed one.' She had heard Johnson use it, for it seems a favourite term with him. See *post*, Letters of March 30, 1776, and July 27, 1778, and *Life*, ii. 106; iii. 419.

Not

Not to come to town while the great struggle continues is undoubtedly well resolved. But do not harass yourself into danger; you owe the care of your health to all that love you, at least to all whom it is your duty to love. You cannot give such a mother too much, if you do not give her what belongs to another.

I am, &c.,
SAM: JOHNSON.

303.

TO MRS. THRALE [1].

[Johnson's Court],
March 20, 1773. The Equinox.

MADAM,

I have now heard twice to-day how the dear lady mends; twice is not often enough for such news. May she long and long continue mending. When I see her again, how I shall love her. If we could keep a while longer together, we should all, I hope, try to be thankful. Part we must at last; but the last parting is very afflictive. When I see her I shall torment her with caressing her [2]. Has she yet been down stairs?

On Tuesday morning I hope to see you. I have not much to tell you, but will gather what little I can.

I shall be glad to see you, for you are much in my head, notwithstanding your negotiations for my master, he has mended his share for one year, you must think of cutting in pieces and boiling him [3]. We will at least keep him out of J—ck—n's copper [4]. You will be at leisure now to think of brewing and negotiating, and a little of,

Madam,
Yours, &c.,
SAM: JOHNSON.

[1] *Piozzi Letters*, i. 78.

[2] On June 18, the day of her death, he recorded in his Diary:—'Yesterday as I touched her hand and kissed it, she pressed my hand between her two hands, which she probably intended as the parting caress.' *Pr. and Med.* p. 128.

[3] This sentence surely is not as Johnson wrote it.

[4] For the impostor Jackson see *ante*, p. 192, *n.* 3. 'He had persuaded Mr. Thrale,' writes Mrs. Piozzi, 'to build a copper somewhere in East Smithfield, the very metal of which cost £2000, for the manufacture of his stuff which should preserve ships' bottoms.' Hayward's *Piozzi*, i. 257.

TO

304.

To Mrs. Thrale [1].

MADAM,   March 25, 1773.

If my letters can do you any good, it is not fit that you should want them. You are always flattering me with the good that I do, without knowing it.

The return of Mrs. Salusbury's appetite will undoubtedly prolong her life; I therefore wish it to continue or to improve. You did not say whether she went down stairs.

Harry will be happier now he goes to school and reads Milton [2]. Miss will want him for all her vapouring.

Did not I tell you that I thought I had written to Boswell? he has answered my letter [3].

I am going this evening to put young Otway to school with Mr. Elphinston [4].

C—— is so distressed with abuse about his play, that he has solicited Goldsmith to *take him off the rack of the newspapers* [5].

M—— is preparing a whole pamphlet against G——, and G—— is, I suppose, collecting materials to confute M—— [6].

Jennens has published Hamlet, but without a preface, and

---

[1] *Piozzi Letters*, i. 79.

[2] The poor boy was but seven years old. He died at the age of ten.

[3] Boswell himself arrived in London a week later. *Life*, ii. 209.

[4] See *ante*, p. 17.

[5] C—— was George Colman the elder, Manager of Covent Garden Theatre. 'His play' was *She Stoops to Conquer*, which he had been 'prevailed on at last by much solicitation, nay a kind of force, to bring on.' *Life*, iii. 320. Johnson wrote on March 4 of this year:—'Dr. Goldsmith has a new comedy in rehearsal at Covent Garden, to which the manager predicts ill success. I hope he will be mistaken. I think it deserves a very kind reception.' *Ib.* ii. 208. According to Mr. Forster, Colman would not go to the expense of new scenes or dresses. 'The actors

and actresses had taken their tone from the manager,' and three of them refused to play. Forster's *Goldsmith*, ii. 334-6. How wrong they were in their forebodings is shown by a sentence in Horace Walpole's Letters (v. 452), who wrote on March 16:— 'There was a new play by Dr. Goldsmith last night, which succeeded prodigiously.'

[6] M—— is Mickle, the translator of the *Lusiad*, and G—— is Garrick. The play that was refused was *The Siege of Marseilles*. Garrick wrote to Boswell on September 14 of this year:—'Your friend —— threatens me much. I only wish that he would put his threats in execution, and, if he prints his play, I will forgive him.' *Life*, v. 349. See also *ib.* ii. 182, *n.* 3, and Appendix D of the present volume.

S——

S—— declares his intention of letting him pass the rest of his life in peace[1]. Here is news.

I am, &c.,
SAM: JOHNSON.

305.

To OLIVER GOLDSMITH[2].

SIR,

I beg that you will excuse my Absence to the Club ; I am going this evening to Oxford.

I have another favour to beg. It is that I may be considered as proposing Mr. Boswel for a candidate of our Society, and that he may be considered as regularly nominated.

I am, Sir,
Your most humble servant,

April 23, 1773. SAM: JOHNSON.

To Dr. Goldsmith.

[1] Charles Jennens published in 1773 an edition of *Hamlet* collated with ancient and modern editions. Lowndes' *Bibl. Man.* iii. 2277. S—— was George Steevens, who assisted Johnson in the revised edition of his Shakespeare (*ante*, p. 168), famous for the malignity of his attacks. *Life*, iii. 281 ; iv. 274. Jennens, the year before, had published anonymously *A vindication of King Lear from the Abuse of the Critical Reviewers*, in which (p. 2) he attacked Johnson and Steevens. Johnson he said 'had tacitly owned that he was the writer of a forged letter in the *Public Advertiser*, wherein the Doctor discovers his knowledge in the geography of his native country, by representing Gopsal (the seat of Mr. Jennens) as some city or large town.'

[2] Published in Croker's *Boswell*, page 255. Corrected by me from the original in the possession of Mr. Alfred Morrison of Fonthill House.

'It is,' says Mr. Forster, 'the only fragment of correspondence between Johnson and Goldsmith that has been preserved.' The Club met on the evening of the day on which this letter was written, and Goldsmith was in the chair. Forster's *Goldsmith*, ii. 367. If Johnson went to Oxford his stay there was brief, as on the morning of April 27 Boswell found him at home. *Life*, ii. 229. It is possible that he gave up his visit on finding that 'several of the members wished to keep Boswell out.' *Ib.* v. 76. For Boswell's election on the 30th see *ib.* ii. 235, 240.

Goldsmith was, it should seem, not given to letter-writing. Grainger, the author of the *Sugar Cane*, wrote to Dr. Percy on March 24, 1764 :— 'When I taxed little Goldsmith for not writing as he promised me, his answer was that he never wrote a letter in his life ; and faith I believe him unless to a Bookseller for money.' Messrs. Sotheby's *Auction Catalogue* for November 27, 1889. Lot 75.

This Letter was sold by Messrs. Christie & Co. on June 5, 1888 for £40. The high price was in part due to the fact already mentioned

To

306.

To Mrs. Thrale [1].

DEAR MADAM,   [Johnson's Court], April 27, 1773.

Hope is more pleasing than fear, but not less fallacious ; you know, when you do not try to deceive yourself, that the disease which at last is to destroy, must be gradually growing worse, and that it is vain to wish for more than that the descent to death may be slow and easy. In this wish I join with you, and hope it will be granted. Dear, dear lady, whenever she is lost she will be missed, and whenever she is remembered she will be lamented. Is it a good or an evil to me that she now loves me [2] ? It is surely a good ; for you will love me better, and we shall have a new principle of concord ; and I shall be happier with honest sorrow, than with sullen indifference ; and far happier still than with counterfeited sympathy.

I am reasoning upon a principle very far from certain, a confidence of survivance [3]. You or I, or both, may be called into the presence of the Supreme Judge before her. I have lived a life of which I do not like the review. Surely I shall in time live better.

I sat down with an intention to write high compliments, but my thoughts have taken another course, and some other time must now serve to tell you with what other emotions, benevolence, and fidelity,

I am, &c.,
SAM: JOHNSON.

307.

To The Reverend W. Bagshaw.

[London,] May 8, 1773. Published in the *Life*, ii. 258.

308.

To Mrs. Thrale [4].

MADAM,   [Johnson's Court], May 17, 1773.

Never imagine that your letters are long ; they are always

that it is the only Letter of Johnson to Goldsmith that is known to exist.

[1] *Piozzi Letters*, i. 81.

[2] See *ante*, p. 196, *n.* 5.

[3] *Survivance* is not in Johnson's *Dictionary*.

[4] *Piozzi Letters*, i. 82.

too

too short for my curiosity. I do not know that I was ever content with a single perusal.

Of dear Mrs. Salusbury I never expect much better news than you send me ; *de pis en pis* is the natural and certain course of her dreadful malady. I am content when it leaves her ease enough for the exercise of her mind.

Why should Mr. • • • • • suppose, that what I took the liberty of suggesting was concerted with you ? He does not know how much I revolve his affairs, and how honestly I desire his prosperity. I hope he has let the hint take some hold of his mind [1].

Your declaration to Miss • • • • is more general than my opinions allow. I think an unlimited promise of acting by the opinion of another so wrong, that nothing, or hardly any thing, can make it right. All unnecessary vows are folly, because they suppose a prescience of the future which has not been given us. They are, I think, a crime, because they resign that life to chance which God has given us to be regulated by reason ; and superinduce a kind of fatality, from which it is the great privilege of our nature to be free [2]. Unlimited obedience is due only to the Universal Father of Heaven and Earth. My parents may be mad or foolish ; may be wicked and malicious ; may be erroneously religious, or absurdly scrupulous. I am not bound to compliance with mandates either positive or negative, which either religion condemns, or reason rejects. There wanders about the world a wild notion, which extends over marriage more than over any other transaction. If Miss • • • • followed a trade, would it be said that she was bound in conscience to give or refuse credit at her father's choice? And is not marriage a thing in which she is more interested, and has therefore more right of choice ? When I may suffer for my own crimes, when

[1] Mrs. Piozzi in a copy of the printed letters has filled up the blank with the name of Thrale, and has added :—' Concerning his connection with quack chemists, quacks of all sorts ; jumping up in the night to go to Marlbro' Street from Southwark, after some advertising mountebank, at hazard of his life.' Hayward's *Piozzi.* i. 65.

[2] ' BOSWELL. "But you would not have me to bind myself by a solemn obligation." JOHNSON (much agitated) : "What! a vow—O, no, Sir, a vow is a horrible thing, it is a snare for sin."' *Life*, iii. 357. See also *ib*. ii. 21.

I may

I may be sued for my own debts, I may judge by parity of reason for my own happiness. The parent's moral right can arise only from his kindness, and his civil right only from his money [1].

Conscience cannot dictate obedience to the wicked, or compliance with the foolish; and of interest mere prudence is the judge.

If the daughter is bound without a promise, she promises nothing; and if she is not bound, she promises too much.

What is meant by tying up money in trade I do not understand. No money is so little tied as that which is employed in trade. Mr. • • • • perhaps only means. that in consideration of money to be advanced, he will oblige his son to be a trader. This is reasonable enough. Upon ten thousand pounds diligently occupied, they may live in great plenty and splendour, without the mischiefs of idleness.

I can write a long letter as well as my mistress; and shall be glad that my long letters may be as welcome as her's.

My nights are grown again very uneasy and troublesome. I know not that the country will mend them; but I hope your company will mend my days. Though I cannot now expect much attention, and would not wish for more than can be spared from the poor dear lady, yet I shall see you and hear you every now and then; and to see and hear you, is always to hear wit, and to see virtue [2].

I shall, I hope, see you to-morrow, and a little on the two next days; and with that little I must for the present try to be contented.

I am, &c.,

SAM: JOHNSON.

[1] Johnson more than once upheld stoutly the right of the child in marriage. See *Life*, i. 346; iii. 377. In *Hudibras* the Lady in her *Answer to the Knight* had maintained much the same, where she says:—

'This is the way all parents prove
In managing their children's love;
That force 'em t' intermarry and wed,
As if th' were burying of the dead:
Cast earth to earth, as in the grave,
To join in wedlock all they have.'
    Hudibras, ed. 1806, ii. 445.
For Miss * * * * see the next letter.

[2] 'Poor Johnson! How careless in examining the nature and the conduct of his Friends!' BARETTI.

To

309.

To Mrs. Thrale [1].

DEAR LADY, [Johnson's Court], May 22, 1773.

Dr. Lawrence [2] is of your mind about the intermission, and thought the bark would be best ; but I have had so good a night as makes me wonder. Dr. Lawrence is just gone. He says I have no fever, and may let bark alone, if I will venture, but it is *meo periculo*.

Make my compliments to the dear lady.

I think Mr. T—— has done right in not prohibiting at least F——'s flight with her lover. There is no danger of Mr. R——'s taking care of his son, and of his son's wife ; and as he is willing to receive a daughter-in-law without a fortune, he has a right to provide for her his own way. The great motive to his consent is, that his son will engage in trade ; and therefore no doubt can be made but he will enable him to do it ; and whether at Midsummer, or Michaelmas, we have no need to care, nor right to prescribe [3].

I am, &c.,
SAM: JOHNSON.

[1] *Piozzi Letters*, i. 88.

[2] Dr. Lawrence was one of the two physicians from whom Johnson got that 'knowledge of physic' which no doubt shortened his life. Boswell describes him as 'the learned and worthy Dr. Lawrence, whom Dr. Johnson respected and loved as his physician.' *Life*, ii. 296, n. 1; iii. 22; *ante*, p. 48. Johnson states in his Diary that he had at this time 'attempted to learn the Low Dutch language. My progress,' he continues, 'was interrupted by a fever, which by the imprudent use of a small print left an inflammation in my useful eye.' *Pr. and Med.* p. 129.

[3] Baretti, who was likely to be well-informed in this case, fills up the three blanks with the names of Thrale, Fanny Plumb, and Rice. In a marginal note on one of Mrs. Thrale's letters (*Piozzi Letters*, i.

95) he says :—' Young Rice, with Mr. Thrale's consent, if not by his advice, went away to France with Fanny, the daughter of Mr. Plumb, brother-in-law to Mr. Thrale, and there married her. The old Gripus would not consent she should marry during his life time.' BARETTI. Mr. Thrale's sisters, 'all eminent for personal beauty,' were, according to Mr. Hayward, Mrs. Rice, Mrs. Nesbitt (afterwards Mrs. Scott), and Lady Lade. Hayward's *Piozzi*, i. 255. Miss Burney (*Diary*, ii. 23) mentions 'a Mrs. Plumbe, one of poor Mr. Thrale's sisters,' so that Mr. Hayward's list is not complete. Mrs. Thrale writing to Johnson begged him 'to settle with Mr. Thrale about these lovers.' *Piozzi Letters*, i. 88. It seems probable that Mr. Plumb was dead, and that Mr. Thrale was Fanny's guardian.

To

To Mrs. Thrale[1].

DEAREST LADY,   May 23, 1773.

Still flatter, flatter! Why should the poor be flattered?
The doctor was with me again to-day, and we both think the
fever quite gone. I believe it was not an intermittent, for I took
of my own head physick yesterday; and Celsus says, it seems,
that if a cathartick be taken the fit will return *certo certius*.
I would bear something rather than Celsus should be detected
in an error. But I say it was a *febris continua*, and had a
regular crisis[2].

What poor • • • • said, is worthy of the greatest mind, since
the greatest mind can get no further. In the highest and the
lowest things we all are equal.

As to Mr. • • • •[3], let him see a couple of fellows within call;
and if he makes a savage noise, order them to come gradually
nearer, and you will see how quiet he will grow.

Let the poor dear lady know that I am sorry for her sorrows,
and sincerely and earnestly wish her all good.

Write to me when you can, but do not flatter me. I am
sorry you can think it pleases me[4]. It is enough for me to be,
as Mr. • • • • phrases it,

MADAM,
Your friend and servant,
SAM: JOHNSON.

311.

To Mrs. Thrale[5].

DEAR MADAM,   May 24, 1773.

My fever has departed; but has left me a very severe
inflammation in the seeing eye. I take physick, and do not
eat.

Recommend me to the poor dear lady, whom I hope to see
again, however melancholy must be the interview[6]. She has

---

[1] *Piozzi Letters*, i. 89.
[2] Boswell justly called Johnson 'a great dabbler in physic.' *Life*, iii. 152.
[3] The man, I conjecture, who was

called A—— in the Letter of March 9; *ante*, p. 211.
[4] *Ante*, p. 200.
[5] *Piozzi Letters*, i. 93.
[6] He recorded in his Diary on now

now quickly to do, what I cannot reasonably hope to put off long,

        Res si qua diu mortalibus ulla est [1];

and which is at no great distance from the youngest. I have the same hope with poor N——.

You do not tell me whither the young lovers are gone. I am glad • • • • is gone with them. What a life do they image in futurity! how unlike to what they are to find it! But to-morrow is an old deceiver, and his cheat never grows stale [2]. I suppose they go to Scotland. Was • • • • • dressed *à la Nesbitienne* [3]?

I shall not, I think, go into the country till you are so kind as to fetch me, unless some stronger invitation should be offered than I have yet found.

The difference between praise and flattery is the same as between that hospitality that sets wine enough before the guest, and that which forces him to be drunk. If you love me, and surely I hope you do, why should you vitiate my mind with a false opinion of its own merit [4]? why should you teach it to be unsatisfied with the civility of every other place? You know how much I honour you, and you are bound to use your influence well.

Do not let your own dear spirits forsake you. Your talk at present is heavy, and yet you purpose to take me; but I hope I shall take from it one way what I add another. I purpose to

---

Friday, June 18:—'This day after dinner died Mrs. Salusbury.' *Pr. and Med.* p. 128.

[1] *Æneid*, x. 861.

'If life and long were terms that
    could agree.'
               DRYDEN.

[2] See Dryden's lines quoted in the *Life*, iv. 303, beginning 'When I consider life, 'tis all a cheat.'

[3] See *post*, Letter of May 25, 1780, where Johnson writes:—'A lady has sent me a vial, like Mrs. Nesbitt's vial, of essence of roses. What am I come to?' Mr. Nesbitt, Thrale's brother-in-law, is mentioned in Goldsmith's lines:—

'So tell Horneck and Nesbitt,
And Baker and his bit,
And Kauffman beside,
And the Jessamy bride.'
   GOLDSMITH, *Selected Poems*,
     ed. Austin Dobson, pp.
     119, 211.

[4] Johnson speaking of the applause which Swift constantly received says:—'He that is much flattered soon learns to flatter himself; we are commonly taught our duty by fear or shame, and how can they act upon the man who hears nothing but his own praises?' *Works*, viii. 217.

watch

watch the *mollia tempora fandi* [1], and to talk, as occasion offer, to • • • •.

I am, &c.,
SAM: JOHNSON.

312.

To the Reverend Dr. Taylor.

[London], June 23, 1773.

In Messrs. Christie & Co.'s Auction Catalogue of June 5, 1888, Lot 44 is a Letter of Johnson to Dr. Taylor, two pages quarto, dated June 23, 1773. 'Friendly letter of condolence. " Do not lie down, and suffer without struggle or resistance. I fancy that neither of us uses exercise enough." '

It was sold for £7 7s.

313.

To James Boswell.

Johnson's Court, July 5, 1773. Published in the *Life*, ii. 264.

314.

To James Boswell.

[London], August 3, 1773. Published in the *Life*, ii. 265.

315.

To James Boswell.

[London], August 3, 1773. Published in the *Life*, ii. 266.

316.

To the Reverend Dr. Taylor [2].

DEAR SIR,

Your solicitude for me is a very pleasing evidence of your friendship. My eye is almost recovered, but is yet a little dim, and does not much like a small print by candle light. You will however believe that I think myself pretty well, when I tell you my design.

I have long promised to visit Scotland, and shall set out to-morrow on the journey. I have Mr. Chambers' [3] company as far

---

[1] ' Mollissima fandi tempora.'
Æneid, iv. 293.
' Himself meantime the softest hours would choose.'
DRYDEN.
No doubt it was to Mr. Thrale that Johnson purposed to talk.

[2] First published in *Notes and Queries*, 6th S., v. 422.
[3] Chambers (*ante*, p. 132), 'who was going a judge, with six thousand a year, to Bengal,' was visiting Newcastle, his native town, to take leave of his relations. *Life*, ii. 264 ; v. 16.

as

as Newcastle, and Mr. Boswell an active lively fellow is to conduct me round the country. What I shall see, I know not, but hope to have entertainment for my curiosity, and I shall be sure at least of air and motion. When I come back, perhaps a little invitation may call me into Derbyshire, to compare the mountains of the two countries.

In the mean time I hope you are daily advancing in your health. Drink a great deal[1], and sleep heartily, and think now and then of

Dear Sir,

Your Most humble Servant,

Aug. 5, 1773.   SAM: JOHNSON.

    To the Rev. Dr. Taylor in Ashbourne, Derbyshire.

317.

To JAMES BOSWELL.

Newcastle, August 11, 1773. Published in the *Life*, ii. 266.

318.

To MRS. THRALE[2].

DEAR MADAM,   [Newcastle], August 12, 1773.

We left London on Friday the sixth, not very early, and travelled without any memorable accident through a country which I had seen before. In the evening I was not well, and was forced to stop at Stilton, one stage short of Stamford, where we intended to have lodged.

---

[1] See *post*, Letter of June 23, 1776, where Johnson writes to Taylor :— 'I hope you persevere in drinking.' He himself was for the larger part of his life a water-drinker. *Life*, i. 103, n. 3.

[2] *Piozzi Letters*, i. 103.

For Johnson's journey to Scotland see *Life*, ii. 265, and the whole of vol. v. and my *Footsteps of Dr. Johnson in Scotland*. The weather was bright and hot, as is shewn by the table given in the *Gentleman's Magazine* for 1774, p. 290. (In that Magazine 'a Meteorological Diary of the Weather' is often given for the corresponding month of the previous year.) The French traveller Faujas Saint-Fond who made the same journey a few years later, writing of the road from London to Stilton says :—' Rien n'est au-dessus de la beauté et de la commodité du chemin pendant ces 63 milles ; c'est l'avenue d'un magnifique jardin.' *Voyage en Angleterre*, ed. 1797, i. 146. Stilton is 75 miles from London. Johnson had seen this country early in 1764 when he visited the Langton family at their seat at Langton in Lincolnshire. *Life*, i. 476.

On

On the 7th, we passed through Stamford and Grantham [1], and dined at Newark, where I had only time to observe that the market-place was uncommonly spacious and neat. In London we should call it a square, though the sides were neither straight nor parallel. We came, at night, to Doncaster [2], and went to church in the morning, where Chambers found the monument of Robert of Doncaster, who says on his stone something like this :—What I gave, that I have ; what I spent, that I had ; what I left, that I lost.—So saith Robert of Doncaster, who reigned in the world sixty-seven years, and all that time lived not one [3]. Here we were invited to dinner, and therefore made no great haste away.

We reached York however that night ; I was much disordered with old complaints. Next morning we saw the Minster, an edifice of loftiness and elegance equal to the highest hopes of architecture. I remember nothing but the dome of St. Paul's that can be compared with the middle walk. The Chapter-house is a circular building, very stately, but I think excelled by the Chapter-house of Lincoln.

[1] Stamford is 89 miles from London by the coach road, Grantham 110, and Newark 124. Paterson's *British Itinerary*, i. 203-6. According to *Tristram Shandy* (ed. 1767, i. 92) between Stilton and Grantham, a distance of 35 miles, there were but two stages. 'These two stages my mother declared were so truly tragi-comical that she did nothing but laugh and cry in a breath from one end to the other of them all the way.'

[2] Doncaster is 160 miles and York 197 miles from London. Smollett describes 'all the windows of all the inns from Doncaster northwards as scrawled with doggrel rhymes, in abuse of the Scotch nation.' *Humphry Clinker*, ed. 1792, ii. 176.

[3] To the kindness of Dr. Sykes of Doncaster I owe the following copy of the inscription. The tomb perished in the fire which destroyed the church in 1853.

'Howe : Howe : who : is : here :
I : Robyn : of Doncaster :
    and : Margaret : my : feare :
That : I : spent : that : I :
    had :
That : I : gave : that : I : have :
That : I : left : that : I :
    loste :

A. D. 1579.

Quod : Robertus : Byrkes :
Who : in : this : world : did :
    reigne :
Threescore : yeares : and :
    seaven :
And : yet : lived : not : one.'
Gibbon quotes much the same epitaph on the grave of Edward Courtenay, Earl of Devon, 'surnamed, from his misfortune, the *blind*, from his virtues, the *good* earl. It inculcates with much ingenuity a moral sentence, which may however be abused by thoughtless generosity.' *The Decline and Fall*, ed. 1807, xi. 263.

I then

I then went to see the ruins of the Abbey, which was almost vanished, and I remember nothing of them distinct.

The next visit was to the jail, which they call the Castle; a fabrick built lately, such is terrestrial mutability, out of the materials of the ruined Abbey. The under jailor was very officious to show his fetters, in which there was no contrivance. The head jailor came in, and seeing me look I suppose fatigued, offered me wine, and when I went away would not suffer his servant to take money. The jail is accounted the best in the kingdom, and you find the jailer deserving of his dignity [1].

We dined at York, and went on to Northallerton, a place of which I know nothing, but that it afforded us a lodging on Monday night, and about two hundred and seventy years ago gave birth to Roger Ascham [2].

Next morning we changed our horses at Darlington, where Mr. Cornelius Harrison, a cousin-german of mine, was perpetual curate. He was the only one of my relations who ever rose in fortune above penury, or in character above neglect [3].

[1] John Howard thus describes York Gaol in 1774 :—'In the spacious area of the Castle is a noble prison for debtors which does honour to the county. The rooms are airy and healthy. The Felons' court-yard is down five steps; it is too small and has no water. The cells are in general about 7½ feet by 6½, and 8½ high; close and dark; having only either a hole over the door about four inches by eight, or some perforations in the door of about an inch diameter; not any of them to the open air, but into passages or entries. In most of these cells hree prisoners are locked up at night; in winter for fourteen to sixteen hours; straw on the stone floors; no bedsteads. A sewer in one of the passages often makes these parts of the gaol very offensive.' The gaolor's pay depended chiefly on the fees, often wrung from the prisoners, and on the profits from the sale of spirituous liquors, for every gaoler was a tapster as well. The allowance of food for each prisoner, whether debtor or felon, was a sixpenny loaf on Tuesday and Friday. (Weight, Nov. 1774, 3 lb. 2 oz.). Howard's *Present State of the Prisons*, ed. 1777, pp. 24, 396.

[2] Northallerton is 222 miles from London. Johnson in his *Life of Ascham* says that 'he was born in the year 1515 at Kirby Wiske (or Kirby Wicke) a village near Northallerton, of a family above the vulgar.' *Works*, vi. 504. Hume spent a night here nearly three years after Johnson, on his last visit to London shortly before his death. *Letters of Hume to Strahan*, p. 320.

[3] Darlington is 238 miles from London. Cornelius Harrison was appointed Perpetual Curate in 1727; he died on October 4, 1748. Surtees' *History of Durham*, iii. 364, and *Gentleman's Magazine*, 1748, p. 476. When Johnson was ten years old he and his brother visited his Uncle Harrison at Birmingham.

The

The church is built crosswise, with a fine spire, and might invite a traveller to survey it, but I perhaps wanted vigour, and thought I wanted time.

The next stage brought us to Durham, a place of which Mr. Thrale bad me take particular notice. The Bishop's palace has the appearance of an old feudal castle [1], built upon an eminence, and looking down upon the river, upon which was formerly thrown a draw-bridge, as I suppose to be raised at night, lest the Scots should pass it.

The cathedral has a massiness and solidity such as I have seen in no other place ; it rather awes than pleases, as it strikes with a kind of gigantick dignity, and aspires to no other praise than that of rocky solidity and indeterminate duration. I had none of my friends resident [2], and therefore saw but little. The library is mean and scanty.

At Durham, beside all expectation, I met an old friend : Miss Fordyce is married there to a physician. We met, I think, with honest kindness on both sides. I thought her much decayed, and having since heard that the banker had involved her husband in his extensive ruin [3], I cannot forbear to think that I saw in her withered features more impression of sorrow than of time.

Qua terra patet, fera regnat Erinnys [4].

'He did not much like us, nor did we like him. He was a very mean and vulgar man, drunk every night, but drunk with little drink, very peevish, very proud, very ostentatious, but luckily not rich.' *Annals*, p. 28. He had, I think, married the sister of Johnson's mother. Cornelius Harrison's son, Cornelius, matriculated at Trinity College, Oxford, on April 28, 1761. *Alumni Oxonienses*.

[1] Durham is 256 miles from London. Pennant thus describes the old powers of the Bishops :—'They had power to levy taxes, make truces with the Scots, to raise defensible men within the bishopric from sixteen to sixty years of age. They could call a parliament, and create barons to sit and vote in it. The Bishop could sit in his purple robes to pronounce sentence of death. He could coin money, hold courts in his own name, and all writs went in his name.' *Tour in Scotland*, ed. 1776, ii. 336. Romilly gives a curious account of 'the grandeur and magnificence and homage' which he [Romilly] enjoyed as Chancellor of Durham. *Life of Romilly*, ed. 1840, ii. 112.

[2] I do not know who were Johnson's friends in the Chapter. He knew Warburton and perhaps Lowth, both of whom, though they were Bishops, were also Prebendaries of Durham. Le Neve's *Fast. Eccl. Ang.* iii. 309, 316.

[3] See *ante*, p. 192, *n*. 3.

[4] Ovid, *Metamorphoses*, i. 241.

He

He that wanders about the world sees new forms of human misery, and if he chances to meet an old friend, meets a face darkened with troubles.

On Tuesday night we came hither; yesterday I took some care of myself, and to-day I am *quite polite.* I have been taking a view of all that could be shewn me, and find that all very near to nothing [1]. You have often heard me complain of finding myself disappointed by books of travels [2]; I am afraid travel itself will end likewise in disappointment. One town, one country, is very like another: civilized nations have the same customs, and barbarous nations have the same nature: there are indeed minute discriminations both of places and of manners, which perhaps are not wanting of curiosity, but which a traveller seldom stays long enough to investigate and compare. The dull utterly neglect them, the acute see a little, and supply the rest with fancy and conjecture.

I shall set out again to-morrow, but I shall not, I am afraid, see Alnwick, for Dr. Percy is not there. I hope to lodge to-morrow night at Berwick, and the next at Edinburgh, where I shall direct Mr. Drummond [3], bookseller at Ossian's head, to take care of my letters.

I hope the little dears are all well, and that my dear master and mistress may go somewhither, but wherever you go do not forget,

Madam,

Your most humble servant,

I am pretty well.   SAM: JOHNSON.

---

[1] Newcastle is 271 miles from London. Johnson had spent five days on the journey, sleeping on Friday at Stilton, on Saturday at Doncaster, on Sunday at York, and on Monday at Northallerton. Pennant, who visited Newcastle the year before Johnson, describes it as 'a vast town. The lower street and *chares*, or alleys, are extremely narrow, dirty, and in general ill-built. The Keelmen are a mutinous race, for which reason the town is always garrisoned. In the upper part are several handsome streets.'

Tour in Scotland, ed. 1776, ii. 303. Wesley who was in the town when the news reached it of the Young Pretender's victory at Prestonpans gives a curious account of the general alarm. Three of the gates were walled up, the walls were mounted with cannon, while most of the best houses in the street outside the walls, in which he lodged, were left without furniture or inhabitants. *Wesley's Journal*, i. 518.

[2] See *ante*, p. 165.

[3] For 'old Mr. Drummond the bookseller' see *Life*, ii. 26 : v. 385.

August 15 [1].

Thus far I had written at Newcastle. I forgot to send it. I am now at Edinburgh ; and have been this day running about. I run pretty well.

319.

To James Boswell.

[Edinburgh], August 14, 1773. Published in the *Life*, ii. 266.

320.

To Mrs. Thrale [2].

DEAR MADAM,   Edinburgh, August 17, 1773.

On the 13th, I left Newcastle, and in the afternoon came to Alnwick, where we were treated with great civility by the Duke : I went through the apartments, walked on the wall, and climbed the towers [3]. That night we lay at Belford, and on the next night came to Edinburgh. On Sunday (15th) I went to the English chapel. After dinner, Dr. Robertson came in, and promised to shew me the place. On Monday I saw their public buildings : the cathedral, which I told Robertson I wished to see because it had once been a church [4], the courts of justice, the parliament-house, the advocates' library, the repository of records, the college and its library, and the palace, particularly the old tower where the king of Scotland seized David Rizzio in the queen's presence. Most of their buildings are very mean ;

---

[1] August 15, which was Sunday, is probably a mistake for the 16th, Monday, on which day Johnson did run about Edinburgh. *Life*, v. 39.

[2] *Piozzi Letters*, i. 108.

[3] Alnwick is 304 miles from London. See *Life*, iii. 271, for 'a scene of too much heat between Dr. Johnson and Dr. Percy' about Pennant's description of Alnwick. 'The Duke' was the first Duke of Northumberland, Sir Hugh Smithson, who had married the great-granddaughter of the eleventh and last Earl of Northumberland, and had assumed the name of Percy. See the *Grenville Papers*, iii. 329, for a curious account of the way in which Lord Chatham was compelled to give the Dukedom. Belford, Johnson's next halting-place, is 319 miles, and Edinburgh 388 miles from London.

[4] 'Come (said Dr. Johnson jocularly to Principal Robertson) let me see what was once a church.' *Life*, v. 41. St. Giles's was at this time divided into four divisions ; the partitions have in late years been swept away, so that Johnson would now probably allow that it is once more a church.

and

and the whole town bears some resemblance to the old part of Birmingham.

Boswell has very handsome and spacious rooms; level with the ground on one side of the house, and on the other four stories high [1].

At dinner on Monday were the Duchess of Douglas [2], an old lady, who talks broad Scotch with a paralytick voice, and is scarce understood by her own countrymen; the Lord Chief Baron [3], Sir Adolphus Oughton [4], and many more. At supper there was such a conflux of company that I could scarcely support the tumult. I have never been well in the whole journey, and am very easily disordered.

This morning I saw at breakfast Dr. Blacklock, the blind poet, who does not remember to have seen light, and is read to, by

[1] Boswell's house was in James's Court. Hume had occupied a flat in the same pile of building—*land* as it is called in Edinburgh—up to the spring of the previous year. *Life*, v. 22; *Letters of D. Hume to Strahan*, p. 118, and *Footsteps of Dr. Johnson in Scotland*, p. 74.

[2] Mrs. Sharpe of Hoddam, who was one of the company, said that 'the impression left on her mind of Johnson was summed up in the laconic verdict of Mrs. Boswell. "He was a great brute." The Duchess of Douglas was there with all her diamonds. She was notable among those of her own rank for her ostentation and her illiteracy. Johnson reserved his attentions during the whole evening almost exclusively for her. The pity was that they did not fall out. The Doctor missed her rebuff and she could be uncommonly vulgar.' Mrs. Sharpe's 'most humorous recollections of the scene were' she says 'the efforts of Boswell, as their go-between, to translate the unintelligible gaucherie of her lady-ship into palatable common-places for his guest's ear.' *Reminiscences of Old Edinburgh* by Sir

Daniel Wilson, ed. 1878, i. 255. See *Life*, v. 43, *n.* 4.

[3] Scotland had at this time a Court of Exchequer with a Chief Baron and four other Barons. The chief Baron was named Ord. It was his daughter who chalked on the wall of Hume's house ' St. David's Street,' and so gave that new street its name. *Letters of Hume to Strahan*, p. 251.

[4] Oughton was Deputy Commander-in-Chief in Scotland. *Life*, v. 45. On November 15 of this year he presided at a general meeting of the Revolution Club, 'and proposed that on purpose to cherish in the minds of the people a just sense of the advantages derived to them from the glorious Revolution .. the members of the Club should for the future on the 15th of November walk in procession to church, where a sermon should be preached on Revolution principles. This proposal was unanimously agreed to.' *Scots Magazine*, 1773, p. 613. In less than twenty years, by the disorders in France, the word *Revolution* in England was entirely to lose its character.

a poor

a poor scholar, in Latin, Greek, and French.   He was originally
a poor scholar himself.   I looked on him with reverence[1].   To-
morrow our journey begins; I know not when I shall write
again.   I am but poorly.

I am, &c.,

Sam: Johnson.

321.

To Mrs. Thrale[2].

Dear Madam,   Banff[3], August 25, 1773.

It has so happened that though I am perpetually thinking
on you, I could seldom find opportunity to write; I have in
fourteen days sent only one letter; you must consider the fatigues
of travel, and the difficulties encountered in a strange country.

August 18th, I passed, with Boswell, the Frith of Forth, and
began our journey; in the passage we observed an island, which
I persuaded my companions to survey.   We found it a rock
somewhat troublesome to climb, about a mile long, and half
a mile broad; in the middle were the ruins of an old fort, which
had on one of the stones—Maria Re. 1564.   It had been only
a blockhouse one story high.   I measured two apartments, of
which the walls were entire, and found them twenty-seven feet
long, and twenty-three broad[4].   The rock had some grass and
many thistles, both cows and sheep were grazing.   There was
a spring of water.   The name is Inchkeith.   Look on your maps.
This visit took about an hour.   We pleased ourselves with being
in a country all our own, and then went back to the boat, and
landed at Kinghorn, a mean town, and travelling through Kirk-
aldie[5], a very long town meanly built, and Cowpar, which

---

[1] 'Dr. Johnson received Dr. Blacklock with a most humane compla-
cency.   "Dear Dr. Blacklock, I am
glad to see you."'   *Life,* v. 47.
Hume magnified him as the Pindar
of Scotland.   Burton's *Hume,* ii. 32.

[2] *Piozzi Letters,* i. 110.

[3] 'We found at Banff but an indifferent inn.   Dr. Johnson wrote a
long letter to Mrs. Thrale.   I wondered to see him write so much so
easily.   He verified his own doctrine,
that "a man may always write when

he will set himself doggedly to it."'
Life, v. 109.

[4] With the remains of the fort a
light-house was built.   *Life,* v. 55.

[5] In Kirkcaldy Adam Smith was
born on June 5, 1723.   Hither he
returned in 1766, and lived in great
retirement for nearly ten years with
study, as he said, for his business,
and long solitary walks by the sea-
side for his amusements.   Here he
wrote his *Wealth of Nations.   Letters of Hume to Strahan,* p. 353.

I could

I could not see because it was night, we came late to St. Andrew's, the most ancient of the Scotch universities, and once the see of the Primate of Scotland [1]. The inn was full, but lodgings were provided for us at the house of the professor of rhetorick, a man of elegant manners, who showed us, in the morning, the poor remains of a stately cathedral, demolished in Knox's reformation [2], and now only to be imaged by tracing its foundation, and contemplating the little ruins that are left. Here was once a religious house. Two of the vaults or cellars of the subprior are even yet entire. In one of them lives an old woman, who claims an hereditary residence in it, boasting that her husband was the sixth tenant of this gloomy mansion, in a lineal descent, and claims by her marriage with this lord of the cavern an alliance with the Bruces. Mr. Boswell staid a while to interrogate her, because he understood her language ; she told him, that she and her cat lived together ; that she had two sons some where, who might perhaps be dead ; that when there were quality in the town notice was taken of her, and that now she was neglected, but did not trouble them. Her habitation contained all that she had ; her turf for fire was laid in one place, and her balls of coal dust in another, but her bed seemed to be clean. Boswell asked her if she never heard any noises, but she could tell him of nothing supernatural, though she often wandered in the night among the graves and ruins, only she had sometimes notice by dreams of the death of her relations. We then viewed the remains of a castle on the margin of the sea, in which the archbishops resided, and in which Cardinal Beatoun was killed.

The professors who happened to be resident in the vacation made a publick dinner, and treated us very kindly and respectfully. They shewed us their colleges, in one of which there is a library that for luminousness and elegance may vie at least

[1] Cupar is 30 miles, and St. Andrew's 37 miles, from Edinburgh. The Professor at whose house they were lodged was Dr. Watson, the author of a *History of Philip II. Life*, v. 58.

[2] 'Dr. Johnson was affected with a strong indignation, while he beheld the ruins of religious magnificence. I happened to ask where John Knox was buried. Dr. Johnson burst out, ' I hope in the highway. I have been looking at his reformations.'' *Life*, v. 61.

with

with the new edifice at Streatham ¹. But learning seems not to prosper among them ; one of their colleges has been lately alienated, and one of their churches lately deserted. An experiment was made of planting a shrubbery in the church, but it did not thrive ².

Why the place should thus fall to decay I know not ; for education, such as is here to be had, is sufficiently cheap. Their term, or, as they call it, their session, lasts seven months in the year, which the students of the highest rank and greatest expence may pass here for twenty pounds, in which are included board, lodging, books, and the continual instruction of three professors ³.

20th, We left St. Andrew's, well satisfied with our reception, and, crossing the Frith of Tay, came to Dundee, a dirty, despicable town ⁴. We passed afterwards through Aberbrothick, famous once for an abbey, of which there are only a few fragments left, but those fragments testify that the fabrick was once of great extent, and of stupendous magnificence ⁵. Two of the towers are yet standing, though shattered ; into one of

---

¹ 'It was the library of St. Mary's College which they saw. 'The doctor by whom it was shewn hoped to irritate or subdue my English vanity by telling me that we had no such repository of books in England.' Johnson's *Works*, ix. 5. Round the library at Streatham were hanging thirteen portraits by Reynolds of Mr. and Mrs. Thrale and their friends. 'It was in this room that the family lived. It used to be the parlour, and there they breakfasted, &c.' Nine years later Johnson was to make his 'parting use' of it, and in the prayer which he composed to mention 'the comforts and conveniences which he had enjoyed in that place.' *Life*, iv. 158, and Prior's *Malone*, p. 259.

² Of the library of St. Salvator's College 'the key,' says Boswell, 'could not be found, for Professor Hill, who was out of town, had taken it with him.' *Life*, v. 65. It was St.

Leonard's College which had been lately alienated, and it was in one of the buildings which had belonged to it that Johnson and Boswell were lodged. The church which had been lately deserted was the College chapel.

³ 'St. Andrew's seems to be a place eminently adapted to study and education. . . . The students, however, are represented as, at this time, not exceeding a hundred. I saw no reason for imputing their paucity to the present professors.' Johnson's *Works*, ix. 4.

⁴ Johnson in his published narrative spares the feelings of the citizens, for he merely says :—'We stopped awhile at Dundee, where I remember nothing remarkable.' *Ib.* p. 8.

⁵ 'I should scarcely have regretted my journey, had it afforded nothing more than the sight of Aberbrothick.' *Ib.* p. 9.

them

them Boswell climbed, but found the stairs broken: the way into the other we did not see, and had not time to search; I believe it might be ascended, but the top, I think, is open.

We lay at Montrose, a neat[1] place, with a spacious area for the market, and an elegant town-house.

21st, We travelled towards Aberdeen, another University, and in the way dined at Lord Monboddo's, the Scotch judge, who has lately written a strange book about the origin of language, in which he traces monkeys up to men, and says that in some countries the human species have tails like other beasts. He enquired for these long-tailed men of Banks, and was not well pleased that they had not been found in all his peregrination. He talked nothing of this to me, and I hope we parted friends; for we agreed pretty well, only we disputed in adjusting the claims of merit between a shopkeeper of London, and a savage of the American wildernesses. Our opinions were, I think, maintained on both sides without full conviction; Monboddo declared boldly for the savage, and I, perhaps for that reason, sided with the citizen[2].

We came late to Aberdeen, where I found my dear mistress's letter, and learned that all our little people were happily recovered of the measles. Every part of your letter was pleasing[3].

---

[1] When last century a town was called *neat* the force of praise was almost exhausted. What the term meant is shown in Johnson's narrative where he describes Montrose as 'well-built, airy and clean.' *Ib.* p. 9. Montrose by the direct road was 70 miles from Edinburgh.

[2] 'Dr. Johnson was much pleased with Lord Monboddo to-day. He said, he would have pardoned him for a few paradoxes, when he found he had so much that was good : but that, from his appearance in London, he thought him all paradox; which would not do. He observed that his lordship had talked no paradoxes to-day. "And as to the savage and the London shopkeeper, (said he) I don't know but I might have taken the side of

the savage equally, had any body else taken the side of the shopkeeper." ' *Life*, v. 83. For Lord Monboddo's strange opinions see *ib.* ii. 74; v. 46, and *Footsteps of Dr. Johnson in Scotland*, p. 111. Banks (afterwards Sir Joseph Banks) had in 1768 accompanied Captain Cook in his first voyage round the world. *Ib.* v. 328, *n.* 2.

[3] Aberdeen is 106 miles from Edinburgh, and 494 from London. Thirteen years later the letters from London to Aberdeen were six days on the road (*Scottish Notes and Queries*, i. 31) ; perhaps in 1773 they were still longer. The next letters which Johnson received were at Glasgow, nearly ten weeks later.

There

There are two cities of the name of Aberdeen : the old town, built about a mile inland, once the see of a bishop, which contains the King's College, and the remains of the cathedral, and the new town, which stands, for the sake of trade, upon a frith or arm of the sea, so that ships rest against the key[1].

The two cities have their separate magistrates, and the two colleges are in effect two universities, which confer degrees independently on each other[2].

New Aberdeen is a large town, built almost wholly of that granite which is used for the new pavement in London[3], which, hard as it is, they square with very little difficulty. Here I first saw the women in plaids[4]. The plaid makes at once a hood and cloak, without cutting or sewing, merely by the manner of

[1] Johnson in his *Dictionary* gives the word both under *Key* and *Quay*. Down to the present year (1891) the two cities have been distinct, each having its own Town Council ; that of the New Town elected by popular vote, but that of the Old Town the same self-elective body that, on the Abolition of Episcopacy, replaced the Bishop's Consistory Court. The oldest charter either city can show is one of 1189 granting right of markets &c. to ('New') Aberdeen. Aberdeen on Don would be naturally called the Old Town, when Aberdeen on Dee had been rebuilt after its burning about 1330 by the English[a].

[2] King's College and Marischal College, which were each a University in itself, were incorporated into one body in 1860.

[3] 'The paving of the streets of London has enabled the owners of some barren rocks on the coast of Scotland to draw a rent from what never afforded any before.' *Wealth of Nations*, ed. 1811, i. 226. William Hutton in his *Journey to London in 1784* (p. 16), describing the improve-

ments made in the previous thirty-five years, says :—'Every street and passage in the whole city and its environs has been paved in one regular and convenient style ; an expense equal in value to the whole dominions of some sovereign princes.' Pennant says that 'the small pieces of granite for the middle of the streets are put on board for seven shillings per ton, the long stones at tenpence per foot.' *Tour in Scotland*, ed. 1774, i. 125.

[4] Ramsay of Ochtertyre says that in 1747 when he first knew Edinburgh, nine-tenths of the ladies there still wore plaids. A few years later, he adds, 'One could hardly see a lady in that piece of dress. In the course of seven or eight years the very servant-girls were ashamed of being seen in that ugly antiquated garb.' *Scotland and Scotsmen in the Eighteenth Century*, ii. 88. Johnson apparently thought that it was a Highland dress only ; in his *Dictionary* he defines *plaid* as 'an outer loose weed worn much by the highlanders in Scotland.'

[a] This information I owe to my friend Mr. John Wight Duff, B.A., of Pembroke College, Oxford.

drawing

drawing the opposite sides over the shoulders. The maids at the inns run over the house barefoot, and children, not dressed in rags, go without shoes or stockings. Shoes are indeed not yet in universal use, they came late into this country. One of the professors told us, as we were mentioning a fort built by Cromwell, that the country owed much of its present industry to Cromwell's soldiers. They taught us, said he, to raise cabbage and make shoes. How they lived without shoes may yet be seen ; but in the passage through villages, it seems to him that surveys their gardens, that when they had not cabbage they had nothing[1].

Education is here of the same price as at St. Andrews, only the session is but from the 1st of November to the 1st of April. The academical buildings seem rather to advance than decline. They shewed their libraries, which were not very splendid, but some manuscripts were so exquisitely penned that I wished my dear mistress to have seen them. I had an unexpected pleasure, by finding an old acquaintance now professor of physick in the King's College[2]: we were on both sides glad of the interview, having not seen nor perhaps thought on one another for many years ; but we had no emulation, nor had either of us risen to the other's envy, and our old kindness was easily renewed. I hope we shall never try the effect of so long an absence, and that I shall always be,

Madam,

Your, &c.,

SAM: JOHNSON.

322.

To Mrs. Thrale[3].

DEAR MADAM,   Inverness, Aug. 28, 1773.

August 23rd, I had the honour of attending the Lord Provost of Aberdeen, and was presented with the freedom of the city, not in a gold box, but in good Latin. Let me pay Scotland one just praise ! there was no officer gaping for a fee ; this could

---

[1] See *Footsteps of Dr. Johnson in Scotland*, pp. 35, 44.

[2] Sir Alexander Gordon. *Life*, v. 86.

[3] *Piozzi Letters*, i. 117.

Inverness by the road through Banff and Aberdeen is 221 miles from Edinburgh.

have

have been said of no city on the English side of the Tweed. I wore my patent of freedom *pro more* in my hat, from the new town to the old, about a mile[1]. I then dined with my friend the professor of physick at his house, and saw the King's College. Boswell was very angry that the Aberdeen professors would not talk[2]. When I was at the English church in Aberdeen I happened to be espied by Lady Di. Middleton[3], whom I had sometime seen in London ; she told what she had seen to Mr. Boyd, Lord Errol's brother, who wrote us an invitation to Lord Errol's house, called Slanes Castle. We went thither on the next day (24th of August), and found a house, not old, except but one tower, built upon the margin of the sea upon a rock, scarce accessible from the sea ; at one corner a tower makes a perpendicular continuation of the lateral surface of the rock, so that it is impracticable to walk round ; the house inclosed a square court, and on all sides within the court is a piazza or gallery two stories high[4]. We came in as we were invited to dinner, and after dinner offered to go ; but Lady Errol sent us word by Mr. Boyd, that if we went before Lord Errol came home we must never be forgiven, and ordered out the coach to shew us two curiosities. We were first conducted by Mr. Boyd to Dunbuys, or the yellow rock. Dunbuys is a rock

---

[1] 'Dr. Johnson was much pleased with this mark of attention, and received it very politely. There was a pretty numerous company assembled. It was striking to hear all of them drinking " Dr. Johnson ! Dr. Johnson !" in the town-hall of Aberdeen, and then to see him with his burgess-ticket, or diploma, in his hat, which he wore as he walked along the street, according to the usual custom.' *Life,* v. 90. John Wesley, who a year earlier had been made a freeman of Perth, in like manner praised the Latinity of his diploma. 'I doubt,' he wrote, ' whether any diploma from the City of London be more pompous or expressed in better Latin.' Wesley's *Journal,* iii. 461. *Pompous,* no doubt, he used much in the sense given in Johnson's Dictionary – *splendid, magnificent, grand.* For Johnson's burgess-ticket see *Life,* v. 90, *n.* 2, and *Footsteps of Dr. Johnson in Scotland,* pp. 18, 116.

[2] 'We had little or no conversation in the morning ; now [i. e. at dinner] we were but barren. The professors seemed afraid to speak.' *Life,* v. 92. The Glasgow professors were almost as timid. *Ib.* p. 371.

[3] She was, perhaps, of the family of the Earl of Middleton who in 1693 threw in his lot with James II. Mr. Boyd, Lord Errol's brother, was also a Jacobite, and had been ' out in the '45.' *Ib.* p. 99.

[4] The house has been rebuilt.

consisting

consisting of two protuberances, each perhaps one hundred yards round, joined together by a narrow neck, and separated from the land by a very narrow channel or gully. These rocks are the haunts of sea-fowl, whose clang, though this is not their season, we heard at a distance. The eggs and the young are gathered here in great numbers at the time of breeding. There is a bird here called a coote, which though not much bigger than a duck lays a larger egg than a goose. We went then to see the Buller or Boulloir of Buchan: Buchan is the name of the district, and the Buller is a small creek or gulf into which the sea flows through an arch of the rock. We walked round it, and saw it black at a great depth [1]. It has its name from the violent ebullition of the water, when high winds or high tides drive it up the arch into the bason. Walking a little further I spied some boats, and told my companions that we would go into the Buller and examine it. There was no danger; all was calm; we went through the arch, and found ourselves in a narrow gulf surrounded by craggy rocks, of height not stupendous, but to a Mediterranean [2] visitor uncommon. On each side was a cave. of which the fishermen knew not the extent, in which smugglers hide their goods [3], and sometimes parties of pleasure take a dinner.

I am, &c.,

SAM: JOHNSON.

I think I grow better.

[1] 'We walked round this monstrous cauldron. In some places, the rock is very narrow; and on each side there is a sea deep enough for a man of war to ride in; so that it is somewhat horrid to move along. However, there is earth and grass upon the rock, and a kind of road marked out by the print of feet; so that one makes it out pretty safely: yet it alarmed me to see Dr. Johnson striding irregularly along.' *Life*, v. 100. 'No man can see the Buller of Buchan with indifference, who has either sense of danger or delight in rarity. . . . He that ventures to look downward sees that, if his foot should slip, he must fall from his dreadful elevation upon stones on one side or into the water on the other.' Johnson's *Works*, ix. 16. Burns thus mentions the place in his *Epistle to Robert Graham :—*

'The stubborn Tories dare to die;
As soon the rooted oaks would fly
Before th' approaching fellers :
The Whigs come on like Ocean's roar,
When all his wintry billows pour
Against the Buchan Bullers.'

[2] Johnson in his *Dictionary* gives as the second meaning of *mediterranean*, 'inland; remote from the sea.'

[3] When I visited this spot nearly

323.

To Mrs. Thrale[1].

DEAREST MADAM,   Skie, Sept. 6, 1773.

I am now looking on the sea from a house of Sir Alexander Macdonald[2] in the isle of Skie. Little did I once think of seeing this region of obscurity, and little did you once expect a salutation from this verge of European life. I have now the pleasure of going where nobody goes, and seeing what nobody sees. Our design is to visit several of the smaller islands, and then pass over to the south-west of Scotland.

I returned from the sight of Buller's Buchan to Lord Errol's, and, having seen his library, had for a time only to look upon the sea, which rolled between us and Norway[3]. Next morning, August 25th, we continued our journey through a country not uncultivated, but so denuded of its woods, that in all this journey I had not travelled an hundred yards between hedges, or seen five trees fit for the carpenter. A few small plantations may be found, but I believe scarcely any thirty years old; at least, as I do not forget to tell, they are all posteriour to the Union[4].

forty years ago I was told that it was often called 'Lord Errol's punch-bowl.' The tradition ran that one of the Earls had seized there a smuggler's cargo of whisky and had had the kegs emptied into the water.

[1] *Piozzi Letters*, i. 120.

[2] See *post*, pp. 244, 252.

[3] 'From the windows the eye wanders over the sea that separates Scotland from Norway, and when the winds beat with violence, must enjoy all the terrifick grandeur of the tempestuous ocean. I would not for my amusement wish for a storm; but as storms, whether wished or not, will sometimes happen, I may say, without violation of humanity, that I should willingly look out upon them from Slanes Castle.' Johnson's *Works*, ix. 15. 'The King of Denmark is Lord Errol's nearest neighbour on the north-east.' *Life*, v. 100. The latitude of Slains Castle is a very little south of the northernmost point of Denmark.

[4] 'To vex the poor Scotch out of mere malignity. Johnson was a real *true-born Englishman*. He hated the Scotch, the French, the Dutch, the Hanoverians, and had the greatest contempt for all other European Nations: such were his early prejudices, which he never attempted to conquer.' BARETTI. 'From the banks of the Tweed to St. Andrews I had never seen a single tree which I did not believe to have grown up far within the present century.' Johnson's *Works*, ix. 7. 'Dr. Johnson persevered in his wild allegation, that he questioned if there was a tree between Edinburgh and the English border older than himself. I assured him he was mistaken, and suggested that the proper punishment would be that he should receive a stripe at

This

This day we dined with a country gentleman, who has in his grounds the remains of a Druid's temple, which when it is complete is nothing more than a circle or double circle of stones, placed at equal distances, with a flat stone, perhaps an altar, at a certain point, and a stone taller than the rest at the opposite point. The tall stone is erected I think at the south. Of these circles there are many in all the unfrequented parts of the island. The inhabitants of these parts respect them as memorials of the sepulture of some illustrious person. Here I saw a few trees [1]. We lay at Banff.

August 26th, We dined at Elgin, where we saw the ruins of a noble cathedral; the chapter-house is yet standing [2]. A great part of Elgin is built with small piazzas to the lower story. We went on to Foris, over the heath where Macbeth met the witches, but had no adventure [3]: only in the way we saw for the first time some houses with fruit trees about them. The improvements of the Scotch are for immediate profit, they do not yet think it quite worth their while to plant what will not produce something to be eaten or sold in a very little time. We rested at Foris.

A very great proportion of the people are barefoot, and if one may judge by the rest of the dress, to send out boys without

every tree above a hundred years old, that was found within that space. He laughed, and said, "I believe I might submit to it for a *baubee!*"' *Life*, ii. 311.

[1] 'We dined this day at the house of Mr. Fraser of Strichen, who showed us in his grounds some stones yet standing of a druidical circle, and what I began to think more worthy of notice, some forest-trees of full growth.' Johnson's *Works*, ix. 17.

[2] Banff by the direct road was 44 miles from Aberdeen, and Elgin 33 miles from Banff. For the curious suppression in Johnson's account of the ruins at Elgin, see *Life*, vol. vi. Addenda, p. xxxiv. At the inn at Elgin they 'fared but ill; Dr. John-

son said that this was the first time he had seen a dinner in Scotland that he could not eat.' *Ib.* v. 115. See *Footsteps of Dr. Johnson in Scotland*, p. 130, for the explanation of this bad dinner.

[3] Hannah More says that the following year Johnson told her 'that when he and Boswell stopt a night at the spot (as they imagined) where the Weird Sisters appeared to Macbeth, the idea so worked upon their enthusiasm, that it quite deprived them of rest. However they learnt the next morning, to their mortification, that they had been deceived, and were quite in another part of the country.' H. More's *Memoirs*, i. 50.

shoes

shoes into the streets or ways[1]; there are however more beggars than I have ever seen in England, they beg if not silently yet very modestly[2].

Next day we came to Nairn, a miserable town, but a royal burgh, of which the chief annual magistrate is styled Lord Provost[3]. In the neighbourhood we saw the castle of the old Thane of Cawdor. There is one ancient tower with its battlements and winding stairs yet remaining; the rest of the house is, though not modern, of later erection[4].

On the 28th, we went to Fort George, which is accounted the most regular fortification in the island[5]. The major of artillery walked with us round the walls, and shewed us the principles upon which every part was constructed, and the way in which it could be defended. We dined with the Governor Sir Eyre Coote[6] and his officers. It was a very pleasant and instructive day, but nothing puts my honoured Mistress out of my mind.

[1] A writer in the *Gentleman's Magazine*, 1802, p. 1111, asks Mrs. Piozzi to explain how this unintelligible passage stands in the original. She replied that as the passage stands in Murphy's edition of Johnson's *Works*, 'the words are well arranged, and the paragraph cleared from all embarrassment. That nevertheless in the original not a particle could be found different from her publication.' *Ib.*, 1803, p. 607. Murphy prints the passage as follows, having apparently conjecturally emended it :— 'A very great proportion of the people are barefoot : shoes are not yet considered as necessaries of life. It is still the custom to send out the sons of gentlemen without them into the streets and ways.' Johnson's *Works*, ed. 1796, xii. 360.

[2] 'In Edinburgh the proportion of beggars is, I think, not less than in London, and in the smaller places it is far greater than in English towns of the same extent.' *Works*, ix. 9.

[3] 'At Nairn we may fix the verge of the Highlands; for here I first saw peat fires and first heard the Erse language.' *Ib.* p. 21. I am informed that 'at each meeting of the Convention of Royal Burghs the Provost of Elgin formally claims to be called the Lord Provost, but that it is not known that Nairn has ever put forward the claim.'

[4] Johnson passes over in silence his visit to Cawdor Manse, where he was entertained by Lord Macaulay's great-uncle, and where he met the Rev. Mr. Grant, the grandfather of Colonel Grant who, with Captain Speke, discovered the sources of the Nile. *Life*, v. 118, and *Footsteps of Dr. Johnson in Scotland*, p. 135.

[5] Wolfe, who saw it in 1751, when it was partly made, writes :—'I believe there is still work for six or seven years to do. When it is finished one may venture to say (without saying much) that it will be the most considerable fortress, and the best situated in Great Britain.' Wright's *Life of Major-General James Wolfe*, p. 178.

[6] Seven years later Coote com-

At

At night we came to Inverness, the last considerable town in the north, where we staid all the next day, for it was Sunday[1], and saw the ruins of what is called Macbeth's castle[2]. It never was a large house, but was strongly situated. From Inverness we were to travel on horseback.

August 30th, we set out with four horses[3]. We had two High-landers to run by us, who were active, officious, civil, and hardy. Our journey was for many miles along a military way made upon the banks of Lough Ness, a water about eighteen miles long, but not I think half a mile broad[4]. Our horses were not bad, and the way was very pleasant; the rock out of which the road was cut was covered with birch trees, fern, and heath. The

manded the army which defeated Hyder Ali at Porto Novo. 'Among the native soldiers his name was great and his influence unrivalled. Nor is he yet forgotten by them. Now and then a white-bearded old sepoy may still be found who loves to talk of Porto Novo and Pollilore. It is but a short time since one of those aged men came to present a memorial to an English officer, who holds one of the highest employ-ments in India. A print of Coote hung in the room. The veteran re-cognised at once that face and figure which he had not seen for more than half a century, and forgetting his salam to the living, halted, drew himself up, lifted his hand, and with solemn reverence paid his military obeisance to the dead.' Macaulay's *Essays*, ed. 1843, iii. 385. It was to Coote and his officers that Johnson, as he afterwards owned to Boswell, 'talked ostentatiously' about granu-lating gunpowder, just as many years later Johnson's editor, Mr. Croker, talked about percussion caps to the Duke of Wellington. John-son perhaps had picked up his information in writing the article on *granulation* in his *Dictionary*.

[1] The Rev. Mr. Grant, who supped with the two travellers this Sun-day, 'used to relate that Johnson, who was in high spirits,' gave an account of the kangaroo, which had lately been discovered in New South Wales, 'and volunteered an imitation of the animal. The company stared; Mr. Grant said nothing could be more ludicrous than the appearance of a tall, heavy, grave-looking man like Dr. Johnson standing up to mimic the shape and motions of a kangaroo. He stood erect, put out his hands like feelers, and gathering up the tails of his huge brown coat so as to resemble the pouch of the animal made two or three vigorous bounds across the room.' Boswell's *Journal*, ed. by R. Carruthers, p. 96.

[2] Of this building nothing re-mains.

[3] 'We might have taken a chaise to Fort Augustus, but, had we not hired horses at Inverness, we should not have found them afterwards : so we resolved to begin here to ride. We had three horses, for Dr. John-son, myself, and Joseph, and one which carried our portmanteaus.' *Life*, v. 131.

[4] Loch Ness is twenty-three miles long, one and three-tenths broad. *Encyclo. Brit.* xiv. 217.

lake below was beating its bank by a gentle wind, and the rocks beyond the water on the right stood sometimes horrid and wild, and sometimes opened into a kind of bay, in which there was a spot of cultivated ground yellow with corn. In one part of the way we had trees on both sides for perhaps half a mile.—Such a length of shade perhaps Scotland cannot shew in any other place.

You are not to suppose that here are to be any more towns or inns. We came to a cottage which they call the general's hut[1], where we alighted to dine, and had eggs and bacon, and mutton, with wine, rum, and whiskey. I had water.

At a bridge over the river, which runs into the Ness, the rocks rise on three sides, with a direction almost perpendicular, to a great height; they are in part covered with trees, and exhibit a kind of dreadful magnificence;—standing like the barriers of nature placed to keep different orders of being in perpetual separation. Near this bridge is the Fall of Fiers[2], a famous cataract, of which, by clambering over the rocks, we obtained a view. The water was low, and therefore we had only the pleasure of knowing that rain would make it at once pleasing and formidable; there will then be a mighty flood, foaming along a rocky channel, frequently obstructed by protuberances and exasperated by reverberation, at last precipitated with a sudden descent, and lost in the depth of a gloomy chasm.

We came somewhat late to Fort Augustus, where the lieutenant governor met us beyond the gates, and apologised that at that hour he could not, by the rules of a garrison, admit us otherwise than at a narrow door which only one can enter at a time. We were well entertained and well lodged, and next morning, after having viewed the fort, we pursued our journey.

Our way now lay over the mountains, which are not to be passed by climbing them directly, but by traversing[3], so that as we went forward we saw our baggage following us below in

[1] It was called after General Wade who had lodged there 'while he superintended the works upon the road.' It was eighteen miles from Inverness, near the modern Foyers Hotel. *Footsteps of Dr. Johnson in Scotland*, p. 150.

[2] It is commonly written Foyers.

[3] Johnson does not give *traverse* in this sense in his *Dictionary*.

a direction

a direction exactly contrary. There is in these ways much labour but little danger, and perhaps other places of which very terrifick representations are made are not in themselves more formidable. These roads have all been made by hewing the rock away with pickaxes, or bursting it with gunpowder [1]. The stones so separated are often piled loose as a wall by the way-side. We saw an inscription importing the year in which one of the regiments made two thousand yards of the road eastward [2].

After tedious travel of some hours we came to what I believe we must call a village, a place where there were three huts built of turf, at one of which we were to have our dinner and our bed, for we could not reach any better place that night. This place is called Enock in Glenmorrison [3]. The house in which we lodged was distinguished by a chimney, the rest had only a hole for the smoke. Here we had eggs, and mutton, and a chicken, and a sausage, and rum. In the afternoon tea was made by a very decent girl in a printed linen; she engaged me so much. that I made her a present of Cocker's arithmetick [4].

> I am, &c.,
>
> SAM: JOHNSON.

[1] 'To make this way the rock has been hewn to a level with labour that might have broken the persever-ance of a Roman legion.' *Works*, ix. 30.

[2] Mr. G. J. Campbell of Inver-ness has kindly made enquiries for me about the old road. It is known to the people of the Glen as the Turnings, and can still be traced. The site of the soldiers' camp can even be distinguished. But of the stone with the inscription on it no-thing is remembered by them. It was probably used for building purposes, or for a hearth-stone. An old shep-herd at Anoch remembers hearing 'the old Bard that was living there speak of the Green Officers' Graves, that is up a bit from our steading.' The new road, along which I drove in the summer of 1889, starts from Invermoriston on Loch Lomond, and following the course of the River Moriston avoids the mountain.

[3] Anoch or Aonach, in Glen-moriston, nine miles from Fort Au-gustus and forty-one from Inverness.

[4] 'One day, when we were dining at General Oglethorpe's, I ventured to interrogate Dr. Johnson. "But, Sir, is it not somewhat singular that you should *happen* to have *Cocker's Arithmetick* about you on your journey? What made you buy such a book at Inverness?" He gave me a very sufficient answer. "Why, Sir, if you are to have but one book with you upon a journey, let it be a book of science. When you have read through a book of entertainment, you know it, and it can do no more for you; but a book of science is in-exhaustible."' *Life*, v. 138. For Johnson's fondness for calculation, see *ib*. iii. 207.

To Mrs. Thrale [1].

DEAREST MADAM, Skie, Sept. 14, 1773.

The post, which comes but once a week into these parts, is so soon to go that I have not time to go on where I left off in my last letter. I have been several days in the island of Raarsa [2], and am now again in the isle of Skie, but at the other end of it.

Skie is almost equally divided between the two great families of Macdonald and Macleod, other proprietors having only small districts. The two great lords do not know within twenty square miles the contents of their own territories.

——[3] kept up but ill the reputation of Highland hospitality; we are now with Macleod, quite at the other end of the island, where there is a fine young gentleman and fine ladies [4]. The ladies are studying Earse. I have a cold, and am miserably deaf,

[1] *Piozzi Letters*, i. 126. This letter was written from Dunvegan Castle, where Johnson was the guest of Macleod of Macleod. The following table of his movements in Skye may be found convenient.

	Life.	*Works.*
Sept. 2-6.		
Armidale .	v. 147-156	ix. 45
Sept. 6-8.		
Corrichata-		
chin . .	„ 156-162	„ 49
Sept. 8-12.		
Raasay . .	„ 162-179	„ 54-62
Sept. 12-13.		
Portree and		
Kings-		
burgh .	„ 180-187	„ 63
Sept. 13-21.		
Dunvegan .	„ 207-234	„ 63-67
Sept. 21-23.		
Ulinish . .	„ 235-248	„ 67
Sept. 23-25.		
Talisker .	„ 250-256	„ 71
Sept. 25-28.		
Corrichata-		
chin . .	„ 257-265	„ 73
Sept. 28-Oct. 1.		
Ostig . .	„ 265-275	„ 73
Oct. 1-3.		
Armidale .	„ 275-279	„ 73

[2] Johnson in his *Journey* calls the island Raasay, as the name is now written; Boswell calls it Rasay. Johnson in his letter was perhaps following Buchanan, who spells it Raarsa.

[3] Sir Alexander Macdonald. For his inhospitality, see *Life*, v. 148, 415, *n.* 4, and *post*, p. 252.

[4] 'Lady Macleod, who had lived many years in England, was newly come hither with her son and four daughters, who knew all the arts of southern elegance, and all the modes of English economy.' Johnson's *Works*, ix. 63. The title which Lady Macleod bore was one of courtesy. Up to this time the wives of Highland lairds and also of Scotch judges were commonly addressed as *Lady*. Ramsay of Ochtertyre, speaking of the year 1769, says that 'Somebody asked Lord Auchinleck before his second marriage if the lady was to be called Mrs. Boswell, according to the modern fashion.' *Scotland and Scotsmen of the Eighteenth Century*, i. 173.

and

and am troublesome to Lady Macleod ; I force her to speak loud, but she will seldom speak loud enough.

Raarsa is an island about fifteen miles long and two broad, under the dominion of one gentleman who has three sons and ten daughters ; the eldest is the beauty of this part of the world, and has been polished at Edinburgh [1] : they sing and dance, and without expence have upon their table most of what sea, air, or earth can afford. I intended to have written about Raarsa, but the post will not wait longer than while I send my compliments to my dear master and little mistresses.

I am, &c.,

SAM: JOHNSON.

325.

To LORD ELIBANK.

Skie, September 14, 1773. Published in the *Life*, v. 182.

326.

To MRS. THRALE [2].

DEAREST MADAM,   Skie, Sept. 21, 1773 [3].

I am so vexed at the necessity of sending yesterday so short a letter, that I purpose to get a long letter beforehand by writing something every day, which I may the more easily do, as a cold makes me now too deaf to take the usual pleasure in conversation. Lady Macleod is very good to me [4], and the place at which we now are, is equal in strength of situation, in the wildness of

[1] See *post*, p. 257, and *Life*, v. 178.

[2] *Piozzi Letters*, i. 128.

[3] The date no doubt, in accordance with Johnson's general custom, came at the end of the letter. The opening lines show that he began to write on September 15—the day after his last letter was posted.

[4] 'September 16. Last night much care was taken of Dr. Johnson, who was still distressed by his cold. He had hitherto most strangely slept without a night-cap. Miss Macleod made him a large flannel one.' *Life*, v. 214. The following anecdote I had from Lady Macleod's grand-daughter when I visited Dunvegan. 'One day he had scolded the maid for not getting good peats, and had gone out in the rain to the stack to fetch in some himself. Lady Macleod went up to his room to see how he was, and found him in bed, with his wig turned inside out, and the wrong end foremost. On her return to the drawing-room she said, "I have often seen very plain people, but anything as ugly as Dr. Johnson, with his wig thus stuck on, I never have seen."' *Footsteps of Dr. Johnson in Scotland*, p. 3.

the

the adjacent country, and in the plenty and elegance of the domestick entertainment, to a castle in Gothick romance[1]. The sea with a little island is before us; cascades play within view. Close to the house is the formidable skeleton of an old castle probably Danish[2], and the whole mass of building stands upon a protuberance of rock, inaccessible till of late but by a pair of stairs[3] on the sea side, and secure in ancient times against any enemy that was likely to invade the kingdom of Skie.

Macleod has offered me an island[4]; if it were not too far off I should hardly refuse it: my island would be pleasanter than Brighthelmstone, if you and my master could come to it; but I cannot think it pleasant to live quite alone.

> Oblitusque meorum, obliviscendus et illis[5].

That I should be elated by the dominion of an island to forgetfulness of my friends at Streatham I cannot believe, and I hope never to deserve that they should be willing to forget me.

It has happened that I have been often recognised in my journey where I did not expect it. At Aberdeen I found one of my acquaintance professor of physick[6]; turning aside to dine with a country gentleman, I was owned at table by one who had seen me at a philosophical lecture[7]; at Macdonald's I was claimed by a naturalist, who wanders about the islands to pick up curiosities[8]; and I had once in London attracted the notice of Lady Macleod. I will now go on with my account[9].

The Highland girl made tea, and looked and talked not inelegantly; her father was by no means an ignorant or a weak man;

---

[1] *Gothick* last century is often the same in meaning as *mediæval* this century. *Mediæval* is not in Johnson's *Dictionary*.

[2] 'It is so nearly entire that it might have easily been made habitable, were there not an ominous tradition in the family that the owner shall not long outlive the reparation.' Johnson's *Works*, ix. 64. See *Life*, v. 233.

[3] It seems odd to find this staircase in Skye described as if it were in an Oxford College or the Temple.

[4] 'There is a beautiful little island in the Loch of Dunvegan, called *Isa*. McLeod said, he would give it to Dr. Johnson, on condition of his residing on it three months in the year; nay one month.' *Life*, v. 249.

[5] 'Your friends forgetting, by your friends forgot.'
FRANCIS. Horace, *Epis.* I. xi. 9.

[6] *Ante*, p. 235.

[7] *Life*, v. 108; *ante*, p. 186.

[8] *Life*, v. 149.

[9] He takes it up from p. 243, at Anoch.

there

there were books in the cottage, among which were some volumes of Prideaux's Connection[1]: this man's conversation we were glad of while we staid. He had been *out*, as they call it, in forty-five, and still retained his old opinions. He was going to America, because his rent was raised beyond what he thought himself able to pay.

At night our beds were made, but we had some difficulty in persuading ourselves to lie down in them, though we had put on our own sheets; at last we ventured, and I slept very soundly in the vale of Glenmorrison, amidst the rocks and mountains. Next morning our landlord liked us so well, that he walked some miles with us for our company, through a country so wild and barren that the proprietor does not, with all his pressure upon his tenants, raise more than four hundred pounds a-year for near one hundred square miles, or sixty thousand acres. He let us know that he had forty head of black cattle, an hundred goats, and an hundred sheep, upon a farm that he remembered let at five pounds a-year, but for which he now paid twenty[2]. He told us some stories of their march into England[3]. At last he left us, and we went forward, winding among mountains, sometimes green and sometimes naked, commonly so steep as not easily to be climbed by the greatest vigour and activity: our way was often crossed by little rivulets, and we were entertained with small streams trickling from the rocks, which after heavy rains must be tremendous torrents.

About noon we came to a small glen, so they call a valley, which compared with other places appeared rich and fertile; here our guides desired us to stop, that the horses might graze, for the journey was very laborious, and no more grass would be found. We made no difficulty of compliance, and I sat down to take notes on a green bank, with a small stream running at my

---

[1] 'Our landlord was a sensible fellow; he had learned his grammar, and Dr. Johnson justly observed, that " a man is the better for that as long as he lives."' *Life*, v. 135. See also Johnson's *Works*, ix. 31.

[2] Adam Smith shows that the Union had raised the price of cattle,

and that this rise had raised the value of all Highland estates. *Wealth of Nations*, ed. 1811, i. 309.

[3] 'As he narrated,' writes Boswell, 'the particulars of that ill-advised but brave attempt I could not refrain from tears.' *Life*, v. 140.

feet,

feet, in the midst of savage solitude, with mountains before me, and on either hand covered with heath. I looked around me, and wondered that I was not more affected, but the mind is not at all times equally ready to be put in motion[1]; if my mistress and master and Queeney had been there we should have produced some reflections among us, either poetical or philosophical, for though *solitude be the nurse of woe*[2], conversation is often the parent of remarks and discoveries.

In about an hour we remounted, and pursued our journey. The lake by which we had travelled for some time ended in a river, which we passed by a bridge, and came to another glen, with a collection of huts, called Auknashealds; the huts were generally built of clods of earth, held together by the intertexture of vegetable fibres, of which earth there are great levels in Scotland which they call mosses. Moss in Scotland is bog in Ireland, and moss-trooper is bog-trotter[3]: there was, however, one hut built of loose stones, piled up with great thickness into a strong though not solid wall. From this house we obtained some great pails of milk, and having brought bread with us, were very liberally regaled. The inhabitants, a very coarse[4] tribe, ignorant

[1] 'I sat down on a bank, such as a writer of romance might have delighted to feign. I had, indeed, no trees to whisper over my head ; but a clear rivulet streamed at my feet. The day was calm, the air soft, and all was rudeness, silence, and solitude. Before me, and on either side, were high hills, which, by hindering the eye from ranging, forced the mind to find entertainment for itself. Whether I spent the hour well, I know not ; for here I first conceived the thought of this narration.' Johnson's *Works*, ix. 36. For my attempt to discover this stream, see *Footsteps of Dr. Johnson in Scotland*, p. 156.

[2] 'The silent heart, which grief assails,
Treads soft and lonesome o'er the vales,
Sees daisies open, rivers run,

And seeks, as I have vainly done,
Amusing thought ; but learns to know
That solitude's the nurse of woe.'
PARNELL. *A Hymn to Contentment.*
Pope in his *Satires of Donne*, iv. 185, has 'wholesome solitude, the nurse of sense.'

[3] Moss-trooper is not in Johnson's *Dictionary*.

[4] Johnson in his *Dictionary* gives as the third meaning of *coarse*, 'rude, uncivil, rough of manners'; but he does not give any instance. It was also applied to weather at this time ; thus May 30, 1772, is described as 'a gloomy, hot morning ; coarse afternoon.'—*Gentleman's Magazine*, 1773, p. 158.

of any language but Earse, gathered so fast about us, that if we had not had Highlanders with us, they might have caused more alarm than pleasure[1]; they are called the Clan of Macrae.

We had been told that nothing gratified the Highlanders so much as snuff and tobacco[2], and had accordingly stored ourselves with both at Fort Augustus. Boswell opened his treasure, and gave them each a piece of tobacco roll. We had more bread than we could eat for the present, and were more liberal than provident. Boswell cut it in slices, and gave them an opportunity of tasting wheaten bread for the first time[3]. I then got some halfpence for a shilling, and made up the deficiencies of Boswell's distribution, who had given some money among the children. We then directed that the mistress of the stone house should be asked what we must pay her: she, who perhaps had never before sold any thing but cattle, knew not, I believe, well what to ask, and referred herself to us: we obliged her to make some demand, and one of the Highlanders settled the account with her at a shilling. One of the men advised her, with the cunning that clowns never can be without, to ask more; but she said that a shilling was enough. We gave her half a crown, and she offered part of it again. The Macraes were so well pleased with our behaviour, that they declared it the best day they had seen since the time of the old Laird of Macleod, who, I suppose, like us, stopped in their valley, as he was travelling to Skie.

We were mentioning this view of the Highlander's life at Macdonald's, and mentioning the Macraes with some degree of pity, when a Highland lady informed us that we might spare our tenderness, for she doubted not but the woman who supplied us with milk was mistress of thirteen or fourteen milch cows.

I cannot forbear to interrupt my narrative. Boswell, with some of his troublesome kindness, has informed this family and

---

[1] 'I observed to Dr. Johnson, it was much the same as being with a tribe of Indians. JOHNSON. "Yes, Sir; but not so terrifying."' *Life*, v. 142, and *Footsteps of Dr. Johnson in Scotland*, p. 162.

[2] Knox recorded a few years later that 'any stranger who cannot take a pinch of snuff or give one is looked upon with an evil eye.' J. Knox's *Tour through the Highlands in* 1786, p. 255.

[3] So uncommon was wheaten bread even a quarter of a century later that Dr. Garnett, after leaving Inverary, tasted none till he reached Inverness. T. Garnett's *Observations on a Tour through the Highlands*, 1800, ii. 12.

reminded

reminded me that the 18th of September is my birth-day[1]. The return of my birth-day, if I remember it, fills me with thoughts which it seems to be the general care of humanity to escape. I can now look back upon threescore and four years, in which little has been done, and little has been enjoyed ; a life diversified by misery, spent part in the sluggishness of penury[2], and part under the violence of pain, in gloomy discontent or importunate distress[3]. But perhaps I am better than I should have been if I had been less afflicted. With this I will try to be content.

In proportion as there is less pleasure in retrospective considerations, the mind is more disposed to wander forward into futurity; but at sixty-four what promises, however liberal, of imaginary good can futurity venture to make? yet something will be always promised, and some promises will always be credited. I am hoping and I am praying that I may live better in the time to come[4], whether long or short, than I have yet lived, and in the solace of that hope endeavour to repose. Dear Queeney's day is next[5], I hope she at sixty-four will have less to regret.

I will now complain no more, but tell my mistress of my travels.

After we left the Macraes we travelled on through a country like that which we passed in the morning. The Highlands are very uniform, for there is little variety in universal barrenness[6];

---

[1] 'Before breakfast, Dr. Johnson came up to my room to forbid me to mention that this was his birth-day ; but I told him I had done it already; at which he was displeased.' *Life,* v. 222. Johnson made the following record in his Diary :—' On last Saturday was my sixty-fourth birthday. I might perhaps have forgotten it had not Boswell told me of it ; and, what pleased me less, told the family at Dunvegan.' *Pr. and Med.,* p. 131. See *Life,* iii. 157, where Boswell four years later again offended Johnson by recalling his birthday, and *post,* Letter of September 16, 1783.

[2] 'Chill penury repressed their noble rage,

And froze the genial current of the soul.'
                    Gray's *Elegy.*

[3] 'Poor Johnson ! All this was too true.' BARETTI.

[4] ' He means little more than that he shall pray more, and go oftener to church.' BARETTI. On July 22 of this year Johnson had recorded :—' Whether I have not lived resolving till the possibility of performance is past, I know not. God help me, I will yet try.' *Pr. and Med.,* p. 130.

[5] She had kept hers the day before. See *Life,* iii. 157, *n.* 3.

[6] 'An eye accustomed to flowery pastures and waving harvests is astonished and repelled by this wide

the

the rocks, however, are not all naked, some have grass on their sides, and birches and alders on their tops, and in the vallies are often broad and clear streams, which have little depth, and commonly run very quick : the channels are made by the violence of the wintry floods ; the quickness of the stream is in proportion to the declivity of the descent, and the breadth of the channel makes the water shallow in a dry season.

There are red deer and roebucks in the mountains, but we found only goats in the road [1], and had very little entertainment as we travelled either for the eye or ear. There are, I fancy, no singing birds in the Highlands [2].

Towards night we came to a very formidable hill called Ratti-ken [3], which we climbed with more difficulty than we had yet experienced, and at last came to Glenelg, a place on the sea-side opposite to Skie. We were by this time weary and disgusted, nor was our humour much mended by our inn, which, though it was built of lime and slate, the Highlander's description of a house which he thinks magnificent, had neither wine, bread, eggs, nor any thing that we could eat or drink. When we were taken up stairs, a dirty fellow bounced out of the bed where one of us was to lie [4]. Boswell blustered, but nothing could be got.

extent of hopeless sterility.' Johnson's *Works*, ix. 35. Beattie describes the Highlands as ‘a picturesque, but in general a melancholy country.' *Essays on Poetry and Music*, p. 169. See *Footsteps of Dr. Johnson in Scotland*, pp. 24-33.

[1] See *Life*, v. 144, for the attempt made by one of his guides to divert him by making the goats jump.

[2] It is odd that he should have looked for singing-birds on the first of September. Goldsmith twenty years earlier describing southern Scotland said :—‘ Every part of the country presents the same dismal landscape. No grove nor brook lend their music to cheer the stranger, or make the inhabitants forget their poverty.' Forster's *Life of Goldsmith*, i. 433. Whether the music was the song of birds or the rustling of the leaves is not clear. Wesley, who visited Inverness early in May, ‘ heard abundance of birds welcoming the return of spring.' Wesley's *Journal*, iv. 275.

[3] Rattachan or Rattagan.

[4] ‘ Out of one of the beds on which we were to repose started up at our entrance a man black as a Cyclops from the forge.' Johnson's *Works*, ix. 44. Macaulay says :—‘ It is clear that Johnson himself did not think in the dialect in which he wrote. The expressions which came first to his tongue were simple, energetic, and picturesque. When he wrote for publication, he did his sentences out of English into Johnsonese. His letters from the Hebrides to Mrs. Thrale are the original of that

At

At last a gentleman in the neighbourhood, who heard of our arrival, sent us rum and white sugar. Boswell was now provided for in part, and the landlord prepared some mutton chops, which we could not eat, and killed two hens, of which Boswell made his servant broil a limb, with what effect I know not. We had a lemon and a piece of bread, which supplied me with my supper. When the repast was ended, we began to deliberate upon bed ; Mrs. Boswell had warned us that we should *catch something*, and had given us *sheets* for our *security*, for —— and ——, she said, came back from Skie, so scratching themselves. I thought sheets a slender defence against the confederacy with which we were threatened, and by this time our Highlanders had found a place where they could get some hay: I ordered hay to be laid thick upon the bed, and slept upon it in my great coat : Boswell laid sheets upon his bed, and reposed in linen like a gentleman. The horses were turned out to grass, with a man to watch them. The hill Rattiken and the inn at Glenelg were the only things of which we, or travellers yet more delicate, could find any pretensions to complain.

Sept. 2nd, I rose rustling from the hay, and went to tea, which I forget whether we found or brought. We saw the isle of Skie before us, darkening the horizon with its rocky coast. A boat was procured, and we launched into one of the straits of the Atlantick ocean. We had a passage of about twelve miles to the point where —— [1] resided, having come from his seat in the middle of the island to a small house on the shore, as we believe, that he might with less reproach entertain us meanly. If he aspired to meanness, his retrograde ambition [2] was completely gratified, but he did not succeed equally in escaping reproach. He had no cook, nor I suppose much provision, nor had the

work of which the *Journey to the Hebrides* is the translation ; and it is amusing to compare the two versions.' Macaulay thereupon quotes these two passages. Macaulay's *Essays*, ed. 1843, i. 404.

[1] Sir Alexander Macdonald. See *ante*, p. 244.

[2] Johnson perhaps had in mind the following passage in Bacon's *Essay on Ambition* :—' If ambitious men be checked in their desires they become secretly discontent, and look upon men and matters with an evil eye, and are best pleased when things go backward. . . Therefore it is good for princes, if they use ambitious men, to handle it so as they be still progressive and not retrograde.'

Lady

Lady the common decencies of her tea-table : we picked up our sugar with our fingers. Boswell was very angry, and reproached him with his improper parsimony; I did not much reflect upon the conduct of a man with whom I was not likely to converse as long at any other time.

You will now expect that I should give you some account of the isle of Skie, of which, though I have been twelve days upon it, I have little to say. It is an island perhaps fifty miles long, so much indented by inlets of the sea that there is no part of it removed from the water more than six miles. No part that I have seen is plain ; you are always climbing or descending, and every step is upon rock or mire. A walk upon ploughed ground in England is a dance upon carpets compared to the toilsome drudgery of wandering in Skie. There is neither town nor village in the island, nor have I seen any house but Macleod's, that is not much below your habitation at Brighthelmstone. In the mountains there are stags and roebucks, but no hares, and few rabbits [1]; nor have I seen any thing that interested me as a zoologist, except an otter, bigger than I thought an otter could have been [2].

You are perhaps imagining that I am withdrawn from the gay and the busy world into regions of peace and pastoral felicity, and am enjoying the reliques [3] of the golden age ; that I am survey-ing nature's magnificence from a mountain, or remarking her minuter beauties on the flowery bank of a winding rivulet ; that I am invigorating myself in the sunshine, or delighting my imagination with being hidden from the invasion of human evils and human passions in the darkness of a thicket ; that I am busy in gathering shells and pebbles on the shore, or contemplative

[1] 'That they have few or none of either [i.e. hares and rabbits] in Sky, they impute to the ravage of the foxes, and have therefore set, for some years past, a price upon their heads, which, as the number was diminished, has been gradually raised, from three shillings and six-pence to a guinea, a sum so great in this part of the world, that in a short time Sky may be as free from foxes, as England from wolves. The fund for these rewards is a tax of sixpence in the pound, imposed by the farmers on themselves, and said to be paid with great willingness.' Johnson's *Works*, ix. 57.

[2] See Johnson's *Works*, ix. 57.

[3] Johnson in his *Dictionary* has *relicks* but not *reliques*. Percy had perhaps made the other spelling familiar by his *Reliques*.

on a rock, from which I look upon the water, and consider how many waves are rolling between me and Streatham.

The use of travelling is to regulate imagination by reality, and instead of thinking how things may be, to see them as they are [1]. Here are mountains which I should once have climbed, but to climb steeps is now very laborious, and to descend them dangerous [2]; and I am now content with knowing, that by scrambling up a rock, I shall only see other rocks, and a wider circuit of barren desolation. Of streams, we have here a sufficient number, but they murmur not upon pebbles, but upon rocks. Of flowers, if Chloris herself were here, I could present her only with the bloom of heath [3]. Of lawns and thickets, he must read that would know them, for here is little sun and no shade. On the sea I look from my window, but am not much tempted to the shore ; for since I came to this island, almost every breath of air has been a storm, and what is worse, a storm with all its severity, but without its magnificence, for the sea is here so broken into channels that there is not a sufficient volume of water either for lofty surges or a loud roar [4].

On Sept. 6th, we left ⸺ [5] to visit Raarsa, the island which I have already mentioned. We were to cross part of Skie on horseback ; a mode of travelling very uncomfortable, for the road is so narrow, where any road can be found, that only one can go, and so craggy that the attention can never be remitted ; it allows, therefore, neither the gaiety of conversation, nor the laxity of solitude ; nor has it in itself the amusement of much variety, as it affords only all the possible transpositions of bog,

[1] See his *Works*, ix. 35, where he enlarges upon this.

[2] 'Upon one of the precipices [on Rattachan] my horse, weary with the steepness of the rise, staggered a little, and I called in haste to the Highlander to hold him. This was the only moment of my journey in which I thought myself endangered.' Johnson's *Works*, ix. 44.

[3] The modern traveller would think that having heath she would have had everything.

[4] 'We had here more wind than waves, and suffered the severity of a tempest, without enjoying its magnificence. The sea being broken by the multitude of islands, does not roar with so much noise, nor beat the storm with such foamy violence, as I have remarked on the coast of Sussex. Though, while I was in the Hebrides, the wind was extremely turbulent, I never saw very high billows.' *Ib.* p. 65.

[5] Armidale.

rock,

rock, and rivulet. Twelve miles, by computation, make a reasonable journey for a day.

At night we came to a tenant's house, of the first rank of tenants, where we were entertained better than at the landlord's [1]. There were books both English and Latin [2]. Company gathered about us, and we heard some talk of the second sight [3], and some talk of the events of forty-five; a year which will not soon be forgotten among the islanders. The next day we were confined by a storm. The company, I think, encreased, and our entertainment was not only hospitable but elegant. At night, a minister's sister, in very fine brocade, sung Earse songs; I wished to know the meaning, but the Highlanders are not much used to scholastick questions, and no translations could be obtained [4].

Next day, Sept. 8th, the weather allowed us to depart; a good boat was provided us, and we went to Raarsa under the conduct of Mr. Malcolm Macleod, a gentleman who conducted Prince Charles through the mountains in his distresses. The Prince, he says, was more active than himself; they were, at least, one night without any shelter [5].

The wind blew enough to give the boat a kind of dancing agitation [6], and in about three or four hours we arrived at

---

[1] Their host was Lachlan Mackinnon, who lived at Corrichatachin, near Broadford (Boswell calls the place Broadfoot). 'We here enjoyed the comfort of a table plentifully furnished, the satisfaction of which was heightened by a numerous and cheerful company; and we for the first time had a specimen of the joyous social manners of the inhabitants of the Highlands.' *Life,* v. 157. On the ruins of Mackinnon's house I saw his initials carved on a stone over the door. *Footsteps of Dr. Johnson in Scotland,* p. 169.

[2] 'I never was in any house of the islands where I did not find books in more languages than one, if I staid long enough to want them, except one from which the family was re- moved.' Johnson's *Works,* ix. 50. He is speaking of 'the higher rank of the Hebridians,' for on p. 61 he says :—' The greater part of the islanders make no use of books.'

[3] See *ib.* p. 104, and *Life,* v. 159.

[4] *Post,* p. 260.

[5] *Life,* v. 161, 191-2, 195.

[6] 'After we were out of the shelter of Scalpa, and in the sound between it and Rasay, which extended about a league, the wind made the sea very rough. I did not like it. JOHNSON. "This now is the Atlantick. If I should tell at a tea table in London, that I have crossed the Atlantick in an open boat, how they'd shudder, and what a fool they'd think me to expose myself to such danger!"' *Ib.* p. 163.

Raarsa, where we were met by the Laird and his friends upon the shore. Raarsa, for such is his title [1], is master of two islands; upon the smaller of which, called Rona, he has only flocks and herds. Rona gives title to his eldest son. The money which he raises annually by rent from all his dominions, which contain at least fifty thousand acres, is not believed to exceed two hundred and fifty pounds; but as he keeps a large farm in his own hands, he sells every year great numbers of cattle, which add to his revenue, and his table is furnished from the farm and from the sea, with very little expence, except for those things this country does not produce, and of those he is very liberal. The wine circulates vigorously, and the tea, chocolate, and coffee, however they are got [2], are always at hand.

I am, &c.,

SAM: JOHNSON.

We are this morning trying to get out of Skie [3].

327.

TO MRS. THRALE [4].

DEAR MADAM,   Skie, Sept. 24, 1773 [5].

I am still in Skie. Do you remember the song?

Ev'ry island is a prison,
Strongly guarded by the sea.

[1] 'It is usual to call gentlemen in Scotland by the name of their possessions, as Raasay, Bernera, Loch Buy, a practice necessary in countries inhabited by clans, where all that live in the same territory have one name, and must be therefore discriminated by some addition.' Johnson's *Works*, ix. 66. The Laird's name was John Macleod.

[2] There was no custom-house on the island. *Post*, p. 271.

[3] This was written on September 21, on which day they left Dunvegan. *Life*, v. 232.

[4] *Piozzi Letters*, i. 143.

[5] It was on September 25 that this letter was written. Boswell records on that day:—'Dr. Johnson remained in his chamber writing a letter, and it was long before we could get him into motion. He did not come to breakfast, but had it sent to him. When he had finished his letter, it was twelve o'clock, and we should have set out at ten. When I went up to him, he said to me, "Do you remember a song which begins,

Every island is a prison
Strongly guarded by the sea;
Kings and princes, for that reason,
Prisoners are, as well as we?"'
Life, v. 256.

The song is by Coffey, and is given in Ritson's *English Songs* (1813), ii. 122. It begins:—

We

o

We have at one time no boat, and at another may have too much wind; but of our reception here we have no reason to complain. We are now with Colonel Macleod, in a more pleasant place than I thought Skie could afford[1]. Now to the narrative.

We were received at Raarsa on the sea-side, and after clambering with some difficulty over the rocks, a labour which the traveller, wherever he reposes himself on land, must in these islands be contented to endure, we were introduced into the house, which one of the company called the Court of Raarsa, with politeness which not the Court of Versailles could have thought defective. The house is not large, though we were told in our passage that it had eleven fine rooms, nor magnificently furnished, but our utensils were most commonly silver[2]. We went up into a dining room, about as large as your blue room[3], where we had something given us to eat, and tea and coffee.

Raarsa himself is a man of no inelegant appearance, and of manners uncommonly refined. Lady Raarsa makes no very sublime appearance for a sovereign, but is a good housewife, and a very prudent and diligent conductress of her family. Miss Flora Macleod is a celebrated beauty; has been admired at Edinburgh; dresses her head very high; and has manners so

[1] Welcome, welcome, brother debtor,
To this poor but merry place,
Where no bailiff, dun, nor setter,
Dares to show his frightful face.'
Perhaps Coffey had read Burton, who says in *The Anatomy of Melancholy* (ed. 1660, p. 339), 'What I have said of servitude I say again of imprisonment. We are all prisoners. What's our life but a prison? We are all imprisoned in an island.' Howell has the same thought in his Letter of August 2, 1643 :—' Let the English people flatter themselves as long as they will that they are free, yet they are in effect but prisoners, as all other islanders are.'

[1] They were at Talisker; *post*, p. 268.

[2] Johnson seems to use *utensils* in much the same sense as Caliban does when he speaks of Prospero's 'brave utensils.' (*The Tempest*, Act iii. sc. 2.) 'In the Hebrides,' he says, 'they use silver on all occasions where it is common in England, nor did I ever find a spoon of horn but in one house.' It was at Grissipol in Coll where the spoons were of horn. *Works*, ix. 53, 119.

[3] ' The drawing-room at Streatham,' writes Dr. Burney, ' if memory does not deceive me, was hung with plain bright sky-blue paper, ornamented with a very gay border, somewhat tawdry.' Prior's *Malone*, p. 259.

OL. I.

lady

lady like, that I wish her head-dress was lower[1]. The rest of the nine girls are all pretty; the youngest is between Queeney and Lucy. The youngest boy, of four years old. runs barefoot, and wandered with us over the rocks to see a mill. I believe he would walk on that rough ground without shoes ten miles in a day.

The Laird of Raarsa has sometimes disputed the chieftainry of the clan with Macleod of Skie, but being much inferior in extent of possessions, has, I suppose, been forced to desist. Raarsa and its provinces have descended to its present possessor through a succession of four hundred years, without any increase or diminution[2]. It was indeed lately in danger of forfeiture, but the old Laird joined some prudence with his zeal, and when Prince Charles landed in Scotland, made over his estate to his son, the present Laird, and led one hundred men of Raarsa into the field, with officers of his own family[3]. Eighty-six only came

[1] ' At a very elegant masquerade at Richmond a gentleman appeared in women's clothes with a head-dress four feet high, composed of greens and garden stuff, and crowned with tufts of endiff nicely blanched. The force of the ridicule was felt by some of the ladies.' *Gentleman's Magazine*, 1776, p. 188. Later on in this same year Foote as Lady Pentweazle in *Taste* wore 'a head-dress stuck full of feathers, in the utmost extravagance of the present mode, being at least a yard wide. Their Majesties, who were present, laughed immoderately. The elegant, becoming manner in which her Majesty's head was dressed was however the severest satire on the present filthy fashion.' *Ib.* p. 334. See *post*, Letter of August 27, 1777. The fashion was not a new one, for on February 10, 1767, Mrs. Osborn, of Chicksands Priory, wrote of a young lady :—' Her dress is the wonder of the town, her head a yard high, and filled or rather covered with feathers to an enormous size, fitter for a mas-querade than a drawing-room.' *Political and Social Letters of a Lady of the Eighteenth Century*. p. 160. According to J. T. Smith in his *Nollekens and his Times*, i. 18, 'it was in 1772 that the head-dress became preposterously high under the fashionable leader of the day, D. Ritchie, hair-dresser and dentist then living in Rupert Street, two doors from Coventry Street.'

[2] Macaulay, as I have shown (*ante*, p. 251), charges Johnson with turning the simple English of his Letters into Johnsonese in his *Journey*. It might be shown that the change was sometimes to greater simplicity. Of this we have an instance here, for he thus paraphrases the above paragraph :—'The estate has not during four hundred years gained or lost a single acre.' *Works*, ix. 55.

[3] Johnson in his *Journey* thus delicately alludes to this :— ' Not many years ago the late Laird led out one hundred men upon a military expedition.' *Works*, ix. 59. See *Life*, v. 171, 4.

back

back after the last battle. The Prince was hidden, in his distress, two nights at Raarsa, and the king's troops burnt the whole country, and killed some of the cattle.

You may guess at the opinions that prevail in this country; they are, however, content with fighting for their king; they do not drink for him [1]. We had no foolish healths. At night, unexpectedly to us who were strangers, the carpet was taken up; the fiddler of the family came up, and a very vigorous and general dance was begun. As I told you, we were two-and-thirty at supper [2]; there were full as many dancers; for though all who supped did not dance, some danced of the young people who did not sup. Raarsa himself danced with his children, and old Malcolm, in his filibeg, was as nimble as when he led the Prince over the mountains [3]. When they had danced themselves weary, two tables were spread, and I suppose at least twenty dishes were upon them. In this country some preparations of milk are always served up at supper, and sometimes in the place of tarts at dinner. The table was not coarsely heaped, but [was] at once plentiful and elegant. They do not pretend to make a loaf; there are only cakes, commonly of oats or barley, but they made me very nice cakes of wheat flour. I always sat at the left hand of Lady Raarsa, and young Macleod of Skie, the chieftain of the clan [4], sat on the right.

[1] 'They disdain to drink for their principles, and there is no disaffection at their tables.' Johnson's *Works*, ix. 103. Johnson was thinking of the English Jacobites. Smollett tells how on the Pretender's march to England 'they were elevated to an insolence of hope which they were at no pains to conceal.' Nevertheless, 'except a few that joined the Prince at Manchester, not a soul appeared in his behalf; one would have imagined that all the Jacobites of England had been annihilated.' Writing of them two years later, he says:-- 'Though they industriously avoided exposing their lives and fortunes to the chance of war in promoting their favourite interest when there was a possibility of success, they betrayed no apprehension in celebrating the memory of its last efforts amidst the tumult of a riot and the clamours of intemperance.' He charges especially men living in the neighbourhood of Johnson's native city, Lichfield, with folly of this kind. *History of England*, iii. 170, 259.

[2] There is no mention of this before.

[3] 'Raasay himself danced with as much spirit as any man, and Malcolm bounded like a roe.' *Life*, v. 166.

[4] Johnson in his *Journey* stated that Macleod of Raasay acknowledged Macleod of Dunvegan as his

After

After supper a young lady, who was visiting, sung Earse songs, in which Lady Raarsa joined prettily enough, but not gracefully ; the young ladies sustained the chorus better.   They are very little used to be asked questions, and not well prepared with answers.   When one of the songs was over, I asked the princess that sat next me, *What is that about?*   I question if she conceived that I did not understand it.   For the entertainment of the company, said she.   But, Madam, what is the meaning of it?   It is a love song.   This was all the intelligence that I could obtain ; nor have I been able to procure the translation of a single line of Earse [1].

At twelve it was bed time.   I had a chamber to myself [2], which, in eleven rooms to forty people, was more than my share.   How the company and the family were distributed is not easy to tell.   Macleod the chieftain, and Boswell, and I, had all single chambers on the first floor.   There remained eight rooms only for at least seven-and-thirty lodgers.   I suppose they put up temporary beds in the dining room, where they stowed all the young ladies.   There was a room above stairs with six beds, in which they put ten men [3].   The rest in my next.

SAM: JOHNSON.

328.

TO MACLEOD OF MACLEOD [4].

DEAR SIR,

   We are now on the margin of the sea, waiting for a boat

chief. For the correspondence which this led to with Raasay see *post*, Letter of May 12, 1775, and *Life*, v. 409.

   [1] It was not till October 16 that he was able to find a translation. On that day he said of a Miss Maclean :— 'She is the first person whom I have found that can translate Erse poetry literally.' *Life*, v. 318. He mentions her in his *Journey* 'as the only interpreter of Erse poetry that he could ever find.' *Works*, ix. 134. See *ante*, p. 255.

   [2] His chamber is still shown. On one of the walls I saw hanging his

likeness. *Footsteps of Dr. Johnson in Scotland*, p. 176.

   [3] Sir Walter Scott, describing Scotland in general at this time, says :—'For beds many shifts were made, and the prospect of a dance in particular reconciled damsels to sleep in the proportion of half-a-dozen to each apartment, while their gallant partners would be sometimes contented with an outhouse, a barn, or a hayloft.' *Quarterly Review*, No. 71, p. 192.

   [4] First published in Croker's *Boswell*, page 356.

   I saw the original in the drawing-

and

and a wind. Boswell grows impatient ; but the kind treatment
which I find wherever I go, makes me leave, with some heaviness of heart, an island which I am not very likely to see again.
Having now gone as far as horses can carry us, we thankfully
return them. My steed will, I hope, be received with kindness ;
he has borne me, heavy as I am, over ground both rough and
steep, with great fidelity; and for the use of him, as for your
other favours, I hope you will believe me thankful, and willing,
at whatever distance we may be placed, to show my sense of
your kindness, by any offices of friendship that may fall within
my power.

Lady Macleod and the young ladies have, by their hospitality
and politeness, made an impression on my mind, which will not
easily be effaced. Be pleased to tell them, that I remember
them with great tenderness, and great respect.

> I am,
> > Sir,
> > > Your most obliged
> > > > and most humble servant,
> > > > > SAM: JOHNSON.

We passed two days at Talisker very happily, both by the
pleasantness of the place and elegance of our reception.

Ostig, Sept. 28, 1773.

329.

TO MRS. THRALE [1].

DEAREST MADAM, Ostich [2] in Skie, Sept. 30, 1773.
    I am still confined in Skie. We were unskilful travellers,
and imagined that the sea was an open road which we could
pass at pleasure ; but we have now learned with some pain, that
we may still wait for a long time the caprices of the equinoctial
winds, and sit reading or writing as I now do, while the tempest
is rolling the sea, or roaring in the mountains. I am now no

---

room of Dunvegan Castle, endorsed
'Dr. Johnston's letter.' By it was
hung a small portrait of him by
Zoffany.

[1] *Piozzi Letters*, i. 148.
[2] Ostig, the residence of the
Minister of Slate. *Life*, v. 265.

longer

longer pleased with the delay; you can hear from me but seldom, and I cannot at all hear from you. It comes into my mind that some evil may happen, or that I might be of use while I am away[1]. But these thoughts are vain; the wind is violent and adverse, and our boat cannot yet come. I must content myself with writing to you, and hoping that you will sometime receive my letter. Now to my narrative.

Sept. 9th[2]: Having passed the night as is usual, I rose, and found the dining room full of company; we feasted and talked, and when the evening came it brought musick and dancing. Young Macleod, the great proprietor of Skie and head of his clan, was very distinguishable; a young man of nineteen; bred a while at St. Andrews, and afterwards at Oxford; a pupil of G. Strahan[3]. He is a young man of a mind as much advanced as I have ever known; very elegant of manners, and very graceful in his person. He has the full spirit of a feudal chief; and I was very ready to accept his invitation to Dunvegan. All Raarsa's children are beautiful. The ladies, all except the eldest, are in the morning dressed in their hair. The true Highlander never wears more than a riband on her head till she is married.

On the third day Boswell went out with old Malcolm to see a ruined castle, which he found less entire than was promised, but he saw the country. I did not go, for the castle was perhaps ten miles off, and there is no riding at Raarsa[4], the

---

[1] Boswell records on this same day :—'There was something not quite serene in his humour to-night after supper, for he spoke of hastening away to London without stopping much at Edinburgh.' *Life*, v. 272. He reproached Boswell later on for indulging in 'an uneasy apprehension' about his wife and children, who were at a distance. *Ib.* iii. 4.

[2] He returns to his account of his visit to Raasay.

[3] In Croker's *Boswell*, ed. 1835, iv. 320, is an interesting fragment of Macleod's autobiography. He says:—'My tutor, Mr. George Strahan,

zealously endeavoured to supply my deficiency in Greek, and I made some progress; but approaching now to manhood, having got a tincture of more entertaining and pleasing knowledge, and a taste for the Latin, French, and English classics, I could never sufficiently labour again as a schoolboy, which I now, and will for ever lament.' He matriculated on November 27, 1770, aged sixteen. *Alumni Oxon.* p. 898. For George Strahan see *ante*, p. 113.

[4] Boswell says that there were a good many horses which were used for works of husbandry, but that he whole

whole island being rock or mountain, from which the cattle
often fall and are destroyed. It is very barren, and maintains,
as near as I could collect, about seven hundred inhabitants,
perhaps ten to a square mile[1]. In these countries you are
not to suppose that you shall find villages or inclosures. The
traveller wanders through a naked desart, gratified sometimes,
but rarely, with the sight of cows, and now and then finds
a heap of loose stones and turf in a cavity between rocks,
where a being born with all those powers which education
expands, and all those sensations which culture refines, is
condemned to shelter itself from the wind and rain. Philosophers there are who try to make themselves believe that this
life is happy[2]; but they believe it only while they are saying
it, and never yet produced conviction in a single mind; he,
whom want of words or images sunk into silence, still thought,
as he thought before, that privation of pleasure can never please,
and that content is not to be much envied, when it has no other
principle than ignorance of good.

This gloomy tranquillity, which some may call fortitude, and
others wisdom, was, I believe, for a long time to be very frequently found in these dens of poverty: every man was content
to live like his neighbours, and never wandering from home, saw
no mode of life preferable to his own, except at the house of the
laird, or the laird's nearest relations, whom he considered as a
superior order of beings, to whose luxuries or honours he had no
pretensions. But the end of this reverence and submission seems
now approaching; the Highlanders have learned that there are
countries less bleak and barren than their own, where, instead of
working for the laird, every man may till his own ground, and
eat the produce of his own labour[3]. Great numbers have been

---

believed the people never rode. *Life,* v.
173. For the old castle see *ib.* p. 172.

[1] The people had never been
numbered, Johnson says. In his
Journey he estimated the population
at nine hundred, basing his calculation on the number of men who had
borne arms in 1745. *Works,* ix. 59.
The population in 1881 was, I was
told, 750.

[2] See *Life,* ii. 74, for his scorn for
'the nonsense' which Rousseau
talked on this subject.

[3] 'The great business of insular
policy is now to keep the people in
their own country. As the world
has been let in upon them they
have heard of happier climates and
less arbitrary government.' Johnson's
Works, ix. 128.

induced

induced by this discovery to go every year for some time past to America. Macdonald and Macleod of Skie have lost many tenants and many labourers, but Raarsa has not yet been forsaken by a single inhabitant[1].

Rona is yet more rocky and barren than Raarsa, and though it contains perhaps four thousand acres, is possessed only by a herd of cattle and the keepers.

I find myself not very able to walk upon the mountains, but one day I went out to see the walls yet standing of an ancient chapel. In almost every island the superstitious votaries of the Romish church erected places of worship, in which the drones of convents or cathedrals performed the holy offices, but by the active zeal of Protestant devotion, almost all of them have sunk into ruin[2]. The chapel at Raarsa is now only considered as the burying-place of the family, and I suppose of the whole island.

We would now have gone away and left room for others to enjoy the pleasures of this little court, but the wind detained us till the 12th, when, though it was Sunday, we thought it proper to snatch the opportunity of a calm day. Raarsa accompanied us in his six-oared boat, which he said was his coach and six. It is indeed the vehicle in which the ladies take the air and pay their visits, but they have taken very little care for accommodations[3]. There is no way in or out of the boat for a woman, but by being carried; and in the boat thus dignified with a pompous name, there is no seat but an occasional bundle of straw. Thus we left Raarsa; the seat of plenty, civility, and cheerfulness[4].

---

[1] Perhaps this was in part due to the fact that 'on the large tract of land possessed as a common every man put upon it as many cattle as he chose.' *Life*, v. 171.

[2] 'It has been for many years popular to talk of the lazy devotion of the Romish clergy; over the sleepy laziness of men that erected churches we may indulge our superiority with a new triumph, by comparing it with the fervid activity of those who suffer them to fall.' Johnson's *Works*, ix. 61.

[3] Johnson commonly says *accom-modations* where we should say *con-veniencies*.

[4] It is not clear in what sense Johnson here uses *civility*, for with him that word included *civilization*. *Civilization* he would not admit into his *Dictionary*. *Life*, ii. 155. He thus takes leave of Raasay in his *Journey*:—'Raasay has little that can detain a traveller except the Laird and his family; but their power wants no auxiliaries. Such a seat of hospitality amidst the winds and waters fills the imagination with a delightful contrariety of images.

We

We dined at a publick house at Port Re; so called because one of the Scottish kings landed there, in a progress through the western isles[1]. Raarsa paid the reckoning privately[2]. We then got on horseback, and by a short but very tedious journey came to Kingsburgh, at which the same king lodged after he landed. Here I had the honour of saluting[3] the far famed Miss Flora Macdonald, who conducted the Prince, dressed as her maid, through the English forces from the island of Lewes; and, when she came to Skie, dined with the English officers, and left her maid below. She must then have been a very young lady; she is now not old; of a pleasing person, and elegant behaviour. She told me that she thought herself honoured by my visit; and I am sure that whatever regard she bestowed on me was liberally repaid[4]. 'If thou likest her opinions, thou wilt praise her virtue.' She was carried to London, but dismissed without a trial, and came down with Malcolm Macleod, against whom sufficient evidence could not be procured. She and her husband are poor, and are going to try their fortune in America[5].

Sic rerum volvitur orbis.

Without is the rough ocean and the rocky land, the beating billows and the howling storm; within is plenty and elegance, beauty and gaiety, the song and the dance. In Raasay, if I could have found an Ulysses, I had fancied a Phæacia.' *Works*, ix. 62.

[1] 'Portree has its name from King James the Fifth having landed there in his tour through the Western Isles, *Ree* in Erse being King, as *Re* is in Italian; so it is *Port Royal.' Life*, v. 181.

[2] *Ib.* v. 183.

[3] By *saluting* Johnson, I believe, meant *kissing*. In his *Dictionary* he gives it as one of the meanings of the word. Topham, writing in 1774, says:—'The Scotch have still the custom of salutation on introduction to strangers. It very seldom happens that the salute is a voluntary one, and it frequently is the cause of disgust and embarrassment to the fair sex.' *Letters from Edinburgh*, pp. 33, 37.

Flora Macdonald was the wife of Macdonald of Kingsburgh.

[4] In his *Journey* he celebrates her as 'a name that will be mentioned in history, and if courage and fidelity be virtues, mentioned with honour.' *Works*, ix. 63.

[5] That after saving the Prince's life she should be driven by poverty to America seems incredible did we not know his character. The Jacobite Dr. King, Principal of St. Mary Hall, Oxford, tells us in his *Anecdotes* (p. 201) that 'the most odious part of the Prince's character is his love of money. I have known him with two thousand Louis-d'ors in his strong box pretend he was in great distress, and borrow money from a lady in Paris who was not in affluent circumstances. His most faithful servants, who had closely at-

At

At Kingsburgh we were very liberally feasted, and I slept in the bed on which the Prince reposed in his distress ; the sheets which he used were never put to any meaner offices, but were wrapped up by the lady of the house, and at last, according to her desire, were laid round her in her grave. These are not Whigs.

On the 13th, travelling partly on horseback where we could not row, and partly on foot where we could not ride, we came to Dunvegan, which I have described already[1]. Here, though poor Macleod had been left by his grandfather overwhelmed with debts[2], we had another exhibition of feudal hospitality. There were two stags in the house, and venison came to the table every day in its various forms. Macleod, besides his estate in Skie, larger I suppose than some English counties, is proprietor of nine inhabited isles; and of his islands uninhabited I doubt if he very exactly knows the number. I told him that he was a mighty monarch. Such dominions fill an Englishman with envious wonder ; but when he surveys the naked mountain, and treads the quaking moor, and wanders over the wild regions of gloomy barrenness, his wonder may continue, but his envy ceases[3]. The unprofitableness of these vast domains can be conceived only by the means of positive instances. The heir

tended him in all his difficulties, were ill rewarded.' Flora Macdonald and her husband returned before the end of the War of Independence. On the way back she showed great spirit when their ship was attacked by a French man of war. Chambers's *Rebellion in Scotland*, ii. 329.

[1] *Ante*, p. 245.

[2] 'Dr. Johnson was much pleased with the Laird of Macleod, who is indeed a most promising youth, and with a noble spirit struggles with difficulties, and endeavours to preserve his people. He has been left with an incumbrance of forty thousand pounds debt, and annuities to the amount of thirteen hundred pounds a year. Dr. Johnson said, "If he gets the better of all this,

he'll be a hero; and I hope he will."' *Life*, v. 176. Macleod, in his *Autobiography*, says that his grandfather, whom he succeeded as Laird, had entered upon his inheritance in the most prosperous condition. 'He was the first of our family who was led by the change of manners to leave the patriarchal government of the clan, and to mix in the pursuits and ambition of the world.' Hence arose his indebtedness. Croker's *Boswell*, ed. 1835, iv. 322.

[3] 'When Mr. Edmund Burke shewed Johnson his fine house and lands near Beaconsfield, Johnson coolly said, "*Non equidem invideo ; miror magis.*"' *Life*, iii. 310. The quotation is from Virgil's *Eclogues*, i. 11.

of *Col*, an island not far distant, has lately told me how wealthy he should be if he could let *Rum*, another of his islands, for two-pence half-penny an acre ; and Macleod has an estate, which the surveyor reports to contain eighty thousand acres, rented at six hundred pounds a-year[1].

While we were at Dunvegan, the wind was high, and the rain violent, so that we were not able to put forth a boat to fish in the sea, or to visit the adjacent islands, which may be seen from the house ; but we filled up the time as we could, sometimes by talk, sometimes by reading[2]. I have never wanted books in the isle of Skie.

We were visited one day by the Laird and Lady of Muck, one of the western islands, two miles long, and three quarters of a mile high[3]. He has half his island in his own culture, and upon the other half live one hundred and fifty dependents, who not only live upon the product, but export corn sufficient for the payment of their rent.

Lady Macleod has a son and four daughters ; they have lived long in England, and have the language and manners of English ladies. We lived with them very easily. The hospitality of this remote region is like that of the golden age. We have

---

[1] It was not for many a year after this that the game on an estate in the Highlands added much to its value. Lord Malmesbury speaking of the year 1833 says :—'At that time a stranger could fish and shoot over almost any part of the Highlands without interruption, the letting value of the *ferae naturae* being unknown to their possessors.' *Memoirs of an Ex-Minister*, ed. 1885, p. 41.

[2] 'It was wonderful how well time passed in a remote castle, and in dreary weather. . . . We were so comfortably situated at Dunvegan that Dr. Johnson could hardly be moved from it. I proposed to him that we should leave it on Monday. "No, Sir, (said he,) I will not go before Wednesday. I will have some more of this good."' *Life*, v. 221, 4.

[3] Johnson must have written, or have meant to write, not *high* but *broad*. The Rev. John Sinclair, Minister of Eigg, in whose parish the island is, informs me that its breadth is about three-quarters of a mile, and its height 372 feet.

'It was somewhat droll,' writes Boswell, 'to hear this Laird called by his title. *Muck* would have sounded ill ; so he was called *Isle of Muck*, which went off with great readiness. The name, as now written, is unseemly, but it is not so bad in the original Erse, which is *Mouach*, signifying the Sows' Island. Buchanan calls it INSULA PORCORUM. It is so called from its form. Some call it Isle of *Monk*. The Laird insists that this is the proper name.' *Life*, v. 225.

found

found ourselves treated at every house as if we came to confer a benefit.

We were eight days at Dunvegan, but we took the first opportunity which the weather afforded, after the first days, of going away, and on the 21st, went to Ulinish, where we were well entertained, and wandered a little after curiosities. In the afternoon[1] an interval of calm sunshine courted us out to see a cave on the shore famous for its echo. When we went into the boat, one of our companions was asked in Earse, by the boatmen, who they were that came with him? He gave us characters, I suppose, to our advantage, and was asked, in the spirit of the Highlands, whether I could recite a long series of ancestors[2]? The boatmen said, as I perceived afterwards, that they heard the cry of an English ghost. This, Boswell says, disturbed him. We came to the cave, and clambering up the rocks, came to an arch, open at one end, one hundred and eighty feet long, thirty broad in the broadest part, and about thirty high. There was no echo; such is the fidelity of report; but I saw what I had never seen before, muscles and whilks[3] in their natural state. There was another arch in the rock, open at both ends.

Sept. 23rd : We removed to Talisker, a house occupied by Mr. Macleod, a Lieutenant-Colonel in the Dutch service[4].

[1] Of the 22nd. *Life*, v. 237.

[2] 'I can hardly tell who was my grandfather,' Johnson once said to Boswell. *Ib.* ii. 261. Of his father's father not even the Christian name is known. It was not, says Boswell, Ulinish's boatmen, but those who rowed them from Sconser, three days later, who asked about the genealogy. Croker's *Boswell*, p. 826.

[3] Johnson only gives this word incidentally in his *Dictionary*. Under *to welk* he says, ' *whilk* is used for a small shell-fish.' *Whelk* he defines as (1) *an inequality; a protuberance;* (2) *a pustule.*

[4] Pennant, writing in the year 1774, thus describes these Scotch regiments in the Dutch service :— 'They were formed out of some independent companies sent over either in the reign of Elizabeth or James VI. At present the common men are but nominally national, for since the scarcity of men occasioned by the late war, Holland is no longer permitted to draw her recruits out of North Britain. But the officers are all Scotch, who are obliged to take oaths to our government, and to qualify in presence of our ambassador at the Hague.' *Voyage to the Hebrides,* ed. 1774, p. 289.

In the war which broke out between England and Holland in 1781, this curious system, which had survived the great naval battles between the two countries in the seventeenth century, at last came to an end. In the *Gentleman's Magazine* for De-

Talisker

Talisker has been long in the possession of gentlemen, and therefore has a garden well cultivated ; and, what is here very rare, is shaded by trees : a place where the imagination is more amused cannot easily be found[1].   The mountains about it are of great height, with waterfalls succeeding one another so fast, that as one ceases to be heard another begins.   Between the mountains there is a small valley extending to the sea, which is not far off, beating upon a coast very difficult of access.

Two nights before our arrival two boats were driven upon this coast by the tempest, one of them had a pilot that knew the passage, the second followed, but a third missed the true course, and was driven forward with great danger of being forced into the vast ocean, but, however, gained at last some other island.   The crews crept to Talisker, almost lifeless with wet, cold, fatigue, and terrour, but the lady took care of them. She is a woman of more than common qualifications ; having travelled with her husband, she speaks four languages.

You find that all the islanders, even in these recesses of life, are not barbarous.   One of the ministers who has adhered to us almost all the time is an excellent scholar[2].   We have now with us the young Laird of Col, who is heir, perhaps, to two hundred square miles of land.   He has first studied at Aberdeen, and afterwards gone to Hertfordshire to learn agriculture, being much impressed with desire of improvement[3] : he likewise has

cember, 1782, p. 595, we read, that on the first of that month 'the Scotch Brigade in the Dutch service renounced their allegiance to their lawful Sovereign, and took a new oath of fidelity to their High Mightinesses.   They are for the future to wear the Dutch uniform, and not to carry the arms of the enemy any longer in their colours, nor to beat their march.   They are to receive the word of command in Dutch, and their officers are to wear orange-coloured sashes, and the same sort of spontoons as the officers of other Dutch regiments.'   Colonel Macleod used the experience he had gained in

Holland in draining the valley-bottom and in making his garden.

[1] 'Talisker is the place beyond all that I have seen from which the gay and the jovial seem utterly excluded ; and where the hermit might expect to grow old in meditation without possibility of disturbance or interruption.'   Johnson's *Works*, ix. 71.

[2] The Rev. Donald M'Queen. *Life*, v. 224.

'I saw not one pastor in the islands whom I had reason to think either deficient in learning or irregular in life.'   Johnson's *Works*, ix. 102.

[3] See *Life*, v. 293, and *post*, p. 277.

the

the notions of a chief, and keeps a piper. At Macleod's the bagpipe always played while we were dining [1].

Col has undertaken, by the permission of the waves and wind, to carry us about several of the islands, with which he is acquainted enough to shew us whatever curious is given by nature or left by antiquity; but we grew afraid of deviating from our way home, lest we should be shut up for months upon some little protuberance of rock, that just appears above the sea, and perhaps is scarcely marked upon a map.

You remember the Doge of Genoa, who being asked what struck him most at the French court, answered, 'Myself [2].' I cannot think many things here more likely to affect the fancy than to see Johnson ending his sixty-fourth year in the wilderness of the Hebrides. But now I am here, it will gratify me very little to return without seeing, or doing my best to see what those places afford. I have a desire to instruct myself in the whole system of pastoral life; but I know not whether I shall be able to perfect the idea. However, I have many pictures in my mind, which I could not have had without this journey, and should have passed it with great pleasure had you, and Master, and Queeney been in the party. We should have excited the attention and enlarged the observation of each other, and obtained many pleasing topicks of future conversation. As it is, I travel with my mind too much at home, and perhaps miss many things worthy of observation. or pass them with transient notice; so that the images, for want of that re-impression which discussion and comparison produce, easily fade away; but

[1] 'The solace which the bagpipes can give they have long enjoyed.' Johnson's *Works*, ix. 100. 'We had the musick of the bagpipe every day, at Armidale, Dunvegan, and Col. Dr. Johnson appeared fond of it, and used often to stand for some time with his ear close to the great drone.' *Life*, v. 315.

[2] Genoa was besieged by the French in 1684. 'Alors, il fallut s'humilier pour prévenir une ruine totale. Le roi [Louis XIV] exigea que le doge de Gênes et quatre principaux sénateurs vinssent implorer sa clémence dans son palais de Versailles... Ce doge était un homme de beaucoup d'esprit. Tout le monde sait que le marquis de Seignelai lui ayant demandé ce qu'il trouvait de plus singulier à Versailles, il répondit : *C'est de m'y voir.*' Voltaire, *Siècle de Louis XIV*, ch. xiv. Johnson quotes this story again in his Letter of April 26, 1784, but substitutes Paris for Versailles.

I

I keep a book of remarks, and Boswell writes a regular journal of our travels, which, I think, contains as much of what I say and do as of all other occurrences together; ' for such a faithful chronicler as Griffith [1].'

I hope, dearest Madam, you are equally careful to reposite proper memorials of all that happens to you and your family, and then when we meet we shall tell our stories. I wish you had gone this summer in your usual splendour to Brighthelmstone.

Mr. Thrale probably wonders how I live all this time without sending to him for money. Travelling in Scotland is dear enough, dearer in proportion to what the country affords than in England, but residence in the isles is unexpensive. Company is, I think, considered as a supply of pleasure, and a relief of that tediousness of life which is felt in every place, elegant or rude [2]. Of wine and punch they are very liberal, for they get them cheap; but as there is no custom-house on the island, they can hardly be considered as smugglers [3]. Their punch is made without lemons, or any substitute.

Their tables are very plentiful; but a very nice man would not be pampered. As they have no meat but as they kill it, they are obliged to live while it lasts upon the same flesh [4].

[1] ' After my death I wish no other herald,
No other speaker of my living actions,
To keep mine honour from corruption,
But such an honest chronicler as Griffith.'
SHAKSPEARE, *Henry VIII, Act IV. Sc.* 2.
Boswell quotes this in the *Life*, i. 24.

[2] ' I was glad to go abroad, and, perhaps, glad to come home; which is, in other words, I was, I am afraid, weary of being at home, and weary of being abroad. Is not this the state of life? But, if we confess this weariness, let us not lament it, for all the wise and all the good say, that we may cure it.' *Life*, ii. 382.

[3] Sir Walter Scott, describing Scotland in general at a period a few years earlier than this time, says :— ' French wine and brandy were had at a cheap rate, chiefly by infractions of the revenue laws, at which the Government were contented to wink rather than irritate a country in which there was little money and much disaffection.' *Quarterly Review*, No. 71, p. 192. In 1786 Knox found a custom-house at Oban. J. Knox, *Tour through the Highlands*, p. 44.

[4] Johnson describing the petty peasants and the tenants says :— ' They seldom taste the flesh of land animals; for here are no markets. What each man eats is from his own

They

They kill a sheep, and set mutton boiled and roast on the table together. They have fish both of the sea and of the brooks; but they can hardly conceive that it requires any sauce. To sauce in general they are strangers; now and then butter is melted, but I dare not always take, lest I should offend by disliking it. Barley-broath is a constant dish, and is made well in every house. A stranger, if he is prudent, will secure his share, for it is not certain that he will be able to eat any thing else[1].

Their meat being often newly killed is very tough, and as nothing is sufficiently subdued by the fire, is not easily to be eaten. Carving is here a very laborious employment, for the knives are never whetted. Table-knives are not of long subsistence in the Highlands; every man, while arms were a regular part of dress, had his knife and fork appendant to his dirk. Knives they now lay upon the table[2], but the handles are apt to shew that they have been in other hands, and the blades have neither brightness nor edge.

Of silver there is no want; and it will last long, for it is never cleaned. They are a nation just rising from barbarity; long contented with necessaries, now somewhat studious of convenience, but not yet arrived at delicate discriminations. Their linen is, however, both clean and fine. Bread, such as we mean by that name, I have never seen in the isle of Skie. They have ovens, for they bake their pies, but they never ferment their meal, nor mould a loaf. Cakes of oats and barley are brought to the table, but I believe wheat is reserved for strangers. They are commonly too hard for me, and therefore I take potatoes to my meat, and am sure to find them on almost every table.

stock. The great effect of money is to break property into small parts. In towns, he that has a shilling may have a piece of meat; but where there is no commerce, no man can eat mutton but by killing a sheep.' *Works*, ix. 98.

[1] 'At dinner [at Aberdeen] Dr. Johnson ate several plate-fulls of Scotch broth, with barley and peas in it, and seemed very fond of the dish. I said, "You never ate it before." JOHNSON. "No, Sir; but I don't care how soon I eat it again." ' *Life*, v. 87.

[2] Dr. Alexander Carlyle, in the year 1742, notices as a sign of increasing refinement, that at the tavern in Haddington, where the Presbytery dined, knives and forks were provided for the table. A. Carlyle's *Autobiography*, p. 64. See *Footsteps of Dr. Johnson in Scotland*, pp. 43, 252.

They

They retain so much of the pastoral life, that some preparation of milk is commonly one of the dishes both at dinner and supper. Tea is always drunk at the usual times ; but in the morning the table is polluted with a plate of slices of strong cheese. This is peculiar to the Highlands ; at Edinburgh there are always honey and sweet-meats on the morning tea-table [1].

Strong liquors they seem to love. Every man, perhaps woman, begins the day with a dram ; and the punch is made both at dinner and supper [2].

They have neither wood nor coal for fuel, but burn peat or turf in their chimnies. It is dug out of the moors or mosses, and makes a strong and lasting fire, not always very sweet, and somewhat apt to smoke the pot.

The houses of inferior gentlemen are very small, and every room serves many purposes. In the bed-rooms, perhaps, are laid up stores of different kinds ; and the parlour of the day is a bed-room at night. In the room which I inhabited last, about fourteen feet square, there were three chests of drawers, a long chest for larger clothes, two closet cupboards, and the bed. Their rooms are commonly dirty, of which they seem to have little sensibility, and if they had more, clean floors would be difficultly kept, where the first step from the door is into the dirt [3]. They are very much inclined to carpets,

---

[1] *Tea-table* had not yet come to mean necessarily the table for the afternoon or evening meal. Addison in *The Spectator*, No. X, boasts that he had brought philosophy out of colleges 'to dwell at tea-tables,' and goes on to advise that every morning his paper should 'be looked upon as a part of the tea equipage.'

[2] 'A man of the Hebrides, for of the women's diet I can give no account, as soon as he appears in the morning, swallows a glass of whisky ; yet they are not a drunken race, at least I never was present at much intemperance ; but no man is so abstemious as to refuse the morning dram, which they call a *skalk.*' Johnson's *Works*, ix. 51. In the earliest *Gaelic Dictionary*, published by W. Shaw in 1780, this word is spelt *sgailc*, 'a bumper of whisky in a morning.' A Highland friend writes to me :—'The practice of the morning dram is dying out very much, but I believe it still not uncommon among farmers, who keep their " keg " very often in the glens, duty unpaid.'

[3] 'With want of cleanliness it were ingratitude to reproach them. The servants having been bred upon the naked earth, think every floor clean, and the quick succession of guests, perhaps not always over-elegant, does not allow much time for adjusting their apartments.' Johnson's *Works*, ix. 97.

and seldom fail to lay down something under their feet, better or worse as they happen to be furnished.

The Highland dress, being forbidden by law, is very little used ; sometimes it may be seen [1], but the English traveller is struck with nothing so much as the *nudité des pieds* of the common people.

Skie is the greatest island, or the greatest but one, among the Hebrides [2]. Of the soil I have already given some account, it is generally barren, but some spots are not wholly unfruitful. The gardens have apples and pears, cherries, strawberries, raspberries, currants, and gooseberries, but all the fruit that I have seen is small. They attempt to sow nothing but oats and barley. Oats constitute the bread corn of the place. Their harvest is about the beginning of October; and being so late, is very much subject to disappointments from the rains that follow the equinox. This year has been particularly disastrous. Their rainy season lasts from Autumn to Spring. They have seldom very hard frosts ; nor was it ever known that a lake was covered with ice stong enough to bear a skater. The sea round them is always open. The snow falls but soon melts; only in 1771, they had a cold Spring [3] in which the island was so long covered with it, that many beasts, both wild and domestick, perished, and the whole country was reduced to distress, from which I know not if it is even yet recovered.

The animals here are not remarkably small; perhaps they

[1] ' I have seen only one gentleman completely clothed in the ancient habit, and by him it was worn only occasionally and wantonly.' *Works,* ix. 47. This gentleman was Macdonald of Kingsburgh. *Life,* v. 184. After the Rebellion of 1745 it had been enacted that no person whatsoever should wear the Highland dress. Any offender 'not being a landed man, or the son of a landed man,' was to be tried before a justice of the peace 'in a summary way, and delivered over to serve as a soldier.' *An Act to Amend the Disarming Act of the* 19 *Geo. II, made in the* 21

Geo. II. Pitt (Earl of Chatham), when he raised the Highland regiments 'to allure men into the army,' allowed the soldiers to wear the national dress. Johnson's *Works,* ix. 94, and *Footsteps of Dr. Johnson in Scotland,* p. 171.

[2] Sky is the largest of the Inner Hebrides, and contains 411,703 acres. Lewis and Harris is the largest of the Outer Hebrides, and contains 492,800 acres. *Encyclo. Brit.,* 9th ed., xiv. 492 ; xxii. 127.

[3] ' It was remembered by the name of the Black Spring.' Johnson's *Works,* ix. 74.

recruit

recruit their breed from the main land. The cows are sometimes without horns[1]. The horned and unhorned cattle are not
accidental variations, but different species, they will however
breed together.

October 3d : The wind is now changed, and if we snatch the
moment of opportunity, an escape from this island is become
practicable[2]; I have no reason to complain of my reception,
yet I long to be again at home.

You and my master may perhaps expect, after this description of Skie, some account of myself. My eye is, I am afraid,
not fully recovered[3]; my ears are not mended ; my nerves seem
to grow weaker, and I have been otherwise not as well as I
sometimes am, but think myself lately better. This climate perhaps is not within my degree of healthy latitude.

Thus I have given my most honoured mistress the story of
me and my little ramble. We are now going to some other
isle, to what we know not, the wind will tell us.

　　　　　　　　　　I am, &c.,
　　　　　　　　　　　　SAM: JOHNSON.

Compliments to Queeney, and Jack[4], and Lucy, and all.

330.

To Henry Thrale[5].

DEAR SIR,　　　　　　　　　　Isle of Mull, Oct. 15, 1773.

　　Since I had the honour of writing to my mistress, we have
been hindered from returning, by a tempest almost continual.

[1] *Life*, v. 380.

[2] They embarked on a small ship
in the hope of reaching Iona that
night, but they were carried by a
storm to the island of Coll. *Ib.*
v. 279.

[3] *Ante*, p. 219, *n.* 2.

[4] Jack, I conjecture, was Thrale's
nephew, John Lade, 'that rich, extravagant young gentleman' on whose
coming of age Johnson wrote some
spirited lines. *Life*, iv. 413.

[5] *Piozzi Letters*, i. 166.

This letter was written at the house
of Dr. Maclean, who lived near

Tobermory, a small harbour in the
Isle of Mull. Boswell, writing on the
same day, says :—'We this morning found that we could not proceed,
there being a violent storm of wind
and rain, and the rivers being im-
passable. When I expressed my
discontent at our confinement, Dr.
Johnson said, " Now that I have had
an opportunity of writing to the
main land, I am in no such haste."
I was amused with his being so
easily satisfied ; for the truth was,
that the gentleman who was to con-
vey our letters, as I was now in-

We tried eight days ago to come hither, but were driven by the wind into the Isle of Col, in which we were confined eight days. We hired a sloop to bring us hither, and hope soon to get to Edinburgh.

Having for many weeks had no letter, my longings are very great to be informed how all things are at home, as you and mistress allow me to call it [1]. A letter will now perhaps meet me at Edinburgh, for I shall be expected to pass a few days at Lord Auchinleck's, and I beg to have my thoughts set at rest by a letter from you or my mistress.

Be so kind as to send either to Mrs. Williams or Mr. Levett [2], and if they want money, advance them ten pounds.

I hope my mistress keeps all my very long letters, longer than I ever wrote before. I shall perhaps spin out one more before I have the happiness to tell you at home that I am

> Your obliged humble servant,
>
> SAM: JOHNSON.

331.

To Mrs. Thrale [3].

DEAR MADAM, Mull, Oct. 15, 1773.

Though I have written to Mr. Thrale, yet having a little more time than was promised me, I would not suffer the messenger to go without some token of my duty to my mistress, who, I suppose, expects the usual tribute of intelligence, a tribute which I am not now very able to pay.

October 3d: After having been detained by storms many days at Skie, we left it, as we thought, with a fair wind; but a violent gust, which Bos.[4] had a great mind to call a tempest, forced us into Coll, an obscure island; on which

---

formed, was not to set out for Inverary for some time; so that it was probable we should be there as soon as he : however, I did not undeceive my friend, but suffered him to enjoy his fancy.' *Life*, v. 314.

[1] *Ante*, p. 129.

[2] 'The obscure practiser in physic'

to whom he gave lodging for many years. *Life*, i. 243.

[3] *Piozzi Letters*, i. 167.

[4] 'Johnson had a way of contracting the names of his friends; as Beauclerk, Beau; Boswell, Bozzy; Langton, Lanky; Murphy, Mur; Sheridan, Sherry.' *Life*, ii. 258.

—— nulla

—— nulla campis
Arbor æstiva recreatur aura [1].

There is literally no tree upon the island [2], part of it is a sandy waste, over which it would be really dangerous to travel in dry weather and with a high wind [3]. It seems to be little more than one continued rock, covered from space to space with a thin layer of earth. It is, however, according to the Highland notion, very populous [4], and life is improved beyond the manners of Skie; for the huts are collected into little villages, and every one has a small garden of roots and cabbage. The laird has a new house built by his uncle, and an old castle inhabited by his ancestors. The young laird entertained us very liberally; he is heir, perhaps, to three hundred square miles of land, which, at ten shillings an acre, would bring him ninety-six thousand pounds a-year. He is desirous of improving the agriculture of his country; and, in imitation of the Czar, travelled for improvement, and worked with his own hands upon a farm in Hertfordshire, in the neighbourhood of your uncle, Sir Thomas Salusbury. He talks of doing useful things, and has introduced turnips for winter fodder [5]. He has made a small essay towards a road.

[1]   'never summer breeze Unbinds the glebe or warms the trees.'
FRANCIS. HORACE, *Odes*, 1. xxii. 17.
[2] 'Perhaps in the whole island nothing has ever yet grown to the height of a table.' Johnson's *Works*, ix. 121. 'We walked a little in the laird's garden, in which endeavours have been used to rear some trees; but, as soon as they got above the surrounding wall, they died.' *Life*, v. 293.
[3] 'We passed close by a large extent of sand-hills, near two miles square. Dr. Johnson said, "he never had the image before. It was horrible, if barrenness and danger could be so." I heard him, after we were in the house of Breacacha, repeating to himself, as he walked about the room,

'And smother'd in the dusty whirlwind, dies."'
[*Cato*, Act ii. sc. 6]. *Ib.* p. 291.
[4] The population was estimated at a thousand. Johnson's *Works*, ix. 123.
[5] 'Col and I rode out this morning, and viewed a part of the island. In the course of our ride, we saw a turnip-field, which he had hoed with his own hands. He first introduced this kind of husbandry into the Western islands.' *Life*, v. 293. Even in the South of Scotland the turnip had only lately been introduced. 'Mr. Drummond, of Blair, sent over one of his ploughmen to learn drill husbandry, and the culture of turnips from Lord Eglinton's English servants. The very next year he raised a field of turnips, which were the first in the country. About the year 1771

Coll

Coll is but a barren place. Description has here few opportunities of spreading her colours. The difference of day and night is the only vicissitude. The succession of sunshine to rain, or of calms to tempests, we have not known ; wind and rain have been our only weather.

At last, after about nine days, we hired a sloop ; and having lain in it all night, with such accommodations as these miserable vessels can afford, were landed yesterday on the isle of Mull ; from which we expect an easy passage into Scotland. I am sick in a ship, but recover by lying down.

I have not good health ; I do not find that travelling much helps me. My nights are flatulent, though not in the utmost degree, and I have a weakness in my knees, which makes me very unable to walk [1].

Pray, dear Madam, let me have a long letter.

> I am, &c.,
>
> SAM: JOHNSON.

332.

To Mrs. Thrale [2].

HONOURED MISTRESS,   Inverary, Oct. 23, 1773.

My last letters to you and my dear master were written from Mull, the third island of the Hebrides in extent [3]. There is no post, and I took the opportunity of a gentleman's passage to the main land.

In Mull we were confined two days by the weather ; on the third we got on horse-back, and after a journey difficult

---

our tenants were well-disposed to the culture of turnips. They begin to have an idea of property in winter as well as in summer.' *Scotland and Scotsmen of the Eighteenth Century*, ii. 231, 272, 277. See *Footsteps of Dr. Johnson in Scotland*, p. 34.

[1] 'Ever since his last illness in 1766, he has had a weakness in his knees, and has not been able to walk easily.' It was this weakness which made him complain so bitterly, the day after he wrote this letter, of the loss of his

walking stick. 'I could not persuade him,' w. es Boswell, 'out of a suspicion that it had been stolen. "No, no, my friend (said he), it is not to be expected that any man in Mull, who has got it, will part with it. Consider, Sir, the value of such a *piece of timber* here!"' *Life*, v. 318.

[2] *Piozzi Letters*, i. 170.

[3] Mull contains about 235,000 acres, of which only about 13,000 are arable. *Encyclo. Brit.*, 9th ed., xvii. 16.

and

and tedious, over rocks naked and valleys untracked, through a country of barrenness and solitude, we came, almost in the dark, to the sea side, weary and dejected, having met with nothing but water falling from the mountains that could raise any image of delight[1]. Our company was the young Laird of Col and his servant. Col made every Maclean open his house where we came, and supply us with horses when we departed ; but the horses of this country are small, and I was not mounted to my wish.

At the sea side we found the ferry-boat departed[2] ; if it had been where it was expected, the wind was against us, and the hour was late, nor was it very desirable to cross the sea in darkness with a small boat. The captain of a sloop that had been driven thither by the storms, saw our distress, and as we were hesitating and deliberating, sent his boat, which, by Col's order, transported us to the isle of Ulva. We were introduced to Mr. Macquarry, the head of a small clan, whose ancestors have reigned in Ulva beyond memory, but who has reduced himself, by his negligence and folly, to the necessity of selling this venerable patrimony[3].

On the next morning we passed the strait to Inch Kenneth, an island about a mile in length, and less than half a mile broad ; in which Kenneth, a Scottish saint, established a small clerical college, of which the chapel walls are still standing[4]. At this place I beheld a scene which I wish you and my master and Queeney had partaken.

---

[1] ' Dr. Johnson said it was a dreary country, much worse than Sky. I differed from him. "O, Sir (said he), a most dolorous country." *Life*, v. 318. He had in mind the march of ' the adventurous bands ' in *Paradise Lost*, Bk. ii. l. 618 :—

' Through many a dark and dreary vale

They passed, and many a region dolorous.'

In his *Journey* he speaks of this tract as ' this gloom of desolation.' *Works*, ix. 136.

[2] They had hoped to cross over to Inch Kenneth, where they were to stay a night on their way to Iona. It was in the Sound of Ulva that poor Col was drowned on September 25 of the following year. *Post*, p. 331, and *Life*, v. 331.

[3] *Life*, iii. 126, 7 ; v. 319.

[4] ' Inch Kenneth was once a seminary of ecclesiastics, subordinate, I suppose, to Icolmkill. Sir Allan had a mind to trace the foundations of the college, but neither I nor Mr. Boswell, who bends a keener eye on vacancy, were able to perceive them.' Johnson's *Works*, ix. 141.

The

The only family on the island is that of Sir Allan, the chief of the ancient and numerous clan of Maclean; the clan which claims the second place, yielding only to Macdonald in the line of battle[1]. Sir Allan, a chieftain, a baronet, and a soldier, inhabits in this insulated desart a thatched hut with no chambers[2]. Young Col, who owns him as his chief, and whose cousin was his lady, had, I believe, given him some notice of our visit; he received us with the soldier's frankness and the gentleman's elegance, and introduced us to his daughters, two young ladies who have not wanted education suitable to their birth, and who, in their cottage, neither forgot their dignity, nor affected to remember it. Do not you wish to have been with us?

Sir Allan's affairs are in disorder by the fault of his ancestors, and while he forms some scheme for retrieving them, he has retreated hither[3].

When our salutations were over, he showed us the island. We walked uncovered into the chapel, and saw in the reverend ruin the effects of precipitate reformation. The floor is covered with ancient grave-stones, of which the inscriptions are not now legible; and without some of the chief families still continue the right of sepulture[4]. The altar is not yet quite demolished; beside it, on the right side, is a bas-relief of the Virgin with her child, and an angel hovering over her. On the other side still stands a hand-

[1] Johnson wrote to Boswell on November 27 of this year :—

'Enquire, if you can, the order of the Clans : Macdonald is first, Maclean second ; further I cannot go.' Boswell replied : 'You shall have what information I can procure as to the order of the Clans. A gentleman of the name of Grant tells me, that there is no settled order among them.' Sir Walter Scott in a note on this passage says :—'The Macdonalds always laid claim to be placed on the right of the whole Clans, and those of that tribe assign the breach of this order at Culloden as one cause of the loss of the day. The Macdonalds, placed on the left wing, refused to charge, and positively left the field unassailed and unbroken.' *Life*, ii. 269.

[2] By *chambers* he means, I conjecture, rooms on an upper floor. Boswell describes the place as 'a commodious habitation, though it consisted but of a few small buildings, only one story high.' He mentions 'little apartments.' *Ib.* v. 323.

[3] *Ib.* v. 343, n. 3.

[4] What Johnson means by *without* in this passage, which at first sight is perhaps not clear, is shown in his *Journey* where he says :—'The ground *round the chapel* is covered with grave-stones of chiefs and ladies; and still continues to be a place of sepulture.' *Works*, ix. 141.

bell.

bell, which, though it has no clapper, neither Presbyterian bigotry nor barbarian wantonness has yet taken away. The chapel is thirty-eight feet long, and eighteen broad[1]. Boswell, who is very pious, went into it at night to perform his devotions, but came back in haste, for fear of spectres. Near the chapel is a fountain, to which the water, remarkably pure, is conveyed from a distant hill, through pipes laid by the Romish clergy, which still perform the office of conveyance, though they have never been repaired since Popery was suppressed[2].

We soon after went in to dinner, and wanted neither the comforts nor the elegancies of life. There were several dishes, and variety of liquours. The servants live in another cottage; in which, I suppose, the meat is dressed.

Towards evening, Sir Allan told us that Sunday never passed over him like another day. One of the ladies read, and read very well, the evening service;—and Paradise was opened in the wild[3].

Next day, 18th, we went and wandered among the rocks on the shore, while the boat was busy in catching oysters, of which there is a great bed. Oysters lie upon the sand, one I think sticking to another, and cockles are found a few inches under the sand.

We then went in the boat to Sondiland, a little island very near. We found it a wild rock, of about ten acres[4]; part naked, part covered with sand, out of which we picked shells; and part clothed with a thin layer of mould, on the grass of which a few sheep are sometimes fed. We then came back and dined. I passed part of the afternoon in reading, and in the evening one

[1] In his *Journey* he makes it about sixty feet in length, and thirty in breath. *Works*, ix. 141.

[2] In the summer of 1889 I saw the fountain still running with a pure stream.

[3] 'You   raised   these   hallowed
        walls ; the desert smil'd,
     And Paradise was open'd in
        the wild.'
   POPE. *Eloisa to Abelard*, l. 134.
 'Dr. Johnson said that it was the most agreeable Sunday he had ever passed.' *Life*, v. 325. See *ib.* for his Latin verses on Inch Kenneth.

[4] 'Even Inch Kenneth has a subordinate island, named Sandiland, I suppose in contempt, where we landed, and found a rock with a surface of perhaps four acres.' Johnson's *Works*, ix. 141. The boatman, who took me to the island, called it, so far as I could catch the sound, Sameilan.

of the ladies played on her harpsichord, and Boswell and Col danced a reel with the other.

On the 19th, we persuaded Sir Allan to launch his boat again, and go with us to Icolmkill[1], where the first great preacher of Christianity to the Scots built a church, and settled a monastery. In our way we stopped to examine a very uncommon cave on the coast of Mull[2]. We had some difficulty to make our way over the vast masses of broken rocks that lie before the entrance, and at the mouth were embarrassed with stones, which the sea had accumulated, as at Brighthelmstone ; but as we advanced, we reached a floor of soft sand, and as we left the light behind us, walked along a very spacious cavity, vaulted over head with an arch almost regular, by which a mountain was sustained, at least a very lofty rock. From this magnificent cavern went a narrow passage to the right hand, which we entered with a candle, and though it was obstructed with great stones, clambered over them to a second expansion of the cave, in which there lies a great square stone, which might serve as a table. The air here was very warm, but not oppressive, and the flame of the candle continued pyramidal. The cave goes onward to an unknown extent, but we were now one hundred and sixty yards under ground ; we had but one candle, and had never heard of any that went further and came back ; we therefore thought it prudent to return.

Going forward in our boat, we came to a cluster of rocks, black and horrid, which Sir Allan chose for the place where he would eat his dinner. We climbed till we got seats. The stores were opened, and the repast taken[3].

We then entered the boat again ; the night came upon us ; the wind rose ; the sea swelled ; and Boswell desired to be set on dry ground : we, however, pursued our navigation, and passed by several little islands, in the silent solemnity of faint moonshine, seeing little, and hearing only the wind and the water.

[1] Iona.

[2] Mackinnon's Cave. *Life*, v. 331, Johnson's *Works*, ix. 142, and *Footsteps of Dr. Johnson in Scotland*, p. 225.

[3] 'We hoped to have procured some rum or brandy for our boatmen and servants, from a publick-house near where we landed ; but unfortunately a funeral a few days before had exhausted all their store.' *Life*, v. 332.

At

At last we reached the island ; the venerable seat of ancient sanctity; where secret piety reposed, and where fallen greatness was reposited[1]. The island has no house of entertainment, and we manfully made our bed in a farmer's barn. The description I hope to give you another time[2].

I am, &c.,
SAM: JOHNSON.

333.

To HENRY THRALE[3].

DEAR SIR,   Inverary, Oct. 23, 1773.

We have gotten at last out of the Hebrides. Some account of our travels I have sent to my mistress; and have inclosed an ode which I wrote in the isle of Skie.

Yesterday we landed, and to-day came hither. We purpose to visit Auchinleck, the seat of Mr. Boswell's father, then to pass a day at Glasgow[4], and return to Edinburgh.

About ten miles of this day's journey were uncommonly amusing[5]. We travelled with very little light, in a storm of wind and rain; we passed about fifty-five streams that crossed our way, and fell into a river that, for a very great part of our road, foamed and roared beside us; all the rougher powers of nature, except thunder, were in motion, but there was no danger. I should have been sorry to have missed any of the inconveniencies, to have had more light or less rain, for their co-operation crowded the scene and filled the mind[6].

I beg, however, to hear from you, and from my mistress. I

---

[1] For the fine passage in which he describes the thoughts which stirred him as 'he trod that illustrious island,' see his *Works*, ix. 145, and *Life*, v. 334.

[2] If the description was given the letter must have been lost.

[3] *Piozzi Letters*, i. 177.

[4] He was not aware apparently that he would have to pass through Glasgow on his way to Auchinleck.

[5] Johnson uses *amusing* in the same sense as Parnell in the passage quoted, *ante*, p. 248. In his *Dictionary* he defines it, 'to entertain with tran-

quillity; to fill with thoughts that engage the mind without distracting it.' See *post*, Letter of April 12, 1781, where writing of his affliction at Mr. Thrale's death, he says :—' I give my uneasiness little vent and amuse it as I can.'

[6] 'The wind was loud, the rain was heavy, and the whistling of the blast, the fall of the shower, the rush of the cataracts, and the roar of the torrent made a nobler chorus of the rough music of nature than it had ever been my chance to hear before.' Johnson's *Works*, ix. 155.

have

have seen nothing that drives you from my thoughts, but continue in rain and sunshine, by night and day, dear Sir,

> Your, &c.,
>
> SAM: JOHNSON.

ODE[1]

Inclosed in the preceding Letter.

Permeo terras, ubi nuda rupes
Saxeas miscet nebulis ruinas,
Torva ubi rident steriles coloni
Rura labores.

Pervagor gentes hominum ferorum,
Vita ubi nullo decorata cultu
Squallet informis, tugurîque fumis
Foeda latescit

Inter erroris salebrosa longi,
Inter ignotae strepitus loquelae,
Quot modis mecum, quid agat, requiro,
Thralia dulcis.

Seu viri curas, pia nupta, mulcet,
Seu fovet mater sobolem benigna,
Sive cum libris novitate pascit
Sedula mentem ;

Sit memor nostri, fideique merces
Stet fides constans, meritoque blandum
Thraliae discant resonare nomen
Littora Skiae.

Scriptum in Skiâ, Sept. 6.

334.

To HENRY THRALE [2].

DEAR SIR,   Inverary, Oct. 26, 1773.

The Duke kept us yesterday, or we should have gone forward. Inverary is a stately place[3]. We are now going to Edinburgh by Lochlomond, Glasgow, and Auchinleck.

I wrote to you from Mull, to send for Mr. Levett or Mrs. Williams, and let them have ten pounds, if it was wanted[4]. I

---

[1] The original manuscript of this Ode with corrections was sold by Messrs. Sotheby & Co., on April 8, 1891, for £19 5s.

[2] *Piozzi Letters*, i. 181.

[3] 'What I admire here,' said Johnson, 'is the total defiance of expense.' *Life*, v. 355.   [4] *Ante*, p. 276.

find

find that the passage of these insular letters is not very certain, and therefore think it necessary now to write again.

I do not limit them to ten pounds; be pleased to let them have what is necessary.

I have now not heard from London for more than two months[1]; surely I shall have many letters in Edinburgh. I hope my dear mistress is well, with all her tribe.

I am, &c.,
SAM: JOHNSON.

335.

To the Duke of Argyle.

Rosedow, Lochlomond, October 27, 1773. Published in the *Life*, v. 363.

This letter is misdated by Boswell, October 29. It was written either on the 26th or 27th.

336.

To Mrs. Thrale[2].

DEAR MADAM,   Glasgow, Oct. 28, 1773.

I have been in this place about two hours. On Monday, 25th, we dined with the Duke and Duchess of Argyle, and the Duke lent me a horse for my next day's journey[3].

26th: We travelled along a deep valley between lofty mountains, covered only with barren heath; entertained with a succession of cataracts on the left hand, and a roaring torrent on the right[4]. The Duke's horse went well; the road was

---

[1] Dr. Percy wrote from Alnwick on October 15 of this year to Sir Robert Chambers:—'By a gentleman who called here last week in his return out of the Highlands I am informed that our friend, Dr. Johnson, together with his conductor, Mr. Boswell, are detained prisoners in the Isle of Sky, and have their return cut off by the Torrents, &c., and that Sir Alexander Macdonald and his Lady (at whose house our Friend is a captive) had made their escape before the floods cut off their Retreat; so that possibly we may not see our Friend till next sum[r] releases him.' From the original in the possession of Mr. W. R. Smith, of Greatham Moor, West Liss.

[2] *Piozzi Letters*, i. 182.

[3] 'The Duke was obliging enough to mount Dr. Johnson on a stately steed from his grace's stable. My friend was highly pleased, and Joseph said, "He now looks like a bishop."' *Life*, v. 362.

[4] The valley was Glen Croe, through which a military road had been made.

good :

good ; and the journey pleasant ; except that we were incommoded by perpetual rain. In all September we had, according to Boswell's register, only one day and a half of fair weather ; and October perhaps not more[1]. At night we came to the house of Sir James Cohune[2], who lives upon the banks of Loch-lomond ; of which the Scotch boast, and boast with reason.

27th : We took a boat to rove upon the lake, which is in length twenty-four miles, in breadth from perhaps two miles to half a mile[3]. It has about thirty islands, of which twenty belong to Sir James. Young Cohune went into the boat with us, but a little agitation of the water frighted him to shore[4]. We passed up and down, and landed upon one small island, on which are the ruins of a castle ; and upon another much larger, which serves Sir James for a park, and is remarkable for a large wood of eugh trees[5].

We then returned, very wet, to dinner, and Sir James lent us his coach to Mr. Smollet's, a relation of Dr. Smollet[6], for whom he has erected a monumental column on the banks of the Leven, a river which issues from the Loch. This was his native place[7]. I was desired to revise the inscription.

When I was upon the deer island, I gave the keeper who

---

[1] In London that year rain fell on eighteen days in September, and on thirteen in October. *Gentleman's Magazine*, 1774, pp. 338, 394.

[2] Johnson writes the name as it is pronounced. It is spelt Colquhoun.

[3] Its length is twenty miles, and its greatest breadth four miles. *Encyclo. Brit.*, 9th ed., xiv. 217.

[4] Just one hundred years later, on the night of December 18, 1873, that very fate befell one of his descendants which the young Colquhoun dreaded for himself. His boat was upset as he was coming home from Yew Island, and he was drowned with three of his gamekeepers and a boy.

[5] 'Eugh. [This word is so written by most writers, but since the original ıp Saxon, or Welsh ywen

more favours the easier othography of *yew*, I have referred it thither.] A tree.' Johnson's *Dictionary*. These yew trees were planted, it was said, on the advice of King Robert Bruce, in order to furnish the Lennox men with bows. Irving's *Book of Dumbartonshire*, i. 347.

[6] Baretti has this curious note on Smollett :—'A Scotch wit, who had some name in his day.' For Johnson's revision of the inscription, see *Life*, v. 367. The copy with the corrections in his handwriting is preserved at Cameron, the seat of the Smolletts. Irving's *Book of Dumbartonshire*, ii. 200.

[7] For Smollett's *Ode to Leven-Water*, see Campbell's *British Poets*, ed. 1845, p. 514.

attended

attended me a shilling, and he said it was too much. Boswell afterwards offered him another, and he excused himself from taking it, because he had been rewarded already.

This day I came hither, and go to Auchinleck on Monday.

I am, &c.,

SAM: JOHNSON.

337.

To MRS. THRALE [1].

HONOURED MISTRESS,   Auchinleck, Nov. 3, 1773.

At Glasgow I received six letters, of which the first was written August 23d [2]. I am now at leisure to answer them in order.

August 23d. Mrs. B——[3] has the mien and manners of a gentlewoman; and such a person and mind as would not be in any place either admired or contemned. She is in a proper degree inferior to her husband: she cannot rival him; nor can he ever be ashamed of her.

Little Miss, when I left her, was like any other Miss of seven months [4]. I believe she is thought pretty; and her father and mother have a mind to think her wise.

Your letter brought us the first certain intelligence of Dr. Beattie's pension [5]. He will now be a great man at Aberdeen, where every one speaks well of him.

August 25th. I am obliged to dear Queeney for her letter, and am sorry that I have not been able to collect more for her cabinet [6], but I shall bring her something.

[1] *Piozzi Letters*, i. 194.

[2] He had not received a single letter since he left Aberdeen on August 24.

[3] Mrs. Boswell. She was alive when this was published by Mrs. Piozzi.

[4] No doubt Boswell's daughter Veronica; but she was only about four months old when Johnson saw her. *Life*, v. 26.

[5] She had written to him:—'Every body rejoices that the Doctor will get his pension; every one loves him but Goldsmith, who says he cannot bear the sight of so much applause as we all bestow upon him. Did he not tell us so himself, who could believe he was so amazingly ill-natured?' *Piozzi Letters*, i. 186. Goldsmith, with immeasurably superior merit and greater need, received no pension. He was indignant moreover at the absurd praise bestowed on Beattie as if he had overcome Hume. *Life*, v. 273, *n.* 4. For the pension see *ib.* ii. 264, *n.* 2; v. 360. Beattie was Professor of Moral Philosophy at Aberdeen.

[6] *Ante*, p. 196.

What

What should · · ·[1] and his wife do at the wrong end of the town, whither they can carry nothing that will not raise contempt, and from which they can bring nothing that will not excite aversion. He is not to be either wit or statesman ; his genius, if he follow his direction, will bid him live in Lothbury, and measure brandy[2].

Sept. 8th. I first saw the account of Lord Littelton's death in the isle of Raarsa, and suspected that it had been hastened by the vexation which his son has given him. We shall now see what the young man will do, when he is left to himself[3].

I am at a loss what to judge of Sir · · ·. To doubt whether six thousand pounds have or have not been paid, as was directed, is absurd and childish ; he to whom they were due can answer the question ; and he by whom they were remitted can confirm or confute the answer. You should surely write to Mr. B——.

Of Sir · · · you had not left me any high notions ; but I supposed him to be at least commercially honest, and incapable of eluding his own bond by fraudulent practices, yet I think Mr. T——'s suspicion not to be slighted. Principles can only be strong by the strength of understanding, or the cogency of religion.

I do not see how you can much offend by putting Harry's life

---

[1] 'Rice.' BARETTI. *Ante*, p. 219.

[2] Mrs. Piozzi publishes a letter of hers written apparently before Johnson's, in which she says :—' * * * * and her husband set out very prettily, and will, I hope, stick to the city. Lothbury, as you say.—How in the world came you to think of Lothbury?' *Piozzi Letters*, i. 186. This passage clearly seems an answer to Johnson's letters. If hers is in any sense genuine, it is, I conjecture, made up of two or three letters written at different times.

[3] Lord Lyttelton died on August 22. *Gentleman's Magazine*, 1773, p. 414. Johnson was at Raasay from September 8-12. Horace Walpole wrote on September 2 : — 'Lord Lyttelton is dead. His worthy son

has added so much to his mass of character by histories too opprobrious to be entertaining, that even this age has the grace to shun him ; but then he is neither a monarch nor a nabob.' *Letters*, v. 499. He was commonly known as 'the wicked Lord Lyttelton.' See *Life*, iv. 298, *n.* 3. Samuel Rogers thus described one of the tricks which he used to play in his boyhood. 'When he knew that the larder at Hagley happened to be illsupplied, he would invite, in his father's name, a large party to dinner ; and as the carriages drove up the avenue, the old Lord (concealing his vexation as much as possible) would stand bowing in the hall, to welcome his unwelcome guests.' *Table Talk of Samuel Rogers*, p. 118.

into

into the lease, it puts no life out, and therefore does not lessen Sir · • ·'s interest [1]. I believe, however, you may depend better for peace upon the indifference of his indolence, than the approbation of his judgment. I think it should not be neglected.

Sept. 14th : I take great delight in your fifteen thousand trees ; the greater, for having been so long in a country where trees and diamonds are equal rarities.

Poor V—— ! There are not so many reasons as he thinks why he should envy me, but there are some ; he wants what I have, a kind and careful mistress ; and wants likewise what I shall want at my return. He is a good man ; and, when his mind is composed, a man of parts [2].

Sept. 28th : When I wrote an account of my intention to return, I little thought that I should be so long the plaything of the wind. Of the various accidents of our voyage I have been careful to give you an account, and hope you have received it. My deafness went away by degrees. Miss Macleod made me a great flannel night-cap, which perhaps helped to set me right.

If Sir · • · [3] goes to Bath, it may deserve consideration whether you should not follow him. If you go, take two footmen, and dress in such a manner as he may be proud to see.

---

[1] On October 7 Mrs. Thrale wrote to Johnson :—'Harry's life *is* put in the lease ; may he hold it, as my father's mother did, for seventy-three years !' *Piozzi Letters*, i. 193. He died in two years and a half from this time. *Life*, ii. 468.

[2] V——, says Baretti, was Vansittart. See *Life*, i. 348 ; v. 460. Johnson is answering the following passage in Mrs. Thrale's letter :—'Meantime I have seen little except the man that saw the mouse. He seems very ill, and very wild ; I fancy *he* wants a governess ; *your* merits, as usual, were talked of ; and he made choice of your *health* as the subject of his eulogium.' *Piozzi Letters*, i. 185. For her confusion of the mouse with the flea in the story to which she here alludes, see *Life*, ii. 194, *n.* 2.

[3] 'Her uncle, Sir Thomas Salusbury.'- BARETTI. See *ante*, p. 193. On the death of his first wife, Mrs. Piozzi writes, 'he *said* he had no kindness but for me. I think *I* did share his fondness with his stud ; our stable was the first for hunters of enormous value.' He yielded however to 'the blandishments' of a widow, the Hon. Mrs. King, whom he married, 'and then scarce ever saw or wrote to me or my husband.' Hayward's *Piozzi*, i. 250-4. He was no doubt going to Bath for his health. He died on the following October 30. *Gentleman's Magazine*, 1773, p. 581.

The

The money that you stake is no great venture, nor will the want of it be felt, whether you gain or lose the purpose of your journey.

My poor little Lucy is, I hope, now quite recovered[1]; for I have brought no little maiden from the Highlands, though I might perhaps have had one of the princesses of Raarsa, who are very pretty people, and in that wilderness of life put me in mind of your little tribe, by the propriety of their behaviour.

Oct. 7th. This is the last letter. I have done thinking of * * *[2] whom we now call Sir Sawney; he has disgusted all mankind by injudicious parsimony, and given occasion to so many stories, that * * * has some thoughts of collecting them, and making a novel of his life[3]. Scrambling I have not willingly left off; the power of scrambling has left me[4]; I have however been forced to exert it on many occasions. I am, I thank God, better than I was. I am grown very much superior to wind and rain; and am too well acquainted both with mire and with rocks, to be afraid of a Welch journey[5]. I had rather have Bardsey than Macleod's island, though I am told much of the beauty of my new property, which the storms did not suffer me to visit[6]. Boswell will praise my resolution and perseverance;

[1] She was his god-daughter. Mrs. Thrale had written to him :—'What ails dear Lucy I cannot guess, but her ear is affected sure enough, and she goes about with her head on one side.' *Piozzi Letters*, i. 188.

[2] Sir Alexander Macdonald. *Ante*, p. 244. He was alive when these Letters were published. It is probable that Johnson wrote, not 'thinking *of*,' but 'thinking *on*.'

[3] * * * * is, no doubt, Boswell, who records on October 15 :—'The penurious gentleman of our acquaintance, formerly alluded to, afforded us a topick of conversation to-night. Dr. Johnson said, I ought to write down a collection of the instances of his narrowness, as they almost exceeded belief.' *Life*, v. 315.

[4] *Ante*, p. 254

[5] Mrs. Thrale on the death of her uncle would become possessed of the Welsh estates of her family. Hayward's *Piozzi*, i. 254. In the following summer Johnson accompanied her and Mr. Thrale when they went to Wales to take possession. *Life*, ii. 281 ; v. 427.

[6] Mrs. Thrale had written :— 'When you sigh for an island of your own, remember that Rasselas could never settle the limits of his imaginary dominion, but when I am grown rich, we will buy Bardsey for you; perhaps a sight of Wales in the mean time may not be amiss.' *Piozzi Letters*, i. 190. Bardsey Island lies off that part of Carnarvonshire where she was born. *Life*, v. 449. For Johnson's island see *ante*, p. 246.

and

and I shall in return celebrate his good humour and perpetual cheerfulness. He has better faculties than I had imagined; more justness of discernment; and more fecundity of images. It is very convenient to travel with him, for there is no house where he is not received with kindness and respect[1].

I wish B—— success in his new mine, and hope that the vein will be as rich as his wants prompt him to wish it[2]. I congratulate you likewise on the rising reputation of the brewery; and hope that the sweets of doing right will so much engage us, that we shall never more allow ourselves to do wrong. Forty shillings is a frightful price for malt, but we must brew on and brew well, and hold out to better times[3].

Thus, Dear Madam, I have answered your six letters, in part too late to be of any use. The regard which you are pleased to express, and the kindness which you always show, I do not pretend to return otherwise than by warm wishes for your happiness.

I will now continue my narrative.

Oct. 29th was spent in surveying the city and college of Glasgow. I was not much pleased with any of the professors[4]. The town is opulent and handsome[5].

30th: We dined with the Earl of Loudon, and saw his mother the Countess; who, at ninety-three, has all her faculties, helps at table, and exerts all the powers of conversation that she ever had[6]. Though not tall, she stoops very much. She had lately a daughter, Lady Betty, whom, at seventy, she used to send

---

[1] See Johnson's *Works*, ix. 1; *Life*, v. 52, and *post*, Letter of June 23, 1784.

[2] She had written to him on October 7:—'Our old friend B——, by the way, has found a vein of lead ore on his estate, and I feel very glad to hear it somehow. You used to hate that poor fellow, because he could not wait for his dinner till four o'clock, but he may have it now to a minute, and I doubt not but the wild fowl will be done to a *turn*.' *Piozzi Letters*, i. 192.

[3] *Ante*, p. 194.

[4] 'The general impression upon my memory,' writes Boswell, 'is that we had not much conversation at Glasgow, where the professors, like their brethren at Aberdeen, did not venture to expose themselves much to the battery of cannon which they knew might play upon them.' *Life*, v. 371.

[5] 'Dr. Johnson told me, that one day in London, when Dr. Adam Smith was boasting of Glasgow, he turned to him and said, "Pray, Sir, have you ever seen Brentford?"' *Ib.* p. 369.

[6] *Life*, iii. 366; v. 371.

after

after supper early to bed, for girls must not use late hours, while she sat up to entertain the company.

31st, Sunday, we passed at Mr. Campbell's, who married Mr. Boswell's sister [1].

Nov. 1st: We paid a visit to the Countess of Eglington, a lady who for many years gave the laws of elegance to Scotland. She is in full vigour of mind, and not much impaired in form. She is only eighty-three. She was remarking that her marriage was in the year eight; and I told her my birth was in nine. Then, says she, I am just old enough to be your mother, and I will take you for my son. She called Boswell the boy: yes, Madam, said I, we will send him to school. He is already, said she, in a good school; and expressed her hope of his improvement. At last night came, and I was sorry to leave her [2].

2nd: We came to Auchinleck. The house is like other houses in this country built of stone, scarcely yet finished, but very magnificent and very convenient. We purpose to stay here some days; more or fewer as we are used [3]. I shall find no kindness such as will suppress my desire of returning home.

I am, &c.,
SAM: JOHNSON.

338.

TO MRS. THRALE [4].

DEAREST MADAM,   Edinburgh, Nov. 12, 1773.

Among the possibilities of evil which my imagination suggested at this distance, I missed that which has really happened. I never had much hope of a will in your favour, but was willing to believe that no will would have been made. The event is now irrevocable, it remains only to bear it [5]. Not to wish it had

---

[1] He had married Mrs. Boswell's sister. *Life*, v. 372.

[2] *Ib.* v. 374, 401.

[3] Boswell, after stating the great differences in character and opinion between Dr. Johnson and his father, adds:—'Knowing all this, I should not have ventured to bring them together, had not my father, out of kindness to me, desired me to invite Dr. Johnson to his house.' *Ib.* v. 376.

Johnson says 'as *we* are used,' being well aware that Boswell himself never was at his ease with his father. *Ib.* ii. 382, *n.* 1; iii. 93, *n.* 1.

[4] *Piozzi Letters*, i. 201.

In the Table of Contents she describes this letter as 'a letter of consolation on her uncle's having bequeathed his estate to another.'

[5] 'We had once expected,' writes Mrs. Piozzi, 'Offley Place in Hertford-

been

been different is impossible ; but as the wish is painful without use, it is not prudent, perhaps not lawful, to indulge it. As life, and vigour of mind, and sprightliness of imaginatoin, and flexibility of attention, are given us for valuable and useful purposes, we must not think ourselves at liberty to squander life, to enervate intellectual strength, to cloud our thoughts, or fix our attention, when by all this expence we know that no good can be produced. Be alone as little as you can ; when you are alone, do not suffer your thoughts to dwell on what you might have done, to prevent this disappointment. You perhaps could not have done what you imagine, or might have done it without effect. But even to think in the most reasonable manner, is for the present not so useful as not to think[1]. Remit yourself solemnly into the hands of God, and then turn your mind upon the business and amusements which lie before you. 'All is best,' says Chene, 'as it has been, excepting the errours of our own free will[2].' Burton concludes his long book upon melancholy with this important precept, 'Be not solitary; be not idle[3].' Remember Chene's position and observe Burton's precept.

We came hither on the ninth of this month[4]. I long to come under your care, but for some days cannot decently get away. They congratulate our return as if we had been with Phipps or Banks ; I am ashamed of their salutations[5].

shire and all its wide domain.' Hayward's *Piozzi*, i. 293. In Chauncy's *History of Hertfordshire*, ed. 1700, p. 407, is a curious print of the old house. 'It is situated,' writes Chauncy, 'on the great ledge of hills which crosses the northerly part of that County, called by some the Alps of England.' See also Cussan's *History of Hertfordshire*, ii. 96. According to Baretti, 'Sir T. Salusbury disinherited Mrs. Thrale on account of her superlative impertinence to his wife.'

[1] *Life*, iii. 136, *n.* 2.

[2] See *ib.* v. 154 for another quotation from Dr. Cheyne.

[3] *Ib.* iii. 415, and *post*, Letter of March 30, 1776.

[4] Boswell records on this day :— 'We arrived this night at Edinburgh, after an absence of eighty-three days. For five weeks together, of the tempestuous season, there had been no account received of us. I cannot express how happy I was on finding myself again at home.' *Life*, v. 385.

[5] 'Every body had accosted us with some studied compliment on our return. Dr. Johnson said, "I am really ashamed of the congratulations which we receive. We are addressed as if we had made a voyage to Nova Zembla, and suffered five persecutions in Japan." ' *Life*, v. 392. For Phipps, see *ante*, p. 210, and Banks, *Life*, ii. 144.

I have

I have been able to collect very little for Queeney's cabinet ; but she will not want toys[1] now, she is so well employed. I wish her success; and am not without some thought of becoming her school-fellow. I have got an Italian Rasselas.

Surely my dear Lucy will recover ; I wish I could do her good. I love her very much ; and should love another god-child, if I might have the honour of standing to the next baby.

                                        I am, &c.,
                                              SAM : JOHNSON.

339.
To MRS. THRALE[2].

MY DEAREST MISTRESS,   Edinburgh, Nov. 18, 1773.

This is the last letter that I shall write ; while you are reading it, I shall be coming home.

I congratulate you upon your boy[3]; but you must not think that I will love him all at once as well as I love Harry, for Harry you know is so rational. I shall love him by degrees.

Poor, pretty, dear Lucy ! Can nothing do her good ? I am sorry to lose her. But if she must be taken from us, let us resign her with confidence into the hands of Him who knows, and who only knows, what is best both for us and her.

Do not suffer yourself to be dejected[4]. Resolution and diligence will supply all that is wanting, and all that is lost. But if your health should be impaired, I know not where to find a

---

[1] By *toys* he does not mean playthings, but the curiosities of her cabinet. She had probably begun the study of Italian under Baretti, and perhaps Johnson means to say that he will take lessons with her. Baretti has the following note on the Italian *Rasselas* :—'And a damned one it is, by a foolish fellow who called himself Cavalier Mei. I knew him a beggar at Padua. He neither knew English, nor Italian, though a Tuscan by birth.'

[2] *Piozzi Letters*, i. 206.

[3] Her second son, Ralph, was born on November 8. 'He died within the year of the inoculated small-pox, during which the mother used to wash him in cold water in consequence of her great skill in physick.'—BARETTI. He lived a year and eight or nine months, and does not seem to have died of inoculation. *Post*, Letters of July 6, 13, 20, 1775.

[4] 'She was not at all dejected at poor Lucy's death, and in a day or two thought no more of her than she would of a puppy-dog.'—BARETTI. The child was buried on the day on which Johnson arrived in London.

                                        substitute.

substitute. I shall have no mistress; Mr. Thrale will have no wife; and the little flock will have no mother.

I long to be home, and have taken a place in the coach for Monday; I hope therefore to be in London on Friday the 26th, in the evening[1]. Please to let Mrs. Williams know.

I am, &c.,
SAM: JOHNSON.

340.

TO JAMES BOSWELL.

[London], November 27, 1773. Published in the *Life*, ii. 268.

341.

TO MRS. MONTAGU[2].

MADAM, Jan. 11, 1774.

Having committed one fault by inadvertency, I will not commit another by sullenness. When I had the honour of your card, I could not comply with your invitation, and must now suffer the shame of confessing that the necessity of an answer did not come into my mind.

This omission, Madam, you may easily excuse, as the consciousness of your own character must secure you from suspecting that the favour of your notice can never miss a suitable return, but from ignorance or thoughtlessness; and to be ignorant of your eminence is not easy, but to him who lives out of the reach of the public voice.

I am, Madam,
Your most obedient and most humble servant,
SAM: JOHNSON.

[1] On Saturday the 27th he wrote to Boswell:—'I came home last night, without any incommodity, danger, or weariness, and am ready to begin a new journey. I shall go to Oxford on Monday.' *Life*, ii. 268.

[2] First published in Croker's *Boswell*, page 410.

For Mrs. Montagu see *Life*, ii. 88; iv. 275.

In the first page of a copy of Johnson's *Dictionary* the following description of him was written this year:—'As to his person he is full six feet high, of an athletic make, but stoops as he walks, which diminishes his stature. He is rather of a sallow complexion, with a cast in his eye, and appears wrapt in contemplation. He is above sixty years of age; but time does not seem as yet to have made any depredations on his constitution. He is very communicative in company, and without any affecta-

TO

To the Reverend Dr. Taylor[1].

Dear Sir,

When I was at Edinburgh I had a letter from you, telling me that in answer to some enquiry you were informed that I was in the Sky. I was then I suppose in the western islands of Scotland; I set out on the northern expedition August 6, and came back to Fleet Street, November 26. I have seen a new region.

I have been upon seven of the islands[2]. and probably should have visited many more, had we not begun our journey so late in the year, that the stormy weather came upon us, and the storms have I believe for about five months hardly any intermission.

Your Letter told me that you were better. When you write do not forget to confirm that account. I had very little ill health while I was on the journey, and bore rain and wind tolerably well. I had a cold and deafness only for a few days, and those days I passed at a good house[3]. I have traversed the east coast of Scotland from south to north, from Edinburgh to Inverness, and the west coast from north to south, from the Highlands to Glasgow, and am come back as I went,

Sir,

Your affectionate humble servant,

Jan. 15, 1774. SAM : JOHNSON.

To the Reverend Dr. Taylor, in Ashbourn, Derbyshire.

To James Boswell.

[London], January 29, 1774. Published in the *Life*, ii. 271.

tion of pedantry. He is a widower, and will probably remain in that state. Add to this that his manner of speaking in conversation is slow, but nervous in delivery, and perfectly correct and elegant in diction.' Quoted in the *Gentleman's Magazine* for 1849, i. 247.

[1] First published in my edition of the *Life*, volume v, page 405, from the original in the possession of Mr. M. M. Holloway of Hillbrow, Streatham. For a fac-simile of this Letter, see *Footsteps of Dr. Johnson in Scotland*, page 308.

[2] Sky, Raasay, Coll, Mull, Ulva, Inchkenneth and Iona.

[3] Dunvegan Castle. *Ante*, p. 245.

To

344.

To JAMES BOSWELL.

London, February 7, 1774.   Published in the *Life*, ii. 272.

345.

To GEORGE STEEVENS.

[London], February 7, 1774.   Published in the *Life*, ii. 273.

346.

To GEORGE STEEVENS.

[London], February 21, 1774.   Published in the *Life*, ii. 273.

347.

To GEORGE STEEVENS.

[London], March 5, 1774.   Published in the *Life*, ii. 273.

348.

To JAMES BOSWELL.

[London], March 5, 1774.   Published in the *Life*, ii. 274.

349.

To [? WILLIAM STRAHAN].

March 7, 1774.

In Messrs. Puttick and Simpson's Auction Catalogue of July 30, 1886, Lot 1109 is a letter of Johnson's, four pages quarto, dated March 7, 1774. 'Containing his ideas as to the laws of literary copyright.'

This use of the word *ideas* Johnson would have censured. *Life*, iii. 196. For copyright see *ib.* i. 437; ii. 259, and Hume's *Letters to Strahan*, pp. 176, 274–281.

350.

To MRS. THRALE [1].

MADAM,   March 11, 1774.

Our master is a very good man, and contrives well for me. I have now a reason for doing on Monday what I might have been persuaded against my will to have delayed till Tuesday. I hope on Monday to be your slave in the morning, and Mrs.

[1] *Piozzi Letters*, i. 208.

Smith's

Smith's[1] in the evening, and then fall again to my true mistress, and be the rest of the week,

Madam,

Your most obedient,

SAM: JOHNSON.

351.

TO MRS. THRALE[2].

MADAM, Thursday.

Master is very kind in being very angry; but he may spare his anger this time. I have done exactly as Dr. Lawrence ordered, and am much better at the expence of about thirty-six ounces of blood[3]. Nothing in the world! For a good cause I have six-and-thirty more. I long though to come to Streatham, and you shall give me no solid flesh for a week; and I am to take physick. And hey boys, up go we. I was in bed all last night, only a little sitting up[4]. The box goes to Calcutta[5].

I am,

Dearest, dearest Madam,

Yours, &c.,

SAM: JOHNSON.

Let me come to you to-morrow.

352.

TO JAMES BOSWELL.

[London], about March 15, 1774. Published in the *Life*, ii. 276.

353.

TO WARREN HASTINGS.

[London], March 30, 1774. Published in the *Life*, iv. 68.

---

[1] Perhaps the Mrs. Smith whom Miss Burney describes two years later as 'very little, ugly, and terribly deformed, but quick, clever, and entertaining.' *Early Diary of Frances Burney*, ii. 138.

[2] *Piozzi Letters*, i. 209. In Mrs. Piozzi's volume this letter follows the last, and therefore I insert it here.

[3] For Dr. Lawrence, see *Life*, ii. 296, and for bleeding, *ib.* iii. 152.

[4] He sat up when he was oppressed by asthma.

[5] Johnson writing to Warren Hastings on March 30, 1774, says that he is sending him a book. *Ib.* iv. 69.

TO

354.

To JAMES BOSWELL.

[London], May 10, 1774.   Published in the *Life*, ii. 277.

355.

To [JAMES BOSWELL] [1].

[May 27, 1774.]

· · · The Lady being interested in some suits desires a letter of introduction to you. That which you have received without understanding it was written for her, and by mistake given to the post.

She flatters me by telling me that when you know that I wish her well, you will be more zealous in her causes. I know that you need no incitements to zeal or fidelity, but are willing to do [rest missing].

356.

To JAMES BOSWELL.

Streatham, June 21, 1774.   Published in the *Life*, ii. 278.

357.

To JAMES BOSWELL.

[London], July 4, 1774.   Published in the *Life*, ii. 279.

358.

To BENNET LANGTON.

[London], July 5, 1774.   Published in the *Life*, ii. 280.

359.

To ROBERT LEVETT.

Llewenny, August 16, 1774.   Published in the *Life*, ii. 282.

[1] From the original fragment in the possession of Mr. G. J. Campbell, of 12 Lombard Street, Inverness. At the foot of the letter is written in a last-century hand, 'original letter and writing of Dr. Samuel Johnson, May 27, 1774.'

In the *Life of Johnson*, ii. 277, is the letter which the lady ought to have delivered, but which 'by mistake was given to the post.' There can be little doubt that this second letter was never delivered, for had Boswell received it he would have published it.

To

360.

To James Boswell.

London, October 1, 1774. Published in the *Life*, ii. 284.

361.

To —— Perkins.

[London], October 25, 1774. Published in the *Life*, ii. 286.

362.

To James Boswell.

London, October 27, 1774. Published in the *Life*, ii. 287.

363.

To James Boswell.

[London], November 26, 1774. Published in the *Life*, ii. 288.

364.

To William Strahan [1].

Sir,

I waited on you this morning having forgotten your new engagement; for this you must not reproach me, for if I had looked upon your present station with malignity I could not have forgotten it [2]. I came to consult you upon a little matter that gives me some uneasiness. In one of the pages there is a severe censure of the clergy of an English Cathedral which I am afraid is just, but I have since recollected that from me it may be thought improper, for the Dean did me a kindness about forty years ago. He is now very old, and I am not young. Reproach can do him no good, and in myself I know not

[1] First published in my edition of the *Life*, vol. vi. *Addenda*, p. xxxiii, from the original in the possession of Messrs. Pearson & Co., 46 Pall Mall.

[2] Strahan, to quote Hume's words (Hume's *Letters to Strahan*, p. 287), the day before Johnson's letter was written, 'had ceased to be a speculative politician, and become a practical one.' He had been chosen member for Malmesbury in the new Parliament which met on November 29, 1774. Johnson was so far from looking on his station with malignity that he always employed him to frank his letters to Scotland, 'that he might have the consequence of appearing a Parliament-man among his countrymen.' *Life*, iii. 365.

whether

whether it is zeal or wantonness. Can a leaf be cancelled without too much trouble? tell me what I shall do. I have no settled choice, but I would not wish to allow the charge. To cancel it seems the surer side [1]. Determine for me.

I am, Sir, Your most humble servant,

Nov. 30, 1774.   SAM: JOHNSON.

Tell me your mind: if you will cancel it I will write something to fill up the vacuum. Please to direct to the borough [2].

---

[1] The leaf which Johnson cancelled contained pages 47, 48 in the first edition of his *Journey to the Western Islands*. It corresponds with pages 19-20 in vol. ix. of Johnson's *Works* (ed. 1825), beginning with the words 'could not enter,' and ending 'imperfect constitution.' The excision is marked by a ridge of paper, which was left that the revised leaf might be attached to it. Johnson describes how the lead which covered the cathedrals of Elgin and Aberdeen had been stripped off by the order of the Scottish Council, and shipped to be sold in Holland. He continues:—
'Let us not however make too much haste to despise our neighbours. Our own cathedrals are mouldering by unregarded dilapidation. It seems to be part of the despicable philosophy of the time to despise monuments of sacred magnificence, and we are in danger of doing that deliberately, which the Scots did not do but in the unsettled state of an imperfect constitution.'
In the copy of the first edition in the Bodleian Library, which had belonged to Gough the antiquary, there is written in his hand, as a foot-note to 'neighbours': 'There is now, as I have heard, a body of men not less decent or virtuous than the Scottish Council, longing to melt the lead of an English Cathedral. What they shall melt, it were just that they should swallow.' It can scarcely be doubted that this is the suppressed passage. The English cathedral to which Johnson refers was Lichfield. 'The roof,' says Harwood (*History of Lichfield*, p. 75), 'was formerly covered with lead, but now with slate.' That Addenbroke, who had been Dean since 1745, had at a still earlier date done Johnson a kindness, I have learnt from a letter of his published in *Notes and Queries*, 6th S., x. 421. It is dated Stafford (of which town he was Rector), May 10 (the year is not given), and is addressed to Thomas Whitby of Heywood, to whom he recommended Johnson as tutor to his son. His services had been required for half a year, 'but,' wrote Addenbroke, 'his affairs won't give him leave to be with your son so long. . . . I can only say that if Mr. Johnson will do what He is capable of doing in that time He will be of more service to your son than a year spent in the usual way at the University.' In a note to this letter, dated November 18, 1824, Mr. T. Whitby, of Creswell Hall, says:— 'I have frequently heard Mrs. Wells, my father's youngest sister, say, that she remembered Mr. Johnson being at Heywood as tutor to her brother, and that he frequently instructed her in the English language.' For an anecdote of Addenbroke and Bentley see Monk's *Life of Bentley*, ii. 212. See *ante*, p. 185.

[2] Johnson was staying at Thrale's

To —— HOLLYER [1].

SIR,

I take the liberty of writing to you, with whom I have no acquaintance, and whom I have therefore very little right to trouble; but as it is about a man equally or almost equally related to both of us, I hope you will excuse it.

I have lately received a letter from our cousin Thomas Johnson complaining of great distress. His distress, I suppose, is real; but how can it be prevented? In 1772, about Christmas, I sent him thirty pounds, because he thought he could do something in a shop : many have lived who began with less. In the summer 1773 I sent him ten pounds more, as I had promised him. What was the event? In the spring 1774 he wrote me, and [2] that he was in debt for rent, and in want of clothes. That is, he had in about sixteen months consumed forty pounds, and then writes for more, without any mention of either misconduct or misfortune. This seems to me very strange, and I shall be obliged to you if you can inform me, or make him inform me, how the money was spent; and give your advice what can be done for him with prudence and efficacy.

He is, I am afraid, not over sensible of the impropriety of his management, for he came to visit me in the summer. I was in the country, which, perhaps, was well for us both : I might have used him harshly, and then have repented.

I have sent a bill for five pounds, which you will be so kind to get discounted for him, and see the money properly applied, and give me your advice what can be done.

I am, Sir,

Your humble servant,

Dec. 6, 1774.   SAM: JOHNSON.

To Mr. Hollyer of Coventry.

town-house in the Borough of Southwark.

[1] First published in Croker's *Boswell*, page 427.

According to Mr. Croker, Hollyer was the son of one of the sisters of Johnson's mother. The tone of the letter however is not that of a man who is writing to so near a relation as his first cousin. For Thomas Johnson see *ante*, p. 154, *n.* 3.

[2] Perhaps for *and* we should read *word*.

To

366.

To John Hoole.

[London], December 19, 1774. Published in the *Life*, ii. 289.

367.

To Warren Hastings.

London, December 20, 1774. Published in the *Life*, iv. 69.

368.

To William Strahan [1].

Sir,

When we meet we talk, and I know not whether I always recollect what I thought I had to say.

You will please to remember that I once asked you to receive an apprentice, who is a scholar, and has always lived in a clergyman's house, but who is mishapen, though I think not so as to hinder him at the case [2]. It will be expected that I should answer his Friend who has hitherto maintained him, whether I can help him to a place. He can give no money, but will be kept in cloaths.

I have another request which it is perhaps not immediately in your power to gratify. I have a presentation to beg for the blue coat hospital. The boy is a non-freeman, and has both his parents living. We have a presentation [3] for a freeman which

---

[1] First published in my edition of the *Life*, vol. vi. *Addenda*, p. xxxv, from the original in the possession of Messrs. Robson and Kerslake, 25 Coventry Street, Haymarket.

[2] The apprentice was young William Davenport, the orphan son of a clergyman. His friend was the Rev. W. Langley, the master of Ashbourne School. Strahan received him as an apprentice. *Life*, ii. 324, *n.* 1. See also Nichols's *Literary Anecdotes*, vol. iii. p. 287.

The 'case' is the frame containing boxes for holding type.

[3] In the original Johnson divides this word *presentati-on*. I am informed by Mr. W. Lempriere, of Christ's Hospital, that 'in 1774 the

Governors were allowed (by Order of Court of the Governors, 1760) to exercise one Presentation in three in favour of a child whose father was not a Freeman of London. Clergymen's children were however accounted free, by Order of Court, 28 March, 1765. The restriction as to Freemen's children has long since been removed.' Boswell writing to Temple in 1789 about another child says, 'I am very sorry to find that it is the most difficult thing you can imagine to get a boy, not the son of a citizen, into Christ's Hospital.' *Letters of Boswell*, p. 269. Coleridge and Lamb obtained presentations in 1782.

we

we can give in exchange. If in your extensive acquaintance you can procure such an exchange, it will be an act of great kindness. Do not let the matter slip out of your mind, for though I try others I know not any body of so much power to do it.

I am, Sir,

Your most humble servant,

Dec. 22. 1774.   SAM: JOHNSON.

369.

TO THE REVEREND DR. TAYLOR[1].

DEAR SIR,

I have upon me in some measure the care of getting a boy into the Bluecoat Hospital, and beg your interest with Mr. Harley[2] or any other man. Our boy is a non-freeman whose parents are both living. We have a presentation for a freeman which we can give in exchange.

Charles Congreve[3] is here, in an ill state of health, for advice. How long he has been here I know not. He sent to me one that attends him as an humble friend, and she left me a direction. He told me he knew not how to find me. He is in his own opinion recovering, but has the appearance of a man much broken. He talked to me of theological points, and is going to print a sermon, but I thought he appeared neither very acute nor very knowing. His room was disordered and oppressive, he has the appearance of a man wholly sunk into that

---

[1] From the original in the possession of Mr. Alfred H. Huth, of Bolney House, Ennismore Gardens, London.

[2] Harley was an Alderman of London. He had been Lord Mayor in 1768, and 'had acted with great spirit against Wilkes.' Horace Walpole called him 'another Sir William Walworth.' *Letters*, iv. 142; v. 92. Junius, writing on July 9, 1771, says that 'the whole interest of government in the City was committed to his conduct.' For the Bluecoat Hospital see last letter.

[3] He had been in the same form as Johnson at Lichfield School. *Life*, i. 45. Johnson gave the following account of him a year or so later : ' He has an elderly woman, whom he calls cousin, who lives with him, and jogs his elbow when his glass has stood too long empty, and encourages him in drinking, in which he is very willing to be encouraged ; not that he gets drunk, for he is a very pious man, but he is always muddy. He confesses to one bottle of port every day, and he probably drinks more.' *Ib.* ii. 460.

sordid

sordid self-indulgence which disease, real or imaginary, is apt to dictate [1]. He has lived, as it seems, with no great frequency of recollection. He asked me, and told me he had forgot, whether I was bred at Oxford or at Cambridge. The mind that leaves things so fast behind it, ought to have gone forward at no common rate. I believe he is charitable, yet he seems to have money much in his thoughts ; he told me that this ilness [*sic*] would cost him fifty pound [*sic*], and told it with some appearance of discontent : he seemed glad to see me, and I intend to visit him again. I rather wonder that he sent to me. I mentioned Hector [2] to him whom I saw about ten weeks ago, but he heard the name without emotion or enquiry, nor has ever spoken of any old companions or past occurrences. Is not this an odd frame of understanding? I asked him how long it was since we had seen one another, and he answered me roundly, fifty years. The greatest pleasure that I have had from him is to find him pious and orthodox ; yet he consorts with John Wesley [3].

You and I have had ill health, yet in many respects we bear time better than most of our friends [4]. I sincerely wish that you may continue to bear it with as little diminution as is possible either of body or mind, and I think, you return the wish to

Dear Sir,

Your most humble servant,

London, Dec. 22, 1774. SAM: JOHNSON.

To the Reverend Dr. Taylor in Ashbourn, Derbyshire.

[1] For Johnson's dislike of the character of a valetudinarian, see *Life*, iii. 152. He had Charles Congreve in his mind when he said :—'There is nothing against which an old man should be so much upon his guard as putting himself to nurse.' *Ib.* ii. 474.

[2] It was to Hector that Johnson gave the account of Congreve quoted above.

[3] Johnson liked Wesley's society. 'His conversation,' he said, 'is good, but he is never at leisure. He is always obliged to go at a certain hour. This is very disagreeable to a man who loves to fold his legs and have out his talk, as I do.' *Ib.* iii. 230.

[4] On his birth-day in 1780 he recorded in his Diary :—

'I am now beginning the seventy-second year of my life, with more strength of body, and greater vigour of mind, than I think is common at that age.' *Life of Johnson*, iii. 440.

370.

To Henry Thrale [1].

DEAR SIR,   Jan. 2, 1775.

I have taken the liberty of enclosing a letter, which contains
a request of which I cannot know the propriety. Nothing, I
suppose, can be done till the present master of the tap [2] has
given notice of his resignation ; and whether even then it is fit
for you to recommend, there may be reason to doubt. I shall
tell Heely [3], that I have laid his letter before you, and that he
must inform you when he is certain of the intended resignation.
You will then act as you judge best. There seems to be nothing
unreasonable in Heely's desire. He seems to have a genius for
an alehouse, and if he can get this establishment, may thank his
friend that sent him to the Marshalsea [4].

[1] *Piozzi Letters*, i. 210.
The date of this letter is there
given as June 2. It is however
printed earlier than the letter dated
February 3. On June 2 moreover
Johnson was in Oxford, and not 'at
home.' It seems likely that *June* is
a misprint for *Jan.*

[2] 'At Ranelagh House,' as we are
told by Mrs. Piozzi in a note. ' Heely,'
writes Hawkins, 'was by Sir Thomas
Robinson made keeper of the Tap at
Ranelagh, but was not able to endure
the capricious insolence with which
he was treated.' Hawkins's *Johnson*,
p. 601. Hawkins merely repeats
Heely's own account. Horace Walpole wrote on April 22, 1742 :—' I
have been breakfasting this morning
at Ranelagh Gardens ; they have
built an immense amphitheatre with
balconies full of little alehouses.'
Letters, i. 158. On June 29, 1744,
he wrote, 'Every night constantly I
go to Ranelagh, which has totally
beat Vauxhall. . . . My Lord Chesterfield is so fond of it, that he says he
has ordered all his letters to be
directed thither.' *Ib.* p. 309. The
'tap' would not be very profitable if

we can trust the account given of
Ranelagh in 1761 in Dodsley's *Environs*, v. 244, where it is stated that
'the regale is tea and coffee.'

[3] Heely's first wife was Johnson's
'near relation'—a first cousin. *Life
of Johnson*, ii. 30 ; iv. 370. He had
married a second time. Nevertheless
Hawkins calls him Johnson's relation, and speaks of the neglect with
which he was treated. Hawkins's
Johnson, p. 599.

[4] The Marshalsea was on St.
Margaret's Hill, Southwark, near to
Thrale's Brewery. It was a prison
for debtors, and for persons who had
committed crimes at sea, as pirates.
Debtors within twelve miles of Westminster (the City of London excepted)
might be carried to this prison for a
debt of forty shillings. Dodsley's
Environs of London, iv. 265. Wesley
described it as 'a picture of hell
upon earth.' *Journal*, ii. 267. Heely's
gratitude was, I suppose, due to the
creditor who had arrested him, because he had brought him so near
Thrale's house that some interest was
taken in his fate.

This,

This, I know, is a happy week ; you will revel with your con-
stituents in plenty and merriment[1] ; I must be kept at home by
my wicked mistress, out of the way of so much happiness. You
shall however have my good wishes. I hope every man will go
from your table more a friend than he came.

I am, &c.,

SAM: JOHNSON.

371.

TO JAMES BOSWELL.

[London], January 14, 1775. Published in the *Life*, ii. 290.

372.

TO THE REVEREND DR. TAYLOR.

[London]. January 14, 1775.
In Messrs. Sotheby and Co.'s Auction Catalogue of June 14, 1870,
Lot 471 is a Letter of Johnson to Taylor, dated January 14, 1775.
'Offers to send him his *Journey to the Western Islands*—mentions his
having been to see Congreve, whom he did not find at home.' On the
same day Johnson wrote to Boswell about his *Journey; Life,* ii. 290.
For Congreve see *ante*, p. 304.

373.

TO JAMES MACPHERSON.

[London], January 20, 1775. Published in the *Life*, ii. 298.
The Letter published by Boswell was dictated to him from memory
by Johnson, who added :— 'This, I think, is a true copy.' The original
was sold for £50, on May 10, 1875, at the great sale of Mr. Lewis
Pocock's *Johnsoniana*, by Messrs. Sotheby & Co. It is dated January
20, 1775. In the Catalogue the opening sentence is quoted. It is as
follows :—
  ' Mr. James Macpherson, I received your foolish and impudent note.
Whatever insult is offered me, I will do my best to repel, and what I
cannot do for myself the law shall do for me. I will not desist from
detecting what I think a cheat from any fear of the menaces of a
Ruffian.'
In the *Life* it stands thus :—
' MR. JAMES MACPHERSON,
  ' I received your foolish and impudent letter. Any violence offered

[1] *Ante,* p. 206.

X 2

me

me I shall do my best to repel ; and what I cannot do for myself, the law shall do for me. I hope I shall never be deterred from detecting what I think a cheat, by the menaces of a ruffian.'

374.

To James Boswell.

[London], January 21, 1775. Published in the *Life*, ii. 292.

375.

To James Boswell.

[London], January 28, 1775. Published in the *Life*, ii. 294.

376.

To Mrs. Thrale [1].

Madam,   February 3, 1775.

So many demands are made upon me, that if you give leave I will stay here till Tuesday. My pamphlet has not gone on at all [2]. Please to send by the bearer the papers on my table ; and give my love to my *brother* and *sisters* [3].

I am, &c.,
Sam: Johnson.

377.

To Dr. Lawrence.

[London], February 7, 1775. Published in the *Life*, ii. 296.

378.

To James Boswell.

[London], February 7, 1775. Published in the *Life*, ii. 296.

379.

To Henry Thrale [4].

Dear Sir,   [London, end of February, 1775.]

I beg that you will be pleased to send me an attestation to

---

[1] *Piozzi Letters*, i. 211.

[2] A fortnight earlier he had told Boswell that ' he was going to write about the Americans.' *Life of Johnson*, ii. 292. The pamphlet was *Taxation no Tyranny*. See *post*, p. 309, *n.* 4, for one cause of delay in its production.

[3] ' Whom he means I cannot guess.' Baretti. Perhaps he playfully alludes to Harry Thrale and his sisters.

[4] *Piozzi Letters*, i. 224. This letter is clearly misplaced in that collection. I have restored it to its proper place.

Mr. Carter's

Mr. Carter's merit[1]. I am going to-morrow; and shall leave the pamphlet to shift for itself[2].

You need only say, that you have sufficient knowledge of Mr. Carter to testify that he is eminently skilful in the art which he professes, and that he is a man of such decency and regularity of manners, that there will be no danger from his example to the youth of the colleges; and that therefore you shall consider it as a favour if leave may be obtained for him to profess horsemanship in the University.

I am, &c.,

SAM: JOHNSON.

Please to free[3] this letter to Miss Lucy Porter in Lichfield.

380.

To JAMES BOSWELL.

[London], February 25, 1775. Published in the *Life*, ii. 309.

381.

To WILLIAM STRAHAN[4].

SIR,

I am sorry to see that all the alterations proposed are

---

[1] Mr. Carter or his affairs are mentioned in the Letters of March 3, April 1, June 1, 6, 7, 11, 23, July 13, and August 1 of this year, and also in the *Life*, ii. 424. Baretti describes him as 'a poor riding-master in the Borough of Southwark.' Viscount Cornbury, Lord Hyde, who died in 1753 (Chester, *Westminster Abbey Registers*, p. 385), left by his will 'divers MSS. of his great-grandfather, Edward Earl of Clarendon, to Trustees, with a direction that the money to arise from the sale or publication thereof, should be employed as a beginning of a fund for supporting a Manage or Academy for riding and other useful exercises in Oxford.' As he died before his father, this bequest did not take effect. His sister, the Dowager Duchess of Queensberry, whose property these MSS. became, complied with his wishes. It was

found however that 'the scheme was not likely to be soon carried into execution, the profits arising from the Clarendon Press being from some mismanagement very scanty.' This set Johnson in his zeal to attempt the reformation of the Press. The scheme for the riding-school dropped through, and the money derived from the publication of the MSS. was allowed to accumulate. By 1860 it amounted to £10,000. In 1872 it was spent in adding the Clarendon Laboratory to the University Museum. See *Life of Johnson*, ii. 424; vi. *Addenda*, p. 1, and *Collectanea*, First Series, i. 305.

[2] It was to Oxford that he was going.

[3] Johnson does not in his Dictionary give *to free*, used in this sense, though he does give *to frank*.

[4] First published in my edition

evidences

evidences of timidity. You may be sure that I do [? not] wish to publish, what those for whom I write do not like to have published. But print me half a dozen copies in the original state, and lay them up for me. It concludes well enough as it is.

When you print it, if you print it, please to frank one to me here, and frank another to Mrs. Aston at Stow Hill, Lichfield.

The changes are not for the better, except where facts were mistaken. The last paragraph was indeed rather contemptuous, there was once more of it which I put out myself.

I am, Sir, your humble Servant,

[Oxford], March 1, 1775.   SAM: JOHNSON.

382.

SIR,   TO WILLIAM STRAHAN [1].

Our post is so unskilfully managed that we can very rarely, if ever, answer a letter from London on the day when we receive it. Your pages were sent back the next post, for there was nothing to do. I had no great difficulty in persuading myself to admit the alterations, for why should I in defense [2] of the ministry provoke those, whom in their own defense they dare

of Boswell's *Life of Johnson*, vol. vi. *Addenda*, p. xxxvi, from the original in the possession of Mr. Frank T. Sabin, of 10 and 12, Garrick Street, Covent Garden. This letter refers to *Taxation no Tyranny*, which was published before March 21, 1775, the date of Boswell's arrival in London. *Life*, ii. 311. Boswell says that he had in his possession 'a few proof leaves of it marked with corrections in Johnson's own hand-writing.' *Ib.* p. 313. Johnson, he says, 'owned to me that it had been revised and curtailed by some of those who were then in power.' When Johnson writes 'when you print it, if you print it,' he uses, doubtless, *print* in the sense of *striking off copies*. The pamphlet was, we may assume, in type before it was revised by 'those in power.' The corrections had been made in the proof-sheets. Johnson asks to have six copies laid

by for him in the state in which he had wished to publish it. It seems that the last paragraph had been struck out by the reviser, for Johnson says 'it *was* rather contemptuous.' He does not think it needful to supply anything in its place, for he says 'it concludes well enough as it is.' I do not know whether any of these six copies are in existence. Boswell had only seen a few proof-leaves with corrections in Johnson's hand-writing. A copy might be found in the possession of one of Strahan's descendants.

[1] From the original in the possession of Mr. Alfred Morrison, of Fonthill House.

It was no doubt written to William Strahan, and refers to the corrections in *Taxation no Tyranny*.

[2] Johnson in his *Dictionary* spells this word *defence*.

not

not provoke.—But are such men fit to be the governours of kingdoms [1] ?

They are here much discouraged by the last motion, and undoubtedly every man's confidence in Government must be diminished, yet if Lives can be saved, some deviation from rigid policy may be excused [2].

I expect to return some time in the next week, perhaps not till the latter end.

Do not omit to have the presentation pamflets [*sic*] done and sent to Mrs. Williams, and lay by for me the half dozen which you print without correction, and please to send me one by the post of the corrected books.

I am, Sir,

Your humble servant,

March 3, 1775.   SAM: JOHNSON.

    University College, [Oxford].

You will send to Mr. Cooper [3] and such as you think proper either in my name or your own.

383.

TO MRS. THRALE [4].

DEAR MADAM,   University College, [Oxford], March 3, 1775.

I am afraid that something has happened to occupy your

---

[1] For his contempt of Lord North's Ministry see *Life*. iii. 1; iv.139.

[2] 'The last motion' was Lord North's Propositions for Conciliating the Differences with America, debated on February 20 and 27. 'He,' said Fox, 'who has been hitherto all violence and war is now treading back his steps to peace.' *Parl. Hist.* xviii. 329. Horace Walpole wrote on February 18 :—'The war with America goes on briskly, that is as far as voting goes. A great majority in both Houses is as brave as a mob ducking a pickpocket.' *Letters*, vi. 191. On the 28th he wrote :—'The gates of Janus's temple

are open and shut every other day ; the porter has a sad time of it, and deserves a reversion for three lives. We are sending the Americans a sprig of olive, lapped up in an Act for a famine next year ; for we are as merciful as we are stout.' *Ib.* The 'Act for a famine' was a Bill to restrain the Trade and Commerce of the New England Colonies, debated on February 24. *Parl. Hist.* xviii. 379.

[3] Perhaps Grey Cooper, Joint Secretary of the Treasury. *Court and City Register*, 1775, p. 93.

[4] *Piozzi Letters*, i. 212. Dr. William Scott (afterwards Lord Stowell), who had been John-

mind

mind disagreeably, and hinder you from writing to me, or think-ing about me.

The fate of my proposal for our friend Mr. Carter will be decided on Monday. Those whom I have spoken to are all friends. I have not abated any part of the entrance or payment, for it has not been thought too much, and I hope he will have scholars.

I am very deaf; and yet cannot well help being much in com-pany, though it is often very uncomfortable. But when I have done this thing, which I hope is a good thing, or find that I can-not do it, I wish to live a while under your care and protection.

The imperfection of our post makes it uncertain whether we shall receive letters, sooner than we must send them; this is therefore written while I yet do not know whether you have favoured me or no. I was sufficiently discontented that I heard nothing yesterday. But sure all is well. I am, dearest Madam,

Your, &c.,

SAM: JOHNSON.

384.

TO [? WILLIAM STRAHAN].

[Oxford], March 6, 1775.

In Messrs. Puttick and Simpson's Auction Catalogue of July 30, 1886, Lot 1111 is a Letter of Johnson, one page quarto, dated March 6, 1775, written, I believe, to William Strahan.

385.

TO THE REVEREND DR. THOMAS FOTHERGILL.

[London], March 26, 1775. Published in the *Life*, ii. 333.

386.

TO MRS. THRALE [1].

MADAM, [Johnson's Court, London], April 1, 1775.

I had mistaken the day on which I was to dine with Mr.

son's companion from Newcastle to Edinburgh, was at this time the senior of the two tutors at University College. His younger brother, John Scott (afterwards Earl of Eldon), was giving lectures on law in the College.

He had lost his fellowship by his marriage, and was generally residing during this period in New Inn Hall. Twiss's *Life of Lord Eldon*, ed. 1846, i. 63-67.

[1] *Piozzi Letters*, i. 213.

Bruce,

Bruce, and hear of Abissinia, and therefore am to dine this day with Mr. Hamilton [1].

The news from Oxford is, that no tennis-court can be hired at any price; and that the Vice-Chancellor will not write to the Clarendon trustees without some previous intimation that his request will not be unacceptable. We must therefore find some way of applying to Lord Mansfield, who with the Archbishop of York and the Bishop of Chester holds the trust. Thus are we thrown to a vexatious distance. Poor ∗ ∗ ∗[2]! do not tell him.

The other Oxford news is, that they have sent me a degree of Doctor of Laws, with such praises in the diploma as, perhaps, ought to make me ashamed; they are very like your praises. I wonder whether I shall ever shew them to you [3].

Boswell will be with you [4]. Please to ask Murphy the way to Lord Mansfield [5]. Dr. Wetherell [6], who is now here, and will be

---

[1] James Bruce had returned to England in June, 1774, after an absence of twelve years. He did not publish his *Travels* till 1790. The stories which he told of Abissinia were often disbelieved. Horace Walpole says that in the spring of 1775 George Selwyn met Bruce at dinner. 'Somebody asked him if the Abyssinians had any musical instruments. "Musical instruments!" said he, and paused—"yes, I think I remember one—lyre." George Selwyn whispered his neighbour, "I am sure there is one less since he came out of the country."' Walpole's *Letters*, vi. 314. Baretti in a note describes him as 'a Scotch impostor, who pretended to have been in Abissinia, of which he gave such accounts as soon to convince everybody that he was nothing but an injudicious and impudent Liar.' Johnson met him at dinner and in the evening gave an account of him to Boswell. *Life*, ii. 333. Miss Burney described him about a month earlier as 'one of the most imperious of men. He entered the room like a monarch, so grand and so pompous.'

He could soften however. *Early Diary of Fanny Burney*, ii. 14, 21.

[2] Carter. See *ante*, p. 309.

[3] He had received his diploma that morning. 'The original,' writes Boswell, 'is in my possession. He shewed me it, and allowed me to read it, but would not consent to my taking a copy of it, fearing perhaps that I should blaze it abroad in his life-time. His objection to this appears from his 99th letter to Mrs. Thrale, whom in that letter he thus scolds for the grossness of her flattery of him.' Hereupon Boswell quotes the passage in the text. *Life*, ii. 332, *n*. 1.

A degree by diploma differs from an honorary degree as 'it confers immediate and full academical privileges.' Cox's *Recollections of Oxford*, p. 6. See *ante*, p. 137, *n*. 5.

[4] Perhaps this refers to that day week when Boswell dined at Mr. Thrale's. *Life*, ii. 349.

[5] Murphy, as a barrister, was likely to know the best way of approaching Lord Mansfield.

[6] The Master of University College, Oxford. *Ib.* ii. 356.

here

herc for some days, is very desirous of seeing the brewhouse ; I hope Mr. Thrale will send him an invitation. He does what he can for Carter.

To-day I dine with Hamilton ; to-morrow with Hoole [1] ; on Monday with Paradise [2]; on Tuesday with master and mistress [3] ; on Wednesday with Dilly [4]; but come back to the Tower [5].

Sic nunquam rediturus labitur annus.

I am, &c.,

SAM: JOHNSON.

Poor Mrs. Williams is very bad, worse than I ever saw her.

387.

To the Reverend Dr. Taylor [6].

DEAR SIR,

When shall I come down to you ? I believe I can get away pretty early in May, if you have any mind of me [7]; If you have none, I can move in some other direction. So tell me what I shall do.

I have placed young Davenport in the greatest printing house in London, and hear no complaint of him but want of size, which will not hinder him much. He may when he is a journeyman always get a guinea a week [8].

The patriots pelt me with answers. Four pamflets [*sic*], I

---

[1] Boswell was one of the guests. *Life*, ii. 334.

[2] *Ib.* iv. 364, *n.* 2. Strange words were sometimes heard at Mr. Paradise's table. 'Nothing could be more elegant or refined than Mrs. Paradise's whole exterior ; her voice was gentle and her manner deliberate. At the head of her table, with a large dinner-party, perceiving that a plate before her was not quite clean, she beckoned the servant, and said to him in an audible whisper :— " If you bring me a dirty plate again I will break your head with it." ' Miss Hawkins's *Memoirs*, i. 72.

[3] Mr. and Mrs. Thrale.

[4] Boswell was one of the guests. *Life*, ii. 338.

[5] Mrs. Piozzi says in a note :— ' The Tower was a separate room at Streatham, where Dr. Johnson slept.' On this Baretti remarks : — ' She dreamt when she wrote this note. The Tower was a part of the house in the Borough, and at Streatham there is no Tower.'

[6] First published in *Notes and Queries*, 6th S., v. 422.

[7] Johnson does not give in his *Dictionary* any instance of this idiom.

[8] *Ante*, p. 303. Johnson had seen the lad a few days before and had given him a guinea. *Life*, ii. 323.

think.

think, already, besides newspapers and reviews, have been discharged against me. I have tried to read two of them, but did
not go through them [1].

Now and then I call on Congreve [2], though I have little or no
reason to think that he wants or wishes to see me. I sometimes
dispute with him, but I think he has not studied.

He has really ill health, and seems to have given way to that
indulgence which sickness is always in too much haste to claim.
He confesses a bottle a day.

> I am, Sir,
>> Your humble Servant,

April 8, 1775.   SAM: JOHNSON.

To the Rev^d Dr. Taylor at Ashborne, Derbys.

388.

TO BENNET LANGTON.

[London], April 17, 1775. Published in the *Life*, ii. 361.

389.

TO THE LAIRD OF RASAY.

London, May 6, 1775. Published in the *Life*, v. 412.

390.

TO MRS. THRALE [3].

May 12, 1775.

And so, my dearest Mistress, you lie a bed hatching suspicions. I did not mean to reproach you, nor meant any thing
but respect, and impatience to know how you did.

I wish I could say or send any thing to divert you ; but I have
done nothing and seen nothing. I dined one day with Paoli [4],

---

[1] Boswell records on April 2 :—
'His *Taxation no Tyranny* being
mentioned, he said, " I think I have
not been attacked enough for it.
Attack is the re-action ; I never
think I have hit hard, unless it re-
bounds." BOSWELL. " I don't know,
Sir, what you would be at. Five or
six shots of small arms in every
newspaper, and repeated cannonad-
ing in pamphlet, might, I think,
satisfy you."' *Life*, ii. 335.

[2] *Ante*, p. 304.

[3] *Piozzi Letters*, i. 215.
Mrs. Thrale eight days earlier had
given birth to a daughter, Frances
Anna, who only lived seven months.

[4] For an account of General Paoli,
the Corsican patriot, see *Life*, ii.
71.

and

and yesterday with Mrs. Southwells[1], and called on Congreve. Mr. Twiss, hearing that you talked of despoiling his book of the fine print, has sent you a copy to frame[2]. He is going to Ireland, and I have given him letters to Dr. Leland[3] and Mr. Falkner[4].

Mr. M——[5] is so ill that the Lady is not visible; but yesterday I had I know not how much kiss of Mrs. Abington[6], and very good looks from Miss * * * the maid of honour.

Boswell has made me promise not to go to Oxford till he leaves London; I had no great reason for haste, and therefore might as well gratify a friend. I am always proud and pleased to have my company desired. Boswell would have thought my absence a loss, and I knew not who else would have considered my presence as profit. He has entered himself at the Temple, and I joined in his bond. He is to plead before the Lords, and hopes very nearly to gain the cost of his journey[7]. He lives

---

[1] A misprint, no doubt, for Southwell. *Ante*, p. 205.

[2] 'An Ideot [*sic*] who wrote his *Travels in Spain*, wherein there was a print by Cypriani and Bartolozzi; very fine, the only thing valuable in that book.' BARETTI. Johnson had been lately reading the book. *Life*, ii. 345. From one of the two copies in the Bodleian this fine print has been stolen—or at least removed. For a lively account of Twiss see the *Early Diary of Fanny Burney*, i. 279–294.

[3] See *Life*, i. 489.

[4] George Faulkner, whom Swift more than forty years earlier had described as 'the prince of Dublin printers.' Swift's *Works*, ed. 1803, xviii. 288. He died in the following August.

Twiss published in 1776 *A Tour to Ireland*. In it he mentions (p. 180) that when he visited Voltaire at Ferney, the talk fell on travelling. Voltaire gave him the following line in his own handwriting :—'An Eng-

lishman who goes to Italy leaves men to see pictures.'

[5] Perhaps the gentleman described in the following passage in one of Mrs. Thrale's letters to Johnson :— 'Mr. M—— was robbed, going home two nights ago, and had a comical conversation with the highwayman, about behaving like a gentleman. He paid four guineas for it.' *Piozzi Letters*, i. 185.

[6] A month earlier he had supped at this actress's house 'with some fashionable people; and he had seemed much pleased with having made one in so elegant a circle.' *Life*, ii. 349. See Walpole's *Letters*, v. 329, for a letter to her full of compliments. Northcote described her as 'the Grosvenor Square of comedy.' *Conversations of Northcote*, p. 298.

[7] To the kindness of Mr. H. W. Lawrence, Sub-Treasurer of the Inner Temple, I owe the following copy of the entries of Boswell's Bonds on admission and call :—

much

much with his friend Paoli, who says, a man must see Wales to enjoy England [1].

The book which is now most read, but which, as far as I have gone, is but dull, is Gray's letters, prefixed by Mr. Mason to his poems. I have borrowed mine, and therefore cannot lend it, and I can hardly recommend the purchase [2].

'Bond on Admission £50

Principals	Securities	Dates
Boswell, James	Johnson, Samuel	8th May 1775

Delivered up on Call Hilary T. 1786.

Bond on Call £100

Principals	Securities	Dates
Boswell, James	Malone, Edmd	11th Febry 1786.

Reced Mr. Boswell's Bond July 26th 1799
    T. D. Boswell.'

[1] T. D. Boswell was James Boswell's brother David, who, when he established himself as a merchant at Valencia, 'assumed the Christian name of Thomas, on account of the Spaniards being prejudiced against the name of David, as of Jewish origin.' Rogers's *Boswelliana*, p. 5.

For Boswell's entering himself at the Inner Temple, see *Life*, ii. 377, *n.* 1, and iii. 178. Baretti in a marginal note says :—'I don't think he will do much there, as he is not quite right-headed in my humble opinion.' It was in a Scotch appeal case that Boswell was this year to plead before the Lords. His fees in all amounted to forty-two guineas, as is shown in Johnson's Letter of May 22.

On the day on which the letter in the text was written Boswell, for the first time, took possession of the room which Johnson had assigned him in his house. *Life*, ii. 375.

[1] Boswell wrote to his friend Temple on June 6 :—'For the last fortnight I was in London I lay at Paoli's house, and had the command of his coach. . . . I felt more dignity when I had several servants at my devotion, a large apartment, and the convenience and state of a coach.' *Letters of Boswell*, p. 200. Paoli had met Johnson and the Thrales the summer before at Carnarvon. *Life*, v. 448. He looked upon Wales as Johnson looked upon Scotland, who said :—' Seeing Scotland is only seeing a worse England. It is seeing the flower gradually fade away to the naked state.' *Ib.* iii. 248.

[2] Boswell wrote to Temple on May 10 :—' Dr. Johnson does not like the book; he however says that one should consider these letters were written in a long series of years, and so might do very well at the time.' *Letters of Boswell*, p. 192. Johnson a year later said of the book :—' I forced myself to read it, only because it was a common topick of conversation. I found it mighty dull; and as to the style, it is fit for the second table.' *Life*, iii. 31. When he wrote Gray's *Life* he thought more favourably, at all events, of the early letters. 'They contain,' he says, 'a very pleasing account of many parts of their journey.' *Works*, viii. 476. Cowper, when he had read half way through them wrote :—' I once thought Swift's letters the best that could be written; but I like Gray's better.' ' His later Epistles,' he adds,

I have

I have offended ; and, what is stranger, have justly offended the nation of Rasay. If they could come hither, they would be as fierce as the Americans [1]. Rasay has written to Boswell an account of the injury done him, by representing his house as subordinate to that of Dunvegan. Boswell has his letter, and I believe copied my answer. I have appeased him, if a degraded chief can possibly be appeased ; but it will be thirteen days, days of resentment and discontent, before my recantation can reach him. Many a dirk will imagination, during that interval, fix in my heart. I really question if at this time my life would not be in danger, if distance did not secure it [2].

Boswell will find his way to Streatham before he goes, and will detail this great affair [3]. I would have come on Saturday, but that I am engaged to do Dr. Lawrence [4] a little service on Sunday. Which day shall I come next week ? I hope you will be well enough to see me often. I am, dearest Madam,

Your, &c.,
SAM: JOHNSON.

391.

TO THE REVEREND DR. THOMAS LELAND.

[London], May, 1775.

A Letter introducing Mr. Richard Twiss. See the Letter of May 12.

392.

TO GEORGE FAULKNER.

[London], May, 1775. A Letter introducing Mr. Richard Twiss. See the Letter of May 12.

'I think are worth little *as such.*' Cowper's *Works*, xv. 38.

Baretti in a note on Mason's name says :—'Poor Mason has much abused Johnson since his death, for the great reason that Johnson always looked on him as a pigmy poet.'

[1] Horace Walpole had written five days earlier :—'All the late letters from America are as hostile as possible ; and unless their heads are as cool as their hearts seem deter-mined, it will not be long before we hear of the overt acts of war.' *Letters*, vi. 208. The Battle of Bunker's Hill was fought on the following June 17.

[2] For the injury done to Macleod of Raasay, see *Life*, ii. 382 ; v. 410, and *ante*, p. 259, *n.* 4.

[3] Boswell wrote to Temple on May 17 :—'I am now at Mr. Thrale's villa at Streatham, a delightful spot.' *Letters of Boswell*, p. 193.

[4] *Ante*, p. 47, *n.* 2.

To

To Mrs. Thrale [1].

DEAR MADAM,   May 20, 1775.

I will try not to be sullen, and yet when I leave you how shall I help it. Bos. goes away on Monday; I go in a day or two after him, and will try to be well, and to be as you would have me. But I hope that when I come back you will teach me the value of liberty.

Nurse tells me that you are all well, and she hopes all growing better. Ralph [2], like other young gentlemen, will travel for improvement.

I have sent you six guineas and an half; so you may laugh at neglect and parsimony. It is a fine thing to have money. Peyton and Macbean [3] are both starving, and I cannot keep them.

Must we mourn for the Queen of Denmark [4]? How shall I do for my black cloaths which you have in the chest?

Make my compliments to every body.

I am, &c.,

SAM: JOHNSON.

I dined in a large company at a dissenting bookseller's yesterday, and disputed against toleration with one Doctor Meyer [5].

---

[1] *Piozzi Letters*, i. 218.

[2] Her second son, who died two months later. *Post*, p. 353.

[3] Two of Johnson's amanuenses when he was writing his *Dictionary*. *Life*, i. 187. The following day he wrote to Bennet Langton :—'I have an old amanuensis in great distress. I have given what I think I can give, and begged till I cannot tell where to beg again. I put into his hands this morning four guineas. If you could collect three guineas more, it would clear him from his present difficulty.' *Ib*. ii. 379. See *post*, Letters of April 1, 1776, and June 26, 1784. 'Peyton was a fool and a drunkard. I never saw so nauseous

a fellow.'—BARETTI. See *post*, p. 385.

[4] She was the youngest sister of George III. Horace Walpole wrote on the 22nd :—' Our papers will tell you that the Queen of Denmark is dead—happily for her, I think, if she had any feeling.' *Letters*, vi. 215. For an account of the plot to restore her to the throne, which was thwarted by her death, see Wraxall's *Memoirs*, ed. by H. B. Wheatley, iv. 176-210.

[5] ' Johnson would have made an excellent Spanish Inquisitor. To his shame be it said, he always was tooth and nail against toleration.'— BARETTI. For Dr. Meyer, see *Life*, ii. 253, *n*. 2.

TO

394.

To Bennet Langton.

[London], May 21, 1775. Published in the *Life*, ii. 379.

395.

To Mrs. Thrale [1].

Dearest Lady,

One thing or other still hinders me, besides what is perhaps the great hindrance, that I have no great mind to go. Boswel went away at two this morning. Langton I suppose goes this week. Boswel got two-and-forty guineas in fees while he was here [2]. He has, by his Wife's persuasion and mine, taken down a present for his Mother-in-law [3].

Pray let me know how the breath does. I hope there is no lasting evil to be feared. Take great care of yourself. Why did you take cold? Did you pump into your shoes?

I am not sorry that you read Boswel's journal [4]. Is it not a merry piece? There is much in it about poor me. Miss, I hear, mentions me sometimes in *her* memoirs [5].

---

[1] *Piozzi Letters*, i. 219. Corrected by me from the original in the possession of Mr. Alfred Morrison. The blanks which Mrs. Piozzi had left I have filled up.

[2] Langton left for Lincolnshire on the 26th. *Life*, ii. 379. Boswell wrote to Temple from Grantham on the evening of the day he left London:— 'Mr. Johnson accompanied me to Dilly's [the bookseller], where we supped; and then he went with me to the inn in Holborn, where the Newcastle Fly sets out; we were warmly affectionate.' *Letters of Boswell*, p. 196. The Newcastle Fly ran six times a week, starting, or professing to start, from London an hour after midnight. It took three days to Newcastle. Grantham, the end of the first day's journey, is 110 miles from London. *Footsteps of Dr. Johnson in Scotland*, i. 59. Boswell wrote in a second letter:—'My father harps on my going over Scotland with a brute

(think, how shockingly erroneous!) and wandering (or some such phrase) to London. In vain do I defend myself; even the circumstance that my last jaunt to London did not cost me £20—as I got forty-two guineas in London—does not affect him.' *Letters of Boswell*, p. 207.

[3] Johnson, I suspect, means his step-mother, with whom Boswell was on bad terms. *Life*, iii. 95, *n.* 1. Johnson calls his own step-daughter, Lucy Porter, his daughter-in-law. *Ib.* i. 370.

[4] On August 27 he wrote to Boswell:—'Mrs. Thrale was so entertained with your Journal that she almost read herself blind. She has a great regard for you.' *Ib.* ii. 383. The words 'Boswel's Journal' had been completely effaced in the original, but had been written in again before the Letter was sent to the printer.

[5] Mrs. Thrale wrote to Johnson a

I shall

I shall try at Oxford what can be done for Mr. Carter [1]. What can be done for his daughter it is not easy to tell. Does her mother know her own distress, or is she out of her wits with pride, or does Betsy a little exaggerate? It is strange behaviour.

The mourning it seems is general [2]. I must desire that you will let somebody take my best black cloaths out of the chest, and send them. There is nothing in the chest but what may be tumbled. The key is the newest of those two that have the wards channelled. When they are at the borough, my man can fetch them.

But all this while, dear and dear lady, take great care of yourself.

Do not buy Chandler's travels [3], they are duller than Twiss's [4]. Wraxal [5] is too fond of words, but you may read him. I shall take care that Adair's account of America [6] may be sent you, for I shall have it of my own.

Beattie has called once to see me. He lives grand at the Archbishop's [7].

---

few weeks later :—' I will keep the story of the fourteen thousand pounds till we meet ; so I will all family concerns, unless little Queeney sends her *country post*, as usual, to give information of a new *sail of ducks*, or some such important intelligence, which will not greatly interfere with my project.' *Piozzi Letters*, i. 269.

[1] *Ante*, p. 309.

[2] For Johnson's compliance with a direction for court mourning see *Life*, iv. 325.

[3] Dr. Richard Chandler's *Travels in Asia Minor*. Horace Walpole, writing of Chandler's *Travels in Greece*, says 'the book is ill-written and unsatisfactory : and yet he revived my visions towards Athens, and made me wish I was a great king, and could purchase to restore it : a great king probably would hold it cheaper to conquer it.' *Letters*, vi. 322.

[4] *Ante*, p. 316.

[5] Nathaniel Wraxall published this year his *Cursory Remarks made in a Tour through some of the Northern Parts of Europe*.

[6] James Adair's *History of the American Indians*, London, 1775. He was a trader with the Indians of the southern states, and resided in their country forty years. In his elaborate book he attempted to prove that they were descended from the Jews. Rose's *Biog. Dict.* i. 85.

[7] I find no mention in Beattie's *Life* of his being at the Archbishop's. In this visit to London, 'I lodged,' he writes, 'the greatest part of the time with my friend, Dr. Porteus, at Lambeth.' Porteus was Rector of Lambeth ; afterwards Bishop, first, of Chester, and then of London. *Life of Beattie*, ed. 1824, p. 218.

Dear

Dear lady do not be careless, nor heedless, nor rash, nor giddy; but take care of your health.

I am, dearest Madam,

Your most humble servant,

May 22, 1775.   SAM: JOHNSON.

Dr. Talbot, which I think I never told you, has given five hundred pounds to the future infirmary.

To Mrs. Thrale.

396.

TO MRS. THRALE.

[London], May 24, 1775.

In Messrs. Sotheby and Co.'s Auction Catalogue of May 10, 1875, Lot 92 is a Letter of Johnson to Mrs. Thrale, dated May 24, 1775, two pages quarto. 'Asking her to send him his "black cloaths,"' of which he says: 'do send the cloaths if you send them in a wheelbarrow.' Mentions the reason of the delay in his departure—indulges in some playful remarks, and in the superscription calls her 'Dearest of all dear Ladies.' It was sold for £6 6s.

397.

TO MRS. THRALE [1].

DEAREST LADY,   May 25, 1775.

The fit was a sudden faintness, such as I have had I know not how often; no harm came of it, and all is well. I cannot go till Saturday; and then go I will, if I can. My cloaths, Mr. Thrale says, must be made like other people's, and they are gone to the taylor. If I do not go, you know, how shall I come back again?

I told you, I fancy, yesterday, that I was well, but I thought so little of the disorder, that I know not whether I said any thing about it.

I am, &c.,

SAM: JOHNSON.

398.

TO JAMES BOSWELL.

[London], May 27, 1775. Published in the *Life*, ii. 379.

[1] *Piozzi Letters*, i. 222.

399.

To Mrs. Thrale [1].

DEAR MADAM, [University College, Oxford], June 1, 1775.

I know well enough what you think, but I am out of your reach. I did not make the epitaph before last night ; and this morning I have found it too long. I send you it as it is to pacify you, and will make it shorter. It is too long by near half. Tell me what you would be most willing to spare [2].

Dr. Wetherell went with me to the Vice Chancellor, to whom we told the transaction with my Lord of Chester, and the Vice Chancellor promised to write to the Archbishop. I told him that he needed have no scruples ; he was asking nothing for himself ; nothing that would make him richer, or them poorer ; and that he acted only as a magistrate, and one concerned for the interest of the University. Dr. Wetherell promises to stimulate him [3].

Don't suppose that I live here as we live at Streatham. I went this morning to the chapel at six [4], and if I was to stay would try to conform to all wholesome rules. Pray let Harry have the penny which I owe him for the last morning.

Mr. Colson [5] is well, and still willing to keep me, but I delight not in being long here. Mr. Smollett of Lochlomond and his Lady have been here. We were very glad to meet [6].

---

[1] *Piozzi Letters*, i. 223.

[2] The epitaph was for the grave of Mrs. Thrale's mother in Streatham Church. *Post*, p. 327.

[3] The Vice-Chancellor was Dr. Fothergill, Provost of Queen's College, known as 'Old Customary.' The night of the great fire in Queen's in 1778, though he and his family escaped with difficulty he contrived nevertheless to get on his wig and gown, 'minus which he would not have been seen abroad for a dukedom.' *Letters of Radcliffe and James*, p. 269.

[4] In the winter no doubt the hour for chapel was later. Nevertheless I was surprised to find a freshman of Queen's College recording on November 21, 1778 : — 'From the convenient and ready breakfast I eat of milk, I am able to sit down to study seriously at nine o'clock, at least half an hour sooner than any body else.' *Letters of Radcliffe and James*, p. 50. In the early part of last century chapel at Trinity College, Cambridge, apparently was at six in the morning all the year round. Monk's *Life of Bentley*, ii. 247, *n.* 2.

[5] Rev. John Coulson, one of the Fellows of University College.

[6] Johnson had visited them at their house on Loch Lomond. *Ante*, p. 286.

Pray

Pray let me know how you do, and play no more tricks; if you do, I can yet come back and watch you.

I am, &c.,

SAM: JOHNSON.

400.

TO MRS. THRALE[1].

MADAME,   [Oxford], June 5, 1775.

Trois jours sont passés sans que je reçoive une lettre ; point de nouvelles, point d'amitié, point de querelles. Un silence si rare, que veut-il ? je vous ai envoyé l'épitaphe, trop longue à la verité, mais on la raccourcira sans beaucoup de peine. Vous n'en avez pas dit un mot. Peutêtre que je serai plus heureux ce soir.

J'ai epuisé ce lieu, ou je n'étudie pas[2], et ou si on ôte l'étude, il n'y a rien, et je ne trouve guere moyen d'echaper. Les voitures qui passent par cy, passent dans la nuit[3]; les chaises de poste me couteront beaucoup. J'envoye querir un passage plus commode.

Je dinerai demain chez le Vice Chancelier[4], j'espere de trouver

---

[1] *Piozzi Letters*, i. 225.

'A poor French letter, and written in a hurry. Johnson never wrote to me French, but when he translated for me the first paragraph of his *Rasselas*.'—BARETTI. Baretti told Malone 'that he never could satisfy himself with the translation of the first sentence, which is uncommonly lofty. Mentioning this to Johnson, the latter said, after thinking two or three minutes, "Well, take up the pen, and if you can understand my pronunciation, I will see what I can do." He then dictated the sentence to the translator, which proved admirable, and was immediately adopted.' Prior's *Life of Malone*, p. 161. There is no copy of Baretti's *Rasselas* in the British Museum, Bodleian, or the National Library at Paris, neither can I find any other mention of it. He published in 1772 *An Introduction to the most useful European languages* (in which by the way German is not included), and in it he gave translations in French, Italian and Spanish of six chapters of *Rasselas*, but the first chapter is not among them.

[2] Twenty-one years earlier, when he was writing his *Dictionary*, he had gone to Oxford ' to visit the libraries.' But though he stayed about five weeks he collected nothing in the libraries for that work. *Life*, i. 270.

[3] Johnson wanted a place in a coach going from London to Birmingham. William Hutton, nine years later, returning from London found all the places taken for two days to come. He left in the evening of a December day. Hutton's *Journey to London*, p. 132.

[4] The dinner was likely to be dull, for the Vice-Chancellor is described as 'a very bashful man. His conversation was pithless and insipid. In his old age he took to himself a

des

des choses un peu favorables à nôtre ami infortuné[1], mais je n'ai nulle confiance. Je suis,

Madame,

Votre tres obeissant serviteur,

SAM: JOHNSON[2].

401.

To MRS. THRALE[3].

MADAM,   [Oxford], June 6, 1775.

Such is the uncertainty of all human things, that Mr. C——[4] has quarrelled with me. He says, I raise the laugh upon him, and he is an independent man, and all he has is his own, and he is not used to such things. And so I shall have no more good of C——, of whom I never had any good but flattery, which my dear mistress knows I can have at home.

That I had no letters yesterday I do not wonder; for yesterday we had no post[5]. I hope something will come to-day. Our post is so ill-regulated that we cannot receive letters and answer them the same day.

Here I am, and how to get away I do not see; for the power of departure otherwise than in a post-chaise depends upon accidental vacancies in passing coaches, of which all but one in a week pass through this place at three in the morning. After

wife, and it was the general wonderment that he had found courage to ask anybody to marry him.' Bentham's *Works*, x. 37.

[1] Mr. Carter. *Ante*, p. 309.

[2] On the day on which Johnson wrote this letter, Horace Walpole, sending Sir Horace Mann news of the fight at Lexington on April 19, where the first blood was shed in the war with our Colonies, continues:—
' So here is this fatal war commenced!
   The child that is unborn shall rue
   The hunting of that day.'
          Walpole's *Letters*, vi. 219.

[3] *Piozzi Letters*, i. 226.

[4] Mr. Coulson. An eye-witness told Mr. Croker that ' Coulson was going out on a country living, and

talking of it with pomp. Johnson chose to imagine his becoming an archdeacon, and made himself merry at his expense. At last they got to warm words, and Johnson concluded the debate by exclaiming emphatically—"Sir, having meant you no offence, I will make you no apology."'
Croker's *Boswell*, p. 458.

[5] 'Yesterday' was Monday. No post left London on Sunday night. A letter posted in London on Monday would be delivered in Oxford on Tuesday; the answer to it would leave by the Wednesday post and be delivered in London on Thursday. At the present day a letter posted in the morning receives its answer in the evening.

that

that one I have sent, but with little hope; yet I shall be very unwilling to stay here another week.

I supped two nights ago with Mr. Bright [1], who enquired after Harry and Queeney, to whom I likewise desire to be remembered.

Suppose I should grow like my mistress, and when I am to go forward, think eagerly how and when I shall come back, would that be a strange thing? Love and reverence have always had some tendency to produce conformity.

Where is Mr. Baretti? Are he and Queeney plague and darling as they are used to be [2]? I hope my sweet Queeney will write me a long letter, when I am so settled that she knows how to direct to me, and if I can find any thing for her cabinet, I shall be glad to bring it.

What the Vice Chancellor says respecting Mr. Carter, if he says any thing, you shall know to-morrow, for I shall probably leave him too late for this day's post.

If I have not a little something from you to-day, I shall think something very calamitous has befallen us. This is the natural effect of punctuality. Every intermission alarms. Dearest dear Lady, take care of yourself. You connect us, and rule us, and vex us, and please us. We have all a deep interest in your health and prosperity.

I am, &c.,
SAM: JOHNSON.

402.

To Mrs. Thrale [3].

DEAREST MADAM,   [Oxford], June 7, 1775.

What can be the reason that I hear nothing from you or from your house? Are you well? Yet while I am asking the question, I know not when I shall be able to receive your answer, for I am waiting for the chance of a place in a coach which will probably be come and gone in an hour.

---

[1] Probably the Abingdon Schoolmaster. *Ante*, p. 157.

[2] 'From the Dialogues I wrote for that same Queeny a true idea may be formed how we were *plague* and *darling* to each other.'—BARETTI.

For these *Dialogues* see *Life*, ii. 449, n. 2.

[3] *Piozzi Letters*, i. 263.

This letter is dated by Mrs. Piozzi, July 7, but it was certainly written on June 7.

Yesterday

Yesterday the Vice-Chancellor told me, that he has written to the Archbishop of York. His letter, as he represented it to me, was very proper and persuasive. I believe we shall establish Mr. Carter the riding master of Oxford.

Still I cannot think why I hear nothing from you.

The coach is full. I am therefore at full leisure to continue my letter; but I have nothing more to say of business, but that the Vice-Chancellor is for adding to the riding-school a house and stable for the master. Nor of myself but that I grieve and wonder, and hope and fear about my dear friends at Streatham. But I may have a letter this afternoon—Sure it will bring me no bad news[1]. You never neglected writing so before. If I have a letter to-day I will go away as soon as I can; if I have none, I will stay till this may be answered, if I do not come back to town.

> I am, &c.,
>
> SAM: JOHNSON.

403.

To Mrs. Thrale[2].

DEAREST LADY,   [Oxford], June 7, 1775.

Your letter which ought to have come on Tuesday came not till Wednesday. Well, now I know that there is no harm, I will take a chaise and march away towards my own country.

You are but a goose at last. Wilton told you, that there is room for three hundred and fifty letters, which are equivalent to twelve lines. If you reckon by lines, the inscription has seventeen: if by letters, five hundred and seventy-nine; so that one way you must expel five lines, the other two hundred and twenty-nine letters. This will perplex us; there is little that by my own choice I should like to spare; but we must comply with the stone[3].

C——[4] and I are pretty well again. I grudge the cost of

---

[1] *Ante*, p. 262.

[2] *Piozzi Letters*, i. 229.

This letter was evidently written on the same day as the last—Wednesday, June 7—after the post from London had come in, and after the

post for London had left.

[3] The stone of her mother's monument. *Ante*, p. 323. The inscription was cut down to 546 letters. Johnson's *Works*, i. 152.

[4] Coulson.

going

going to Lichfield, Frank and I in a post-chaise[1]; yet I think
of thundering away to-morrow; so you will write your next dear
letter to Lichfield.

This letter is written on Wednesday after the receipt of yours,
but will not be delivered to the post till to-morrow. I wish
Ralph better, and my master and his boys well[2]. I have pretty
good nights.

I am, &c.,
SAM: JOHNSON.

404.

To Mrs. Thrale[3].

DEAR MADAM,   [Lichfield], June 10, 1775.

On Thursday morning I took a post-chaise, and intended
to have passed a day or two at Birmingham, but Hector[4] had
company in his house, and I went on to Lichfield, where I know
not yet how long I shall stay, but think of going forward to Ashbourne in a short time.

Neither your letters nor mine seem to have kept due time; if
you see the date of the letter in which the epitaph was inclosed,
you will find that it has been delayed. I shall adjust the epitaph
some way or other. Send me your advice.

Poor Miss Porter has been bad with the gout in her hand. She
cannot yet dress herself.

I am glad that Ralph is gone; a new air may do him good.
I hope little Miss promises well.

I will write you a longer letter on Monday, being just now
called out according to an appointment which I had forgotten.

I am, &c.,
SAM: JOHNSON.

---

[1] See *post*, Letter of June 24, 1779, where he says that to go from London to Lichfield had cost him seven guineas. The charge for a chaise and pair was ninepence a mile; in some districts more. There was a duty on each horse of one penny per mile. The driver expected at least a shilling or eighteen pence for each stage of ten or twelve miles. There were heavy tolls to be paid at the turn-pikes. See Mostyn Armstrong's *Actual Survey*, &c., p. 4; and Paterson's *British Itinerary*, vol. 1, preface, p. vii. Frank was Johnson's black servant.

[2] Ralph was one of Mr. Thrale's two sons. Who are meant by 'his boys' I do not know.

[3] *Piozzi Letters*, i. 230.

[4] *Ante*, p. 41.

TO

405.

To Mrs. Thrale [1].

DEAREST LADY,   [Lichfield], June 11, 1775.

I am sorry that my master has undertaken an impracticable interest ; but it will be forgotten before the next election. I suppose he was asked at some time when he could not well refuse.

Lady Smith [2] is settled at last here, and sees company at her new house.—I went on Saturday. Poor Lucy Porter has her hand in a bag, so disabled by the gout that she cannot dress herself. She does not go out. All your other friends are well.

I go every day to Stowhill : both the sisters are now at home [3]. I sent Mrs. Aston a *Taxation*, and sent it nobody else, and Lucy borrowed it. Mrs. Aston since that enquired by a messenger when I was expected. I can tell nothing about it, answered Lucy ; when he is to be here I suppose she'll know [4].

Every body remembers you all. You left a good impression behind you. I hope you will do the same at ﹡﹡﹡﹡﹡ [5]. Do not make them speeches. Unusual compliments, to which there is no stated and prescriptive answer, embarrass the feeble, who know not what to say, and disgust the wise, who knowing them to be false, suspect them to be hypocritical [6]. Did I think when I sat down to this paper that I should write a lesson to my mistress, of whom I think with so much admiration ?

As to Mr. Carter, I am inclined to think that our project will succeed. The Vice-Chancellor is really in earnest. He remarked

---

[1] *Piozzi Letters*, i. 231.
Mrs. Thrale had spent three days at Lichfield in the summer of the year before. She would know the people and places mentioned. *Life*, v. 428.

[2] She is mentioned, *post*, p. 335, and in the Letter of May 29, 1779.

[3] Mrs. Gastrell and Mrs. Aston. *Ante*, p. 160, *n.* 4.

[4] 'She' is Mrs. Aston, of whom Lucy Porter was jealous on account of her copy of *Taxation no Tyranny*.

[5] Probably Lewes, *post*, p. 332, *n.* 1.

[6] Johnson recorded in his *Diary of a Journey into Wales* :—'August 3. Talk with Mistress about flattery.' On this Mrs. Piozzi has the following MS. note :—' He said I flattered the people to whose houses we went. I was saucy, and said I was obliged to be civil for two, meaning himself and me. He replied nobody would thank me for compliments they did not understand.' *Life*, v. 440.

to me how necessary it must be to provide in places of education a sufficient variety of innocent amusements, to keep the young men from pernicious pleasures[1].

When I did not hear from you, I thought whether it would not be proper to come back and look for you. I knew not what might have happened.

Consider the epitaph, which, you know, must be shortened, and tell what part you can best spare. Part of it, which tells the birth and marriage, is formulary[2], and can be expressed only one way; the character we can make longer or shorter; and since it is too long, may choose what we shall take away. You must get the dates for which you see spaces left.

You never told me, and I omitted to enquire, how you were entertained by Boswell's Journal. One would think the man had been hired to be a spy upon me[3]. He was very diligent, and caught opportunities of writing from time to time. You may now conceive yourself tolerably well acquainted with the expedition. Folks want me to go to Italy[4], but I say you are not for it. However write often to, Madam,

Your, &c.,

SAM: JOHNSON.

[1] 'Jeremy Bentham,' who entered Queen's College, Oxford, in 1760, 'sometimes went to fish as a relief from the weary monotony of existence. To catch a minnow was an interruption to the dulness of the day. But even the fishing sports partook of the system of neglect with which all education was conducted. Generally a poacher was hired to go with a casting-net. He caught the fish, and the youths went and got it dressed at a neighbouring inn.' Bentham's *Works*, x. 40. Burke talking about games 'said that as there are so few who will exercise their minds by the study of books, it is better they should employ it [*sic*] this way than let it get no energy or exercise at all ; for all games are regular, and require some reflection or combination of thought. Education should ever be considered in the light of mitigated and moderate restraint.' Burke's *Table Talk. Miscellanies of the Philobiblon Society*, vii. 22.

[2] *Formulary* as an adjective is not in Johnson's *Dictionary*.

[3] It seems very improbable that Johnson wrote this.

[4] The following year all was arranged for a journey to Italy with the Thrales, when it was cut short by young Henry Thrale's sudden death. *Life*, iii. 19, 27.

To

406.

To Mrs. Thrale [1].

DEAREST LADY,   Lichfield, June 13, 1775.

I now write at Mr. Cobb's [2], where I have dined and had custard. She and Miss Adey send their compliments. Nothing considerable has happened since I wrote, only I am sorry to see Miss Porter so bad ; and I am not well pleased to find that after a very comfortable intermission, the old flatulence distressed me again last night. The world is full of ups and downs, as I think I once told you before.

Lichfield is full of box-clubs [3]. The ladies have one for their own sex. They have incorporated themselves under the appellation of the Amicable Society ; and pay each twopence a week to the box. Any woman who can produce the weekly twopence is admitted to the society; and when any of the poor subscribers is in want, she has six shillings a week ; and I think when she dies five pounds are given to her children. Lucy is not one, nor Mrs. Cobb. The subscribers are always quarrelling ; and every now and then a lady in a fume withdraws her name ; but they are an hundred pounds before hand.

Mr. Green [4] has got a cast of Shakespeare, which he holds to be a very exact resemblance.

There is great lamentation here for the death of Coll [5]. Lucy is of opinion that he was wonderfully handsome.

Boswell is a favourite, but he has lost ground since I told them that he is married, and all hope is over [6].

---

[1] *Piozzi Letters*, i. 234.

[2] A misprint for Mrs. Cobb's. She was a widow lady; Miss Adey was her niece. *Life*, ii. 466.

[3] Friendly or Provident Societies. In the *Gentleman's Magazine* for 1736, p. 353, is the following entry:— 'The demurrer to a bill filed by a Society of Weavers in Spittle-fields, against Mr. Sutton, landlord of the house where their club was kept, for a sum of £30 lent him out of the box, was argued before the Barons of the Exchequer, when the Court were

of opinion that they were not a legal society, and therefore could neither sue nor be sued.' See *ib.* for 1770, pp. 422, 524, for the formation of a Provident Society open 'to all persons of either sex, *Jews excepted.*' I was told in Lichfield that ' when a man is sick it is still commonly said that he goes upon the box.'

[4] The owner of the Lichfield Museum. *Ante*, p. 161.

[5] *Ante*, p. 279, *n*. 2.

[6] Boswell had been married nearly six years. *Life*, ii. 140, *n*. 1.

B e

Be so kind as to let me know when you go to Lewes[1], and when you come back, that I may not fret for want of a letter, as I fretted at Oxford. Pay my respects to my dear master.

> I am, &c.,
> SAM: JOHNSON.

407.

TO MRS. THRALE[2].

DEAR MADAM,   Lichfield, June 17, 1775.

Write to me something every post, for on the stated day my head runs upon a letter[3]. I will answer Queeney. Bad nights came again ; but I took mercury, and hope to find good effects. I am distressfully and frightfully deaf. *Querelis jam satis datum.*

So we shall have a fine house in the winter, as we already have in the summer[4]. I am not sorry for the appearance of a little superfluous expence. I have not yet been at Ashbourne, and yet I would fain flatter myself that you begin to wish me home ; but do not tell me so, if it be not true, for I am very well at Stowhill.

Mrs. Porter will be glad of a memorial from you, and will keep the work-bag carefully, but has no great use for it ; her present qualifications for the niceties of needlework being dim eyes and lame fingers.

---

[1] They knew Dr. Delap the Rector of Lewes. Mrs. Piozzi describes how one morning in the year 1766, when Johnson was suffering from melancholy, she and Mr. Thrale 'heard him in the most pathetic terms beg the prayers of Dr. Delap, who had left him as we came in. I felt excessively affected with grief, and well remember my husband involuntarily lifted up one hand to shut his mouth, from provocation at hearing a man so wildly proclaim what he could at last persuade no one to believe ; and what, if true, would have been so very unfit to reveal.' *Piozzi Anec-dotes*, p. 127, and Murphy's *Johnson*, p. 99.

[2] *Piozzi Letters.* i. 236.

On the morning of the day on which this letter was written the Battle of Bunker's Hill was fought.

[3] Lichfield is not in the list of the towns to which mails were sent every night but Sunday. On Tuesday, Thursday, and Saturday, mails were sent to all parts of England. Dodsley's *Environs of London*, v. 221.

[4] Mr. Thrale was going to build, as is shown in the next paragraph but one.

the

Of the harvest about us it is said that much is expected from the wheat, more indeed than can be easily remembered. The barley is promising enough, but not uncommonly exuberant. But this is of itself a very good account, for no grain is ever dear, when wheat is cheap. I hope therefore that my master may without fear or danger build this year, and dig the next. I do not find that in this part of the country rain has been much wanted.

If you go with Mrs. D—— [1], do not forget me amidst the luxuries of absolute dominion, but let me have kind letters full of yourself, of your own hopes, and your own fears, and your own thoughts, and then go where you will. You will find your journey however but a barren business; it is dull to live neither scolding nor scolded, neither governing nor governed. Now try.

I expected that when the interest of the county had been divided, Mawbey would have had very little difficulty, and am glad to find that Norton opposes him with so much efficacy; pray send me the result [2].

> I am, &c.,
>
> SAM: JOHNSON.

[1] Perhaps the wife of Dr. Delap (*ante*, p. 332, *n.* 1) or a Mrs. Davenant, who, as Mrs. Thrale's letter of June 24 shows, accompanied her to the Regatta. *Piozzi Letters*, i. 248. See Mme. D'Arblay's *Diary*, ed. 1842, ii. 41. 'She was by birth a Cotton, as was Mrs. Thrale's mother.' *Early Diary of Fanny Burney*, ii. 266, *n.* 1.

[2] Sir Joseph Mawbey had been Thrale's colleague for Southwark in the last parliament. *Parl. Hist.* xvi. 443. A vacancy having occurred in Surrey this year he had stood, and had been elected two days before Johnson's letter was written. *Gentleman's Magazine*, 1775, p. 301. On August 17 an action was brought against him by a Guildford shopkeeper for the sum of £117 6s. for ribbons at the last general election. He paid £30 into Court, and the jury gave a verdict for £29 only. *Ib.* p. 404. He is the 'Sir Joseph' of the following lines from the *Rolliad* in the description of the Speaker:—

'There Cornewall sits, and oh! unhappy fate !
Must sit for ever through the long debate.
Painful pre-eminence ! he hears, 'tis true,
Fox, North, and Burke, but hears Sir Joseph too.'

I thought when I saw my friend Mr. Leonard H. Courtney, sitting as Chairman of Committees, that to him, as Member for a division of Cornwall, these lines might be aptly applied.

To

To Mrs. Thrale[1].

DEAR MADAM,   Lichfield, June 19, 1775.

I hope it is very true that Ralph mends, and wish you were gone to see him, that you might come back again.

Queeney revenges her long task upon Mr. Baretti's hen, who must sit on duck eggs a week longer than on her own. I hope she takes great care of my hen, and the Guinea hen, and her pretty little brood[2].

I was afraid Mawbey would succeed, and have little hope from the scrutiny. Did you ever know a scrutiny change the account?

Miss A——[3] does not run after me, but I do not want her, here are other ladies.

Invenies alium, si te hic fastidit Alexis[4].

Miss • • • • grows old, and Miss Vyse[5] has been ill, but I believe she came to me as soon as she got out. And I can always go to Stowhill. So never grieve about me. Only flatu-lencies are come again.

Your dissertation upon Queeney is very deep. I know not what to say to the chief question. Nature probably has some part in human characters, and accident has some part; which has most we will try to settle when we meet[6].

Small letters will undoubtedly gain room for more words, but words are useless if they cannot be read[7]. The lines need not all be kept distinct, and some words I shall wish to leave out, though very few. It must be revised before it is engraved. I always told you that Mr. Thrale was a man, take him for all in all, you ne'er will look upon his like[8]; but you never mind him

---

[1] *Piozzi Letters*, i. 238.

[2] 'It was one of the Streatham whims to call the cocks and hens by the name of some acquaintance or other of the family, and so we roasted Johnson to-day and boiled Baretti or somebody else to-morrow.' BARETTI.

[3] Perhaps Miss Adey. *Ante*, p. 331, *n.* 2.

[4] VIRGIL. *Eclogues*, ii. 73.
'And find an easier love though not so fair.' DRYDEN.

[5] *Life*, iii. 124.

[6] For 'the original difference in minds and the influence of education,' see *ib.* ii. 436.

[7] He is speaking of the epitaph to Mrs. Thrale's mother. *Ante*, p. 323.

[8] 'He was a man, take him for all in all,
I shall not look upon his like again.'
Hamlet, Act i. sc. 2.

nor

nor me, till time forces conviction into your steely bosom. You will, perhaps, find all right about the house and the windows.

Pray always suppose that I send my respects to Master, and Queeney, and Harry, and Susey, and Sophy.

Poor Lucy mends very slowly, but she is very good-humoured, while I do just as she would have me.

Lady Smith has got a new post-chaise, which is not nothing to talk on at Lichfield. Little things here serve for conversation. Mrs. Aston's parrot pecked my leg, and I heard of it some time after at Mrs. Cobb's.

> ——We deal in nicer things
> Than routing armies and dethroning kings.

A week ago Mrs. Cobb gave me sweetmeats to breakfast, and I heard of it last night at Stowhill.

If you are for small talk:

> ——Come on, and do the best you can,
> I fear not you, nor yet a better man.

I could tell you about Lucy's two cats, and Brill her brother's old dog, who is gone deaf; but the day would fail me. *Sua-dentque cadentia sidera somnum* [1]. So said Æneas. But I have not yet had my dinner. I have begun early, for what would become of the nation if a letter of this importance should miss the post? Pray write to, dearest Madam,

Your, &c.,

SAM: JOHNSON.

409.

To Mrs. Thrale [2].

DEAR MADAM,   Lichfield, June 21, 1775.

Now I hope you are thinking, shall I have a letter to-day from Lichfield? Something of a letter you will have; how else can I expect that you should write? and the morning on which I should miss a letter would be a morning of uneasiness, notwithstanding all that would be said or done by the sisters of

---

[1] *somnos.* VIRGIL, *Æneid*, ii. 9 and iv. 81.

'The setting stars to kindly rest invite.' DRYDEN.

[2] *Piozzi Letters*, i. 241.

Stowhill

Stowhill [1], who do and say whatever good they can. They give me good words, and cherries, and strawberries. Lady ＊ ＊ ＊ ＊[2] and her mother and sister were visiting there yesterday, and Lady ＊ ＊ ＊ took her tea before her mother.

Mrs. Cobb is to come to Miss Porter's this afternoon. Miss A—— comes little near me. Mr. Langley of Ashbourne was here to-day, in his way to Birmingham, and every body talks of you [3].

The ladies of the Amicable Society are to walk, in a few days, from the town-hall to the cathedral in procession to hear a sermon. They walk in linen gowns, and each has a stick with an acorn, but for the acorn they could give no reason, till I told them of the civick crown [4].

I have just had your sweet letter, and am glad that you are to be at the regatta [5]. You know how little I love to have you

---

[1] Mrs. Gastrell and Mrs. Aston.

[2] 'Lady Smith.'—BARETTI. Mrs. Thrale replied :—' Lady ＊ ＊ ＊ should not have taken the tea before her mother, that's certain, as her husband is dead, and all pretence of supporting the rank he had given her is past. I can find no excuse for her conduct except too attentive an observation to dear Mr. Johnson's odd speeches against parental authority.' *Piozzi Letters*, i. 247.

[3] There is an omission here, as is shown both by the structure of the sentence, and also by Mrs. Thrale's reply, where she refers to a compliment paid her by some pedantic gentleman. *Piozzi Letters*, ii. 246. Mr. Langley was the Master of Ashbourne School. *Ante*, p. 189.

[4] For the Amicable Society see *ante*, p. 331. Within the last ten years the women's club in Lichfield used to go to church on an appointed day; in Stafford till very lately they carried staves in their procession to church.

[5] 'March 24, 1775. The *Savoir vivre* Club are going to give quite a new thing on the Thames; all the river from Blackfriars Bridge to some way above Westminster Bridge is to be filled with gondolas, barges, &c., leaving a space as wide as the centre arch of Westminster Bridge quite clear for a boat-race, and all the company are to go by water to Ranelagh to dine, and to sup at Vauxhall.' *Letters of the First Earl of Malmesbury*, i. 298. See also *ib.* p. 311.

'June 23, 1775. An entertainment called a Regatta, borrowed from the Venetians, was exhibited partly on the Thames and partly at Ranelagh.' *Annual Register*, 1775, i. 133. 'It was beautiful,' writes Horace Walpole, 'to see the Thames covered with boats, barges, and streamers, and every window and house-top loaded with spectators. I suppose so many will not meet again till the day of judgment, which was not to-day. In the middle of the river was a street of lighters and barges covered with pent-houses like a carpenter's yard, which totally prevented all the other millions seeing anything. The rowers passed through this street, and so we never beheld them at all.' Walpole's *Letters*, vi. 223. See also Walpole's *Journal of the*

left

left out of any shining part of life. You have every right to
distinction, and should therefore be distinguished. You will see
a show with philosophick superiority, and therefore may see it
safely. It is easy to talk of sitting at home contented, when
others are seeing or making shows. But not to have been where
it is supposed, and seldom supposed falsely, that all would go if
they could ; to be able to say nothing when every one is talking ;
to have no opinion when every one is judging ; to hear exclama-
tions of rapture without power to depress ; to listen to falsehoods
without right to contradict, is, after all, a state of temporary inferiority, in which the mind is rather hardened by stubbornness,
than supported by fortitude [1]. If the world be worth winning,
let us enjoy it [2] ; if it is to be despised, let us despise it by conviction. But the world is not to be despised but as it is compared
with something better. Company is in itself better than solitude,
and pleasure better than indolence. *Ex nihilo nihil fit,* says the
moral as well as natural philosopher. By doing nothing and by
knowing nothing no power of doing good can be obtained. He
must mingle with the world that desires to be useful. Every
new scene impresses new ideas, enriches the imagination, and
enlarges the power of reason, by new topicks of comparison.
You that have seen the regatta will have images which we who
miss it must want, and no intellectual images are without use [3].
But when you are in this scene of splendour and gayety, do not
let one of your fits of negligence steal upon you. *Hoc age,* is the
great rule whether you are serious or merry [4] ; whether you are
stating the expences of your family, learning science or duty

---

Reign of George III, i. 493, ed. 1759,
and *Gentleman's Magazine,* 1775, p.
314.

[1] 'I said there was not half a
guinea's worth of pleasure in seeing
this place [the Pantheon].—JOHN-
SON. "But, Sir, there is half a
guinea's worth of inferiority to other
people in not having seen it."' *Life,*
ii. 169.

[2] 'If the world be worth thy winning,
    Think, O think it, worth enjoying.'
DRYDEN, *Alexander's Feast,* st. v.

[3] 'Dr. Johnson asked me if I would
lose the recollection of our Tour to
the Hebrides for five hundred pounds,
I answered I would not ; and he ap-
plauded my setting such a value on
an accession of new images in my
mind.' *Life,* v. 405.

[4] 'Remember the *hoc age* ; do
what you are about, be that what it
will ; it is either worth doing well or
not at all.' Chesterfield's *Letters to
his Son,* i. 290. Chesterfield never
tires of insisting on *hoc age.*

from a folio [1], or floating on the Thames in a fancied dress. Of the whole entertainment let me not hear so copious nor so true an account from any body as from you.

I am, dearest Madam,

Your, &c.,

SAM: JOHNSON.

410.

To MRS. THRALE [2].

DEAR MADAM,   June 23, 1775

So now you have been at the regatta, for I hope you got tickets somewhere, else you wanted me, and I shall not be sorry, because you fancy you can do so well without me; but however I hope you got tickets, and were dressed fine and fanciful [3], and made a fine part of the fine show, and heard musick, and said good things, and staid on the water four hours after midnight, and came well home, and slept, and dreamed of the regatta, and waked, and found yourself in bed, and thought now it is all over, only I must write about it to Lichfield.

We make a hard shift here to live on without a regatta. The cherries are ripe at Stowhill, and the currants are ripening, and the ladies are very kind to me. I wish, however, you would go to Surry, and come back, though I think it wiser to stay till the improvement in Ralph [4] may become perceptible, else you will be apt to judge by your wishes and your imagination. Let us in the mean time hope the best. Let me but know when you go, and when you come back again.

If you or Mr. Thrale would write to Dr. Wetherell about Mr. Carter, it will please Wetherell, and keep the business in motion. They know not otherwise how to communicate news if they have it.

As to my hopes and my wishes, I can keep them to myself. They will perhaps grow less if they are laughed at. I needed

---

[1] 'Reading James's *Medical Dictionary* to learn how to administer antimonial wine to a boy.'—BARETTI.

[2] *Piozzi Letters*, i. 244.

[3] Mrs. Thrale writing in 1781 says

that the trimming of her Court dress was to cost £65. Mme. D'Arblay's *Diary*, ii. 7.

[4] Her second son.

not

not tell them, but that I have little else to write, and I needed not write, but that I do not like to be without hearing from you, because I love the Thrales and the Thralites.

I am, &c.,

SAM: JOHNSON.

411.

To MRS. THRALE[1].

DEAR MADAM, June 26, 1775.

That the regatta disappointed you is neither wonderful nor new[2]; all pleasure preconceived and preconcerted ends in disappointment[3]; but disappointment, when it involves neither shame nor loss, is as good as success; for it supplies as many images to the mind, and as many topicks to the tongue. I am glad it failed for another reason, which looks more sage than my reasons commonly try to look; this, I think, is Queeney's first excursion into the regions of pleasure, and I should not wish to have her too much pleased[4]. It is as well for her to find that pleasures have their pains; and that bigger misses who are at Ranelagh when she is in bed, are not so much to be envied as they would wish to be, or as they may be represented.

So you left out the · · · ·s, and I suppose they did not go. It will be a common place for you and Queeney fourscore years hence; and my master and you may have recourse to it sometimes. But I can only listen. I am glad that you were among the finest[5].

[1] *Piozzi Letters*, i. 255.

[2] The wind had been high and the water rough so that they had not ventured on to the river. They had gone to a friend's house in the Temple, where they had struggled for places at a window and 'discomposed their head-dresses.' They had hastened thence in a boat to Ranelagh; but the wind roared and the rain fell. The screams of the frighted company were heard as they were tossed about at the moment of getting to shore. The Rotunda was not to be opened till twelve o'clock, and they crowded into the new building, whence they drove the carpenters.

The supper was said to be execrable. They did not return home till about five or six in the morning. *Piozzi Letters*, i. 248-254.

[3] 'Nothing is more hopeless than a scheme of merriment.' *The Idler*, No. 58.

[4] 'I have a notion that Queeny has listened too much to his gloomy lessons, as now that she is three and twenty, though rich and independent, she is already too gloomy herself.'— BARETTI.

[5] According to Horace Walpole (*Letters*, vi. 223), 'A great deal of the show was spoilt by everybody being in black; it looked like a

Nothing

Nothing was the matter between me and Miss • • • •[1]. We are all well enough now. Miss Porter went yesterday to church, from which she has been kept a long time. I fancy that I shall go on Thursday to Ashbourne, but do not think that I shall stay very long. I wish you were gone to Surry and come well back again, and yet I would not have you go too soon. Perhaps I do not very well know what I would have; it is a case not extremely rare. But I know I would hear from you by every post, and therefore I take care that you should every post day hear from me.

I am, &c.,
SAM: JOHNSON.

412.

To RICHARD GREEN.

[Lichfield or Ashbourne], June 29, 1775.

In Messrs. Puttick and Simpson's Auction Catalogue of March 10, 1862, Lot 363 is 'a Letter of Johnson to Mr. Green, one page quarto, making an appointment, dated June 29, 1775.'

For Mr. Green, see *ante*, p. 161.

413.

To MRS. THRALE[2].

DEAR MADAM,   Ashbourne, [Saturday], July 1, 1775.

On Thursday I came to Dr. Taylor's, where I live as I am used to do, and as you know. He has gotten nothing new, but a very fine looking glass, and a bull-bitch[3]. The less bull is

general mourning for Amphitrite rather than for the Queen of Denmark.' Yet Mrs. Thrale wrote :— 'It had been agreed that all [of our party] should wear white; but the ornaments were left to our own choice. I was afraid of not being fine enough ; so I trimmed my white lute-string with silver gauze, and wore black ribbons intermixed. You will be told I was too fine, and 'tis partly true ; but the other extreme would have been worse.' *Piozzi Letters*, i. 248, 253.

[1] Mrs. Thrale had asked :—' Why does Miss * * * never find a place in the letters from Lichfield ? I thought her a mighty elegant amiable country lady.' *Ib.* i. 246. Perhaps Miss Seward is the lady.

[2] *Piozzi Letters*, i. 257.

[3] See the *Life*, iii. 190, for Johnson's criticism of Dr. Taylor's bull-dog, which had not ' the quick transition from the thickness of the fore-part to the *tenuity* – the thin part—behind— which a bull-dog ought to have.'

now

now grown the bigger. But I forgot; he has bought old Shake-speare, the racehorse, for a stallion[1]. He has likewise some fine iron gates which he will set up somewhere. I have not yet seen the old horse.

You are very much enquired after, as well here as at Lich-field.

This I suppose will go after you to Sussex[2], where I hope you will find every thing either well or mending. You never told me whether you took Queeney with you; nor ever so much as told me the name of the little one[3]. May be you think I don't care about you.

I behaved myself so well at Lichfield, that Lucy says I am grown better; and the ladies at Stowhill expect I should come back thither before I go to London, and offer to entertain me if Lucy refuses.

I have this morning received a letter from Mrs. Chambers of Calcutta[4]. The Judge has a sore eye, and could not write. She represents all as going on very well, only Chambers does not now flatter himself that he shall do much good.

> I am, &c.,
> SAM: JOHNSON.

414.

TO MRS. THRALE[5].

[Ashbourne, July 1775.]

Now, thinks my dearest Mistress to herself, sure I am at last gone too far to be pestered every post with a letter: he knows that people go into the country to be at quiet; he knows too that when I have once told the story of Ralph, the place where I am affords me nothing that I shall delight to tell, or he will wish to be told; he knows how troublesome it is to write letters about

[1] See *post*, Letter of Michaelmas Day, 1777.

[2] The Thrales went to Brighton. *Post*, p. 345.

[3] *Ante*, p. 315, *n.* 3.

[4] Johnson on March 5 of the previous year had written to Bos-well:—'Chambers is either married, or almost married, to Miss Wilton, a girl of sixteen, exquisitely beautiful, whom he has, with his lawyer's tongue, persuaded to take her chance with him in the East.' *Life*, ii. 274. Her chance apparently was a good one, for she lived till 1839. *Dict. of Nat. Biog.*, article Sir Robert Chambers. See also *ante*, p. 222, *n.* 3.

[5] *Piozzi Letters*, i. 258.

nothing:

nothing; and he knows that he does not love trouble himself, and therefore ought not to force it upon others.

But, dearest Lady, you may see once more how little knowledge influences practice, notwithstanding all this knowledge, you see, here is a letter.

Every body says the prospect of harvest is uncommonly delightful; but this has been so long the Summer talk, and has been so often contradicted by Autumn, that I do not suffer it to lay much hold on my mind. Our gay prospects have now for many years together ended in melancholy retrospects[1]. Yet I am of opinion that there is much corn upon the ground. Every dear year encourages the farmer to sow more and more, and favourable seasons will be sent at last. Let us hope that they will be sent now.

The Doctor and Frank are gone to see the hay. It was cut on Saturday, and yesterday was well wetted; but to day has its fill of sunshine. I hope the hay at Streatham was plentiful, and had good weather.

Our lawn is as you left it, only the pool is so full of mud that the water-fowl have left it. Here are many calves, who, I suppose, all expect to be great bulls and cows[2].

Yesterday I saw Mrs. Diot[3] at church, and shall drink tea with her some afternoon.

I cannot get free from this vexatious flatulence, and therefore have troublesome nights, but otherwise I am not very ill. Now and then a fit, and not violent. I am not afraid of the waterfall[4]. I now and then take physick; and suspect that you were

---

[1] *Ante*, p. 194.   [2] *Ante*, p. 166.

[3] Johnson mentions seeing her when he and the Thrales visited Ashbourne the year before. *Life*, v. 430. Mr. J. Coke Fowler, Stipendiary Magistrate of Swansea, says that about the year 1837 he met in a country-house in Leicestershire, 'a very aged lady, a Miss Dyott, who had more than once dined with Dr. Johnson at Lichfield. At one dinner he was talking on some interesting subject. A dish of Brussels sprouts or broccoli was on the table before

him. She saw a footman take a plate to him to receive a helping of the vegetables, and to her horror she saw the great man, as he was talking, dive his hand mechanically into the dish, and effect the helping with his fingers.' *Recollections of Public Men* in *The Red Dragon*. p. 239.

[4] See *ante*, p. 198. Mrs. Thrale, I conjecture, had expressed a fear lest, while he was at the waterfall, a sudden faintness might overcome him such as he had had a few weeks earlier. *Ante*, p. 322.

not

not quite right in omitting to let blood before I came away[1]. But I do not intend to do it here.

You will now find the advantage of having made one at the regatta. You will carry with you the importance of a publick personage, and enjoy a superiority which, having been only local and accidental, will not be regarded with malignity. You have a subject by which you can gratify general curiosity, and amuse your company without bewildering them. You can keep the vocal machine in motion, without those seeming paradoxes that are sure to disgust; without that temerity of censure which is sure to provoke enemies; and that exuberance of flattery which experience has found to make no friends. It is the good of publick life that it supplies agreeable topicks and general conversation. Therefore wherever you are, and whatever you see, talk not of the Punick war[2]; nor of the depravity of human nature; nor of the slender motives of human actions; nor of the difficulty of finding employment or pleasure; but talk, and talk, and talk of the regatta, and keep the rest for, dearest Madam,

Your, &c.,

SAM: JOHNSON.

415.

TO MRS. THRALE[3].

DEAR MADAM,   Ashbourne, July 6, 1775.

Dr. Taylor says he shall be very glad to see you all here again, if you have a mind of retirement[4]. But I told him that he must not expect you this summer; and he wants to know why?

---

[1] *Ante*, p. 298, and *post*, p. 354.

[2] 'Sooner than hear of the Punic War,' Murphy writes, 'Johnson would be rude to the person that introduced the subject.' Murphy's *Life of Johnson*, p. 138. Mrs. Piozzi says (*Anec.*, p. 80) that 'no kind of conversation pleased him less, I think, than when the subject was historical fact or general polity. "What shall we learn from *that* stuff?" said he. "He never," as he expressed it, "desired to hear of the *Punic War* while he lived."' The *Punic War*, it is clear, was a kind of humorous catchword with him. She wrote to him in 1773:— 'So here's modern politics in a letter from me; yes and a touch of the *Punic War* too.' *Piozzi Letters*, i. 187. He was no doubt sick of the constant reference made by writers and public speakers to Rome. For instance, in Bolingbroke's *Dissertation upon Parties*, we find in three consecutive Letters (xi–xiii) five illustrations drawn from Rome. See *Life*, iii. 206 *n*.

[3] *Piozzi Letters*, i. 261.

[4] See *ante*, p. 314, *n*. 7.

I am

I am glad you have read Boswell's journal [1], because it is something for us to talk about, and that you have seen the Horneeks [2], because that is a publick theme. I would have you see, and read, and hear, and talk it all, as occasion offers.

Pray thank Queeney for her letter. I still hope good of poor Ralph ; but sure never poor rogue was so troubled with his teeth. I hope occasional bathing, and keeping him about two minutes with his body immersed, may promote the discharge from his head, and set his little brain at liberty. Pray give my service to my dear friend Harry, and tell him that Mr. Murphy does not love him better than I do [3].

I am inclined to be of Mr. Thrale's mind about the changes in the state. A dissolution of the Parliament would, in my opinion, be little less than a dissolution of the government, by the encouragement which it would give to every future faction to disturb the publick tranquillity [4]. Who would ever want places and power if perseverance in falsehood and violence of outrage were found to be certain and infallible means of procuring them ? yet I have so little confidence in our present statesmen, that I

---

[1] *Ante*, p. 320.

[2] 'The Horneeks were and are still two Ladies no less beautiful than modest and sensible. Both have been my pupils ; but Madam never liked them much, because few would take notice of her where they were.'— BARETTI. Boswell describes them as 'two beautiful young ladies, one of whom married Henry Bunbury, Esq., and the other Colonel Gwyn.' Goldsmith accompanied them and their mother on a tour in France. *Life*, i. 414. His nickname for the eldest was Little Comedy, and for the youngest, the Jessamy Bride. 'Burke, who was their guardian, tenderly remembered in his premature old age the delight they had given him from their childhood. The youngest died in 1840.' Forster's *Goldsmith*, ii. 147. 'I don't know why she is so kind as

to come to see me,' said Northcote in 1830, 'except that I am the last link in the chain that connects her with all those she most esteemed when she was young— Johnson, Reynolds, Goldsmith—and remind her of the most delightful period of her life.' Northcote's *Conversations*, p. 94.

[3] When nine months later Johnson heard of poor Harry's death he exclaimed :—' I would have gone to the extremity of the earth to have preserved the boy.' *Life*, ii. 469. It was Arthur Murphy who introduced Johnson to the Thrales. *Ib.* i. 493. Miss Burney writing in May, 1779, says :—'Mr. Thrale and Mr. Murphy are very old friends ; and I question if Mr. Thrale loves any man so well.' Mme. D'Arblay's *Diary*, i. 210.

[4] Parliament was not dissolved till 1780.

know

know not whether any thing is less likely, for being either absurd
or dangerous.   I am, dearest Lady,

Your, &c.,

SAM: JOHNSON.

416.

To Mrs. Thrale [1].

DEAR MADAM,   Ashbourne, July [? 9], 1775.

I am sorry that my poor little friend Ralph goes on no
better.   We must see what time will do for him.

I hope Harry is well.   I had a very pretty letter from
Queeney; and hope she will be kind to my hen and her ten
chickens, and mind her book.

I forget whether I tell some things, and may perhaps tell them
twice, but the matter is not great, only, as you observe, the more
we write the less we shall have to say when we meet.

Are we to go all to Brighthelmstone in the Autumn, or have
you satiated yourself with this visit?   I have only one reason for
wishing you to go, and that reason is far enough from amounting
to necessity.

That • • • •'s simplicity should be forgiven, for his benevolence
is very just; and I will not now say any thing in opposition to
your kind resolution.   It is pity that any good man should ever
seem, or ever be ridiculous.

This letter will be short, for I am so much disordered by indigestion, of which I can give no account, that it is difficult to
write more than that I am, dearest Lady,

Your, &c.,

SAM: JOHNSON.

417.

To Mrs. Thrale [2].

DEAR MADAM,   Ashbourne, [July 11, 1775].

I am sure I write and write, and every letter that comes
from you charges me with not writing.   Since I wrote to Queeney
I have written twice to you, on the 6th and the 9th, be pleased
to let me know whether you have them or have them not.   That

---

[1] *Piozzi Letters*, i. 273.   [2] *Piozzi Letters*, i. 264.

of

of the 6th you should regularly have had on the 8th, yet your letter of the 9th seems not to mention it; all this puzzles me.

Poor dear • • • • [1]! He only grows dull because he is sickly; age has not yet begun to impair him; nor is he such a chameleon as to take immediately the colour of his company. When you see him again, you will find him reanimated. Most men have their bright and their cloudy days, at least they have days when they put their powers into act. and days when they suffer them to repose [2].

Fourteen thousand pounds make a sum sufficient for the estab-lishment of a family, and which, in whatever flow of riches or confidence of prosperity, deserves to be very seriously considered [3]. I hope a great part of it has paid debts, and no small part bought land. As for gravelling and walling and digging, though I am not much delighted with them, yet something, indeed much, must be allowed to every man's taste. He that is growing rich has a right to enjoy part of the growth his own way. I hope to range in the walk, and row upon the water [4], and devour fruit from the wall.

Dr. Taylor wants to be gardening. He means to buy a piece of ground in the neighbourhood, and surround it with a wall, and build a gardener's house upon it, and have fruit, and be happy.

[1] Perhaps Mr. William Seward is meant, described in the *Life*, iii. 123, *n.* 1. He was very intimate with the Thrales. In Mme. D'Arblay's *Diary*, ii. 71, he is described as 'quacking both himself and his friends. "When he was at my place," said Mr. Crutchley, " he did himself up pretty handsomely; he ate cherries till he complained most bitterly of indigestion, and he poured down Madeira and Port most plenti-fully, but without relief. He went on to ask for peppermint-water, ginger, brandy, and a dose of rhubarb. I advised him to take a good bumper of gin and gunpowder, for that seemed almost all he had left untried."' Edge-worth mentions his hypochondria-cism. *Memoirs of R. L. Edgeworth*, ed. 1844, p. 117. He was the son of a wealthy brewer, partner in the house of Calvert and Seward. In the *Ann. Reg.* for 1760, i. 174, that firm is returned as the largest brewers in London; they having brewed 74,700 barrels against Thrale's 32,700. His name was pronounced Suard, as is shown by Charlotte Burney thus writing it. *Early Diary of Frances Burney*, ii. 287. See *post*, Letter of September 18, 1777.

[2] *Life*, i. 332, *n.* 2.

[3] Mrs. Thrale replied:— 'I will keep the story of the £14,000 till we meet.' *Piozzi Letters*, i. 269. It may have been the year's profits of the Brewery. See *post*, Letter of August 23, 1777, where he looks forward to their soon amounting to £15,000. It may have come by in-heritance. See *post*, p. 351.

[4] *Post*, p. 360.

Much

Much happiness it will not bring him ; but what can he do better ? If I had money enough, what would I do ? Perhaps, if you and master did not hold me, I might go to Cairo, and down the Red Sea to Bengal, and take a ramble in India [1]. Would this be better than building and planting ? It would surely give more variety to the eye, and more amplitude to the mind. Half fourteen thousand would send me out to see other forms of existence, and bring me back to describe them [2].

I answer this the day on which I had yours of the 9th, that is on the 11th. Let me know when it comes.

I am, &c.,
SAM: JOHNSON.

418.

To Mrs. Thrale [3].

DEAR MADAM,   Ashbourne, Wednesday, July 12, 1775.

On Monday I was not well, but I grew better at night, and before morning was, as the doctors say, out of danger.

We have no news here, except that on Saturday Lord Scarsdale [4] dined with the Doctor. He is a very gentlemanlike man. On Sunday Mr. • • • • paid a visit from Lichfield, and having nothing to say, said nothing, and went away.

Our great cattle, I believe, go on well, but our deer have died ; all but five does and the poor buck. We think the ground too wet for them.

I have enclosed a letter from Mrs. Chambers [5], partly, perhaps wholly, for Mr. Baretti's amusement and gratification, though he has probably a much longer letter of his own, which he takes no care to send me.

Mr. L——[6] and the Doctor still continue at variance ; and the

---

[1] See *Life*, iii. 453, for Johnson's eagerness for travelling.

[2] Mrs. Thrale replied : — 'Mr. Thrale said when we read the last paragraph of your letter together, that you should not travel alone, if he could once see this dear little boy quite well, or see me well persuaded (as many are) that nothing ails him.'

Piozzi Letters, i. 269. They went to France together this Autumn. *Life*, ii. 384.

[3] *Piozzi Letters*, i. 266.

[4] For Johnson's visit to his house at Keddlestone, see *Life*, iii. 160.

[5] *Ante*, p. 341.

[6] Mr. Langley, the Head Master of Ashbourne School. *Ante*, p. 189.

Doctor

Doctor is afraid, and Mr. L—— not desirous of a reconciliation. I therefore step over at by-times, and of by-times I have enough.

Mrs. Dale[1] has been ill, and, at fourscore, has recovered. She is much extenuated, but having the summer to favour her, will, I think, renew her hold on life.

To the Diots[2] I yet owe a visit. Mr. Gell is now rejoicing, at fifty-seven, for the birth of an heir-male[3]. I hope here is news. Mr. • • • • and • • • • seem to be making preparations for war.

Now I flatter myself that you want to know something about me. My spirits are now and then in an uneasy flutter, but upon the whole not very bad.

We have here a great deal of rain; but this is a very rainy region. I hear nothing but good of the harvest; but the expectation is higher of the wheat than of the barley, but I hope there will be barley enough for us, and Mr. S——, and Lady L——[4], and something still to spare. I am, dearest sweetest Lady,

> Your, &c.,
>
> SAM: JOHNSON.

419.

TO MRS. THRALE[5].

DEAREST MADAM, July 13, 1775.

In return for your three letters I do not find myself able to send you more than two; but if I had the prolixity of an emperour, it should be all at your service[6].

Poor Ralph! I think what they purpose to do for his relief is right, but that it will be efficacious I cannot promise.

Your anxiety about your other babies is, I hope, superfluous. Miss and Harry are as safe as ourselves[7]; they have outlived the age of weakness; their fibres are now elastick, and their

---

[1] Mrs. Thrale had seen her the year before. *Life*, v. 431.

[2] *Ante*, p. 342, *n.* 3.

[3] Philip Gell of Hopton, Derbyshire. A younger son, born in 1777, was Sir William Gell, author of *The Topography of Troy*. The Thrales had dined with Mr. Gell in 1774. *Life*, v. 431.

[4] Probably Mr. Scrase and Lady Lade of whom Mr. Thrale had bor-rowed money. *Ante*, p. 192, *n.* 3.

[5] *Piozzi Letters*, i. 274.

[6] 'DOGBERRY. But truly, for mine own part, if I were as tedious as a king, I could find it in my heart to bestow it all of your worship.' *Much Ado About Nothing*, Act iii. sc. 5.

[7] Harry died the following March, *Post*, p. 381.

headachs,

headachs, when they have them, are from accidental causes, heat or indigestion.

If Susy had been at all disposed to this horrid malady[1], it would have laid hold on her in her early state of laxity and feebleness. That native vigour which has carried her happily through so many obstructions to life and growth, will, I think, certainly preserve her from a disease most likely to fall only on the weak.

Of the two small ladies it can only be said, that there is no present appearance of danger; and of fearing evils merely possible there is no end. We are told by the Lord of Nature, that ' for the day its own evil is sufficient[2].'

Now to lighter things, and those of weight enough to another. I am still of opinion, that we shall bring the Oxford riding-school to bear. * * * * * * *[3] is indeed *un esprit foible*, and perhaps too easily repressed, but Dr. Wetherell is in earnest. I would come back through Oxford, but that at this time there is nobody there. But I will not desist. I think to visit them next term.

Do not let poor Lizard be degraded for five pounds. I sent you word that I would spend something upon him; and indeed for the money which it would cost to take him to Taylor or Langton and fetch him back, he may be kept, while he stands idle, a long time in the stable[4].

Mrs. Williams has been very ill, and it would do her good if you would send a message of enquiry, and a few strawberries or currants.

Mr. Flint's[5] little girl is alive and well, and prating, as I hope yours, my dear Lady, will long continue.

---

[1] Many of them died of some kind of fit. Mrs. Thrale had written to Johnson:—'The illness of this boy frights me for all the rest; if any of them have a headach it puts me in an agony, a broken leg would less affect my peace.——So many to have the same disorder is dreadful. What can be the meaning of it?'

[2] 'Sufficient unto the day is the evil thereof.' *St. Matthew*, vi. 34.

[3] Perhaps Dr. Fothergill, the Vice-Chancellor. *Ante*, pp. 323, *n*. 3, 324, *n*. 4.

[4] Lizard was perhaps ' Mr. Thrale's old hunter on which Johnson rode with a good firmness ' at a fox-chase. Piozzi's *Anec.*, p. 206, and *Life*, v. 253. See *Life*, iv. 248, 250, about the treatment of ' old horses, unable to labour.'

[5] The Thrales visited Mr. Flint The

The hay harvest is here very much incommoded by daily showers, which, however, seem not violent enough to beat down the corn.

I cannot yet fix the time of coming home. Dr. Taylor and I spend little time together, yet he will not yet be persuaded to hear of parting [1].

I am, dearest Lady,
Your, &c.,
SAM: JOHNSON.

420.

To Mrs. Thrale [2].

DEAR MADAM,   Ashbourne, July 15, 1775.

You are so kind every post, that I now regularly expect your favours. You have indeed more materials for writing than I. Here are only I and the Doctor, and of him I see not much. You have Master, and young Master, and Misses, besides geese, and turkies, and ducks, and hens [3].

The Doctor says, that if Mr. Thrale comes so near as Derby without seeing us, it will be a sorry trick. I wish, for my part, that he may return soon, and rescue the fair captives from the tyranny of B——i [4]. Poor B——i! do not quarrel with him;

---

in 1774. *Life*, v. 430. He is often mentioned in Johnson's Letters to Taylor in 1782. *Post*, Letter of July 22, 1782.

[1] *Ante*, p. 184.

[2] *Piozzi Letters*, i. 277.

[3] 'Susan Burney, describing Streatham in August 1779, says :— 'As a *place* it surpassed all my expectations. The avenue to the house, plantations, &c., are beautiful; worthy of the charming inhabitants. It is a little Paradise, I think. Cattle, poultry, dogs, all running freely about, without annoying each other.' *Early Diary of Frances Burney*, ii. 256. Sir James Prior thus writes of it :—' Its site perhaps is too low, but Tooting Common opens pleasantly in front; and often while resident for several years in the vicinity have I lingered around it for hours as venerated ground.' *Life of Malone*, p. 259. On the Common still stands an oak known as Johnson's oak.

[4] 'If B—i means Baretti, God knows what lies the woman wrote to Johnson! The girls were never so happy as when their mother was away, who did nothing but scold or beat them for the most trivial faults or omissions. As to me, when I had done teaching Queeny I made them run merrily about, and nobody checked their mirth but their beastly mother. However I suspect that this gabble is not Johnson's but her own.' BARETTI. See *Life*, iii. 49,

to

to neglect him a little will be sufficient. He means only to be frank, and manly, and independent, and perhaps, as you say, a little wise. To be frank he thinks is to be cynical, and to be independent is to be rude. Forgive him, dearest Lady, the rather, because of his misbehaviour, I am afraid he learned part of me. I hope to set him hereafter a better example.

Your concern for poor Ralph, and your resolution to visit him again, is too parental to be blamed. You may perhaps do good; you do at least your duty, and with that we must be contented; with that indeed, if we attained it, we ought to be happy: but who ever attained it?

You have perceived, by my letters, that without knowing more than that the *estate* was unsettled, I was inclined to a settlement. I am likewise for an entail. But we will consult men of experience, for that which is to hinder my dear Harry from mischief when he comes to age may be done with mature deliberation.

You have not all the misery in the world to yourself; I was last night almost convulsed with flatulence, after having gone to bed I thought so well—but it does not much trouble me when I am out of bed. To your anxiety about your children I wrote lately what I had to say. I blame it so little, that I think you should add a small particle of anxiety about me; for

> I am, dearest Madam,
>> Your, &c.,
>>> SAM: JOHNSON.

421.

To Mrs. Thrale [1].

DEAR MADAM,   July 17, 1775.

The post is come without a letter; how could I be so

n. 1, 96, and *post*, Letter of June 3, 1776. Miss Burney describes Baretti in 1772 as 'a very good-looking man.' *Early Diary of Fanny Burney*, i. 169. Twiss, the traveller, mimicked to her his utterance. 'I think I never knew a foreigner,' he said, 'who spoke English so well as Baretti does; but so very slow' (in a drawling voice, turning to me) 'that if he — were — to — make — love — it — would — take — him—*tree*—hours—to utter a declaration.' *Ib.* p. 286.

[1] *Piozzi Letters*, i. 279.

sullen

sullen—but *he must be humble who would please*[1]. Perhaps you
are gone to Brighthelmstone, and so could not write; however
it be, this I feel, that I have no letter; but then I have sometimes had two, and if I have as many letters as there come
posts nobody will pity me if I were to complain.

How was your hay made?[2] The Doctor has had one part
well housed, another wetted and dried till it is hardly worth the
carriage; and now many acres newly mown, that have hitherto
had good weather. This may be considered as a foreign article;
the domestick news is, that our bull-bitch has puppies, and that
our six calves are no longer to be fed by hand, but to live on
grass.

Mr. Langley has made some improvements in his garden.
A rich man might do more; but what he has done is well[3].

You have never in all your letters touched but once upon
my master's Summer projects. Is he towering into the air, and
tending to the centre? Is he excavating the earth, or covering
its surface with edifices? Something he certainly is doing, and
something he is spending. A genius never can be quite still.
I do not murmur at his expences; a good harvest will supply
them.

We talk here of Polish oats, and Siberian barley, of which
both are said to be more productive, to ripen in less time, and
to afford better grain than the English[4]. I intend to procure

[1] 'Ten thousand trifles such as
these
Nor can my rage nor anger
move;
She should be humble who
would please;
And she must suffer who can
love.'
Cloe Jealous. Prior's *Poetical
Works*, 1858, p. 78.

[2] 'I don't know why, but people
are always more anxious about their
hay than their corn, or twenty other
things that cost them more. I suppose my Lord Chesterfield, or some
other dictator, made it fashionable to
care about one's hay. Nobody be-
trays solicitude about getting in his
rents.' Horace Walpole's *Letters*,
viii. 382.

[3] 'After breakfast, Johnson carried
me to see the garden belonging to
the school of Ashbourne, which is
very prettily formed upon a bank,
rising gradually behind the house.
The Reverend Mr. Langley, the
head-master, accompanied us.' *Life*,
iii. 138.

[4] 'We are credibly informed that
a gentleman at Kilmarnock in Scotland had the curiosity to plant three
grains of Siberian barley. Their produce was 2585 grains.' *Gentleman's
Magazine*, 1771, p. 520. See *ib.* 1783,
p. 852, for a comparison of 'Tartarian
and Poland oats.'

specimens

specimens of both, which we will try in some spots of our own ground.

The Doctor has no great mind to let me go. Shall I teaze him, and plague him till he is weary of me ? I am, I hope, pretty well, and fit to come home. I shall be expected by all my ladies to return through Lichfield, and to stay there a while ; but if I thought you wanted me, I hope you know what would be done by,

Dearest, dearest Madam,

Your, &c.

SAM: JOHNSON.

422.

To MRS. THRALE [1].

DEAR MADAM,   Ashbourne, July 20, 1775.

Poor Ralph ! he is gone; and nothing remains but that you comfort yourself with having done your best. The first wish was, that he might live long to be happy and useful ; the next, that he might not suffer long pain. The second wish has been granted. Think now only on those which are left you. I am glad that you went to Brighthelmstone, for your journey is a standing proof to you of your affection and diligence. We can hardly be confident of the state of our own minds, but as it stands attested by some external action ; we are seldom sure that we sincerely meant what we omitted to do.

Dr. Taylor says, that Mr. Thrale has not used us well, in coming so near without coming nearer [2]. I know not what he can say for himself, but I know that he can take shelter in sullen silence.

There is, I think, still the same prospect of a plentiful harvest. We have in this part of the kingdom had rain to swell the grain, and sunshine to ripen it. I was yesterday to see [3] the

---

[1] *Piozzi Letters*, i. 281. Mrs. Thrale fresh from the loss of her little boy, might surely, as she read this strange letter, have exclaimed with Constance in *King John*:—

'He talks to me that never had a son.'

There is nothing to show that in her mood there was anything that was jarred upon by the childless Johnson's natural ignorance of the feelings of a parent.

[2] *Ante*, p. 350.

[3] This idiom, a very common one in the writers—especially in the early

Doctor's Poland oats. They grow, for a great part, four feet high, with a stalk equal in bulk and strength to wheaten straw. We were of opinion that they must be reaped, as the lower joints would be too hard for fodder. We will try them.

Susy was always my little girl [1]. See what she is come to; you must keep her in mind of me, who was always on her side. Of Mrs. Fanny [2] I have no knowledge.

You have two or three of my letters to answer, and I hope you will be copious and distinct, and tell me a great deal of your mind; a dear little mind it is; and I hope always to love it better as I know it more.

I am, &c.

Sam: Johnson.

423.

To Mrs. Thrale [3].

Dear Lady.   Ashbourne, July 21, 1775.

When you write next direct to Lichfield, for I think to move that way on Tuesday, and in no long time to move homewards, when we will have a serious consultation, and try to do every thing for the best.

I shall be glad of a letter from dear Queeney, and am not sorry that she wishes for me. When I come we will enter into an alliance defensive at least [4].

Mr. B——i very elegantly sent his pupil's letter to Mrs. Williams without a cover, in such a manner that she knows not whence it was transmitted [5].

I do not mean to bleed but with your concurrence [6], though I am troubled with eruptions, which I cannot suppress by frequent physick.

---

writers—of the century, is very uncommon in Johnson.

[1] 'Little did he care for Susy, or for any of the rest. I find he mentions them often in writing, but scarce ever took notice of any when present.' Baretti. See *post*, Letter of Oct. 6, 1777, where Johnson says:—'I was always a Susy, when nobody else was a Susy.'

[2] The last baby, eleven weeks old. *Ante*, p. 315, *n*. 3.

[3] *Piozzi Letters*, i. 283.

[4] An alliance against Baretti. *Ante*, p. 350.

[5] 'I don't know what this gabble means, and what letter they are speaking of.' Baretti. The *cover* was the piece of paper in which the note should have been inclosed. It answered the purpose of the modern envelope, and was secured by either wax or a wafer.

[6] *Ante*, p. 343.

As

As my master staid only one day [1], we must forgive him, yet he knows he staid only one day, because he thought it not worth his while to stay two.

You and B——i are friends again [2]. My dear mistress has the quality of being easily reconciled, and not easily offended. Kindness is a good thing in itself; and there are few things that are worthy of anger, and still fewer that can justify malignity.

Nothing remains for the present, but that you sit down placid and content, disposed to enjoy the present, and planning the proper use of the future liberalities of Providence [3]. You have really much to enjoy, and, without any wild indulgence of imagination, much to expect. In the mean time, however, life is gliding away, and another state is hastening forwards. You were but five-and-twenty when I knew you first [4]. What I shall be next September I confess I have *lacheté* [5] enough to turn aside from thinking.

I am glad you read Boswell's journal [6]; you are now sufficiently informed of the whole transaction, and need not regret that you did not make the tour of the Hebrides.

You have done me honour in naming me your trustee, and have very judiciously chosen Cator [7]. I believe our fidelity will not be exposed to any strong temptations.

I am, &c.,

SAM: JOHNSON.

[1] At Derby. *Ante*, p. 350.

[2] Baretti, describing Mrs. Thrale by the word which gave Mrs. Jonathan Wild such just offence, says that she 'has suppressed the letter that made Johnson write these idle words, therefore I cannot even have a guess at their meaning.' In all probability she had it not in her possession to suppress, for Johnson burnt all of her letters that he could find. *Life*, iv. 339, *n*. 3.

[3] Her little son had been dead four or five days.

[4] She was born on January 16, 1740, O.S., or January 27, 1741, N.S.

Hayward's *Piozzi*, i. 33. See *Life*, i. 520, for the date of Johnson's first acquaintance with the Thrales.

[5] Johnson in these letters does not show himself strong in his French accents. Perhaps the fault was the printer's. Goethe in a letter which he wrote in French in 1774 equally neglected the accents. G. H. Lewes's *Life of Goethe*, ed. 1890, p. 210.

[6] *Ante*, p. 320.

[7] Cator was a timber-merchant. Mrs. Piozzi says in her *Anecdotes*, p. 304 :—'I mentioned two friends who were particularly fond of looking at themselves in a glass. "They do

424.

To Mrs. Thrale[1].

Dear Madam,   July 24, 1775.

Be pleased to return my thanks to Queeney for her pretty little letter. I hope the peacock will recover. It is pity we cannot catch the fellow; we would make him drink at the pump. The victory over the poor wild cat delights me but little. I had rather he had taken a chicken than lost his life.

To-morrow I go to Lichfield. My company would not any longer make the Doctor happy. He wants to be rambling with his Ashbourne friends. And it is perhaps time for me to think of coming home. Which way I shall take I do not know.

Miss says, that you have recovered your spirits, and that you all are well. Pray do not grudge the trouble of telling me so your ownself; for I do not find my attention to you and your sensations at all lessened by this time of absence, which always appears to my imagination much longer than when I count it.

Now to-morrow I expect to see Lucy Porter and Mrs. Adey, and to hear how they have gone on at Lichfield; and then for a little I shall wander about as the birds of passage circle and flutter before they set out on the main flight.

I have been generally without any violent disorder of either mind or body, but every now and then ailing, but so that I could keep it to myself.

Are we to go to Brighthelmstone this Autumn? I do not enquire with any great solicitude. You know one reason, and it will not be easy to find another, except that which brings all thither that go, unwillingness to stay at home, and want of power

not surprise me at all by so doing (said Johnson); they see reflected in that glass men who have risen from almost the lowest situations in life, one to enormous riches, the other to everything this world can give—rank, fame, and fortune. They see likewise men who have merited their advancement by the exertion and improvement of those talents which God had given them; and I see not why they should avoid the mirror."'

Mrs. Piozzi states in a marginal note that these two men were Cator and Wedderburne. Hayward's *Piozzi*, i. 154, 294. Cator is, perhaps, the man mentioned in the *Life*, iv. 83, 'who had acquired £4,000 a year in trade, but was absolutely miserable because he could not talk in company.' He was one of Mr. Thrale's executors. *Ib.* iv. 313.

[1] *Piozzi Letters*, i. 285.

to

to supply with either business or amusement the cravings of the day. From this distress all that know either you or me, will suppose that we might rescue ourselves, if we would, without the help of a bath [1] in the morning and an assembly at night.

I am, &c.,

SAM: JOHNSON.

425.

To Mrs. Thrale [2].

DEAR MADAM,   Lichfield, July 26, 1775.

Yesterday I came hither. After dinner I went to Stowhill [3]; there I was pampered, and had an uneasy night. Physick to-day put me out of order; and for some time I forgot that this is post night.

Nothing very extraordinary has happened at Lichfield since I went away. Lucy Porter is better, and has got her lame hand out of the bag. The rest of your friends I have not seen.

Having staid long enough at Ashbourne, I was not sorry to leave it. I hindered some of Taylor's diversions, and he supplied me with very little. Having seen the neighbouring places, I had no curiosity to gratify: and having few new things, we had little new talk.

When I came I found Lucy at her book. She had Hammond's Commentary on the Psalms [4] before her. He is very learned, she says, but there is enough that any body may understand.

Now I am here I think myself a great deal nearer London than before, for though the distance is not very different, I am here in the way of carriages, and can easily get to Birmingham, and so to Oxford [5]; but I know not which way I shall take, but some way or other I hope to find, that may bring me back again to Streatham; and then I shall see what have been my master's goings on, and will try whether I shall know the old places [6].

---

[1] 'The man who dipped people in the sea at Brighthelmstone seeing Mr. Johnson swim in the year 1766, said, "Why, Sir, you must have been a stout-hearted gentleman forty years ago."' Piozzi's *Anecdotes*, p. 113.

[2] *Piozzi Letters*, i. 287.

[3] *Ante*, p. 160, *n.* 4.

[4] *Paraphrase and Annotations upon the Book of Psalms*, London, 1659, folio. Johnson recorded on Good Friday, in 1782:—'Read Hammond on one of the Psalms for the day.' *Pr. and Med.*, p. 211.

[5] *Ante*, p. 183.

[6] *Ante*, p. 346.

As

As I lift up my head from the paper. I can look into Lucy's garden. Her walls have all failed. I believe she has had hardly any fruit but gooseberries; but so much verdure looks pretty in a town.

When you read my letters I suppose you are very proud to think how much you excel in the correspondence; but you must remember that your materials are better. You have a family, and friends, and hopes, and fears, and wishes, and aversions, and all the ingredients that are necessary to the composition of a letter. Here sit poor I, with nothing but my own solitary individuality; doing little, and suffering no more than I have often suffered; hearing nothing that I can repeat; seeing nothing that I can relate; talking, when I do talk, to those whom you cannot regard; and at this moment hearing the curfew, which you cannot hear[1]. I am,

Dearest, dearest Lady,

Your, &c.,

SAM: JOHNSON.

426.

TO MRS. THRALE[2].

MADAM,   July 29, 1775.

The rain caught me at Stowhill, and kept me till it is very late; I must however write, for I am enjoined to tell you how much Mrs. Lucy was pleased with your present[3], and to entreat you to excuse her from writing. because her hand is not yet recovered. She is very glad of your notice, and very thankful.

I am very desirous that Mr. • • • • should be sent for a few weeks to Brighthelmstone. Air, and vacancy, and novelty, and the consciousness of his own value, and the pride of such distinction and delight in Mr. Thrale's kindness, would, as Cheney[4]

---

[1] The curfew still rings in Lichfield, every evening at eight o'clock.

[2] *Piozzi Letters*, i. 291.

[3] *Ante*, p. 332.

[4] 'The learned, philosophical and pious Dr. Cheyne,' as Boswell calls him, whose books on Health and the English Malady were recommended to him by Johnson. *Life*, i. 65; iii. 26.

The 'English Malady' was melancholy or hypochondria. There is some comfort in knowing that so long ago as 1733 Cheyne pointed out how the conditions of modern life 'have brought forth a class and set of distempers, with atrocious and frightful symptoms, scarce known to our ancestors. These nervous dis-

phrases

phrases it, afford all the relief that human art can give, or human nature receive. Do not read this slightly, you may prolong a very useful life.

Whether the pine-apples be ripe or rotten, whether the Duke's venison be baked or roasted, I begin to think it time I were at home. I have staid till perhaps nobody wishes me to stay longer, except the ladies on the hill[1], who offer me a lodging, and though not ill, am unsettled enough to wish for change of place, even though that change were not to bring me to Streatham ; but thither I hope I shall quickly come, and find you all well, and gay, and happy, and catch a little gaiety, and health, and happiness among you[2].

I am, dearest of all dear Ladies,

Your, &c.,

SAM: JOHNSON.

427.

TO MRS. THRALE[3].

DEAR MADAM,   August 1, 1775.

I wonder how it could happen. I forgot that the post went out yesternight, and so omitted to write ; I therefore put this by the by-post[4], and hope it will come, that I may not lose my regular letter.

This was to have been my last letter from this place, but Lucy says I must not go this week. Fits of tenderness with Mrs. Lucy are not common ; but she seems now to have a little paroxysm, and I was not willing to counteract it. When I am to go I shall take care to inform you. The lady at Stowhill says, how comes Lucy to be such a sovereign, all the town besides could not have kept you[5].

orders are computed to make almost one third of the complaints of the people of condition in England.' *The English Malady*, ed. 1733, Preface, p. ii. Fielding spells Cheyne's name as Johnson does, *Cheney*; no doubt in accordance with the way it was pronounced. He says : 'The learned Dr. Cheney used to call drinking punch pouring liquid fire down your throat.' *Tom Jones*, Bk. xi. ch. 8.

[1] Stowhill. *Ante*, p. 329.

[2] 'That he never caught. He thought and mused at Streatham as he did habitually everywhere, and seldom or never minded what was doing about him.'—BARETTI.

[3] *Piozzi Letters*, i. 292.

[4] I conjecture that he sent his letter by a cross-post either to Birmingham or Derby, from each of which towns a mail was sent to London six days a week.

[5] *Ante*, p. 329.

America

America now fills every mouth, and some heads, and a little of it shall come into my letter. I do not much like the news. Our troops have indeed the superiority; five-and-twenty hundred have driven five thousand from their intrenchment; but the Americans fought skilfully; had coolness enough in the battle to carry off their men; and seem to have retreated orderly, for they were not pursued[1]. They want nothing but confidence in their leaders, and familiarity with danger. Our business is to pursue their main army, and disperse it by a decisive battle; and then waste the country till they sue for peace[2]. If we make war by parties and detachments, dislodge them from one place, and exclude them from another, we shall by a local, gradual, and ineffectual war, teach them our own knowledge, harden their obstinacy, and strengthen their confidence, and at last come to fight on equal terms of skill and bravery, without equal numbers.

Mrs. Williams wrote me word, that you had honoured her with a visit, and *behaved lovely*.

Mr. Thrale left off digging his pool, I suppose, for want of water. The first thing to be done is by digging in three or four places, to try how near the springs will rise to the surface; for

[1] He is referring to the Battle of Bunker's Hill, *ante*, p. 332, n. 2. Horace Walpole wrote two days later :—' I did not send you immediate word of our victory at Boston, because the success not only seemed very equivocal, but because the conquerors lost three to one more than the vanquished. The last do not pique themselves upon modern good breeding, but level only at the officers, of whom they have slain a vast number. We are a little disappointed indeed at their fighting at all, which was not in our calculation. . . . Well! we had better have gone on robbing the Indies; it was a more lucrative trade.' Walpole's *Letters*, vi. 235.

[2] See Boswell's account of the dinner at Mr. Dilly's, where Johnson roared out : ' " I am willing to love all mankind, *except an American* ; " and his inflammable corruption bursting into horrid fire, he "breathed out threatenings and slaughter; " calling them, " Rascals—Robbers—Pirates;" and exclaiming, he'd "burn and destroy them." ' *Life*, iii. 290.

Horace Walpole wrote on August 7 :—' Is not our dignity maintained ? have not we carried our majesty beyond all example ? When did you ever read before of a besieged army threatening military execution on the country of the besiegers ! *car tel est notre plaisir.* But alack ! we are like the mock Doctor ; we have made the heart and the liver change sides ; *cela était autrefois ainsi, mais nous avons changé tout cela !*' *Letters*, vi. 237. See also Hume's *Letters to Strahan*, p. 289.

though

though we cannot hope to be always full, we must be sure never to be dry.

Poor ∗ ∗ ∗ ∗! I am sorry for him. It is sad to give a family of children no pleasure but by dying. It was said of Otho: *Hoc tantum fecit nobile quod periit.* It may be changed to ∗ ∗ ∗ ∗: *Hoc tantum fecit utile.*

If I could do Mr. Carter any good at Oxford, I could easily stop there; for through it, if I go by Birmingham, I am likely to pass; but the place is now a sullen solitude[1]. Whatever can be done I am ready to do; but our operations must for the present be at London.

I am, &c.,
SAM: JOHNSON.

428.

TO MRS. THRALE[2].

MADAM,   Lichfield, August 2, 1775.

I dined to-day at Stowhill, and am come away to write my letter. Never surely was I such a writer before. Do you keep my letters? I am not of your opinion that I shall not like to read them hereafter; for though there is in them not much history of mind, or any thing else, they will, I hope, always be in some degree the records of a pure and blameless friendship, and in some hours of languour and sadness may revive the memory of more cheerful times.

Why you should suppose yourself not desirous hereafter to

---

[1] When Johnson was an undergraduate the place was by no means a sullen solitude in the beginning of August. The books of Pembroke College show that on August 15, 1729, there were twenty-five members in residence out of a maximum of little more than fifty. On September 12 the number sank to sixteen. *Life*, i. 63, *n.* 1. Gibbon, writing of the year 1752, says:—'The long recess between the Trinity and Michaelmas terms empties the Colleges of Oxford as well as the courts of Westminster.' Gibbon's *Misc. Works*, i. 56. A young undergraduate of Queen's, who re-

mained in residence most of the Long Vacation of 1779, writing on October 7, says:—'The University is yet thin and desolate. A few solitary tutors, that drop in one by one, are all you meet in an evening, and these by a certain woefulness of countenance seem not too well pleased with the exchange of a good table and merry circle of friends for spare diet and prayers twice a day.' *Letters of Radcliffe and James*, p. 85. For Mr. Carter, see *ante*, p. 309.

[2] *Piozzi Letters*, i. 295.

read

read the history of your own mind, I do not see[1]. Twelve years, on which you now look as on a vast expanse of life, will probably be passed over uniformly and smoothly, with very little perception of your progress, and with very few remarks upon the way. That accumulation of knowledge which you promise to yourself, by which the future is to look back upon the present, with the superiority of manhood to infancy, will perhaps never be attempted, or never will be made; and you will find, as millions have found before you, that forty-five has made little sensible addition to thirty-three[2].

As the body after a certain time gains no increase of height, and little of strength, there is likewise a period, though more variable by external causes, when the mind commonly attains its stationary point, and very little advances its powers of reflection, judgment, and ratiocination[3]. The body may acquire new modes of motion, or new dexterities of mechanick operations, but its original strength receives not improvement; the mind may be stored with new languages, or new sciences, but its power of thinking remains nearly the same, and unless

[1] Johnson advising Boswell in 1773 to keep a journal of his life, said:—'The great thing to be recorded, is the state of your own mind; and you should write down every thing that you remember, for you cannot judge at first what is good or bad; and write immediately while the impression is fresh, for it will not be the same a week afterwards.' *Life*, ii. 217. Five years later Boswell spoke of publishing the Autobiography of Sir R. Sibbald, of which he had the manuscript:—'Mrs. THRALE. "I think you had as well let alone that publication. To discover such weakness, exposes a man when he is gone." JOHNSON. "Nay, it is an honest picture of human nature. How often are the primary motives of our greatest actions as small as Sibbald's, for his re-conversion." MRS. THRALE. "But may they not as well be forgotten?" JOHNSON. "No, Madam, a man loves to review his own mind. That is the use of a diary, or journal."' *Ib.* iii. 228. See *post*, p. 441.

[2] She was thirty-four. *Ante*, p. 355, *n.* 4.

[3] See *Life*, iv. 115, *n.* 4, for an account of 'a pretty smart altercation' between Johnson and Dr. Barnard, which gave rise to some pleasant verses, of which the following are the first two stanzas :—

'I lately thought no man alive
Could e'er improve past forty-five,
   And ventured to assert it;
The observation was not new,
But seem'd to me so just and true,
   That none could controvert it.

"No, Sir," says Johnson, "'tis not so;
That's your mistake, and I can show
   An instance, if you doubt it;
You, Sir, who are near forty-eight,
May *much* improve, 'tis not too late;
   I wish you'd set about it."'
                              Ib. iv. 432.

it

it attains new subjects of meditation, it commonly produces
thoughts of the same force and the same extent, at very distant
intervals of life, as the tree, unless a foreign fruit be ingrafted,
gives year after year productions of the same form and the same
flavour.

By intellectual force or strength of thought is meant the degree
of power which the mind possesses of surveying the subject of
meditation, with its circuit of concomitants, and its train of de-
pendence.

Of this power, which all observe to be very different in different
minds, part seems the gift of nature, and part the acquisition of
experience.   When the powers of nature have attained their intended energy, they can be no more advanced.   The shrub can
never become a tree.   And it is not unreasonable to suppose,
that they are before the middle of life in their full vigour.

Nothing then remains but practice and experience; and perhaps why they do so little, may be worth enquiry.

But I have just now looked, and find it so late, that I will enquire against the next post-night.

I am, &c.,
SAM: JOHNSON.

429.

TO MRS. THRALE [1].

DEAR MADAM,   Lichfield, August 5, 1775.

Instead of forty reasons for my return, one is sufficient,—that
you wish for my company.   I purpose to write no more till you
see me.   The ladies at Stowhill and Greenhill [2] are unanimously
of opinion, that it will be best to take a post-chaise, and not to
be troubled with the vexations of a common carriage.   I will
venture to suppose the ladies at Streatham to be of the same
mind.

You will now expect to be told why you will not be so much
wiser as you expect, when you have lived twelve years longer.

It is said, and said truly, that experience is the best teacher;

---

[1] *Letters*, i. 298.
[2] The ladies at Stowhill were Mrs.
Aston and Mrs. Gastrell (*ante*, p.
329); those on Green-hill were,

I think, Mrs. Cobb and Miss Adey
(*ante*, p. 331).   For Green-hill Bower
see *post*, Letter of May 29, 1779.

and

and it is supposed, that as life is lengthened experience is encreased. But a closer inspection of human life will discover that
time often passes without any incident which can much enlarge
knowledge or ratify judgment. When we are young we learn
much, because we are universally ignorant; we observe every
thing, because every thing is new. But after some years, the
occurrences of daily life are exhausted; one day passes like
another, in the same scene of appearances, in the same course
of transactions; we have to do what we have often done, and
what we do not try, because we do not wish to do much better;
we are told what we already know, and therefore what repetition
cannot make us know with greater certainty.

He that has early learned much, perhaps seldom makes, with
regard to life and manners, much addition to his knowledge [1];
not only because as more is known there is less to learn, but
because a mind stored with images and principles turns inwards
for its own entertainment, and is employed in settling those ideas
which run into confusion, and in recollecting those which are
stealing away; practices by which wisdom may be kept but not
gained. The merchant who was at first busy in acquiring money,
ceases to grow richer, from the time when he makes it his business
only to count it.

Those who have families or employments are engaged in
business of little difficulty, but of great importance, requiring
rather assiduity of practice than subtilty of speculation, occupying the attention with images too bulky for refinement, and
too obvious for research. The right is already known, what
remains is only to follow it. Daily business adds no more to
wisdom, than daily lesson to the learning of the teacher. But of
how few lives does not stated duty claim the greater part.

Far the greater part of human minds never endeavour their
own improvement. Opinions once received from instruction, or
settled by whatever accident, are seldom recalled to examination;
having been once supposed to be right, they are never discovered

---

[1] 'Sir,' said Johnson, 'in my early years I read very hard. It is a sad reflection, but a true one, that I knew almost as much at eighteen as I do now. My judgment, to be sure, was not so good; but I had all the facts.' *Life*, i. 445.

to be erroneous, for no application is made of any thing that time
may present, either to shake or to confirm them.   From this ac-
quiescence in preconceptions none are wholly free ; between fear
of uncertainty, and dislike of labour, every one rests while he
might yet go forward [1] ; and they that were wise at thirty-three,
are very little wiser at forty-five.

Of this speculation you are perhaps tired, and would rather
hear of Sophy.   I hope before this comes, that her head will be
easier, and your head less filled with fears and troubles, which
you know are to be indulged only to prevent evil, not to encrease it.

Your uneasiness about Sophy is probably unnecessary, and at
worst your other children are healthful [2], and your affairs prosperous.   Unmingled good cannot be expected ; but as we may
lawfully gather all the good within our reach, we may be allowed
to lament after that which we lose.   I hope your losses are at
an end, and that as far as the condition of our present existence
permits, your remaining life will be happy.

I am, &c.,

SAM: JOHNSON.

430.

To MRS. DESMOULINS [3].

MADAM,   Lichfield, August 5, 1775.

Mr. Garrick has done as he is used to do.   You may tell
him that Dr. Hawkesworth and I never exchanged any letters

---

[1] 'A man who has settled his
opinions does not love to have the
tranquillity of his conviction disturbed ; and at seventy-seven it is
time to be in earnest.' Johnson's
Works, ix. 118.   When Mr. Murray
maintained that 'truth will always
bear an examination,' Johnson replied :—'Yes, Sir, but it is painful to
be forced to defend it.   Consider,
Sir, how should you like, though
conscious of your innocence, to be
tried before a jury for a capital crime
once a week.' *Life*, iii. 11.

[2] Her baby died four months later,

and her only surviving son in the
following March.

[3] First published in the *Garrick
Correspondence*, ii. 72.

In the same *Correspondence* is
a letter by Mr. D. Wray, dated only
three days earlier than Johnson's, in
which he informs Garrick that he
must 'leave to those ingenious gentlemen who had the happiness of Dr.
Goldsmith's friendship the pleasing
task of paying those honours to his
memory,' &c. *Ib.* p. 71.   Perhaps
Wray's letter refers only to the pro-
jected memorial to Goldsmith, in

worth

worth publication. Our notes were commonly to tell when we should be at home, and I believe were seldom kept on either side. If I have anything that will do any honour to his memory, I shall gladly supply it, but I remember nothing.

I am, Madam,

Your humble servant,

SAM: JOHNSON.

431.

TO JAMES BOSWELL.

London, August 27, 1775. Published in the *Life*, ii. 381.

432.

TO MRS. THRALE [1].

MADAM, [London], August 29, 1775.

Here is a rout and bustle; and a bustle and a rout; as if nobody had ever before forgotten where a thing was laid. At last there is no great harm done; both Colson and Scot have copies; and real haste there is none [2]. You will find it some day this week, and any day will serve, or perhaps we can recollect it between us.

About your memory we will, if you please, have some serious

Westminster Abbey (*post*, Letter of June 21, 1776). It is possible however that Garrick planned Memoirs both of Goldsmith and Hawkesworth. He may have repented of his malicious epitaph on the poet (Forster's *Goldsmith*, ii. 409) and of a cold letter in the third person which, only six months before Hawkesworth's death, he sent to that writer in reply to one subscribed, 'Your truly affectionate.' Hawkesworth's letter and the copy of Garrick's answer are endorsed:—'Letter of Dr. Hawkesworth. My answer to his about his breach of Correspondence.' *Garrick Corres.* i. 536.

[1] *Piozzi Letters*, i. 306.

[2] It is probable that the mislaid paper was connected with the scheme of the riding-school. *Ante*, p. 309. For Coulson see *ante*, p. 325, n. 4, and for Scott, *ante*, p. 311, n. 4. Scott was the elder brother of John Scott, afterwards Earl of Eldon. Johnson in spelling the name Scot perhaps was paying a delicate compliment. Lord Eldon records that he once 'found himself seated at dinner near a gentleman who claimed to be his namesake, though he spelt his surname with but a single *t*. "I allow you," added he, in a strong northern accent, "that Scott with two *t*'s may sound rounder in the mouth, but Scott with one *t* has more of quality in it."' Twiss's *Life of Eldon*, ed. 1846, i. 141.

talk.

talk. I fret at your forgetfulness, as I do at my own[1]. We will try to mend both; yours at least is I should hope remediable. But, however it happens, we are of late never together.

Am I to come to-morrow to the Borough[2], or will any one call on me? This sorry foot! and this sorry Dr. Lawrence, who says it is the gout! but then he thinks every thing the gout[3]; and so I will try not to believe him. Into the sea I suppose you will send it, and into the sea I design it shall go.—Can you remember, dear Madam, that I have a lame foot? I am sure I cannot forget it; if you had one so painful, you would *so* remember it. Pain is good for the memory.

I am, &c.,
SAM: JOHNSON.

433.

To Mrs. Porter[4].

DEAR MADAM, London, Sept. 9, 1775.

I have sent your books by the carrier, and in Sandys's Travels[5] you will find your glasses. I have written this post to the ladies at Stowehill, and you may, the day after you have this, or at any other time, send Mrs. Gastrell's books.

Be pleased to make my compliments to all my good friends. I hope the poor dear hand is recovered, and you are now able to write, which, however, you need not do, for I am going to Bright-

---

[1] Two years later Boswell records: —'I mentioned an old gentleman of our acquaintance whose memory was beginning to fail. JOHNSON. "There must be a diseased mind, where there is a failure of memory at seventy. A man's head, Sir, must be morbid, if he fails so soon."' *Life*, iii. 191. Nevertheless the following year Johnson entered in his *Journal*: —'My memory is less faithful in retaining names, and I am afraid, in retaining occurrences.' *Pr. and Med.*, p. 170. For Mrs. Thrale's inaccuracy see *Life*, i. 416, *n.* 2 ; iii. 226, 404.

[2] Mr. Thrale's house in Southwark.

[3] It is some satisfaction to know that more than a hundred years ago there was an eminent physician who thought everything the gout.

[4] First published in Croker's *Boswell*, page 459.

In Johnson's last preceding letter to his step-daughter, dated May 29, 1770, he addresses her as Miss Porter. We now and henceforth find her dignified as Mrs. Porter. She was born in November 1715. The matronly title therefore seems to have been assumed between the ages of fifty-five and sixty.

[5] George Sandys, the traveller and poet, who in 1615 published *A Relation of a Journey begun in* 1610. Johnson included it in a list of books which he drew up for a student. *Life*, iv. 311.

helmstone.

helmstone, and when I come back will take care to tell you.   In the mean time take great care of your health, and drink as much as you can [1].

I am, dearest love,

Your most humble servant,

SAM: JOHNSON.

434.

TO MRS. ASTON AND MRS. GASTRELL.

London, September 9, 1775.

In the last Letter Johnson says that by the same post he had written to the ladies at Stowhill—Mrs. Aston and Mrs. Gastrell.

435.

TO JAMES BOSWELL.

[London], September 14, 1775.   Published in the *Life*, ii. 384.

436.

TO ROBERT LEVETT.

Calais, September 18, 1775.   Published in the *Life*, ii. 385.

437.

TO ROBERT LEVETT.

Paris, October 22, 1775.   Published in the *Life*, ii. 385.

438.

TO JAMES BOSWELL.

[London], November 16, 1775.   Published in the *Life*, ii. 387.

439.

TO MRS. PORTER.

[London], November 16, 1775.   Published in the *Life*, ii. 387.

440.

TO THE REVEREND DR. TAYLOR [2].

DEAR SIR,

I came back last Tuesday from France [3].   Is not mine

---

[1] She had been suffering from the gout. *Ante*, p. 328. See *post*, p. 408, where Johnson attributes his own attack of the gout to his abstinence from wine, and Letter of March 4, 1779, where he a second time urges his step-daughter 'not to forget to drink.'

[2] First published in *Notes and Queries*, 6th S., v. 422.

[3] For his trip to France, see *Life*, ii. 384.

a kind

a kind of life turned upside down ? Fixed to a spot when I was young, and roving the world when others are contriving to sit still, I am wholly unsettled. I am a kind of ship with a wide sail, and without an anchor.

Now I am come home, let me know how it is with you. I hope you are well, and intend to keep your residence this year. Let me know the month, and I will contrive to be about you. Our friendship has now lasted so long, that it is valuable for its antiquity. Perhaps neither has any other companion to whom he can talk of his early years. Let me particularly know the state of your health. I think mine is the better for the journey.

The French have a clear air and fruitful soil, but their mode of common life is gross and incommodious, and disgusting. I am come home convinced that no improvement of general use is to be gained among them [1].

I am, dear Sir,

Your affectionate servant,

London, Nov. 16, 1775.   SAM: JOHNSON.

441.

TO EDMUND HECTOR [2].

DEAR SIR,

On Tuesday I returned from a ramble about France, and about a month's stay at Paris. I have seen nothing that much delighted or surprised me [3]. Their palaces are splendid, and their churches magnificent in their structure, and gorgeous in their ornaments, but the city in general makes a very mean appearance.

When I opened my letters, I found that you had very kindly complied with all my requests. The Bar (?) may be sent in a box directed to me at Henry Thrale Esq., in Southwark. The whole company that you saw went to France together, and the Queen was so pleased with our little girl, that she sent to enquire who she was [4].

[1] *Life*, ii. 389, 402 ; iii. 352 ; iv. 237.

[2] First published in *Notes and Queries*, 6th S., iii. 401.

[3] Johnson recorded in his journal at Paris :—' The sight of palaces, and other great buildings, leaves no very distinct images, unless to those who talk of them. As I entered, my wife was in my mind : she would have been pleased. Having now nobody to please, I am little pleased.' *Life*, ii. 393.

[4] The Thrales and Johnson on their return from their tour in Wales

We are all well, but I find, my dear Sir, that you are ill. I hope it does not continue true that you are almost a cripple. Would not a warm bath have helped you? Take care of yourself for my sake as well as that of your other friends. I have the first claim on your attention, if priority be allowed any advantages. Dear Mrs. Careless[1], I know, will be careful of you. I can only wish you well, and of my good wishes you may be always certain, for

I am, dear Sir,

Your most affectionate

Fleet Street, Nov. 16, 1775.   SAM: JOHNSON.

442.

To Mrs. Montagu[2].

MADAM,   Dec. 15, 1775.

Having, after my return from a little ramble to France, passed some time in the country, I did not hear, till I was told by Miss Reynolds, that you were in town; and when I did hear it, I heard likewise that you were ill. To have you detained among us by sickness is to enjoy your presence at too dear a rate. I suffer myself to be flattered with hope that only half the intelligence is now true, and that you are now so well as to be able to leave us, and so kind as not to be willing.

I am, Madam,

Your most humble servant,

SAM: JOHNSON.

443.

To Mrs. Montagu.

MADAM,   Dec. 17, 1775.

All that the esteem and reverence of mankind can give you has been long in your possession, and the little that I can add

had stayed at Birmingham and there had breakfasted with Hector. In examining at the British Museum the original MS. of Johnson's *Journey into North Wales*, I find that in the record of September 19, 20 and 21, *Hector* has been wrongly copied as *Wheeler*. *Life*, v.458. Johnson wrote to Levett on October 22, 1775:—
'We came yesterday from Fontainbleau, where the Court is now. We went to see the King and Queen at dinner, and the Queen was so impressed by Miss, that she sent one of the Gentlemen to enquire who she was.' *Ib.* ii. 385.

[1] Hector's sister. *Ante*, p. 164, *n.* 1.

[2] This and the next two letters were first published in Croker's *Boswell*, page 470. For Mrs. Montagu see *ante*, p. 87, *n.* 3.

to

to the voice of nations will not much exalt; of that little, however, you are, I hope, very certain[1].—I wonder, Madam, if you remember *Col* in the Hebrides[2]? The brother and heir of poor *Col* has just been to visit me, and I have engaged to dine with him on Thursday. I do not know his lodging, and cannot send him a message, and must therefore suspend the honour which you are pleased to offer to,

Madam,

Your most humble servant,

SAM: JOHNSON.

444.

To MRS. PORTER.

[London], December 17, 1775. Published in the *Life*, ii. 388.

Boswell gives only the date of December, 1775, but Mr. Croker, who perhaps had seen the original, adds the day of the month.

445.

To MRS. MONTAGU.

MADAM, Thursday, Dec. 21, 1775.

I know not when any letter has given me so much pleasure or vexation as that which I had yesterday the honour of receiving. That you, Madam, should wish for my company is surely a sufficient reason for being pleased;—that I should delay twice, what I had so little right to expect even once, has so bad an appearance, that I can only hope to have it thought that I am ashamed.—You have kindly allowed me to name a day. Will you be pleased, Madam, to accept of me any day after Tuesday? Till I am favoured with your answer, or despair of so much condescension, I shall suffer no engagement to fasten itself upon me[3].

I am, Madam,

Your most obliged and most humble servant,

SAM: JOHNSON.

---

[1] Mr. Croker quotes a letter (*Boswell*, p. 458) from Mrs. Williams to Mrs. Montagu, dated June 26 of this year, in acknowledgment of a pension which that great lady had just conferred on her. Johnson's flowery language was no doubt in part due to his gratitude for this kindness to his poor blind friend.

[2] He means of course, not the island of that name, but the young Laird of Col mentioned in the *Journey to the Hebrides, ante,* p. 279.

[3] A few years later he said to Bos-

446.

To James Boswell.

[London], December 23, 1775.   Published in the *Life*, ii. 411.

447.

To James Boswell.

[London], January 10, 1776.   Published in the *Life*, ii. 412.

448.

To James Boswell.

London, January 15, 1776.   Published in the *Life*, ii. 415.

449.

To the Reverend Dr. Taylor.

[London], January 15, 1776.

In Messrs. Sotheby and Co.'s Auction Catalogue for April 10, 1885, Lot 590 is a Letter of Johnson, dated January 15, 1776, franked by Thrale to Dr. Taylor, respecting his (Taylor's) law-suit.

For the law-suit see *post*, pp. 375, 390, and *Life*, iii. 44, *n.* 3 ; 51, *n.* 3.

450.

To James Boswell.

[London], February 3, 1776.   Published in the *Life*, ii. 416.

451.

To the Reverend John Wesley [1].

SIR,   Feb. 6, 1776.

When I received your Commentary on the Bible, I durst not at first flatter myself that I was to keep it, having so little claim to so valuable a present ; and when Mrs. Hall [2] informed me of your kindness, was hindered from time to time from returning you those thanks which I now entreat you to accept. I have thanks likewise to return you for the addition of your

---

well :—' Mrs. Montagu has dropt me. Now, Sir, there are people whom one should like very well to drop, but would not wish to be dropped by.' *Life*, iv. 73.

[1] First published in the *Gentle-* *man's Magazine*, 1797, i. 455.

[2] She was Wesley's sister. Her worthless husband had died on January 2 of this year ' in deep repentance.' Wesley's *Journal*, iv. 64. See *Life*, iv. 92, *n.* 3.

important

important suffrage to my argument on the American question. To have gained such a mind as yours may justly confirm me in my own opinion¹. What effect my paper has upon the public, I know not ; but I have no reason to be discouraged. The lecturer was surely in the right, who, though he saw his

¹ On June 14, 1775, Wesley had written to the Earl of Dartmouth :— 'All my prejudices are against the Americans, for I am an High Churchman, the son of an High Churchman, bred up from my childhood in the highest notions of passive obedience and non-resistance ; and yet in spite of all my rooted prejudice I cannot avoid thinking (if I think at all) that an oppressed people asked for nothing more than their legal rights, and that in the most modest and inoffensive manner which the nature of the thing would allow.' *Hist. MSS. Comm.*, vol. xi, App. 5, p. 378.

In his *Calm Address to our American Colonies*, published near the end of 1775, he tells the Americans that they are 'the dupes of a few designing men in England, who are determined enemies to monarchy. Vainly,' he continues, 'do you complain of "unconstitutional exactions, violated rights, and mutilated charters." Nothing is exacted but according to the original constitution both of England and her Colonies.' He warns them against the danger of a republic : 'No governments under heaven are so despotic as the republican ; no subjects are governed in so arbitrary a manner as those of a commonwealth. If any one doubt of this, let him look at the subjects of Venice, of Genoa, or even of Holland. Should any man talk or write of the Dutch government as every cobler does of the English, he would be laid in irons before he knew where he was. And then wo be to him ! Republics shew no mercy.'

A Calm Address, pp. 13, 16, 17, 21. In his *Journal*, iv. 59, he gives also a Letter published by him in *Lloyd's Evening Post* near the end of 1775, in which he maintains that 'the Americans are not contending for liberty, but for the illegal privilege of being exempt from parliamentary taxation.'

The *Gent. Mag.* for Dec. 1775 (p. 561) contains an admirable reply to the *Calm Address*. 'You are surely, Sir, too well acquainted,' says the writer, 'with the nature and workings of human passions to expect any good to arrive from a calm address to men (as you say the Americans are) under the dominion of enthusiasm. The experience of your whole life has been the influence of enthusiasm over the calm. . . . I have seen, Mr. Wesley, near a hundred persons, whose consciences or understandings were affected under your ministry, fall into convulsions, see angels and demons by turn, converse alternately with God and the devil . . . When a chimera, without a substantial basis or a visible object, can thus triumph over the reason and the will, and laugh argument to scorn, can it be hoped, Mr. Wesley, that men acting upon the known and established systems of human policy, irritated to enthusiasm in the contention for everything that is dear, will turn aside to listen to your Address ? Can it be hoped that the two-penny pamphlet of a Lay Methodist preacher will influence the camps of the Americans, or the Congresses of New Senators ?'

audience

audience slinking away, refused to quit the chair while Plato staid[1].

I am, reverend Sir,

Your most humble servant,

SAM: JOHNSON.

452.

TO JAMES BOSWELL.

[London], February 9, 1776.   Published in the *Life*, ii. 419.

453.

TO ARCHIBALD HAMILTON[2].

DEAR SIR,   Feb. 13, 1776.

    I am afraid that by altering the first article of the *Dictionary* at your desire I have given occasion to an unhappy difference between you and Dr. Calder, who has been with me, and seems to think himself in danger of losing the revision of the work. For this consequence I should be very deeply sorry. I considered the redundance which I lopped away, not as the consequence of negligence or inability, but as the [3] of superfluous diligence, naturally exerted on the first article. He that does too much soon learns to do less. By his own account however it appears that [he] has shown what I think an improper degree of turbulence and impatience. I have

---

[1] 'Plato enim mihi unus instar est omnium millium.' CICERO, *Brutus*, chap. 51. See *post*, Letter of March 18, 1779, where Johnson writes :— 'Plato is a multitude.'

[2] First published in Nichols's *Literary Anecdotes*, ix. 805.
Archibald Hamilton was a printer, one who had long 'kept his coach. "He was in the right," said Johnson ; "life is short. The sooner that a man begins to enjoy his wealth the better."' *Life*, ii. 226. A new edition of Ephraim Chambers's *Cyclopædia* had been undertaken by the booksellers and a contract had been made in 1773 with Dr. Calder for its preparation. He set to work, 'and, as was his usual custom, soon overstocked himself with materials. In 1776 the first sheet, by general consent, was submitted to Dr. Johnson, who made many remarks on it; which,' adds Nichols, ' I have in his own hand-writing.' Calder, to judge from the correspondence published by Nichols, does not seem to have been a judicious editor. The result was that the contract was dissolved, and the *Cyclopædia* placed in the hands of Dr. Rees, who did very well for the proprietors. Nichols's *Lit. Hist.* iv. 800–819.
According to Percival Stockdale, Johnson regretted that he had not himself undertaken the editorship. ' Sir, (said he) I like that muddling work.' *Life*, ii. 204.

[3] A word has been omitted in the original.

advised

advised him, and he has promised, to be hereafter less tenacious
of his own determination, and more pliable to the direction of
the Proprietors, and the opinion of those whom they may consult.
I entreat therefore that all the past may be forgotten; that he
may stand where he stood before, and be permitted to proceed
with the work in which he is engaged. Do not refuse this
request to

Sir,

Your most humble servant,

SAM: JOHNSON.

454.

To JAMES BOSWELL.

[London], February 15, 1776. Published in the *Life*, ii. 420.

455.

TO THE REVEREND DR. TAYLOR [1].

DEAR SIR,

The Case which you sent me contains such vicissitudes of
settlement and rescission that I will not pretend yet to give
any opinion about it. My advice is, that it be laid before some
of the best Lawyers, and branched out into queries, that the
answer may be more deliberate, and the necessity of considering
made greater.

Get it off your hands and out of your head as fast as you
can. You have no evidence to wait for: all that can be done
may be done soon.

Your health is of more consequence. Keep yourself cheerful.
Lye in Bed with a lamp, and when you cannot sleep, and are
beginning to think, light your candle and read [2]. At least light
your candle; a man is perhaps never so much harrassed [*sic*]
by his own mind in the light as in the dark.

Poor Caled [3] Harding is dead. Do's [*sic*] not every death of

---

[1] First published in *Notes and
Queries*, 6th S., v. 423.

For Taylor's law-case see *post*,
p. 390.

[2] Johnson in his last illness 'lamented much his inability to read
during his hours of restlessness.
"I used formerly (he added) when
sleepless in bed to read like a Turk."'
Life, iv. 409.

[3] A misprint, I conjecture, for
Caleb.

a man

a man long known begin to strike deep? How few dos [*sic*] the Man who has lived sixty years now know of the friends of his youth! At Lichfield there are none but Harry Jackson[1] and Sedgwick, and Sedgwick, when I left him, had a dropsy.

I am, I think, better than usual, and hope you will grow better too.

I am, Sir,

Your most affectionate,

Febr. 17, 1776.   SAM: JOHNSON.

Rev^d Dr. Taylor, Ashbourn, Derbyshire.

456.

To the Reverend Dr. John Calder[2].

SIR,   Feb. 19, 1776.

I saw Mr. —— on Saturday, and find that Mr. Hamilton had shown him my letter. Mr. —— is, as I feared, so angry and so resolute that I could not impress him in your favour, nor have any hope from him. If anything is done it must be with the other Proprietors. I am sorry for it.

I am, Sir,

Your very humble servant,

SAM: JOHNSON.

457.

To James Boswell.

[London], February 24, 1776. Published in the *Life*, ii. 422.

458.

To James Boswell.

[London], March 5, 1776 Published in the *Life*, ii. 423.

[1] 'We dined at our inn [at Lichfield], and had with us a Mr. Jackson, one of Johnson's schoolfellows, whom he treated with much kindness, though he seemed to be a low man, dull and untaught. He had a coarse grey coat, black waistcoat, greasy leather breeches, and a yellow uncurled wig; and his countenance had the ruddiness which betokens one who is in no haste to "leave his can."' *Life*, ii. 463. Johnson wrote to Boswell on September 1, 1777:— 'When I came to Lichfield I found my old friend, Henry Jackson, dead. It was a loss, and a loss not to be repaired, as he was one of the companions of my childhood.' *Ib*. iii. 131.

[2] First published in Nichols's *Literary History*, iv. 811; see *ante*, p. 374.

To

To the Reverend Dr. John Douglas [1].

SIR,

This gentleman has been approved by the Vice-Chancellor and Proctors of Oxford, as a man properly qualified to profess Horsemanship in that place. The Trustees of the Clarendon legacy have consented to issue money for the credit of a Riding house, and the Bishop of Chester delays the payment till he knows the state of the account between the Trustees and the University, for he says very reasonably that he knows not to give, till he knows how much they have.

Upon application to the Dean of Hereford, I was told that you, dear Sir, have in your hand the accounts between them. If you would be pleased to examine them, and appoint this Gentleman a time when he may wait on you for the result to carry to the Bishop, you will put an end to a business in which I have interested myself very much, as it will restore prosperity to a family that has suffered great difficulties a long time.

I am, dear Sir,

Your most humble servant,

SAM: JOHNSON.

March 6, 1776.

To the Reverend Dr. Douglas.

460.

To Edmund Hector [2].

DEAR SIR,   March 7, 1776.

Some time ago you told me that you had unhappily hurt yourself; and were confined, and you have never since let me hear of your recovery. I hope however that you are grown, at least are growing well. We must be content now to mend

---

[1] From the original in the British Museum, *Egerton MSS.* 2182.

Dr. Douglas was made Bishop of Carlisle in 1787, of Salisbury in 1791. He had exposed Lauder's literary fraud about Milton (*Life*, i. 228) and had helped to expose the Cock Lane Ghost (*ib.* i. 407). Goldsmith introduces him in *Retaliation* :—

'Here Douglas retires from his toils to relax,
The scourge of impostors, the terror of quacks.'

For the subject of the letter see *ante*, p. 309.

[2] First published in *Notes and Queries*, 6th S., iii. 401.

very

very gradually, and cannot make such quick transitions from sickness to health, as we did forty years ago. Let me know how you do, and do not imagine that I forgot you.

I forget whether I told you that at the latter end of the summer I rambled over part of France. I saw something of the vintage, which is all I think that they have to boast above our country, at least, it is their great natural advantage. Their air, I think, is good, and my health mended in it very perceptibly.

Our schoolfellow Charles Congreve [1] is still in town, but very dull, very valetudinary, and very recluse, willing, I am afraid, to forget the world, and content to be forgotten by it, to repose in that sullen sensuality, into which men naturally sink, who think disease a justification of indulgence, and converse only with those who hope to prosper by indulging them. This is a species of Beings with which your profession must have made you much acquainted, and to which I hope acquaintance has made you no friend [2]. Infirmity will come, but let us not invite it ; indulgence will allure us, but let us turn resolutely away. Time cannot always be defeated, but let us not yield till we are conquered [3].

I had the other day a letter from Harry Jackson, who says nothing, and yet seems to have something which he wishes to say. He is very poor. I wish something could be done for him [4].

I hope dear Mrs. Careless is well, and now and then does not disdain to mention my name. It is happy when a Brother and Sister live to pass their time at our age together. I have nobody to whom I can talk of my first years—when I go to Lichfield

---

[1] *Ante*, p. 304.

[2] Hector was a medical man.

[3] Johnson, not long before he died, when 'talking of his illness, said, "I will be conquered ; I will not capitulate."' *Life*, iv. 374. See also *post*, Letter of March 14, 1782.

[4] For Harry Jackson, see *ante*, p. 376. Hector, as well as Johnson, had been his school-fellow. 'He had tried to be a cutler at Birmingham, but had not succeeded ; and now he lived poorly at home, and had some scheme of dressing leather in a better manner than common ; to his indistinct account of which Dr. Johnson listened with patient attention, that he might assist him with his advice.' *Life*, ii. 463.

I see

I see the old places, but find nobody that enjoyed them with me.   May she and you live long together[1].

I am, dear Sir,

•   Your affectionate humble servant,

SAM: JOHNSON.

To Mr. Hector in Birmingham.

461.

TO THE REVEREND DR. TAYLOR[2].

DEAR SIR,   March 7, 1776.

You will not write to me, nor come to see me, and you will not have me within reach long for We are going to Italy in the spring[3].

I called the other day upon poor Charles[4], whom I had not seen for many months.   He took no notice of my absence, nor appeared either glad or sorry to see me, but answered everything with monosyllables, and seemed heavy and drowsy, like a man muddled with a full meal ; at last I enquired the time, which gave him hopes of being delivered from me, and enabled him to bounce up with great alacrity and inspect his watch.   He sits in a room about ten feet square, and though he takes the air every day in his chaise, fancies that he should take cold in any other house, and therefore never pays a visit.

Do you go on with your suit ?   If you do, you had surely better come to town and talk with Council [*sic*].   Unless skilful men give you hopes of success, it will be better not to try it, you may still triumph in your ill-success[5].   But supposing that by the former compact between you and ——[6], She had it

---

[1] For Mrs. Careless, see *ante*, p. 164, *n*. 1. Johnson wrote to Bennet Langton in 1758 :—' I, who have no sisters nor brothers, look with some degree of innocent envy on those who may be said to be born to friends ; and cannot see, without wonder, how rarely that native union is afterwards regarded.' *Life*, i. 324.

[2] From the original in the possession of Messrs. J. Pearson & Co. of

[5] Pall Mall Place, S.W.

[3] *Post*, p. 384.

[4] Charles Congreve. *Ante*, p. 378.

[5] This paragraph is scored through in the original.

[6] The name is effaced. It appears to be Wood. According to Nichols (*Literary Anecdotes*, ix. 63), Taylor's heir was a young gentleman in his own neighbourhood of the name of Webster, about 12 or 14

for

for her life, She had as much as She ought to have. I never well understood the settlement he and you concerted between you [1]. Do you know what is become of her, and how She and the   [2] live together? What a wretch it is!

I should be glad to take my usual round, and see my friends before I set out, but I am afraid it will hardly be convenient, therefore write to me.

I am, dear Sir,

Your most humble servant,

SAM: JOHNSON.

462.

TO JAMES BOSWELL.

[London], March 12, 1776. Published in the *Life*, ii. 424.

463.

TO THE REVEREND DR. WETHERELL.

[London], March 12, 1776. Published in the *Life*, ii. 424.

464.

TO THE REVEREND DR. TAYLOR [3].

DEAR SIR,

I came hither last night, and found your Letters. You will have a note from me on Monday, yet I thought it better to send a Messenger to-day. Mr. Boswel is with me, but I will take care that he shall hinder no business, nor shall he know

years old. I am informed however by the Rev. Francis Jourdain, Vicar of Ashbourne, that 'Taylor left all his property to his shoe-black, with the proviso that he might take any name but that of Taylor.' Perhaps this lad was his illegitimate son, and 'She' was the boy's mother.

[1] The last six words of this sentence are scored through.

[2] This word is not only effaced but defaced.

[3] From the original in the possession of Mr. Alfred Morrison of Fonthill House. Boswell had accompanied Johnson on a visit to Lichfield. He writes on Monday, March 25 :—'Johnson had sent an express to Dr. Taylor's, acquainting him of our being at Lichfield, and Taylor had returned an answer that his post-chaise should come for us this day.' *Life*, ii. 468.

more

more than you would have him. Send when you please, we shall be ready.

I am, Sir,

Your humble servant,

SAM: JOHNSON.

Lichfield, Saturday, March 23, 1776.

If you care not to send let me know, we will take a chaise.

465.

TO MRS. THRALE[1].

DEAR MADAM,   Lichfield, March 25, 1776.

This letter will not, I hope. reach you many days before me ; in a distress which can be so little relieved, nothing remains for a friend but to come and partake it.

Poor dear sweet little boy ! When I read the letter this day to Mrs. Aston, she said, ' Such a death is the next to translation[2].' Yet however I may convince myself of this, the tears are in my eyes, and yet I could not love him as you loved him, nor reckon upon him for a future comfort as you and his father reckoned upon him.

He is gone, and we are going ! We could not have enjoyed him long, and shall not long be separated from him. He has probably escaped many such pangs as you are now feeling.

[1] *Piozzi Letters*, i. 307.

While Johnson and Boswell sat at breakfast at Miss Porter's house the post came in and brought news of the death of little Harry Thrale. ' He died on March 23, suddenly, before his father's door.' *Life*, ii. 468. Baretti has the following malignant note : ' Here our Madam has sunk the letter to which this is an answer. Did she own in it that she herself poisoned little Harry, or did she not ? I think she suppressed that particularity, and attributed his death to convulsions, or some other complaint of that kind, as Johnson seemed the remainder of his life ignorant of the accident that caused the boy's death, and I would not tell him lest his attachment to her should make him discredit my words, and of course cause a serious quarrel between us.' BARETTI. In later notes (*Piozzi Letters*, pp. 316, 319, 338) he says that she had been in the habit of giving 'tin-pills' to Queeny, and that ' he was obliged to be very violent to keep her from sending Hetty where she had just sent poor Queeny.'

[2] Johnson does not give in his Dictionary *translation* as used in this sense, though it is used in *Hebrews* xi. 5.

Nothing

Nothing remains, but that with humble confidence we resign ourselves to Almighty Goodness, and fall down, without irreverent murmurs, before the Sovereign Distributer of good and evil, with hope that though sorrow endureth for a night yet joy may come in the morning [1].

I have known you, Madam, too long to think that you want any arguments for submission to the Supreme Will ; nor can my consolation have any effect but that of showing that I wish to comfort you. What can be done you must do for yourself. Remember first, that your child is happy; and then, that he is safe, not only from the ills of this world, but from those more formidable dangers which extend their mischief to eternity. You have brought into the world a rational being ; have seen him happy during the little life that has been granted him ; and can have no doubt but that his happiness is now permanent and immutable.

When you have obtained by prayer such tranquillity as nature will admit, force your attention, as you can, upon your accustomed duties and accustomed entertainments. You can do no more for our dear boy, but you must not therefore think less on those whom your attention may make fitter for the place to which he is gone.

I am, dearest, dearest Madam,

Your most affectionate humble servant,

SAM: JOHNSON.`

466.

TO MRS. THRALE [2].

[London], March 30, 1776.

DEAR MADAM,

Since, as Mr. Baretti informs us, our dear Queeney is grown better, I hope you will by degrees recover your tranquillity.

---

[1] 'Heaviness may endure for a night, but joy cometh in the morning.' *Psalms,* xxx. 5.

[2] *Piozzi Letters,* i. 309.

Johnson and Boswell left Lichfield for Ashbourne on Tuesday, March 26 ; leaving it the next evening they rested Wednesday night at Loughborough, and Thursday night at St. Alban's, reaching London on Friday morning, March 29. Johnson at once hurried away to Mr. Thrale's house

Only

Only by degrees, and those perhaps sufficiently slow, can the pain of an affliction like yours be abated [1]. But though effects are not wholly in our power, yet Providence always gives us something to do. Many of the operations of nature may by human diligence be accelerated or retarded. Do not indulge your sorrow; try to drive it away by either pleasure or pain; for, opposed to what you are feeling, many pains will become pleasures. Remember the great precept, *Be not solitary; be not idle* [2].

But above all, resign yourself and your children to the Universal Father, the Author of Existence, and Governor of the Universe, who only knows what is best for all, and without whose regard not a sparrow falls to the ground [3].

That I feel what friendship can feel, I hope I need not tell you. I loved him as I never expect to love any other little boy; but I could not love him as a parent. I know that such a loss is a laceration of the mind. I know that a whole system of hopes, and designs, and expectations, is swept away at once, and nothing left but bottomless vacuity [4]. What you feel I have felt, and hope that your disquiet will be shorter than mine.

Mr. Thrale sent me a letter from Mr. Boswell, I suppose to be inclosed [5]. I was this day with Mrs. Montague, who, with everybody else, laments your misfortune.

I am, dearest Madam,

Your, &c.,

SAM: JOHNSON.

in the Borough, where he found the coach at the door to take Mrs. and Miss Thrale and Baretti to Bath. *Life*, ii. 473, iii. 6. The funeral had taken place the day before.

[1] 'The most unaccountable part of Johnson's character was his total ignorance of the character of his most familiar acquaintance. Far from recovering by slow degrees, on our arrival at Bath the first thing that the woman did was to buy black feathers for her hat.' BARETTI.

[2] *Ante*, p. 293.

[3] *St. Matthew*, x. 29.

[4] See *ante*, p. 212, *n.* 4, and *post*, Letter of July 27, 1778, where we find much the same thoughts and words.

[5] By the kindness of Mrs. Thomas, of Eyhorne House, Hollingbourne, near Maidstone, who is in possession of the original, I am able to give a copy of Boswell's letter :—

'DEAR MADAM,—Allow me to assure you and Mr. Thrale that I very sincerely regret your present affliction, and very sincerely wish it were in my power to alleviate it. Were you as sure as I am of my concern for you, I doubt not that it would be

To

467.

To Mrs. Thrale [1].

Dearest Madam,   [London], April 1, 1776.

When you were gone, Mr. Thrale soon sent me away [2]. I came next day, and was made to understand that when I was wanted I should be sent for ; and therefore I have not gone yesterday or to-day, but I will soon go again whether invited or not.

You begin now I hope to be able to consider, that what has happened might have had great aggravations. Had you been followed in your intended travels [3] by an account of this afflictive [4] deprivation, where could have been the end of doubt, and surmise, and suspicion, and self-condemnation ? You could not easily have been reconciled to those whom you left behind, or

some relief. You have now with you Dr. Johnson, whose friendship is the most effectual consolation under heaven. I wish not to intrude upon you ; but as soon as you let me know that my presence will not be troublesome, I shall hasten to your house, where as I have shared much happiness, I would willingly bear a part in mourning.

I ever am, Madam,
Your obliged humble servant,
JAMES BOSWELL.

Mr. Dillys in the Poultry,
Friday, 29 March, 1776.'
It was at the house of Messieurs Dilly, the booksellers in the Poultry, that Johnson and Boswell alighted on their return to London. *Life*, iii. 5.

[1] *Piozzi Letters*, i. 311.

[2] 'Mr. Thrale who was a worldly man, and followed the direction of his own feelings with no philosophical or Christian distinctions, having now lost the strong hope of being one day succeeded in the profitable Brewery by the only son he had left, gave himself silently up to his grief,

and fell in a few years a victim to it.' BARETTI. When the news had first arrived of the boy's death, Boswell had ' said it would be very distressing to Thrale, but she would soon forget it, as she had so many things to think of. JOHNSON. "No, Sir, Thrale will forget it first. *She* has many things that she *may* think of. *He* has many things that he *must* think of." ' *Life*, ii. 470. This, though true as a general remark, was not true in this case.

[3] They had been on the point of starting with Johnson for Italy.

[4] Johnson avoided the use of the present participle as an adjective. He would not have said 'afflicting deprivation.' Mrs. Piozzi in her *British Synonomy* (ii. 139), which was no doubt to a great extent founded on what she had learnt from him, distinguishing between *prevalent* and *prevailing*, says :— ' *Prevailing* being a participle is in common use, of course, and I think it lies a whole shade nearer to vulgarity than *prevalent*.' She calls both words *adverbs* !

those

those who had persuaded you to go. You would have believed that he died by neglect, and that your presence would have saved him. I was glad of your letter from Marlborough[1], and hope you will try to force yourself to write. If grief either caused or aggravated poor Queeney's illness, you have taken the proper method for relieving it. Young minds easily receive new impressions.

Poor Peyton[2] expired this morning. He probably during many years, for which he sat starving by the bed of a wife, not only useless but almost motionless, condemned by poverty to personal attendance, and by the necessity of such attendance chained down to poverty—he probably thought often how lightly he should tread the path of life without his burthen. Of this thought the admission was unavoidable, and the indulgence might be forgiven to frailty and distress. His wife died at last, and before she was buried he was seized by a fever, and is now going to the grave.

Such miscarriages, when they happen to those on whom many eyes are fixed, fill histories and tragedies; and tears have been shed for the sufferings, and wonder excited by the fortitude of those who neither did nor suffered more than Peyton.

I was on Saturday at Mrs. Montague's, who expressed great sensibility[3] of your loss; and have this day received an invitation to a supper and a ball; but I returned my acknowledgment to the ladies, and let them know that I thought I should like the ball better another week[4].

I am, dear Madam,

Your, &c.,

SAM: JOHNSON.

---

[1] Marlborough is 74 miles from London, and 33 from Bath on the main road between those cities. It was at Marlborough that Matthew Bramble halted to dine on his way from Bath to London, on the day when Humphry Clinker comes first upon the scene. *Humphry Clinker*, ed. 1792, i. 169.

[2] *Ante*, p. 319.

[3] Johnson does not in his *Dic-*

tionary give *sensibility* as used in this sense.

[4] He had however attended the Lichfield Theatre on the day on which the news arrived of the boy's death. Boswell says:—'We were quite gay and merry. I afterwards mentioned to him that I condemned myself for being so, when poor Mr. and Mrs. Thrale were in such distress. JOHNSON. "You are wrong,

468.

To Mrs. Thrale [1].

DEAREST MADAM,   April 4, 1776.

I am glad to hear of pretty Queeney's recovery, and your returning tranquillity. What we have suffered ought to make us remember what we have escaped. You might at as short a warning have been taken from your children, or Mr. Thrale might have been taken from us all.

Mr. Thrale, when he dismissed me, promised to call on me; he has never called, and I have never seen him. He said that he would go to the house [2], and I hope he has found something that laid hold on his attention.

I do not wish you to return, while the novelty of the place does any good either to you or Queeney, and longer I know you will not stay; there is therefore no need of soliciting your return. What qualification can be extracted from so sad an event, I derive from observing that Mr. Thrale's behaviour has united you to him by additional endearments. Every evil will be more easily borne while you fondly love one another; and every good will be enjoyed with encrease of delight *past compute,*

Sir; twenty years hence Mr. and Mrs. Thrale will not suffer much pain from the death of their son. Now, Sir, you are to consider, that distance of place, as well as distance of time, operates upon the human feelings. I would not have you be gay in the presence of the distressed, because it would shock them; but you may be gay at a distance."' *Life*, ii. 471.

'See the sensibility of Mrs. Montague that invited Johnson to a ball on such an occasion! Oh, these learned Ladies, how sensible they are of other people's afflictions.' BARETTI.

[1] *Piozzi Letters*, i. 313.

[2] The House of Commons, I conjecture. On April 1, if he attended, he heard a debate on ' Mr. Hartley's Motion for Estimates of the probable expenses of the War with America.' *Parl. Hist.* xviii. 1302. Lord North replied that ' Mr. Hartley looked for impossibilities; he could not divine what the expenses of the campaign would amount to.' *Ib.* p. 1315. Could it have been foreseen that the National Debt would be raised by the war from 129 to 268 millions, even Gibbon might have hesitated about supporting throughout this memorable contest 'with many a sincere and silent vote the rights, though not perhaps the interest, of the mother country.' Gibbon's *Misc. Works*. i. 220. For the increase in the debt see *Penny Cyclo.*, ed. 1840, xvi. 100.

to

to use the phrase of Cumberland [1].   May your care of each other always encrease!

I am, dearest Madam,
Your, &c.,
SAM: JOHNSON [2].

469.

TO THE REVEREND DR. TAYLOR.

London, April 4, 1776.

In Messrs. Sotheby and Co.'s Auction Catalogue of April 8, 1891, Lot 61 is a letter of Johnson to Dr. Taylor, two pages quarto, dated April 4, 1776, containing ' frequent references to Boswell.' It was sold for £6 15*s*.

470.

TO MRS. THRALE [3].

DEAR MADAM,   April 9, 1776.

Mr. Thrale's alteration of purpose is not weakness of resolution; it is a wise man's compliance with the change of things, and with the new duties which the change produces.

---

[1] Probably Richard Cumberland, the playwriter. *Life*, iv. 384, *n*. 2.

[2] Arthur Murphy, who had made Johnson and the Thrales acquainted (*Life*, i. 493), wrote to Mrs. Thrale the following letter, the original of which is in the possession of Mrs. Thomas, of Eythorne House, Hollingbourne, Maidstone. 'March 6' is a misdate for 'April 6':—

'DEAR MRS. THRALE,

I was heartily glad to hear that you had set out for Bath. The best Effort we can make upon trying occasions is as much our Duty, as submission to the Supreme Will. I hope that your Journey has had every good Effect. I long much to see you, and at the same I dread it. I have never gone near Mr. Thrale, for I thought I should only hinder his wounds from healing. It is, in my opinion, lucky that you are all going to change the scene. Your absence will be felt by me, but if

I hear from you occasionally it will be a real pleasure. Your present is melancholy, but I receive it with that pleasure which melancholy affords, and I shall wear it with that sensibility which is due to you, and to all belonging to you.

I will not Endeavour to tell you the Sentiments, with which I am,
Dear Madam,
Your most obliged
humble servant,
ARTHUR MURPHY.

Lincoln's Inn,
6th March, 1776.'

[3] *Piozzi Letters*, i. 314.
This letter, if it is rightly dated, must have crossed Mrs. Thrale on her way back, for we find her dining at her own house on April 10. *Life*, iii. 29. Soon afterwards she returned to Bath with her husband and Johnson. *Ib*. p. 44. Mr. Thrale's alteration of purpose was the abandonment of the journey to Italy.

Whoever

Whoever expects me to be angry, will be disappointed[1]. I do not even grieve at the effect, I grieve only at the cause.

Your business for the present is to seek for ease, and to go where you think it most likely to be found. There cannot yet be any place in your mind for mere curiosity. Whenever I can contribute to your tranquillity, I shall readily attend, and hope never to add to the evils that may oppress you. I will go with you to Bath, or stay with you at home.

I am very little disappointed. I was glad to go to places of so much celebrity, but had promised to myself no raptures, nor much improvement[2]: nor is there any thing to be expected worth such a sacrifice as you might make.

Keep yourself busy, and you will in time grow cheerful. New prospects may open, and new enjoyments may come within your reach. I surely cannot but wish all evil removed from a house which has afforded my miseries all the succour which attention and benevolence could give. I am sorry not to owe so much, but to repay so little. What I can do, you may with great reason expect from,

Dearest Madam,

Your, &c.,

SAM : JOHNSON.

[1] This passage seems to be an answer to a passage in Mrs. Thrale's letter to him, where she says:— 'Baretti said you would be very angry because this dreadful event made us put off our Italian journey, but I knew you better.' Her letter however is dated May 3, more than three weeks later; on which day, to add to the perplexity, Johnson was with her till about eleven at night, when he left for London (*post*, p. 391). I suspect that her letter is either wholly or in part a fabrication.

[2] The following day, Johnson said to Boswell :—'" I am disappointed, to be sure; but it is not a great disappointment." * * * I perceived that he had so warmly cherished the hope of enjoying classical scenes, that he could not easily part with the scheme; for he said, " I shall probably contrive to get to Italy some other way. But I won't mention it to Mr. and Mrs. Thrale, as it might vex them." ' *Life*, iii. 28. 'Johnson was not fit to travel as every place was equal to him. He mused as much on the road to Paris as he did in his garret in London, as much at a French Opera as in his room at Streatham. With men, women, and children he never cared to exchange a word, and if he ever took any delight in any thing it was to converse with some old acquaintance. New people he never loved to be in company with, except Ladies, when disposed to caress and flatter him.' BARETTI.

To

To Miss Reynolds [1].

DEAREST MADAM,   April 11, 1776.

To have acted, with regard to you, in a manner either unfriendly or disrespectful, would give me great pain ; and, I hope,
will be always very contrary to my intention. That I staid away
was merely accidental. I have seldom dined from home ; and I did
not think my opinion necessary to your information in any pro-
prieties of behaviour. The poor parents of the child are much
grieved, and much dejected. The journey to Italy is put off, but
they go to Bath on Monday [2]. A visit from you will be well
taken, and I think your intimacy is such that you may very
properly pay it in a morning. I am sure that it will be thought
seasonable and kind, and I wish you not to omit it.

I am,

Dear Madam, &c.,

SAM: JOHNSON.

472.

To the Earl of Hertford, Lord Chamberlain [3].

MY LORD,

Being wholly unknown to your lordship, I have only this
apology to make for presuming to trouble you with a request,—
that a stranger's petition, if it cannot be easily granted, can be
easily refused. Some of the apartments are now vacant in which
I am encouraged to hope that by application to your lordship I
may obtain a residence. Such a grant would be considered by
me as a great favour ; and I hope that to a man who has had the
honour of vindicating his Majesty's Government, a retreat in one
of his houses may not be improperly or unworthily allowed [4].

[1] First published in Croker's *Boswell*, page 505.

[2] Monday was the 15th.

[3] First published in the *Gentleman's Magazine* for 1850, part i.
page 292.

Lord C. stands for Lord Chamberlain. The Earl (afterwards first
Marquis) of Hertford was at one
time Hume's patron. Hume's *Letters*
to *IV. Strahan*, p. xxx. He was the
grandfather of the third Marquis,
who was born within a year of the
date of Johnson's letter, and who is
supposed to be the original of the
Marquis of Steyne in Thackeray's
Vanity Fair. The endorsement
does not agree in date with the
letter.

[4] Johnson 'complained that his

I therefore

I therefore request that your lordship will be pleased to grant such rooms in Hampton Court as shall seem proper to

My Lord,

Your lordship's most obedt. and

most faithful humble servant.

Bolt court, Fleet street,   SAM: JOHNSON.
   April 11, 1776.

Indorsed—'Mr. Samuel Johnson to the Earl of Hertford, requesting apartments at Hampton Court. 11th May, 1776.' And within, a memorandum of the answer :—'Lord C. presents his compliments to Mr. Johnson, and is sorry that he cannot obey his commands, having already on his hands many engagements unsatisfied.'

473.

To the Reverend Dr. Taylor [1].

DEAR SIR,

I have not yet carried the cases. I would have the value of the Estate truly told. This trial takes up the Attorney general for the present ; and there is little hope of his attention to anything else. And upon the whole, I do not see that there is any haste. The opinion is as good and as useful a month hence, unless you found [name obliterated] alienating the land. I am going with Mr. Thrale to Bath on Monday. Our Italian journey

pension having been given to him as a literary character he had been applied to by administration to write political pamphlets.' On another occasion speaking of them he said :— 'Except what I had from the bookseller, I did not get a farthing by them.' This letter however shows that Boswell went too far when he asserted that 'he neither asked nor received from government any reward whatsoever for his political labours.' *Life*, ii. 147, 317. Wraxall asserts that in the struggle with America, 'with the exceptions of Johnson and Gibbon all the eminent or shining talents of the country, led on by Burke, were marshalled in support of the Colonies.' Wraxall's *Memoirs*, ed. 1815, ii. 81.

[1] Copied by me from the original in the possession of Mr. Alfred Morrison, of Fonthill House.

For the first mention of Taylor's law case, see *ante*, p. 375. Boswell wrote to Temple on May 1 :— 'Luckily Dr. Taylor has begged of Dr. Johnson to come to London, to assist him in some interesting business, and Johnson loves much to be so consulted and so comes up.' *Letters of Boswell*, p. 234. The Attorney-General was Thurlow. The trial on which he was engaged was that of 'Elizabeth, styling herself Duchess of Kingston, for bigamy.' It began on April 15 and ended on the 22nd with a verdict of guilty. *Gentleman's Magazine*, 1776, p. 179.

is

is deferred to another year, perhaps totally put off on their part. They are both extremely dejected. I think, his grief is deepest. If you put off your coming to town, I will give you notice when we return, but if your coming is necessary, I will come from Bath to meet you.

I am, Sir,

Your most humble servant,

SAM: JOHNSON.

Bolt court. (not Johnson's court), Fleet street.
    April 13, 1776.
To the Reverend Dr. Taylor in Ashburne, Derbyshire.

474.

To MISS REYNOLDS [1].

DEAREST MADAM,   April 15, 1776.

When you called on Mrs. Thrale, I find by enquiry that she was really abroad. The same thing happened to Mrs. Montagu, of which I beg you to inform her, for she went likewise by my opinion. The denial, if it had been feigned, would not have pleased me [2]. Your visits, however, are kindly paid, and very kindly taken. We are going to Bath this morning; but I could not part without telling you the real state of your visit.

I am, dearest Madam, &c.,

SAM: JOHNSON.

475.

To JAMES BOSWELL.

[Bath, April, 1776.]   Published in the *Life*, iii. 44.

476.

To MRS. THRALE [3].

DEAREST MADAM,   [London, Monday], May 6, 1776.

On Friday night, as you know, I left you about eleven

[1] First published in Croker's *Boswell*, page 508.

[2] 'Johnson would not allow his servant to say he was not at home when he really was. "A servant's strict regard for truth (said he) must be weakened by such a practice. A philosopher may know that it is merely a form of denial; but few servants are such nice distinguishers. If I accustom a servant to tell a lie for *me*, have I not reason to apprehend that he will tell many lies for *himself*."' *Life*, i. 436.

[3] *Piozzi Letters*, i. 320.

o'clock.

o'clock. The moon shone, but I did not see much of the way, for I think I slept better than I commonly do in bed. My companions were civil men, and we dispatched our journey very peaceably. I came home at about seven on Saturday very little fatigued[1].

To-day I have been at home. To-morrow I am to dine, as I did yesterday, with Dr. Taylor. On Wednesday I am to dine with Oglethorpe; and on Thursday with Paoli[2]. He that sees before him to his third dinner, has a long prospect.

My political tracts are printed, and I bring Mr. Thrale a copy when I come. They make but a little book[3].

Count Manucci is in such haste to come, that I believe he will not stay for me; if he would, I should like to hear his remarks on the road[4].

[1] Johnson took twenty hours in travelling in the stage coach a distance of 107 miles. In 1772 it had taken him twenty-six hours from London to Lichfield—a distance of 116 miles. *Ante*, p. 191. In 1783 the journey from London to Salisbury—82 miles—took him nearly fifteen hours. *Life*, iv. 234, *n.* 3. From about 4½ to 5½ miles an hour was, it seems, at this time the rate at which a stage-coach travelled. By a Parliamentary Return in 1836 it was shown that in that year the greatest speed travelled by the mail-coaches was 10⅘ miles an hour, the slowest 6; the average being 8⅐. *Penny Cyclo.* ed. 1840, xviii. 458. In Dickens's *Tale of two Cities* mail-coaches are described as running in 1775. They did not begin till nine years later, as is shown by the following entry in the *Gentleman's Magazine* for 1784, p. 634 :—'Monday, August 2, 1784. Began a new plan for the conveyance of the mail between London, Bath, and Bristol, by coaches constructed for that purpose. The coach which left London this evening at 8 o'clock arrived at Bristol the next morning

before eleven; and the coach that set out from Bristol at 4 o'clock in the afternoon got into London before 8 o'clock next morning.'

Horace Walpole on July 4, 1788, wrote to Hannah More :—'As letters, you say, now keep their coaches, I hope those from Bristol will call often at my door.' *Letters*, ix. 129.

[2] Boswell records :—'I dined with him at Dr. Taylor's, at General Oglethorpe's, and at General Paoli's.' *Life*, iii. 52. Boswell was indolent in keeping his Journal at this time, and has left us scarcely any account of the talk. *Life*, iii. 52. For Oglethorpe see *ib.* i. 127, and for Paoli *ib.* ii. 71.

[3] His four pamphlets, *The False Alarm, Falkland's Islands, The Patriot,* and *Taxation no Tyranny* he collected into one volume with the title of *Political Tracts.* Boswell says that on the title-page is added:— '*By the Authour of the Rambler*' (*Life*, ii. 315); but these words do not appear in my copy of the first edition.

[4] Boswell says that Manucci was a Florentine nobleman. *Life*, iii.

Mr. Baretti

Mr. Baretti has a cold and hoarseness, and Mrs. Williams says that I have caught a cold this afternoon.

I am, &c.,

SAM: JOHNSON.

477.

To Mrs. Thrale [1].

DEAR MADAM,   [London], May 11, 1776.

That you may have no superfluous uneasiness, I went this afternoon to visit the two babies at Kensington, and found them indeed a little spotted with their disorder, but as brisk and gay as health and youth can make them. I took a paper of sweet-meats, and spread them on the table. They took great delight to shew their governess the various animals that were made of sugar; and when they had eaten as much as was fit, the rest were laid up for to-morrow.

Susy sends her duty and love with great propriety. Sophy sends her duty to you, and her love to Queeney and Papa. Mr. Evans [2] came in after me. You may set your heart quite at rest, no babies can be better than they appear to be. Dr. Taylor went with me, and we staid a good while. He likes them very much. Susy said her creed in French.

Dr. Taylor says, I must not come back till his business is adjusted; and indeed it would not be wise to come away without doing what I came hither only to do. However, I expect to be dismissed in a few days, and shall bring Manucci with me.

I dined yesterday with • • • •. His three children are very lovely. • • • • longs to teach him a little economy. I know

---

89. Baretti describes him as 'a good and most pleasing man, who had read very little in his language and next to nothing in any other.' Johnson did not return to Bath. Had he done so he might have come across Hume, who had gone there on May 8, in the vain hope that the waters might relieve the illness of which he was dying. *Letters of Hume to Strahan*, p. 323.

[1] *Piozzi Letters*, i. 321.

[2] Mr. Evans is mentioned *post*, Letter of April 25, 1780, and *Life*, iii. 422. He was, I believe, 'the Rev. Mr. Evans,' mentioned in Miss Hawkins's *Memoirs*, i. 65, 'who having the living of St. Olave's, Tooley Street, was frequently a guest at Mrs. Thrale's table.'

not

not how his money goes, for I do not think that Mrs. Williams and I had our due share of the nine guineas [1].

He begins to reproach himself with neglect of • • • •'s education, and censures that idleness, or that deviation, by the indulgence of which he has left uncultivated such a fertile mind. I advised him to let the child alone; and told him that the matter was not great, whether he could read at the end of four years or of five, and that I thought it not proper to harass a tender mind with the violence of painful attention. I may perhaps procure both father and son a year of quiet; and surely I may rate myself among their benefactors [2].

> I am, &c.,
> SAM: JOHNSON.

478.

To Mrs. Thrale [3].

DEAR LADY, May 14, 1776.

Since my visit to the younglings, nothing has happened but a little disappointment in Dr. Taylor's affairs, which, he says,

---

[1] It was with Bennet Langton, no doubt, that Johnson dined. See *Life*, iii. 48, *n.* 4 for criticisms on his mode of living. On November 16 Johnson wrote to Boswell :—'Do you ever hear from Mr. Langton? I visit him sometimes, but he does not talk. I do not like his scheme of life; but as I am not permitted to understand it, I cannot set any thing right that is wrong. His children are sweet babies.' *Ib.* iii. 93.

Mrs. Thrale, I conjecture, had heard that Langton had received nine guineas from some unusual source. It might have been expected that the dinner which he had given to Johnson and Mrs. Williams would have been better than usual on account of this windfall, but it was not. Johnson later on complained that his table was 'rather coarse.' *Ib.* iii. 128.

[2] 'Endeavouring to make children prematurely wise,' said Johnson, 'is

useless labour. Suppose they have more knowledge at five or six years old than other children, what use can be made of it? It will be lost before it is wanted, and the waste of so much time and labour of the teacher can never be repaid. Too much is expected from precocity, and too little performed.' *Life*, ii. 407. According to Mrs. Piozzi (*Anecdotes*, p. 24) he had persuaded Dr. Sumner, the Head Master of Harrow School, to give up the practice of setting holiday-tasks. 'He told me,' she adds, 'that he had never ceased representing to all the eminent schoolmasters in England the absurd tyranny of poisoning the hour of permitted pleasure, by keeping future misery before the children's eyes, and tempting them by bribery or falsehood to evade it.' Unfortunately for 'the children' Dr. Sumner died before the next vacation.

[3] *Piozzi Letters*, i. 323.

must

must keep me here a while longer.   Mr. Wedderburn [1] has given
his opinion to-day directly against us.   He thinks of the claim
much as I think.   We sent this afternoon for a solicitor, another
Scrase [2], who gave the same sentence with Wedderburn, and with
less delicacy.   The Doctor tried to talk him into better notions,
but to little purpose, for a man is not much believed in his own
cause.   At last, finding the Doctor somewhat moody, I bid him
not be disturbed, for he could not be injured till the death of
Mrs. Rudd [3], and her life was better than his.   So I *comforted
and advised him* [4].

I know not how you intend to serve me, but I expect a
letter to-morrow, and I do not see why Queeney should forget
me.

Manucci must, I believe, come down without me.   I am
ashamed of having delayed him so long, without being able to
fix a day; but you know, and must make him know, that the
fault is not mine.

 . . . . goes away on Thursday, very well satisfied with his

---

[1] Wedderburne (at this time
Solicitor-General, afterwards Lord
Chancellor, Lord Loughborough and
Earl of Rosslyn) had been consulted
by Taylor. *Life*, iii. 44.

[2] Mr. Scrase, an old solicitor, who
lent money to Mr. Thrale has been
mentioned before, *ante*, p. 348, *n.* 4.
Mrs. Piozzi says that he had told her
that in the neighbourhood of Brighton
' he had made gentlemen's wills when
they left the county of Sussex ;
describing the leave-takings, &c., as
if they had been setting out for a discovery of the North Pole.' Hayward's *Piozzi*, ii. 244.   She says
that he was eighty-six years old in
1765, but this probably is an exaggeration as he was still living in
1777. By ' another Scrase ' Johnson
means, I conjecture, a man of his
character.

[3] This can scarcely refer to ' the
celebrated Mrs. Rudd, who had been

much talked of this spring.' She had
been tried for forgery with the two
brothers Perreau.   She was acquitted
and they were hanged.   Boswell
' talked to Johnson a good deal of
her ' the day after the date of the
letter in the text.   *Life*, ii. 450 ;
iii. 79.

[4] This was, it should seem, a
common quotation in the Streatham
set.   Mrs. Thrale wrote to Miss
Burney in 1779 :— ' And so, as Mowbray the brutal says of Lovelace the
gay, " We comforted and advised
him." ' Mme. D'Arblay's *Diary*, i.
159.   The original passage is found in
Mr. Mowbray's Letter of September
7, to John Belford, Esq. (*Clarissa*,
ed. 1810, viii. 95) : —' The conquest
did not pay trouble ; and what was
there in one woman more than
another? Hey, you know, Jack ! –
And thus we comforted him and advised him.'

journey.

journey. Some great men have promised to obtain him a place, and then a fig for my father and his new wife[1].

I have not yet been at the Borough[2], nor know when I shall go, unless you send me. There is in the exhibition of Exeter Exchange[3], a picture of the house at Streatham, by one Laurence, I think, of the Borough. This is something, or something like.

Mr. Welch[4] sets out for France to-morrow, with his younger daughter. He has leave of absence for a year, and seems very much delighted with the thought of travelling, and the hope of health.

I am, &c.,
SAM: JOHNSON.

479.

TO MRS. THRALE[5].

DEAR MADAM, May 16, 1776.

This is my third letter. Well, sure I shall have something to-morrow. Our business stands still. The Doctor[6] says I must not go; and yet my stay does him no good. His solicitor says he is sick, but I suspect he is sullen. The Doctor, in the mean time, has his head as full as yours at an election. Livings and preferments, as if he were in want with twenty children, run in his head[7]. But a man must have his head on something, small or great.

---

[1] 'New wife' seems a strange term to apply to a woman more than six years after her marriage. For Boswell's disagreement with his step-mother, see *Life*, ii. 377, *n.* 1. He too often nursed hopes of promotion through great men. On March 18, 1775, he wrote:—'I have hopes from Lord Pembroke. How happy should I be to get an independency by my own influence while my father is alive!' *Letters of Boswell*, p. 182. On May 1, 1776, he wrote:—'I am going to sup with Lord Mountstuart [the Earl of Bute's eldest son] my Mæcenas. You know how I delight in patronage.' *Ib.* p. 234.

[2] Mr. Thrale's house at Southwark.

[3] 'Exeter 'Change, an edifice in the Strand, erected for the sake of trade, consisting of a long room with a row of shops on each side, and a large room above, now used for auctions.' Dodsley's *Environs of London*, ii. 290. On its site stands Exeter Hall.

[4] Saunders Welch, Fielding's successor as one of the Magistrates for Westminster. He went abroad for his health's sake, having through Johnson's influence obtained leave of absence. *Life*, iii. 216.

[5] *Piozzi Letters*, i. 325.

[6] Dr. Taylor.

[7] For Taylor's eagerness for preferment see *ante*, pp. 12, 156.

For

For my part, I begin to settle and keep company with grave
aldermen. I dined yesterday in the Poultry with Mr. Alderman
Wilkes, and Mr. Alderman Lee, and Counsellor Lee, his brother[1].
There sat you the while, so sober, with your W——'s and your
H——s[2], and my aunt and her turnspit; and when they are
gone, you think by chance on Johnson, what is he doing? What
should he be doing? He is breaking jokes with Jack Wilkes
upon the Scots[3]. Such, Madam, are the vicissitudes of things[4].
And there was Mrs. Knowles, the Quaker, that works the futile[5]
pictures, who is a great admirer of your conversation. She saw
you at Mr. Shaw's[6], at the election time. She is a Staffordshire
woman, and I am to go and see her. Staffordshire is the nursery
of art, here they grow up till they are transplanted to London[7].

Yet it is strange that I hear nothing from you; I hope you

[1] This was the famous dinner at
Messieurs Dilly's, 'my worthy booksellers and friends,' as Boswell calls
them, where Johnson met Wilkes.
'Counsellor Lee' was Arthur Lee,
who, says Boswell, 'could not but
be very obnoxious to Johnson, for
he was not only a *patriot*, but
an *American*. He was afterwards
Minister from the United States at
the Court of Madrid.' *Life*, iii. 68.
He was a son of Thomas Lee, of
Virginia. One of his brothers was
the author of the Resolution of June
10, 1776, for the Independence of the
Colonies; another brother was the
ancestor of Robert Lee, the famous
General of the Slave States in the
War between the North and South.
Memoirs of Robert E. Lee, by A. L.
Long, 1886, p. 19. According to
Franklin's *Memoirs*, ed. 1833, ii. 42;
iii. 407, Arthur Lee was at this time
'employed by Congress as a private
and confidential agent in England,'
receiving his letters by private hand
under cover to his brother, the Alderman. I have not been able to identify
the Alderman (whose Christian name
was William) in the *Memoirs of
Robert Lee*.

[2] W——, I conjecture, was one
Woodward. See *post*, p. 400, where
he and H—— are mentioned.
[3] See *Life*, iii. 73, 76, for the jokes
of Johnson and Wilkes against Boswell.
[4] *Life*, v. 117, *n.* 3.
[5] Johnson wrote *sutile*; his initial
s being always formed like an *f* was
here absurdly taken for one. In the
Idler, No. 13, he describes some
rooms as 'adorned with a kind of
sutile pictures which imitate tapestry.'
For Mrs. Knowles see *Life*, iii. 78,
299, *n.* 2. Nichols (*Lit. Hist.*, iv.
830) says that 'her grand undertaking was a representation of the
King in needle-work—which she
completed to the entire satisfaction
of their Majesties.' Mr. Lort wrote
to Bishop Percy about *futile*:—'I
desired a sight of the original letter
in order to determine a wager. There
it plainly appeared that a dash had
been put across the long *s*, perhaps
by the printer or corrector of the
press.' Nichols's *Lit. Hist.*, vii. 494.
[6] Mr. Shaw is mentioned, *post*
Letter of August 14, 1780.
[7] Johnson, it must be remembered,
came from Staffordshire.

are

are not angry, or sick. Perhaps you are gone without me for spite to see places. That is natural enough, for evil is very natural, but I shall vex, unless it does you good.

Stevens seems to be connected with Tyrwhitt in publishing Chatterton's poems; he came very anxiously to know the result of our enquiries, and though he says he always thought them forged, is not well pleased to find us so fully convinced [1].

I have written to Manucci to find his own way, for the *law's delay* [2] makes it difficult for me to guess when I shall be able to be, otherwise than by my inclination, Madam,

Your, &c.,

SAM: JOHNSON.

480.

To Sir Joshua Reynolds.

[London], May 16, 1776. Published in the *Life*, iii. 81.

481.

To Mrs. Boswell.

[London], May 16, 1776. Published in the *Life*, iii. 85.

482.

To Mrs. Thrale [3].

DEAR MADAM, May 18, 1776.

Then you are neither sick nor angry. Don't let me be defrauded of Queeney's letter. Yesterday Seward [4] was with me, and told me what he knew of you. All good. To-day I went to look into my places at the Borough [5]. I called on Mr. Perkins

---

[1] Steevens on the publication of these Letters inserted an unsigned letter in the *Gentleman's Magazine* (1788, p. 187) in which he asserted that he always thought the poems forged, and that Mr. Tyrwhitt, before he printed them, had arrived at the same conclusion. Nichols, however, in a note on this statement says that 'Mr. Tyrwhitt changed his opinion after his volume was actually com-

pleted at the press; and cancelled *several sheets* which had been printed to demonstrate that the poems were genuine.' *Lit. Anec.* ix. 530.

[2] *Hamlet*, Act iii. sc. 1.

[3] *Piozzi Letters*, i. 333.

[4] *Ante*, p. 346, *n.* 1.

[5] His room, or rather the receptacles in it, in Mr. Thrale's house in Southwark.

in

in the counting-house[1]. He crows and triumphs, as we go on we shall double our business. The best brown malt he can have laid in at thirty and sixpence, and great stores he purposes to buy[2]. Dr. Taylor's business stagnates, but he resolves not to wait on it much longer. Surely I shall get down to you next week.

B—— went away on Thursday night, with no great inclination to travel northward; but who can contend with destiny? He says, he has had a very pleasant journey. He paid another visit, I think, to · · · ·, before he went home[3]. He carries with him two or three good resolutions; I hope they will not mould upon the road. Who can be this new friend of mine[4]? The letter you sent me was from Mr. Twisse, and the book, if any come, is Twisse's travels to Ireland, which you will, I hope, unty and read[5].

[1] 'Mr. Perkins was the worthy superintendant of Mr. Thrale's brewery, and after his death became one of the proprietors. . . . He hung up in the counting-house a fine proof of the admirable mezzotinto of Dr. Johnson, by Doughty; and when Mrs. Thrale asked him somewhat flippantly, "Why do you put him up in the counting-house?" he answered, "Because, Madam, I wish to have one wise man there." "Sir," (said Johnson,) "I thank you. It is a very handsome compliment, and I believe you speak sincerely."' *Life,* ii. 286.

[2] *Ante,* p. 192, *n.* 3.

[3] B—— is Boswell. It was perhaps Mrs. Rudd (*ante,* p. 395, *n.* 3) to whom he paid another visit. That he had visited her more than once he tells us. *Life,* iii. 79; vi. *Addenda,* p. li.

[4] This is in answer to the following passage in Mrs. Thrale's letter of May 16:—'We have a flashy friend here already, who is much your adorer; I wonder how you will like *him?* An Irishman he is; very handsome, very hot-headed, loud and lively, and sure to be a favourite with you, he tells us, for he can live with a man of *ever so odd a temper.* My master laughs, but likes him, and it diverts me to think what you will do when he professes that he could clean shoes for you; that he could shed his blood for you; with twenty more extravagant flights.' *Piozzi Letters,* i. 329. He was a Mr. Musgrave. *Life,* ii. 343, *n.* 2; iv. 323, *n.* 1.

[5] For Mr. Twiss see *ante,* p. 316, *n.* 2. His *Tour in Ireland* in 1775 is reviewed in the *Gentleman's Magazine* for September, 1776, p. 420. Twiss, who had travelled, describes 'the poverty of the common Irish as much greater than that of the Spanish, Portuguese, or even Scotch peasants.' The gentry, he says, have three, and only three peculiar customs. They always have boiled eggs for breakfast; they always have potatoes at every meal; and they pretty universally forge franks. *Ib.*

I enclose

I enclose some of the powders, lest you should lose your patient by delay.

I am, &c.,

Sam: Johnson.

483.

To Mrs. Thrale [1].

Dear Madam,   May 22, 1776.

On Friday and Saturday I dined with Dr. Taylor, who is in discontent, but resolved not to stay much longer to hear the opinions of lawyers who are all against him. Who can blame him for being weary of them?

On Sunday I dined at Sir Joshua's house on the hill, with the Bishop of St. Asaph. The dinner was good, and the Bishop is knowing and conversible [2]. Yesterday at the Doctor's again— very little better.—In the evening came in Dr. Crane, who enquired after you.

All this while • • • • [3] is hurt only in his vanity. He thought he had supplanted Mrs. W——, and Mrs. W—— has found the means of defeating him. He really wanted nothing more than to have the power of bequeathing a reversion to Mr. G——'s son, who is very nearly related to W——. This purity of intention however he cannot prove; and the transaction in itself seems *pactum iniquum*. I do not think that he can, or indeed that he ought to prevail.

Woodward, I hear, is gone to Bristol, in deep dudgeon at Barret's declaration against Chatterton's productions. You have now only H——, whom you can only make a silent admirer [4].

[1] *Piozzi Letters*, i. 334.

[2] Sir Joshua had a house on Richmond Hill, 'where in the summer season it was his frequent custom to dine with select parties of his friends.' Northcote's *Reynolds*, i. 304. The Bishop of St. Asaph was Dr. Shipley. Boswell quotes in the *Life*, iv. 246, Johnson's praise of him. He was one of the two Bishops with whom Johnson dined one Passion Week. *Ib.* iv. 88.

[3] No doubt Dr. Taylor. See *ante*, p. 379, where it is stated his suit was with a woman, and *post*, p. 408.

[4] Johnson and Boswell had visited Bristol on April 29, and examined into the authenticity of Chatterton's poems:—'We called on Mr. Barret, the surgeon, and saw some of the *originals* as they were called, which were executed very artificially; but from a careful inspection of them, and a consideration of the circum-

I hope

I hope my friend buzzes a little about you to keep me in your head, though I think I do my part pretty well myself; there are very few writers of more punctuality.

I wish Queeney joy of her new watch[1]; and next time I write, intend myself the honour of directing my letter to her. Her hand is now very exact, and when use has made it free, may be very beautiful.

I am glad of Mr. Thrale's resolution to take up his *restes* in person[2]. He is wise in keeping the trade in his own hands, and appearing on proper occasions as the principal agent. Every man has those about him who wish to sooth him into inactivity and delitescence[3], nor is there any semblance of kindness more vigorously to be repelled than that which voluntarily offers a vicarious performance of the tasks of life, and conspires with the natural love of ease against diligence and perseverance[4].

While I was holding my pen over the last period, I was called down to Father Wilks the Benedictine, and Father Brewer a Doctor of the Sorbon, who are come to England, and are now wandering over London. I have invited them to dine with me to-morrow[5]. Father Cowley is well; and Mrs. Strickland is at

stances with which they were attended, we were quite satisfied of the imposture.' *Life*, iii. 50. H—— was perhaps Dr. Harington of Bath, or his son who published the *Nugae Antiquae. Ib.* iv. 180.

[1] Hawkins in his *Life of Johnson*, p. 460, says that he believes Johnson never had a watch of his own before 1768, when he was in his fifty-ninth year.

[2] 'When the master brewer goes round to his victuallers once a year, in order to examine the state of the trade, and the stock left on the hands of the alehouse-keeper, the expression used in the profession is, *that he takes up his restes*; a word borrowed from the French, and means the remainder —*les restes.*' Note by Mrs. Piozzi.

[3] *Delitescence* is not in Johnson's *Dictionary*.

[4] 'There is nothing,' said Johnson, 'against which an old man should be so much upon his guard as putting himself to nurse.' *Life*, ii. 474. See also *ib.* ii. 337; iii. 176, *n.* 1. Baretti says that the passage in the text 'is a stroke against poor Perkins who contributed much to make Mr. Thrale rich by his skill and assiduity as his chief clerk; but no dependent can constantly shun censure.'

[5] Johnson recorded in his French Journal:—' October 31. I lived at the Benedictines.... I parted very tenderly from the Prior and Friar Wilkes.' *Life*, ii. 399. He visited the Sorbonne (*ib.* ii. 397), but he does not mention Brewer. See *post*, Letter of September 25, 1777. Had these men officiated as priests in England, if they were foreigners, their act was felony, and if natives, high treason.

Paris¹. More than this I have not yet learned. They stay, I think, here but a little time.

I have sent your last parcel of powders, and hope soon to come myself.

I am, &c.,

SAM: JOHNSON.

484.

TO THE REVEREND DR. ADAMS².

SIR,

The Gentleman who brings this is a learned Benedictine, in whose monastery I was treated at Paris with all the civilities which the Society had means or opportunity of shewing. I dined in their refectory, and studied in their library³, and had the favour of their company to other places, as curiosity led me. I, therefore, take the liberty of recommending him to you, Sir, and to Pembroke college, to be shewn that a lettered Stranger is not treated with less regard at Oxford than in France, and hope that you and my fellow collegians will not be unwilling to acknowledge some obligations for benefits conferred on one who has had the honour of studying amongst you.

I am, Sir,

Your most humble servant,

SAM: JOHNSON.

May 29, 1776.

Lord Shelburne, in 1778, said that when he was in office (1766–1768) a priest was brought to trial by an informer. 'The Court was reluctantly obliged to condemn him to perpetual imprisonment. Though every method was taken by the Privy Council to give a legal discharge to the prisoner, neither the laws would allow of it, nor dared the King himself to grant him a pardon. Lord Shelburne and his colleagues ventured to give him his liberty at every hazard.' *Parl. Hist.*, xix. 1139, 1145. It was the proposal to mitigate these cruel laws which led to the Gordon Riots of 1780.

¹ For Father Cowley, the Prior of the Benedictines, see *post*, Letter of September 25, 1777, and for Mrs. Strickland see *Life*, iii. 118, *n.* 3.

² First published in Mr. Morrison's *Catalogue of Autographs*, ii. 342. Dr. Adams was the Master of Pembroke College, Oxford. See *post*, Letter of July 11, 1784.

³ Johnson made the following record in his Journal of their refectory and library:—' Meagre day; soup meagre, herrings, eels, both

To

485.

To Henry Thrale [1].

Dear Sir, [Bolt Court], June 3, 1776.

You are all, I suppose, now either at one home or the other [2], and all I hope well. My mistress writes as if she was afraid I should make too much haste to see her. Pray tell her that there is no danger. The lameness, of which I made mention in one of my notes, has improved to a very serious and troublesome fit of the gout [3]. I creep about and hang by both hands. Johnny Wilcocks might be my running footman. I enjoy all the dignity of lameness [4]. I receive ladies and dismiss them sitting. *Painful pre-eminence* [5].

Baretti is at last mentioned in one of the Reviews, but in a manner that will not give him much delight. They are neither angry nor civil [6].

with sauce; fryed fish; lentils, tasteless in themselves. In the library; where I found *Maffeus's de Historiâ Indicâ: Promontorium flectere, to double the Cape.' Life*, ii. 399. He does not in his *Dictionary* give *meagre* used in this sense. Like *transpire*, it is 'a sense innovated from France without necessity.' *Life*, iii. 343.

[1] *Piozzi Letters*, i. 337.

[2] Streatham or the Borough.

[3] The note in which he mentions this is not in Mrs. Piozzi's Collection. Johnson wrote to Boswell on July 6 that he was attacked by the gout on May 29, and was not quite recovered. *Life*, iii. 89.

[4] ' What dignity attends the solemn Gout !
What conscious greatness if the heart be stout.'
Mr. R. Pitt to his Brother C. Pitt. Johnson's *English Poets*, ed. 1790, lii. 119.

[5] ' Am I distinguished from you but by toils,

Superior toils, and heavier weight of cares ?
Painful pre-eminence !'
Addison's *Cato*, Act iii. sc. 5.
See *Life*, iii. 82, *n.* 2.

[6] He had this spring published an *Essay on Phraseology, for the Use of Young Ladies who intend to learn the Colloquial Part of the Italian Language. Gentleman's Magazine*, 1776, p. 132. Under the date of June 4 he has recorded in a marginal note: 'On this day I quitted Streatham without taking leave, perfectly tired with the impertinence of the Lady, who took every opportunity to disgust me, unable to pardon the violent efforts I had made at Bath to hinder her from giving tin-pills to Queeney. I had by that time been in a manner one of the family during five years and a half, teaching Queeney Spanish and Italian from morn to night, at her earnest desire originally, and Johnson who had made me hope that Thrale would at last give me an annuity for my pains; but never

D d 2 Catcot

Catcot has been convinced by Barret, and has written his recantation to Tyrwhitt, who still persists in his edition of the poems, and perhaps is not much pleased to find himself mistaken[1].

You are now, I suppose, busy about your *restes*[2]; I heartily wish you, dear Sir, a happy perambulation, and a good account of the trade ; and hope that you and my mistress, as you come by, will call upon, Sir,

Your, &c.,

SAM : JOHNSON.

486.

TO MRS. THRALE[3].

DEAR MADAM,   June 4, at night [1776].

The world is indeed full of troubles, and we must not chuse for ourselves. But I am not sincerely sorry that in your present state of mind you are going to be immediately a mother[4]. Compose your thoughts, diversify your attention, and attend your health[5].

If I can be of any use, send for me ; I think I can creep to the end of the court, and climb into a coach, though perhaps not very easily; but if you call me, very willingly. If you do not send for me, let me, pray let me know as oft as you can how you do.

receiving a shilling from him or from her, I grew tired at last, and on some provocation from her left them abruptly.'

[1] 'George Catcot, the pewterer, who was as zealous for Rowley, as Dr. Hugh Blair was for Ossian, attended us at our inn, and with a triumphant air of lively simplicity called out, "I'll make Dr. Johnson a convert."' *Life*, iii. 50. Horace Walpole wrote on February 17, 1777 :—'Mr. Tyrrwhit has at last published the Bristol poems. He does not give up the antiquity, yet fairly leaves everybody to ascribe them to Chatterton if they please.' Walpole's *Letters*, vi. 412. See *ante*, p. 398.

[2] *Ante*, p. 401, *n.* 2.

[3] *Piozzi Letters*, i. 338.

[4] Her next child was born on February 8, 1777, more than eight months later. I should have thought that the Letter (of which the year apparently was not given) had been misplaced by Mrs. Piozzi, had there not been mention of the gout and the *restes* which had been mentioned in the previous letter.

[5] This use of *attend* as a transitive verb was not common in Johnson's time.

I am

I am glad that my master is at his *restes* [1], they will help to fill up his mind.

Pray let me know often how you do.

I am, dearest Lady,

Your, &c.,

SAM: JOHNSON.

487.

To Mrs. Thrale [2].

DEAREST LADY, June 5, 1776.

You will have a note which I wrote last night. I was thinking, as I lay awake, that you might be worse; but I hope you will be every moment better and better. I have never had any overpowering pain, nor been kept more awake than is usual to me; but I am a very poor creeper upon the earth, catching at any thing with my hands to spare my feet. In a day or two I hope to be as fit for Streatham as for any other place. Mr. Thrale it seems called last night when I was in bed, and yet I was not in bed till near twelve, for I sit up lest I should not sleep. He must keep well, for he is the pillar of the house [3]; and you must get well, or the house will hardly be worth propping.

I am, dearest Madam,

Your, &c.,

SAM: JOHNSON.

488.

To Mrs. Thrale [4].

MY DEAR LADY, June 6, [1776].

How could you so mistake me? I am very desirous that the whole business should be as you would have it, only cheerfulness at that time is reckoned a good thing [5].

My feet grow better, and I hope, if you send a carriage, to mount it on Monday. This gout has a little depressed

[1] *Ante*, p. 401, *n.* 2.
[2] *Piozzi Letters*, i. 339.
[3] See *post*, Letter of November 4, 1779, where he calls Mr. Thrale
'*columen domus.*'
[4] *Piozzi Letters*, i. 340.
[5] He is apparently referring to her approaching confinement.

me,

me, not that I have suffered any great pain; I have been teized rather than tormented; but the tediousness and the imbecillity [1] have been unpleasant. However I now recover strength, and do not yet despair of kicking the moon [2].

Could not you send me something out of your garden? Things have been growing, and you have not been consuming them. I wish I had a great bunch of asparagus for Sunday.

Take great care of our Queeney, and of yourself, and encourage yourself in bustle, and variety, and cheerfulness. I will be ready to come as soon as I can, but the pain is now twinging me. Let me know, my sweetest lady, very often how you do. I thought it late before I heard to-day.

I am, dear Madam,

Your, &c.,

SAM: JOHNSON.

489.

TO MRS. THRALE [3].

DEAR MADAM, June 8, [1776].

My feet disappointed me last night; I thought they would have given me no disturbance, but going upstairs I fancy fretted them, and they would not let me be easy. On Monday I am afraid I shall be a poor walker, but well enough to talk, and to hear you talk. And then, you know, what care we?

Mr. Norton called on me yesterday. He is at Sayer's print-shop in Fleet-street; and would take an invitation to dinner very kindly.

Poor Mr. Levet has fallen down, and hurt himself dangerously [4].

Of the monks I can give no account. I had them to dinner, and gave each of them the *Political Tracts*, and furnished Wilkes

---

[1] Johnson defines *imbecility* as 'weakness; feebleness of mind or body.'

[2] In *Drunken Barnaby's Journal*, ed. 1818, p. 18, we find 'salientem contra lunam.'

[3] *Piozzi Letters*, i. 342.

[4] Johnson said that 'Levett was perhaps the only man who ever became intoxicated through motives of prudence.' *Life*, i. 243, n. 3. Perhaps he had fallen in one of these fits of prudential intoxication.

with

with letters, which will, I believe, procure him a proper reception at Oxford [1].

I am, dearest Lady,

Your, &c.,

SAM: JOHNSON.

490.

TO MISS REYNOLDS [2].

DEAREST MADAM,   June 21, 1776.

You are as naughty as you can be. I am willing enough to write to you when I have any thing to say. As for my disorder, as Sir Joshua saw me, I fancied he would tell you, and that I needed not tell you myself. Of Dr. Goldsmith's Epitaph, I sent Sir Joshua two copies, and had none myself. If he has lost it, he has not done well. But I suppose I can recollect it, and will send it to you.

I am, Madam, &c.,

SAM: JOHNSON.

P.S.—All the Thrales are well, and Mrs. Thrale has a great regard for Miss Reynolds.

491.

TO SIR JOSHUA REYNOLDS.

[London], June 22, 1776. Published in the *Life*, iii. 82.

[1] *Ante*, p. 402.

[2] First published in Croker's *Boswell*, p. 519.

This letter was in answer to one from Miss Reynolds, given by Mr. Croker in full, in which she says:— 'You saw by my last letter that I knew nothing of your illness, and it was unkind of you not to tell me what had been the matter with you ; and you should have let me know how Mrs. Thrale and all the family were ; but that would have been a sad transgression of the rule you have certainly prescribed to yourself of writing to some sort of people just such a number of lines. Be so good as to favour me with Dr. Goldsmith's Epitaph ; and if you have no objection, I should be very glad to send it to Dr. Beattie ... My brother says he has lost it.' Goldsmith died on April 4, 1774. It was Reynolds who first proposed the erection of his monument. He went to Westminster Abbey, and selected the place where it should be set up. Northcote's *Reynolds*, i. 326. The 'two copies' which he so carelessly lost were two distinct epitaphs. *Life*, iii. 82.

To

To the Reverend Dr. Taylor [1].

DEAR SIR,   June 23 [? 26], 1776.

The Gout is now grown tolerable ; I can go up stairs pretty well, but am yet awkward in coming down.

Some time ago I had a letter from the Solicitor [2], in which he mentioned our cause with respect enough, but persists in his opinion, as I suppose, your Attorney has told you. He is however convinced that nothing fraudulent was intended : I would be glad to hear what the Attorney says.

Mr. Thrale would gladly have seen you at his house. They are all well.

Whether I shall wander this Summer, I hardly know. If I do, tell me when it will be the best time to come to you.

I hope you persevere in drinking. My opinion is that I have drunk too little, and therefore have the gout, for it is of my own acquisition, as neither my father had it nor my Mother [3].

Wilkes and Hopkins have now polled two days, and I hear that Wilkes is two hundred behind [4].

Of this sudden Revolution in the Prince's household, the original cause is not certainly known. The quarrel began between Lord Holderness, and Jackson, the part of Jackson was taken by the Bishop, and all ended in a total change [5].

I am, Sir,

Your affectionate, &c.,

SAM: JOHNSON.

To the Reverend Dr. Taylor in Ashbourne, Derbyshire.

[1] First published in *Notes and Queries*, 6th S. v. 423.

[2] See *ante*, p. 395, for 'the solicitor who gave the same sentence with Wedderburne, and with less delicacy.' Johnson, I think, means to say that Taylor was not suspected of any fraudulent intention. See *ante*, p. 400, *n.* 3.

[3] *Ante*, p. 368, *n.* 1, and *Life*, i. 103, *n.* 3.

[4] The poll was for the Chamberlain of the City of London. Hopkins received 2610 votes and Wilkes 1513. As the show of hands was taken on June 24 (*Gent. Mag.*, 1776, p. 285), the date of this letter—June 23—as given in *Notes and Queries* seems to be wrong.

[5] Horace Walpole describes on June 5 'the very singular revolution which has happened in the Penetralia and made very great noise. Yesterday se'nnight it was declared that

To

493.

To James Boswell.

[London], July 2, 1776. Published in the *Life*, iii. 86.

494.

To James Boswell.

[London,] July 6, 1776. Published in the *Life*, iii. 88.

495.

To Francis Fowke [1].

Sir,   [London], July 11, 1776.

I received some weeks ago a collection of papers which contain the trial of my dear friend, Joseph Fowke ; of whom I

the Bishop of Chester and Mr. Jackson, preceptor and sub-preceptor to the Prince of Wales, were dismissed, and that Lord Holdernesse and Mr. Smelt, governor and sub-governor, had resigned their posts. . . . It is now known that on Lord Holdernesse's return from the south of France he found a great alienation from him in the minds of his royal pupils, which he attributed to Jackson,' &c. *Letters*, vi. 346. As the Bishop of Chester (Markham) was made Archbishop of York a few months later (*Gent. Mag.*, 1776, p. 580), and Jackson was made Dean of Christ Church in 1783, they did not apparently lose the favour of the King. The ' royal pupils ' were George IV and the Duke of York.

[1] First published in *Original Letters*, ed. by Rebecca Warner, 1817, p. 205.

Joseph Fowke, she tells us, was born about 1715, and entered the service of the East India Company at the age of seventeen. He returned to England in 1748 and remained there till 1771. According to Mr. Croker, ' he went to India in 1736 as a writer, and served in

several subordinate offices till he was appointed, in 1751, fifth member of Council at Madras. He had been, however, for some years a dissatisfied man, and in 1752 resigned the service and came to England. In 1770 he was permitted to return as a free merchant to Calcutta. He was afterwards re-appointed to office in India, but finally resigned the Company's service, and returned to England in 1790, when a vote of the House of Commons, moved by Mr. Burke, forced the reluctant Court of Directors to grant him a pension. He died in Bath, in 1806, æt. 84.'

He is no doubt the gentleman described by Johnson on April 5, 1776, from whom he had lately received a letter from the East Indies, and whom he had once had some intention of accompanying thither. *Life*, iii. 20. Fowke used to tell anecdotes of Johnson. ' One morning, on calling on him, he found him,' he said, ' somewhat agitated. On inquiring the cause, "I have just *dismissed* Lord Chesterfield," said he ; " if you had come a few moments sooner I could have shown you my letter to him." Johnson cannot

cannot easily be induced to think otherwise than well, and who seems to have been injured by the prosecution and the sentence. His first desire is that I should prepare his narrative for the press ; his second, that if I cannot gratify him by publication, I would transmit the papers to you.   To a compliance with his first request I have this objection, that I live in a reciprocation of civilities with Mr. H. [1], and therefore cannot properly diffuse a narrative intended to bring upon him the censure of the public. Of two adversaries it would be rash to condemn either upon the evidence of the other ; and a common friend must keep himself suspended, at least till he has heard both.

I am therefore ready to transmit to you the papers which have been seen only by myself ; and beg to be informed how they may be conveyed to you.   I see no legal objection to the publication ; and of prudential reasons Mr. Fowke and you will be allowed to be fitter judges.

told him that Chesterfield had sent him a present of £100 to induce him to dedicate the *Dictionary* to him ; "which I returned," said he, "to his Lordship with contempt ;" and then added, "Sir, I found I must have gilded a rotten post. Lord C., Sir, is a wit among lords, but only a lord among wits."' *Original Letters*, p. 204. Boswell's version of Johnson's saying is different : — ' This man I thought had been a Lord among wits, but I find he is only a wit among Lords.' *Life*, i. 266. The story of the present of £100 is not supported by any other evidence and is very improbable.

Fowke did not think much of the various *Lives* of his friend. 'Ah ! where shall I find another Johnson ?' he wrote ; 'I am sorry his biographers cannot be brought upon their trial for murder ; it would be no difficult matter to convict them.' *Original Letters*, p. 215. See also *Life*, iii. 71, *n.* 5 ; iv. 34, *n.* 5, for other anecdotes.

[1] Warren Hastings. Johnson, very likely, wrote the name in full. For their 'reciprocation of civilities' see *Life*, iv. 66. In India, Fowke had taken an active part against Warren Hastings, when Governor-General. In April, 1775, he and Nuncomar— so famous in Macaulay's *Essay*— were charged with having conspired with others to force one Comaul Uddien Khan to write a petition against the Governor-General, Mr. Barwell, and others. They were acquitted on the charge of conspiracy against Hastings, and convicted on the charge of conspiring against Barwell. The sentence on Fowke was almost nominal—a fine of fifty rupees. Hastings before the trial wrote : — ' In my heart and conscience I believe both Fowke and Nuncomar to be guilty.' This opinion Sir Fitzjames Stephen thinks justified by the trial. Stephen's *Nuncomar and Impey*, i. 82, 101, 203, 215. Johnson, so far as he knew the facts, sided with Fowke and Nuncomar. *Post*, Letter of April 19, 1783.

If

If you would have me send them, let me have proper directions ; if a messenger is to call for them, give me notice by the
post, that they may be ready for delivery.

To do my dear Mr. Fowke any good would give me pleasure ;
I hope for some opportunity of performing the duties of friendship to him, without violating them with regard to another.

I am, Sir,

Your most humble Servant,

SAM: JOHNSON.

496.

To SIR JOSHUA REYNOLDS.

[London], August 3, 1776. Published in the *Life*, iii. 90.

497.

To MRS. REYNOLDS [1].

DEAREST MADAM,

To do what you desire with your restrictions is impossible.
I shall not see Mrs. Thrale till Tuesday in the afternoon. If
I write, I must give a stronger reason than you care to allow.
The company is already very numerous, but yet there might,
I suppose, be found room for a girl, if the proposal could be
made. Even writing, if you allow it, will hardly do ; the penny
post does not go on Sunday, and Mr. Thrale does not always
come to town on Monday. However let me know what you
would have done.

I am, Madam,

Your most humble servant,

SAM: JOHNSON.

August 3.

To Mrs. Reynolds.

[1] First published in the Catalogue
of Mr. Alfred Morrison's Autographs,
ii. 342.

Mrs. Reynolds was Sir Joshua's un-
married sister, who, like Miss Porter
and others of Johnson's friends, had
reached an age when she took ' bre-
vet-rank.' This letter was written
either on a Saturday or Sunday.
In some of the years in which
Johnson was in London in the beginning of August the 3rd fell on neither
of those days. I have assigned it,
therefore, to 1776, in which year
August 3 was Saturday. It is not
unlikely that it was sent with the

TO

To John Ryland [1].

SIR,

I have procured this play to be read by Mrs. Thrale, who declares that no play was ever more nicely pruned from the objection of indelicacy.

If it can be got upon the stage, it will I think succeed, and may get more money than will be raised by the impression of the other works.

In selling the copy to the printer, the liberty of inserting it in the volumes may be retained.

I am, Sir,

Your most humble servant,

SAM: JOHNSON.

Sept. 21, 1776.
To Mr. Ryland.

499.

To William Strahan [2].

SIR,

I wrote to you about ten days ago, and sent you some copy [3]. You have not written again, that is a sorry trick.

I am told that you are printing a Book for Mr. Professor Watson of Saint Andrews, if upon any occasion I can give any help, or be of any use, as formerly in Dr. Robertson's publication,

previous Letter to Sir Joshua Reynolds, dated August 3, 1776. What 'the company' was I do not know.

[1] From the original in the possession of Mr. Alfred H. Huth, of Bolney House, Ennismore Gardens, London.

This Letter and that of November 14 of this year are explained by a third in the same series, dated April 12, 1777. Ryland was brother-in-law of Dr. Hawkesworth (*ante*, pp. 56, 60), who had died on November 17, 1773. He was, it should seem, proposing to publish that author's Collected Works for the benefit of the widow. Hawkesworth had had

some success as a play-writer; Murphy's *Life of Garrick*, pp. 226, 236. I cannot find that the publication ever took place.

This Letter was sold by Messrs. Sotheby & Co., on May 10, 1875, for £5 15s. (Lot 93).

[2] First published in my edition of the *Life of Johnson*, vi. *Addenda*, p. xxxvii.

[3] The 'copy' or MS. that Johnson sent was, I conjecture, *Proposals for the Rev. Mr. Shaw's Analysis of the Scotch Celtick Language. Life*, iii. 107. This is the only acknowledged piece of writing of his during 1776.

I hope

I hope you will make no scruple to call upon me, for I shall be glad of an opportunity to show that my reception at Saint Andrews has not been forgotten [1].

I am, Sir,

Your humble servant,

Oct. 14, 1776.   SAM: JOHNSON.

500.

To ROBERT LEVETT.

Brighthelmstone, October 21, 1776.   Published in the *Life*, iii. 92.

501.

To JOHN RYLAND [2].

DEAR SIR,

The selection made in this parcel is indicated partly in a catalogue by the words *print* or *omit*, and partly by the same words written in red ink at the top of those pieces which are not in the catalogue. I purpose to send the rest very soon, and I believe you and I must then have two or three interviews to adjust the order in which they shall stand.

I am, Sir,

Your most humble servant,

Nov. 14, 1776.   SAM: JOHNSON.

[1] The book printing for Professor Robert Watson was his *History of the Reign of Philip II.* Johnson's offer of assistance seems to have been accepted. *Post*, Letter of May 20, 1779.

In the *Annual Register* for 1776, sixteen pages are given to a review of this work, while for the *Wealth of Nations*, which came out in the same year, little more than two pages is spared. Carlyle, reading the *History* when he was a young man, calls it 'an interesting, clear, well-arranged, and rather feeble-minded work.' *Early Letters of T. Carlyle*, ed. Norton, i. 187. For Watson's hospitality to Johnson at St. Andrews, see *Life*, v. 58.

I do not think that it was known till this letter was published, that Johnson had given any help in Dr. Robertson's publication.   Strahan, as we know from Beattie, 'had corrected the phraseology of both Hume and Robertson.' Forbes's *Beattie*, ed. 1824, p. 341.   His long residence in England had enabled him, no doubt, to detect many Scotticisms ; but he seems, at all events in the case of Robertson, to have had Johnson's help.

[2] From the original. I have, I regret to say, mislaid the reference to the owner of this letter, It was sold for six guineas by Messrs. Sotheby & Co., on May 10, 1875, (Lot 94), and for £2 8s. by Messrs. Christie & Co., on June 5, 1888, (Lot 45).   See *ante*, p. 412.

To

502.

To James Boswell.

Bolt-court, November 16, 1776.   Published in the *Life*, iii. 93.

503.

To the Reverend Dr. Percy [1].

Dear Sir,

Mr. Langton and I shall wait on you at St. James's [2] on Tuesday.

I must entreat your attention to a business of more importance.   The Duke [3] is President of the Middlesex Hospital; could you obtain from him the admission of a Patient, the Son of Mr. Thomas Coxeter [4], a Gentleman and a Man of Letters? The unhappy Man inherits some claim from his Father to particular notice; and has all the claims, common to others, of disease and want.

I shall apply no where else till I hear from you: be pleased to answer this request as soon as you can.

I am, Sir,

Your most humble Servant,

Sam: Johnson.

Dec. 1, 1776.

To the Reverend Dr. Percy.

504.

To the Reverend Dr. Percy [5].

Thomas Coxeter of little Carter lane, in Doctors Commons.

---

[1] From the original in the Dyce and Forster Collection, South Kensington. I owe this copy to the kindness of Mr. R. Forster Sketchley.

[2] 'In 1769, Percy was appointed Chaplain to George III. About the same time Mrs. Percy was appointed nurse to Prince Edward, the infant son of the King, afterwards Duke of Kent, and father of Her present Majesty.' Wheatley's Percy's *Reliques*, ed. 1876, i. Preface, p. 76. I conjecture that the Percies had rooms in St. James's.

[3] Percy's patron, the Duke of Northumberland.   *Court and City Register*, 1775, p. 228.

[4] See *ante*, p. 170.

[5] From the original in the possession of Mr. Mitchell Henry, Kylemore Castle, Galway.

Dr. Percy, it is clear, had asked for further information, which this letter supplies.

His

His disease I could not gather from his sister's accounts so as to name it. He has had a scorbutick humour which I believe has fallen back upon his vitals.

I have got a cold which, I hope, will not hinder me from dining at your table, and returning you thanks for this favour.

Dec. 2, [1776].

To the Reverend Dr. Percy.

505.

To James Boswell.

[London], December 21, 1776. Published in the *Life*, iii. 94.

APPENDIX A.

(*Page* 7.)

THE draft of a letter written by Johnson in the name of Lewis Paul to the Duke of Bedford, President of the Foundling Hospital [1].

'MY LORD,

'As Beneficence is never exercised but at some expense of ease and leisure, your Grace will not be surprised that you are subjected, as the General Guardian of deserted Infants, and Protector of their Hospital to intrusion and importunity, and you will pardon in those who intend though perhaps unskilfully the promotion of the charity, the impropriety of their address for the goodness of their intention.

'I therefore take the liberty of proposing to your Grace's notice a Machine (for spinning cotton) of which I am the inventter [*sic*] and Proprietor, as proper to be erected in the Foundling Hospital, its structure and operation being such that a mixed number of children from five to fourteen years may be enabled by it to earn their food and clothing. In this machine thus useful and thus appropriated to the publick, I hope to obtain from Parliament by your Grace's recommendation such a right as shall be thought due to the inventer.

'I know, My Lord, that every Project must encounter opposition, and I would not encounter it but that I think myself able to surmount it. Mankind has prejudices against every new undertaking, which are not always prejudices of ignorance. He that only doubts what he dos [*sic*] not know, may be satisfid by testimony, at least by that of his own eyes. But a Projector, my Lord, has more dangerous enemies, the envious and the interested, who will neither hear reasons nor see facts and whose animosity is more vehement as their conviction is more strong.

'I do not implore your Grace's Patronage for a work existing only in possibility, I have a Machine erected which I am ready to exhibit to the view of your Grace or of any proper judge of mechanical performances whom you shall be pleased to nominate. I shall decline no trial, I shall seek no subterfuge; but shall shew not by argument but by practical experience that what I have here promised will be easily performed.

'I am an old Man oppressed with many infirmities and therefore cannot

[1] By the kindness of Miss Cole of Teignmouth, who has lent me a fac-simile of the original document, which was in her father's collection of autographs, I am able to give the letter exactly as Johnson wrote it.

pay that attendance which your Grace's high quality demands, and my respect would dictate, but whenever you shall be pleased to assign me an audience, I shall explain my design with the openness of a man who desires to hide nothing, and receive your Grace's commands with the submission which becomes

'My Lord,

'Your Grace's most obedient

'and most humble servant.'

The result of this application is not known.

APPENDIX B.

(*Page* 14.)

AMONG the Hume Papers in the Royal Society of Edinburgh I found the original of the following letter to David Hume about the expenses &c. of an education at Oxford. The write was Archibald Macdonald, a younger brother of Sir James and Sir Alexander Macdonald of Sky. (*Life*, v. 154.) He matriculated at Christ Church in 1764, and took his degree of B.A. in 1768. He was Solicitor-General from 1784 to 1788, Attorney-General from 1788 to 1793, and Lord Chief Baron of the Exchequer from 1793 to 1813. He died in 1826.

'DEAR SIR,   'Oxford, July 27, 1769.

'The day before yesterday your letter was transmitted to me from Lincoln's Inn, which I am afraid you will think I should have answered sooner, not knowing that I had set out for this place some days before it was written; conscious of great dissipation and idleness during the course of the winter, I have retired to these deserted abodes for the vacation to make up my arrears.

'I cannot desire any better method of leading you to a solution of the question you put to me, than by stating to you what is required of the members of the different orders of Commoner and G[entleman] Commoner, and in what the greater expense of the latter consists. Since the accession of our present Dean, Dr. Markham, late Master of Westminster School, the independent members (by which I mean all such as are not of the foundation) have been put upon the same footing precisely in respect of the exercises required of them; these are a quarterly examination in certain authors and an essay upon a given subject in their turn. There is, I must own, a way of shuffling in these performances too often successful, but at the same time they may be, and often are, done with credit. Their attendance is required indiscriminately in the Hall and Chapel, and the Dean is very strenuous in

support

support of this rational plan of government. By the constitution of the University every man not having a degree in it is required to have one of the college tutors; from him very little is to be expected. He does not interfere at all with the expense of his pupil, not a great deal with his Latin and Greek, far less with his progress in the sciences. These advantages and disadvantages are common to all independent members. The difference in their expense is owing to this. The Gent. Commoner pays his Tutor 20 guineas per annum. The Commoner eight; the one stands to a higher ordinaing [? ordinary] in the College Hall than the other by about 15 or £20 a year at the utmost, and the College fees are all more considerable to the former than the latter, so that the *necessary* difference in expense may be about 50 or £60 a year. But these are not the great sources of expense, it is the Cook's shop and the Coffee House (which are here in the nature of taverns) that consume so large a sum of money; together with many other *voluntary* extravagancies. These last it is the continual object of our governors to restrain, but to little purpose; all ranks of people give into such expenses, Commoners as well as Gent. Commoners. It so happens in this place that what is called the best company consists of the most expensive people, of those who entertain most, and are most extravagant in their amusements. Whoever keeps their company is obliged to share in their expenses, let his gown be of what shape he pleases. I speak at present of Christ Church only. In short it seems to be the general opinion that the difference of the expense of these orders, admitting that they live much together (which will be Mr. Hume's case particularly) consists chiefly in the difference of their *necessary* expense. This you must take along with you, that a young man is left to his own discretion as much in the one order as the other. There are, in fact, two different sorts of Commoners in this College, one that enjoys a considerable exhibition left to the natives of certain counties, the other, differing in nothing that I can distinguish, from a Gent. Commoner but in the necessary addition to the college fees which I have stated above.

My own situation was the most advantageous possible. I was elected from Westminster School in a capacity correspondent to a fellow in other colleges; which fashion has rendered one of the genteelest things in the University. Our order consists of 101, and is filled by the younger sons of people of fashion in a great degree; our College expenses are all paid by Queen Elizabeth, and a small balance divided among us. In this situation I partook of the advantages of both orders; and could keep the best company upon a smaller income than will be necessary for one of any other order, and still I spent little less than £200 a year. The £50 I state as the necessary expense added to this £200 will with common attention be a genteel allowance for any Gentleman; and as a Commoner keeping the best company I really believe his expense will be full two hundred pounds a year; though many of that order live retiredly for the half of it; the expense of this place being regulated more by the company one keeps than by any other circumstance I know.

· Many of those Gentlemen who are now here were Mr. Hume's companions at Edinburgh, particularly Messrs. Elliot, Mr. Adam. and some others. The former are indeed in point of discretion, application, and good sense superior to most young people I meet with. These are all Gent. Commoners, which perhaps may have its weight with you in your determination.

'Upon the whole the advantages and disadvantages are in this society common to both orders. The College expense differs in about £50 or £60, and a little more the first year. The unnecessary expense of the same *set* is nearly the same to every individual composing that set, the most reputable and genteelest is the most extravagant; in this set you would wish him to be, so that it is reduced to this, whether for the sake of an appearance somewhat genteeler, you would wish him to spend a third more than is absolutely necessary, from which he reaps no other benefit but that of dining with his old friends upon a better dinner, and having the use of a very fine library from which the Commoners are excluded.

'In this College few people enter Commoners but such [as] are designed for a profession—In others it is more common. But if Christ Church is set aside, the College of all others the most attractive to its young members is University College, the Master an illiberal man, the tutor, I am informed, a very useful ingenious man. His name is Scott [afterwards Lord Stowell]. Ours being the largest Society affords of course a greater choice of company, which gives it a preference in the eyes of many over every other, especially for men of fortune.

'The expense of a Commoner keeping the best company is certainly near £200, that of a Gent. Commoner at least £250.

'I propose being here till November. If Mr. Hume should arrive before that time, my utmost endeavours shall be used to be of any sort of use to him. In answer to that dreadful accusation with which you conclude your letter, I shall only observe that I go to prayers ' seven every morning, sometimes in the evening, consistently with which you will get no one to believe I have the smallest flaw in me.

'I remain, dear Sir,
'With great sincerity,
'Your obd. ser^t,
'A. MACDONALD.'

'To David Hume, Esq.,
Brewer's Street,
London.'

Hume had consulted also Sir Gilbert Elliot whose sons were at Oxford; the answers were not satisfactory. 'My brother,' Hume wrote on October 16, 1769, 'thinks his son rather inclined to be dissipated and idle; and believes that a year or two at Oxford would confirm him thoroughly in that habit, without any other advantage than the acquiring of a little better pronunciation.' Burton's *Life of Hume*, ii. 430.

APPENDIX C.

(*Page* 187.)

By the kindness of Captain Alfred C. Christopher, of the Seaforth Highlanders, who possesses the originals, I am able to publish the two following sets of verses by David Garrick. The first was addressed to Captain Christopher's great-great-grandfather, Henry Wilmot, Esq., of Farnborough Place, Hants, grandson of Robert Wilmot, M.P. for Derby, in the Reign of William and Mary. Henry Wilmot was Secretary to Lord Chancellor Camden. He died in 1794, aged 84.

'HAMPTON, Saturday.

My Wilmot dear,
Your Garrick hear,
With friendship steady,
Beds are ready,
One, two, or three,
For men like thee ;
Our joys of life,
Are you, and wife,
Babes, sister too,
And all from you :
So come away,

On marriage day,
With cares unmixt,
(Tis Tuesday next :)
And let us laugh,
Good liquor quaff,
Our friends will toast
(Our love and boast)
To fill our cup
Of transport up —
Camden, imprimis,
To him no Rhyme is,

Nor equal neither—
Haste you hither,
To eat and drink,
Till eyelids wink,
Then lay your heads,
On well aired beds ;
To you and spouse
My loving wife insures,
Herself, heart, house,
And husband wholly
yours.

'D. G.'

The second set of verses was addressed to Valentine Henry Wilmot, Henry Wilmot's only son. 'At Farnborough Place,' Captain Christopher informs me, ' there is a white marble tablet in the garden, on which are lines very similar to those I enclose in memory of " Hoppy." It was accidentally discovered a few years ago, on the removal of some ivy, on an old wall. I think there can be no doubt they were by Garrick.'

'TO MASTER WILMOT UPON THE DEATH OF HIS FAVOURITE
CAT HOPPY.

No more dear Youth shall Hoppy scratch and purr,
O never fondle animals like her ;
From every naughty Puss, guard well thy mind,
Wicked and wanton all are after kind :
Would'st thou shun cats, and Sire-like love the Law,
Thou'lt ne'er be clawed or scratched, but scratch and claw.

'GARRICK.'

APPENDIX D.

(*Page* 214).

By the kindness of Miss Mickle of Toronto, and of William Julius Mickle, Esq., M.D., of Grove Hall, Bow, London, I have copies of some letters of James Boswell to their ancestor, the translator of the Lusiad. Boswell 'had recommended,' he said, 'to Garrick's patronage the *Siege of Marseilles.*' When he heard of the poet's wrath on its rejection he wrote the following letter :—

'TO MR. WILLIAM MICKLE.

'Edinburgh, 1 December, 1772.

'DEAR SIR,

'As I was much afraid of Mr. Garrick's oracular response with regard to the Siege of Marseilles, and foresaw that you might be hurt by it, I was at pains all along to prepare you for it, and I am persuaded you will remember that so was the case. I am sincerely sorry that he does not think your Tragedy fit for the stage. But as I said again and again, as I am a very incompetent judge of a dramatick performance, and believe him to be a very good one, I cannot but acquiesce in a Decision pronounced by him not only impartially, but with a strong weight of favour to ballence [*sic*] him on the side of what he has rejected. I am sensible how very difficult it is for *you* to think as I do ; but I would fain hope that I may have some influence with you. I declare to you upon honour that Mr. Garrick spoke very highly of your poetry, and of the poetry of this very play ; and I believe he was sincere ; for I have always found him to be an honest honorable [*sic*] man. At the same time, I am persuaded of the truth of what he has frequently told me, that the most exquisite poetry will not be sufficient to make a successful Theatrical representation, and that inferior Poetry *will*, when arranged with that art which is necessary to keep alive the attention of an audience. I saw Mr. John Home to-day, and was regretting to him that your Play was refused. I think his words were "not from its deficiency in *spirit* but in *form*, and which a longer acquaintance with the Theatre will teach him." This was just what I have been echoing to you from Mr. Garrick. Mr. Home observed that many of the modern Plays which Mr. Garrick has brought on are so poor in poetry, that one cannot read them to an end, and yet the disposition and variety of the scenes and changes in them is such that they have gone very well off when acted. Your play it seems has not those requisites. Mr. Garrick sees this ; and therefore though he admires your genius, he will not bring your play upon the stage. Let me as a sincere friend expostulate with you closely. Mr. Garrick brings out some plays every year. The interest used in behalf of yours has been strong. I know from Mr. Garrick himself that he has felt it to be so. I am vain enough to think that even my warm recommendation

must

must have had weight with him. Would he not then have let your Play be one of the number had he not been firmly of opinion that it could not be carried through? Supposing him then to be firmly of this opinion, is it reasonable to think that he should lay out considerable expence and throw away much time, and in short hurt the interests of himself and partner by making an attempt which he is sure would only expose him? Let me add too on the same supposition, would it not be doing a real injury to you, to bring on a Play written by you, which he is sure would be damned, the consequence of which would be to hurt your reputation as a Writer in other departments of literature where real genius independant [*sic*] of mechanism has its just applause? These, Sir, are my views of the matter, and therefore it vexes me to find you taking up the same tone which numbers have done before. If I might advise you, I would have you be in no hurry to print your Play; and if you do print it, pray repress any reflections against Mr. Garrick.

'As a certain proof that you are at present chagrined and not a fair judge of his conduct, I take the Anecdote of the Bookseller calling on him for his 20 subscriptions to the Lusiad and his desiring the Bookseller to call again, at which you are much offended. Now, my dear Sir, will you only consider that here was nothing more than what happens upon almost every occasion, when money is asked without any . . . .'

The rest of the letter is missing.

In the List of Subscribers to the Lusiad, published in 1776, Garrick's name is entered for twenty copies.

END OF VOL. I.